IMMORTAL QUEEN

ELIZABETH BYRD

IMMORTAL QUEEN

BALLANTINE BOOKS

NEW YORK

813.54
B99i

Second Printing

34 227
October, 1956

Library of Congress Catalog Card No. 56-10189

Printed in the United States of America
American Book–Stratford Press, Inc., New York

To my parents
Emma Howard Byrd and Joseph Hunter Byrd
and to my
husband – editor – critic
Don Phares

IMMORTAL QUEEN

PROLOGUE

"In my end is my beginning."
—Mary Stuart, Queen of Scotland,
Feb. 8, 1587

I.

SHE LAY ON THE BED staring into the pale taperlight, watching the slow shift of shadow on stone walls. At the barred window a north wind pushed the crimson hangings, and she heard the long sigh of banners in the courtyard. There were other sounds—the muted prayers of her servants, voices caught on sobs as they told their beads. Halberdiers clanged along the corridor outside, and below in the Great Hall workmen hammered the scaffold.

She watched the dripping rushlights as dawn grayed the bed-chamber. Her body was captive, but her mind journeyed beyond the fortress of Fotheringay, out of Northamptonshire into this final day. She thought of dawn silvering the disputed heatherline between England and Scotland, of mosstroopers waiting for news of her, waiting to ride the miles of wind to Edinburgh. There at Holyrood House was her son James, King of Scotland, heir to the throne of England, and she visioned him deep in a wine-sleep with hounds at his feet. Two days would pass before the news reached him: "Queen Mary is dead . . . Long live the King!" And he would weep and curse (so facile an actor at twenty-one), then write a properly threatening letter to Queen Elizabeth demanding satisfaction for the outrage. And Elizabeth would read it briefly, wrinkle her beaky nose and laugh.

But was Elizabeth laughing now, seventy miles away across this dawn? Or pacing her apartments at Greenwich Manor with her conscience screaming? Or deep in guilty nightmare, hands twitching the coverlid? Or praying?

I must pray for her, Mary thought. I must pray for her immortal soul.

And my own.

[1]

She prayed as she had all the long night, asking forgiveness of her sins. "Surely there is mercy at the throne of heaven even for such as I. For Thou knowest I have kept the faith, defended the true church with all my heart and all my armies—and now will die for it. Thou knowest the mockery of my trial, that I never conspired against Elizabeth's life . . ."

The clock struck six.

Her attendants rose from their knees. The dying fire bloomed suddenly and blazed. At the far end of the room tapers were lit against the chill gloom of the morning.

The hammering below had stopped.

Terror rose in her, spreading like ice through her veins. I am a coward, she thought, despite my outward composure and my fine bravado before Elizabeth's envoys. As I fear hell-fire so do I fear death by the sword. The headsman of London is said to be skilled, swift, and precise as a surgeon. But if he blunders, God grant me the strength to clamp my mouth tight, swallow my screams, and bear the agony.

For pride—courage to die—is all that is left me. Such courage may justify my existence, even expiate my sins. May it not be said, "Her life was evil," but rather, "Her death was brave."

She was shivering uncontrollably. "God, help me still my trembling so that no one may guess . . ."

Gradually she calmed, extended her hands and found them steady. She parted the red velvet bed curtains and looked out. Elizabeth Curle and young Marie Paget stood near the hearth in their black mourning gowns, clinging together for comfort. Jane Kennedy opened the wardrobe, brought out the dark ceremonial robes and placed them on a chair. Her sandy hair was drawn under a severe white cap, which accentuated the long narrowness of her face, and her eyes were puffed red from weeping. As she turned she saw the Queen and hurried over to her.

"Madam, what may I do?"

Mary said, "I shall dress."

She had lain all night in yesterday's gown, and the women removed it, then her undergarments. They brought a vessel of water and she bathed. Jane slipped a scarlet satin camisole over her shoulders and helped her into a scarlet velvet petticoat.

"Perhaps red is not seemly at such a time," Mary said, "but my blood against it will not be so conspicuous."

Jane fell to her knees and kissed the velvet skirt. Elizabeth and Marie cried softly, chins sunk into their stiff collars. Tear-blinded, they moved to and from the wardrobe with green garters, white jersey stockings, shoes of soft Spanish leather. Shoes that had been

[2]

specially ordered; they would not creak as Mary walked the steps to the scaffold.

Finally she stood arrayed as she wished to be, tall and wide-shouldered in a black velvet gown stamped with gold. The puffed upper sleeves were purple velvet, the lower sleeves black, buttoned with pearl-trimmed jet. Lined with sable, they fell full to her feet. From her belt swung a rosary and scapular. There was a high pleated ruff for her throat, a brown wig for her hair. Jane fastened in place a peaked white crepe headdress, its lace-edged veil sweeping to the floor. Mary asked for a mirror and looked into the polished metal.

"You have never been more beautiful, Madam," Elizabeth said.

Mary shook her head. At forty-four she was regal, elegant, but no longer beautiful. Nineteen years of imprisonment had thickened her slender body, and her legs were swollen with rheumatism. Her hair had lost its dark fire and curled white under the wig. Crimson salve covered a bloodless mouth. Only the eyes were unchanged, eyes made legend by poets. Long and heavily lashed, they shaded from brown to hazel to golden amber. Now they were tearless as she told her face farewell, darkened the satiny eyebrows and perfumed them for the last time.

"Summon my household," Mary said.

She went to the window and looked at the barred world. There was drifting fog, a slate-colored sky, nothing to see but flat winter-bound earth and the corpse-boughs of the oaks. None of her prisons had been so grim as this one.

She turned as the men of the household came in, and she gave her hand to Dominique Bourgoing, her physician. He caught it to his gray-bearded lips, then studied her anxiously.

"Was Your Majesty able to sleep?" he asked.

"The hours were too precious for sleep. I spent them in prayer; and I finished my will."

She went to her writing desk and removed some papers from a small casket. "I have tried to make provision for all of you, but as you know I was stripped of my jewels and most of my money."

She sank into an armchair by the fire and bade her attendants be seated. There was Andrew Melville, Master of the Household; Gurion, her surgeon; Gervais the apothecary; and Martin the chef. The women were sobbing again and Mary's pity for them thrust deep. She had so little to leave them.

"The Queen of England is rapacious," she said. "She has taken all my valuables. There are my garments to divide among you women, some trinkets, and such furnishings as you see before you." She handed the will to Bourgoing. "Read this aloud so that it may be witnessed."

[3]

His voice trembled. *I, Mary, by the Grace of God Queen of Scotland and Dowager Queen of France, being on the point of death, and having no means of making my will, have myself committed these articles to writing . . . I will that the wages and sums due my household, for the last and the present year, be paid them before all other things . . . Further, I ask pensions for these people and safe-conduct back to their countries . . . As for myself, I wish to be buried in France beside my mother, so that this poor body of mine may find at last the rest it never knew when joined to my soul . . .*

As he read, Mary wondered if there was the remotest chance that her will would be honored. These English could look you in the eye and swear on their Bibles, then turn and break their word. She had no assurance that her Catholic servants would not be murdered before the day was over. Would the gaunt, gray Bourgoing ever see France again? What would happen to pretty pert-nosed Marie, to gentle Elizabeth Curle, to her favorite, Jane Kennedy?

I must not show uneasiness, she thought, *nor hint my fears for them. Better that they make their plans in hope.*

After the will had been signed and sealed, Mary distributed small purses containing a few French crowns, and mementos for the women.

"My dear friends," she said, "I beg all of you to help me at my death, to testify to my devotion to my religion. I shall not have my priest—he is prisoned in his room."

Bourgoing's voice was shocked. "Madam! You are not to have extreme unction?"

"No. They offer me the heretic Dean of Peterborough, a gentleman deeply enamored of the sound of his own voice." Her smile was contemptuous. "However, I have a consecrated wafer sent me by the Pope with a unique dispensation to administer the Eucharist myself."

"Thank God," Bourgoing said. But she realized that her triumph was lost upon the others. Pious though they were, they could not see beyond the present darkness. Perhaps, she thought, they are still too close to life.

Mary rose and went to a cabinet. From its hiding place she brought the gold and jeweled ciborium which contained the holy wafer. Her attendants bowed as she passed into the oratory. There she knelt before her altar, the long velvet train a path of black on the stone floor.

She did not hear the clock strike seven, eight, nor the weeping in the next room. Striving for peace of heart, she prayed for friends and enemies. Friends—there were so few! Her brother-in-law Henry III of France might well send his armies against Elizabeth to avenge this crime. Philip of Spain—his vast armada now building with high-pooped galleons to crash their might against the English fleet. But friends who had no political motives? Only a handful. The truest of these were waiting in the next room, simple folk who had tended her these endless months.

She prayed for her son James, for the Scottish lords in league with Elizabeth, and for all her other enemies. And at last she prayed for the soul of James Hepburn, Earl of Bothwell, dead these nine years —and better so. Remembrance of him slashed at her serenity even as she prayed. At the feet of God, and so near to his mercy, carnal thoughts were blasphemous. "Forgive me," she whispered, "that even now, in thy presence, I sin in my memory."

Folk said that passion for Bothwell had brought her to ruin. But she wondered if the seeds of her ruin were not sown at birth, a Stuart heritage planted in the darkness of her mother's womb. The monstrous growth might have flowered had Bothwell never drawn breath.

She felt the touch of a hand on her shoulder and Bourgoing lifted her to her feet. "You must take some wine, Madam. You must preserve your strength."

She followed him into the bedchamber and was sipping the wine when the Sheriff of Northampton knocked loudly on the door and was admitted.

He swept off his cap and bowed low. "Your Majesty, my lords are waiting."

Jane Kennedy brought the long sable-lined black velvet cloak and drew the white veil across Mary's face. They gave her an ivory crucifix to hold and a gold-bordered handkerchief with which to bind her eyes at the block. They kissed her feet and the hem of her skirt and her hands. Then they followed her out of the room, Mary's white terrier romping ahead into the corridor. Guards armed with swords and pistols waited at the staircase with the Earls of Kent and Shrewsbury.

As they bowed, Mary drew back the veil from her eyes. "My lords," she said, "I beg you to provide for my servants according to my will, which is on my desk. And I trust in your honor that they will not be molested after I am gone."

"Your Majesty's trust is not misplaced." Shrewsbury, deadly pale, did not meet her eyes.

"I also ask that they be present at my death, so that they may testify to my behavior when they return to their countries."

The Earl of Kent frowned. "That we cannot risk. Your women will moan and wail and dip their handkerchiefs in your blood."

"I give you my word they will do no such things."

"How can you know what they will do, Madam?"

"Because we have discussed this and I have their promises." Mary appealed to Shrewsbury. "Surely your mistress will not want it said that none save her own people witnessed my death? It might well be whispered abroad that I was denied prayer, or even tortured!" She paused and added significantly, "Such rumors would greatly disturb Their Majesties of France and Spain."

She saw that she had troubled them, for the earls went to the stair landing and consulted. When they returned they told her that six of her household might accompany her, and she chose her best-loved servants and warned them against any outcry. "Do not approach me at any time unless I ask it," she said, "but pray for me every moment."

Mary walked slowly toward the stairs. Her glance dropped to her crucifix. She veiled her face and moved past the guards, past the stained gold tapestries, down the long staircase.

II.

The Great Hall of Fotheringay was draped in black from wall to wall. Near the huge Gothic fireplace stood the scaffold, raised two feet from the floor, measuring twelve feet square. Black serge was stretched over it, and serge covered the cushion at the block and the small stool placed for Mary's use.

Beyond the scaffold railing stood three hundred armed halberdiers and two hundred chattering nobles, armored, jeweled, and plumed. Outside in the courtyard a troop of cavalry held back a mob. Farmers and villagers from miles around had come to push and pummel for a glimpse of royalty.

Musicans in wine velvet cloaks took their places in the gallery above the hall and tuned their instruments. Then Robert Beale, Clerk of the Council, shouted for silence as Mary appeared in the doorway, Melville bearing her train.

She was prepared for jeers and curses, but the company was orderly. Perhaps, she thought, they are too avid for the spectacle to waste time with accusations. But she knew the accusations in their hearts: Murderess. Conspirator. Adulteress. The Scottish Whore. Years ago she had raged and sobbed at such labels. Now they no longer mattered.

Sir Amyas Paulet, her jailer, offered Mary his arm and helped her up the steps of the scaffold. Her rheumatic legs were painful and she sank gratefully onto the stool. Near the block stood swarthy, massive-chested Bulle, the headsman of London. He and his assistant wore black velvet gowns, white aprons, and black masks.

Angrily Mary whispered to Sir Amyas. She had expected to be executed with the respect due an anointed queen—by a sword. Instead, an axe with a short handle rested on the block, crude as a woodcutter's. More insulting, if possible, was the music—a dirge commonly played at the execution of witches. And all Elizabeth's doing . . .

"How dare she?" Mary asked Sir Amyas. "It is shameful enough to be denied a priest—am I also to be publicly humiliated?"

"You wished it public, Madam," he reminded her coldly.

"So that my death in the true faith be witnessed. But not only does she refuse to witness it—she wants me hacked like a tree and dirged like a heathen granny!"

"The black mass," he said, smirking, "would be more to your liking?"

She turned away, sick with her long loathing of him, sick too that he had destroyed her peace. For months, expecting this hour, she had woven with God a strong fabric of faith and now it was fraying. God would not abide where there was hatred. He would rightly desert her when she needed him most. She kissed her crucifix and prayed for Sir Amyas, and that her heart be purged of anger.

She felt capable of martyrdom but not of saintliness, for she knew that her concern with pride and posterity was all too human. A saint would not seek to impress Elizabeth's nobles with a magnificent end. Assuredly a saint would not die in red satin undergarments fragrant with French musk.

She raised her head and looked about her. Her attendants were grouped close to the railing, a tiny island in a hostile sea. On her right stood the Earls of Kent and Shrewsbury, on her left the Sheriff of Northampton. She saw familiar faces—Sir Ralph Sadler and Sir Francis Walsingham, the spy-master. Robert Beale came toward her and read aloud the Royal Commission for the Execution.

"God save the Queen!" The shout for Elizabeth rang to the high-vaulted ceiling and the mob outside took up the cry and flung it skyward.

Mary's hands tightened on her crucifix. *"Judica me, Deus, et discerne causam meam . . ."*

"Madam," said Shrewsbury, "you hear what we are commanded to do."

"Then do your duty."

As he hesitated, she rose and faced the crowd, who pushed close for a glimpse of her. She could see in the rear small children held high in their fathers' arms.

"My lords," she said, "I was born a queen, a sovereign princess not subject to your laws, a cousin to Queen Elizabeth, and her

[7]

legitimate heir." She emphasized the word "legitimate," tasting it sweet on her tongue. For not one here could deny that Elizabeth was Henry VIII's bastard daughter by Anne Boleyn. Thus she, Mary, granddaughter of Henry VII, was rightful Queen of England.

"After being long and wrongfully imprisoned in this country I am now, through force, about to close my life. I thank my God that he has permitted me to die for my religion . . . before a company who will be witness that I die Catholic."

She locked her eyes with the Dean of Peterborough's and lifted her chin. "As to the crime which they have fixed upon me—conspiracy against the Queen's life—I never suggested it nor consented to it nor to anything against her person. You, my lords, and you, Beale, know this."

She paused, glancing from one bearded face to another. They avoided her scrutiny, and she smiled and continued:

"But I forgive my enemies with a good heart. After my death it will be known and seen to what end they have desired and procured my death. I accuse no one any more than I have done previously; my tongue shall harm no one."

She sat down. The Dean of Peterborough puffed out his blue velvet chest and bowed his way to her—a big, square-jawed man with gray-streaked yellow hair.

"At the command of Her Majesty Queen Elizabeth, I come to prepare you for death, Madam." He rolled the words, mindful of his distinguished audience. "Let it not be said that through ignorance one soul was denied the path to heaven. However late be the hour, it is not too late to—"

"Peace, sir," Mary interrupted gently. "I have nothing to do with you. I do not wish to hear you."

"—to embrace the true faith. Change your opinion and repent your former wickedness—"

"I will not listen. Be silent, if you please, and go."

"—and lay aside those unclean dregs of superstition which you have about you. Settle your faith only in Jesus Christ."

"I *am* so settled—you are presumptuous!" She turned her back on him, but he continued exhorting her until the Earl of Kent interrupted.

"Madam, accept Christ to your heart and leave these trumperies." He indicated the crucifix she held. "What does it avail you to hold in your hands this vain image of Christ if you do not bear him in your heart?"

"How is it possible," she asked softly, "to have such an image in one's hand without the heart being profoundly touched by it?"

Kent snorted in contempt. The Dean knelt on the scaffold steps

[8]

and prayed in English that God would grant long life to Elizabeth, victory over her enemies, and the triumph of the Protestant religion.

Mary slid to her knees and prayed aloud in Latin—for the Pope and pastors of the church, for all gathered in the hall, for Queen Elizabeth—"so that she may worship Thee in the truth—and for my son's conversion to the Catholic faith."

It was a counterpoint of prayer, but the clash was ill-matched. English swelled from five hundred throats, Latin from seven. Our small voices are lost, Mary thought, except to God.

"Amen." The Dean of Peterborough rose from the steps and dusted his blue hose. "Amen."

Mary's terrier snuggled against her and licked her cheek. She held it close for a moment, then stood up.

"My lords, I am ready."

Bulle came forward to remove her cloak and gown, but Mary shook her head. "Let me do this," she said. "I understand this better than you." She smiled at the big masked face. "I never had such a groom of the chamber before."

She took the pins from her headdress, the gold cross from her neck. "I wish this cross to be given Jane Kennedy."

Bulle grabbed the cross and put it in his boot. "It is my right."

"She will give you more than its value in money. Please—"

"It is my right," he repeated.

Mary laid her veil and ruff on the stool. Then she beckoned her attendants and they climbed to the scaffold, where she kissed and blessed them, making the sign of the cross on their foreheads. The executioners knelt to ask forgiveness for what they were about to do. When it was granted, Mary's women removed her cloak and gown and bound her eyes with the gold-bordered handkerchief.

The crowd milled, whispering, as she stood bare-armed in her petticoat. The red satin camisole embroidered in gold was laced in the back with strips of black velvet and fell low on her shoulders. For a moment she swayed, as if dizzy, and put a hand to her bound eyes. Then she stood erect. Proudly she raised her head. Bulle took her hand and led her to the block.

She knelt and he forced her to the floor while his assistant held her. The Earl of Shrewsbury raised his sword to give the signal.

Mary gripped her crucifix. Praying, she wove the weakened fabric tight, tighter, until there was only God and herself; neither fear nor hatred nor regret. She saw in an instant how her entire life had hurried to this ending, how she had forged her own shackles with link after fatal link. Catherine de Medici, Chastelard, Elizabeth; John Knox, Darnley, Rizzio; James, Bothwell, Babington. The life begun at Linlithgow one wind-torn morning was ending on another such at Fotheringay forty-four years later.

Yet she could escape death, even now. She had only to scream, "Wait!" If she confessed to conspiracy she would be pardoned and sent back to the larger prison of Protestant Scotland with her son James as her jailer. For Elizabeth wanted her confession far more than her death. Elizabeth wanted her alive, broken of pride and begging grace, a coward Queen to throw in the face of the Pope.

But was it cowardice to cling to life?

The room was utterly silent. Far off she heard the growl of thunder and in her mind a lion roared across time, and time swept her back to a summer afternoon in her childhood. Even then, she thought, on a day drenched in sunlight, there was omen of the dark.

CHAPTER ONE

I.

IN THE COURT GARDENS of St. Germain-en-Laye, a young lion paced his golden chain, eying the peacocks that preened on the terraces below. Sometimes he nosed the earth or snapped at a bee, but always he resumed his pacing, back and forth, to and fro, wearing away the grass.

Mary watched him from a nearby bench. "He must be so unhappy here," she said to her governess. "Each day he grows more restless."

Madame de Paroy grimaced. "Each day he grows fustier. The Master of Beasts should perfume him."

At the end of his chain the lion paused and looked at them. Mary could see his eyes—green-gold with flecks of brown, not savage but soft, moist, despairing. He begs to be free, she thought, he wants to return to his own land, to his friends . . .

Madame rose. "Come, we must get to our lessons. The children are waiting and doubtless in mischief."

"His eyes," Mary said. "Look at his eyes!"

Her own eyes were suddenly wet. "See, he asks me to help him— and I can do nothing! Unless I ask the King to free him—"

"Your Majesty is talking nonsense." Madame took her firmly by the arm and pulled her off the bench. "You must not annoy the King with such a foolish request."

She is right, Mary thought. After all, I am only a visitor in France and Mama would not want me to ask favors. And yet . . . the lion was begging, tawny head to one side, a cushiony paw raised as though in supplication. Tears spilled down Mary's nose onto her ruff.

"I can't bear it!" she sobbed, hands to her face.

Madame looked down at her in astonishment, felt her forehead. "You seem to have no fever, yet I vow you must be ill." Her voice turned querulous. "Your Majesty knows weeping is not permitted— I am shocked by your loss of dignity." She picked up her ivory staff. "Come, forget the silly beast and let us join Their Highnesses."

Tear-blinded, Mary followed her, groping down a flight of steps to a checkerboard terrace of white and ebony marble.

"Dry your eyes." Madame gave her a handkerchief. "Mon Dieu, suppose someone sees you—twelve years old, and in tears!"

"I wouldn't care," Mary sniffled. "The lion—"

"The lion, the lion! Jesu! What ails you? Why should the filthy animal make you weep?"

"Because—I don't know." Mary shivered in the warm sun. "It is —I cannot explain, Madame. I only know I will never look at him again, never!"

They crossed the terrace. Water lilies floated in the moat beneath the long, sun-goldened palace. Between the trees Pan and his white stone nymphs stared eyeless at splashing fountains. As far as Mary could see, green lawns sloped to shimmering terraces of pink and blue and sea-green marble.

Down another flight of steps, they took a wooded path bordered by wild flowers. Set among them were little silver unicorns, jade monkeys, onyx panthers. They passed the royal dovecote and its bowing attendants.

Far in the distance hunting horns shivered through the forest of St. Germain, echoing back to the walled town that faced the Seine valley.

"Their Majesties should find good sport," Madame said. "The stags are fat on blossoms."

The lion roared, and Mary said, "Perhaps he will break his chain and hide in the forest."

Madame groaned. "Forget him!"

Farther down the path that sloped toward the river they entered a pink marble summerhouse, its columns spiraled with rambler roses, its roof an arch of willows. On satin cushions three royal children of France ate honeyed almonds and pretended to read their lessons.

They smiled at Mary and nodded politely to Madame as she sat down on a bench.

"Your Majesty will be seated." Madame reached for a book. "We will resume *The Odyssey*."

Mary sat in the swing suspended from willow boughs. Gently she swayed, buttercup skirts ballooning above her round-toed slippers.

Madame droned the verses of Homer. Her voice and the hum of bees in the rhododendron drowsed Princesses Claude and Elizabeth to sleep. The Dauphin Francis yawned and slid farther down on his cushion. An epic became a lullaby.

Presently Madame looked up, lifted her thin gray eyebrows, and poked Francis with her staff. "Your Highness! One can forgive inattention in your sisters but you—you are nearly eleven years old. There is no excuse for your dullness."

Francis roused, loose-lipped, blinking. He mumbled an apology and glanced appealingly at Mary. She smiled at him sympathetically. Tutors nagged him from morning mathematics to evening lute lesson with variations of the same complaint: "The future King of France is sluggish . . . The future King of France does not use the mind God gave him . . ." Always they set him in the future, pushing him beyond his capabilities. For Mary knew that God had not gifted Francis with a great mind, only a great heart. And sometimes the heart was lanced by ridicule.

Madame adjusted her black gabled headdress, folding back the lappets from her ears to cool her face. She turned to Mary. "I trust that Your Majesty is paying attention. I have known you to dream with your eyes wide."

"I've followed every word, Madame."

Madame resumed the verses and Mary sighed as the flat monotonous voice deadened Homer. How different when her uncle the Cardinal read *The Odyssey!* Then she could hear the grind of oars against surf, the breeze-borne sirens' song, the clash of spears. Under the spell of his voice she was Penelope, white-robed and silver-sandaled, good and beautiful beyond compare.

Wistfully she looked down at her slender body in the full-spreading yellow silk skirts. Her legs were too long—Madame Diane called her a little colt. Earnest prayer had not thinned her round cheeks, though they had a fashionable pallor. Her hip-length dark hair with its copper lights was satisfactory but the widow's peak, though slight, was unlucky. She had asked the Virgin to remove it lest Francis die before she did. She could not bear the thought of living without him.

They would be married in three years, when she was fifteen, and then they could do as they pleased. No more nagging tutors, no more hated science and sums. She would devote her time to verse-making and stories of King Arthur, and embroidery. With Francis she would swim in the Seine and ride, and dance the night through. Being married would be a constant playtime. They would hunt with the King at Amboise and Blois and drift down the Loire on the royal barge. Best of all, Francis would be free of his mother's domination, her desperate whims, her strange, scornful possessiveness. Queen Catherine de Medici stalked her childrens' love as if it were prey.

"Your Majesty will kindly stop swinging."

Mary came to earth with a flutter of skirts.

"You will please explain—in Greek—what I have just read."

[13]

"My thoughts were elsewhere, Madame," Mary said humbly.

"Then—" Madame's smile was malicious—"perhaps His Highness will explain for you."

Mary saw the familiar fear spring to Francis' eyes as he shook the dark head that was too large for his body. His pox-scarred skin reddened. He tried to move his lips, tried to help her, but no words came.

Mary defended him. "His Highness is not well today."

"Both of you overate at noon. Gluttony is a sin . . ."

Mary half-listened as Madame warmed to her favorite theme. It was gluttony, she said, that caused Mary's fainting spells and nightmares. And Francis, who had had a delicate stomach all of his life, seemed bent on ruining it. They used no judgment or discretion. They behaved like babies. "How can you expect to rule France and Scotland when you cannot even rule your appetites?"

"I am sure," Mary said coolly, "that Madame does not mean to be impertinent."

She saw color flare in the bony yellow cheeks and was instantly sorry. One must be especially patient with servants for they were helpless and dependent. Yet there were times when Madame de Paroy came close to insolence, particularly with Francis. He could not help it if his body was puny and misshapen, if his mind was sometimes slow and strange. Madame could not know how entertaining he was when adults were not present. He understood staghounds and horses better than the Master of Horse. He could ride as well as his grooms. But sometimes he raced his horse too fast, played tennis too violently, and his face purpled and she feared for his life. Then the physicians ordered him to bed, purged and bled him. Priests hung sanctified amulets at his belt and the Cardinal conducted ceremonies of exorcism. But it was no devil that plagued Francis. It was his desperation to be a man worthy of her. He drove his frail body to extremes, while his tutors prodded his mind and his mother ridiculed it.

Madame said stiffly, "I am sorry if I have displeased Your Majesty. It is my duty to protect you and His Highness from overindulgence. If you overeat and then dream away the afternoon we will never progress according to the Cardinal's schedule."

"Surely," Mary teased, "it is dangerous to exercise the mind on such a warm day."

"No," Madame said seriously, "it is imperative to exercise it constantly. It is not I who rush your education—it is destiny. Royal children *must* learn more quickly than humble folk and their knowledge must be vast. Who knows when Your Majesty and the Dauphin

[14]

may be called upon to rule? The King is well, God be praised." She crossed herself. "But you must be prepared."

Francis spoke timidly. "If I were King tomorrow Mary would know enough for us both."

"I would not depend upon that," Madame said grimly. "To govern wisely one needs more than a talent for verse-making and the stitching of altar cloths." She rose and bent over the little princesses. Chins sunk in ruffled collars, caps askew, they curled together like puppies. "Come," she said, shaking them awake. "I shall take Your Highnesses indoors."

She pulled them to their feet, brushed grass burs from their petticoats and tidied their mouse-brown curls. Like Francis they were thin and sallow-skinned, nervous, frequently ill. Though eight and nine years old they were treated as babies, allowed neither privacy nor initiative. Now they stood patiently, waiting to be returned to the nursery.

"May Mary and I play tennis?" Francis asked hopelessly.

"You will remain here until I return." Madame handed them books from the bench. "I suggest you review yesterday's grammar."

Taking a princess by each of her hands, she moved off into the glare of the sun. Francis watched until they disappeared in a bend of the path. "I don't like Madame de Paroy," he said. "She's nasty and she doesn't explain things. I wish we had Lady Fleming back again."

"I miss her too," Mary said. "She was my favorite aunt."

"Why did they send her back to Scotland?"

"I don't know." Mary wound a tendril of hair from under her gold lace snood and curled it absently around her finger. "But I know your mother didn't like her."

"My mother likes no one but my father."

"Your mother was angry one day and I heard her call my aunt a commonwhore."

"What is that?"

Mary shrugged. "I don't know. I asked the Cardinal, but he flushed red as his robe and wouldn't tell me."

"Commonwhore," Francis mused. Then he brightened. "Perhaps it means Protestant."

"My aunt would not be Protestant!" Mary said, shocked.

"But many people in Scotland are—even some of your own nobles."

"But my family isn't. And as soon as my mother wins help from your father she'll wipe out the traitor nobles. It will take much gold and many men, and right now your father can't spare soldiers from the Italian campaign."

"When I'm King," Francis said, "your mother shall have all the help she needs. I'll put the Protestants to the rack and the boot." He slipped a silver-handled dagger from his belt and unsheathed it. Hissing through his teeth, he slit imaginary throats and decapitated clovers. Mary watched, swinging, until he had tired of the game. Sometimes she felt years older . . .

"Remember the time," he asked, "when we saw the tailor burned at the stake in the Rue St. Antoine and you were sick all over your gown?"

"I was only seven," she said defensively. "I wouldn't behave so now."

"I was only five, but I didn't get sick." He stretched full length on the cushions, staring up at the willows. "It was the first time I ever saw anyone burned. The tailor deserved it, though. My father says Huguenots are even worse than other Protestants."

"They are all godless." Mary left the swing and shook out her skirts. Far in the distance they heard hunting horns and the baying of hounds. "Listen!" she said. "Listen—how beautiful . . ."

"It's just my parents hunting," Francis said. "I wish I could have gone, but my mother forbade it. She's angry with me." He dug the dagger violently into the grass. "I hate her."

Mary sat down on the cushion beside him. "I know."

His chin trembled. "You don't know! You only see her when people are present. You don't know how she talks to me. Sometimes she says I will go mad and never rule, and other times she kisses me and her arms hurt me. Last night she was furious—" He moved closer to Mary and clutched her hand. "Will you keep a secret?"

"Of course."

He whispered, "Last night I awakened with a nosebleed, and I went to my mother's bedchamber. It was very late. As I opened the door I noticed that her bed was empty. At first I didn't see her, for the room was dim. She was on her knees, crouching down on the floor with her head and shoulders under the perfume cabinet in the corner."

Mary stared at him. Sometimes when they daydreamed of the future his fancies ran away with him. But he never lied.

"What was she doing, Francis?"

"I don't know. She heard me and jumped up in a rage and slapped me for spying on her."

Mary stroked his thin brown hair. "My poor Francis! Perhaps she was searching for something under the cabinet."

"She was not searching. She was staring."

"One can't stare through the floor."

[16]

"My mother has the Evil Eye. She can see in the dark. She can see in back of her without turning."

It was true. All the court knew that Catherine de Medici was supernaturally gifted.

"Did she explain what she'd been doing, Francis?"

"No. She slapped me and pushed me from the room and called her attendant to rouse the physician." He touched his flat little nose. "He stopped the bleeding."

Mary sat silent a moment. "I wonder what she was doing, looking at the floor . . . Even if she can see through the floor, there are only Madame Diane's apartments beneath."

He nodded. "Madame Diane's bedchamber."

"Francis!" She spoke so explosively that he jumped. "Do you suppose there is a trap door and secret stairway from that corner, and your mother was about to climb down into Madame Diane's bedchamber?"

"Why would she do that? She hates Madame Diane."

"Enough to kill her?"

His mouth formed a little O. Mary lowered her voice sepulchrally. "I think there *is* a trap door, and I think Madame Diane is in dire peril."

"Perhaps," he said uncertainly.

"Of course she's in peril!" Everyone knew the hostility between Queen Catherine and Madame Diane de Poitiers. Mary understood it readily. For the King preferred to hunt with Madame Diane, to dance with her. He sought her company at pall-mall and wore her colors at tournaments. He was always consulting her regarding court appointments and affairs of state. And the Queen was jealous . . .

Mary said, "We must tell Madame Diane, warn her. No—first we must make sure there is a trap door."

"How can we? We dare not look, for if my mother caught us . . ." They shuddered.

"Besides," he said, "Madame Diane is not worth such a risk."

"She is too! She is the most beautiful, the kindest—"

"She is kind to you because you're Queen of Scotland and will be Queen of France. My mother says she's only kind to people for what they can give her."

"You believe your mother?" she asked incredulously.

"Perhaps sometimes she is right."

"She is not right about Madame Diane," Mary said sharply. "She is jealous—so are many people. But I know Madame Diane better than anyone else. And I shan't rest if she's in danger."

"You love her more than you do me," he pouted.

"I do at this moment. For you're not behaving as a prince nor a knight nor even a gentleman." She tucked her hair into its net, rose and picked up her Greek grammar. Moving to a bench she sat down and opened the book, ignoring him.

"Mary, please . . ."

"I'm sorry you told me your secret. Next time keep such secrets to yourself."

"I'll never have secrets from you—not even state secrets. When we are married—"

"I'm not so sure I'll marry you." She stuck her nose in the air. "Perhaps I'll marry Prince Philip of Spain."

"You can't! He's betrothed!"

"Poo! Queen Mary Tudor is a hag. He'll change his mind."

"But Philip's an enemy of France!"

"So are you." She snapped the book shut. "So are you if you don't help me rescue Madame Diane."

He looked at her helplessly, made a little pleading gesture with his hands.

"And I thought you so brave," she sighed.

"How can we risk it? Even when my mother leaves her chamber one of her ladies is always there in attendance."

"Not on a fête night!" Mary jumped up and came to kneel beside him. "Tomorrow night is the Fête of the Roses for the Venetian Ambassador. Your father has commanded the entire court, so your mother and her ladies will be there. I will go into her bedchamber—"

"There is always a guard outside."

"Never mind the guard—you invent trouble. Now listen carefully. I shall go into her bedchamber. You will stay close to your mother in the rose gardens. Should she start to return to the palace before I appear, you must detain her—perhaps feign illness. Do you understand?"

"Yes," he said. He frowned and passed his hand across his eyes. "But you speak so fast . ."

Patiently she explained again. Sometimes his mind grew weary and she had to repeat things. But she broke off in mid-sentence as Madame de Paroy came down the path. Hastily she thrust a book into Francis' hand and grasped her grammar. Madame's shoes squeaked up the steps, and swallows in the willows took flight in a blue sweep across the sunlight.

II.

For an hour Madame drilled Mary and Francis in Greek grammar. Then as the sky tarnished into a gray-gold sunset, they left the summerhouse and took the wooded path through the terraced gardens.

A great rose gate had risen at the entrance. Workmen were hammering arbors and trellises, placing green boughs on papier-mâché floats. The fountains were drained of water, to be replaced by wine.

Madame bent to fluff the ruff at Mary's throat. "What will Your Majesty wear to the fête tomorrow night?"

"A rose-colored gown," Mary said. "Madame Diane designed it for me."

With Francis and Madame, Mary crossed the flower-pleated paths to the palace that rose in arched tiers of pale yellow stone. From the courtyard, bells tolled for evening prayers and they followed the sound toward the Chapel of St. Louis. Behind them, coming from forest paths and terraces, dawdled ladies and gentlemen of the court, their pages swinging picnic baskets and tennis racquets, bows and arrows. Others came through the Gothic arches of the palace, the women's skirts a great satin whisper along the cobbled walks. They wore pale brocades—pink and lilac and ivory, the great full-hanging sleeves lined with gold and silver cloth or seed-pearl embroidery. Their eyebrows were thin plucked arcs, their lips were painted and their eyelids heavy with kohl. Hair was smoothed into coifs of lace surmounted by golden circlets or hidden under roofed headdresses with long side lappets of tinsel cloth. The men, beards curled and perfumed, carried brimmed berets banded with gold to match the heavy necklaces that reached to the belts of their padded doublets.

It was a beautiful crowd, Mary thought, as she nodded to bows and curtsies. The attendants of the Venetian Ambassador and Queen Catherine's Florentine retinue were somberly splendid in wine damasks and purple brocades. There were hooded monks from the court of Tsar Ivan the Terrible, nuns from Chartres and Orléans and officers of the guard in their dress uniforms, slender swords in jeweled scabbards. Ladies formed a cooing group around Duke François de Guise, Mary's soldier-uncle. Their fans fluttered about him, their voices chirped predictions of a quick victory against the Spanish in Italy. And assuredly, they said, he would regain Calais from the greedy English.

English, too, was spoken in the crowd that swelled the courtyard —the burred Scots-English of Mary's own noblemen, Lords Erskine and Livingstone. Their bold wool tartans looked crude, she thought, beside the silks and velvets of the French and Italians. Their manners lacked elegance. But because they were hers, and because she knew that the court made fun of their awkwardness, Mary smiled on them with particular graciousness and gave them her hand to kiss.

Hunting horns announced the King's return from the forest. Stable grooms scooped up coins and dice and straightened their brown trunk hose. In the great stone kitchens butchers sharpened game knives and cooks sweated at the fireplaces, where calves and lambs spitted over the coals. Lark and pigeon pies were crusted, cakes ornamented with sugar fleurs-de-lis. The Master of the Cellars selected hogsheads of burgundy and claret, and scullions wrestled them up the narrow stone stairs.

In the pantry butlers inspected a line of footmen in forest-green liveries. Serving maids in ankle-short skirts and holland aprons were slapped or smiled upon. The Master of the Household entered the banqueting hall to scatter azalea blossoms on the King's table and direct the placing of the gold service. Above in the gallery musicians set up the virginals and cithers. A tumbler in flame-striped pantaloons practiced a cartwheel.

In the royal apartments Catherine de Medici's ladies awaited her return from the hunt. On the vast canopied bed were laid amber satin bodice and oversleeves, a brown velvet petticoat embroidered in topaz. A tall wooden corset with leather laces was propped against the headboard. Vials of sweet oils lay ready on the perfume cabinet to conceal the smell of horse and sweat.

In the adjoining nursery at a small table the Princesses Claude and Elizabeth ate bread and roast ox. Grease ran down their chins and spotted their embroidered collars. From time to time a maid filled their wine goblets and fanned away flies. Under the table four-year-old Prince Charles and three-year-old Prince Henry played hide-and-seek below their sisters' dangling feet.

In the corridors cressets were lit. The guard was changed. Sentries paced the arched galleries that overlooked the rose gardens. A crescent moon hung in the long blue twilight.

The chapel bells rang out again. From the altar, the Cardinal of Lorraine blessed the congregation, his arms raised, red robes flaring back from jeweled wristbands. Tapers sparkled the diamonds on his fingers.

The crowd rose from its knees. Mary whispered to Madame de Paroy, "I shall stay here for a while."

Francis tugged at her hand. "Why?"

"To be alone," she said.

III.

It was not easy to be alone at St. Germain—or in any of the royal palaces. Thirty-seven children, sons and daughters of noblemen, shared Mary's play and certain of her studies. In her private apartments there were always four maids of honor. Tutors and governesses and guards were forever watching. Sometimes she felt stifled and the chapel was a haven.

She moved through the empty aisle toward the altar where her uncle the Cardinal knelt in prayer. She imagined that God must resemble the Cardinal—tall, fair, with a halo of golden wavy hair, and with white compassionate hands. God and the Cardinal were close to her, protective as shawls. Sometimes they were remote if she was naughty, but when she repented they were always here to listen to confession and forgive.

They had much to forgive, she reflected. There was her quick temper, only recently controlled. Her pranks—unseemly and unqueenly. The sins of gluttony and vanity. It was difficult not to believe the courtiers' compliments or the sonnets of Monsieur Ronsard which praised her lips and eyes. It was impossible to pose for Monsieur Clouet without being aware of his admiration. "I am painting an angel," he had told her, "who has not yet tried her wings."

The Cardinal rose and moved through the oaken door into his study. It was there that Mary spent two hours each morning learning history, philosophy, politics. He explained the world of the court, the world outside and the world beyond death. He made death so beautiful that sometimes she prayed to die, particularly when seized with the strange gnawing pain in her side. To die was to meet God and Our Lady and the angels and to live forever, traveling on clouds. To die was to be reborn in perfection.

The Cardinal examined her thoughts as the physician had examined her body. When she had a new thought she was sworn to tell him, lest it be heresy. And sometimes, to her horror, it was. Like the time she had said, "Since God made Protestants they cannot be bad." And he had explained that though God made them the devil corrupted them. It was the same with serpents and vultures and all evil creatures.

Mary's smallest act was supervised by the Cardinal. He read the letters she wrote to her mother before they were sent to Scotland. The tiniest gift to her ladies must be approved by him. And where his guidance ended, Madame Diane's began. In matters of dress and behavior Madame Diane ruled Mary as she ruled the etiquette of the court.

Theirs was a loving domination and Mary loved them in return. She was sure that their decisions were for her own good and for the good of Scotland and France. Yet sometimes—more often, of late— there had been moments of rebellion. In the past few weeks she had hoarded certain thoughts from the Cardinal, daydreamed strangely. Once in the orchard, reading of Sir Lancelot, she had imagined his kiss on her lips, gentle as the fall of petals. There was a time of dying sunset when she had wept without reason, filled with a sort of ecstatic sadness. She could not get close enough to the springtime;

to touch a bud, a leaf, was not enough. She wanted to wrap the forest in her arms, France, the new green world. There was the snowy day in Blois when from under her hood she had caught a page's sidelong glance and memorized it . . .

Guiltily she hugged the secrets. They were sweet, yet they brought a sharp new loneliness. With each week she slipped further from the Cardinal's gentle hands, more deeply into her own thoughts.

Questions crowded her mind, questions too revealing to ask him. Would it be sinful to spy against Queen Catherine, to try to protect Madame Diane? Could such an act of love be wrong?

For a moment she was tempted to run to the Cardinal and ask him, to confide her plan. But she had sworn secrecy to Francis. A vow was sacred—except, of course, when made to Spain or England. That was another confusing matter. In politics sin became diplomacy. One accepted both the teachings of Christ and the writings of Machiavelli and often the two dueled in her mind. The Cardinal said that she would understand when she grew up, that one must live both spiritually and practically. "You must keep your feet on the ground and your eyes on heaven."

There were some who whispered that the Cardinal's feet were on the King's neck and his eyes on the crown—but that was vilely untrue. It hurt her that the people she loved most were targets for slander. She tried vainly to forget the hateful little jingles sung by drunken students on the court's last visit to Paris. Sung as the golden coach of the Cardinal rolled through the Boulevard St. Michel:

> *The Cardinal rules as the Cardinal pleases.*
> *The Pope amens when the Cardinal sneezes.*
> *The King bows low at the Cardinal's snore,*
> *And God's own throne isn't safe any more.*

She had expected God to send a thunderbolt that very instant to annihilate the students, and bowed her head and waited in terror. But nothing happened. When another group of rowdies insulted Madame Diane, the Queen, sitting beside Mary, had said, "Cover your ears." But somehow the Queen had looked pleased as a cat at milk, and so Mary had listened.

> *Diana's prey, hi he, hi ho,*
> *Is caught in bed, hi he, hi ho,*
> *It wears a crown, hi he, hi ho,*
> *Upon its head, hi he, hi ho.*

Mary had not understood the verses but she felt their venom. The captain of her guard had looked at Madame Diane, hand at his sword, but she had shaken her sleek black head and lifted her chin. Mary was proud of her. So gentle that she would not unleash her soldiers on these swine. So forgiving, so wholly above revenge.

Mary knelt. "God protect her. And I thank Thee for protecting me."

She left the chapel, feeling cleansed and happy. God had been good to her. Some of his goodness she remembered and the Cardinal had told her the rest—how God had wrought a miracle, championed a seemingly hopeless cause. The story was like a romance, she thought, only it was true. It was history—*her* history.

IV.

She was born to the sound of wind on a wild December night in 1542. Wind raved across the Firth of Forth to the briared hills of Linlithgow, battering the palace walls. The midwife placed Mary in her mother's arms and Mary of Guise wept and turned her face to the gusted bed curtains. She had prayed for a son, for a male heir to the Stuart throne. And now, in Scotland's most desperate hour, while her husband fought the English somewhere in the tree-tossed darkness, she had borne a daughter.

James V never saw that daughter. Twenty miles to the north in Falkland Castle he lay dying, delirious from wounds. At Solway Moss his troops had panicked and been butchered. The corpses of ten thousand Scots froze on the banks of the Esk or in its waters. Twelve hundred soldiers were captive at Carlisle. The English had lost seven men.

A messenger arrived to deal him the final blow. "The Queen has borne a daughter, Sire."

A daughter—a puling girl-child! The Stuarts had seemed cursed ever since they inherited Scotland through marriage with Margery Bruce. "The devil take it," he sobbed. "It came with a lass and it will go with a lass."

Mary Stuart became Queen on her sixth day. Queen of a land plundered by the English and the traitor Scots in their pay. Across the border Henry VIII dipped his hands in the bloodied gold of looted monasteries and bribed Mary's nobles to do his will.

His will was made clear. Mary Stuart was to journey to England and receive her education. At the age of twelve she would marry his son, Prince Edward. Otherwise he would send his armies and his fleet to crush Scotland to dust.

Mary of Guise, though widowed and virtually helpless, had the heart of a tigress. She would not send her daughter to this heretic, this wife-killer, this monstrous strutting Bluebeard. She doubted that he wanted a bride for his son—he wanted the Scottish crown for himself. Once in England Mary would likely be murdered. A "fall" from a staircase, a poisoned cup—and a neat little corpse in Westminster.

There was an uneasy peace while Henry VIII poured gold into Scotland—gold that changed Catholics to Protestants and Stuart sympathizers to Tudor toadies. Mary of Guise put off Henry with promises, sparring for time. Time to raise a rabble army, time to beg soldiers of Spain and Rome. To Henry II of France and her brother, Charles de Guise, Cardinal of Lorraine, she wrote: *If you do not send help, Scotland will fall to the new religion and Catholic blood will clot your consciences.*

Suddenly, savagely, Henry VIII lunged sixteen thousand soldiers across the border. A fleet of two hundred warships joined in massacres from the Tweed to the Forth. Peasants were trapped and burned alive in their huts, or axed in the fields where English Borderspears played football with severed heads. Along the roads lay the corpses of mutilated women and children.

Wading boot-deep in gore, the Butcher Hertford moved toward the fortress of Stirling on orders to kidnap the little Queen. Mary of Guise seized her child and fled north. For the next four years there were wild night rides over the moors into the dripping hills and mountains, to elude the English. Mary shivered against a mosstrooper's steel chest, clung to the scarfed neck of a laird, clutched a spearman's mailed arms. Dunkeld in the Highlands . . . brief safety on the Isle of Inchmahone . . . and finally, Dumbarton.

There in the rocky port waited a rescue fleet—the galleys of Henry II of France and their laughing, swaggering captains. They had tricked the prowling English warships and maneuvered safely into harbor to take aboard the fugitive Queen. She would be educated in France and betrothed to the Dauphin Francis.

Mary remembered the day of departure—the tall ships riding at anchor, the men with earrings and curled beards whose plumed hats swept the decks as they bowed to her. Her mother's lovely face under a black hood, her gentle admonitions: "Trust in God . . . Obey the King and the Cardinal . . . Love the Dauphin Francis, for you will some day be his Queen."

Mary was not yet six years old; she clung to her mother, begging her to accompany her. But Mary of Guise shook her head. "I must stay here to guard your throne. To hold Scotland . . ."

Hastily she pushed Mary into safe French arms. Waving from the rocks, she waited until the galleys were bobbing dots in the sea mist. Then she turned and swung onto her horse, riding off into twelve long years of violence and heartbreak.

The King's own galley, bright with banners, carried Mary to Roscoff. Safe on French soil in the sword-bright August sunshine she journeyed from Brittany to Touraine. Crowds pelted her with flowers as her litter, borne by two palfreys, swayed over the dusty roads. Six knights held aloft a gold cloth canopy to shield her from the sun. Bell-capped jesters pranced by to amuse her. Behind her on horses caparisoned in green brocade rode French courtiers, smiling behind their hands at Mary's kilted attendants. The bagpipes of the Scots Guard brought startled peasants from orchards and vineyards, lured villagers from taverns and huts and shops. Towns were decorated in Mary's honor, wine gushed from fountains in market squares. Men and women who had never heard of Scotland came to gape at the little Queen who would someday be theirs; to hear her laugh, to marvel at her eyes.

And Mary marveled too. The sunlight, so wan in Scotland, dazzled her. The farm-plenty astonished her. Never were apples so round and red nor pears so plump. Grapes weighted the vines. Fat deer scampered through birchwood thickets. Her French escorts tarried for hunting, for a feast of venison by torchlight.

She fell in love with France on that first journey, with the white chateaux mirrored in the Loire where swans drifted among the water lilies. Some of those chateaux became home to her, for the court moved from Chinon to Amboise, from Blois to Orleans at the King's whim.

King Henry II greeted her as if she were his daughter. His court welcomed her as a novelty, amused and delighted by her poise, her pride of position and her instant affection for Francis. The ambassadors to France were charmed. Only Catherine de Medici found her "haughty and arrogant, precocious to a degree."

Each year Mary learned to love more deeply the Cardinal and Madame Diane. She missed her mother whose one year's visit to France had seemed painfully brief; but she was not homesick. Scotland was an old gray dream that flickered, half-remembered. A barbarous place, to rule from the safe, sunny distance of Paris or Rouen or Fontainebleau. Some day, she thought, Francis and I will go there to show ourselves to the people and perhaps hunt boar in the Highlands. But France will be our home.

V.

Mary awakened in her canopied bed of pink-and-silver damask. Sunlight fingered the pale brocade window hangings, jeweled the crucifix in the altar niche. Benignly the Virgin in her cold stone robes looked down from a frame of white roses.

[25]

Peering out from the bed curtains Mary saw that her maids of honor were already astir, moving about the great room with under-garments and hose and slippers. Four white-capped beruffled little girls her own age who had come with her from Scotland. They had all been christened Mary in her honor and to avoid confusion she addressed them by their last names.

As she greeted them they turned and curtsied, spreading blossom-colored skirts. Only in name were they alike. Beaton was mischie-vous from red-gold curls to tiny feet, and often had to be chided. Fleming, tall for her age, was a languid blonde already accustomed to admiration from the younger nobles. Seton, also blond, shared Mary's love for play-acting and romantic verse. Long-nosed Living-stone, like a plump mother hen, protected them from their own rash-ness. Pranks were inevitable, but when Livingstone could not prevent them, she took the blame.

Mary swung off the bed in her wide white nightdress and the girls followed her into the dressing room. They helped her into a long-sleeved violet shift, then laced her into a leather corset that covered her from armpits to thighs. "Some day," she gasped, "I shall create a law against this. No corsets—"

"The corset," said a soft voice from the doorway, "must come off. And the shift."

They whirled and sank into deep curtsies as Diane de Poitiers came into the room. As usual she wore white—white in summer, black in winter. A satin robe, falling in classic folds, was clasped at her slender waist with a gold-and-diamond girdle. Crescent moons of diamonds on onyx combs held back her smooth black hair.

"Your Majesty," she accused gently, "has neglected to bathe. Where is the vessel of water, the drying linen?"

Livingstone said, "Your Grace, it is my fault. I forgot."

"Four cannot forget so easily nor so often. It is my wish that Her Majesty bathe in water—*cold* water—every morning."

Mary said, "Your Grace, no one else—"

"I do." Diane seated herself on a carved gilt chair near the win-dow. "Nothing preserves youthfulness like cold water."

Fleming and Seton bowed out of the room for the water while Beaton and Livingstone helped Mary out of the corset. Diane said, "You are unhappy now, but in years to come you will thank me."

"I am sure of that, Madame," Mary said, "but I'll never be beauti-ful as you are."

"Not as I am, no. Your features are not as precise as mine. You lack the patience for perfection. You will laugh and love too much, and emotion creates wrinkles. But I think you will be beautiful like

[26]

a candle that flares magnificently for a short while and then glows steadily."

"I thought you were going to say 'dies.'" Mary laughed, standing in her shift. Beaton brought a shawl and covered her shoulders.

"We need not die early," Diane said, "if we live properly. How old do you think I am?"

Mary knew that she was very old—probably twenty-eight, or even thirty-five like Queen Catherine. Tactfully she asked, "Twenty-six, Madame?"

"Another guess," Diane teased.

Mary studied her. One shoulder, bared in the Grecian style, was satiny smooth—the shoulder of a young girl. Her skin was a fine transparent white, unwrinkled as Mary's own. No paint outlined the rosy lips nor tinted the eyelids. The ink-black hair was shining and luxuriant.

"Twenty-one," Mary said impulsively.

"I am fifty-five."

The three Marys gaped at her. Why, folk were dead at fifty-five! Or wizened, ailing, shivering by the fire. And this lady rode and hunted, swam and played pall-mall better than any at court. It was witchery.

"Do you," Mary gulped, "use a potion?"

"I have told you. Water."

"But there must be something else."

"Rest. I rise early, earlier than you. But after a ride at sunup I sleep until the noon meal. Even if there is a fête I am early abed. I guard my sleep jealously. I avoid the drying sun and exercise only at sunup or sundown. I use no creams nor paints."

"But your hair," Mary said, worshiping, "there isn't a thread of gray, yet you do not tint it?"

"Never. Gray hairs grow with worry, but I allow nothing to disturb me. I indulge neither anger nor grief. It is harmful to weep, but tears refresh the eyes, so each morning with gloved hands I peel an onion close to my face. I never frown. I do not often smile."

"But you smile at me!"

"Sometimes I cannot help it. You are a comic blend of child and woman. You shall wrinkle me yet."

The girls laughed, and Diane's eyes twinkled. Then Seton and Fleming entered with a huge iron pot, followed by maids with vessels of water who filled it and retired.

The bath, Mary knew, was a test of her discipline. Under Diane's commanding eye she moved toward the pot. The Marys watched in dismay as Her Majesty removed her shift and stood like a nymph on the edge of disaster.

[27]

"Puir lass," blurted Seton, lapsing into Scots, "I'm praying for ye."

Mary glanced pleadingly toward Diane but her goddess wore a cold mask. Hurriedly she put one leg, then the other, in the pot and sat down. Her teeth were clenched. She would not squeal.

They gave her soap and scrubbed her back with a rough cloth. Diane sent Beaton to her apartments for scent and when Mary emerged she was rubbed with oil of roses and wrapped in a sheet.

Diane nodded approvingly. "I am pleased. You behaved exceedingly well."

"Oh, thank you, Madame!" A compliment from Diane was rare, thus doubly cherished. Mary's skin tingled. She wanted to throw off the sheet and dance, turn cartwheels. Instead she pulled the sheet more tightly and sat down with dignity on the petit-point hassock.

"I believe Your Majesty will grow up to your colt legs," Diane said. "You will be slender and round, and probably tall. You will have your mother's wide shoulders and her grace."

"I thank—"

"However, Madame de Paroy tells me you overeat. From now on you will ignore gravies and sweet pastries. You may eat all the fruit you like."

"As you wish, Madame." Plague take Madame de Paroy for tattling!

"Rich foods may be responsible for the pain in your side, and for the fainting spells after meals. That, and lacing." Diane turned to the Marys. "Discard that corset—it is not necessary. I myself wear none."

Again they stared at her, at the graceful fluid figure checked only by the diamond girdle. To Mary she said, "I shall see you at the fête tonight. You and the Dauphin may stay up until midnight."

Diane rose and moved to the door. Seton hurried ahead to open it and the girls curtsied deeply.

Mary arranged the sheet so that one arm was bared and strutted to the chair Diane had occupied. "I shall be exactly like her," she said dreamily. "It's my command that you never forget the cold water even if I ask you to. And when I smile or frown you are to correct me immediately."

The Marys nodded, awed.

"Beaton, bring me an onion."

As Beaton scurried off toward the kitchens the others dressed Mary in the shift and two petticoats. Over these went a gown of blue-and-silver brocade, the bell-topped sleeves slashed to reveal the violet silk of the shift. Blue jersey hose were fastened above the knee with gold cord and a rosette. There were white leather shoes, a violet coif for her hair.

"Bring me gloves. And Beaton—the onion."

Clumsily, in the gloves, Mary peeled the onion close to her face and tears dribbled down her cheeks.

Livingstone said hesitantly, "I'm afraid you torture yourself needlessly, Madam. Whatever she may say, Madame Diane's beauty is unnatural. To be so beautiful at fifty-five is a gift of God."

Fleming's hand went to her mouth. "Fifty-five! Jesu! Are you sure?"

"She told us when you were out of the room," Mary said.

Fleming said, "Then she is more than twenty years older than the King—yet he has loved her, they say, for sixteen years."

"That is not true," Mary said. "A husband loves only his wife. Madame Diane is the King's best friend."

"Others say differently . . ."

"Others don't know. The King himself told me that Madame Diane is like his own sister, Madame Margaret. A wise sister, cool-headed where the Queen is emotional. Both have their places."

"I thought Your Majesty disliked the Queen," Seton said.

"I do. She is fearsome. But—she is the Queen, and none of you are to belittle her, do you understand?"

They understood. Royalty defended royalty. Even Emperor Charles of Spain—tyrant and mortal enemy of France—must be spoken of respectfully lest anarchy and Protestantism spread the world over. Kings and Queens ruled by Divine Right, though sometimes God wrought strangely.

"Madame Diane is really the queen of France," Fleming said. "She has more authority than any other lady. She owns the crown jewels, the best horses and falcons, the chateau of Chenonceaux——"

"Fleming! How dare you say such things?"

"Your Majesty frowns."

"Oh! So I do! I have probably started a wrinkle!" Mary ran to the chest and looked into the new glass mirror given her by the Venetian Ambassador. Her brow seemed unmarred but she realized hopelessly that she would never resemble Diane. Her lips were too full, her cheeks too roundly babyish. Tears glistened in her eyes. How absurd, she thought, how comical! The Queen of Scotland peeling an onion!

"Your Majesty laughed," Fleming said.

VI.

After Mass Mary breakfasted in her own apartments, then returned to the chapel for lessons in the Cardinal's study. This morning as she knelt to kiss his ring he patted her cap and said, "I have a surprise for Your Majesty."

She looked at his empty hands, wondering if the surprise was hidden in his robes or somewhere in the somber gray-tapestried room. He said, "Sit down and I will tell you of it."

She sat in the oaken-armed chair across from his desk.

"I have heard from your mother in Edinburgh. She graciously accedes to my request that you be declared of age."

"Of age!" Mary leaned forward. "Of age to marry?"

"No." He smiled. "Of age to make certain decisions regarding Scotland. You are twelve years old. Your mind, in many ways, is mature."

She wanted to jump up, to pirouette in delight. Instead she managed a proper gravity. "I shall do as Your Eminence wishes."

"We must strive for a united Scotland—united against Protestantism. That will be impossible as long as the Earl of Arran remains Regent."

"But he has been Regent since I was born."

"Precisely. Henry VIII placed him in power and bribed him to Protestantism along with the rest of the Scottish Parliament. But Henry has been dead these seven years and the wind begins to blow fair. Mary Tudor, the new English Queen, is strongly Catholic." He pressed the tips of his slender fingers together. "I am told that she is beginning to shed heretic blood."

"So she will not support Arran?"

"She will support none of her father's puppets. So the time seems feasible for us to rid Scotland of Arran and appoint a new Regent."

"My mother!" Mary said quickly.

"An excellent choice. The Regency is her right."

"But what will Arran do? He might be so furious that he'd try to murder my mother!"

"My dear child, you are melodramatic. Arran is a weakling, a mean-spirited oaf. He will be quite satisfied with a French dukedom."

"You would grant him that?"

"The King has decided to create him Duke de Chatelherault, provided Arran will relinquish the Regency without a struggle. And without the help of England he cannot struggle long."

Mary felt very grown-up, very important. "Do you have papers for me to sign, appointing my mother?"

"Not until we have Arran's acceptance of terms. I foresee no difficulties. And now there is another matter to discuss. Your mother agrees with me that you shall have your own establishment. Next week you will move from the children's quarters to a separate wing of the palace. Your Marys, of course, will remain with you. Your other Scots attendants now lodged in the village shall become part of your household."

Again she strove for composure. Her own establishment, removed from Queen Catherine and the nursery down the corridor! "I thank Your Eminence," she said, "with all my heart."

"You have always had precedence over the Valois children but I wish to offer this advice: do not flaunt your new privileges."

"I've never flaunted any."

"I am sure you have not meant to. But for all her goodness and grace Her Majesty Queen Catherine is, shall we say—touchy. She realizes only too keenly that eventually you will usurp her position. If the King dies before she does, you, not she, will be Queen of France. Further, there is her motherly heart to consider. You are taking away her first-born child. In fact, Francis is already your slave, and that must hurt her deeply."

Mary had not thought of it this way. She could feel sorry for Catherine de Medici—almost.

"She loves you dearly," the Cardinal continued, eyes hooded under his long fair lashes, "but with your ascendancy her own star wanes. Remember that and be tactful."

"I shall be." Guiltily she thought of tonight's plan.

"The Duchess de Valentinois (he used Madame Diane's formal name) and I shall continue to advise you. Nothing shall change as regards your education." He rose. Evidently there would be no lesson this morning. "Is there anything you wish to ask?"

"Yes," she said shyly. "Is it possible to kiss one's uncle even though he is a Cardinal? I never have, you know."

He laughed. "You had only to command."

She went to him and he bent to receive her kiss. His cheek was smooth and cool. He smelled of sandalwood, and its fragrance followed her out into the courtyard. Proudly she walked between the privet hedges, feeling her new importance like an invisible cloak. She was beginning to rule at last . . .

After supper, dressed for the Fête of Roses, Mary found Francis alone on the second-floor gallery watching workmen testing the torchlighting of statues in the garden. He wore a white satin doublet over puffed sleeves of gold brocade, and his long trunk hose ended in netherstocks of puffed gold velvet.

"You look splendid," she said. "See? I am dressed as a rose." She whirled so that he could see the leaf-patterned petticoat of vine green under the rose-colored gown. "And my cap is petaled!"

"You're beautiful!" he said.

"I'm not very beautiful yet, but I'm mature." She told him of her talk with the Cardinal. "Imagine—my own establishment!"

Francis was happy for her, as she had known he would be, but wistful. "If only I could get away from my mother too! Next door to the nursery I'm practically her prisoner."

"It isn't forever," she comforted. Then she lowered her voice. "Francis, about our plan for tonight—"

"Plan?" His mouth went slack.

"You have forgotten so soon!" Sometimes when he forgot things she felt an aching loneliness, as though he had journeyed far away from her. "Don't you remember about the trap door in your mother's chamber which I must find?"

"Oh," he said vaguely. "I—what is it I must do, Mary?"

She told him again. "You will stay with your mother in the gardens and somehow keep her there until I join you."

"I don't know," he said dubiously. "When my mother wishes to go somewhere, nobody can stop her."

Mary shrugged. "Well, if you don't want to help me—"

"But I do! I will. Only—Mary, if she catches you she'll put the Evil Eye on you for life."

It was a possibility she had not fully considered. Francis saw her shiver. "You're afraid too," he said triumphantly.

Her chin lifted. "Afraid? I?" She laughed. "Now you are absurd. That is child's talk." She moved haughtily away from him to the next archway, taking care that her skirts did not touch him.

"Mary," he said miserably, "I'm sorry. I didn't mean it. You are very brave—braver than I."

She drummed her fingers on the stone balustrade, touched an azalea blossom in a silver urn.

He crept toward her timidly, placed a hand on her shoulder. "Please forgive me."

Still she did not turn and her shoulder was rigid.

His voice quavered. "I love you so much. You're the only one I have to love."

She turned slightly.

"Without you I would want to die."

She faced him, saw the pain-tightened face, the big head bent on its reedy neck. He was so little, so abject. But her pride had been hurt. No one, not even Francis, could call the Queen of Scotland a coward.

Francis groveled closer, fell on one knee.

She extended her hand for him to kiss, and felt it wet with tears.

VII.

Torches set in pyramids of roses illuminated St. Germain from river to hill. Above the Seine, roses bloomed in fireworks. Red buds sped skyward, bursting against the darkness and hissing down to die in moonlit water. Swan-prowed barges moved slowly through floating petals as players from Paris re-enacted the journey of Antony and Cleopatra down the Nile.

Wearying of the play, the royal family moved up the hill on rose-canopied litters. As they reached the gardens trumpets sounded. The crowd bowed as if bent to a great wind. A path was made to the throne of roses.

Their Majesties mounted the throne—a couch of yellow roses roofed with tinsel of gold. At the King's right, as guest of honor, sat the Venetian Ambassador. At the Queen's left, Mary and Francis shared a love seat of blossoms.

Horse-drawn floats passed in review—a gondola of roses flying the banners of Venice; a French war galley with pink satin sails and a crew of court ladies representing mermaids; tableaux of vine-chained nymphs on Pan's rose bed. A white horse bridled in roses bore the Master of Revels, followed by tumblers and jesters on garlanded mules.

In the Temple of Diana troubadours from Provence serenaded the eyes and lips of Diane de Poitiers. Monsieur Clouet sketched her as she lay on satin pillows in a robe fashioned of white roses. Her black hair, unbound, waved to her knees and her legs were bared to show an anklet of buds. The crescent moon—her symbol in diamonds—hung on a velvet band from her throat. And the troubadours sang of the jealous moon that could not match her beauty.

Couples drifted into the music-haunted shadows of the forest. At the wine fountain servants filled goblets and passed platters of petal-shaped pastries and marchpane. At the palace entrance peasants and beggars peered through iron-latticed gates, sniffing the grease of boars that roasted in the forest pits. Guards impaled bread on spears and tossed it to the mob, laughing as men and dogs tore it to pieces. Kegs of sour red wine were lifted over the gates. The Master of the Household proclaimed the King's bounty and promised largesse at midnight.

The King left his throne to watch a dagger match, and Mary and Francis, free to join the crowd, wandered the gardens as they pleased. Nibbling honeyed rose leaves, they watched the fireworks from the hill, the gypsy wrestlers, the sword-swallower. Diane de Poitiers, as was her custom, retired early, followed by her ladies. Catherine de

Medici with the Venetian Ambassador joined the grave court dances on the terrace.

"Would you like to dance?" Francis asked.

Mary shook her head. "No. I don't feel well." Apprehension made her head ache and chilled her body. She could not enjoy the fête until she had explored the Queen's chamber. "I think I'll go to the palace now." But as she spoke the King was departing and she waited until his litter had passed out of sight. The King might ask why she was leaving and she wanted to avoid questioning.

"Are you going to faint?" Francis asked. "I'll catch you."

"No." She drew him behind a tree and whispered. "Your mother has just stopped dancing and is walking toward the fortune teller's arbor. Go there and wait. Don't let her out of your sight until I return."

As she started toward the palace her four Marys came running behind her but she commanded them to remain. "I shan't need you," she said. "And I'll be back."

She hurried on and was caught in a whirl of maypole dancers, and when she escaped them the young poet Pierre de Chastelard lured her to a bench to read his new sonnet. Ordinarily she would have been flattered that so handsome a lad praised her in verse but now she listened impatiently. No fourteen lines had ever seemed so long.

"It's lovely," she told him. "Now I must—"

"But I cannot capture the magnificence of Your Majesty's eyes. There are no words for your eyes."

"Thank you. But now I must go—"

"To meet a lover," he said morosely.

Even through her impatience she was pleased with him. Chastelard made her feel grown up and his devotion was touching. Guiltily she compared him with Francis. If only Francis had fat blond curls and smooth white skin and a perfect Grecian nose! True, Chastelard was short and slightly knock-kneed but his eyes were wonderful—a dark, tragic blue. He looked precisely as a poet should.

"I have no lover—yet," Mary said. "But I become mistress of my own household next week, so perhaps I'll be allowed one."

"Do let me know," he said gravely.

"I shall." She rose and gave him her hand to kiss. It would be nice to have Chastelard in her household. Lovers added a certain tone. They sat about sighing, writing verses, treasuring one's lace handkerchiefs and occasionally threatening suicide. One rewarded them with plumes and doublets or even a kiss. She must get a lap dog too, and perhaps an African slave or a dwarf like Queen Catherine's. She had asked the Queen about the dwarf, purchased from Holland. "Is he more amusing than other jesters?"

And the Queen had sneered, looking at Francis, "More amusing than most dwarfs."

Mary had wanted to scream, "He's not a dwarf! He's just little and ill-formed!" Instead she had sought to divert Francis by prattling of a trained poodle she had seen. If the Queen could be so cruel to her own son, how must she feel toward Madame Diane, what might she do if given the opportunity?

Mary hurried on toward the palace but was stopped again by obsequious courtiers. Was Her Majesty bored? Retiring early? Ill? She smiled at them and said she wished to change her gown; it was the only excuse she could think of.

Safe in the courtyard, she entered the palace and climbed the staircase to the second floor. Halberdiers guarded the corridor, one at each end. Walking slowly, eyes lowered as though searching for something on the floor, Mary paused by the guard at the Queen's bedchamber.

"Have you found a pearl earring?" she asked.

"No, Your Majesty."

"I have lost one—this morning, I think, when I left the Queen's bedchamber." The fib was a safe one for the guard had been changed at dusk. "Her Majesty gave me the earrings herself and if she finds I have lost one she will be furious."

"I am sorry, Your Majesty. I have not seen it."

Mary pointed to the closed oak door. "I'm sure I was wearing it in there. May I go and look?"

He hesitated. "It is against orders for anyone to enter Her Majesty's apartments."

Mary bent her head. Her shoulders slumped. "I don't know what to do."

"But since it is Your Majesty who asks . . ." He opened the door for her and stood aside.

She thanked him effusively and went in, closing the door behind her. The room smelled of oak polish and a heavy Italian fragrance used by the Queen. The brown velvet bed curtains were drawn back and a stiff brocaded nightdress lay across the spread, so suggestive of a woman's body that Mary caught her breath and stepped back.

From the carved oak chest she picked up a lighted taper in its iron holder and went to the perfume cabinet at a far corner of the room. There she knelt, placing the taper on the floor. Under the cabinet was a length of blue tapestry and she pulled it aside. Her fingers searched an intricate pattern of stone medallions. She pushed with both hands but nothing moved.

There was a sound behind her and she turned, terrified. Then she realized it was only rats scampering in the walls. Again she bent to the floor. One medallion seemed slightly higher than the others and she pressed down on it, but nothing happened. She pried it up with her fingernail and it came loose and rolled on its side. There was a small opening. Faint light came through it and she lay flat on her stomach and put her eye to it.

Below, at an angle, she saw a great bed, its oak headboard shaped like a crescent moon, its white velvet curtains open on one side. Madame Diane lay nude on black satin sheets, arms clasped behind her head. Beside her, in a purple dressing robe a man turned a book toward the flickering taperlight and the murmur of his voice reached Mary faintly. There was no mistaking that voice, nor the massive body nor the curly brown beard. Nor his little white dog, Fleurette, who lay on the end of the bed and nuzzled her master's feet.

Slowly Mary straightened. She sat on the floor with the image of the scene in her mind and tried to adjust to it. Madame Diane brazenly unclothed—and with the King! Her thoughts tangled, piling up on themselves, and her head ached painfully. She could not understand what she had seen, yet it had shocked her. How could Madame Diane, the epitome of propriety, entertain the King in such fashion? Even supposing she had not expected his visit, surely she could have grasped a robe to cover herself! Did his sister Margaret receive him so? Did the Queen?

At thought of the Queen, Mary started to rise but her legs were shaking and she sat down again. Miserably she told herself that she had been mistaken in what she saw—from the ceiling the scene was naturally distorted. But when she lay down again and put her eye to the crevice it was the same, except that Madame Diane had turned on her side and put her head on the King's shoulder. Her eyes stared up at the ceiling, almost as if she could see the peephole, and Mary drew back again. It surprised her that her face was wet. She had not known she was weeping.

The Italian scent in the room seemed heavier and Mary's heart jumped frantically. Someone was close, watching her. She felt the presence as surely as she felt the tears on her cheeks, and a chill ran down between her shoulder blades. She dared not turn.

A voice, husky as a man's, sidled through the silence. "Well, Maria. Have you found a new amusement?"

Only one person called her by the Italian name, spoke the French language with that accent. Slowly Mary turned, afraid to raise her eyes beyond the topaz-embroidered hem of the velvet skirt. For if she looked up into Catherine de Medici's face the Evil Eye would mark her. She would be forever possessed by demons.

Mary was jerked to her feet. She tried to cover her eyes but Catherine pulled her hands away, gripping them in one of her own. With the other hand she slapped Mary across the mouth.

"So the Queen of Scotland is a common spy!"

Mary forgot the danger of those eyes. She looked full into their bulging blackness and spat defiance. "How dare you slap me? How dare you—a merchant's daughter—slap *me?*"

Mary was shouting and Catherine bent suddenly to the perfume cabinet and swiftly replaced the medallion on the floor. "She will hear you!"

"What do I care? You will apologize for your insult or I'll go to the King this minute!"

"You will not go to the King nor anywhere else." But the harsh voice wavered, there was a flicker of uncertainty in the eyes. Catherine sat down stiffly on the bed, sank her thickening chin into the pleats of her ruff. Suddenly her voice turned gentle, fawning through the shadows between them. "Come here, Maria. We must talk quietly."

"I demand an apology!"

"Very well. I am sorry I slapped you."

Mary moved cautiously toward her.

"How did you find the hole in the floor, Maria? Who told you of it?"

When she is sly and still, Mary thought, she is most dangerous. God help me to protect Francis.

"No one told me, Madame. I have lost one of my pearl earrings. I was afraid to tell you. I thought perhaps I had lost it in here— you recall I was admiring your perfumes a few days ago. So I looked under the cabinet and by chance I found the hole."

"And the earring?"

"No, Madame."

"Do you think for a moment I believe such a tale?"

"It's the truth."

"Shall we go to your chamber and look in your jewel chest, Maria?"

"Shall I also tell the King that you think me a liar?"

"No! You certainly will not go to the King."

She is frightened, Mary thought—even more frightened than I. Catherine chewed her thick painted lips and the sallow folds of her skin were moist with sweat. Her hands ground together. "We must talk, Maria. You are old enough to understand certain matters. And if you will tell me the truth I swear I will not punish Francis."

"Francis?" Mary simulated surprise.

"He saw me at the cabinet two nights ago—he must have sus-

[37]

pected something." She leaned forward. "I must know if it was he who told you of it—or someone else."

"It was he who told me," Mary said, and saw the strained shoulders slacken in relief. "But if you dare to break your vow—if you mistreat Francis in any way—I shall go to the King and tell him that you spy on him."

"That is not true. The hole was made years ago when the nursery was below so that I might keep an eye on the babies."

"Yet now you keep an eye on others. Francis saw you."

"And you? What did you see, Maria? The King abed with his slut? What did he give her tonight—my rubies? The pearls he promised me on the birth of the last child? What did he say to her—could you hear? Ah, sometimes when they talk, provinces change hands, titles and castles and blooded horses." Catherine rose from the bed and paced the length of the room and back. Softly she cursed in Italian. "Do you know what they say, Maria? Do you know the court joke? That the King treats Diane as his wife—and that I bear their children. Have you heard that, Maria?"

"No, Madame." Mary watched her, horrified. Catherine's eyes held an insane glitter, and blood ran from her bitten lip. She jerked off her headdress and oily brown hair tangled witchlike about her shoulders. She was panting and her words came in gasps. "Have you heard me called a breed-sow? Good enough to bear a child a year but not fit to sleep with, once the seed is sown?"

"Madame, I must go," Mary said desperately.

Catherine caught her arm as she started for the door. "Do you know what the slut does? *She sends him to me!* They need children for France, so exactly three months after my baby is born she sends him to me for another quick mating—"

"Madame," Mary said miserably, "I won't listen. You shouldn't make me listen—"

"Do you know," said Catherine de Medici, "that he has never kissed me?"

"For shame, Madame! You lose your dignity!"

"What dignity? What is left me? My children?" Catherine smashed her hand down on the oak table. "Six children, all stolen from me at birth—she chooses their christening robes, their nurses, their tutors. She has all the pleasures of motherhood while I stand by and wait to bear a new brat—"

"*Madame!* You had best tell your priest these things; I don't understand them, they are horrible!" Mary shook off Catherine's arm but again the Queen stopped her, and this time her eyes were narrowed to slits.

"You repeat one word of this and I'll have you packed off to Scotland like your aunt—and for the same reason."

"For what reason?"

"Your aunt was immoral. I will discover that you are too—and it will not be difficult to arrange proof. When that becomes apparent, the King will not want you for Francis. No prince in Europe will want you for a wife. Do not underestimate me, Maria. Others have made that error."

And they were dead or disgraced. Mary could name half a dozen of the Queen's enemies who had met with fatal accidents or been executed or exiled.

"If you keep your promise not to hurt Francis, I will say nothing."

"Not even to Francis?" Catherine asked.

"Not even to him."

"Does he know you came here tonight, Maria?"

"No, Madame," she lied.

"And why, precisely, did you come here? I want the truth this time."

"When Francis told me about seeing you under the cabinet I thought perhaps there was a trap door. I wanted to explore it." She tried to smile. "It seemed like an adventure, Madame."

"What you did was treasonable."

"Perhaps, Madame. If that is so, you are guilty too."

"You have a unique way of twisting the facts."

"The King would see them as I do. He would find us equally at fault."

Catherine shook her head wonderingly. "Your wits are sharp. The Cardinal has taught you sophistry. I will teach you fear."

"I do not fear you, Madame," Mary said—and surprisingly it was true. She had seen the Queen's own fear too clearly. She was revolted but unafraid. "I will keep my promise to you just as long as you keep yours to me."

"Very well. But take care, Maria. For all your cleverness you are still a child."

"I am a queen," Mary said. "And so are you—but only by marriage. You are not my equal in royal blood. Remember that, Madame."

She went to the door.

Catherine's voice was heavy with threat. "I shall remember that, Maria."

CHAPTER TWO

I.

IN HER LILAC-AND-SILVER PARLOR Mary embroidered a shift for her trousseau. From the window seat she could see the winter-weary gardens of Fontainebleau, rain flushing dead leaves into the moat. But the dismal weather troubled her far less than the talk she had just had with the Cardinal in his study.

"You are fifteen now, and soon to be wed," the Cardinal had said. "Should an accident befall the King, you and Francis will rule France. Thus you must share the burden of world problems and I shall not minimize them." He unfolded a map of Europe on his desk. "Religious war spreads like a vast bloodstain . . ."

That winter of 1557-58 England's mad Queen Mary Tudor exterminated Protestants, while her husband Philip II purged them from Spain. Torture-crippled refugees crawled into Scotland where Mary of Guise held a tottering Catholic throne. Her nobles, converts to the new religion, plotted to seize power and proclaim a Protestant Scotland. Her lairds feuded among themselves. English hackbuteers massed at Carlisle on orders to burn the Border towns to ash. "Spare no living creature," went Mary Tudor's ultimatum, "neither man, woman nor child."

Scots watching from peel towers saw the English tide moving darkly through the hill passes. Women and children pulled the straw roofing from their huts and piled it in the fields, making giant stacks. The balefires were lit. Ancient warning of English attack, they flamed in the night skies at Kirkcudbright to the west. At Lockerbie on mid-Border. To the east in Alnwick. The signal fires burned northward on the wind, streaking past Glasgow and Edinburgh, sweeping through panicked towns to the far Highlands.

Out of the blazing Borderlands rode the young Earl of Bothwell to champion Mary of Guise. He rallied his men and raised a rabble army. With a knife in his teeth and an axe in his fist he terrorized the English, guerrilla-fashion, in surprise attacks from the hills, intercepting gold bound for the rebels and seizing horses and arms. He smoked traitor Scots from their peel towers and carried their treasure to the Queen. He chased Protestant refugees back into England, and they fled to the dubious safety of France.

France was one-third Protestant but the Cardinal's spies nosed them out of their hiding places in Paris cellars and burned them at the stake. Peasants suspected of heresy were clubbed to death or carted through villages as examples to the people. Others fled to Geneva, where the Scottish preacher John Knox welcomed them into his congregation.

From his pulpit Knox defied the Catholic Church "and the Pope's whores who rule Scotland and England." Mary of Guise had denounced him and ousted him from his church at Berwick. Mary Tudor had banished him from England. His dream of uniting the two countries in Protestantism seemed remote. But he continued his exhortations, his writing. His pamphlets, translated into French, fanned sparks of courage in Huguenot leaders. His words, whispered from Paris to the farthest fields, became action. Cathedrals were sacked, altars toppled and burned. Men spat on holy relics and stamped on the wooden faces of saints. In the names of Luther, Calvin and Knox they smashed the symbols of Catholicism, proclaimed their freedom from superstition. They needed no idols nor images, no intermediary saints nor priests. The path to God was through Christ alone.

This morning the Cardinal had shown Knox's pamphlet to Mary. "I have inked out words too gross for a lady," he said. "Read it and give me your opinion."

She read the pamphlet in his presence, finding it more lunatic than shocking. Knox stripped the symbolic beauty from religion and substituted nothing in its place. His God was vengeful, his Christ so jealous of the saints that he could not endure their images in his churches. Our Lady the Queen of Heaven was ignored. In Knox's own words, "Women are weak, frail, impatient, feeble and foolish ... Queens are repugnant to nature. All queens are thus traitoresses and rebels against God ..."

"Ridiculous!" Mary said. "Who could take such blather seriously? I warrant he will be in a madhouse within the year."

"You cannot dismiss him so blithely. He threatens your very existence and the rights of your future children and their children." The Cardinal tossed the pamphlet in the fire. "But enough of this. Madame Diane will have my head for causing you worry wrinkles."

Now as she stitched her shift she forgot politics and turned to thoughts of her wedding. In three months she would be married. Already workmen were erecting scaffolding to accommodate crowds outside Notre Dame. That gloomy, drafty pile of stone seemed designed for funerals, and she had begged to be married in the Cathedral of Chartres that rose like a shaft of gray lace on the plains of Touraine. But the Cardinal decreed otherwise. There must be the pomp and pageantry of Paris. A royal bride could not be hidden away in a small town like a peasant girl.

But in some ways, Mary thought, peasant girls were more fortunate than queens. Even the humblest had the right to plan the details of her wedding, choose her attire. For three years Mary had visioned her bridal gown—pure white silk, unadorned, angelic. A white velvet robe embroidered in silver thistles entwined with fleurs-de-lis. The crown of Queen-Dauphine would be her only jewel.

But Madame Diane and the Cardinal had wrecked the dream. The simple silk had turned to heavy damask and blazed from throat to hem with pearls, rubies and diamonds. The white robe became blue and the train a solid mass of jeweled embroidery. She thought, I am to be a showcase for the treasures of France, a peacock on display. Mobs will gabble and gape. The most sacred hours of my life will become a fête.

She had hoped at least that her mother would be present but Mary of Guise wrote that it would be impossible. "However, I am sending eight Scottish commissioners—bishops and lords. Among them your half-brother Lord James Stuart, Prior of St. Andrews . . . I trust that you can lure him from his flirtation with Protestantism. In most respects you will find him shrewd, intelligent and possibly valuable . . ."

Mary marveled at her mother's tolerance for the illegitimate James. Long ago her father had had a mistress, Margaret Douglas, who had borne him six children. James, the eldest, had been raised by Margaret and her husband, the Laird of Lochleven. Nicknamed "The Bonniest Bastard," James was said to be a young man of great wit, and Mary was curious about him. Doubtless he used the new religion as an intellectual toy—many young nobles found it fashionable and daring. If she could win him back to the true faith he might be an ideal choice for the Regency—a Stuart to guard the throne at her mother's death.

The thought of death brought back a worry she had kept in the back of her mind. A month ago, in December, Francis had taken his horse from the stables and ridden its heart out. Frantic attendants had found him crumpled on the dead animal in the snowy woods that bordered the road to Soissons. For hours he was unconscious. The last rites were given him. It seemed a miracle when he recovered from chills and high fever.

It was not the first time Francis had ridden recklessly, but the adventures had never before seemed suicidal. Mary found it impossible to lift him out of his depression. Unless commanded by the King he avoided masques and revels and remained secluded in his apartments. When they met, his smile was wan. Several times she had caught him looking at her with such hurt wistfulness that she had turned away, unable to bear his glance. When she questioned him he was evasive.

"Is it your mother?" she asked. "Has she said or done something to upset you?"

"No."

"Do you swear that, Francis?"

"Yes." But he had avoided her eyes. She felt for the first time that Francis had lied to her. Only his mother was capable of inflicting such hurt. His father ignored him, the court held politely aloof. No one really cared about a shy fourteen-year-old boy. Only when he became king would the fawning and flattering begin. Disgustedly she thought, They save their love for his crown.

She threw down her embroidery. She would demand immediate audience with Queen Catherine and get to the root of the matter. During the past three years they had not once been alone; in the presence of others they had maintained a courteous if cool relationship. Only in Catherine's eyes had she detected hostility, a sly watchfulness. But she believed the Queen had kept their bargain—until now.

Summoning Beaton, Mary sent her to the Queen with a note requesting private audience. It seemed impetuous and she regretted it the moment Beaton had left. To ask a favor of Catherine was galling, possibly dangerous. She would have to be very careful.

At the long jewel-framed mirror, a birthday gift from Pope Paul IV, Mary straightened her coif, pulled its peak to the exact center of her forehead. She fluffed her mink-lined sleeves, smoothed the pointed bodice of her green velvet gown. I am no child now, she thought grimly, remembering Catherine's taunt. I am as tall as she.

Slender, fine-boned, she paraded her new stateliness before the mirror. Without egotism she saw the beginning of beauty in her face, its promise in her figure. Though boyishly flat in the hips and chest, she scorned padding as blowsy and inelegant. She outlined her lips with rose salve, her eyelids with smoky kohl. To look older would give her confidence.

Nervously she waited, resuming her embroidery. But she ruined a border and tore out the stitches. The Rouen clock ticked off fifteen minutes.

Beaton returned out of breath. "I'm so sorry, Your Majesty. I was kept waiting in the nursery. The Queen will receive you in her parlor."

The parlor, Mary thought as she entered, reflected Catherine's vulgarity. It was a jangling mixture of mosaics, ivories, tassels, beaded embroidery. The walls were painted with overblown cupids cradled in the fat arms of Venus. Catherine's lap dog waddled from a window nook, smelling of suet and Italian scent.

Catherine sat on a purple velvet love seat, the charts of Nostradamus scattered about her. She nodded to Mary, and indicated the chair opposite. Her attendant withdrew and closed the door.

Still Catherine said nothing. Her heavy-jowled face—like an animal's muzzle, Mary thought—was expressionless. Only the popeyes burned darkly, steadily, under the painted eyebrows. Tightly corseted fat bulged from the sides of her velvet sash.

Mary said, "I've come to ask you about Francis." To her embarrassment her voice cracked childishly. "He behaves so strangely that I worry about him."

"He has always behaved strangely," Catherine said.

"He seems hurt."

Catherine shrugged. "He is your responsibility."

"Not yet," Mary said. "He still remains in Your Majesty's charge. You have never permitted him freedom—his apartments adjoin your own."

"What is it you hint—that I have hurt him?"

"I am only wondering, Madame."

"Why don't you ask Francis?"

"I have—he won't tell me. He must be afraid to. Have you broken your sworn vow?"

"If you come to me with questions you may learn an unpleasant truth."

"Whatever it is, I must know. I must help him."

"Already the devoted wife!" Catherine flipped her pudgy hands in mock astonishment. "Such unselfishness in one so young is touching."

"Please, Madame, there is no cause for levity. You are his mother —I shall be his wife. Surely if you know what troubles him you will tell me."

"Is it not apparent?"

Mary shook her head. "Not to me."

"Then you are obtuse. He rides off by himself in the hope of death. He survives, but is greatly depressed." Catherine smiled. "I have seen you following him about as he used to follow you— pestering him with questions. That's no way to rekindle love, Maria. You'd best let him alone."

"Rekindle . . . but he loves me! I've never doubted that."

"Consider carefully, Maria. How long has it been since his ride?"

"A month."

"And on what day did that occur?"

"December ninth—the day after my birthday."

"And what happened on your birthday?"

"Our marriage was announced. But I don't see—"

"Don't you?" Catherine polished her rings on the palm of her hand. "Does a boy in love try to kill himself the day after his wedding date is set?"

"But he *is* in love with me; we have always been in love. Why, in the autumn he was as happy as I, making plans and . . ." Mary struggled to keep the tears from her eyes, her voice. "Are you trying to tell me that Francis loves someone else?"

"Doubtless he finds you priggish. God knows you keep men at a distance."

"And you know why! If I flirted with anyone, you would delight in misconstruing it. You'd twist the most innocent word or look to vileness."

"Considering the immorality in your family—"

"I shall not brawl with you, Madame. Talk of family ill becomes you. I'm concerned only with Francis and how to help him. I can't believe he loves someone else. But if he does I'll release him from his pledge."

"A noble sentiment! I myself should like nothing better. But the King and the Cardinal are set on this marriage. If Francis has a dozen mistresses, you will still be his wife."

"Mistresses!"

"He is fourteen. My husband was scarce older than that when Madame de Poitiers snatched him from nursery to boudoir. Perhaps she is equally generous to Francis."

"No! I shan't listen—"

"After all, Madame de Poitiers always has an eye to the future. My husband will not live forever. As the next King of France, Francis would be her obvious choice."

With the salt of illness in her mouth Mary rushed to the door, opened it, fled across the corridor and out onto the long arcaded gallery. Standing in the shelter of an archway she took deep breaths of cold air. Rain beat down on the stone balustrade. In the courtyard below, the fountain was spilling over and she watched as though it were important, centering all her attention on the drowning stone cherubs. She began to shiver; she wore no cloak. Like a sleepwalker she moved to the end of the gallery, turned into the corridor and down the flight of stairs to her own apartments.

Seton and Livingstone jumped up from hearth cushions as Mary came into her parlor, and Beaton turned from the book cabinet to regard her curiously. She hurried past them to the window and stood with her back to them. They must not see her face until she had calmed it. A queen must be disciplined. One wept in private or screamed in one's pillow but never in the presence of others.

Mary turned and said, "Light the tapers."

Seton brought a spill from the fire and lighted the wall candelabra. Beaton said, "Your Majesty is so pale. Have you seen a spookie?"

A Scots word in a French phrase had always amused Mary. They expect me to laugh, she thought. Obediently she set a smile on her lips. "No spookie."

"Fleming saw one—" Seton began, then put her hand to her mouth as Livingstone looked at her warningly.

Mary intercepted the look. "Fleming saw what?"

"Nothing, Madam. Just a shadow on the wall—a guard probably. Torches sometimes carry a shadow along a corridor before one sees the man . . . Would you care for some hot wine?"

"No. Where was this shadow seen, and when?"

"Last night, on the first stair landing. But it was nothing."

"Send Fleming to me."

Down through the years the Stuarts had whispered the dark omens that presaged disaster. James I and James III had seen a blood-red hand in an armored sleeve the day before they were murdered. James II had seen it and died in battle. The vision had come to Mary's grandfather before Flodden, to her father at Falkland. It would come to her too, she thought. If not now, later.

Fleming, under Livingstone's stern eye, insisted that it meant nothing. "A shadow can frighten one, Madam. Besides, last night I was quite tipsy on Bordeaux."

"You are never tipsy. Was the shadow of a man—or part of a man?"

"An entire man, Madam." Fleming smothered a giggle and dug her mouth deep into her high-spreading ruff. The Marys began to snicker, and to her astonishment Mary joined them, knowing her laughter was half-hysterical, uncaring that tears poured down her cheeks. She clung to the bedpost, hiding her face against it until her vision began to darken. Swaying, she felt soft bodies break her fall . . .

She opened her eyes to the delicately painted ceiling, to the familiar lilac-and-silver wall draperies. She lay on the floor, a cushion under her head. Seton held a vinegar cloth to her nose, and Livingstone and Beaton were chafing her hands.

"Thank God," Fleming said, kneeling beside her.

Mary raised up on one elbow. "You remembered your promise?" she asked them.

They nodded. The physician was not to know of these fainting spells that came seemingly without reason. Mary might be happy or morose, wise or unwise in eating—the spells continued. Sometimes once, sometimes four or five times weekly. She found them a mystery.

"We have promised," Livingstone said, "but don't you think you should see Queen Catherine's new Florentine physician? He might be able to do something. A new herb—"

"He would be like all the rest. I have nearly retched to death on medicines, and the bleeding only weakens me."

Fleming said, "But Madam, when you faint we are terrified. We could never forgive ourselves if—"

"I know that I place a grave responsibility on you," Mary said, "but among my papers in that onyx casket on the chest there is a note absolving you of blame in case of my death."

She rose and moved to the window seat, smiling at the tear that rolled down Livingstone's long nose. "Livvy, I shall plague you for years yet. The fainting worries you far more than it does me."

"We love Your Majesty far more than you love yourself."

"Not more than I love you." Mary stretched out her arms and the four girls came to embrace her. Don't change, she begged them silently. Don't ever change . . .

II.

For others had changed. Mary's time of worshiping was over. Never again would Madame Diane be quite a goddess nor the Cardinal God. She had seen them both too clearly. One on black satin sheets; the other at a blaze reeking of Protestant flesh.

The scene in Diane's bedchamber three years ago had softened with time and understanding. Mary could even think of it as vaguely romantic. It could be rationalized, dignified. The King and Madame Diane resembled Launcelot and Guinevere, Tristram and Iseult. Their relationship was sinful of course, but elegantly so.

The Cardinal she could not forgive, though she tried nightly in prayer. She had scarcely been able to look at him since October. Four Protestants caught inciting a mob in Orléans had been dragged to the palace and tied to stakes in the courtyard. Faggots were piled on mounds of dead leaves. The Cardinal demanded Mary's presence on the balcony beside him. She had not failed the test of discipline, had not cringed nor hidden her eyes. She had watched the poor writhing wretches, then turned to her uncle for a moment's respite. "How long must I stay?" she asked him.

But he did not hear her. From his vestments he brought a lacy handkerchief scented with sandalwood and held it to his nose. Suddenly he leaned forward, laughing, and she followed his gaze. A Protestant was dancing grotesquely on one charred leg. The other had burned away.

Mary fainted. Guards carried her to her apartments and the Cardinal followed soon after to reprimand her for her squeamishness. She told him the truth. "It was Your Eminence that sickened me. You laughed!"

"I was amused. But I cannot condone your behavior. Such display of emotion is vulgar."

She turned away. God would have wept—even for Protestants.

Mary tried to put the incident from her mind, but it returned as nightmare. Timidly she told Madame Diane what had happened, but was met with frosty silence—a hint that the Cardinal was above criticism. Francis seemed genuinely puzzled by her attitude. "It was not amusing to you," he said, "but it was to His Eminence. It's like a jest, appealing to some but not to others. Why should you be so upset?"

It was impossible to explain to him. He would laugh if she said, "Because I had thought of the Cardinal as God."

God did not torture—and assuredly God did not lust. One dawn as Mary approached the Cardinal's study on an unscheduled visit, the door opened suddenly and a court lady came out, her hair down her back, a fur cloak barely concealing her nightrobe. She looked at Mary, gasped, curtsied and fled. A penitent, Mary thought, who had needed prayer in the night. But when she entered the Cardinal's study he was rubbing paint from his face and the couch was littered with golden hairpins.

She did not cease to love him, but she ceased to adore. He was no longer infallible. The more bitterly he branded Protestants, the more tolerant she became. But she kept her thoughts to herself, and there was little time for brooding. She met the ambassadors to France, the papal representatives. She sat in Justice Court. There were Scottish affairs to discuss; her mother as Regent was placing Frenchmen in important posts and the Scots Lords were resentful. Mary softened their anger with notes explaining the political value of French friendship. She learned to pacify without promises.

The King asked Mary to attend his audiences. Her relations with him had always been amiable, but only of late had he honored her in private conference. "We are molding you to French dimensions," he told her. "You will be both king and queen."

"I—king? What do you mean, Sire?"

"My son is a dullard. He will be of no help to you. God knows we have tried to create a brain from wood. Your wits must serve two." He tried in his heavy-humored way to make a jest. "Francis favors his mother."

"The Queen is shrewd," Mary said carefully, "and Your Majesty is the world's greatest ruler. If Francis and I fail it will not be for lack of inspiration."

He shook his massive head. "Only divine inspiration will help you. But—" He struggled out of his gloom—"whatever the future brings we shall give you happiness now. Your frivolity is our pleasure— and command."

Thereafter, Mary was invited to all the King's revels, to his hunting parties and intimate suppers. Usually sullen and introspective, he brightened in her company. She polished his clumsy jests to wit, encouraged his timid attempts at play-acting, introduced new ideas for masques. In the coolly elegant aura of Diane de Poitiers he had never known genuine, uninhibited gaiety. Mary was not afraid to smile.

The watching court, jaded by sophistication, suddenly discovered the charms of innocence. Voluptuous beauties studied Mary and paid her the compliment of imitation. Bosoms were bound, hips flattened, stilt-shoes worn to lend an illusion of slender height. Farthingales were discarded as figure-thickening and narrower skirts were adopted. Mary's demure heart-shaped caps that came to a point between her eyebrows became the rage. On cold winter nights Scottish tartans shawled bare shoulders, and Highland dress was worn on hunts.

Mary danced through the heavy syrup of flattery in satin slippers. But she avoided flirtatious entanglements. Chastelard pleaded in vain for a stroll in the gardens, a ride in the forest. Young noblemen found her enchanting—but never alone. She kept her Marys around her like a bouquet, and she dreamed vicariously through their amorous adventures. Sometimes in bed after an evening's revel she thought of one man's eyes or lips, another's words. She was curious enough to ask the more sophisticated Fleming a great many questions but not curious enough to find her own answers. A queen—especially a queen betrothed—could not risk the slightest impropriety. She would not forget Catherine's warning. She could not ignore Francis' humble, adoring eyes.

For Francis was defenseless. He had no weapons against her attraction of other men. He could not write her poems nor compliment her on the lute. No matter how splendidly he dressed he always looked awkward—big-headed, puffy-faced, thin-necked, with narrow sloping shoulders and spindly legs. But she did not find him ugly. If the little brown button eyes were dull, they were spaniel-soft for her. The loose-lipped mouth spoke only kindness. Francis was worth a hundred pretty lads.

Queen Catherine did not shake her faith in him. Not for a moment did Mary believe Francis had a mistress or that Madame Diane had designs on him. The idea was preposterous. Instead of running from the Queen's apartments she should have laughed, ridiculed the lie.

For surely it was a lie. Francis loved her. His avoidance of her was only because of ill health. The shock of his accident had naturally depressed him. But perhaps Catherine was right about one matter —she should not follow him about or plague him with questions. He would come to her.

But he didn't. He sat in his apartments close to the fire, maneuvering his toy soldiers on endless campaigns. He hung about the stables with the grooms, eying the horses he was forbidden to ride. At banquets and balls he gave Mary his arm and his sad little smile. But not his confidence.

Her own confidence reached its lowest ebb. She moved through the brilliant prenuptial entertainments as mechanically as she rehearsed her part in the wedding ceremony. Public appearances were less difficult than the moments alone with her Marys. Their affection weakened her self-control. Four pairs of eyes watched her wistfully, ready to weep with her, crinkle in laughter, or harden in indignation. But she resisted the temptation to confide in them. Not only would it be unqueenly; it would serve no purpose. Only Francis could reassure her.

On a dark February afternoon, while Mary was being fitted for trousseau gowns, a page announced the arrival of the Scottish commissioners. Mary dismissed the embroidering nuns and seamstresses, and sent Seton to request Lord James Stuart in private audience.

Perhaps, she thought as she waited for him in her parlor, she should have received the eight commissioners together—Archbishop, Bishop and noblemen. Doubtless the Cardinal would chide her but she did not care. James Stuart might be misguided by the new religion, but he was her half-brother. The same proud blood beat in them both. She felt desperately in need of a friend in whom she could confide. Perhaps she could even tell James about Francis and ask his advice.

She dismissed her Marys, poured glasses of wine. She must put James at ease, show him she was his sister as well as his Queen. When she heard footsteps approaching along the corridor she ran to the door, her hands outstretched in welcome.

III.

In some ways, Mary thought, James resembled a portrait of her father. At twenty-six, he had the same long sleepy-lidded eyes, the passionate mouth with its full underlip. But her father's face had been delicate and merry. James's was strong, sensuous, intensely grave. A sparse beard curled darkly against pallid skin, and she saw that his eyes were green as a cat's. A strange face, she thought, noble yet sinister. So might Lucifer have looked after his fall.

Douglas of Lochleven had raised him well, Mary decided. His French was fluent, unmarred by a Scots accent. He had a courtier's grace of expression, a suavity unusual among the Scots nobility. Her concern over putting him at ease proved unnecessary. Evidently his illegitimacy was a source of pride rather than embarrassment. In the chair across from her his slim body was relaxed, his eyes bright and watchful under the heavy lids.

Mary served him wine. They talked of his journey, the health of her mother, plans for Mary's coming marriage. James said Edinburgh would observe the event by the firing of cannon from Castle Rock on her wedding day. There would be bonfires from Dumfries to Inverness.

"And entertainments?" she asked. "Dancing, feasts?"

"The people will celebrate according to their means, Madam."

She sensed reproof. "It costs nothing to dance, to sing."

"No," he agreed, "but the people are not wholly in favor of the French alliance."

"Then what do they want? God knows Scotland cannot survive without outside help."

James said nothing. As he lifted his wine glass she noticed his ruby-heavy fingers, the jeweled border of his sleeve. His padded doublet was somber black damask, but richly brocaded. Heavy jade chains hung from his neck.

"You are a prior," she said, "but you do not wear your robes."

"No, Madam, because the Priory of St. Andrews is merely an honorary office inherited from our father. Were it not for the revenues it brings me, I would gladly relinquish it."

"For what?"

"For the Earldom of Moray."

She smiled. "The richest earldom in Scotland! You are ambitious!"

"Would Your Majesty wish me otherwise?"

"No," she said. "But regarding religion I would prefer you otherwise for I hear you flirt with Protestantism."

"The flirtation ended months ago. I have wed it."

She stared at him, shocked. "You are a follower of John Knox?"

"Yes, Madam."

"You would destroy the faith of your father—and your Queen?"

"Not through violence. I differ with Knox on that score. The smashing of altars is a wasteful business—gold and sculpture tossed to a mob does nobody good. The murder of priests only creates martyrs. I believe Catholicism will die of itself like a gouty man bloated with years of self-indulgence. It has nothing to offer the intellectual and is too expensive for the rabble."

"But you would not outlaw it?" Sarcastically she added, "You would be generous enough to allow me my Mass?"

"Of course, I would defend Your Majesty's right to Mass. But I would not like to see your personal faith thrust down the gagging throats of your subjects."

"My lord! You forget yourself."

"My apologies. I assumed Your Majesty wished me to speak frankly."

He had placed her in the wrong, and she wriggled uncomfortably. "Is my mother aware of your views?"

"Yes, Madam. She knows that I do my utmost to prevent bloodshed and destruction of holy property. She would tell you there is no man more loyal to the Crown."

"Except," Mary blurted, "the Earl of Bothwell."

His pale cheeks flushed and his body tensed. "Bothwell is depraved, an opportunist, an adventurer."

"Indeed he came to my mother's aid at an opportune moment—to defend her almost single-handedly against her enemies."

He shrugged. "He is most unpopular in Scotland, Madam."

"He would be unpopular in traitorous circles," she said angrily.

Hatred ran darkly in his eyes, flicked down a corner of his mouth and was gone. Expressionless he said, "I have offended you. I am sorry."

"You may criticize my faith," she said. "You may defend your own. But you may not in my presence belittle the only man who has truly served me and my mother. Lord Bothwell has my respect and my gratitude."

From his chair he made an ironic little bow.

Mary rose and went to him. He stood, slender as she, only slightly taller. Impulsively she put her hand on his shoulder.

"Forgive me if I am harsh, but we differ so greatly." She strained hard for tolerance. "Of course your religion is *fashionable*."

Embarrassed by his silence she added, "I suppose my religion appalls you too."

His voice was cool, clipped. "I should not dream of criticizing Your Majesty."

"Come," she said, "it is our first meeting and I have not yet seen you smile!"

His smile did not reach his eyes.

"We must talk again soon," she said, dismissing him.

"I thank Your Majesty for receiving me," he said stiffly.

As he bowed backward to the door she thought, I welcomed him as a brother but he leaves me as an enemy.

IV.

No Dauphin had been married on French soil for more than two hundred years and the Cardinal of Lorraine took full advantage of international interest. He would dazzle Protestant eyes with a blaze of Catholic pageantry, show the world how the French-Scottish alliance would block the march of the Reformation. The peasants, starved for bread and lentils, would eat figs and cream. Mobs would drink free wine under the bannered spires of Paris.

Paris swarmed with workmen hammering pavilions, theaters, vending booths. Goldsmiths, armorers and jewelers worked throughout the gusty nights of March, and candles burned until dawn in the shops of wigmakers and dressmakers. The Palace of the Louvre was scoured and newly tapestried for the ceremony of handfasting— the private betrothal ceremony that preceded the public wedding. Cartloads of flowers were brought in from the fields, waxed, and sewn to satin ribbons to flutter from balconies. In the great square at the Place du Parvis facing Notre Dame rose an open pavilion of blue Cyprus silk spangled with fleurs-de-lis. Over the cobblestones stretched a giant blue carpet stamped with gold.

Fontainebleau was crowded with royal visitors and the Pope's ambassadors from Rome. The court slept by day and danced the nights through. Wedding gifts piled up in palace storerooms—the treasures of Catholic Europe boxed in ivory, ebony and mother-of-pearl.

Mary and Francis were never alone. She could not penetrate his indifference. He was publicly attentive, obedient to his duties. Congratulated on the beauty of his bride-to-be, he mumbled polite agreement. He helped Mary from cushions, onto horses, down flights of stairs, into litters. They moved correctly into the pink-petaled days of early April, weighted with honors and misery.

Mary could see his misery, though apparently the court did not. Sometimes she thought it was akin to embarrassment. Aware of her glance, he would redden and become suddenly busy with wrist frills or buttons. At other times he stared into some private grief, chin buried in the pleats of his ruff. The antics of jesters and trained dogs brought only a wan smile. Mary longed to comfort him. She would have set her pride aside, but to pursue him was to risk the notice and the speculation of the court. She dared not make their estrangement conspicuous.

As the day of handfasting approached she grew panicky. Toward the end of an evening's masque, standing beside Francis in the Salle du Bal, she whispered, "Meet me under the oak near the stables." Her mouth smiled, but her eyes pleaded through the little mask of black Brussels lace. "It's important."

She thought he had not heard her for he said nothing.

"Francis, I *must* see you alone."

His voice was reluctant. "Very well—the oak."

Mary hurried to her chamber for a cloak, evaded the questions of the Marys and, still masked, slipped out through the courtyard past the guards. She did not care if they recognized her—no gossip could hurt her as these past weeks had hurt her. She walked beyond the torchlit gardens into the green-black of the woods. Marble statues loomed up in ghostly whiteness along the path. The stars were faint between scudding clouds.

Francis waited under the spread of the great oak, his face muffled in the folds of his cloak. "What is it?" he asked. "Is anything amiss?"

"That's what I must know," she said. "What has happened to you? Have I offended you?"

He spoke on a sigh. "No. You asked me that before. I told you it is nothing."

"Are you ill? Are you concealing some illness?"

"No."

She put her hand on his arm. "You force me to lose all dignity, you make me plead. If you no longer love me I have a right to know before the handfasting."

Francis pulled away from her. "Why do you say you love me? Because they tell you to? Because I'll be King some day?"

She gasped. "How can you doubt me? What have I done?"

"Nothing. But you've had other proposals—dozens. It would be better for you to marry someone else. The King of Denmark—"

"Francis! Do you love someone else?"

"No." His voice was choked. "I love you. I don't love anyone else in the world. Only I'm—not worthy of you. I see other men, I hear them talk, and I know I'm not like them."

"Thank God," she said. She grasped his hand and held it tightly, then brought it to her lips. "What do I care about other men? They mean nothing."

Francis turned his face away.

"If you were a cobbler, a peasant, I'd marry you! I'd marry you even if you were Protestant!"

She could not make him smile, but for the moment her own relief was sufficient. When they were married she would prove her devotion, and once away from his mother he would change and turn merry. As they walked back to the palace she chattered as she had longed to, sharing her excitement about wedding gifts and trousseau. "Wait until you see my nightcaps—one has a tassel on top. I've shoes with pearl heels . . . a nightrobe embroidered with butterflies, the nuns say it is shocking . . . Oh Francis, we will be so happy!"

In the shadows of the courtyard he kissed her hand, smiled his pinched little smile and said, "I must go in, Mary. My mother will wonder where I've been."

"In two weeks," she said, "your mother will not matter."

V.

On the morning of April 24, 1558, Paris scuffled for space in the square of Notre Dame. People leaned from the windows of the Hotel de Ville, from balconies and turrets and scaffoldings to watch the arrival of the bridal party. First came musicians in crimson-and-yellow uniforms with trumpets, bass viols and flageolets. Two hundred of the King's cavaliers rode behind them, followed by the princes, princesses and their attendants. On white palfreys came bishops and abbots holding their miters and crosiers; the Cardinal of Lorraine and the high-capped papal legate—archbishops and priests bearing great golden crosses.

Francis, his narrow shoulders heavy with ermine, shuffled slowly between his two young brothers and the King of Navarre. The mob shouted to hoarseness, then hushed in awe as Mary Stuart appeared with the King at her side.

Sunlight sheathed her in flame from golden shoe buckles to the great coronet of sapphires, rubies, pearls, emeralds and diamonds. A diamond necklace circled her throat and her blue velvet robe glittered with diamond-and-silver lilies. Four little girls staggered under the massed jewels of her six-yard train. Plodding under the weight of her magnificence, Mary held her head high so that the crown, too large for her, would not slip down over her eyes. The muscles of her neck ached from the strain. Her body was soaked with sweat under the layers of damask and velvet, the ground-sweeping ermine sleeves. But she could bear the sharp fire of the sun, the momentary discomfort. All of her life had been channeled toward this moment, this first long step to power. Proudly, eagerly, she walked toward the entrance of Notre Dame.

The mob broke its silence in a roar of delight, pelting blossoms, blowing kisses from grubby fingers. Mary had dreaded the mob, but now she felt the intoxication of its approval. Women fell to their knees, blessing her. A man shouted, "An angel passes!" She felt the sting of tears against her eyelids. She would be worthy of their love; she longed to tell them so.

Behind her walked Catherine de Medici in stiff yellow brocade, with the Prince de Condé. Then Madame Margaret, the King's sister. Diane de Poitiers in pearl-embroidered white satin, a little pearl cap on her dark hair. They led a parade of ladies that stretched clear to the Bishop's palace. Last came Lord James Stuart, the Scottish commissioners and their attendants with a skirl of bagpipes.

At the church door the Archbishop of Rouen slipped the King's jeweled ring on Mary's finger, blessing it as Francis placed his limp hand in hers. Then they moved to the open pavilion of blue silk. In the beating sun Mary felt faint and the ceremony seemed interminable. Gratefully she followed the Archbishop into the cool stone of the cathedral, where nobles and magistrates had waited since dawn.

Mary and Francis walked a gold-cloth path to the sanctuary. Incense puffed from braziers under the great petals of stained glass, and the air was heavy with thousands of lilies. Fighting dizziness, Mary bore herself rigidly through Solemn High Mass. The tapers of the choir boys, like fireflies in the far darkness, blurred alarmingly. She forced her eyes wide, set her teeth and prayed for strength.

Finally she spoke to Francis the gracious little phrase she had planned. "I salute you, my beloved husband—King of Scotland."

She sensed rather than heard a stir among her countrymen. Francis was only King-Consort. But she wished to think of him as King of her land, and she saw pleasure and surprise in the timid brown eyes. Later she would grant him the Crown Matrimonial.

Trumpets sounded. The ceremony was over and Mary Stuart was Queen-Dauphine of France. The wedding party left the cathedral for the Bishop's palace. As the procession passed out of sight, heralds on the cathedral porch threw gold down to the mob. In the scramble for coins children were trampled, women kicked to their knees. Men fought with fists and drew daggers. The screaming mob panicked, pushing futilely against its own tight-packed weight, moving in a ghastly embrace. Some pleaded with the heralds to stop the flow of gold lest they perish. But their voices were lost in the stomping, shouting terror of five thousand.

From her litter Mary heard the anguished roar behind them and

turned to the Cardinal beside her. "What is it? What is happening?"
"Gold lust," he smiled. "A disease of the rabble."

For hours the bridal party feasted and danced in the Bishop's palace. Late in the afternoon they journeyed on open litters to the Palais de Justice where Duke François de Guise had arranged supper and pageants. The excitement that had sustained Mary through the long ceremonies had dulled to exhaustion. Dutifully she danced in slippers that seemed leaden, ate the fantastically beautiful food, drank from a goblet of pearls. Through two hours of hot taperlight she watched the Procession of the Seven Planets, the march of wicker hobby-horses bearing the young princes, a pageant of ships. Each miniature gold ship, satin-sailed and propelled by a hidden mechanism, voyaged the polished floor, and each carried a royal passenger. The King, as his ship approached Mary's table, extended his hand and drew her aboard. To the soft music of harps and cithers the fleet sailed the vast hall and came to port at the open windows that faced the Seine.

The King helped Mary out of the ship and she swayed, dizzy from its motion. For a moment she leaned out to look at the river where fireworks streaked comet tails of gold. With an enormous effort of will she turned to the King, smiled and started the long parade back to her table, her head held painfully high.

She was conscious of a thousand eyes—eyes so easily escaped. She had only to crumple, sink to the shining floor and the dark velvet of unconsciousness . . .

Eyes . . . She saw the black eyes of Catherine de Medici veiling their hatred, then widening in triumph. Catherine knows, Mary thought. She expects me to sprawl, disgracing myself before the most illustrious company in Europe.

Mary's hands clenched so tightly that the great jeweled ring cut into her palm and she felt the trickle of blood. She moved toward Catherine, passed her, sat down between the high, antlered candelabra at her table.

The crown toppled her head forward. The muscles of her neck corded, rigid in pain. For fifteen hours she had worn the crown, battling it back from her eyes.

Deliberately, with both hands she removed it and blood from her palm spilled down her arm into the ermine sleeve.

VI.

At the Palace des Tournelles, in a bedchamber hung with white pearled brocade, Mary awaited her bridegroom. She sat on the edge

[57]

of the satin-sheeted bed, willing herself to wakefulness. The piled pillows, stamped with the crests of France and Scotland, tempted her aching head. But Francis must find her awake and attentive.

She forced her eyelids open and walked to the window. Fireworks still sparked the paling night sky—the wedding celebrations would last fifteen days. But tomorrow she and Francis would escape to the chateau in Villiers-Cotterets for a month of country peace. She would sleep at least a week.

Again she eyed the bed. If she stole a nap Francis was sure to catch her and perhaps be offended. She wondered what could be delaying him in his apartments. It was over an hour since her Marys had brought her bath and dressed her in the white transparent gown of gauze. Baring her shoulders, it fell in a long train of embroidered lilies. A fragrant lily was tucked in her hair, which waved unbound to her hips.

There was a timid knock on the door and Francis, dismissing his taper-bearers, came in and closed the door behind him. He was pale, she thought, pale as his white damask robe. He looked everywhere but at her—at the bed with its jeweled headboard, at the lily-massed table set with wine and cakes.

"They have thought of everything," he said.

"Yes." She moved toward him from the window. "Will you take wine?"

"No." He went to the bed and sat down, removing his white sandals. "I am very tired, Mary. Couldn't we sleep a few hours? No one need know."

"I wish we could, but we dare not risk it. Nothing escapes the Cardinal." She blushed. "You know the custom at dawn."

"Oh." He played with the fringe on the bed curtain and she stood, miserably embarrassed, at the end of the bed. Not once had he raised his eyes and looked at her.

"Francis," she said finally, "I am as weary as you. But it is our wedding night. Didn't the Cardinal explain to you what is expected of us?"

He nodded.

"We cannot lie to the Cardinal from a bed blessed with holy water. At least," she said, "I cannot."

"Since you feel it your duty," he said stiffly, "you had best come here."

He looked at her then and caught his breath, and his eyes turned soft with wonder. In the dim taperlight he rose to meet her, took her hands in his and kissed each slender finger. Clumsily he pulled her into his arms. She bent her head and kissed his lips. Together they trembled, moved shyly to the bed.

As Francis blew out the tapers and pulled the curtains around the bed, Mary removed her gown and slid under the satin sheets. She heard the rustle of his robe as it fell to the floor. In sudden terror she lay rigid. *It is Francis,* she told herself. *Francis, your husband, whom you love.*

Nine years of love for him unrolled like a spool in her mind. Francis in a tiny suit of armor wearing her colors in a mock tournament at Chinon. Francis, aged eight, to the English Ambassador: "No one is so beautiful as the Queen of Scots." They had embraced, as puppies cuddle; kissed as playmates. They had clung together through years of secrets, two against the grownup world. But never a love like this. Never his kiss on her mouth, never his arms, never a thought of this. . . .

This was not love, she knew. For her it was an utter collapse of dignity, and the threat of pain; for him a blundering frenzy. For both, panic. Instinctively she tried to relax, but her body seemed paralyzed. Suddenly she felt his tears spill down her neck and he moved, sobbing, to the far side of the bed.

"Francis . . ." She groped toward him. "What is it?"

He pressed his face into the pillow, but she heard the shuddering sobs. She turned on her side and put her hand on his shoulder. "Are you ill? Have I offended . . . won't you tell me?"

"I tried to." His voice was muffled and she strained to hear him. "I tried to warn you."

"Warn me? I don't understand. What has happened?"

He cursed. "Nothing! Nothing has happened. I cannot give you a child, Mary. It is impossible!"

"But why? Is there something wrong with me? If there is I didn't know—my physician didn't tell me—"

"My mother told me years ago," he said. A torrent of words poured out with his tears. "I've known since I was eleven, twelve. But I wasn't sure until last year when I lay with a serving wench. It was the same with a dancer in Paris, a girl in Chantilly. I could do nothing; my mother was right all along. Second sight, magic, whatever it is, she knows. Long ago she told me I would be incapable, impotent. And it is true."

"Then—" Mary felt the plunge of her heart—"we can never have children?"

"Never."

Her heart seemed to stop beating and she thought, I might as well die if I cannot justify my life. Never to have heirs . . . the throne of Scotland to pass from the Stuarts to the weakling Protestant Arrans. The Valois line barren until Francis' death. The shame seemed too great to bear.

Francis sat up, wiping his eyes. "Can you understand, Mary? I tried to tell you, but I couldn't. Besides, my mother said if I ever told anyone she would kill me. She said my brother Charles would make a much better king than I and she would welcome the chance to get rid of me."

"She said that? When?"

"Two years ago."

So the Queen had broken her sacred vow, Mary thought. She had been naïve to expect otherwise. For only Catherine's façade was royal. Lower than a peasant, she was an animal, plucking and tearing. "She has put a curse on you," Mary said.

"I should have told you. Can you ever forgive me? I'm stupid—I know it. I'm ugly. I'm not even a man."

Angrily she turned over, flinging aside her hair. "How can you debase yourself? You are Dauphin of France. You are a Valois. You will be King. And you are my husband, King-Consort of Scotland. You should be proud! Instead you whimper."

"Mary—"

"Never again come crying to me. It is not your fault you are unlike other men—your mother has cursed you. But we will not bend to her. Not once, by the flicker of an eyelash, will we show her that she has hurt us." She raised up on one elbow and cupped his chin in her hand. "A moment ago I wanted to die. Now I want to live if only to show her that we are one, that she cannot wreck us in this or anything else . . ."

They heard footsteps in the corridor and Mary lay back on the pillows, pulling Francis down beside her. Hastily he dragged the covers over him. There was a tap on the door, a long pause. Slowly the door opened and the Cardinal of Lorraine and the Archbishop of Glasgow tiptoed into the room.

The Cardinal pulled aside a bed curtain, smiling at the children clasped close in the tumbled sheets. The Archbishop smiled too, pointing to the nightrobes on the floor, the lily petals on the pillows, the blown tapers. They knelt at the end of the bed and prayed as the sun goldened the window draperies.

Mary stirred, yawned, snuggled closer to Francis. Then she opened her eyes and sat up blinking, pretending astonishment at the sight of the priests. Demurely she brought the sheet high to her chin.

"My child." The Cardinal's voice blessed her. "We have prayed for a fruitful union. Has your marriage been consummated in obedience to divine and royal law?"

She did not hesitate. "It has been consummated, Your Eminence."

VII.

Marriage was like a birthday, Mary discovered. One awakened expecting to look different, feel different, but one was the same. The honeymoon in the country near Soissons was only a withdrawal from court; there was little change in her life.

The lazy days sunned by, one like another. The nights were less happy. In spite of their prayers Francis' attempts at manhood failed. God did not see fit to remove the curse. Perhaps, Mary thought, he was still angry with her for confusing him with the Cardinal.

As a bride Mary remained under the Cardinal's surveillance. He shared the honeymoon chateau, and a few weeks after the marriage her studies were resumed. The Scottish commissioners arrived for a final conference but Mary did not receive James Stuart alone. Politely, in the presence of others, they bade each other a cool farewell before he left for Edinburgh.

Then the King ordered Francis to military training at a camp near Amiens. Peace was being negotiated with Spain but the Dauphin must learn the strategy of war.

Mary felt guilty relief at his absence. Much as she loved Francis she had found the nights nerve-racking, and now she was spared his grim attempts at love-making. Contentedly she passed the flowering days with books and music; composed some romantic ballads. Versemaster Ronsard had them bound in pink velvet with silver scrolling.

In July she rejoined the court, trailing the swan path of the Loire which reflected the dunce-cap spires of Touraine chateaux. Catherine de Medici received Mary at Chambord with quick appraisal of her flat stomach, and suppressed a smile behind her hand. What a shame, Catherine said, that the bride was bereft of a bridegroom. How frustrating the fortunes of war!

Mary smiled and prattled of Francis; of his goodness, his generosity, of the sapphire necklace he had given her, the diamond stomacher, the ruby crucifix. "We are almost too happy," she said in assumed guilelessness, "almost too much in love!"

"Of course you are," Catherine purred in her tomcat voice, "of course . . ."

Francis returned from camp in October. In November the dead leaves of Touraine whirled under pounding hoofbeats. Couriers gasped out news from England: Mary Tudor was dead and with her the hopes of Catholic Europe. The torture fires of Smithfield were extinguished and Protestant prisoners stumbled to freedom.

London was draped in black. The funeral cortege gloomed toward Westminster. At Hatfield red-haired Elizabeth Tudor proclaimed herself Protestant, tore off her rosary and spat upon it.

CHAPTER THREE

I.

In the king's audience chamber at St. Germain the English Ambassador, Sir Nicholas Throckmorton, bowed backward from the throne.

"Your Majesties—" He glanced from King Henry to Mary, who sat below the dais on a love seat—"my mistress, Queen Elizabeth, was crowned January fifteenth at Westminster . . ."

As he described the coronation and the procession through London Mary visioned Elizabeth ramrod-stiff in purple velvet and diamonds, riding under wind-whipped banners. She had never seen her cousin but knew her face from portraits. At twenty-five Elizabeth had a taut, hard-boned beauty, the cheeks and mouth thin, the blue eyes dagger-sharp, the hair a glorious reddish gold. And she knew Elizabeth's history as well as she knew her own. Spawned of Henry VIII and the executed adulteress Anne Boleyn, Elizabeth had been declared illegitimate by Parliament and imprisoned by her half-sister Mary on charges of Protestant sympathy. For years she had walked the perilous tightrope of other people's whims. Now she could indulge whims of her own.

Throckmorton said the mob was swollen with Protestants snatched from the stake and the whipping posts. Stump-fingered men and breastless women cheered Elizabeth's passage through confetti-choked streets. The tongueless blessed her with streaming eyes.

"Her Majesty has appointed Sir William Cecil Secretary of State. She surrounds herself with wise counselors. We believe she will be a great queen, for her mind is keen as a man's."

"We are delighted," King Henry said heavily. "Please convey to Her Majesty our felicitations and best wishes for a long and prosperous reign. I have instructed my ambassador to present gifts."

Mary said, "I am sending her a golden heart bordered by white sapphires. Please tell her I am overjoyed that she is Queen."

But she lied. Elizabeth was a threat, certain to persecute Catholics and strengthen Protestantism in Scotland. Doubtless she would encourage John Knox in priest-baiting and abbey-wrecking.

King Henry's sluggish voice expressed her thought. "We trust she will not persecute Catholics."

"She does not intend to persecute anyone." Throckmorton smoothed his handsome gold beard. "But she does intend that the true faith be spread, to God's glory."

"That," said the King drily, "is also our intention."

"We feel sure," Throckmorton continued suavely, "that France and England will enjoy the most harmonious relations." He turned to Mary. "The Queen sends Your Majesty her greetings and belated congratulations on your sixteenth birthday. She regards you as her dear sister and always refers to you so."

"She does, sir? Really?"

"Yes, Madam. Her own sister proved her bitterest enemy. Her Majesty lived a lonely girlhood. To her you are the epitome of all a true sister should be—gentle, understanding, beautiful."

"I am flattered beyond words," Mary said. The interview minced to its end.

The King detained Mary. "I have come to an important decision. A decision, in fact, that may halt the spread of Protestantism. We shall not act upon it for several months, but since it involves you, the Cardinal and I believe you should know at once."

He motioned her to the throne dais. "Come. Sit here with me."

She settled herself in a rustle of satin skirts. Under the square-cut bodice she could feel the skipping beat of her heart.

"In 1536 the English Parliament barred Elizabeth Tudor from succession to the crown on grounds of illegitimacy. Their act of 1544, though it restored succession, did not remove the stigma of bastardy. Therefore, she cannot be England's rightful Queen."

"But she *is* Queen."

"She has grasped the throne but she is not entitled to it—no more than your brother James is entitled to rule Scotland. You, however, are the granddaughter of Margaret Tudor, the great-granddaughter of Henry VII. By legal and divine right you are the true Queen of England."

Mary knew her own history but she had not translated it into such ambitious terms, and thrill brought her to her feet. "I am! I am Queen of England!"

"Spain and Rome and the provinces of Italy so regard you. Every Catholic country agrees—and even Elizabeth cannot deny her illegitimacy."

"What will we do? Proclaim my rights and invade England?"

"That is one course, but we shall not take it. We cannot risk full-scale war with England, when Spain may pounce on us again in spite of peace talk. But we will proclaim you rightful Queen and sow the seed of rebellion among Elizabeth's subjects."

Mary could not argue with the King—it was inconceivable to question his authority. But to proclaim her Queen and not enforce the proclamation with arms seemed absurd. Such an action could only infuriate Elizabeth and cut the tenuous strings of friendship between England and Scotland.

"The Cardinal sanctions this?" Mary asked warily.

"It was his sug—it has his full approval," the King amended hastily.

Mary hesitated. The Cardinal was the shrewdest politician in Europe. Who was she to mistrust his judgment? Perhaps the proclamation was sufficient after all. Elizabeth's subjects had no years of loyalty to her. It was possible they would rebel against this obvious usurper. At worst, Mary thought, I have nothing to lose and a kingdom to gain.

"Does my mother know of this decision?" Mary asked.

"Not yet. But she will certainly agree. The move would encourage wavering Catholics in Scotland, demonstrate to Protestants the power and solidity of Catholicism. Surely you can see the benefits to your own country?"

She supposed she did. "Yes, Sire."

"We will wait for the strategic moment. Meanwhile I shall order your coat of arms combined with England's on a single escutcheon, your shields and seal decorated." His rare smile came. "The crown of France above—Scotland and England and Ireland below. One empire, indivisible . . ."

I am Queen of England, she thought. It is true whether I rule or not. And I should be jubilant.

But as she left the audience chamber to seek Francis she was uneasy. Sooner or later her kingdoms would know she was doomed to barrenness—unless God wrought a miracle.

II.

In late June, King Henry II commanded a triple celebration in Paris. His sister Margaret was betrothed to the Duke of Savoy. His daughter Elizabeth was married to widower Philip II of Spain. Spain and France were finally at peace.

In the Rue St. Antoine, in the shadow of the Bastille, the third day of a tournament was about to begin. Lists were set up, galleries looped in crimson velvet and cloth of gold. Most of the royal family, the court and its distinguished visitors were assembled.

Trumpets blared. Heralds preceding a gold and purple litter shouted, "Make place! Make place for the Queen of England!"

English Ambassador Throckmorton leaned forward as Mary and Francis were carried to the royal box. Their servants wore purple uniforms stamped in gold with the arms of England and Ireland, France and Scotland. Their guards wore the crest emblazoned on breastplates and mailed sleeves. A shout rose from the great field and Mary kissed her hand to the crowd.

Again trumpets sounded. King Henry entered the lists on a big bay war horse. His arm plates and the trappings of his horse flaunted the black-and-white silks of Diane de Poitiers, her moon-symbol curved in diamonds on the pommel of his saddle. Brilliantly he jousted through the morning and the long afternoon. Horses' hoofs thundered the dust, crushing flowers and favors flung from the Ladies' Galleries. Catherine de Medici, surrounded by her younger children, watched stolidly as her husband galloped across the field to receive a white rose from Diane. The joust resumed. Over the shock and clash of lances Mary and Francis screamed encouragement.

The sunlight waned but the King was buoyant, tireless. He challenged Captain Montgomery of the Scots Guard to tilting. The Captain tried to refuse but the King commanded him. Catherine de Medici sent two messengers to her husband with notes asking him to end the sport. "I have a premonition," she wrote. "I had a fearful dream last night . . ." But the King ignored his wife. He held Diane's rose in one iron-gauntleted hand.

The trumpets pealed across the lengthening shadows. The King dug jeweled spurs into his horse. Lances leveled, he and Montgomery charged toward each other but missed. They circled the field, pounded close in a swirl of dust, missed again, passed. On the third charge there was a shattering crash as both lances splintered. Montgomery failed to drop his in time and the jagged edge of the stump pierced the King's visor.

The King clutched his saddle pommel, reeled. Grooms rushed to break his fall. They placed him on the ground and raised his visor to a face drowned in blood.

He was carried to the nearby Palace des Tournelles, where surgeons removed five splinters from his temple and eye. They could not remove the one that penetrated the brain. For ten agonized days the King screamed for Diane de Poitiers. But Catherine de Medici blocked the entrance to his apartments. On his deathbed he was hers.

Within an hour after Henry's death Francis and Mary, King and Queen of France, were hurried from the palace to the Louvre, where Catherine, the Cardinal and high nobles paid them homage. Dazed, weak from successive fainting spells, Mary stood on the dais of the

Great Hall. Francis' hand in hers was moist with sweat. He too had been ill this past week, feverish, stricken with shock.

Through the ceremony of allegiance Mary's thoughts wandered: I loved the King—I wonder if he knew . . . Francis is ill, he should be abed . . . Poor Madame Diane, may heaven comfort her . . . Queen Catherine looks ghastly . . .

Catherine's face was waxen and tear-puffed but her eyes were dry. Supported by the Cardinal, she moved like a puppet on the strings of his solicitude, kneeling to Francis and Mary, rising, stepping backward. After the ceremony the new King and Queen led the procession through the huge cobbled courtyard to the street. In the breeze-flared torchlight the royal coach waited. A footman opened the door and Mary stepped aside for Catherine to enter.

"No, Madam," Catherine said. "You now take precedence."

In sudden overwhelming pity, Mary put her arm around the thick, rigidly corseted waist. "Please, Your Majesty. I wish you to go first."

Mutely Catherine obeyed.

The weight of Catherine's grief touched Mary as no peace offering could have. She put herself in Catherine's place and forgave her much. Love redeemed sin—Christ had said so. Catherine's futile, unreciprocated love for the King surely negated her evil. Or did it? Once she emerged from shock would she turn on Madame Diane in furious reprisal?

The court wondered, waiting uneasily, ladies on pearl-heeled tiptoe, gentlemen attentive. Diane remained secluded at Chenonceaux, venturing out only to attend the King's funeral in the deepest shadows of Notre Dame and the splendid, mournful coronation of Francis and Mary at Rheims.

But Catherine was too crushed, too apathetic to care about Diane. The venom of twenty years was watered with tears. Diane was asked to return the crown jewels, to trade the magnificent Chenonceaux for Catherine's Chateau of Chaumont. These things accomplished, Diane, retaining all of her other properties, was dismissed from court.

She left regally, in a canopied litter of black velvet emblazoned with crescent moons of diamonds. Ahead rode her guard in black hose and white satin doublets, her ladies, her pages. Behind her trailed seven lovelorn cavaliers following her to the south of France.

As the retinue passed the Palace des Tournelles Mary waved from a balcony. Diane looked up, raised her arm, fluttered a handkerchief.

She will not smile for me, Mary thought. Even at sixty. Even in farewell.

III.

To Mary new power brought new responsibilities. To Francis it brought the opportunity to do as he pleased, and his pleasure was hunting. She was helpless to stop his frantic punishment of his body. Falconing, running rabbits and foxes, he was sometimes twenty hours in the saddle. He would command races, and often his attendants had to drag him forcibly off his horse, pour wine through his blue lips as he gasped for breath. Mary pleaded and scolded in vain. His physicians threatened and were ignored. In the six months since his father's death he had shot up suddenly to gangling height and was frighteningly thin. Pox-scars showed red on a pallid, nerve-twitching face.

Often feverish, he would rise from his bed, stagger to the stables and ride off into the forest of St. Germain, spurring his horse viciously. Mary would follow, sometimes futilely, sometimes heading him off through a short cut. Splashing through brooks, jumping hedgerows, she rode with a prayer; she felt that only God could prevent disaster.

"The Devil drives him," Queen Catherine said to Mary one day after Francis was carried to his apartments by frightened grooms. They were alone in Mary's parlor. "He is possessed."

"Possessed by the drive to be a man," Mary blurted. She saw Catherine's smile. "I mean he wishes to be sportive and strong like his father."

"Your first statement was more accurate," Catherine said. "You have no heir, yet you have been married well over a year." Her eyes probed and Mary thought, She never looks me in the face—only in the stomach.

"May I remind Your Majesty," Mary said, "that you were barren eleven years before you bore Francis?"

"What does that have to do with you?" Catherine asked sharply.

"God's will guides us both."

"There is a devil in Francis," Catherine persisted. "He should be exorcised again. The physicians should hang him from his heels and beat the demon from him; that is the only cure."

"That," Mary said furiously, "would likely kill him. Is that what you want? So that you may rule through your son Charles?"

"Take care, Maria. I told you long ago not to underestimate me."

"I estimate you as vicious and dangerous. I thought grief had softened you but I was wrong, your suffering taught you nothing. I won't trust Francis in the same palace with your physicians. I am taking a small court to Blois as soon as he is fit to travel. I am taking Francis away from you."

[67]

"You took him away from me when you were six years old. And what do you have?" Catherine laughed, the coarse laughter of a man.

"I have the King of France," Mary said, "and I am Queen—which you seem to forget. One more word of disrespect and you will leave court."

"You would not dare!"

"Don't test me." Mary turned from her. "You may go to your apartments now."

"Dismissed like a maid!"

"I dismiss you like the peasant you are."

Catherine strode to the door, then paused. "You will pay for that."

In Blois Francis' health improved. He seemed content to sit at the great map in his study, conquering the world with toy soldiers. Mary, free to deal with government matters, consulted with the Cardinal and Duke François de Guise, bringing state papers to Francis for his obedient signature.

Then Francis fell ill again. He complained of severe headaches and was unable to leave his bed for Mary's seventeenth birthday celebration in December. In churches throughout France, loyal subjects prayed for his recovery. At the insistence of her uncles Mary reluctantly summoned Queen Catherine from St. Germain.

The Huguenot Protestants, led by adventurer Godfrey de Barry, used Francis' illness to foment rebellion against the Cardinal and "royal Catholic despotism." Rumor was spread that the King had leprosy, that in attempts to cure himself he bathed in the blood of newborn infants. When Francis was able to rise and attend New Year's Mass in the cathedral, peasants swept their children from his path or locked them indoors. Cries of "Monster!" followed his carriage.

The Cardinal acted quickly. Priests were encouraged to spy on the people, the people on one another. In large towns "heretic traps" were set—portable altars were placed in the streets and persons who refused to buy a candle were arrested and imprisoned. Secret agents of the Cardinal disguised as beggars mingled with the Paris mobs and ferreted out Protestants, dooming them to the rats of the Bastille.

But the Protestant cause swept forward like a great tide, swelled by the backwash of the Spanish war. Returned veterans found action and excitement in the movement, and their swords were for hire. Famine victims of Picardy and Touraine, bled penniless by renegade priests, found the new religion appealing because it cost nothing. One could pray for rain without paying. One could get to heaven free.

[68]

But Godfrey de Barry needed money to hire swords, to draw his scattered forces into an efficient organization. He needed money to execute a murder plot against the de Guise brothers, against Catherine de Medici, King Francis and Mary Stuart.

De Barry went to London. On the fog-laden bastion of Hampton Court Queen Elizabeth reproved him sternly for the murder plot, subtly suggested a better one, and gave him gold.

Elizabeth's gold armed cobblers and tailors, students and street vendors. It hired war veterans and professional assassins. It encouraged Huguenot noblemen to join forces with the rabble. Godfrey de Barry sent his recruits into Touraine in innocent-appearing groups of two and three, and their number swelled to thousands. Fanlike they spread around Blois, some in the surrounding villages, others in the deep woods. On the night of March 10th they were to attack the palace and seize the royal family and the hated de Guises.

They reckoned without Des Avenelles, a Paris magistrate in whose lodging house de Barry had hatched the plot. Riding to Blois, he warned the Cardinal, and the court prepared to move to the high-walled fortress of Amboise.

Mary, after weeks of sickroom duty, found the journey up the Loire exhilarating. The royal barges provided a gay escape from Huguenots and court formality. The ladies wore peasant dresses and after dark swam in their shifts, for the weather was unusually warm. The men fished and played at cards and dice. There were pageants aboard, and dancing. Not once did Mary worry—was not her uncle Duke François de Guise the greatest military genius in the world? In Amboise they would be safe, perched high on the rocky cliff above the town.

But the dusty fortress had few guards and supplies, and Duke François, with only a handful of Swiss and Scottish halberdiers, sent couriers riding for help to the scattered castles of loyal nobles. He could depend on peasants' greed if not their loyalty, and his gold, sprinkled throughout Touraine, bought men from the fields.

It was a time of tension for Mary, of waiting, of reassuring Francis. All around her men jumped at shadows, women trembled in prayer. She did not share their fright. God was with them, the fortress was impregnable and reinforcements arrived hourly.

The royal patrols captured some Protestant stragglers in the woods. They were tortured for information and revealed the names and whereabouts of their leaders. Godfrey de Barry was shot by a royal servant and his corpse stretched batlike on the bridge at Amboise as a warning to his men. Duke François routed six hundred Protestants a mile from town and took prisoners. The back of the conspiracy was broken; each hour saw more captives choking the jails, the dungeons, spilling into the subterranean corridors of the fortress.

"What will we do with them all?" Mary asked, as she sat in the council chamber with Francis and the brothers de Guise. "There are far too many to execute."

The Cardinal raised a gray-gold eyebrow. "There are never too many Protestants to execute."

"But it must be done lawfully," Francis said. It had hurt and bewildered him that among the Protestants were noblemen. "Throw the rabble in the river, but execute the gentlemen with axe or sword according to their rank."

"It will take a month to dispose of them all," said Duke François.

And it did take thirty days. Some humble folk were tied in sacks, in bunches of ten and twenty, and drowned in the Loire. Others were hanged. But the Cardinal did not feel their deaths were sufficiently dramatic. The Protestant world must hear of a vivid vengeance at Amboise, the Huguenots must learn a grisly lesson.

In the presence of ambassadors and high-ranking papal dignitaries the public tortures began—and for years afterward blood ran in Mary's dreams. She could not avoid the ceremonies even on plea of illness—and she was ill many times, in many places, during that month. In a field she saw four horses roped together to form a square. A man was slung across their backs, face upward, a leg and an arm bound to each. Grooms prodded the horses with hot lances and they stampeded, breaking their ropes. She saw the man's face convulsed in agony as his legs and arms were ripped from his trunk. Saw the torso fall in the dust as the horses pounded by. White horses, chosen to show blood to best advantage. White horses racing across the bridge into the soft April sunlight. And the man's face still aware, the eyes knowing . . .

In the market square Mary watched victims bound to iron stakes lowered gradually into bonfires—raised and lowered, raised and lowered. Men begged for death, but it came slow and searing. On white-hot spikes. In trenches of sizzling oil. Groups of ten were tied to horses' tails and dragged to shreds over cobblestones.

On the last day, from the castle's high iron balcony, Mary watched the executions in the courtyard. The Protestants sang psalms as the scaffolds were draped with white.

"God be merciful and bless us . . ."

Duke François called the first name: "Jean Louis Alberic."

Refusing the aid of monks, Alberic, earless and half-blinded from torture, stumbled to the block and put his head upon it. The headsman swung the axe.

"Receive us, oh God . . ."

The afternoon wore on, and the psalms grew thin as the prisoners diminished. The headsman threw down his blunted axe and called for another . . . and another. He demanded wine, and by twilight was butchering drunkenly. It took seven strokes to sever the head of a boy.

On the balcony Mary stood rigidly. Clinging to sanity she thought, *They are our enemies—they would have killed us.* But as the fifty-sixth head rolled to the wet grass she was screaming soundlessly behind blood-bitten lips.

On the turrets above her, heads grinned from pikes, carcasses swung from the battlements. Below, scattered on railings and along the town walls, were toes and fingers, ears and genitals. Spring flowered in the carnage and petals fell to the stained cobbles. The corpse-crammed woods blossomed with yellow violets. The Loire, sluggish with bodies, moved red to the sea.

IV.

Amboise reeked, and the court, noses covered with lace, left for the Chateau of Chenonceaux. Queen Catherine sent servants ahead to air and scour it. She supervised the landscaping of Italian gardens and grottoes. But Mary walked with the wraith of Diane de Poitiers, visioned her in every mirror, every forest pool. The galleries seemed to whisper her satins, and on nights of crescent moon her symbol hung above the castle spires.

Mary, struggling out of the horror of Amboise, was plunged into new problems. Couriers brought news that John Knox was in Edinburgh spreading rebellion against her mother. From the pulpit of St. Giles he swayed the Lords of Scotland to an act deposing Mary of Guise as Regent. He encouraged Queen Elizabeth to hurl troops against Leith, the port of Edinburgh.

Beleaguered by land and sea, Leith fell. Mary of Guise, surrounded by traitor Scots, shut herself inside Edinburgh Castle and fought with her back to its walls. She had the weathercock allegiance of a few Catholic nobles and a small band of French mercenaries. She had the Earl of Bothwell and his men. Together, incredibly, they recaptured Leith and drove the English back.

Bothwell, for the first time, wrote to Mary Stuart: "We cannot hope to hold out for long nor weather another attack. I ride to the Highlands tonight to raise men, thence sail to Denmark to plead a fleet from King Frederick . . . If Your Majesty values your mother's life you will connive, beg or threaten help from France."

And so Mary begged and won Francis' approval of troops for Scotland. But the Cardinal objected. He was distressed, he said, at his sister's plight. But he needed French troops on French soil. The Protestants were too strong. A second conspiracy led by nobles jealous of de Guise power might result in disaster.

Mary faced him furiously. "You brought disaster upon us! You blundered stupidly by insisting that I display the emblems of England—it has only enraged Elizabeth and unified her subjects. At Amboise you blundered horribly—your bloodlust revolted our nobility and turned many to Protestantism. You shall not blunder now and lose me my mother and my kingdom. You will carry out our orders. My husband and I rule France, not you."

"I have ruled France these twenty years." He smiled at her contemptuously. "I take no orders from sick children."

"I am seventeen!"

"Queen Catherine and I rule France. Make no mistake."

His voice was the gentle voice she had once loved. But his face was thin and evil as a devil's mask, his eyes cold as sapphires. Mary threatened, but she knew she was helpless. The halberdiers, the sentries were his. The troops were his brother's. To ask her Scottish Guard, a pitiful few, to seize the de Guises would be madness. Nor could she rouse their enemies, for they were her enemies—Protestants.

In June her mother died. James Stuart wrote: *She was taken with a loathsome swelling of her arms and limbs . . . There was a touching scene at her bedside where we wept. Her Majesty asked for a priest but our minister, John Willock, was tolerant in her last hours. He brought his Bible to the castle and counseled her to embrace the true faith. She admitted there was no salvation save through Christ . . .*

Mary crumpled the letter and threw it on the floor. James Stuart would pay for this—allowing a Protestant preacher at her mother's deathbed, refusing her the comfort of the last rites. A woman too weak to protest, forced to listen to heresy. ". . . She admitted there was no salvation save through Christ." Of course she admitted it! Did the Protestants claim sole ownership of Him? Were they so abysmally ignorant of Catholic doctrine that they believed Catholics denied Christ?

Mary raged through her apartments, as yet too angry for grief. Francis, shocked, scurried from her path. The Marys prayed for her. She could neither eat nor sleep, and she grew so thin that the physicians feared she was dying of consumption. A morsel of bread or a sip of broth caused nausea, and weeping ravaged her—to a hag, Catherine said. Then, gradually, she turned to prayer. To Francis. Like her dogs he followed her about with moist brown eyes. When she finally took to her bed he ordered special masses throughout France. If she died, he said, he would kill himself.

As Mary recovered he brought her gifts—fabulous jewels. A Persian kitten collared in diamonds. A saddle wrought in emeralds and silver. But a clumsy sonnet he wrote himself brought sudden light to her eyes.

On her first public appearance in mid-August at St. Germain she wore black and the Cardinal gently reproved her at the banquet table. "Black is not seemly for young girls."

Heedless of listeners Mary said, "It is not seemly that you forget I mourn my mother. Your Eminence will respect my grief."

"I meant no disrespect, Your Majesty." Publicly he was her humble servant. Suave, charming, he played the role of guardian priest. Privately he kept her in a pink brocaded jail.

Mary had scarcely recovered when Francis fell ill again. He complained of pain in his right ear and excruciating headaches. Not only is there a curse laid on Francis, she thought—there is one upon me too. Barren, orphaned, politely imprisoned. Without a friend save a helpless boy and servants. Always she had blithely expected the best, because it had come to her so easily. Crowns had fallen into her lap like blossoms. But the crown of Scotland was bloody. The crown of France was borrowed. The crown of England, rightfully hers, was worn by a Protestant bastard.

The weather was oppressive—a hot, dry August brewing storms that never broke. The poplars were dusty as lint, the pools dried in the forest, the gardens parched. Day after day she sat at the window of Francis' bedchamber, helpless to ease his pain, staring down at the sun-baked courtyard. One morning she saw Scottish couriers gallop in and she rushed downstairs to the Cardinal's study, where messages were always delivered.

She found him studying a copy of the Treaty of Edinburgh. Scotland, England and France were at peace.

"All foreign troops," the Cardinal said, "shall be barred from Scotland. Your Majesty shall 'in all times coming abstain from bearing the title, emblems and arms of the Kingdom of England and Ireland.' "

He took a pinch of snuff from a gold-and-ruby box. "Your own Parliament recognizes Elizabeth's claim to the English throne. They lick her slipper-soles."

"They might as well give her Scotland and be done with it," Mary said bitterly.

"Your Majesty of course will refuse to ratify this treaty. But the damage is done. Elizabeth knows her power now—the Scottish Parliament bows to her bidding. It is also obvious that her people are strongly behind her. None have rallied to your cause."

"For all of which I am indebted to you," she said. "If only I had had the wit to use my own judgment!"

He did not seem to have heard her. "We may expect a total demoralization of Catholic power in Scotland," he said.

On a chill October day in St. Germain Mary sat at her parlor hearth rereading her mother's last will and testament. The bequests were pitifully small and few. But, Mary thought, she bequeathed to the world a matchless example of courage. For seventeen years, one woman against thousands of rebels, opportunists, fanatics. But there was no bitterness in her last letter to Mary, written with pain-cramped fingers. *I forgive my enemies but they do not forgive me. I leave you a heritage of hatred . . .*

Fleming tapped on the door and entered. Her eyes were wide and shining, and a gold curl had crept from her cap. "Madam, the Earl of Bothwell is here! He arrived from Flanders but an hour ago and is lodged at the Inn of the Three Brothers. He desires private audience."

"Bothwell!" Mary jumped up. "Send a page to tell him I'll receive him in half an hour. You will help me dress."

As she changed from the informal robe to a stiff black velvet dress she thought of James Stuart. With just such excitement she had prepared to welcome him. In disillusionment she had dismissed him. Perhaps it would be the same with Bothwell. She needed a friend desperately. But she wondered, with her new cynicism, what favor he wanted from her.

"Is he a barbarian?" she asked, as Fleming spread the long sable-lined train, "or a gentleman?"

Fleming giggled. "Both, I think. He walked into the palace as if he owned it and his glance is dreadfully bold. But I think he is a gentleman. He has Scots attendants and a French page. His clothes are old but of elegant style."

Mary looked at her sharply, saw the fluttering lashes, the blush, the nervous adjustment of frilled cap. "You bridle like a schoolgirl. He must be attractive."

"Yes, Madam. But his reputation! He can't be over twenty-five, yet they say he has been a rake for ten years. Beaton's aunt in Edinburgh wrote that a woman is not safe with him alone."

"Some women are not safe with any man." Mary smoothed the high silver-lace ruff that flared back from the gown's deep neckline. "I would ignore such gossip."

"I thought perhaps I should be near—in case Your Majesty needs me."

"My husband is in the bedchamber. There are guards in the corridor. But I appreciate your offer of protection." Mary smiled. "I think you need it more than I!"

Reluctantly Fleming left her, and Mary went to her tapestry frame. Outside the wind gusted bright leaves and the sky darkened in storm. The room was suddenly grayed, and she took a spill from the fire and lit the candelabra on the table. There was a tap at the door and she called "Come in."

Mary turned as the door opened. In the dim hallway, in the flare of a guard's torch, she saw the gigantic shadow before she saw the man.

V.

James Hepburn, Earl of Bothwell, was six-feet-two in boots that were worn at the heel. He came to Mary swiftly, cat-lithe for all of his big-boned height, and knelt at her feet. She offered her hand, which he touched but did not kiss.

"You are welcome, my lord," she said, sinking wide-skirted onto a love seat. "You may sit down."

He looked about at the fragile chairs, selected the sturdiest and sat experimentally on its edge. Then, easing back, he crossed long legs—magnificent legs, she thought, in beautifully fitting dark blue hose. But his silver-laced doublet was old, as Fleming had said. His scarlet wool cloak, tossed over one wide shoulder, showed a frayed blue lining.

He appraised her frankly, without guile or insolence, and she sensed his thought: Here is my Queen. Does she measure to her mother? Does she have her mother's courage? Is she truly a Stuart in mind and heart?

Her body did not interest him—she knew it instinctively and was shocked by her own resentment. Doubtless, she thought, he would admire some buxom Scottish wench with hay in her hair or the plum-ripe beauties of Italy. But his glance lingered for a moment on her eyes and lips and paid them tribute.

She matched his stare, examined him from scuffed leather toes to waving dark red hair. His face was built on high cheekbones and the lips were strongly sensual, the chin arrogant. From Border lore she knew his type—weathered and wary-eyed, tense, swift-moving. The absurd little chair could not frame him—his dimensions were moors and mountains and the desolate stretch of the Border March.

"Well?" she asked finally. "Am I an impostor?" She laughed. "Or am I indeed your Queen?"

"I apologize," he said. "I did not mean to gawk. But Your Majesty dazzles me."

The compliment was a courtier's. She did not believe it. "You disappoint me, my lord. I had hoped to find the truth in you."

He threw back his tawny head, and his laugh boomed through the room. "By God, I'm glad you said that. Now we are free of pretense. There's little time for it."

"So," she said, smiling but piqued, "I do not dazzle you."

"You're not old enough. You're a young lass, fragile as Venice glass. Do you know you are a legend?"

"A legend? I?"

"It's said in Scotland that your skin is so white and transparent that one can see the red wine move down your throat when you drink."

"Really?" she asked, delighted. "What else do they say?"

He hesitated.

"Come," she said. "We have a bond of frankness. Tell me the worst."

"That you are a doll Queen, puppet of the de Guises."

"No," she said. "Not puppet. Prisoner."

She was immediately appalled—she had confided to this stranger something she had not even told her husband. No one knew of her conflict with the Cardinal; she had not fully admitted her plight even to herself. Yet she blurted it out to a man she had known three minutes.

"A prisoner—you?"

She told him, haltingly, of the Cardinal's blunders, of Queen Catherine's enmity, omitting nothing except the curse on Francis and their barrenness. "The Cardinal and Queen Catherine rule. He admitted it."

It pleased her that his eyes held no pity for her.

"I suspected as much," he said. "You're a pawn of the de Guise ambition. The Cardinal uses you to the glory of his family."

"When I think," she said violently, "how I loved the very people who duped me! I thought my uncles were perfect—I worshiped them as heroes. Only Francis is worth my love."

The reddish eyebrows raised. "He can protect you?"

"No, not precisely. You see, he does not know of my quarrel with the Cardinal. I simply told him we could not send troops to Scotland. Francis is so frail, so frequently ill. I cannot upset him by matters beyond his control."

"I see. You protect him."

"No!" She felt impelled to defend Francis to those grimly narrowed eyes. "He would protect me if he could—I mean—" She floundered. "He is still a lad, not yet seventeen."

"We were to be frank, Madam, remember? What of his mind? I have heard that he isn't normal."

She was silent, hands clenched in her lap, eyes to the rain-washed window. In all fairness she should answer the question, for she knew Bothwell was not taunting her. Finally she said, very low, "It is true. He is not normal. I have never admitted that to anyone."

Bothwell rose and went to the hearth, stared into the firelight. He was taut as a pulled bow, she thought, and he moved like someone she knew long ago. She could not think who among the mincing courtiers walked like this Border lord.

"I am not here to counsel you," he said. "I'm no diplomat. But I could be your watchdog. If you are afraid, I am at your service for a court appointment."

"Thank you," she said stiffly. "But I am not afraid."

"Spoken like your mother!" He smiled, and she noticed how unusually white and even his teeth were. "But I wasn't suggesting that you are cowardly. I was thinking you need an ally."

"I do," she said gratefully. "But a watchdog your size would be conspicuous." And cause scandalous tongues to wag, she added silently. "Besides, I can't picture you here at court, padding about as Gentleman of the King's Chamber or even as an officer of the guard."

"I'm your servant—at your command."

"You were not sure of that when you came in, were you?"

"No," he said frankly, "but I am now."

Mary was tempted to accept his offer. He inspired confidence because he had defended her mother. To have Bothwell about would be like having a regiment near, alert, trained to danger and accustomed to fighting against odds.

"I think," she said slowly, speaking half to the fire, "that Scotland needs you more than I. You are Lord High Admiral, Lieutenant of the Border. You belong there."

She saw agreement in his fox-brown eyes and a grudging admiration. A thought flicked through her mind: He will learn I am more than a child, an image in Venice glass.

"Tell me the news from Scotland," she said.

He told her tersely that the Protestant Lords of the Congregation controlled the country, that there was talk of appointing as regent the young Earl of Arran or her half-brother James Stuart. "What is your opinion of your brother, Madam?"

She weighed her answer. "I found him shrewd. He seems gentle, frankly ambitious. But he has aligned himself with my enemies."

"He leads them, Madam."

"With John Knox?"

"Aye, with Knox, Arran and Maitland of Lethington. Those four rule Scotland."

"And I am its Queen," she said bitterly.

"In name only, Madam. That's the blunt truth. There's peace now with England, but in a year Elizabeth may have the land tight in her claws. That woman has a genius for management—if she *is* a woman."

"What do you mean?"

"I wouldn't risk flipping her petticoat." He slapped his hand to his mouth in such self-astonishment that Mary laughed as she had not for weeks.

Bothwell was delighted. "Thank God you're no prude. But I should not have said that. Haven't you heard the talk about Elizabeth?"

"What talk?"

"They say that when she was small, Princess Elizabeth was sent to Overcourt to escape an epidemic. For months Henry VIII practically forgot her. Then, impulsively, he sent word to Overcourt that he planned to visit his daughter. But—so the tale goes—Elizabeth died of fever while he was en route. Her governess and Thomas Parry, a steward, were afraid Henry would execute them for negligence if he found a dead Princess. So they substituted a village lad in Elizabeth's place, fooled Henry, and played the game to the end."

"Where did you hear this?" Mary asked.

"In Denmark at Frederick's court. In Germany. In Carlisle. In Flanders. It is everywhere. I doubt its truth, but for a fact Elizabeth forbids her physicians to examine her nude. She is skittish, you note, about marriage. And a bonier, broader-shouldered wench never straddled a throne."

"You have seen her?"

"Yes, she received me last winter at your mother's request. For all the world she put me in mind of a filly with the bit between her teeth. Nervous! She cannot sit still. She plucks at her gown, frets her wig, bites her lips, chews her nails. Something nags her conscience for certain."

"Did she mention me?"

"With dripping sweetness, as her 'dear sister.' She did not blame you, she said, for displaying her emblems. She blamed the Cardinal."

"Perhaps I have done her a grave wrong," Mary said. "And yet—in my heart—I consider myself Queen of England."

"Naturally, as a Catholic you do."

"You are not Catholic?" she asked sharply.

"No, Madam."

"A Protestant!" she said. She had betrayed herself, confided her secrets to an enemy.

"A freethinker," he corrected.

Mary was shocked, yet relieved. "You subscribe to no religion?"

He shrugged his wide shoulders. "I see nothing but hypocrisy in organized religion. Or perhaps I should say 'disorganized religion.' Catholics and Protestants mouthing the love of Christ and slashing each other to ribbons. How God must laugh—if he appreciates irony."

"You are blasphemous!"

"I am realistic. I hear of the Cardinal's blood bath at Amboise; I see Knox howling for blood in St. Giles's. What's the difference? I find priests and ministers equally presumptuous. Is God so weak that he needs men to interpret him?"

"Then you do believe in God?"

"Do you take me for a fool, Madam? Of course I believe in God."

"Interpreting him," she said, "*your* way."

"I'm authorized as well as another. I wager I've read more books than the Cardinal has diamonds . . . I'm sorry, Madam. My mouth is as big as my boot."

"Let us not argue," she said. "We would never convince one another." She rose and went to the table, poured a glass of wine and brought it to him. "Now, tell me why you are here."

"Shortly before her death your mother commissioned me to deliver messages and final requests to her few loyal nobles in the north of Scotland, to Denmark, Germany and Flanders." He took a letter from the pouch at his belt. "This, Madam, she sent to you."

Mary struggled against tears as she saw the familiar lacy handwriting and put the letter on her desk to read in privacy.

Bothwell burst out, "We'll never see her like again!"

He said it so passionately, with such sincerity, that Mary forgot their differences. No man who worshiped her mother could be evil or treacherous.

"You are not Catholic," she said, "yet you fought for my mother. Why?"

"I'd fight for any woman trapped by a pack of scoundrels." He took a gulp of his wine. "When I was a lad of eleven I rode from Crichton to Linlithgow to offer your mother my sword. She didn't laugh. She told me she would have need of men like me—later. She was in the courtyard on horseback. She wore a black hood lined with ermine. And I wanted to slay dragons for her."

"You loved her," Mary said.

"A lad's romancing."

"But you loved her, nonetheless. That is good to know. I feel so alone in my love for her. Even Francis—" She bit her lip. "After all, he was only six years old when my mother visited us here. He did not really know her."

"Nor did you. You knew her principally through letters. I was more fortunate."

"Yes," she agreed. "I can't repay what you did for her, my lord. But I hope we can maintain our frankness in a delicate matter."

"Which is?"

"Money."

"I can think of nothing less delicate than money," he smiled.

"I noted in my mother's will that she bequeathed you additional land near your castle in Liddesdale, with the stipulation of future grant of two disputed abbeys. I should like to add six hundred crowns."

"I didn't come here for that," he growled.

"I know. Now, stop scowling. I too can be practical. I will not have my Lord High Admiral, my Lieutenant of the Border embarrassed because he has spent his fortune defending my crown."

Bothwell did not argue. She could see that money meant little to him, neither impressed nor distressed him. He said, "Your Majesty is generous. Thank you."

"What are your plans? Will you stay here at court awhile? I'll arrange accommodations for you."

"I'd appreciate that. But I can't stay long. Someone must represent your interests in Scotland."

"You shall," Mary said warmly. She rose and he stood too, placing the empty goblet on the table. "Later we must discuss Scottish affairs in more detail."

Again he knelt, again she extended her hand. It was odd, she thought, that he did not kiss it. But then he was an odd combination of independence and deference, roughness and suavity. As he left she watched the proud lithe walk and remembered from long ago the young lion stalking a golden chain in the gardens of St. Germain. Bothwell wore the chains of civilization, she thought—but lightly.

The letter Bothwell had brought from Mary of Guise was a document of Scottish treachery. Under "Traitors" was a list heartbreakingly long. James Stuart's name was there with a question mark: "There is evidence that he is a tool of Queen Elizabeth as the others are. Yet I believe that deep in his heart he supports our cause. Win him from the Protestant religion, and I think you will have a powerful ally."

And under "Allies" a list that scarcely covered a page. Bothwell's name headed it: "Trust this man with your life. He is irreligious, immoral, but honest and forthright. Give him military but not political power. Since the nobles hate and fear him you would never unite Scotland under Bothwell. But you may, with God's help, save it with his sword."

Mary received Bothwell several times during the following week, once at Francis' bedside. Francis, who worshiped warriors, listened entranced to tales of Border brawls and guerrilla strategy. But suddenly he lay back upon the pillows and screamed of an agonizing pain in his ear. Bothwell ran for the physician.

Mary did not see Bothwell again until a week later, when they held a final conference in her parlor. "You must forgive me," she said, "but I am so worried about the King that other problems seem remote. His health is my sole concern."

"Of course, and I shan't intrude. I'm off for Scotland tonight. But when His Majesty is better it might be advisable for you to come to Edinburgh, even if for a brief time. Your people have never seen you; your nobles don't know you. A young and beautiful Queen might perform miracles, rally thousands. The longer you delay, the more precarious your situation is."

"The Cardinal would never let me go."

"He can't prevent the Queen of Scotland from returning to her own domain."

"But—"

"Are you afraid?" Bothwell asked incredulously.

Deep in her heart she knew that she was. Scotland was a wild barbarian country, a hundred years behind the rest of Europe. Yet her fear of Scotland was not as strong as her love for France. She said, "France is my country. I shall not leave it."

His face turned hard. "I see." He picked up his cloak from a chair and swirled it around his shoulders.

"You must not misunderstand me, my lord. I shall do my best for Scotland, wrangle what money I can for its defense." She found herself apologizing. "After all, I was raised here. Everything I love is here."

Bothwell nodded curtly. "May I go now, Madam?"

"Not like this," she said miserably. "What about . . . our frankness? I'd rather you say what you think than leave me like this."

"I'd best go, Madam."

"You think I am selfish—"

Bothwell glared at her. "Selfish and spoiled and pampered rotten! I hoped to find a Queen—and I find a French doll. It isn't courage you lack—it's compassion. What do you care for your people? Have you once thought of them, huddled in huts, starving, plundered and pillaged by the English, rebuilding and replanting only to be smashed

[81]

down again? No, you haven't. Not a word, not a question about their welfare. Only 'What of my nobles? What of my crown? How can I save my throne?'"

"Go," she gasped, "immediately."

"I will—and gladly. You are not even honest. You plead for frankness but when you get it you take cover behind your rank."

He started for the door, but her voice whipped him motionless. "You'll go with no commissions of mine!"

"As you wish. What I do in Scotland is my own concern."

"You are still my Lord Lieutenant. I demand to know your intentions."

"They wouldn't interest you, for I love the damned land—every bracken-strangled inch of it. I'll defend it my way, against invasion or civil war." He moved closer to her, and his voice was rough with contempt. "And against neglect."

Her eyes were drawn to his as though magnetized and she tried to speak, but no words came. She was forced to look up to his arrogant height, and the physical inferiority outraged her. Then swiftly he went to the door and turned, mocking courtliness.

"I trust that the King recovers speedily. And I thank Your Majesty for an illuminating interview."

He was gone.

Mary forgot Bothwell the moment she returned to Francis' chamber. His ear was abscessed, and she had a quick consultation with the physicians. One wanted to amputate the ear, another to press a leech to it. Mary took the advice of the third: in the milder climate of Orléans the King might improve. A litter was made ready and a small court commanded to accompany them.

Orléans was knifed with wind, and the sky threatened snow. Mary was uneasy as they entered the city, for the townspeople remembering the old tales of Francis' depravity, were superstitiously fearful of him and openly hostile to the Cardinal and Duke François. At the Place de l'Etape a small boy ran out of an alley, and a woman screamed and rushed after him. She picked up the child and carried him into a house. Francis put his face in his thin hands.

On the way to the palace Francis insisted on stopping for prayer in the Church of the Jacobins, and Mary could not dissuade him. The church was bitterly cold, drafty. On his knees at the altar Francis took Mary's hand, and she felt his fingers jerking in spasms of chill. His forehead poured sweat. Mary turned to Queen Catherine behind her. "We must get him to bed at once."

They took him to the nearest shelter, the Hotel Groslot, where he shivered under piled blankets. Daily he grew worse, and the abscessed ear caused such severe pains in his jaw that he could not eat. Broth and wine were liquid lances. He pleaded to be left alone with Mary, but for seven hours each day Queen Catherine, the Cardinal and Duke François sat at his bedside—sharp-eyed, patient. Like vultures, Mary thought. Then as the days passed they were not so patient. Gradually they retreated to chairs at the far end of the room. The rotting ear offended them. Mary looked at the three faces, and found disdain for a boy dying obnoxiously and too slowly.

Mary heard of a famed physician who was passing through Rheims and she sent a courier to fetch him. He examined Francis and shrugged. Only one treatment was possible, he said—a thin, hot iron in the ear to probe the devil out. Over the objections of Catherine and the de Guises, Mary sent the physician on his way.

Night after night Mary kept vigil, dozing when she could at the foot of Francis' bed. He could no longer open his mouth, and his eyes begged forgiveness as pus trickled down the side of his neck. "I can't help it," the eyes told her. "Don't look at me. I've always been ugly and now I'm revolting. This is the final indignity . . ."

She thought, You are my beloved, and to me you were never ugly. I see only gallantry and goodness. You were cursed, ridiculed, but you plodded on as best you could. You think you failed me but you didn't. The shrewd, the brilliant failed me. Never you.

Even now she did not weep. The long training in discipline was too deeply rooted. *A queen weeps alone.* Besides, she must not let him suspect she had given up hope.

The draperies were drawn against the night air. The room was hot with firelight and putrid with poison. But the begging eyes held Mary to the bed. "I love you," she said aloud. "I love you," over and over again until the eyes grew calm. "I will never love another man. Never . . ."

She leaned forward, took him in her arms. Gently she raised his head and kissed his lips.

A week later the Cardinal took Francis' confession, a guttural whimper. On the night of December 5th he returned to the bed-chamber with Queen Catherine and Duke François. They sat looking at the floor, fingering their crosses.

The Cardinal rose and moved to the foot of the bed, standing in prayer. Mary, dragging with weariness, went to the table at the far end of the room and poured herself a cup of wine. She had taken no nourishment for forty-eight hours. Miraculously God had sustained her.

She heard a gasp and a rattle. The Cardinal's voice, bright with relief: "The King is dead."

[83]

Mary dropped the wine cup to the floor and rushed toward the bed, but Catherine blocked her way. Bewildered, Mary tried to push past her and was flung violently off balance.

"I take precedence now, Madam." Catherine's voice clawed through the shadows. "*I am Queen of France.*"

VI.

On her eighteenth birthday Mary Stuart, Dowager Queen of France, attended her husband's interment. For fear of Protestant agitation there was no funeral. Without ceremony, without pallbearers, the corpse was hurried to St. Denis, four miles from Paris, and buried in the basilica.

Mary returned to Orléans. For forty days she kept to her apartments at the Hotel Groslot. By custom, no daylight was permitted. There were no visitors save the Cardinal, Queen Catherine and her son, ten-year-old King Charles IX. To Charles, Mary ceremoniously returned the crown jewels of France.

Charles was a vicious-faced child, impudent and precocious. He sat on Mary's lap and covered her face with wet kisses, proposing that they marry and rule France together. Under Catherine's cold eyes Mary tried to humor the boy, but it only encouraged him to sly indecencies. One afternoon she pushed Charles off her lap in disgust and turned to his mother. "Madame, I am poor company. Please allow me my solitude."

Catherine called Charles to her. "Come here, Sire. You displease Her Majesty."

"No," Mary said, "it is just that I am so tired . . ."

"You do not like children," Catherine said. "Perhaps that is why you refused Francis an heir." She held Charles close to her, stroking his thin black curls.

Mary said nothing, too grief-stricken to defend herself.

"He told me you were cold, unfaithful to him . . ."

I will not be goaded. She wants me to lose my temper and my place at court. She seeks an excuse to be rid of me.

"Francis was sick unto death when he discovered your intrigue with Lord Bothwell . . ."

Bothwell . . . Mary had not thought of him in weeks. As Catherine's words flowed on and on, soft and obscene, Mary closed her mind to the accusations and barricaded herself with memories. Bothwell might have been her friend, she thought wistfully, if she had not behaved like a haughty child. He had wrongly accused her of heartlessness, but he had been right about one thing—after she had encouraged his frankness she had taken cover in her superior

ank. Thus she had cheated him, and herself. She had thrown away
potentially strong friendship because she preferred flattery.

"Can you deny it?" Catherine asked.

Mary turned to her indifferently. "Deny what, Madame?"

"You have not even heard me!"

"I am sorry, Madame." Wearily Mary rose, trailing the long white
mourning robes to the hearth. Charles broke away from Catherine
and ran to Mary, grabbing her hand and slobbering kisses on it.

"Give me a kiss," he said. He tugged at her arm, trying to bend
her down to his height. "Francis is dead. You can kiss me now . . ."

Nauseated, Mary jerked away from him and turned to Catherine.
"Madame, in your bereavement I was sympathetic—you know that
in your heart. Am I not even to be allowed the privacy due a widow?
Each day you come and I—I am not well. I cannot sleep or eat.
I faint—"

"Ah, the fainting is interesting. Let us see, Lord Bothwell has
been gone two months . . . They say he may wed his Norwegian
mistress, Anna Throndsen. She's in Scotland with him now. She
too is with child . . ."

And so it went, day after day. Mary could not deny the King and
Catherine access to her apartments, so she endured Catherine's
insults and Charles's perversities. The boy was deranged, she thought,
but his mind was shrewd and subtle. Adult lust raged in a child's
body, and she found him frightening.

At night Mary sought the peace of prayer, tried to store up resistance against the attacks by day. She read scripture and the lives of
the saints, heard Mass in her apartments each dawn. But she found
no comfort. With the loss of Francis she seemed to have lost God
too.

She touched the holy symbols and found them merely wood and
gold. The Mass was only words. Pacing the dark tapestried room,
she tried to find assurance in Jesus' promise: "I will not leave you
comfortless. I will come to you."

But when? How? She needed Him now. She had no one else.

There were the Marys, serving her on tiptoe, eyes soft with
sympathy. But she felt a world removed from their innocence, their
beauty. In the mirror she saw a tall, willow-thin figure with eyes
almost black, circled by deep gray shadows. White lips blurred into
white face under white widow's veil. She thought, Lord Bothwell
was right. I am frail as Venice glass.

But she would not break—not for Catherine. She would not yield
to the Cardinal's will unless the future he planned for her suited
her own desires. She did not yet know what he had in mind, but
she was aware of her value as prize pawn on Europe's chessboard.

The Cardinal would move her shrewdly to the glory of his family—always the de Guises would come before France. He would allow her these days of mourning and then place her to his advantage—perhaps in Spain. Philip II's fourteen-year-old son Don Carlos was marriageable—and a brutal imbecile.

She thought, I will enter a convent. There I will be safe. There in time I will find God.

Often she wakened in the night, reaching for Francis across the great bed, retreating from a cold expanse of silken sheet. Sleep was her only refuge. Sleep was a form of death.

The black candles were snuffed, the dark window tapestries parted to admit wan winter sunlight. From a deep chair by the hearth the Cardinal said, "Your Majesty's mourning is officially over. I suggest you dress more attractively to receive the ambassadors."

"Grief is not regulated by the calendar," Mary said. She looked down at her simple white crepe gown. "I shall receive the ambassadors as I am."

"You deliberately hurt your chances. The ambassadors will return to their sovereigns and report that your beauty has been exaggerated, your portraits falsified."

"Let them."

"Where is your ambition?"

"Your Eminence has sufficient for us both."

"How can you speak to me in such fashion, my child?" His voice, she thought, was a priest's. His eyes were rapacious.

She said, "You don't care what becomes of me so long as I bring glory to you. It has always been that way; you brought me to France not out of goodness but to strengthen your own power."

He shrugged. "Let us not waste time in recrimination. Your future must be settled, a marriage arranged. The Kings of Sweden and Denmark are negotiating for your hand. You will, of course, encourage their ambassadors to think you are interested. The King of Navarre would divorce his wife for you. But we are concerned with only two of the suitors, principally your brother-in-law, King Charles."

"I would sooner kill myself than marry Charles."

He ignored her. "Marriage to him would restore to you the power you lost when Francis died. You would no longer live in Queen Catherine's shadow."

"I do not intend to live in her shadow. Nor in yours."

"May I remind Your Majesty that as Queen Dowager of France you are no more than a guest here? And guests must be civil?"

"Guests may leave."

"Where would you go?"

"To a convent."

He shook his head. "Not on French soil."

"You give me no choice," she said.

"Ah, but I do. If you are so violently opposed to Charles—and doubtless the Queen would also oppose the match—there is Don Carlos. Married to him, heiress to the Empire of Spain and the New World, you would recover your lost prestige. With Philip II for father-in-law you could rule Scotland by armed force."

That much, she thought, was true. Marriage to Don Carlos would be a brilliant political move. Spain would snatch Scotland back to Catholicism from under the greedy claws of Elizabeth.

"Elizabeth," he said, as if reading her thought, "would be furious."

"I shall not devote my life to infuriating Elizabeth but to pleasing myself. Don Carlos is said to be a degenerate idiot. Our courtiers have returned from Spain with tales of horror—he tortures children in his private apartments—"

"Nonsense. He dismembered a few Protestants in a dungeon—the tale has been exaggerated. You say he is an idiot—the late King whom you mourn so touchingly was no intellectual giant."

"My husband was neither an idiot nor a beast."

"I am beginning to lose patience," the Cardinal said, still gently. "Your Majesty forgets that you are dependent on the generosity of France—and I am France."

A voice spoke from the doorway. "Are you indeed, Your Eminence?"

Catherine de Medici stalked unannounced into the parlor and settled her fat body in a chair as Mary and the Cardinal started to rise.

"So," she addressed the Cardinal in a voice bright with interest, "you are France?"

"A mere figure of speech."

"And the speech has become tiresome." She spoke through tight-clenched teeth. "My son is France. As Regent I shall rule through him. The house of de Guise has had a long and dazzling day. Now it is sunset."

The Cardinal inclined his head, his face expressionless.

Catherine turned to Mary. "Downstairs the public room is thronged with ambassadors awaiting audience with Your Majesty. You will not receive the envoy of Don Carlos. I am negotiating for his marriage to my daughter Princess Marguerite."

Despite her relief, Mary was angry. "You do not rule Spain, Madame."

"No? I have told Philip that if he allows his son to marry you

I will form an alliance with Elizabeth of England, and the Protestants."

Under their shocked stares she smiled, lip rouge scarlet against ivory teeth. To Mary she said, "My son Charles wishes to marry you. But I have forbidden him."

"For once," Mary said sarcastically, "Your Majesty is gracious."

"You may have six months to arrange your affairs."

"And then?" Mary lifted her chin.

"Take whatever suitor pleases you—the match will be of no consequence. Go to Sweden, Denmark, where you will. You too are in sunset, Madam."

You are wrong, Mary thought. There is only the dark.

Mary lingered in Orléans, taking a small house. There she received the emissaries of her royal suitors, who came and went through the late winter and early spring. She encouraged none of them. Better to remain the second lady of France than first lady of a foreign land. The thought of journeying to an unknown husband, an unknown country, terrified her.

Catherine de Medici moved the court to Fontainebleau. The Cardinal retreated to his diocese in Rheims. Mary, accompanied by her Scottish attendants and a few French courtiers, hunted stags in Touraine and memorized the springtime.

Some of her impressions she wrote in verse. Others she stored in her mind to hold against the future. Whatever happened, she thought, they could not take France from her. For France was neither a crown nor a scepter. It was not the endless gardens of Fontainebleau, formal as a pavan, or the full-skirted fir trees that curtsied to the checkerboard terraces of St. Germain. France was grayed villages dozing in lilac-plumed walls. It was the Loire framed in willows, a looking glass for swans. It was woods so wildly romantic that unicorns pawed the dead leaves of the past. If France is my past, she thought, I shall keep it close, close as my heartbeat.

In June she attended the coronation of King Charles in Rheims. In July at Fontainebleau she received English Ambassadors Throckmorton and Bedford. For them she dressed with special care, though she would not relinquish her mourning white. There must be no reports to Elizabeth of a frayed hag. She greeted them in a gown of white satin, the sleeves slashed to reveal seed-pearl embroidery. She wore a coronet of pearls on her smooth, dark hair.

"Your Majesty was always beautiful," Throckmorton said, kissing her hand. "Now there is soul in the beauty."

"Suffering," she said, remembering Madame Diane, "only creates wrinkles."

[88]

"Your Majesty's skin is like cream. The poets grope for adjectives."

"And the suitors grasp from their thrones," smiled the Earl of Bedford. "Has Your Majesty made a decision yet?"

"No," she said. "I hope by fall to have definite plans." She changed the subject, asking of Elizabeth's health.

"She is blooming," Throckmorton said, "but extremely disturbed by Your Majesty's failure to ratify the Treaty of Edinburgh."

Mary knew that to do so was to relinquish all claim to the English throne. "I cannot ratify the treaty without advisors," she hedged. "The Cardinal is in Rheims. My Scots counselors are not at hand."

"Her Majesty is prepared to give you unstinting love, friendship and protection if only you will yield in this one matter."

"It should reassure Her Majesty that since King Henry's death I have assumed neither the title nor emblems of England. It was by his order that I did so."

Bedford said, "Her Majesty appreciates that. She realizes you were a young girl under the King and the Cardinal's domination, not to be blamed for their ambitions. But now you are a woman, free to follow your own heart and judgment."

And to make my own mistakes, she thought.

Throckmorton drew the treaty from a case of Florentine leather. "A scrap of paper. Shall it stand between queens who should be close as sisters?"

Mary took the treaty, unfolded it. "What troubles me, my lords, is one specific sentence. That I shall 'in all times coming abstain from bearing the title, emblems and arms of England and Ireland.' That would preclude any heirs of mine from succession to the throne."

She blushed. "If God grants me a child in my next marriage—and if your mistress remains a spinster—my child must inherit the English throne. You may tell Queen Elizabeth that I will ratify this treaty only when she acknowledges me and my children as her successors."

Mary likened that summer of 1561 to walking a path of roses on the edge of an abyss. The most desirable young woman in Europe, gifts from hopeful suitors overflowed her jewel chests, and the whole of Europe flattered her. But she knew Catherine's enmity would force her to a decision that might be disastrous.

She had been trained to regard marriage as a political duty and would have wed Francis, unmurmuring, even had she hated him. But now, mourning him, she considered only her heart. I have tasted love, she thought, a dangerous brew, a luxury most royal folk never know. Henceforth I must whip myself to be satisfied with less.

In July, Mary and her uncles visited at St. Germain. She found Catherine openly hostile and publicly sarcastic. Early one morning after Mass she was summoned to the Queen's audience chamber with the Cardinal and Duke François.

"You have had more than six months to settle your affairs," Catherine said. "We wish to know Your Majesty's intentions."

Mary looked at her uncles, but they did not meet her glance. She thought, Since I cannot marry Charles or Don Carlos they have no further interest in me. I am valueless.

"I have considered various proposals of marriage, Madame," Mary said. "But none seems feasible. I am still too attached to Francis' memory to seek another husband."

"You babble nonsense."

Mary controlled her temper. "In time, Madame, a politically suitable marriage may present itself."

"And what are your immediate plans?"

"I beg leave to remain in France, living as a simple dowager on my dowry of Touraine and Poitou." Mary turned away for a moment, feeling tears mass behind her eyes. "I would not interfere in matters of state. I ask only haven until I—I find a proper husband."

"*Jesu!*" Catherine rose in a flare of wine-red skirts and stood facing Mary, hands on hips. "You want the impossible; the wealth and power of Spain, the brain of a genius, the body of Adonis—and a Catholic. You wish to wait in France until this paragon appears. Months, years . . . Well, you shan't. You forget, Madam, that you have a country of your own."

Duke François took his cue. "It would be advisable to return to Scotland at once. It slides from Your Majesty's grasp with each passing month."

"I am aware of that," Mary said. "But how am I to protect it without support, without an army? Foreign troops are barred. I have no money to bribe back the rebel lords from Elizabeth—"

"That," Catherine cut in, "is your puzzle, not ours. It is time that you solve it."

Mary appealed to the Cardinal. "You know that my enemies control Scotland. Surely you do not advise me to go there without an army, with no defense, few friends—"

"There is nothing for you here," he said coldly. "In Scotland you must try to rally your nobles and contrive a marriage that will hold your throne."

She looked into the three faces, so hard, so closed to her. And then, because she felt the tears humiliatingly close, she raised her head defiantly. Lightly, gayly, she said, "Very well. I shall leave as

soon as I am able to pack my belongings—in three weeks, perhaps
. . . I could sail in August."

"I shall have galleys ready to leave from Calais," Duke François
said. "Your Majesty had best ask Throckmorton for Elizabeth's
assurance of safe-conduct should the winds blow you to the English
coast."

"That I shall do immediately," Mary said.

"We are only sorry," Catherine mocked, "that your youth and
inexperience must be tested in such a barbaric land." The popeyes
gloated. "You will find Scotland vastly different from France."

She wants me to weep and plead. "Oh," Mary said airily, "Scotland
will be an adventure. I am young and the thought of freedom, of
being my own mistress, is altogether pleasing." She steadied her
hands, then perked the frills of her ruff. "I must go to Paris tomorrow and order some new gowns."

"Gowns! You'd best buy weapons," Catherine said grimly.

"I shall," Mary smiled. "Plumes and petticoats and ruby-heeled
slippers. Kirtles and caps and waist-cords. Fans and ruffles and
grosses of sparkly buttons. Do you know of better weapons to win
men?"

The Cardinal said, "Your Majesty's frivolity is astonishing."

Catherine's coarse laughter bellied out. "To rally your nobles you
need only appear in a ballgown? Convert Protestants with a flip of
your fan? Win Knox with a ruffle?"

"And impale Elizabeth's Borderspears on a ruby heel," Duke
François chuckled.

The Cardinal joined in their laughter. "The strategy of satin—
your enemies will smother in frills."

"I am glad," Mary said, "that I have amused you." Her voice
trembled on the edge of a sob. "Of course—" She turned to the
Cardinal—"my legs are not charred. I am not so comical as the
Protestant."

She rose abruptly and walked to the door.

Catherine spluttered, "Wait until you are dismissed. I did not
give you permission to leave my presence."

"I do not ask permission, Madame. Not now. Not ever again."
Mary looked at her uncles for a long moment. "God forgive you,"
she said, "for you know what you do."

VII.

In Calais four galleys rode at anchor. Two were loaded with
Mary's household goods—furniture and silver, tapestries and bolts
of cloth, carpets, barrels of wine, china, books and bric-a-brac.

Another awaited Mary's palfreys, the royal stud, falcons and hunting dogs. A white passenger ship, scoured and shining, flew the banners of France and Scotland.

At an inn near the docks, surrounded by the retinue that was to accompany her, Mary awaited notification of the safe-conduct from Queen Elizabeth. She had an honor guard of French noblemen, the poet Pierre de Chastelard and the poet-historian Sieur de Brantôme. Priests, altar boys, pages, musicians, tiring women, chefs, a secretary, her four Marys and other Scottish attendants. The small court, magnificently dressed, crowded the inn's public rooms, passing the time with chess and music.

Mary wrote farewell notes to Charles, Catherine and the Cardinal, thanking them for their past kindnesses. Regretting her outburst, she had patched a truce before she left them, and relations were polite if not warm. Once in Scotland she would desperately need friends—powerful friends who would help her against Elizabeth.

To Mary the four days' wait in Calais was a reprieve. The stone inn, lichened with age, was her last home on French soil and she cherished every age-grayed rock from dormered attic to wine cellar. Lingering wistfully in the kitchen one morning, she watched the innkeeper's wife in her kingdom of bubbling pots and kettles. Here brewed nothing more formidable than leek soup and rabbit stew, here were serenity and safety. She would remember sun on white-washed walls, strings of red onions trailing from blackened beams, a cat with kittens on a burlap nest. There were smells to remember —dried basil and rosemary, new-baked bread. But she knew her presence awed and embarrassed the kitchen help. Reluctantly she sought her own quarters, where her Marys told her that Monsieur Chastelard had left a sonnet for her.

It was a graceful sonnet, Mary thought—the theme being the transplanting of France's fairest flower—but she was in no mood for flirtation and when she saw Chastelard at the noon meal she thanked him briefly and turned away. He was handsome, well educated, talented. But any man's admiration was an intrusion on her grief. No one had ever taken her love for Francis seriously; people had persisted in thinking it a marriage of convenience, and now that he was dead she was expected to toss off his memory like a shawl.

"Are you not pleased that Monsieur Chastelard follows you all the way to Scotland?" Beaton asked Mary that afternoon as she dressed for a walk to the docks. "He has loved you so faithfully these six years."

"And I loved Francis for twelve years." Mary slipped on gloves that were slit to reveal her rings. "I cannot think of other men."

"Of course not, Madam. But if Edinburgh is as dour as they say, Chastelard will be merry company."

"That's why I permitted him to come with us. My mind looks ahead. My heart looks back."

When Mary descended the staircase, Chastelard was waiting in the hallway, hopeful of a smile or a word. She had given him little encouragement these past years. There had been her fear that Francis might be jealous or unhappy; her fear of Queen Catherine's watchfulness. Then in the tragedy of double bereavement she had forgotten Chastelard altogether. He had been a decorative fixture, nothing more.

I have been selfish, she thought. He leaves the court of France— a favored poet—to follow me to desolation, even danger. He is due more than civility.

And so she smiled. "Will you accompany me to the docks, Pierre?"

"With the greatest pleasure." His face was alight, where shadows had been, his voice boyishly eager. But his boyish prettiness had hardened to manliness, the pale blond hair darkened in burnished waves. He was Mary's height and she thought, When I feel like dancing again, Chastelard will be my favorite partner. If I ever feel young again he will be a pleasant playfellow.

Trailed by Mary's Scots guard they walked toward the docks, avoiding puddled mud and tar on the cobbles. A crowd gathered, curious but respectful, and followed them to the wharves. A huddle of galley slaves roped to a pier gaped as Mary passed, and she smiled and waved at them.

"Your Majesty is gracious," Chastelard said, "even to those poor wretches."

"Why shouldn't I be? They are whipped to their knees."

"Some rise from their knees to whip others. You recall John Knox was a galley slave years ago, captured by the French and put to the oar for eighteen months."

"I wonder," she mused, "if chaining Knox like a beast caused him to behave like one? They say when he preaches he slavers at the mouth, a red-eyed animal."

"I confess to Protestant sympathies," Chastelard said. "I have made no secret of my Huguenot heritage. But Knox appalls me. How can he presume to call himself a man of God?"

"His God is a God of vengeance. But I think I understand Knox. I shall not make the mistake my mother made of antagonizing him. I hope to win him with gentleness and tolerance. Love begets love."

"I wish," Chastelard said softly, "that were true."

"Look!" Mary said, pointing. "The sailormen are loading my mirrors. Heaven grant that none crack!"

The captain, supervising the loading, turned and saw them, hurried to meet them. He was a plump grizzle-bearded Breton, red with the sun.

"I am honored." He bowed low, plumed helmet in big fist, earrings swinging. "But we did not expect Your Majesty. We thought you would send a messenger when you were ready to sail."

"I'm not ready to sail. The safe-conduct permit has not arrived. But I expect it hourly."

"Are you not worried, Madame?"

"No. Queen Elizabeth has no reason to deny me her protection. Scotland and England are officially at peace."

"We've good weather wasting," the captain grumbled. "It won't hold forever."

"We won't wait forever. But I came to ask a favor. I want a couch made up for me on deck when we sail. I shall watch the coast of France as long as I can."

"Certainly, Madame." His voice turned gentle. "To leave France is one's first death."

"It is surely mine. And I ask another favor—that the galley slaves shall be unchained and allowed to row freely."

"But that is impossible. It is against the law of France."

"Then it's my wish that none be lashed or struck while I am aboard."

She saw his open-mouthed astonishment and added wryly, "Yes, I am the Cardinal's niece. But the Queen of Scotland does not permit torture."

"Then there shall be none."

"The voyage takes five days?"

"With favorable winds, Madame."

"I shall send a messenger as soon as we receive the safe-conduct."

She assured herself that there was not the least cause for worry. But when she returned to the inn, Throckmorton was waiting for her and she knew at once that his news was bad.

"Her Majesty refuses the safe-conduct." He was tired, dusty and wretchedly embarrassed. "I could do nothing."

Mary was furious. "I am sorry that I so far forgot myself as to ask a favor of her."

"Her Majesty will grant it only on condition that you ratify the Treaty of Edinburgh. If you would do that, she not only would offer you haven on English soil but receive you and entertain you as a sister."

"I shall not sign the treaty until she acknowledges me her successor."

"Madam," he said softly, "believe me I am your friend. I have come to admire and respect you more than I can say. May I speak freely—not as a diplomat?"

She said, "You are known as an honest man. I should like to hear you speak freely."

"Then as myself may I remind you that you are very young and without advisors. When you reach Edinburgh you will be surrounded by men politically and religiously hostile. Some will masque as friends, but you will not be sure until they have proven themselves. Meanwhile, you may lose your crown."

"What you say is true. My enemies control Scotland."

"Do not make the most powerful enemy of all, Madam. My mistress could be your friend. You can remedy the harm that has been done by King Henry and the Cardinal with a flick of the quill."

She hesitated. He was so obviously sincere . . .

"Try to understand as a woman," he said, "the blow that was given my mistress's pride. Unlike yours, her young life was a long fear. She had no security, no affection. Then suddenly she becomes Queen and the world opens bright as a flower—until you assume her title and taunt her most vulnerable point—an accident of birth."

"I meant no taunt, sir."

"I am sure you didn't. You could not be so petty, nor so cruel." He smiled at her. "Sign the treaty and sail with her blessing, Madam. If you wish, she will meet you at any port you designate or send an escort to take you to London."

Mary remembered the price of Elizabeth's friendship: *"In all times coming to abstain from bearing the title . . ."*

"No," she said. "I cannot relinquish what I believe to be my right—at the very least, my future right. You may tell Her Majesty that I will consult with advisors in Scotland when I find those whom I can trust. Until then no treaty will be signed."

His shoulders slumped. "Then you sail without her permission?"

"The seas are free. If the ship chances to blow to English soil your mistress may do with me as she pleases. Perhaps I would be better dead. God will know. God will guide me."

But at dawn the next day on the ship's high deck Mary had no feeling of God's guidance—only his power. Wind heaved the harbor, tugging tall masts, ballooning sails. It whipped her cloak about her legs and lifted the hood from her hair. As the ship moved out toward the North Sea, she raised her eyes to the cloud-torn sunlight. *God help me. I am afraid.*

She did not fear the journey. She feared the journey's end. *Strengthen me and give me courage . . .*

But God seemed remote as the far green hills of France, cold as the sea ahead. Out of unspeakable loneliness she stretched her mind on tiptoe, waiting, listening. If God would give only the tiniest touch of his warmth, the faintest flicker of his presence . . . She held her breath.

Someone screamed. Mary turned and saw her courtiers crowding the rails. Then she followed their glance. Across the harbor, too distant to be helped, a fishing boat was foundering on the rocks. Carried on the wind were faint despairing cries. Men struggled in the water and were sucked under. The boat vanished.

"Oh God!" she said, "what omen is this?"

She fumbled for the crucifix at her throat and clutched it tight.

CHAPTER FOUR

I.

On the fourth day of the voyage, as the galleys neared Leith, fog met them. Borne up the Firth of Forth on an east wind, it settled for miles along the shoreline, heavy, impenetrable. All night the galleys floundered outside the harbor, announcing their positions with drumbeats.

At dawn the pall lifted briefly, and three ships crept into harbor. The courtiers were rowed ashore in small boats. But as Chastelard helped Mary onto Leith Landing the fog was so thick she could not see him nor the attendants who groped with her along the wooden pier.

The fog billowed and swirled—a witch's brew, Mary thought, with the chill of the grave stirred in. A ghastly yellow-gray, it smelled of rotting fish and sea spawn. She extended her hand and could not see her jeweled fingers.

"Jesu!" She heard the fat fluttering voice of Monsieur Brantôme. "Now I know how my shroud will feel."

Another voice spoke authoritatively, and Mary recognized the Scots-French of Arthur Erskine, Captain of the Guard. "Your Majesty, it is dangerous for you to move about in this; it's the worst haar I've seen in my fifty years. Remain here, and I'll try to find your escort. They're probably at the other end of the quay."

Mary and her ladies huddled together for warmth. Her white velvet cape and ermine hood had been chosen for elegance rather than warmth—she wanted to look her best for the entry into Edinburgh. Teeth chattering, she said, "If this is Scottish weather in August, God help us in the wintertime!" She sneezed. "My father's first wife, Queen Madeleine de Valois, died a month after she arrived here from France; she couldn't endure the climate."

Mary felt someone fumble a wool cloak around her shoulders.

"Thank you," she said, turning. But she could see nothing. The fog was a frightening blindfold. "Who are you?"

[97]

There was no answer. She heard the thump of boots departing along the quay, the slap of water against the pier, the curses of her French courtiers, who stood shivering in the wet swirl. Five minutes passed, ten. The fog frayed in a gust of knifing wind, and Mary turned for her first glimpse of Scotland.

Through drifting yellow vapor she saw the fire-blackened bones of a warehouse. A roofless tavern, open to the sky, its wooden shutters slapping in the wind. Ropes coiled like snakes on the rotting wharves among torn fishing nets and splintered barrels. There was no one on the long desolate quay. As far as the eye could see, only rubble and ruin under a granite sky.

Fleming echoed Mary's thought. "It is like hell . . ."

"But I'd sooner burn than freeze," Chastelard said, pulling his cloak tighter about him. He peered anxiously at Mary. "Is it possible that Your Majesty's messages didn't reach Edinburgh, that they don't expect us?"

"The messages were acknowledged by my brother," Mary said. "I am positive we are expected. They have known we were coming since late July."

Erskine returned and hurried to Mary's side. "Your escort is not here, Madam. But I took the liberty of sending a courier to Edinburgh Castle—it is only two miles or so."

"Good," she said. "But now we must find shelter. Is there a suitable house nearby or a city hall?"

"Madam, the English left scarcely a building standing. But I know my friend Andrew Lamb will be honored to receive you. His lodgings are poor but his heart and his hearth are warm."

"I will be grateful. Leave word with the captain where we will be."

Following Erskine, Mary and her retinue walked through the torn, trenched town of Leith. A few early-risen townspeople stared at them curiously, but there was no cheering, no greeting from provost or magistrate. She had expected arches of flowers over a path of gold cloth from pier to city hall, an escort of Scottish lords and pipers. Instead she stumbled along weed-grown cobbles between Chastelard and Brantôme, standing aside as a sheep farmer blundered through the procession, driving his herd to market.

Mist turned to rain, and mud began where cobbles ended. Mary refused the gentlemen's offer to carry her. It would be undignified. Holding up her skirt, she sloshed through the mud. Her white satin slippers were black by the time they passed through the Kirkgate and reached Andrew Lamb's small stone house.

Mary and her ladies were escorted to a squalid parlor with rock walls and a dirt floor. She tossed her two cloaks to Fleming and went to the turf fire. On the inglenook bench she removed slippers and stockings and placed them near the hearth to dry.

"Whose is this blue cloak, Madam?" Fleming asked.

"I don't know. Someone put it about my shoulders in the mist—probably one of the ship's officers."

"If so," Fleming said, examining the heart-shaped gold clasp at the collar, "he has a devoted admirer." She carried the cloak to Mary. "See? A locket forms the fastening."

Mary opened it. "How romantic—a miniature of a lady."

The girls gathered to look at the tiny portrait in oils. The woman's skin was olive, the mouth lush, the curls blackly abundant under a steeple headdress. "She is beautiful, isn't she?" Beaton said.

"Yes—Spanish or Italian, I think." Mary snapped the locket shut and Fleming hung the cloak on a nail with Mary's white one.

"Your Majesty had best wear the gentleman's cloak into Edinburgh if this rain continues," Livingstone said.

"I suppose I should. But I will look ridiculous. And I'd sooner enter the city barefoot than in dirty shoes."

"When they dry I will try to brush them," Seton said.

A servant entered, placed a tray with ale, barley bread and herring on the scarred deal table, drew up stools and left. The Marys nibbled suspiciously. The bread was dry and hard, the texture of pounded pebbles. Accustomed to wine, they found the ale harsh and bitter. They could not get the herring past their noses.

"We cannot hurt Master Lamb's feelings by returning this food uneaten," Mary said.

Livingstone lifted her herring by the tail. "Could we burn it in the fireplace?"

"And reek the house with fish?" Mary bit into hers grimly. "If I can eat it, you can."

They ate the wretched meal, and after the servant had removed the tray and departed, Mary said, "I'm sorry . . . but if herrings are our only trial we'll be fortunate."

"It isn't the herring," Beaton said hotly, "it's the idea of Your Majesty being inconvenienced. Perhaps I shouldn't say so, but I think it outrageous of your brother to make you wait like this. If he was in doubt of your arrival it was he who should have arrived early and waited for you."

"You are right," Mary said. "But my way must be conciliation. I cannot afford to lose my temper or I may lose my crown."

Never before had she confided her troubles to the Marys, but now in this dour parlor, in a land completely strange to her, she blurted out the truth. "I am Queen in name only. To win back my rights will be a battle. I should not ask you to share the hazards of such a life."

Mary moved back to the bench in the inglenook and stretched her bare feet to the fire. "Perhaps you will wish to leave me and return to your families. If so, I will arrange for it and provide suitable dowries for your future marriages."

Livingstone spoke through a shocked silence. "I will never leave Your Majesty save by your command."

"I'd sooner die!" said Seton.

Fleming and Beaton went to Mary and knelt at the bench, assuring her they wanted to stay.

"In fact," Fleming said, "none of us shall leave you until you are married again. We made that vow last January."

"We have sworn it," Beaton said.

"I would never hold you to such a vow. You are young and lovely and I may not marry for years."

But they were stubborn, and finally Mary said, "Just remember that you are free to go at any time. My court will be no bed of plumes." She put her head in her hands. "I . . . it is difficult for me, and it will be for you. We are spoiled. We have had everything. For me it is more than a change of climate; it will be an entire change of personality." She peeped through her fingers and tried to smile. "I must learn to eat herring and humble pie."

"What may we do to help?" Seton asked.

They gathered around her on the hearth floor, skirts billowing over one another's laps.

Mary raised her head. "You can help me; of course you can!" She remembered the Cardinal's phrase—"The strategy of satin"—and wondered why she hadn't thought of that strategy before. "The French court was not mine," she said, "so you had little influence. But in Scotland your position is established; all of you bear noble names. As my maids of honor you will have high place."

"But how may we help you?" Fleming asked.

"By winning men to our side. It is as simple—and difficult—as that. The Scots lords are hostile. But no matter how crude or cold or arrogant they may be, I ask you to flatter them, humor them within propriety, and curtsy to their moods. In other words—charm them."

"That should not be difficult," Seton said. "We have never lacked for admirers."

"But these are not soft French fops. These are men who would snuff out a life as casually as a candle. My brother James is a gentleman. So, I understand, is William Maitland of Lethington, and you may recall the Earl of Arran at King Henry's court some years ago—

he and his father are educated. The rest are barbaric tribesmen. Few of them can read, or write more than their names."

"All the better," Beaton said, perking a curl. "We have more wit than they."

"But we must have the wit not to flaunt our wit," Livingstone added.

Mary smiled. "And you, Fleming? Do you care to contribute to this strategy?"

"Oh, yes, Madam! I may not have great wit, but I am fortunate in looking more susceptible than I am."

They laughed and Mary said, "Heaven help the poor clods. Together, and in battle dress, you are formidable."

They were not beautiful, she thought, but all were unusually attractive. Golden-blond Fleming was moodily seductive, sometimes languid, sometimes sparkling. She wore her gowns low at the bosom and a beauty patch to accentuate her violet eyes.

Seton, also blond, arranged her pale silvery hair madonna-fashion, parted in the center and braided across the back with blue ribbons. Wide blue eyes were deceptively guileless, and her air of fragility sent men running for cushions and shawls.

Brown-eyed Beaton was a merry contrast. Her red curls bounced from golden side combs, her nose was tilted and freckle-dusted. Vivacious, mischievous, she looked the youngest of the four.

Livingstone, once plump, had become statuesque. French court painters had posed her against classic temples, robed her as Juno. Her black eyes and hair were magnificent, but she mourned her long nose and dark skin and referred to herself as "The weed in the Queen's bouquet."

Livingstone said, "It is not the clods that need worry us. It is the four gentlemen."

"Her Majesty can handle all four," Beaton said confidently, "with one smile."

"Save your flattery for the gentlemen," Mary laughed.

"We could portion them out," Beaton teased, "and save Your Majesty's efforts for a husb—for someone more attractive." She looked into the fire. "Wouldn't it be odd if we fell in love—all four of us—with the four gentlemen?"

"Very odd," Fleming said tartly, "considering that they are Her Majesty's enemies."

Mary bent and kissed her cheek. "We mustn't think of the lords as enemies, rather as pawns in a game that I must win."

There was a tap at the door, and the girls sprang to their feet. Fleming went to the door, opened it a crack and whirled to Mary. "It's Lord Bothwell, Madam!"

[101]

"Bothwell!" Mary curled up on the bench with her bare feet under her. "Admit him."

Bothwell stooped to avoid the low doorframe, his touseled red head just missing the ceiling beams. Rain spotted his blue wool doublet, dripped from the blue-feathered cap he held in his hand. He bowed deeply to Mary and nodded to her ladies, who sat down on the battered window seat.

"I am happy to see you," Mary said. "Come to the fire—you are drenched."

He went to the hearth and faced her with his elbow on the mantelpiece. "Welcome to Scotland, Your Majesty."

She smiled up at him. "You are the first to welcome me, my lord."

"I suppose I should have rehearsed a speech with the proper platitudes. Instead, I bring bad news. Your captain tells me that the galley bearing the animals is missing."

"But it was with us yesterday! We sighted it in the morning, to the east of us."

"So did I, at nine o'clock yesterday morning. Then the fog set in and I lost sight of your fleet."

Surprised, she said, "You were at sea with us?"

"Should your Admiral be ashore at such a time? I sailed to meet you. When I sighted you three days ago I circled, prowling for English warships off the coast. I saw none, but they may have trapped your galley in the fog. I don't doubt Elizabeth would welcome the royal stud. She has an eye for fine horses."

"Plague take it! My dogs and falcons—and my favorite palfrey was aboard. I was going to ride her into Edinburgh. I had everything planned, even to the trappings—the Stuart colors of yellow and crimson, a sidesaddle worked in emeralds."

"I'm sorry, Madam . . . Now I'd best be off to search for the ship."

"Wait a moment. Did my brother tell you I was coming?"

"No, Lord James doesn't honor me with his confidence. But I heard you were sailing from Calais in mid-August."

"Who told you?"

"Among my agents there's a clever page, an imp named Paris. He knows all that goes on in Edinburgh—and accurately. I don't doubt he could tell you to the hour how many wenches have sneaked to Knox's bed since Whitsuntide—if you care."

"I would care if we could prove it," she smiled. "But tell me, my lord, do you think my brother is deliberately humiliating me by making me wait here?"

"I don't know. I had certainly thought him cleverer than to antagonize you."

"But you do not trust him?"

"I would not trust him were we to meet in heaven, which is unlikely. I'm sorry I can't escort you to Edinburgh myself."

"Will you come there to bring me news of the galley?" Mary asked.

"Yes, Madam. But I won't linger. Too much is brewing on the Border. Besides, I am not precisely popular in Edinburgh. The lords call me 'Satan's Spawn.' " He chuckled. "But actually they approved my father—he too licked English boots."

"Your father proposed to my mother once," Mary said. "How odd, to think you might have been my half-brother."

"I'm glad she didn't accept him," he said.

"You would not like to be my brother?" Mary asked, glancing at him through heavy lashes.

"Hell no, Madam. My father was no good. Your mother was wise in rejecting him."

"Oh," she said stiffly. Her small attempt at flirtation had been dismissed so bluntly that she was embarrassed. Hastily she added, "You had no love for your father?"

"As a child I scarcely knew him. I was raised by my great-uncle, the Bishop of Moray."

"Bred religious, yet you lack faith. Was the Bishop too strict with you?"

"On the contrary, Madam. He is a whoremonger."

Aghast at what he had blurted, he stared at them, slowly reddening. Mary tried hard to appear shocked but it was impossible—his expression was too comical. The Marys joined in her laughter as Bothwell looked at them helplessly. Finally he said, "Believe me, ladies, I meant no offense. But he *is* a —" Their laughter burst out again—"a scoundrel."

"Are you sure," Mary asked, "you are not judging the Bishop too harshly?"

"No, Madam, he is a known procurer. And it's a fact that he has children by different women sprinkled throughout Aberdeenshire. He legitimized them in batches, but there were so many that he ran out of names. Thus there are two Johns, two Patricks, and two Agneses. His motto—most suitably—is 'Expecto.' "

Again they laughed. "And what is your motto?" Mary asked.

" 'Keep Trust.' " He sent her a grim little smile. "An anachronism, Madam. But now with your permission, I must go."

She granted permission, and as he moved past the wall where the blue cloak hung she said, "Is that your cloak? Was it you who put it about me in the mist?"

"Yes, Madam. Please keep it; I have another aboard ship."

"But how did you recognize me in the fog?"

"By your voice. And I've eyes like an owl."

"But you did not speak."

"I was hurrying to gather my crew for this trip. They're waiting for me now."

"I will keep the cloak for you in Edinburgh. It must be valuable, with that clasp."

He shrugged. "A lady's whim."

"She is lovely," Mary prodded. "A bit foreign-looking."

"Yes, Madam." He went to the door. "I hope that all fares well with you. And if I may suggest—assert your authority. Otherwise the lords may trample you."

"Thank you for the warning. And for your protection at sea."

"I wish it had been more effective." He bowed and left, closing the door behind him.

Seton pouted. "He wouldn't say who the foreign lady is."

"That is his business," Mary said. "I don't really care who she is."

Fleming imitated a swoon. "Ah," she said dreamily, "he is fascinating! No wonder the ladies capitulate."

"They have no choice," Beaton snapped. "He takes them by force. He abducted my poor Aunt Janet to Hermitage Castle."

"To a fate more delightful than death?" Fleming asked.

"Your flippancy is not amusing. Aunt Janet was frightened out of her wits."

"So frightened," Fleming drawled, "that she remained Bothwell's mistress for months and followed him everywhere. I too received letters from Scotland, lass. Yours must have been censored. Or else you are incredibly naïve."

"I know more about my own aunt than you do!"

Mary half-listened to their squabble. The rain beat steadily against the shuttered windows and she stretched out on the bench and closed her eyes. The girls fell silent. The turf fire crackled. Mary dozed.

II.

Four of the Scots lords and their attendants reached Leith at noon, and Mary received them in the gloomy parlor. Suspicious though she was of James she was objectively proud of him. He wore magenta velvet with casual grace. His manners were elegant. There was just a trace of condescension, as if he were her host extending hospitality to a respectable but slightly tattered poor relation.

He immediately apologized for not meeting her at the dock. "It is difficult to calculate voyages, Madam. We did not expect Your Majesty until the end of August."

His cat-green eyes were direct, his manner forthright, yet she did not believe him. She thought of Bothwell's advice. If she failed to demonstrate her authority from the start she could expect to be trampled. Yet she had nothing with which to defend a show of authority. Conciliation was her only course.

"Don't apologize," she said gaily. "The haar was an adventure. Now will you please present my lords?"

They came to her grimly—graceless, shabby, none too clean: Swollen-jowled, big-bellied Huntley, Lord High Chancellor of Scotland, Chief of the powerful Gordon clan, in kilt and Highland bonnet. The old evasive-eyed Duke de Chatelherault, once Regent of Scotland, next in line to the throne. Mary took particular notice of his son, the Earl of Arran, thinking, God forbid that I die without issue and the throne pass to this oaf.

Arran ogled her. "Does Your Majesty recall that I once visited the court of France?"

Mary remembered him vaguely as a boor. "How could I forget, sir?" As he bent to kiss her hand, she smelled sheep grease, which she supposed he used to restore his thinning hair. His sandy beard was matted, his linen dirty. Weak-chinned, pasty-faced, he had the flabby body of an ale-bibber. Though she knew he was only five years older than she, lines of dissipation were cut deep at mouth and eyes.

"And do you also remember, Madam, that I wrote you last January about a certain matter?"

He had had the effrontery to propose marriage immediately after Francis' death. Too grief-stricken to bother with him, Mary had told her French secretary to write him a polite rejection.

"During my mourning," Mary said, "I did not engage in personal correspondence."

Softly he said, "We must discuss that matter later."

Her smile concealed her disgust. Arran would be easy to manage. But James was an enigma, Chatelherault and Huntley coldly reserved. She turned to them.

"My lords," she said, "I wish first to apologize for my appearance. I had planned to be elegant for you and look—I am in ruin!"

She raised the grayed hem of her skirt to show them the stained slippers. "And my petticoat ruffle—is it not a disgrace?" Deliberately, she held it high above her ankle.

There was an appreciative silence, and then Huntley spoke gruffly. "You don't lack for looks, Madam."

She clutched the rude compliment gratefully. "Thank you. I was afraid you'd be ashamed to take me into Edinburgh. And to make matters worse, we have no horses." She told them of the missing galley and of Bothwell's search for it. "I wanted to make an impressive entry, and now there are not even pack mules for my clothing and furniture."

Their interest in the mishap broke the tension. Lackeys were sent to local stables and neighborhood farms and by early afternoon had rounded up enough animals for the journey.

It was a ludicrous procession—ox-drawn wagons piled with household goods, the exquisitely dressed French courtiers on mules and Highland ponies. Mary on a wretched sway-backed bay was preceded by the Scots Guard.

"I would gladly lend Your Majesty my own horse," James said, "but it would not be safe for you."

"Ours are too spirited for a lady," Huntley said.

Mary's horsemanship was one of her prides. "No horse is too spirited for me. I ride as well as a man." She bit her lip, controlling angry tears. "Surely you would not have me enter Edinburgh on this mangy nag?"

"It is gentle," James insisted. "We will not risk your neck for the sake of appearances."

She tried to penetrate what lay behind the calm mask of sparse brown beard and sleepy green eyes. Perhaps he really was concerned for her safety—or he could be repaying her for her outburst at Fontainebleau.

"Very well," she sighed. As she turned in the scarred saddle she saw shocked sympathy in the faces of her courtiers. Grimly she dug her heels in the horse's ribs and moved off beside James's lustrous stallion.

The rain had stopped but the sky was overcast. As they trotted out of Leith and galloped into open country, wind tugged the blue cloak, whipping it back from Mary's shoulders.

"In this weather," James said, "Your Majesty is wise to wear a man's cloak."

She said pointedly, "I was fortunate to meet Lord Bothwell." James must know at once that he could not dictate her friendships.

They rode through dreary moors that sponged soddenly under their horses' hoofs. A few thin sheep grazed the low folds of the hills, nosing the dark-gold gorse. Passing a ruined monastery Mary saw skeleton arches rising grotesquely above strewn rock and tumbled tombstones. Crows flapped cawing from the wounds, wings black against the slate of the sky.

Wind mourned through the dark purple heather, clawed through a rising mist. They passed a gibbet where the vulture-picked corpse of a man swung to and fro. Further on, posted on tree bark, was a warning to witches written on human skin.

James shouted above the wind and pointed with his whip to a

great glow in the distance. "Calton Hill, Madam—and bonfires in your honor."

They rode up the steep hill. The wind-fanned smoke was choking, eye-smarting, and Mary hid her face in her cloak collar. Firelight glared against her closed lids, but she was grateful for its warmth. At the summit she opened her eyes, gasped, and reined in her horse.

Across a deep ravine lay the walled city of Edinburgh, dominated by a fortress crouching like a mammoth on the rocky roof of the world. Its battlements shouldered an iron sky, and clouds like black rags drifted above its turrets. Far below, forming a natural moat, stretched the wide waters of North Loch. Down the rocky spine of the castle huddled the high-piled red-roofed town, a ragged outline of gable-ends through which St. Giles Cathedral thrust its spire into murk. The town ended at the base of towering black crags and the sky-hung crest of Arthur's Seat.

On their side of the ravine James pointed out the Lang Gait, a wide road of furze and broom that bordered the north side of the lake. Beyond it were a few hovels, a desolate moor. In the distance Mary could see the vague outline of the Firth of Forth. To the west, fog shrouded the mountain peaks that guarded the Highlands.

James said, "Well, Madam, what do you think of it?"

She thought it the edge of nightmare. But she said, "It is awesome. It looks as though giants had flung it together from broken mountains."

He shrugged. "I admit it is not pretty—what battleground is? We have built on blood and bones . . . Smile, Madam—the crowd has found us."

They came running across the hilltop from the bonfires, a scarecrow pack of men and women, children and dogs. Mary swept off Bothwell's cloak and laid it across her saddlebow—if she perished from cold she would look as queenly as possible. In her white velvet cape and ermine hood she smiled down on them, one white-gloved hand on the reins, the other waving a lacy handkerchief.

There were scattered cheers—from Catholics, she supposed—but for the most part the crowd received her gravely, with respect rather than enthusiasm. The upturned faces were curious, cautious, as though deferring judgment. I am on trial, she thought . . .

In the light of the fires the poverty of the people was cruelly revealed—patched cloaks, faded outmoded doublets and kirtles. In Paris, she thought, the mob flaunted its tatters lightly, like old plumes raised in bravado. The people of Edinburgh wore their rags like armor. The women, shawled in hodden gray, stared at Mary's painted eyes and lips, at the snowy ermine hood, the diamond earrings, the kidskin gauntlets embroidered in pearls. But there was neither resentment nor envy in their scrutiny—only wonder. She had seen that look on the faces of French peasants at the jeweled altars of cathedrals.

James leaned toward her. "Speak to them, Madam."

But Mary did not know how. The Cardinal had never permitted her to address the mobs of France. Trained to converse with the most brilliant men in Europe, she was tongue-tied in the presence of cobblers and chimney sweeps, kailwives and fisherwomen. But she smiled and bowed from the saddle as they rode down the hill past a hostelry and tilting yard.

Mary halted the procession at the ravine and turned to James, pointing to the castle. "I hope you are not taking me to that monstrosity. From what I've heard of it I'd prefer to stay at Holyrood House."

"Neither place is properly prepared for you," he said, "but you will find Holyrood less gloomy. I sent servants there this morning."

"Then let us go there."

They crossed the wind-blustered ravine that stretched high above the lake and turned down the foot of the High Street. It was a steep straight thoroughfare running from Edinburgh Castle to Holyrood House, the Royal Mile made famous by Mary's ancestors. Bonfires burned at the Tron corner, where a dense crowd shuffled near the salt-weighing beam and the gibbet.

"Here," James said, "we hang minor criminals and punish petty offenders."

In iron frames with holes for head and hands sat two debtors wearing the yellow bonnets of their shame. Next to them on a wooden pedestal a drunkard was chained to a post from which a brown jug swung temptingly just out of reach. Small boys, pelting the trio with stones and rotten eggs, turned with the mob and pushed close for a glimpse of Mary.

The crowd hemmed in the procession on three sides, leaving just enough space ahead for the guard to ride slowly forward. Mary smiled and waved, heartsick that so few smiled back at her. An occasional cheer was so conspicuous that heads turned at the sound. Even the children were subdued, fingers in mouths, eyes wide.

On both sides of the street people leaned from diamond-paned windows and forestairs. Mary looked up. The houses were narrow stone but rose in projecting timber galleries to ten and twelve stories, each gallery jammed with spectators clear to the crow-stepped gables.

Tradesmen occupying the first floors took advantage of the crowd to hawk merchandise displayed on canvas-roofed stalls: "Bolster feathers . . . fine Flemish tapestry . . . eggs, ten a penny . . ." The city dung cart trundled by, holding up the procession at a crossing. Huddled in the filth sat a punished cobbler with a sign around his neck: MAKER OF DISHONEST SHOES. Mary caught a glimpse of two girls slinking through an alley. Their heads were shaven, and she turned to James in astonishment.

"Are they nuns who have forsaken the faith?" she asked.

"They are bawds," he said, "who have forsaken virtue. By law they may not wear their caps until their hair grows in."

"I never heard of such a law."

"It is new—and Presbyterian."

Evidences of Protestant pillage shocked her. She saw women in aprons made from altar cloths and brocaded cloaks fashioned from priests' vestments. And then, far behind her, a psalm began.

At first it was the merest thread of sound. It built slowly as people joined in, gathering strength and power until it soared down the High Street on a thousand voices: *"The Lord is my rock and my fortress and my deliverer . . ."*

It beat harshly against Mary's ears, then gradually faded. Ahead of her she saw a black-robed choir gathered on a corner below a gabled house. Holding open psalmbooks, they stared up as though awaiting a signal from the man who stood above them on the forestairs.

As she rode toward the group Mary looked up into the fierce hard-carved face of a prophet. His nose was long and narrow, his mouth full-lipped above a goatish beard, which straggled limply, a dirty gray, to the waist of his black Geneva cloak. He leaned forward with his fists clenched on the stair rail, his black eyes burning savagely into Mary's from deep red-rimmed sockets. As their glances clashed, he raised his hand to the singers below:

". . . O daughter of Babylon, who art to be destroyed; happy shall he be who rewardeth thee as thou hast served us. Happy shall he be who taketh and dasheth thy little ones against the stones."

The threat of the psalm and the glaring eyes infuriated her. In this case, she decided, conciliation would be cowardice. She checked her horse, halting the procession. Still looking up, she pulled from under her collar a ruby crucifix on a golden chain. It lay like a splatter of blood on her white velvet cape.

Mary saw rage in the face above her. She stared for a moment, shrugged, and then as though dismissing him, slapped her horse lightly with the reins and moved slowly on.

The crowd murmured, and James leaned from his horse to whisper in Mary's ear, "For God's sake, Madam, that was Master Knox!"

"One of my subjects," she said lightly, "who must learn respect."

"Apparently you don't understand, Madam. That was John Knox . . ."

"I know," she said impatiently. "Am I to cower? Prostrate myself?"

"I pray you, Madam, lower your voice . . . the people . . ."

She looked down into the moving sea of faces—faces clearly shocked by what they had witnessed. Probably, she thought, they expected divine wrath to descend upon her, and she felt sudden tenderness for their innocence. If ever she was to speak to them, now was the time. They had a waiting look, a wide-eyed open look that had not yet hardened to suspicion or anger.

God help me find the words.

Again she reined her horse, looked into the faces nearest her and spoke impulsively, confidentially, as if she had known these men and women all of her life.

"I have been away too long and I have much to learn," she said humbly. "I am only eighteen and in my ignorance I shall probably make mistakes. So I am going to need your help and your faith. And though your faith may be different from mine, our God is the same and he has commanded us to love one another."

She smiled at them. "You can help me now if only you will. Tell your friends and neighbors that I have no intention of interfering with your worship in any way. You have absolute freedom to attend any church you wish. But I insist on the same freedom for myself."

They stared at her uneasily, and she thought, In the shadow of Knox they are fearful. I could not have chosen a worse place than this. And perhaps they resent that I speak the Scots tongue poorly, with a French accent.

One of the men mumbled to his neighbor, "The Queen speaks fair enough."

"Aye, that she does."

Two women nodded agreement, and she saw heads wag in a widening circle of approval. An old man holding a child on his shoulder smiled toothlessly and said, "The Queen is fair to hear, and marvelous fair to look upon."

Mary smiled, glancing from face to face. "May God bless you."

"May God bless Your Majesty," they chorused.

She rode forward with new confidence. It was a tiny triumph—perhaps not more than twenty people had heard her clearly—but it showed her how she might win thousands. Not by rhetoric declaimed from a pinnacle but with friendly informality. She had flattered this small group by addressing them confidentially, as friends. She had no doubt that before midnight the thirty thousand people of Edinburgh would know what she had said.

At the massive turreted Netherbow Port gate the mob was halted by sentries, and the procession entered the Burgh of the Canongate, a continuation of the High Street beyond the city limits. They passed a church and a great grim Tolbooth that served as council place, law court and jail. Riding through the slowly falling twilight Mary saw elegant gray stone houses with Baltic timber fronts, armorial bearings carved above the doorways. But few heads were poked from the latticed windows, and the area seemed virtually deserted.

"These are nobles' homes," James said, "but since the court has been at Edinburgh Castle most of them have moved within its walls."

"And you?" she asked. "Where do you live?"

"Back through the Netherbow in Blackfriar's Wynd."

He explained that a wynd was a sort of thoroughfare, open at each end. And what appeared to be alleys between the houses were called "closes"—open at one end during the day and closed at night, being private property.

This street, Mary thought, was like a dignified wide-bosomed matron walking a straight path while her children, the wynds and the closes, capered off on adventures of their own. Purple mist filtered through the gardens back of the houses, softening the lines of gables and forestairs. Mary remembered tales told of her merry father, James V—how he had roamed these nooks and crannies in disguise, and one night, returning late to Holyrood from some romantic gallantry, had been refused entrance through the Netherbow Port and climbed the spiked city wall with its grisly row of severed heads.

As dusk deepened and they approached the stables of Horse Wynd, wind cut the mist and Mary saw Holyrood House ahead.

Towered and pinnacled, with crenelated battlements, it brooded in foggy meadows at the base of blackened hills. Eastward from high crags bonfires flamed like burnt sacrifice to the summit of Arthur's Seat which reared lion-shaped above a vast oak forest. To the west of the palace stood a huge, partially demolished abbey, lichened with years. Bats flew from a ruined arch, circling the broken roof.

Mary reined her horse. "Did the Protestants do that?" she asked angrily, pointing to the abbey.

"No, Madam," James said. "The English. In the invasion of '44 the Butcher Hertford swept through here on his way to Stirling to kidnap Your Majesty, and three years later returned for final looting. This is nothing compared with the damage he did on the Border—more than three thousand abbeys lie in ruins there."

She had heard of those ruined abbeys, but now, seeing the second one within the hour, Scotland's mutilation became a personal outrage. She thought of the loot that fattened England, of golden altars melted into coins, and jewels torn from crucifixes to adorn the gowns of Elizabeth.

"A groat for your thoughts, Madam."

"Never," she said, "will I bow to Elizabeth or England's greed. Hearsay is one thing—to see with my own eyes, another."

She pulled Bothwell's cloak about her, and they rode on. The miles of wild forest to the right warmed Mary's huntress heart, but the thought of werewolves and vampires there alarmed her. She looked up at the flaming crags and imagined Saxon tribes huddled on their ledges, the Knights of the Round Table riding up the heights to Arthur's Seat. The Roman Legions had known this place. So had Robert the Bruce and the seven Stuart Kings. The twelfth-century abbey had been founded on a miracle, and she thought, The air is so heavy with history it curdles the living blood.

They rode across the drawbridge. Sentries saluted and unbolted a massive iron gate that led into the outer courtyard. Mary had expected a welcoming blaze of candlelight, but there was only a dim glow from the high windows. No regal carpet stretched from the columned entrance, no herald appeared to trumpet her arrival. James's lackeys swung off their horses and went inside, reappearing with torchbearers, awkward lads in shabby blue jerkins and wrinkled hose.

James helped Mary dismount, and they followed bobbing torches through the entrance into the inner courtyard. A straggling line of maids and kitchen help curtsied and bowed along the arcaded walk.

Mary smiled at them and asked if there was a Master of the Household.

"No, ma'am." A man in a cook's apron came forward. "I am John Turner, in charge of the kitchen, and Mistress McDoon here orders the maids."

"And a green lot of country lasses they are." Mistress McDoon put her hands on her broad hips and leaned confidentially toward Mary. "Some has never seen a chimney nor inside privy, pardoning my honesty. But they was rounded up so hasty it's a wonder they got caps on their heads and shoes on their feet."

"Never mind," Mary said. "They will probably do for the present." She turned to the cook. "We will sup as soon as possible."

"I have planned a feast," James said. "Maitland of Lethington wishes to be presented, Lords Morton and Argyll and others."

"Good," she said. Then she turned to her courtiers, who trailed through the entrance by twos and threes, windblown and shivering. "Welcome to Holyrood House."

The French, she thought, were superb actors. They admired the grim courtyard as if it were an anteroom to heaven. It reminded him, said Monsieur Brantôme, of the lovely loggias of Italian palaces. All one needed were lemon trees to complete the illusion.

Moths shriveled in the high-held torches, and the Gothic arches were green with mold. There was a rank smell of dampness and decay, of years of trapped meadow fog. James said, "No one has cared for this place since our father's time and parts of it are fire-blackened. Your mother rarely visited here except to hunt."

"Then no one has lived here since her death?"

"Only a caretaker, Master Pye, and his family, and the Hunt Master. Here are kept the royal falcons and staghounds . . . But now Your Majesty will wish to go to your apartments. I thought you would want the suite your mother occupied in the west wing."

"I would, sir. Is there room there for my ladies?"

"No, but the king's suite below yours is prepared for them. The courtiers may lodge in the east wings."

The torchbearers separated into two groups, one conducting the courtiers across the yard, the other preceding Mary, her ladies and the Scots lords to a staircase at the left. At the top of the first flight Mary caught a glimpse of a long, narrow chamber hung with the banners of Scotland. "The Great Hall," James said. "Adjoining it are the five rooms we have prepared for your Marys." They continued up the stairs and at the second landing stopped at the threshold of a large apartment.

"Your Majesty's audience chamber," Huntley said.

It was lit by dripping rushlights fastened to tall wooden blocks. Wind from an open window stirred the rotting gray tapestries so that hunters and horses moved to eerie life. The graceless oak furniture was sparse—a round table, five chairs with worn gray velvet cushions. In the east wall under a stained-glass window was a small recess for prayer.

Spider webs hazed the ceiling, which was paneled with the crowned initials of Mary of Guise and James V and the armorial bearings of Scotland. As the Marys crossed the stone floor to the dark oak fireplace, their skirts rustled a carpet of dusty rushes.

"Mon Dieu," Mary blurted. "Am I to receive ambassadors here, or spookies?"

"This suite was fine enough for your forebears, Madam," Huntley said gruffly. "Scotland is not France."

"Fortunately we have brought a bit of France with us." Mary stared nervously at the moving tapestries. "Seton, close that window. I am chilled."

But not with cold, she thought—with apprehension. No wraiths had dared the pale, brocaded light of French chateaux, but here they seemed close as her heartbeat. It was as if the presence of the living intruded on a room long dead. She touched her crucifix.

"The bedchamber is smaller," James said, "but perhaps you will find it cosier."

It was as cosy as a small tomb, a dirge of a room that overlooked the outer courtyard and the end of the Canongate. Here too were cobwebs, and Mary wondered what Mistress McDoon and the maids had been doing all day. The plastered walls were green with mildew through which she could see faded murals of fruit and flowers. There was a fireplace with a narrow oak mantel and two hearth chairs. A high bed with a sagging mattress was canopied and curtained in stained gold velvet, and a sprig of dried berries lay on the bolster. Near the bed in a corner was a curtain of ragged tapestry. Mary drew it aside, revealing a narrow spiral staircase of stone.

"Private stairs," Arran said. "They lead below to the king's apartments." He looked at Mary and smirked. "A romantic domestic arrangement."

Arran was behaving annoyingly, as if they shared some secret, and Mary spoke coldly. "My ladies can make use of it, since they have the king's apartments." To avoid him she stepped into the tiny unfurnished room beyond the stairs in the tower turret. Except that it had a fireplace she would have thought it a large closet, and she sighed and turned back through the bedroom to a tiny dressing room that had neither fireplace nor furniture.

As she returned to the bedchamber, James said, "Will this suite be suitable?"

Mary remembered the spacious apartments at Fontainebleau and St. Germain, eight- and ten-room suites, golden with sunlight. These four rooms—two of them doll-sized—seemed a mockery of royal dignity.

"It is so small," Mary said. She removed her cloaks, and Fleming laid them on the bed. "Perhaps I should consider Edinburgh Castle after all."

"The rooms there are even smaller," Huntley said. She thought he sounded grimly pleased. "Darker, too."

"Is this the largest suite in the palace?" Mary asked.

"There is the king's, but this being higher is lighter—"

"Ah, well," she said, "if my mother could stay here so can I."

"I admit Holyrood is small. With a court of any size it is crowded, but at least you have the advantage of hunting. Five miles of forest thick with deer and boar."

"And wolves," added the Duke of Chatelherault. "Last winter hunger drove them clear into the Canongate. Our winters are fearful, Madam—on beasts and men alike."

[114]

He looked at her with his cold, pale eyes, so light a blue they seemed almost white. She thought: His glance measures me for a coffin. He notes my slenderness and hopes I will not survive the winter, for I am all that stands between him and the throne. For eighteen years he must have prayed for my death, and now he is old and his time runs out . . .

Lightly, she said, "I've dozens of swan's-down puffs and quantities of warming pans, Your Grace. Now if you will excuse me, I wish to dress before supper."

James said, "We will await you in the Great Hall at nine, Madam."

The lords bowed out, and a procession of servants bowed in. Maids with trays of wine, pitchers of warm water, towels. Lackeys staggering under dozens of chests and boxes. The Marys supervised their placement and pounced on those containing Mary's newest Paris gowns. They begged her to wear the cherry brocade or the sea-green lace with the golden underskirt.

"No!" Mary said above the clamor of voices. "The black velvet with the jet embroidery."

"You exchange mourning white for mourning black," sighed Seton. "And we wanted you to dazzle—" She bit her lip. "Yes, Madam, I'll just take a pokestick to the ruff. It needs perking."

Mistress McDoon bustled in as the last of the servants trudged out. "Now what will Your Majesty be needing?"

"Nothing at present. But tomorrow we must begin a thorough scouring from cellar to turrets. I shall not live in spiderwebs and mold. Then I plan to redecorate this place and chase the gloom from it."

"I'm thinking you'll not chase it far, Ma'am. Your mother tried, but the moisture creeps through and rots both wood and fabric."

"In any case I will make improvements." Mary wriggled out of her white gown and went to the earthen basin on the hearth. Beaton brought her scented soap and a sponge and she knelt and washed her face and hands.

Mistress McDoon pointed to the soap. "I have heard of that but never seen any. They say it is wondrous slippy."

Mary smiled at the round, inquisitive face—like a winter apple, harsh-skinned and rosy. A white cap puffed atop her gray curls, and her thick waist was belted with jangling keys. She gaped at the soap with such fascination that Mary said, "I will give you some soap when we unpack the rest. I brought a great deal from France."

"Thank you, Ma'am! Here we use wood ash to get clean, but it smarts the skin. Is it the soap that makes your skin so white?"

"I don't think so. It is naturally pale."

"Imagine that, now! Why, fine ladies all over Edinburgh are swallowing gravel ashes and tallow trying to be as white as you."

Mary laughed over the edge of a towel. "Are my portraits circulated in Edinburgh?"

"Indeed, yes, the artists do a busy trade in copying. And the ladies copy your gowns down to the last button, even after Master Knox preached against it."

"Why should he care?"

"They have tails—'Satan's Tails' he calls them—that drag the dust in back. He says it's wasteful of cloth." Mistress McDoon chuckled. "So the ladies pin them up under their cloaks when they venture on the High Street and set them down again when they're safe inside." She watched as Beaton helped Mary into a tight-bodiced, square-necked velvet gown with a sweeping train. "Ah, that's beautiful—with a tail to enrage the old goat! But you shouldn't wear black, Ma'am, not at your age. Why, it makes you thin as a stalk."

"I am a widow," Mary said sharply, "though none seem to remember it."

"I was a widow too, Ma'am, but I put on red before the month was out, and what do you think?" She cocked a bright blue eye. "I caught another husband within a fortnight. A fleshmonger," she added triumphantly.

Mary could not help but smile. "I'm glad of your conquest. But I shall wear black until I wed again." She sat down in the hearth chair, and Beaton arranged her hair and pinned on a jet cap, its heart-shaped peak bordered in diamonds.

"Husbands," said Mistress McDoon, "are a prime necessity. I wouldn't be without one, particularly here. You'll find out, Ma'am, when the wind rises and the corbies start croaking in the turrets. A man can be downright cheerful at such times. I mind your mother thought so."

"You knew my father?"

"Indeed I did." She winked. "Many's the time I helped him off with his boots of a dawn when he tiptoed into your mother's chamber. He frolicked, the King did, and though he loved the Queen —but I'll not be telling *that* story."

"Now that you've started," Mary said, "You'd best proceed."

"Well—there was a bonny blacksmith's wife lived in a wynd near the Cowgate, t'other side of the city wall. It was her I got the story from. The King saw her one day while his horse was being shod, and that very night he visited her in disguise of a simple laird while her husband was at the tavern. Jenny had no idea he was the King but she liked him well, for he was merry and full of grace while her husband was a burly, black-bearded dolt and surly as a bloodied cock.

The King took to coming to Jenny's house at midnight, and when she heard the Tolbooth clock strike the hour she would creep from her husband's bed and greet the King and take him across the hall to another room which had only chickens in it and maybe the goat. It was all cosy as could be, until one dawn, when the King was preparing to leave, Jenny saw the royal crest on his underlinen. And he confessed who he was.

"Well, naturally she was overjoyed and proud to bursting. As she said to me, 'I was bursting to tell somebody,' so she ran into the next room and roused her husband and told him. The King heard her and picked up his boots and doublet and lit out like a comet for Holyrood, but the sentry at the Netherbow wouldn't let him pass, not recognizing him, so the poor man had to climb the city wall and got all bloodied from the heads there, and when he returned the Queen was waiting up with a tart tongue. But the tragedy was what happened to Jenny."

"Did her husband kill her?" Mary asked.

"Kill her? Mercy, no. He wouldn't believe her! She's talked and talked and talked these twenty years, and he *still* doesn't believe her. It's sad," she said, "when a woman's only triumph in life is disallowed."

The Marys laughed and Mistress McDoon said, "You, Ma'am, should have a man in your bed for protection."

"Protection? Against what?" Mary asked.

"The dead."

"Jesu Maria!" Beaton crossed herself.

So I was right, Mary thought—we intrude on the dead. Fleming and Livingstone turned from their unpacking to stare at Mistress McDoon with frightened eyes.

Mistress McDoon pointed to the bed bolster. "Mark those rowan berries? I put them there this morning, but with no priest to bless them I'm not sure they'll protect you."

Anxious to spare her ladies the grisly stories she knew were coming, Mary said, "You must go to your apartments and tidy yourselves for supper. Hurry now!"

"But Madam," Seton said, "May we not hear what Mistress McDoon—"

"I said go!"

Livingstone took a candle from the mantel and lit it from the fire. The others, with jewel cases and reticules, followed her down the spiral staircase.

"Now," Mary said, "who are these dead?"

"Queen Madeleine rises from her vault and moans with the cold on winter nights. There's a gumple-faced nun weeps in the abbey aisle, and on All Saints' Eve she does penance. A monk walks the herb garden—I saw him by full moon, plain as I see your face, and you know as well as I that no live monks walk Edinburgh *these* days, nor nuns either for that matter. They'll not bother you inside here. It's the King does that, and no door can bar him, bolted or not."

"The King—my father?"

Mistress McDoon pursed her lips. "Why, no—it would be your great-grandsire, the third James. Him that was murdered at Sauchieburn, some say by a priest, the knavish Protestants. Anyway he was stabbed. And as he walks—" She shuddered—"he drips blood."

Mary said, "You mustn't spread these tales among my court. I want no panicked servants afraid to walk the halls after dusk."

"I'll be mum as a cod. You won't find *my* tongue rattling." She curtsied and said, "God bless and keep you, Ma'am."

Alone, Mary rose and went to the window. A few pale stars lifted above the crags, and mist rose from the meadows like lazy white smoke. Far off she heard the clop of horses' hoofs. Gradually the horizon lightened and torches cut the darkness, bobbing and plunging down the Canongate. The long shadows of spears streaked past gray gables, and she saw the glitter of steel helmets, a swirl of crimson plaids and plumes. The cavalcade pounded into the courtyard in a shouting, whinnying, spur-jangling uproar.

Mary turned from the window into the moth-circled light. Slowly she walked from the bedroom through the dim gray audience chamber toward the main staircase. A rat scuttered from the whisper of her train in the brittle rushes.

III.

The Great Hall, paneled in dark oak, was lit by five iron chandeliers set with fat tallow candles. Rotting blue tapestry covered one wall, and along another, in window embrasures facing the courtyard, hung tarnished boar spears and the banners of Scotland. Scots and French musicians played behind a shredding silk screen. Hooded falcons perched on ceiling beams, and at the huge hearth staghounds gnawed bones flung from the tables.

Mary sat at a small table on a dais under a moth-eaten canopy that bore the arms of Scotland and Lorraine. Behind her chair stood a guard who tested each dish for poison by ordering the servant who carried it to swallow a mouthful before proffering it to Mary. At her right sat James and the Duke de Chatelherault. At her left, Sir William Maitland of Lethington and the Earl of Arran.

Below her another table extended the length of the room. Nearest her, at the upper end, French and Scots nobles sat on benches according to their rank—earls, barons, knights, ladies, bonnet lairds and French gentlemen. The great pewter saltcellar divided these privileged guests from humbler folk who sat "below the salt"—priests, tiring women, pages, gentlemen of the chamber, falconers, laundresses, grooms, lackeys, sweepers and all kitchen help not engaged in serving the supper. None of these dared speak to their neighbors above the salt, nor presumed to share the more elaborate food and wines. At their end of the table stood a stone bowl where scraps were placed for beggars and the poor.

No cloths covered the scarred oak tables, there were no flowers. Clumsy maids passed wooden platters heaped with roast pork and mutton, boiled and spitted beef, grilled herring. On the tables were trenchers of turbot, wood pigeon, rabbit stew, porpoise pudding. Earthen jugs of malmsey, claret and elderberry wine stood between every two persons and pint leather mugs of ale were set at each place.

Never before had Mary seen food served like fodder for horses—crudely piled on earthen plates without sauce or garnish. Accustomed to subtle French cooking, she found it inedible and was thankful for her foresight in bringing two chefs from Paris. The French courtiers nibbled at huge slabs of beef and chicken, staring helplessly at their greasy hands. Mary demanded napkins and was brought torn strips of Holland cloth.

She noticed that all the men present, from lords to chimney sweeps, wore hats. She remarked it to James. "I see our French fashion of displaying elegant headgear at meals has reached Scotland."

James grimaced. "It is not a fashion, Madam, but a precaution. Should the men remove their hats, lice and other lively creatures might fall into the food."

Appalled, she stared at his own feathered hat.

"Fear not," he chuckled. "Lethington and I are fastidious."

They alone of the Scots nobles ate and drank as gentlemen. Mary shuddered as Arran lifted a whole pigeon to his mouth, then wiped his greasy beard on his sleeve. Lords Huntley, Ruthven and Lindsay gobbled and slobbered, grabbed and tore. Spilled grease puddled the table, and wine from overturned jugs spread along the oak like the flow of blood. This is a nightmare, she thought, and I am back in Saxon times at a tribal feast.

The lords grew merrier as the wine jugs emptied, pounding the tables and calling for whisky. The rush-carpeted floor was a shambles of bones, bread crusts and discarded belts. Staghounds snapped and rolled and chased each other through the debris.

Nowhere else in the world, Mary thought, would one find noblemen belching and spitting in a queen's presence. She caught Chaste-lard's understanding glance and held it wistfully. For he symbolized at that moment the grace and chivalry she might never know again. Reluctantly she turned from him as Lethington offered her a goblet.

"It is whisky, Madam—a brew of barley."

"Thank you." She took a sip, gasped, feeling a run of fire from throat to stomach.

"It is a tonic you will come to appreciate, Madam. Without whisky to warm the long winters there'd be many a dead Scot."

"Since it is August," she smiled, "I will wait."

Black-bearded Lindsay lurched to his feet with a flagon in his hand. "Up, all! A toast to the most beautiful woman in the world—the Queen of Scotland!"

The court rose and turned toward Mary with lifted glasses.

"A long and prosperous reign . . ."

Glasses lifted higher, glowing red and amber in the candleblaze.

"Strong sons and fair daughters . . . to the glory of God and Scotland!"

Lindsay tipped back his head and drank from the flagon, then hurled it toward the fireplace where it crashed on the stone hearth. Glasses followed, shattering, and hounds ran yelping under the tables.

There were more toasts. They drank to Mary's ancestors back through the long line to King Fergus, in 330 B.C. They drank to Mary's eyes and lips, her hair, her exquisite hands. As the toasts began to verge on bawdiness, Chastelard sent for his lute and saluted her in verse. It was a poem of praise, deft and delightful, but she sensed the Scots' scorn of such delicacy, and before the last notes had died away they began a series of ribald ballads, accompanying themselves with thumping mugs and pounding feet.

The songs did not shock her—she had heard verses as frank at King Henry's soirées—but she found them dull and boorish. The Scots could not play with a risqué situation. They bludgeoned it.

James leaned toward her. "They grow rowdy, Madam. Shall we end this?"

"No. They are gay, let them be."

Lethington said, "Your Majesty is accustomed to professional entertainment. This must seem grossly amateur."

"My policy," she smiled, "is tolerance."

"A mark of exquisite worldliness, Madam. I have never known a fanatic who was not naïve."

She wondered if he referred to Knox and if he meant to slur him. But this was not the time or place to explore Lethington's religious convictions. Later she would have a frank talk with him.

So far, and to her surprise, Lethington impressed her favorably. Courtly, soft-spoken, he was neither condescending nor arrogant. He was about forty, she thought, and his face was long and narrow with peaked hairline and pointed black beard—a fox face, full of craft yet not unpleasing. His thin height was accentuated by black velvet clothes embroidered in silver thread, and he wore gold and silver chains around his neck. He and her brother were by far the best-dressed Scots, and she wondered if Elizabeth's gold had purchased their mink sleeves and jewel-hilted daggers. In any case they were preferable to the ruffians who had turned the Great Hall into a tavern.

Arran, glaze-eyed, leered at her, and she stared at him coldly. He mumbled incoherent flattery, and she whispered to Lethington, "Lord Arran is either very drunk or very stupid."

"Must one necessarily be drunk or stupid to compliment a beautiful woman?"

She smiled, but she thought, That is the pity. They regard me first as a woman, secondly as Queen. They have no conception of the divine right of kings and queens, no understanding of the philosophy behind the pomp.

A queen did not demand reverence for herself, but for her position. God had designated her ruler of Scotland in his name, and as his servant she held the highest rank. When that rank was not recognized, when men treated her as a mere woman, her entire concept of herself was shattered.

After years of self-discipline she had made the woman subordinate to the queen; the impulse to tears and temper had been rigidly controlled. But now that she had come to claim her kingdom, men knelt not in awe but in fascination. They honor the least part of me, she thought—the façade of beauty. And in doing so they force me to use it as a weapon against them.

"It is a curious thing," she said, as James and Lethington leaned close to hear her above the din, "but with all the toasts, no one has asked me to speak. Do they think I have no words, no wit—only a face and form?"

"The face and form are sufficient to the moment, Madam. Would you waste your words on wine-brains?" Lethington asked.

"Clever," Mary smiled, "and evasive. You remind me of Throckmorton, Elizabeth's envoy."

"Indeed? Which in turn reminds me—I received word this afternoon that Elizabeth is sending Thomas Randolph as her permanent ambassador to your court."

"Plague upon her! I wanted Throckmorton. He was my friend."

"So naturally Elizabeth assumes he is in love with you and sends Randolph instead. She is a jealous cat, Madam. But you know that."

Cautiously she said, "Why should Elizabeth be jealous of me? I am queen of a poor country, a widow, with bleak prospects of a wealthy or powerful alliance."

"I doubt that she is politically jealous, except of your claim to her throne. I think she is spitefully and personally jealous of a younger and more beautiful woman."

"But that is absurd! I have never been her rival in a romance or mocked her beauty."

"Elizabeth is obsessed with being the most beautiful and accomplished royal lady in Europe. You, Madam, wreck her dream."

"I had not thought her so immature."

"She does display a childish greediness, possibly because she was denied luxuries as a girl. She has acquired three thousand dresses and is building a 'wardrobe manor,' since her palaces will not hold them all. And there is such a drive for possession—objects, people, land. It is revealed even in casual conversation. It is never 'the palace' or 'the table' or 'the forest.' It is 'my palace,' 'my table,' 'my forest.' Yet with all her extravagance to collect and own, she is a miser, the despair of her ministers who must wrest pennies from a tight fist."

Perhaps, Mary thought, you are personally disillusioned. The hand once open to you is now closed.

"It appears that you have made a study of Elizabeth," she said.

"I think I understand her better than her own advisers," Lethington said. "She is a most fascinating puzzle; I prefer her to chess. Some winter night when Your Majesty is bored I will show you the notes I have kept on Elizabeth since her coronation. Nine times out of ten you will see that I anticipated her moves."

"So that you could outmaneuver her if you wished?"

He nodded.

"Later we must talk at length," she said. She needed time to consider what his motives might be. At the moment she was too weary to be on guard against a man who might be Elizabeth's spy.

A shout went up from the Scots as two young men appeared in the doorway, booted and spurred, in scarlet cloaks. Lindsay rose and reeled toward them, trying to draw them into the ballad singing. They laughed and pushed him back into his chair, ignored the mugs that were waved as lures and crossed the room to kneel at Mary's feet.

"Our brothers," James said. "Lord Robert and Lord John Stuart."

Mary looked down on the fair, curly heads and extended her hand for them to kiss. They raised merry brown eyes and John blurted, "Lord, Madam, you're lovelier than your portraits!"

"Thank you," she said, bidding them rise. "Come, we will make room for you."

A servant brought chairs and they sat down—long-legged, handsome, thoroughly at ease.

"We were hunting at Falkland," Robert said, "and returned to town but an hour ago. Otherwise we would have been here to welcome you."

"Do you live in Edinburgh?" she asked. She knew little of her natural brothers except that, like James, they drew a generous income left by her father.

"I live in Coldingham," John said, "but we move about, subject to the whims of our creditors."

"You are in debt?"

"To everyone," Robert said blithely. "Bootmakers, goldsmiths, falconers, innkeepers, weavers, saddlers—everyone. It makes for lively living, Madam."

"You are scamps," she said.

"Villains, Madam. But old James here—a veritable rock. The soul of propriety, industry and thrift."

James mocked a bow.

"Yet we have talents that James lacks," Robert said. "And they are at Your Majesty's disposal. May I enumerate them? Our goshawks are the best trained in Scotland. We brew as fine a brandywine as ever staggered a bishop. We can outdrink any man in the land, except, perhaps, Lord Bothwell."

"But we take our drinking more seriously than he," John said. "We are dedicated men."

"I can see that," Mary said, "and I believe your talents may be utilized. But let me test you. You see before you a dying revel. What would you do to revive it?"

They looked down the long table, at the French with their fixed polite smiles, at the drunken Scots. Lindsay lay with his head on the table, one arm sprawled across a platter of fish. Argyll and Ruthven snored, hunched on their benches, chins sunk into their collars. The other nobles, half-asleep, softly caterwauled the ballads.

"Did Your Majesty bring French wine?" Robert asked.

"A great deal."

"Then I would order it opened and served to those bored gentlemen who, being sober, cannot be Scots. The pretty girls I would scatter among us. Lindsay, Argyll and the others I would not attempt to revive. I'd have their servants carry them to bed."

"I agree in all particulars," John said, "save that I would perch the ash-blonde upon my knee."

"Kneel," Mary said.

They knelt and she pulled a silver hairpin from under her cap. "Do you solemnly swear fidelity to frivolity?"

"We do."

"Then I dub you, Lord Robert, and you, Lord John, Masters of Revels of Holyrood House." She touched them with the hairpin. "You may rise."

James said drily, "Your Majesty is evidently unaware that our brothers already hold office. John is Commendator—Prior—of Coldingham. Robert is Abbot of Holyrood."

Shocked, she said, "Dignitaries of the Church! And you romp unfrocked!"

"These offices are hereditary," Robert said. "Apparently I looked round and innocent and abboty at the age of two months, so our father gave me the title. Neither John nor I disgrace our robes, for we don't wear them."

James chuckled. "Does Your Majesty begin to see why Scotland turned Protestant?"

She turned to Robert and John. "Have you also turned Protestant?"

"It is fashionable, Madam." Robert shrugged. "So, in our way, we subscribe to it. I grant you Protestantism is austere—we weather-chilled Scots are like to catch our death of cold in it. But for men of our debts Catholicism is far too expensive."

From the courtyard came a sudden skirl of bagpipes, a wailing banshee cacophony that startled the court into utter silence. Never had Mary heard such dissonance, and she rose and went to a window while her courtiers crowded to others. Outside, a bonfire blazed on the cobblestones and in its light she saw about two hundred men with pipes, rebecs and fiddles. At sight of her they stopped playing and cheered, lifting ragged caps. Then the music resumed with vilely screeching violins accompanying psalm singers.

"Jesu Maria!" Monsieur Brantôme retreated from window to table, plump hands to his ears. "They murder Orpheus!"

The courtiers laughed, groaned, grimaced. But Mary leaned further from the window, touched to tears. These were her people, serenading her as best they could, greeting her in the only way they knew. She longed to toss them gold, to give tangible proof of her appreciation, but that would be in poor taste. Instead, at a merciful pause in the din, she blew them a kiss and called to them, "Please continue—it is beautiful, and I cannot conceive of a more delightful welcome."

She sent servants down to them with wine, whisky and platters of honeycakes. They drank her health, then resumed sawing on violins and yelling tuneless hymns. She stood at the window fifteen minutes, half an hour.

"Madam." James touched her shoulder. "You are exhausted. You had best dismiss them."

"Dismiss them! After all their trouble? The court has my permission to retire but I shall stay here as long as one man is in the courtyard."

Servants carried the drunken lords to bed. One by one the courtiers disappeared, until only Livingstone and James remained in the guttering candlelight.

Forty minutes later the scratching violins sent a final shiver down Mary's spine and, the serenaders prepared to leave. She called to them again, her hands outstretched.

"Please come back again . . . You have made me so happy."

She turned from the window, stumbling a little. James picked her up in his arms, and Livingstone, with a candle, lit their way up the staircase. Cuddled against James's shoulder, Mary thought sleepily how pleasant it was to have a strong protective brother whom she could . . . almost . . . trust . . .

IV.

The next morning an east wind whipped in from the sea and the haar returned, murking the forest, the meadows, the gardens of Holyrood. Mary breakfasted in bed. Then with Fleming she followed Mistress McDoon on a tour of the palace.

The chill candlelit darkness lent an illusion of midnight. They climbed to dripping bat-blackened turrets, wound down through small melancholy rooms that bordered the drafty corridors. The king's apartments which the Marys occupied were walled with peeling plaster painted with fading frescoes. Chairs veered drunkenly on two legs; tapestries were ravaged by moths, rats and mold. They groped across the fog-filled courtyard to the northeast wing.

In the State Chamber the great gold throne was tarnished black. Purple hangings were in shreds, and the magnificently carved ceiling was gray with cobwebs. Tight-lipped, Mary followed Mistress McDoon past the apartments of the courtiers. Through an open door she caught a glimpse of strewn luggage, clothing hung on pegs and a straw pallet laid on the rushes.

Mary paused, shocked. "Did one of my courtiers sleep on that pallet last night?"

"Yes, Ma'am. The plump gentleman with the yellow whiskers."

"Monsieur Brantôme slept on the *floor?*"

"They all did. There is only nine beds in the palace. You and your ladies had five and the rest we gave your brothers and the Duke of Chatelherault."

"You mean that everyone—my nobles and my priests—slept on those wretched pallets?"

"Yes, Ma'am."

Mary thought of the great golden featherbeds of France to which they were accustomed; the perfumed hangings and satin sheets. "I wouldn't blame them if they set sail tomorrow!"

"Well, they was a little fleabit, but what was we to do? The rushes are free to the dogs, and there was no time to lay new ones."

"Jesu!" Mary turned to Fleming. "If this tale reaches Queen Catherine I'll be the laughing stock of Europe."

"Who would write her, Madam? These are your friends."

"Monsieur Brantôme is first an historian and secondly a friend. I've no doubt his notebook lists every fleabite, every humiliation since we landed." Mary went to the threshold of the room and poked her head in. "The place reeks! The rushes must be fifty years old."

Fleming said, "They should be burnt at once."

"We never burn them," Mistress McDoon said cheerfully. "We just lay new ones on top to make a nice carpet."

Mary said, "The rushes will be swept out and burned. The floors will be scoured. Then we will lay down the Turkey carpets I have brought from France—there are thirty-six. My forty-five beds will be uncrated this very day. If you haven't sufficient servants, hire more. But if my guests are not sleeping in comfort tonight, you will be sleeping in the kirkyard."

Mistress McDoon hurried off to the servants' quarters, and Mary sighed, looking after her. "She is not efficient. What I need is a Mistress of the Household who understands how to achieve elegance, who can train servants."

"Madam," Fleming said eagerly, "I could do that."

"Of course you could. But it would leave you little time for pleasure."

"I would take the greatest pleasure in making the palace orderly and beautiful."

"If you find it drudgery will you promise to tell me?"

"Yes, Madam. But I will love it! Just tell me what you want, and it will be done."

"First we will change the food. That Scots cook must either be ruled by my chefs or perpetrate his crimes elsewhere."

Seeking the kitchen they went to the end of the corridor and descended a staircase. Down a long stone passage they came to another staircase which led to cold, green-dripping rooms rubbled with whitened bones.

The candle in Fleming's hand began to shake. "Dungeons, Madam."

There were instruments of torture rusty with age—an iron boot with clamps, a body press, thumbscrews. From somewhere came the slow-splashing sound of water on stone.

"These must lead to the abbey vaults," Mary said.

A rat slithered across their path, and they ran back the way they had come, continuing up a passage that led to the wine cellar. Bottles lay flat on high shelves, and they squeezed past barrels of ale to climb steps that brought them into the kitchen.

It was a vast rock-walled room, the earth floor hardened with bullocks' blood, and mud. From the black-beamed ceiling hung flitches of bacon, hams, dried herring. Tall stone cupboards held sheep-bone cutlery and earthenware. At opposite ends of the room were huge fireplaces. One, used for boiling, was fitted with hooks and cranes, and soup simmered in big-bellied pots. At the roasting fire a boy turned a lamb on long spits, and in the deep recess an ox held by iron spikes sizzled above the coals.

Nearby a woman prepared rushlights, peeling off the green fiber and dropping the rushes to soak in troughs of sheepgrease, then removing them to dry on the warm hearthstones. Another woman fastened the finished rushes into wooden holders. Mary and Fleming paused to watch them, then crossed to the long oak table in the middle of the room where scullery maids were rolling dough under the direction of Henri and Gaston, Mary's French chefs.

The servants bowed and curtsied.

"Where is the Scots cook?" Mary asked.

"Departed, Madame," Gaston said. "He would not abide our instructions."

"Good riddance," Mary said. She turned to the maids. "Gaston and Henri are in complete charge of the kitchen. Lady Fleming is Mistress of the Household."

While Fleming was instructing the maids, Mary called the boy from the spit. He was about thirteen, a freckled redhead with an engaging grin.

"What is your name?" she asked.

"Peter Pye." He bowed awkwardly, his patched brown hose wrinkling loose at the knees. "Your Majesty," he added.

"A fine sturdy lad like you should not be a turnspit. You shall lose your work to a dog."

He gaped at her.

"In France we train dogs to turn the spits with their paws. My poodle is lost at sea, but if she is not found I will send for another, and she will take over your duties." Mary patted his spiky red hair. "How well do you know the palace? Have you explored it?"

"Yes Ma'am. My uncle is caretaker here—I have known my way about since I was wee."

"Then perhaps you can instruct my French pages. They understand Scots but they are sure to lose themselves in the maze of corridors. Will you take charge of them and show them around, Peter?"

"Yes, Ma'am—Your Majesty!"

"One of the maids will turn the spits. You shall guide Lady Fleming and me to the places we haven't seen."

Peter led them through the kitchen door along an arcaded walk gray with fog. Where the cobbles ended were a cluster of small stone huts—buttery and brewery, laundry and bakehouse. Across the backyard were timber houses with thatched roofs where the servants lived within the palace walls.

"Back of those houses there's a lion's den," Peter said. "Only there's no lion there now, just a big muck pit."

"Muck?" Fleming asked. "You mean refuse is piled there?"

"Yes'm. It stinks something terrible. If the wind was south you'd smell it now."

"We'll have it burned regularly," Fleming said. "And Peter, we're going to hire a ratcatcher with a ferret pack, and you may show him all the places to hunt."

"Rats are everywhere, but mostly in the abbey."

"That reminds me," Mary said. "I want the abbey swept out and the floor covered with my gold cloth. We will hear Mass on Sunday."

"Mass?" Peter lowered his voice to a whisper. "It's forbidden, Ma'am. Why, the people would *murder* a priest if they caught him holding Mass."

"They'll not murder my priest," Mary said grimly.

"Just the same," Peter warned, "you'd best keep him guarded. To hear Mass is against the law, and anybody who does can be flogged, or even hanged." He hesitated, reddened. "You be careful, Your Majesty. Master Knox is terrible hard on witches."

"Witches! Does he say I am a witch?" Mary asked.

"Well, last Sunday he said you'd come here and cast spells. He said you were a enchant—enchant—"

"Enchantress?"

"Yes'm."

She laughed. "He is a silly old man."

They turned back along the cobbled walk and separated in the courtyard, Peter and Fleming to seek the French pages and Mary to return to her apartments. The floors had been swept clean of rushes, and pale gray carpets stamped with gold fleur-de-lis were spread in audience chamber and bedroom. Beaton was smoothing satin sheets on the gold-and-ebony bed brought from St. Germain. Mary's initials were embroidered in pearls on rose damask bed curtains, and a pearl coronet roofed the canopy.

"A vast improvement," Mary said.

It would cost money to refurbish Holyrood with more furniture and tapestries, but she could well afford it. Her dowries had been generous. Francis had granted her lifetime revenues from Touraine and Poitou. Her many jewels from him and from suitors could be sold or pawned for splendid sums. She was a rich queen of a poor country.

"Madam," Beaton lowered her voice. "There's something I think I should tell you."

"What, cherie?"

"This morning I was alone in the State Chamber behind the throne pulling the worn velvet off the dais, when Lord James and Sir William Lethington came in. They did not see me. Lord James said, 'I never really believed that she would come.' And Lethington said, 'Nor I. She is sure to raise wonderful tragedies.' "

"Wonderful tragedies!" Mary said. "Are you sure you heard aright?"

"Positive, Madam."

"Did Lethington sound as though he was jesting?"

"No, Madam. He was quite serious."

Lethington's phrase haunted Mary through the dark afternoon, while she and her ladies unpacked and arranged her jewels and gowns. *She is sure to raise wonderful tragedies.* It had the solemn ring of prescience and confirmed her own uneasiness.

At four o'clock she summoned Lethington to the audience chamber.

Already it was a different room. Rose and gray tapestries hung on frames set a foot from the walls to prevent contact with the damp stone. The pale gray carpet stretched the width of the room, and her white velvet love seats and rose-cushioned chairs bloomed under tall candelabra of gold and ebony.

Lethington exclaimed at its loveliness. "You have exquisite taste, Madam."

"Thank you. But it will take weeks of work before Holyrood looks as it should."

She indicated a chair, and Lethington sat down, crossing spidery black-hosed legs. Contrasted with the dark pointed beard, his skin was pallid, almost bloodless. In his somber black velvet doublet and onyx neck chains he had an austere elegance. He is civilized, she thought, polished to a hard brilliance. He is probably attractive to women who are challenged by coldness. He would be a fitting mate for Madame Diane . . .

"You should have joined us at dinner, Madam, if only to see the French perk and the Scots gape. Your chefs are magnificent. It is one reformation I approve."

"Do you not approve Master Knox's reforms?"

"I do not approve of Master Knox. No man who mistrusts beauty can believe in God."

"He mistrusts beauty?"

"I saw how he ruined St. Giles. There was no cathedral in Europe to match it, save, possibly, Chartres. Deep topaz hangings jeweled into the palest primrose against unbelievably delicate oak carving. As a boy I visioned heaven as amber and oak and golden light because St. Giles was thus. Knox stripped it, and whitewashed it."

"He hated the Catholic symbols."

"That was his excuse. I think it was the beauty he hated, just as he hates the sight of a comely woman trailing her silks along the High Street, be she Protestant or Catholic. Does he shake his fist at sunsets? Curse the springtime? I wonder . . ."

"I gather that you are Catholic."

"No, I am not. Catholicism requires devout imagination, and I am not sufficiently mystic. In fact, religion does not interest me."

"Perhaps you are somewhat like Lord Bothwell—"

"God forbid!" He threw up his hands in mock horror, and black satin spilled back from his wrists. "I live neither by my sword nor by my appetites."

"None of you will ever forgive Bothwell's loyalty to my mother."

"I fear you romanticize a rogue. Are you aware that Bothwell, before the Siege of Leith, intercepted and stole a shipment of more than three thousand crowns from England?"

Mary laughed. "I am indeed. My mother thought it delightful irony that he gave her money which Queen Elizabeth herself had counted out to pay Scots traitors."

"Traitors, Madam? That is a harsh word."

"Rebels, then." Gently she said, "You were one of them—a rebel against my mother's authority, against the crown. Why?"

"Because I wanted, and still want, a strong alliance with England. Scotland cannot survive without it."

"You would give Scotland to Elizabeth in order to achieve this union?"

"No. I would effect the union by insuring Your Majesty's succession to the English throne."

"You actually think you can persuade Elizabeth to name me her successor?"

"Yes, Madam. I have told you that I can outmaneuver her."

"Even if you could, there is her Secretary of State. I hear Cecil is wilier than she."

"They are a clever pair. But, though it may sound boastful, I am their match. Let me prove it, Madam, and empower me to negotiate with Elizabeth in your behalf."

"I don't understand your motives," she said. "You were once allied with Elizabeth against my mother. You now wish to work against Elizabeth in my interests. Why?"

"Because Scotland's only hope of survival lies in Your Majesty's succession to the English throne."

"Come, sir—Scotland's survival cannot be your principal concern. Spare me the high-flown phrases and tell me the truth."

"The plain truth is so simple that you may not believe it, Madam. My only passion is diplomacy. I'd like the satisfaction of outwitting Elizabeth and Cecil. Not for spite—for sport. I would take the same pleasure in a difficult game of chess."

"That," she smiled, "I can understand. I have known men like you; the Cardinal of Lorraine loves diplomatic intrigue. But he has an obsession for power."

Lethington shrugged. "Not I. Power entails responsibilities that would bore me. I want only power to negotiate in your behalf. I would like to approach Elizabeth as your Secretary of State."

"First I must appoint a Privy Council." She looked him in the eye. "Without advisers I might raise wonderful tragedies."

She had hoped to puncture his poise, but he smoothed his mustache and smiled. "If Lord James quoted me he failed to explain my use of a stage term, Madam. I used the word 'tragedies' in the sense of 'dramas.' You will, inevitably, create wonderful dramas in Scotland."

"Clever," she laughed. "Your diplomatic qualifications are evident."

"Thank you, Madam. Together we can accomplish great things. Believe me . . ."

She wished that she could believe him. His self-assurance impressed her. If any man on earth could outwit Elizabeth, she felt that this man could. On the other hand he might be Elizabeth's spy.

"We both want the same thing," he said, "for different reasons. You want the English crown—I want the alliance it would bring about. Why should we not work toward a common goal?"

"I shall consider your proposal."

She rose and accompanied him to the door, extending her hand for him to kiss. As he straightened he said, "A word of warning, Madam. Always keep a guard at your door."

"I do at night. Is there any special reason—"

"It is merely a precaution that I strongly urge you to take."

Abruptly he opened the door. His taperbearer waiting on the landing bowed and preceded him down the staircase. Below in the Great Hall Mary heard the clink of mugs and voices off-key:

The Pope in his chapel instructed a nun
Till she was great with piety and swollen with a son . . .

V.

On Sunday morning the haar lifted—a happy omen, Mary thought, for the hearing of her first Mass in Scotland. While the abbey chapel was being prepared with her portable altar and gold-cloth carpet, she walked with her courtiers in the damp weed-tangled gardens.

Dead honeysuckle bushes retained a faint fragrance and early asters raised shaggy heads in neglected flower beds. The surrounding meadows were purpled with heather that shaded from lavender to dark violet. Above the oak forest the crags climbed red against the sun. In the distance she heard cowbells and the deeper-throated bells of St. Giles.

Chastelard maneuvered her deftly away from the others, and they walked slowly toward the abbey. "Your Majesty has been avoiding me," he said. "Have I offended you?"

"Of course not, Pierre. I have been busy—it is no small task to unpack the accumulations of a lifetime and find room for them. Besides, you know I've been besieged with visitors. First Randolph, the English Ambassador. Then the nobles riding in from the Border and the Highlands. It seems every man in Scotland wants audience."

"They come to protest your religion, and leave protesting love for you. You smile on barbarians, yet you have no time for me. Am I a log, a bit of furniture to be taken for granted?"

Mary paused in the grassy path. Decidedly, she thought, he is no longer a pretty boy to be pacified by a nod. The soft jaw had hardened, there were shadows under the dark blue eyes and tiny lines in the corners. He looked almost haggard.

"I have heavy duties at present," she said. "Later there will be time for frivolity."

"You think of me only in that regard," he said glumly. "Someone to amuse you, little better than a fool."

"That's not true. You are one of my favorite gentlemen. Or you were before you caught the Scots grimness."

"Why should I not be grim? I see the way the lords lust for you, I could cut their hearts out. I am in love with you. No," he said as she frowned, "I shall not be silent. For five dark days I have been closed in with my thoughts and now I shall speak my mind—"

A high animal scream shrilled up and gurgled into silence. Outside the abbey door in a crowd of Scots lords Mary saw Father Black trying to help an altar boy whose head poured blood over his white smock. As she and Chastelard ran forward, the boy fell to the grass over spilled candles. Lindsay bent above him with a dripping sword.

Over the babble of voices Arran roared, "Death to idolaters! Burn the priest!"

James stepped between Lindsay and the cowering priest with drawn sword and shouted to his men to carry the wounded boy into the palace. Mary's Scots halberdiers came running to their assistance, and Lords John and Robert escorted Father Black into the abbey and slammed the door shut.

"So you protect idolaters!" Lindsay shook his sword at James. "You'd infect decent folk with Romish filth!"

"No Protestant shall enter the abbey," James said, his voice calm and cold. "But the Queen and her Catholics shall hear Mass—now and forever, if they wish."

Mary pushed forward to James's side. "Thank you," she said. She turned to Lindsay. The fist holding the sword gradually lowered until it was level with her heart.

"Sheath that sword," she commanded.

Lindsay scowled at her. His arm jerked out and the crowd gasped. Then, slowly and sullenly he sheathed the sword in its scabbard.

"God help you," she said, "if that boy dies."

"He won't," Arran babbled. "He won't, he won't; it was a flesh wound in the forehead." He began to laugh hysterically and tears streamed down his cheeks. Ignoring him, Mary turned again to Lindsay.

"Men have been executed for less than this," she said. "Another such attempt and your rank will not save you. It is all that saves you now."

He said nothing, sulking under the lash of her voice. "This terror of the Mass is childish," she said. "You accuse Catholics of superstition—yet you are so deep in it you have lost reason."

She took James's arm. "I am ready to hear Mass now."

"I shall guard the door," he said. "You will not be disturbed."

[133]

Impulsively, Mary put both arms around James and kissed his cheek. Then, followed by her courtiers, she entered the vast broken abbey and walked the gold path to the altar where Father Black stood in prayer. Looking back she saw that Lord Robert and Lord John had shut the door and bolted it from the inside.

Mary knelt on the hard stone. Through the shattered roof came the trill of bird song. Wood pigeons cooed in the high Gothic arches. Lifting her head she saw a flight of doves above the fire-blackened columns. Never before had she worshiped in church without pageantry. But in these gray ruins the Mass seemed most precious—and poignant. For though she prayed with a full heart she felt no responding presence. It was as though her plea winged into vacant sunlight, unheard, ungrasped.

When the Mass ended she accompanied Father Black to his quarters, where a physician was attending the altar boy. The scalp wound was not serious, and Mary, reassured, returned to her apartments, where she found James waiting for her in the audience chamber. They sat by the sunlit window.

"I am deeply grateful for what you did," Mary said.

"So am I," James smiled. "It won me my first kiss from a queen."

She thought he looked young, almost boyish in the dappling sun. Amber lights danced in the dark brown beard, in the wavy hair. Again she was reminded of the portraits of her father.

"I am afraid I made an enemy of Lindsay," she sighed, "but he could spark a powder keg. Did you note Arran screaming for a burning?"

"Arran." He dismissed him with a wave of his hand. "Weak and unstable, half-bully, half-mouse. He and Lindsay are violent against the Mass but basically unpredictable. You do not know these weathercock lords, Madam. They change allegiance as often as you change jewels."

"And every one a Protestant," she sighed, "except Huntley. And he resents me for some reason."

"Huntley has good reason. As Lord High Chancellor and head of the Catholic party in Scotland he had great prestige. Now you head the Catholics, and he sees his power usurped. In the Highlands he rules as a king—'Cock o' the North' they call him. Were I you I would handle him with particular care." He smiled. "He is too old for your present lures."

"Lures?" she asked innocently.

"My dear sister, I am not blind. You have set out to captivate, and your progress has been remarkable. In a scant five days you have all but Huntley and Lindsay nibbling from your hand. Arran, despite his outburst this morning, is in love with you."

"I cannot bear Arran. He is the most revolting man I've ever met."

"There's a maggot in his brain that makes him act strangely at times. He longs for his father's death so he will be heir to the throne, yet the old man hangs on, robust as a winter apple."

"I am thinking of Lethington as Secretary of State."

He nodded. "A block of ice animated by a shrewd brain."

"James—" She hesitated, for the question might seem to him naïve. "You are virtual ruler of Scotland, are you not?"

His green eyes crinkled with amusement. "In a manner."

"I have spoiled your dream?"

"It was never a dream." His eyes, so like her own in their heavy-lidded length, were direct. "A bastard cannot dream of the crown. But your father's blood also runs in me. I would not be content in the shadows. I am half a king."

Touched, she leaned toward him and put her hand on his. For a moment they sat in silence, hands clasped.

"I am no longer frightened," she said, "now that I have you. I need someone to love." She turned away for a moment, pretending to adjust her silver gauze cap. "I did love Francis. No one knew how much."

"You loved a child, Mary. Some day you will love a man."

"There is only one man I could imagine loving," she said, thinking aloud. "But of course I *don't* love him," she added quickly.

"Who?"

"Lord Bothwell."

She felt his hand tense under her own. "I pray that you never will," he said. "Aside from political reasons and my own dislike of him, he is too violent for a woman of your breeding. He has no regard for convention, no gentleness. Bothwell is as close to a brute as a man can be."

"I would say Lindsay and Arran are far more brutish. Bothwell has manners, he is clean. He can read and write, he has opinions. Perhaps he lacks the wit of Lethington but he is accepted in the courts of Europe—"

"He has a surface culture which he maintains in your presence. But I have drunk with him, gamed with him—I know him well."

"But what do you mean by 'brutish'? Cruel?"

"Ruthless. Women are his prey. Why, for example, did he choose Janet Beaton for his mistress, a woman nearly twice his age? Because he wanted her lands. He persuaded the infatuated fool to deed everything to him. And then he left her for a tavern slut in Jedburgh."

"How do you know this?"

"He bragged of it. But that is merely one instance; there are many. His most recent dupe is Anna Throndsen. He took her from her family in Norway on the promise to marry her when they reached Flanders. But he didn't. Once her dowry was spent and she had sold her last jewel, he left her and went to France to see what he could wheedle from you."

Mary did not mention the money she had given Bothwell. Some stubborn loyalty to him kept her silent. But she thought about Anna Throndsen, wondering if she was the dark beauty pictured in the locket clasp of his cloak. "Where is Anna now?"

"She followed him here to Scotland. But I expect he will pack her back to Norway—returning used merchandise."

"If this is true he is contemptible."

"It is true. Your mother knew his nature, but she turned the tables. She used him."

Perhaps I can too, Mary thought. Use the best in Bothwell—the courage and the strength—and leave the rest to foolish women.

"You could not do that," James said, and she looked up guiltily. "You are too soft, too romantic. Or perhaps I should say Bothwell is too practiced a lover."

"If my mother could resist him, I can."

"The circumstances of your mother's life forced her into armor. She was a fortress—you are a woman."

Mary withdrew her hand from his with a little pat. "Believe me, Bothwell means nothing to me. I just thought—in the future—merely to dally—"

"You cannot dally with such a man. You would be a moth to fire. Play with a Chastelard if you like until a suitable husband presents himself. You must choose someone who will help you unite Scotland."

"I know, and I shall." Mary sighed. "Meanwhile I must try to unite it myself—with Knox pulling the people against me."

"You must pacify Knox. Show him that you are neither sorceress nor Jezebel. I am loath to tell you, but in a sermon last week he referred to you as 'The Cardinal's whore.' "

"He is mad," she said. "I cannot persuade a deranged brain."

"If he is mad, it is the madness of titans—of Moses, of Paul."

She would not argue the point. "Should I send for him? I fear he will make an embarrassing scene, perhaps publicly."

"His intent is not to embarrass you but to convert you. I'm sure he would be glad to come if you summon him."

"Then I shall," she said. "Early this week. And I wish you to be present."

He nodded. "If I may suggest—do not wear lip paint or color your eyelids."

"No! He will see me as I am. I would be a hypocrite to masquerade as a country bumpkin."

"Please reconsider. It is such little things that change the course of history."

"To be myself is no little thing," Mary said.

CHAPTER FIVE

I.

MARY DRESSED CAREFULLY to receive John Knox—not to impress him, for she felt he would be impervious to physical appeal—but to bolster her confidence. She chose a gown of black Spanish lace, the square neck bordered in pearls, the bell sleeves pearl-buttoned at the tight wrists. When she moved, the overskirt rippled back to reveal velvet fringe, and on her head she wore a half-veil of black lace. Pearl and onyx butterflies held her hair in place.

"Which ruff, Madam?" Seton asked. "The new enormity?"

"No. Nineteen yards of linen would likely choke me. The small one of black gauze."

"The ruffs are so big in Spain," Livingstone said, "that ladies can't dine in comfort. Monsieur Brantôme says they eat soup from spoons two feet long."

"It is scarce sillier than the new fashion for men," Beaton said. "Have you noted Master Randolph's enormous puffed and padded breeches? They would be grotesque on anyone else. But he is attractive; I'm surprised Queen Elizabeth sent him to us."

"I too," Mary said. She sprinkled scent on her hair and wrists. "I expected a snoopy old man. He snoops, of course—that is his duty—but for a man of thirty-seven he is marvelously preserved."

Beaton said, "Did Randolph tell Your Majesty that Queen Elizabeth has no glass mirror?"

"No!"

"Not one. When she heard Your Majesty had three face mirrors and one full-length she was livid, for she has only polished metal."

Mary laughed. "She would do well to turn Catholic and cultivate the Venetians. But Beaton, this seems an odd thing for Randolph to tell you. As Elizabeth's ambassador he should not admit her rages and her frustrations."

Beaton sat down on a hearth cushion, her hands clasping her knees. "Randolph may be her ambassador but he is my admirer.

Lord John's brandywine has inspired him to admit several things he would not have mentioned otherwise. But it is difficult to lead him off the subject of my curls. He seems to find them more fascinating than Elizabeth."

"And does he fascinate you?"

"No, I encourage him only for Your Majesty's sake, trying to pry Elizabeth's secrets from him." She smiled. "He in turn asks questions about you—some fearfully personal when the wine is at work."

"Such as?"

"He asked if you padded your bosom. Evidently Elizabeth does, and she cannot bear the thought that Your Majesty does not need to. I think she is as concerned about that as she is about political matters."

"What a strange, vain creature she must be!" Mary glanced at the clock. "You and Livingstone had best go into the audience chamber and await Master Knox and Lord James. I wish you to remain throughout the interview—for spiritual support. A little prayer will do no harm."

They curtsied and left. Seton smoothed Mary's train. "I would be shaking in your place, Madam."

"Knox blames me for everything," Mary sighed, "from 'Satan's tails' to the haar. He says God heralded my arrival by darkening the heavens."

"God lifted the darkness for our Mass," Seton said.

"So he did! I shall point that out if I can get a word in edgewise." She fastened the ruby crucifix to her belt. "I wish I were not so young. He is fifty-seven, old in cunning."

Livingstone tapped at the door and poked her head in. "The gentlemen are here, Madam."

Mary paused for a final glance in the long amethyst-framed mirror. She tried to see herself through Knox's eyes. Her somber dignity he could not question. The dark gown and smoky kohl deepened her eyes to blackness, contrasting with the dead white of skin and pearls. Perhaps her mouth would offend him—crimson and curving, voluptuously underlipped. But she was thankful for such a mouth, for eyes full of light and fingers elegantly tapered. This portrait in black and white and scarlet was truly herself at her best. She would not alter it.

She opened the door to the sun-shadowed audience chamber and smelled the fragrance of juniper wood burning in golden wall braziers. The Marys curtsied from the window recess, and James and Knox stood near the unlit fireplace. They turned as Mary came forward, and Knox bowed, sweeping off a narrow-brimmed black velvet hat.

She had thought him a big man, but to her surprise he was not as tall as she. Thin but not gaunt, his face was powerfully defined. Heavy gray brows tufted over the eyes she remembered so well—deep set and blackly burning. The lips were red and full, the skin sallow, like wrinkled parchment. A limp gray beard streaked with yellow flowed to the waist of his rusty black doublet. Though the day was warm, he wore a black Geneva cloak, the full sleeves banded in velvet.

"Please sit down," Mary said.

Knox sat stiffly on the edge of a rose velvet sofa, James beside him. Livingstone and Beaton shared a window seat, and Mary chose a chair near the men. She was conscious of Knox's unflickering stare that traveled slowly from her lacy headdress down to the pearl-embroidered tips of her slippers. Though accustomed to the scrutiny of men, she was resentful. No man of God should make such bold examination of a woman, but she smiled at him and kept her voice soft, sweet.

"Master Knox," she said, "I have read your writings and heard so much of you that I am glad to see you—"

"Your Majesty saw me on the High Street," he said, his eyes on her crucifix, his mouth sneering.

"Ah, yes," she said. "I meant I am glad to meet with you. Though we differ in faith we both have Scotland's good at heart—"

"The heart, Madam, is of the body and thus inclined to evil. We will consider the soul." He leaned forward, pointed two long fingers at her. "What of yours?"

She felt like a schoolgirl lax in her lessons. "S-s-soul?" she stammered. "Why, my—"

"Aye, your soul." He seemed grimly pleased. "I warrant Romish tutors neglected it to verse you in sophistry."

"You are wrong," she said, still patiently. "But I wish to speak of Scotland. You know the needs of the people as I do not, and I would welcome your counsel. Together, we—"

"The people will not tolerate the Mass, Madam!" He half-rose from his chair. "Nor will I!"

"Pray, sir, let us not battle!" Again she smiled at him. "I have told the people they may worship as they please, but so shall I. I've no wish to split my realm but to be tolerant—"

"To tolerate evil is to deny Jesus Christ!"

She glanced at James, begging his help with her eyes, hoping he would intervene to help her. But he sat expressionless, toying with his rings.

"There can be no compromise between good and evil," Knox said.

Nor between us, she thought sadly. It is hopeless. He makes it impossible.

"You shall not poison a clean well," Knox said. "You shall not—"

"Peace, Master Knox!" Her voice shook with anger. "It is you who spread poison. I am told that the Sunday before my arrival you accused me of sorcery and dubbed me an enchantress. That is not true. It is you who use sorcery. You stir my people to priest-flogging and abbey-wrecking through the use of necromancy."

"Whoever says that lacks ears." His voice was a deep bass, harshly resonant. "I have preached against necromancy since my first pastorate at Berwick. But seeing that my Master, Jesus Christ, was said to practice the black arts I must patiently bear such accusations."

"Do you compare yourself to Jesus Christ?" she asked. "Did he ever instigate sedition and slaughter as you have done in England and Scotland? Did he foment rebellion against lawful rulers as you have done and flout the authority of queens as you have flouted Mary Tudor's, my mother's and my own?"

"If your people accept your authority I am content to live under Your Majesty's regimen, as the Israelites lived under Pharaoh, as Paul lived under Nero."

His bland egotism disgusted her. "You are no Paul, but a rabble-rouser. You inflame my people to adopt a faith contrary to my own."

"Daniel was subject to Nebuchadnezzar, yet he prayed publicly, as I do, against the commandment of the King."

"But how can your doctrine be God's, since God commands subjects to obey their rulers?

Knox hesitated. She knew he dared not deny the divine right of kings.

"Madam, religion takes neither strength nor authority from rulers, but from the Eternal God alone. Subjects are not bound to frame their beliefs according to the appetites of their princes."

"But neither Paul nor Daniel raised the sword against their princes."

"You cannot deny that they resisted them."

"But not by the sword," Mary insisted.

"God had not given them the power and the means!"

Mary stared at him incredulously. "Do you mean," she asked, "that subjects having power may resist their princes?"

"Yes, Madam!" His voice boomed through the room. "If princes exceed their bounds they may be resisted. Think of a prince as a father. God has commanded us to honor our father and our mother, but if the father fall into a dangerous frenzy and would slay his own children, may not the children resist him? It is so with princes who would murder the children of God. Their blind zeal is a mad frenzy; and therefore to take the sword from them and bind their hands

[141]

and cast them into prison till they be brought to soberness agrees with the will of God."

Mary was speechless. Such a doctrine shattered all existing law, smashed every belief by which she had been spiritually, emotionally and intellectually trained. She put her head in her hands. Never before had she panicked at an idea. Yet never before had she heard anarchy and insurrection expounded. Her universe had been orderly. Now it reeled as though torn by the birth of a monstrous star.

The room was silent, save for the ticking of the gold filigree clock on the mantel. James stirred uneasily, then rose and went to Mary, touching her arm.

"Madam," he asked anxiously, "are you all right?"

She looked up and nodded. Tears trembled in her eyes, but she flung her head high. "Master Knox, you advocate that my subjects shall obey you and not me."

Evasively, he said, "God commands queens to be nurses unto his people and unto his troubled Church."

"Yes—but yours is not the church that I shall nurse. I will defend the Church of Rome, for I believe it is the true Church of God."

"Your belief does not make the Roman harlot the true and immaculate spouse of Jesus Christ!" he shouted.

He is mad, she thought—raving. She jumped up, and James stepped between her and Knox.

"You shall not use such language in my presence!" Mary said.

"Rome is polluted with spiritual fornication—"

"Master Knox!"

"—and harlotry."

"My conscience does not say so."

He sneered. "Conscience, Madam, requires knowledge; and I fear you have none."

"The simplest shepherd in the fields may have conscience," she said, "but I have read and studied—"

His harsh roar drowned her out. "So did the Jews who crucified Christ read and study the law and the prophets. You have been taught only what is allowed by the Pope and his cardinal."

Wearily she said, "You interpret the scriptures one way, they another. Whom shall I believe? And who shall be judge?"

"You shall believe God, Madam. Does not his word plainly assure us that Jesus neither said nor commanded Mass at his Last Supper? Mass is not mentioned in the entire Scripture. It is an invention of man and an abomination before God . . ."

He ranted on as though the chamber were St. Giles and the sofa his pulpit, oblivious to her attempts to break in. If she and James and her ladies left the room she was sure he would not realize it but would continue declaiming to the tapestried nymphs on the wall. Perhaps he was not mad but insensitive, shelled with self-righteousness. To dismiss him as a fanatic was too simple. She felt that he was a passionate man who had chanced upon Calvinist doctrine and seized upon it as another might seize a woman, elementally, in a torrent of emotion.

Mary studied his face, searching in vain for the smallest hint of spirituality. But the storm-black eyes were fierce, the mouth sensual, the chin stubborn. Even the prophet-like beard had a pagan, goatish look. She thought, Kindness, humility, gentleness are not in him. If he loves God, then it is a God of his own invention who mirrors himself.

She marveled at his hold upon the people, for even James had admitted that Knox had contempt for the rabble. There was no known instance of his having visited the poor, the sick, or the wretched folk in almshouses. He did not minister to his flock—he bullied them with threats of hellfire. Probably, she thought, he provides a fine, blazing show of oratory. The poor, with few amusements, might find shuddering excitement in his declamations, a spark in the drabness of their lives. But assuredly he held his congregation through fear, not love.

Mary pounced as Knox caught his breath. "This argument is futile. I am as strong in my faith as you are in yours. But there is a final matter I should like to discuss. Why do you take it upon yourself to arbitrate such trivial matters as fashion? I am told you prohibit tails on women's gowns and such things as lip paint."

"The man of God protects his flock against Jezebels. I do not call you a whore, Madam—"

"How generous of you," she said scathingly, "to change your opinion!"

"—but tails and paint are whorish."

"If you cannot perceive the heart of a woman beneath the cover of her dress then you are no true man of God."

"I perceive that women are by nature frail and lustful. Thus God has placed man above woman."

"Master Knox," she said in sudden assumed sweetness, "I read your blast against 'The Monstrous Regiment of Women' and know in what low opinion you hold my sex. But in writing that book you unwittingly spread before the world your intense jealousy of women. It is obvious that you feel beneath us, perhaps because some woman once rejected your love. In France we ladies used to speculate as to what so embittered you."

Knox sprang to his feet, and for a moment Mary thought that he was going to strike her. His face was gray, almost convulsive with rage, and she thought, No theological argument could penetrate his conceit. But by womanly spite I have struck his vulnerable point.

He spluttered, momentarily incoherent with fury, and she said, still sweetly, "I am sorry if I chanced to revive a tragic memory . . . Good day, Master Knox."

She nodded coolly to him, smiled at James and trailed slowly into the bedchamber. Beaton and Livingstone followed her and closed the door behind them.

"Madam," Beaton burst out, "You were magnificent!"

"No, I was not." Mary sank onto a hearth cushion. "I was no match for him in theological argument. I could not even defend our faith."

Livingstone said, "But you had the last word. He was speechless!"

Mary smiled wanly. "I should have convinced him. Instead I enraged him. It is small triumph to prod a man's wounds, Livvy. Were he not so dangerous I could almost pity him. But since he is ruthless, then so must I be."

"Could you not have him seized for treason and imprisoned?"

"No. That would dignify him to martyrdom and split the country more widely. Since my nobles support him I cannot fight him with arms. Today I learned I cannot fight him with words."

"Then how shall you fight him, Madam?"

Mary sighed. "In the way of a cat."

II.

Heat lightning flickered through the broken arches of the abbey and snaked above the palace turrets. Thunder growled, bombarded, rolled along the Canongate and reverberated to the massive rock of Arthur's Seat.

Alone in the small library on the first floor, Mary lit a taper on her desk and continued her letter to Elizabeth.

". . . and I very much appreciated the messages you sent by Master Randolph, and the safe-conduct permit—" Mary smiled wryly as she dipped her quill in the ink—"which did not reach me until yesterday."

A guard tapped on the door and opened it. "Lord Arran desires audience, Madam."

"I will see him." Resignedly Mary pushed back the letter, wishing that Arran and his father would return to their castle and leave her in peace. Since the Mass a week ago both had been sullen, and their sour faces irritated her.

"Yes, my lord?" Mary sighed, as Arran bowed. She did not ask him to sit down.

"Bothwell is in Edinburgh." He spat the words. "My men saw him in a tavern. He plans to come here this afternoon."

"Why shouldn't he?" she asked, controlling her temper. "I asked him to come."

"Holyrood is too small to hold us both, Madam."

"This feud is foolish. I am told that years ago your father and his quarreled because both wished to wed my mother. What does it profit you and Bothwell to continue it?"

"If Bothwell comes here, I and my father go."

Mary shrugged. "Then that is your decision, not mine. Go if you wish." She returned to her letter.

But he would not be dismissed. "Come, Madam, let us not maintain this pretense."

She looked up, puzzled. He was smiling fatuously, preening his sandy mustache. "You pretend indifference to me to deceive the others. But now we are alone."

"You had best explain yourself," she said coldly.

"I know it is only your mourning that prevents our immediate marriage."

"Have I," she asked incredulously, "given you the slightest encouragement?"

"Your eyes have, Madam."

"Your conceit astounds me. Never once have I considered you as a husband. To put it bluntly, what could you bring me? Power? That I have. Wealth? That you do not have."

He turned pettish. "Why must you tease me so? You know as well as I that you love me . . ."

He is unbalanced, she thought. What was it James had said? *There is a maggot in his brain that makes him act strangely at times.* Well, she would not waste words on him. She rose and, avoiding him, took a circuitous path to the door. She called the guard and asked him to summon the Duke de Chatelherault.

"Why send for my father?" Arran whined. "He will give his blessing. He is anxious for our marriage."

Mary said nothing. Standing near the open door she listened to Arran's blather, bored to the point of exasperation. She had invited his attentions, he insisted, with secret smiles and fluttering lashes. The entire court suspected her infatuation.

"Your Grace," she said as the old Duke appeared in the doorway, "your son is not well. I request that you take him to your castle of Dumbarton, or some other place in the country, until he recuperates."

The pale eyes were frigid. "I understand, Madam. Nor do we wish to remain at a court that celebrates the Romish sacrilege. We will leave tomorrow."

[145]

"You will leave at once," she said.

Chatelherault bowed and took Arran by the arm. Mary had expected some resistance but there was none. Like a small boy, slump-shouldered, Arran allowed himself to be guided through the door.

Mary closed it and returned to her desk. For an hour she wrote, then tore up the pages. Lethington had advised a friendly, flattering letter in reply to Elizabeth's but she could not achieve the correct tone. She thought, Such hypocrisy requires practice. She began again . . .

Late in the afternoon Bothwell arrived. As he tossed his dripping cloak on a chair Mary saw that he wore a broadsword, rapier and dagger at his belt, and the stiff breadth of his chest suggested armor under his doublet. Spurs jangled on his muddied boots as he came to bow before her.

"Please sit down, my lord."

He did so. "Your Majesty's galley is safe. I found it anchored off Cumberland. The English had seized it on the excuse that it lacked proper passport. They released it to me and it is now being unloaded at Leith."

"I am most grateful," Mary said. "I have missed my dogs and horses. Since they let you have them, perhaps Elizabeth has changed her humor."

"Perhaps."

"I was just writing her to thank her for the safe-conduct permit, which arrived yesterday." She laughed. "It was forwarded from Calais."

"I had not thought her so transparent."

"Nor I. She pretends it was all Throckmorton's fault, that he misunderstood her orders. In any case she seems amiable."

He said, "I'm more curious as to how you find your nobles. Are they amiable?"

"James and Lethington appear to be and save for Huntley and Lindsay the rest are pleasant enough. Arran I have temporarily dismissed from court." She told him what had happened. "I think Arran is mad."

"He feeds on fantasies. But his father can control him. The spells come and go—some think by the moon." He turned to the storm-swept window. "Or sparked by lightning."

"At least I am rid of him. What are your plans, my lord?"

"There's an outbreak of cattle thievery on the Border. I should go there."

"And thereafter?"

He smiled. "A little piracy is never amiss. The English provide lively sport at sea."

[146]

"And Randolph asking me just today to control Scots privateers! If I gave you a post here you would not be content, would you?"

"What is there for me in Edinburgh? It's peaceful enough at the moment."

"I must appoint a Privy Council. I want you among my advisers."

He stared at her. "Are you daft, Madam? I'm no statesman."

"But you are an honest man. I believe you are the only one who places Scotland's welfare above his own ambitions."

"You have been here more than two weeks. By now you must have heard me reviled—yet you still have faith?"

"As my mother did," she said.

The rain cascaded at the window, and he was silent for a moment, staring out at the flooding moat. Finally he said, "Are you willing to renew our bond of frankness?"

"With pleasure," she said. "And this time I shan't cheat."

"What do James and Lethington say of me?"

"That you are a rogue, a knave, an adventurer. That you are violent and headstrong." She smiled. "James says you are ruthless with women and incapable of fidelity."

"He should not bore Your Majesty with matters that do not concern you."

It was a slap but she felt it was justified. Bothwell was right, his romantic affairs did not concern her and her curiosity was unbecoming. Anxious to regain her dignity she said, "Indeed he should not have told me. I pointed out that your amorous adventures were extremely dull."

He tilted his tawny head. "Sleep-provoking."

She was sure he was about to laugh, and she felt a schoolgirl blush warming her cheeks. To cover her confusion she said, "Perhaps you should marry and dispel this notoriety."

"If you think so I shall give the matter consideration. Have you a lady in mind?"

Plague take him, she thought, he allows me no escape. "I have met few ladies in Edinburgh as yet. But next month I plan a large reception to become acquainted with them."

"Is Lady Mary Fleming attached?" he asked.

"No." Her twinge of jealousy was absurd.

"Would she strike you as a suitable wife for me?"

She could not tell whether he was joking. "Fleming would make a fine wife for any man. She is of noble birth, well educated, charming—"

"And beautiful," he said.

"Well, yes. But being a devout Catholic she would not marry outside her religion."

"A kiss has converted many a lass."

"To freethinking?"

"Oh, I'm past that now, Madam. I am interested in the new religion."

"I don't believe it! Why, last year—"

"Last year I had not been in Geneva. I had not heard Calvin preach. I had not dug to the source and studied the writings of Luther. They make spiritual sense, Madam—to me."

She sighed. "So Knox has won another of my lords."

"God, no! If I turn Protestant it will be despite Knox. He harms the faith, shaping God to his own mad image. But even Knox cannot obscure the basic truth—that between God and man is a current so powerful that it needs neither Mass nor priest nor churchly trappings."

"Then," she said sadly, "in your heart you are Protestant."

"Aye. But I'll worship in no damned churches. I can't regulate my need for prayer by bells that ring at four o'clock of a morning and five o'clock in the afternoon. I refuse to sit, pray, rise and sing God's praises at the order of any man. There's something indecent in public exhibition of faith—it's more personal than lovemaking and should be as secret."

"I marvel," she said, "that you are even interested in religion."

"It's true that I live by brawls of one kind or another. But between them are the long night watches at sea or on the Border March— times when the fog closes in and only the mind can work. We Scots are mystics, perhaps because our land is the strangest on earth. But that," he smiled, "you will find out for yourself when you travel your kingdom."

"I hope to travel soon. But there is this matter of the Privy Council. I plan to appoint James, Lethington, and seven or eight others. All but Huntley will be Protestant. That will prove to the people my tolerance and confound Knox, who least expects it. And I want you."

"My presence would infuriate the others, Madam."

"It is my Council and I want you on it. In times of crisis you are naturally free to go where there is trouble, but I should like you to have a part in my government."

"Then I am honored."

"Good," she said gaily. "Tonight you will sup with James and Lethington and me, and there will be no murder at table. Is it agreed?"

He laughed. "The role of peacemaker comes easily to you. You are so young that you cannot comprehend the bloody years between the lords and me. You would wipe them out in an evening."

"I hope to." She rose, and he picked up his cloak. "We will sup in my apartments at nine."

When he had left she reread her letter to Elizabeth, but her thoughts were not on it. She puzzled Bothwell's intentions toward Fleming and asked herself angrily why she should care. Determinedly she drew quill and paper toward her ". . . I appreciate Your Majesty's kindness in sending the . . ."

She threw down the quill, and ink spattered across the page. Locking the papers in her desk she left the library and went to her apartments. The guard saluted and she hurried through the audience chamber into her bedroom.

"Seton!" she called. "Unpack the black satin ball gown."

It was daringly cut, totally unsuitable as mourning attire.

III.

Mary had made an informal supping room of the tiny turret chamber off the bedroom. Cosier than the Great Hall, it provided a place to entertain her favorite courtiers privately. There was just room for a table and benches. Servants climbing the private staircase proffered dishes from the doorway.

The room was draped with ruby velvet, and a portrait of Mary's mother hung above the fireplace. Tonight the tablecloth of Brussels lace glittered with silver plates and goblets. White asters bloomed between tall silver candelabra.

James sat at one end of the table, Mary at the other. Her black gown bared her shoulders in Italian fashion, sloping into long skin-tight satin sleeves. Her hair, parted in the center with madonna-innocence, waved low at her neck, caught into a mesh of rubies. Long ruby earrings that matched her lips caught the fire of the candlelight.

On her left sat Lethington, on her right Bothwell. She had placed Fleming next to him—partly to watch his reaction, partly to convince him and herself that she was not jealous. Indeed, she thought, if they find each other attractive I will push the flirtation toward marriage. He might turn Catholic for love.

The other guests were Beaton and Chastelard. Of the four men he was the only one who behaved naturally. Bothwell, James and Lethington were coolly reserved. Mary knew how to dissipate the chill but she did not intend to mix politics with Poulet en Champignons and the exquisite white wine of the Loire valley.

Fleming prattled valiantly against the weight of masculine moodiness. "Lord James, how do you like this preserve we brought from France?"

"Excellent," he said unenthusiastically.

"When Her Majesty was ill last year at St. Germain the chef sought to tempt her appetite with some new creation, and he went about the kitchens racking his brain for an idea. 'Marie est malade,' he mumbled, 'Marie is ill.' Then he remembered that she loved Spanish oranges, and viola—the preserve. We call it 'Mariemalade.' "

"Indeed?" James said, absently.

Men! Mary thought disgustedly—the least adaptable creatures on earth, clamping chips to their shoulders, brooding and sulking over old differences. She had expected better of Bothwell but he was as grim as the others. Fleming beside him might have been old or ugly for all the attention he paid her.

Beaton built bridges of talk but the men would not cross them. Chastelard questioned Lethington about the merits of Irish hunting mares and was answered in monosyllables. After the tarts and sweet wines were served, Mary looked down the table at James.

"Would you be happier, my lord, if you knew that I intend to appoint you chief adviser on my Privy Council?"

"Happier?" he stammered. "Why—"

She turned to Lethington. "And you, my lord, could you contrive a smile at the prospect of being Secretary of State?"

"Madam, I am honored. I have no words—"

"Mon Dieu!" she said in mock exasperation, "are you to remain wordless all evening?"

"Your Majesty's decision is so sudden," James said. "Naturally we hoped, but we were not sure—"

"Neither was I. And my decision is not sudden. I have lain awake nights wondering whom to entrust with the most important posts in my government. Nor was I motivated by sentiment, my dear brother. I feel that you and Lethington have the ablest political minds in Scotland, and that though our motives may differ we seek the same goals."

She paused. "In tolerating the new faith I demand in return complete tolerance for mine, and your protection of holy Catholic property."

James and Lethington bowed from their chairs.

"Now," she said bluntly, "you have the plums you coveted. Under the circumstances I believe you will find it expedient to cooperate with Lord Bothwell, whom I am appointing with you to my Privy Council."

James frowned, and she said, "The plain truth is that in years past Bothwell outmaneuvered you. Hurt vanity has a long memory, has it not? He tricked you by seizing gold and arms sent you from Elizabeth. He upset your conspiracy with her and defended my mother against you. To brand him a rogue is patently absurd—in war all men are rogues.

"But that is history. We begin a new era. I will not have the dead past dragging me. If you, my lords—" She turned to include Bothwell—"are unable to patch your differences for my sake, then I must conclude that your pride is greater than your patriotism."

Bothwell looked down the table at James and rasped, "For Her Majesty's sake I'm willing to forget our enmity."

Mary thought, Never were soft words so harshly spoken.

"And I," James said, "pledge you my friendship."

Lethington said, "We will drink to it."

The three men rose, gathered at James's end of the table, and clinked goblets. As they drank they clasped hands, then shattered the goblets in the fireplace.

"Thank you, gentlemen," Mary said. "You have eased me. We will leave you to talk in private."

With Chastelard and the two Marys she went through the bedroom into the audience chamber, where lackeys were setting up a long Chinese brocade screen. Musicians entered with flutes, violins and lutes to take their places behind it. Pages were sent to summon Seton, Livingstone, Brantôme and the English Ambassador Randolph. It would be an intimate evening, a serene and civilized gathering.

Fleming went down to the kitchen to inspect the evening's crop of strolling entertainers and returned with a gypsy fortuneteller, a juggler and a ballad peddler. They were ragged folk grateful for pennies, and as Mary paid them generously and sent them behind the screen with the musicians, she thought wistfully of the entertainments at St. Germain and Blois. There exquisitely costumed mimics and troubadours came to present tragedies and pageants under diamond-glittered pavilions. The finest voices of Europe sang the verses of great poets. The castles of Scotland would never know such marvels.

Poor Holyrood, Mary thought—try as I may I cannot change its mood. The rose room had a surface elegance. But behind the tapestry lay the cold slime of old walls and the juniper must burn forever in its golden braziers to fight the musty smell of age. The ratcatcher had worked for a week throughout the palace and abbey, yet in dark corners Mary caught the gleam of bright eyes, and there was a scuffling and chittering in the night. Carpeting and furniture did not change a place that was determined to hold its dead and mock its living.

The men returned from the supping room and seemed in good humor. They gathered about the buffet table, where whisky and wines stood in crystal decanters. James, his hand on Bothwell's shoulder, was laughing about something and Mary thought, God has granted a miracle . . .

The musicians began to play, and the guests seated themselves on chairs and cushions. Mary, sharing a sofa with Chastelard, watched as Bothwell carried a wine glass to Fleming and sat down on the window seat beside her. Her flowery blue gown puffed out over his legs and she smiled at him above the edge of the wine glass, her head tilted coquettishly.

Mary clapped her hands for silence. The music stopped and she called for the ballad peddler.

In doggerel verse, accompanied by his ill-tuned lute, he brought them news and gossip of England and Scotland. They learned to Randolph's embarrassment that Queen Elizabeth had been publicly pinched on the buttocks by Sir Robert Dudley—"and none could find that she did mind." A jury had pronounced Dudley innocent of murder when his wife Amy Robsart was found dead at the foot of a flight of stairs, but "most people think he caused her death so he could wed Elizabeth." In Scotland at a cottage near Hawick a laird had caught an Englishman abed with his wife:

> *In punishment for it*
> *The husband turned him on a spit*
> *And basted him with brandywine*
> *Then forced his wife to sit and dine.*

The musicians resumed the plaintive love songs of France, and Bothwell whispered something to Fleming. Mary saw her dimple and laugh. And presently Fleming laid her hand on his, and Mary turned hastily away, unable to watch them. As Chastelard prattled of the Dudley scandal she thought, I am stupidly, illogically jealous. And why? I do not love Bothwell. I scarcely know him. There is no excuse for me, none.

"In all your life Your Majesty has never looked so beautiful," Chastelard said. "Always before you have had the beauty of buds, an April look. Tonight you are midsummer, lush as an opened rose . . ."

She listened to the love talk and the love songs, but from the corner of her eye she was miserably aware of Bothwell and Fleming. She saw them in profile as they leaned toward each other, Fleming's face raised to his or lowered behind her fan in assumed shyness. She is a practiced coquette, Mary thought, each gesture studied—the lazy sweep of lashes, the widened violet eyes, the pout. No man can resist her—none ever has.

". . . beg that Your Majesty will grant me an evening alone," Chastelard was saying.

"What?" Mary had completely forgotten him. "An evening alone? That is impossible, Pierre. I am still in mourning."

"That gown mourns nothing. It celebrates your loveliness . . ."

Lethington was also watching the couple in the window seat, and Mary wondered if he too was attracted to Fleming. It would be awkward if he and Bothwell, so recently pledged in friendship, wanted the same woman. Presently Lethington rose and sauntered over to the window, and Fleming beckoned to him. To Mary's relief Bothwell rose, obviously insisting that Lethington sit down in his place. The three talked for a few moments, then Bothwell turned and Mary saw him coming toward her.

Hastily she leaned toward Chastelard's astonished face and touched his hair lightly. "Whatever would I do without you, Pierre?"

He caught her hand and kissed it. Bothwell sees us, she thought, but I cannot continue to flirt and raise Chastelard's hopes falsely.

"Do forgive me, Pierre," she said, "but I have important matters to discuss with Lord Bothwell. Will you ask him to come here?"

Reluctantly he bowed and left her, and presently Bothwell came to her.

"You sent for me, Madam?"

"Sit down." She tried to think of some legitimate business she might discuss with him, and questioned him more thoroughly on the Border situation. He told of the English cattle thieves, of rebellious Scots who had set up their own tiny monarchies in protest of Mary's rule. His mission was to catch, try, and hang thieves and traitors.

His eyes are the strangest color, she thought—brown with red glints, and his hair is the dark red-gold of oak leaves in October. Usually redheads are freckled or pasty-white but his skin is tanned, weathered but smooth . . .

"In Jedburgh I hold Justice Court in Your Majesty's name."

. . . And his hands, big, strong, yet slender-fingered . . .

"Your Majesty will visit the Border soon, I hope."

"Next week James and I ride to Linlithgow and Stirling and St. Andrews. Later I wish to see the Border and the far Highlands. Is it true that men in the Highlands still wear bear pelts?"

He laughed. "Literally, no—metaphorically, yes. They are the most backward folk in 'civilized' Europe. Huntley is king there—suitably."

"My Catholics hold firm only in primitive areas," she said with a sad little smile.

"It is more accurate to say that Protestantism has not yet penetrated the wilder country. You'll still find many Catholics on the Border too."

"When do you wish to go there?" she asked.

"This week, if you have no objection."

She nodded, already feeling bereft. "If we need you here I will send for you."

"The first important decision of the Council must be your marriage. Lethington feels—and I agree—that your choice of a husband must humor Elizabeth. If we are to work for your succession, we must choose a man acceptable to her as future king of England. It might be wise to send Lethington to London immediately."

"I shall do so. But whatever she says I'll not wed a Protestant. And I shan't rush. It is not a year since my husband's death."

He grinned. "If you can dally with Chastelard your heart is healing."

"My flirtation with Pierre has always been literary," she said. "We embrace in sonnets."

"I'd hate to be constrained to fourteen lines," he said. "But to return to your marriage . . ."

He spoke of her suitors, evaluating them, and she thought, I cannot bear it. He talks as if I were merchandise to be shipped to the highest bidder—as indeed I am.

"I must see you before you go to the Border," she said. "Come to me tomorrow evening." Hastily she added, "I should know every detail of the—the sheep thievery."

She fancied a flicker of amusement in his eyes before he inclined his head. "I shall wait upon Your Majesty tomorrow evening."

But the next evening Mary waited for Bothwell. Strolling in the misty gray-green garden, glancing impatiently up the Canongate, she puzzled how to be alone with him. Assuredly not here, trailed by six halberdiers and her archer guard. Nor trammeled in a chamber with the Marys near . . .

A pumpkin-colored moon edged above Arthur's Seat as Bothwell clattered into the courtyard, and as he swung down from his horse Mary called, "I've a whim to ride to Arthur's Seat. It's said the view is fine by moonglow."

Bothwell bowed and came toward her. "Shall I order Your Majesty's horse?"

"I'll ride with you." She sought to efface her boldness as he lifted her to his saddle. "I'm wearing slippers, not boots."

To the guards she said, "No need to follow us."

As Bothwell mounted behind her, her pearl-meshed snood caught on the top button of his doublet, and to dislodge it she pulled off the headdress and her hair rippled down, blowing against his face as they galloped around the palace through the Royal Park.

[154]

"I'm sorry," she said, grasping her hair and bringing it back over one shoulder. "I'll try to put on my snood."

"Don't trouble," he said. "No one will see you."

Could it be, she wondered, that he liked the silky mass of her hair, its fragrance of crushed rose petals? Nonsense, his arm about my waist is dispassionate as rope; he has no interest in me of that sort. Even if he did, what could come of it? He has neither power nor wealth and my husband must have both. It would be wrong from every standpoint, including religion.

They climbed a sharply rising road and passed Hunter's Bog—"a lively hawking ground," Bothwell said. As the path turned, Mary looked down on a lake of swans, their heads wing-tucked in sleep. There was a tiny village of thatched rooftops and to the south Bothwell pointed out Cragmillar Castle and the distant line of the Moorfoots, the Pentlands and the Lammermuirs. Up they wound, and up, spiraling high above the dark roofs of Edinburgh, higher than Mary had ever been. In the moonlight the crags were a deep orange and Holyrood a toy castle pinpricked by lights.

At the summit of Arthur's Seat Bothwell checked the horse. The North Loch was a long glitter below the bulked blackness of Castle Rock, and then a cloud obscured the moon and there was only the dark star-spattered sky and rising mist. Far off and forlorn, Mary heard the barking of a dog and somewhere on the Forth a foghorn.

"When I was a boy," he said, "and my uncle brought me to Edinburgh I used to climb up here during storms, tethering my horse down the hill. I'd stand there on the edge and command the thunderbolts and the lightning and laugh like a demon when a tree went down or a hut caught fire."

"A sort of exultation," she said. "The way I feel on a fast horse on a gusty day."

"You'll have your gusty days here, Madam. And a kingdom to ride."

"But I wonder if I will ever feel at home in Scotland, if I ever will be happy here."

He said nothing, and she leaned back to look up at the sky, her head touching his shoulder. She felt the quick jolt of her heartbeat as his arm tightened around her waist. Their solitude, their closeness and his strength both pleased and panicked her. She remembered the tales she had heard of him and cursed herself for a fool to climb to the edge of nowhere with such a man. Yet she did not want to break the moment.

The moon reappeared, blurred in a trail of cloud. A sudden wind lifted her hair, and she raised both hands to catch it back and looked up at him. His eyes, deeply lit, stared down into hers. He bent his

[155]

head slightly, and she raised her mouth toward his and closed her eyes.

Gruffly he said, "We'd best get back, Madam."

As she opened her eyes and jerked her head straight, the horse lunged forward and they started the long climb down. She could feel her cheeks flame in shame and fury. I can never face him again—never. Like the easiest bawd I begged for a kiss, and he scorned it. Perhaps he is laughing to himself at his newest conquest. Yet when he spoke he sounded angry—bored by my eagerness, bored and disgusted. And it is my own fault, for he never encouraged me. He is intrigued by Fleming. He urges me to marry . . .

They reached level ground and cantered through the park, the horse's hoofs crunching yellow-green leaves. I must say something, she thought desperately, lest he take my silence for the miserable humiliation that it is.

"Apparently there will be an early autumn," she said.

"Yes. It's unfortunate you didn't come in the spring. Then you could forgive our winter."

"The winters are so hard?" she asked, grateful for the cloak of talk.

"Killing to some. But you will adjust quickly. It's old bones that are troubled."

At Holyrood gate the sentries admitted them, and Bothwell rode to the entrance, dismounted, and helped Mary to the ground. He tethered the horse to a tree and followed Mary into the inner courtyard. She swept up her hair and stuffed it into her snood, too miserable to care what the guard thought.

"I still have your blue cloak," she said as they started up the staircase. "I will have Fleming find it for you."

"Thank you."

"And thank you for the ride," she said.

"Sometimes Your Majesty speaks like a little lass mindful of her manners."

"I rarely forget my manners," she said, "but when I do I am careful never to repeat the offense. Wait in the audience chamber. Fleming will bring your cloak."

She hurried up the stairs ahead of him through the audience chamber to the bedroom. Fleming rose from a cushion near the window and curtsied.

"Please find Lord Bothwell's blue cloak and give it to him," Mary said. "He waits in the outer chamber."

"Yes, Madam. It is below in the wardrobe room. Shall I help you to bed first?"

"No. I wish to be alone."

Fleming started toward the spiral staircase.

"Wait," Mary said. "Lethington seemed quite attentive last night. Can it be that you are melting our block of ice?"

"He is thawing, Madam." Fleming smiled. "I've told him he has a fascinating mind, and since he agrees, we have much in common."

"Minx!"

"Of course he is subtle and slippery, but eventually I hope to gain his confidence."

"And Bothwell," Mary said casually, removing her snood. "Do you find him amusing?"

"I am afraid of him."

"Why?"

"Even if I did not know his reputation I would be wary. He would rouse fire in a woman, but she would be consumed—not he."

Wistfully Fleming added, "I could almost follow Lord Bothwell to hell, but *he* would come back."

They laughed together, and then Mary dismissed her. She undressed herself and climbed into bed. She said her prayers mechanically, without hope that they were heard. Tonight she could understand God's desertion of her. He had witnessed her shame. She turned over and buried her face in the pillow as if she could bury the memory of what had happened. Bothwell must wonder how often she had offered her lips—and been rejected. Perhaps he now believed what Knox had been telling Edinburgh for months—that the Queen of Scots was a wanton.

She sat up, shaking back her hair, her hands clasped about her knees. She had not learned self-discipline in vain. As surely as she controlled her emotions in public, so she could control them in private. Never again would she allow herself to think of Bothwell romantically.

I swear it, she whispered.

IV.

November wind flogged Edinburgh. In the tree-shaken dawn, the last leaves scuttered along dead bracken and browned heather, whirled on the High Street, swept into the moat at Holyrood House. Seton brought warmed undergarments, and Mary dressed by the fire in her bedchamber.

Teeth chattering, she said, "I never thought to receive a suitor's ambassador in a wool kirtle. But it's warm, and I'd rather be a frump than freeze."

Seton placed a wide fringed shawl around Mary's shoulders. "Now, Madam, you'd best eat before your porridge cools."

"It is probably frozen solid." Mary sat in the hearth chair and Seton put a tray on her lap. "No one could have told me two months ago that I would come to like porridge—and even herring if it is grilled properly."

"Gaston says the way to time a herring is to repeat a Paternoster and two Ave Marias—then it is done to perfection." Seton heated a long-handled iron spoon in the fire until it glowed red, then plunged it into a mug of brandied milk that stood on the hearth. "Here, Madam; this will warm you."

Mary took the mug. "Nothing will warm me. My veins run ice water."

They had done so for three weeks. Holyrood's great-mouthed fireplaces roared from kitchen to turret chambers, but the creeping cold lurked just beyond the hearths. Mary and her courtiers never crossed a room or traveled a corridor without good reason, and their cloaks and shawls were removed only at the fireside. If the banshee winds calmed, then clammy fog settled down, penetrating the warmest clothing.

Mary said, "Did Ambassador Moretta bring a large retinue?"

"I do not know, Madam. But I saw considerable luggage downstairs in the hall."

"Then tell Fleming to lodge him at a guest house in the Canongate." Mary sighed. "If my suitors only realized how much it costs to entertain their ambassadors, they would understand why I am so quick to reject their proposals. By saying no instead of perhaps, I save money."

"Maybe it will be yes this time, Madam."

"The Duke of Ferrara is no catch. The only inducement would be the warmth of Italy." Mary handed Seton the tray. "Well . . . I shall go now to receive Cupid."

In the audience chamber a slender, elderly man turned from the fire as Mary entered and announced himself formally: "Sieur de Moretta, Ambassador of Savoy, greets Your Majesty in the name of His Grace the Duke of Ferrara."

She extended her hand and Moretta kissed it. "Sit down, sir. I regret I was not awake when you arrived. Have you breakfasted?"

"Divinely, Madam." He sat down across from her. "Your chef pampered us."

"I am glad. How many attendants did you bring?"

"Only twenty-two. And musicians and jesters."

"We have need of jesters here," she said.

He bent toward her in soft-eyed concern. "His Holiness the Pope and the Duke have been deeply worried about Your Majesty.

We hear of atrocities committed against the Church that we can scarcely credit."

"They are true," she said bitterly. "I have seen them with my own eyes."

She discussed the September tour she had made with James and Huntley. In Perth she had gasped at the ruins of abbeys and monasteries, at foul words painted on images of the Virgin. The Protestant pageants she saw there had so offended her that she had fallen from her horse in a faint. At St. Andrews with her hood drawn over her face she had wept at the shattered cathedral. Throughout her journey she had seen earless monks and nuns with broken jaws. There were sickening tales of priest-baiting—a new Protestant sport supplanting the Robin Hood masques banned by Knox.

"And John Knox is responsible for all this?" Moretta asked angrily.

"Yes." She told him that when she returned to Edinburgh she was greeted with a proclamation from the town Provost and bailiffs reiterating that "all monks, frairs, priests, nuns, adulterers, fornicators and all such filthy persons remove themselves from this town within twenty-four hours under pain of carting, burning on the cheek, or banishing forever."

"I dared not arrest Knox," Mary said, "though I know he instigated it. But I dismissed the Provost and bailiffs from office. Knox was doubly furious because my Council approved the action." She smiled. "Knox howled from the pulpit that night that I 'bewitch all men from their right senses.'"

"That," said Moretta gallantly, "I am aware of." He picked up a portfolio next to his chair and said, "Here is another you have bewitched." From a linen wrapping he uncovered the portrait of a young man. "His Grace of Ferrara."

Mary studied it. God knows, she thought, I am not so shallow as to demand good looks, but here is a veritable pig. If the artist has painted him this plump, then I may be sure he weighs three times as much. And if one wart is allowed on his nose, then there may be a dozen.

Mary said, "What character!" She peered at the head. "Is his hair black or brown, sir?"

"That is a cap," Moretta said reluctantly.

So he was bald too!

"His Grace is in love for the first time. Day and night he keeps a candle burning below Your Majesty's portrait. He cannot sleep or eat . . ." Moretta paused to let the latter point sink in.

"He feels that Your Majesty would adorn his court as no other lady could. In our customs we are more French than Italian. Picture if you will a pink marble pallazia surrounded by olive groves . . ."

As she listened to the familiar pattern of persuasion she considered her other matrimonial prospects. The King of Sweden persisted in his suit. Slow-moving Philip II had cautiously indicated that negotiations for the marriage of his son Don Carlos to Catherine de Medici's daughter had fallen through. Thus Mary might yet become heiress to Spain if she could bring herself to marry an imbecile.

"Later," she said, rising, "we will discuss this in detail. Tonight we will feast and dance in your honor."

Moretta bowed to the door. "My musicians are at your disposal, Madam."

Mary sent for Fleming and discussed preparations for the evening. "We might have fireworks in the courtyard if it is not too windy."

"And attract Master Knox's fury?" Fleming asked. "He would see them from the High Street and say we were orgying again."

"He will say that anyway. Huntley tells me Knox peers from his window every night to see what guests ride by to Holyrood, whether they are drunk, sober, masqued or in ball dress. If he has a soul it is an old woman's."

"But his sermons do you great harm, Madam. It is not my place to advise you, but should we flaunt this occasion with fireworks? Each revel adds fuel to Knox's fury and we have entertained so much lately."

That was true, Mary thought. Throughout the autumn Holyrood's rushlights had blazed until dawn for masques, balls, feasts, musicales. She had given a reception for the nobles, their wives and prominent citizens which lasted from sundown All Hallows' Eve until sunup three days later. Knox, outraged, had attacked Mary for dancing the French Brawl and the Arch of Love, for playing Rag Man's Roll and Bob the Apple and Hoodman Blind. Night after night, watching from his forestairs on the High Street, Knox had seen torches flare as masqueraders pounded toward the palace wearing dragon heads and peacock feathers and donkey tails. "Holyrood has become a brothel," he thundered, "filled with wanton debaucheries."

"Nevertheless," Mary said, "I intend to continue our revels. I will not bow to Knox. If I stopped them he would think me intimidated and shout to the world that he commands my court." She pushed Fleming gently to the door. "See to the fireworks, lass!"

After noon dinner Lethington came to Mary in the library to discuss the latest news from Elizabeth. "She wishes you to marry Arran, Madam."

"She insults my wits!"

"The shabbier the match, the happier she will be. It's essential that if we negotiate for your marriage to Don Carlos we keep it secret. Otherwise she will try to block it."

Mary frowned. Don Carlos was a depraved lunatic. But it was unthinkable to balk at such a marriage. Queens had endured worse for the sake of their countries . . .

"Your Majesty would be heiress to the most fabulous empire in Europe. You could look down on Elizabeth from an Olympian height —buy and sell England ten times over. She dreads nothing so much as your possible alliance with Spain." He spread his long white fingers in a sweeping gesture. "Think of it—such wealth and power as Elizabeth and Catherine de Medici would give their immortal souls for."

Lethington roused her dream. "Under Spain, Scotland would be forced to Catholicism, Knox hanged or driven from power. Philip would use this country as a base from which to attack England—it is strategically perfect for him. Invading England, he would depose Elizabeth, place you on her throne and proclaim a Catholic Britain."

Still she was silent, and he said, "I understand your reluctance. But I feel sure the horror tales you have heard of Don Carlos were cleverly fabricated by Catherine to kill your interest in the marriage."

Mary brightened. "I had not thought of that. The people who told me of Don Carlos' brutality *were* Catherine's courtiers. And she was anxious enough for her own daughter to marry him—though God knows she would sacrifice her children to her power-lust."

Lethington said, "Philip moves like a turtle. It might be a year or two before he agrees to the marriage. Meanwhile we will continue to work for your succession to the English throne. Elizabeth has nearly agreed to meet you sometime next summer. If she will, I am sure Your Majesty can do more with her than a dozen ambassadors. Vain and stubborn and whimsical though she is, Elizabeth is human. And no human being seems able to resist your charm."

"Except Knox," Mary said.

And Bothwell, she added silently. She had kept her vow not to think of him romantically, yet when she received his reports from the Border she could not help searching them for some personal message, which she never found. But my infatuation is a passing illness, she thought, and each day I grow stronger. By the time he returns to Edinburgh at Yuletide I will be cured.

"Your Majesty has a victory over Knox. He is unable to ban your Mass or to rouse sufficient public indignation to stop it by force. Each day he sees your conquest of the Protestant nobles."

"Since my Council is almost entirely Protestant, how can it approve my marriage to Don Carlos?"

"With all respect to Lord James and the rest—I know no Scots Protestant who would not approve the marriage in return for Spanish gold."

Only Bothwell cannot be bribed . . .

[161]

"If Knox gets wind of this, or Elizabeth, the marriage is doomed, Madam. I leave it to you to mislead Randolph."

As Lethington bowed from her presence, Mary thought how different she was from him. He thrived on intrigue, she wilted. He found the devious path fascinating, she found it tiresome. In France conspiracy had tentacled around her but she had not been forced to it. Here in Scotland she must conspire, to rule.

It was not that lying and deception shocked her. But both bored her to exasperation. She would like to be forthright but she must play by Elizabeth's rules, and her resentment toward Elizabeth mounted accordingly.

At the banquet that night Mary shivered in her ballgown and sent for her sable cloak. The one fireplace was inadequate to heat the Great Hall that stretched a hundred and fifty feet, and even the French and Italians drank whisky to warm themselves. At eleven o'clock the tops and trestles of the dining tables were laid against the wall and the carpet rolled to one end. Musicians set up their instruments, and Mary and Ambassador Moretta opened the dancing.

She danced with her three brothers, with Lord Ruthven, with Kerr and Lords Morton and Argyll. But Chastelard was her favorite partner. They were so accomplished that the court preferred to watch rather than join them. In the gold candlelight they performed the Canary, circling arm in arm, playful, flirtatious, bending and dipping, kissing lightly at the end of each measure. Mary was conscious of Randolph's sharp-eyed interest in those kisses, but she did not care. Elizabeth would believe the worst, but then Elizabeth was not the paragon of chastity she pretended to be. Her affair with Sir Robert Dudley was common gossip, though just how far it had gone was a matter of speculation. It was reported that the Virgin Queen was more queenly than virgin.

Monsieur Brantôme confirmed those reports. He drew Mary to a bench by the fire and whispered that he was in correspondence with Dudley's physician. "Dudley told him that Elizabeth is ardent, in fact, insatiable. But her pleasures must be unnatural. She can only play at love."

"I have heard she is unlike other women," Mary said, "that there is some anatomical difference."

Brantôme nodded, plump cheeks wobbling. "She is unable to be mistress or mother. I thought Your Majesty would like to know that since she is aware she cannot bear children she will never marry. You need not fret that she will have heirs."

"Perhaps this lack taunts her into her frenzies, her tantrums, her bursts of hysteria." Mary looked up as Moretta came to the fire, toasting his back at the blaze of oak logs. "Sit down with us, sir."

"Thank you, Madam, but I came to ask permission to present my most talented musician, a singer from Piedmont. May I ask him to perform?"

"Of course."

Mary called for silence. Pages snuffed the tapers so that only fire-light gleamed on the apple-green hunting tapestries and copper-handled boar spears that crisscrossed the wall. Mary turned on the bench with her back to the room. When she listened to music she liked to watch the fire.

Lute strings were softly plucked, and a voice like deep velvet sang of a lover's loneliness. The words were banal, the tune haunting, the voice magnificent. The last notes ended on a sigh, and Mary, with tears in her eyes, turned to applaud.

She had expected the singer to be big and deep-chested, as fit the bass voice, but a small man smiled and bowed to the clapping, cheering court. Mary beckoned him, and as he approached she saw that though he was not humpbacked his shoulders were hunched, his legs too short for his frame. He was black-jowled, thick-lipped, and only great luminous black eyes saved him from ugliness. She thought that he looked like a goblin.

He knelt before Mary, his yellow-ribboned lute in one hand. With the other he drew the hem of her skirt to his lips.

As he rose she said, "Thank you for the finest music I have heard since I left France."

His English was heavily accented. "Your Majesty does me great honor."

Her heart skipped a beat. How odd, she thought, how very odd . . . He did not resemble Francis. He looked ten years older than Francis, yet there was a poignant similarity. The eyes held the same spaniel-soft expression; there was the same shy smile. And the poor mal-formed body . . .

"What is your name, sir?"

"David Rizzio, Madam."

She thought, In just such a way Francis looked at me with his humble heart in his eyes. When she spoke her voice trembled. "I know you have had a long journey and a tiring day, Signor Rizzio, else I would ask you to sing again. Do you play other instruments?"

He said that he did but the lute was his favorite. As they talked she realized the court was watching her with surprise. A musician was considered little better than a page or a valet. With the other servants he ate in the kitchen and supplemented his performances with menial duties. Mary had three male singers, who also washed windows in her apartments, swept the carpets and tended the fires. But she perceived at once that Rizzio was educated and intelligent.

He was witty at the expense of the new Italian composers, knew more than she of contemporary literature. In one unmistakable way, she thought, he is unlike Francis. He has a mind.

She had been hungry for this sort of talk, for new ideas in the intellectual desert of Edinburgh. The French courtiers parroted the old cliches of art and philosophy she had known all her life, and the Scots had not yet heard of Plato.

Fascinated, she forgot about dancing, about her other guests, about the late hour. Impulsively she asked, "Would you accept a permanent post as musician here after Signor Moretta leaves? I need a bass for my quartet, a soloist."

"I would be delighted, Madam. But—" His black eyes twinkled— "you seem sure you are not voyaging to Italy to be married."

"I was sure," she whispered, "when I saw the Duke's portrait. When my French courtiers leave after Christmas I shall be bored; that is why I want you to stay. With music and books I can create a world of my own—"

She broke off abruptly. Captain of the Guard Erskine had entered the hall and hurried to James, whispering something in his ear. She saw James's incredulous expression change to alarm.

Mary excused herself from Rizzio and went to James. "What is amiss?"

James said, "Captain Erskine has heard a rumor from town that Arran and his father have left Dumbarton and are riding here with two thousand men to abduct Your Majesty and kill me."

"Kill . . ." It was incredible. No, she thought, it was entirely possible. Arran's desperation had unhinged his mind. Perhaps his father, unable to control him, was coming with him in a final attempt to seize power.

"It may be the wildest rumor," James said.

"But we will take no chances." Mary called for silence and explained the situation to the courtiers. Then she issued orders for the defense of the palace. "Lord Robert will send out scouts and post sentinels at the Netherbow Port and around the palace grounds. Captain Erskine will command my halberdiers and my archers at the gate and drawbridge. Lord Ruthven will arouse the Town Watch and summon men from Edinburgh Castle. Lord John will organize and arm the menservants and set up inner defenses . . ."

As she spoke the men were already moving to the door to obey instructions. Chastelard and the French noblemen went to their apartments for swords and pistols to supplement their daggers. James, Lethington, Moretta and Brantôme remained in the Great Hall with the ladies and the frightened maids.

From the kitchen Mistress McDoon commanded a battalion of

lackeys who lugged in great covered pots of hot water to the window embrasures should the attackers try to climb up from the courtyard. Peter Pye collected broken goblets and distributed them along with heavy sticks to the pages and scullery boys. Boar spears were torn from the wall, and up from the dungeons came boxes of ammunition, rusted dags and broadswords.

Mary paced the Great Hall like a cooped lioness. She wished she could ride to the Castle herself and summon help. Why must the men have all the excitement?

"Holyrood is indefensible if Arran really has a force," James said. "The moment they are sighted we will ride to Stirling."

"And let them take Holyrood?" Mary gasped.

"Better to lose Holyrood than our lives."

He was right. Admittedly she knew little of defense tactics, although she had seen her uncle's strategy at Amboise. But this was not Amboise. Holyrood in its low-lying meadows was all too vulnerable.

They waited. From time to time Lord Robert or Captain Erskine sent up a trooper to report the progress of the defenses. Men arrived from Edinburgh Castle to take up positions in the outer courtyard or behind the palace. Chastelard, Brantôme and Mary played a game of Primero, stopping to listen, the cards forgotten in their hands. James and Lethington sat silently at chess.

The candles burned low and the sky paled. A pink dawn grayed into rain. Lethington said, "I think we are victims of a ruse. If Arran were counting on a surprise attack, he would have been here long before now."

"Why would anyone play such a pointless trick?" Mary asked.

"Rumors do not start without reason," Lethington said. "And no town idiot started this one. Someone wished to discredit Arran at court and took this means to deepen suspicion of him."

"But who hates Arran so much?" Mary asked.

James and Lethington spoke in unison. "Bothwell."

"Ridiculous! He's on the Border—"

"With agents all over town, Madam."

"But Bothwell knows I sent Arran away."

"And he takes no chances that you will restore him to favor." James made a little pleading gesture. "You do not know Bothwell. Do not allow your loyalty to blind you to his ruthlessness. He has loathed Arran these ten years—"

"But I discussed Arran with him. He seemed merely contemptuous."

Lethington and James exchanged superior smiles.

"Very well," she said curtly. "That is your opinion. To me it is incredible. I am going to bed."

In bed, sleepless, she stared at the dripping window and wondered if she was a fool, if James and Lethington spoke the truth. Or if this was their means to drive a wedge between her and Bothwell. She thought how often her mother must have lain awake, weighing one man against another, sifting and sorting evidence, never quite sure who was friend, who was foe.

My mother knew James and Lethington better than I do, she thought. And the last words she wrote to me were "Trust Bothwell."

V.

From the Castle of Falkland
this 29th day of March 1562

Madam my good "sister" Elizabeth:

As always I take pleasure in addressing Your Majesty as "sister," for I feel as you do that we should be so in spirit. My heart is full of affection and the hope that you may have a pleasant Eastertide.

I wish to thank you for the exquisite diamond ring, made even more precious by the message that accompanied it . . .

Mary set down her quill and reread Elizabeth's message. *Should Your Majesty ever be in any extremity you have only to return this diamond as token and I will come to your assistance.* Doubtless another insincerity, Mary thought, but the pear-shaped diamond was beautiful and rarely left her finger. She continued the letter.

. . . I have spent an apprehensive winter. First there was the rumor that Lord Arran planned to attack Holyrood House which, as you know, proved false. Then on Christmas Eve while my court was merrymaking, a great brawl began between Lord Arran and Lord Bothwell on the High Street. They and their men—eight hundred in all—would have battled to death with swords and pikes had not my brother James intervened with the palace guard. Fortunately there were no casualties, but Christmas Day was spoiled for I was forced to banish both Arran and Bothwell to their estates, warning them not to return to court until after the Twelfth Night revels. A few days ago I learned that Master Knox had patched the quarrel between them and that they are now on excellent terms—a most surprising and happy turn of events. However, Arran's mind is very strange. You, Madam, will be the first to agree that I cannot consider him in marriage as you suggested . . .

Marriages we have had a-plenty. My natural brother Lord John was wed in December to Janet Hepburn, Lord Bothwell's sister, and they will live at Coldingham. My brother Lord Robert also wed

*in December, and my eldest brother James, after long love of Lady
Agnes Keith, married her in St. Giles last month. I gave them a
vast reception with feasting and dancing and casting of firespears.
As a wedding gift I created James Earl of Mar and knighted several
others. Weary of entertaining, I have come here to Fife for country
peace.*

*The hawking is excellent and I am in the forest from sunup until
sundown if the weather permits. Lord James and his wife and Sir
William Maitland are with me, but all save one of my French
courtiers have returned to Queen Catherine's court. Monsieur
Chastelard remains as my Court Poet.*

*Nothing so gratifies me as Your Majesty's indication that you
may meet me this summer in the north of England. I will gladly
travel wherever you designate. I share your belief that it is the
blundering of envoys that has caused our former misunderstand-
ings and that when we meet matters may be happily adjusted.*

I pray God to grant you, Madam, health and long life.

> Your most affectionate sister,
> Mary R.

In the Great Hall of Falkland Mary reread the letter and waxed
her seal upon it. She felt it was exactly right—gossipy, guileless,
friendly without fawning. But she would show it to Lethington for
his approval. In her dealings with Elizabeth she trusted his judgment implicitly. She put on a shawl, picked up the letter and started
for the library.

The palace was dismal. Wind from the Lomond Hills whistled
through chinks in the rock walls and she had neither tapestry nor
carpeting to spare. Like Holyrood, Falkland was somber, seeming to
hug old tragedies. Here in 1402 the young Duke of Rothesay, heir
to the Stuart throne, was starved on his uncle's orders and died after
fifteen days of agony. Here as a boy Mary's father, disguised as a
stable lad, escaped from the power-mad Douglases to the safety of
Stirling. And here, delirious with the mental and physical wounds
of Solway Moss, he had died.

In the library James and Lethington were examining a sheaf of
papers at the long oak table and Mary thought they looked worried.

"Good afternoon," she said.

"I am afraid it is not too good, Madam," James said. "A letter
from Arran has arrived from Edinburgh. It was delivered to me, but
when I opened it I found it was also addressed to Your Majesty."
He handed it to her. "It has taken us nearly an hour to decipher it."

She glanced at the letter—blotted, lines crossed out, crumpled as
though the writer had sought to destroy it and changed his mind.

[167]

"I can scarce make out his writing," she said impatiently. "What is the gist of it?"

"It seems to be the confession of a plot which Arran and Bothwell have hatched against us. The plan was to kill Lethington and me, imprison Your Majesty in the fortress of Dumbarton and seize power."

Furiously she said, "How dare that maniac try to implicate Bothwell in treason? I am sick unto death of Arran—his plots, his delusions, his very name. It is my command that he be apprehended immediately, brought here and confined in chains. His madness may lead to murder."

"I agree that he should be confined," James said, "But—"

"I wish you to ride to Edinburgh or wherever he is and take a strong force of men. Bring him here—and his father too."

"And Bothwell?"

"Bothwell should be summoned here to defend himself against the charge."

A voice spoke from the doorway behind the guard's shoulder. "That won't be necessary, Madam."

"Bothwell!" Mary said. "Come in, my lord."

Bothwell pushed past the guard, smiling as James and Lethington stepped closer to Mary, their hands at their swords. "No," he said, "I have not come to abduct the Queen or to kill you. It is not my habit to attack in broad daylight with an army of two servants. But since you seem apprehensive, you'd best search the grounds and see for yourself."

"They will take your word for it," Mary said, "but we are somewhat upset. A letter from Arran—"

"He told me he planned to write it," Bothwell said, "and with tears in his eyes he also implored me to pull a devil from his head that was prodding his temple with a pitchfork."

"Where was this?"

"In a Canongate tavern three nights ago. I presume he went to his lodgings and wrote a confession of treason. He suffers the delusion that he and I plotted to seize power. I tried to reason with him, but it was futile."

Mary turned to James. "Please go and bring him here. God knows what tales he is spreading."

James bowed. "I shall go. And I expect Lord Bothwell to be here when I return."

"Would I come here of my own will if I didn't intend to stay?" Bothwell asked angrily.

James strode over to him. "Why did you make peace with Arran? Why after ten years of enmity do you suddenly seek Arran's friendship? Is it because you would push his deranged brain to violence, fill his mind with a plot to seize power, have him do your murders for you—and then pretend innocence?"

"Do you know," Bothwell said quietly, "that only your relationship to the Queen prevents my killing you here and now?"

Lethington sprang between them. "This is childish! This matter will be tried by the Council, not in combat." Gently he held Mary back as she tried to reach James. "It is all right, Madam."

But she was terrified. Bothwell had not touched his weapons, yet she knew how quickly he could move, swifter than a cat. And James's face was mottled red as though he would burst a blood vessel.

Mary said, "My lords, I command you to sit down. I should not like to embarrass you by ordering the guard to lay hands on you."

Slowly, glaring at each other, they separated and sat down.

Mary went to the table and poured wine, bringing them each a glass. "Now," she said, "I shall ask Lord Bothwell to tell *me* why he made peace with Arran."

"The answer is simple, Madam," he said. "I had a practical reason. For the past ten years I have spent a fortune feuding the bast—" He bowed to Mary, then mockingly to James—"My apologies. I couldn't appear in Edinburgh without a large protective force because Arran's men lay in wait for me. Each time I came to court I housed and fed and armed five hundred rogues. Then I saw Arran's mind fail. At Christmas I realized the feud was pointless. I was damned if I'd waste time and blood and money on a madman."

Mary turned to James. "How can you possibly hold Lord Bothwell responsible for Arran's behavior? But this will all come out in Council meeting. It cannot be decided here."

James rose. "Very well. I'm off to get Arran. You have commanded my actions, Madam, but you do not command my thoughts." He bowed and left the room.

It was Mary's first clash with her brother and she found it distressing. In the back of her mind was a reluctance to test her power over James for fear of discovering she had none. If she allowed an open break she knew that Lethington and her nobles would side with James against her, that Knox would seize on the disunity to her ruin. Only lately had she been able to ride through Edinburgh to smiles and cheers. Her small gains in popular favor must not be lost.

Lethington said, "Considering the gravity of the charges against Lord Bothwell he should be placed under guard, Madam."

"When he has come here of his own will? No. He is a guest, not a prisoner."

Lethington asked to be excused, saying he had heavy correspondence, and Mary gave him her letter to Elizabeth. She asked him to instruct Fleming to arrange apartments for Bothwell. As the door closed Bothwell said, amusedly, "He is doubtless alerting the guard and placing extra men on watch. By God, I think he's terrified."

"What a sinister reputation you have," she teased, "to come alone to a castle and cause such consternation."

"My reputation doesn't appear to frighten you, Madam." He went to the table and refilled his wineglass.

She said, "Somehow I feel safer with you than with any man in the world."

He stared at her curiously. Then, almost curtly, he said, "Thank you," and drained his glass, setting it down on the table with a clink.

"What of the Spanish marriage negotiations?" he asked.

"Philip is cautiously encouraging. By the time he makes up his mind I may find someone who suits me better than Don Carlos."

"I hope so. I'd hate to see the Inquisition set up in Scotland."

"But you don't care if I marry an imbecile." She regretted the words as soon as they were out. Why, indeed, should he care?

"It's a risk you seem willing to take," he said.

Mary went to the window and looked out on the wind-tossed gardens, drumming her hand against the pane. "I cannot think only of myself," she said.

"Why not? You always have."

She turned to him in astonishment. Smiling, he stood by the fire, tamping coltsfoot weed into his pipe. "Doesn't our bond of frankness still hold, Madam?"

"You accuse me of selfishness!"

"I state a fact. Most of us are selfish. I know of no one who does not place his own interests first. Except, oddly enough, Elizabeth."

"You think Elizabeth unselfish?" she asked incredulously.

"She is the only person I know who sets the wishes of others above her own. What her people want, Elizabeth grants. Were there to be a clamor for Catholicism tomorrow, Elizabeth would turn Catholic in a wink. There is absolutely nothing she would not do to please her subjects."

"Except marry."

He chuckled. "How neatly she avoids it. 'I cannot wed an Englishman because he is a subject and I cannot marry a foreigner because my people would resent him.' Actually, I believe she balks because she knows she is barren. But you no longer hear her people screaming for marriage. They take a certain pride in her spinsterhood."

"And compared to Elizabeth I am willful and self-centered?"

"You don't have her love for the people, Madam."

"They have shown me no love. I believe they accept me now and perhaps they find me a pretty pageant. But they do not love me."

"Perhaps they realize you are not genuinely concerned about them. You don't travel as Elizabeth does, stopping in remote villages to learn their needs. You don't visit almshouses or hospitals. Hers is a new concept of rulership, I grant you—mother to the people."

"I think it an affectation. How can one care about masses of humans? What sentimentality to say 'I love the peat-cutter and the candle-maker.'"

"Yet you love your servants," Bothwell said. "From the Marys down to the scullery help you've shown real devotion. You are no snob."

"And I am no hypocrite." She spread her jeweled hands, and emeralds winked in the firelight. "The people are merely faces, voices. How could I learn to love them?"

"That is something James and your other councilors hope you will never learn—yet it's simple. You will begin to love your people when you begin to help them—and then they will be your safeguard against treachery."

"Perhaps."

"You have the training, the wit, the courage to be a great queen. All you lack is the heart."

"You have said that before."

"And you hated me for it."

"I don't hate you now."

Nor do I love you, she thought triumphantly. I am attracted to you and perhaps always will be, but such infatuation I can control. Never again will you sense my desire for your arms or your lips. I learned my lesson well . . .

"I could not hate you," she repeated primly, "after all you did for my mother. And I am pleased with your work on the Border. Even James admits you have accomplished wonders there."

"I have brought disorder out of chaos," he smiled.

Fleming tapped at the door and came in, curtsying as Bothwell bowed to her. "Your apartments are ready, my lord. I am sorry there is only hay for the floors and a rag mattress, but we have done the best we can."

"Your best could not be excelled," Bothwell said.

Mary noted the way his glance followed Fleming as she crossed the room and bent to poke the fire. She thought, He never looks at me like that, as though admiring hair and bosom and sweep of gown. And yet in all humility I am more beautiful than she.

They talked trivialities—weather and hunting—and Mary became increasingly uncomfortable. Bothwell's and Fleming's awareness of each other flowed like a current between them, excluding her. Bothwell may not love Fleming, she thought, but he wants her. Fleming may not want Bothwell but she is stirred by him, probably against her will. And I am intruding.

As twilight grayed the room Mary could bear it no longer. "I must dress for supper. No," she said as Fleming started to the door with her, "Seton will help me. Entertain Lord Bothwell while I am gone."

She left them in the dying firelight. As she passed through the bannered hall she heard the wind try the door. She felt its chill through the rock walls—and the deeper, sharper chill of loneliness.

VI.

Two days later Arran was dragged into the guardroom at Falkland Castle, weeping and incoherent. Confronted by Bothwell, he appeared at first terrified, then sullen. When his father arrived that evening, he did not recognize him, staring at the old Duke with mildly curious blue eyes as though regarding a stranger.

Disgusted, Mary summoned James and Lethington to private conference in her apartments. "What information can you expect to gain from a man who babbles like a babe?" she asked. "Obviously he is not fit for trial. Perhaps he never will be. Meanwhile, Bothwell is kept from important work—"

"He is indeed," James said grimly. "While you were at supper I ordered him confined."

"Bothwell—*confined?*"

"In the dungeon, Madam. I am appalled at your recklessness, entertaining an accused traitor as honored guest, risking your life and ours. How do you know but what he has men in the hills awaiting his signal to attack? How do you know his arrival here was not part of a clever plan?"

"There is not one scrap of evidence against him! He is accused by a madman. Even Arran's father, who has no love for Bothwell, thinks him innocent of any plot. The plot is entirely in Arran's imagination."

"If Bothwell did not have a long history of violence I might agree with you, Madam. But unfortunately he is capable of creating and executing such a plot."

"That is your opinion."

"And mine, Madam," Lethington said.

"But you are only two of my councilors. I want the nine others summoned here and an immediate trial for Bothwell."

"I am sorry," James said, "but Bothwell cannot be tried. If he were acquitted, then by law Arran must automatically be put to death."

"And why not? A madman is as good as dead."

"But you forget," Lethington explained, "Arran is in line to the throne. To execute him would have serious consequences."

She had not thought of that. "Then why not acquit Bothwell and keep Arran imprisoned?"

"I have explained the law, Madam," Lethington said impatiently. "It is impossible to acquit one without executing the other."

She looked at them, hating their bland faces, their smugness, their evident enjoyment at having outmaneuvered her. It took all of her will power not to lash out at them. But defiance would gain her nothing. She would have to move carefully, feeling her way like a blind woman through the twists and turns of their conspiracy.

For she knew now that it was a conspiracy. They had used Arran's demented confession as a means to get rid of Bothwell once and for all. Having failed to turn her against him they had found this excuse to remove him.

"If Bothwell went free it would encourage treason," James said. "I've sent a messenger to Edinburgh Castle with orders to prepare cells for both Bothwell and Arran and send a heavy force here to escort them."

Edinburgh Castle—a living death, she thought. Even on her state visits, with the rooms tapestried and the lights aglow, it had horrified her—mean-roomed, iron-barred, incredibly high above the earth. In all its recorded history of more than five hundred years only one man had escaped, and he had had inside help.

"You plan to hold them indefinitely?" she asked.

"Until Arran recovers and Bothwell confesses," James said.

She sat with her fists clenched, the nails digging her palms, afraid she would rise and strike the full sneering mouth. Yes, she thought, you will be rid of Bothwell for years, rid of my only defender, my only friend. And sooner or later, in one way or another, you will dispose of me too, unless I appear to conform to your pattern of rule. For, despite your fair words, you consider yourself king of Scotland.

"I am glad that Your Majesty seems to appreciate our position," Lethington said. "We were afraid you would misunderstand our motives."

"Not at all," she said. "You feel responsible for my safety, of course."

She saw them examining her face for sarcasm, and smiled reassuringly. Tears or tantrum could be dangerous. To defend Bothwell, to plead for his freedom might cost him his life.

Lethington brought papers from his waist pouch. "Instructions to the Commander of Edinburgh Castle for the incarceration of Arran and Bothwell," he said. "We prepared them hoping Your Majesty would agree."

Knowing I would have to agree . . .

She took the papers to her desk, read and signed them.

"Who is the castle commander?" she asked.

"Lord Erskine."

Bothwell's enemy, one of the lords he had tricked at the Siege of Leith. How well conceived this plan, how neatly arranged. Sickened, she said, "You will excuse me now I wish to retire."

Smilingly they left her. Hour after hour she sat in thought while the tapers burned low in their iron holders. She considered sending Peter Pye down to the dungeons with a message for Bothwell, but it was too risky. If only Bothwell could know he has my secret support, she thought, it would at least encourage him. But James has likely told him this was my idea, and when he reaches Edinburgh Castle and learns that I signed the incarceration order he will loathe me . . . If I could get word to his men—but I don't know who they are or where. Likely they're scattered from Border to Highlands.

Her thoughts tangled, circled. A log fell into embers, a tiny sound of finality. Wearily she prepared for bed.

She would miss Bothwell's guidance through the darkness ahead. He was more than a watchdog for Border and seas. She saw him as the one strong thread in the rotting fabric that was her kingdom. Without him it would fall to treachery. James, Knox and Elizabeth maneuvered it cynically. The Border lairds knifed its weakest spots. In the Highlands, Huntley strained the seams, setting up a Catholic hierarchy with himself and his sons as rulers.

From the bed table Mary took her crucifix and knelt in the dusty straw.

Late the next afternoon, watching from her window, Mary saw the prisoners start toward Edinburgh under heavy guard. Arran was chained to a mule-drawn litter. Bothwell rode a shaggy horse, and in the sun his hair was the burnished red-gold of the tall surrounding spears.

Trumpets shrilled, horses jostled forward. On high-held lance the ragged banners of Scotland whipped up in swirls of yellow and crimson. Mary stood at the window until the hoofbeats were lost in the long sigh of wind from the Lomond Hills.

CHAPTER SIX

I.

ABOVE THE SPIRES of Inverness Castle the harvest moon cruised among wind-gusted clouds. Alone in the watchtower, Mary could see the surrounding humps of the Highlands and far below on the banks of the River Ness the campfires of her soldiers.

She leaned from the open turret, wind lifting the plumes on her steel helmet. Somewhere out in the heaving dark, Huntley's clansmen, the wild, kilted Gordons, were racing their shaggy ponies toward this stronghold. But they could not recapture it. Her forces were too strong. With James she was breaking Huntley's hold on the Highlands—swiftly, surely bringing the north to her emerald-spurred heel.

It was her one triumph in five months of failure. Bothwell was still imprisoned two hundred miles across the hills in Edinburgh, and she had been unable to communicate with him. Knox pounded persecution from the pulpit. Hope of meeting Elizabeth was gone; all summer the English Queen had found excuses to postpone the rendezvous. She never intended to see me, Mary thought. Her jealousy, her hatred go too deep . . .

And so, with the dream of succession remote as the stars, this battle trip to the north had been a boon, a break in the pattern of failure. Riding with James at the head of two thousand men, gathering support in each village, she won personal as well as military victories. Mindful of Bothwell's advice she mingled among her people, joining in their pageants, their carnivals and fairs. She visited almshouses and tolbooths, fishing hovels and moorland farms. For the first time in her life she saw poverty in its grisly nakedness, the swollen-bellied hunger of children. She gave generously. Her saddlebag, heavy with coins when she left Edinburgh, was nearly empty. Protestant prayers followed her north, and in the ruins of Catholic churches rushlights glowed her name toward God.

Now, looking out on lands newly won, she thought of the people who gathered the bleak harvests of the hills, who tended thin flocks and sent their frail boats against the sea. She visioned them asleep on cob pallets by banked turf fires. Never again would the mob be merely faces. She knew names, she had touched wounds and looked into hearts.

Below her she saw the sprawl of horses and wagons in the firelight and the peaked tents of the soldiers. Two months ago these men had belonged to James. Although she maintained them from her own funds it was he who commanded them. But now . . . She smiled in the darkness. James would be furious if he knew what she had done.

On the long, hard trip from Edinburgh he had been too pre-occupied with Lady Agnes, his pretty, whining bride, to realize how often Mary left his side to gallop back to the troops. She wanted to win their confidence, but they were difficult to approach, close-mouthed and obviously fearful of being patronized. Although the young recruits seemed flattered by her attention, the veterans were stony-eyed and she was a little afraid of them. Savage-faced, tangle-bearded, they hunched in their leather coats cursing the fog, and when she spoke to them they had the look of cornered boars, half-hostile, half-suspicious. Contemptuously, their eyes measured her slim body and she thought, They see me frail as a fern, they expect me to whimper like James's wife and order a litter. They think I should have remained at Holyrood with Chastelard and Rizzio and the spaniels.

Through Perth and Aberdeenshire the weather turned raw, the skies emptied of light. Moors stretched limitless, purple-gray folds of briared heather. Dust-colored curlews moved above the death of the land, and in hill farms crow flocks bent like black cloaks to the stubs of corn.

Rains swept down on the wolf-howl of the wind, slowing the army to eight miles a day. At night Mary and her courtiers were enter-tained in dreary wayside castles or burghers' homes while the soldiers camped in courtyards or gardens. Often she slept in a blustered tent pitched in a mountain cut. At dawn she was in the saddle again, weighted by armor that rusted under her damp cloak. Rain pounded her steel helmet, dripped down her face, blurred her vision. She caught a head cold and suspected that she had the New Acquaint-ance, a feverish disease that ached every muscle in her body. But she plodded on smiling, shaking the rain like a terrier.

Wearily, she thought, My rank is too high, and the men have a peasant mistrust of a foreigner. For though I wear Scots wool and speak Scots and ride a Highland pony, I am forever French to them. I cannot go further on the path of friendship. I will not beg.

And then one icy dusk, whisky jugs were passed surreptitiously behind the officers' backs. Mary, pretending not to notice, turned her head. But a mosstrooper nudged her and held out a tattered cloak. Carefully she took it, feeling a jug inside. She unplugged it and drank. Wrapping it in the cloak she passed it to the man on the other side of her. A spear touched her lightly on the shoulder, and she turned in the saddle. As far back as she could see, pikes were raised in salute. Her army was smiling.

I will never understand, she thought. I will never know at what point they ceased to tolerate and started to love. But that they love me is enough . . .

Afterward, men fought to rag her jingling stirrups, to lift her to or from the saddle, to tend her pony, to ride beside her. Shyly, gruffly they presented gifts—a woolen cutting scarf to bind her throat against enemy steel, a two-edged sword, a Glasgow buckler. As she clattered into the rain-glittered granite of Aberdeen riding beside James, Captain Erskine handed her a bouquet of heather. It was preposterously large and cumbersome. But she held it proudly, ignoring the smiles of her ladies, the guffaws of Lords Ruthven and Morton. She saw James's speculative stare and thought, He suspects, but he will not know for sure unless his arrogance pushes him to outright defiance of me, and then it will be too late. Without the loyalty of the army he is helpless, just as I was.

"Mary!"

She heard James's voice from the level below and called down to him. He came up the narrow stone stairs to the tower with a lantern in his hand, setting it down on the dirt floor.

"Bothwell has escaped," he said.

It was a miracle that she accepted in silence, in utter awe. She stood staring at James, her hands limp at her sides. Then tears flooded her face and she turned, felt blindly for the wall and leaned against it, pressing her cheek against the rock.

"Are you ill?" he asked sharply.

She rubbed her wet face on her sleeve and turned to him. "No," she said. "Is he safe? Was he hurt?"

"You no longer trouble to conceal your love."

"Answer me!"

"Yes, my dear, duped sister, the traitor is safe on the Border, safe and swaggering in Liddesdale. He escaped August 28th, between two and four in the morning. They found his window stanchion broken in the tower and a length of rope on the rocks."

For a moment she visioned that dizzy descent down the sheer

[177]

face of Castle Rock. She could see him on a wind-swayed rope high above the darkened city, clinging, swinging . . .

"God damn him!" James exploded.

She laughed exultantly. "God protects him."

"So your deception is over," James said, "if indeed you ever deceived anyone. A woman in love is transparent as water."

She laughed again. "One can admire a man without loving him."

"He must be recaptured."

"No," she said gaily, "We cannot spare one soldier from this campaign."

"You fool!" he said furiously, "You're so blind in love you cannot see what stares you in the face. None of us is safe if he is free."

"James," she said quietly, "I agree on one point. I have been a fool. I have allowed you to override my authority. That will not happen again. Neither you nor any of my lords shall move one man to recapture Bothwell. That is my command."

He was silent, whether from anger or surprise she could not tell. She thought, He wonders how far he dares to go. He probably realizes that the bouquet of heather was something more than an officer's gallantry.

"You have changed," he said at last. "Your hardness appalls me."

"I have no doubt," she said, wryly amused.

He asked the question she had been expecting. "What has happened to you?"

"What should have happened when I first reached Scotland—I realize that I am Queen. I take no orders, I give them. And I have given you a great deal. In less than a year you have received the highest position on my council, a royal wedding and the Earldom of Mar. These are not puny gifts, even for an ambitious man, are they?"

"No one ever questioned your generosity," he said sullenly.

"You have said that you are ambitious, and I find that natural to a man of your birth and your talents. But insatiable greed is something else. If I cannot give you power without imperiling my own, then I shall have to relieve you of all power."

"And place it in the hands of an adventurer?"

"If you refer to Bothwell, no. He is a military, not a political expert. He would fret at the reins of government. But you, James, you are suited to help me govern. It is unfortunate that you cannot govern your own appetite."

"If that is true, would I not be demanding more lands, more titles?"

"I expect you to," she said. "In the next few days we will likely seize Huntley's richest lands—the Earldom of Moray. You have coveted that title for years. But you cannot get it without my signature. And unless you cooperate fully with me there shall be no signature."

"You have honored me freely in the past. You led me to think that you loved me, trusted me."

"I did. Until I saw an obvious conspiracy against the man I trusted beyond all others."

"There was no conspiracy against Bothwell," James said. "I truly felt he was a threat to your safety. But if you want him back at court what can I say or do?"

You can instigate a new conspiracy against him—murder. Aloud she said, "I shall not summon Bothwell to court. It would be foolish."

"It is up to you, of course. But if you wish him back I will see that the Council accepts him."

With newly sharpened daggers? "Thank you, James. You need not trouble. For appearances, I shall send a small force to search for him—in the wrong places. He will be the most unimpeded fugitive in history."

She started toward the steps, and he picked up the lantern and followed her, then paused a moment.

"I hope that our differences are forgotten, Mary."

"Very well."

"I could not be happy if I thought you no longer loved me."

She turned and smiled into the bland, bearded face. "Rest assured that I love you, James, just as you love me."

That night she wrote to Bothwell explaining her unwilling submission to his imprisonment. *It is dangerous for you to remain in Scotland. Go to France and seek service with the Cardinal of Lorraine. I will summon you when the time seems right. Until then, do not try to communicate with me . . . God's blessing always.*

She stamped her seal in wax, and turned to Peter Pye. "From here to the Border is a terrible journey for a boy—for a man to make. It's nearly three hundred miles. Are you sure you want to go?"

"Nothing can stop me, Ma'am."

She went to her reticule and transferred some money into a leather pouch. "Be careful of this, and of your horse. Stay at good hostelries on the way."

"I can do twenty miles a day easy, Ma'am. I'll be in Liddesdale in less than two weeks."

"If I know Bothwell," she said, "he's more likely hunting than hiding. Try Hermitage Castle first, but inquire discreetly. Bothwell has a page named Paris. You might pretend to be looking for him." She winked. "Paris is a distant cousin of yours."

"Yes, Ma'am," he grinned. "On my mother's side."

"Give no one this letter but Bothwell himself. And after you have delivered it, go to Holyrood and await me there."

She gave him the money, the letter and a sentry pass to permit him through the portcullis. Then from an ivory box she took a jewel-hilted dag worked in rubies and fleurs-de-lis. "This is too conspicuous for you to take with you," she said, "but it will be waiting for you. It belonged to my husband, the King of France."

He touched the pistol with gentle, stubby fingers and she heard his indrawn breath. Then he looked up at her, opened his mouth and closed it again.

"For extraordinary gallantry," she said.

II.

Snow fell on Holyrood, forming white dunce caps on the turrets. In the Great Hall, rushlights burned in holly holders, and evergreen boughs hung on the wall between the crossed boar spears. At the hearth Peter Pye poked at the remnants of a giant Yule log.

Mary, seated by the fire with her embroidery, sent Peter an approving smile as he left the room. He had delivered her letter and returned with Bothwell's assurance that he would leave the country. By now he was probably at sea or safe in France.

Across from her, Lady Jean Gordon, her new lady-in-waiting, worked a tapestry in silk and wool. Her face was unusual, Mary thought, fine-boned, clean-cut as a young lad's. Her eyes were gray and forthright, widely spaced under gold brows. Freckles sprinkled her nose; her mouth, too generous for prettiness, was unpainted. Straight fair hair was caught into a black snood as though pushed there rather than arranged. She had a boy's wide shoulders and narrow waist, and the ugly wool mourning robes could not conceal the lovely lines of throat and bosom and thigh.

Poor lass, Mary thought, I must make her life as pleasant as possible. Because of me her father, Lord Huntley, is dead. One of her brothers was executed, another imprisoned, and her clansmen routed on the field of Corrichie. My Highland victory tore her world apart.

"I hope," Mary said, "that in time you will come to forgive us."

The gray eyes opened wide. "What else could you do, Madam? We were rebels against the crown. You were entirely justified."

"How can you be so objective?"

"I never approved my father's defiance; I felt it was morally wrong." Her chin trembled. "One can love one's father, but one worships one's Queen."

Touched, Mary said, "Such devotion is rare."

"But it isn't, Madam. On our journey here from Strathbogie I saw how the crowds cheered you."

"True, but that was in the north where Knox's voice is scarcely heard. Here in Edinburgh he bellows. In my absence he roused the people to such resentment that I lost what popularity I had."

Jean said, "His flouting of your authority is the one thing I cannot condone. Otherwise I think him a great man."

"You, a Catholic, say that?"

"I am Protestant, Madam."

"You astonish me! I thought all the Gordons were Catholic."

"I've a mind of my own."

Mary smiled. "In that case how will we ever catch you a husband? I cannot imagine you curtsying to a man's whims."

"If I loved him," Jean said, "I would grovel."

"Suppose," Mary teased, "your husband forbade you to hear Knox preach?"

"I'd not marry a man so intolerant."

"I do not mean to pry," Mary said, "but I heard you were promised to Alex Ogilvie of Boyne."

"We had planned to marry, but last month he met Mary Beaton. Since then he has had eyes for no one else."

"Beaton! I had no idea. Why, she flirts with Randolph and a dozen others. I am sure she is not serious or she would have mentioned the matter to me. I will speak to her—"

"No, Madam, I beg you not to. If you force the issue I will never know Alex's true feelings. I don't want him back unless he comes of his own free will."

"Very well, Jean. But I hope he returns to you. Beaton is a butterfly, and from my scant acquaintance with Alex I'd say he is too grave for her. We who were raised in France find Scotsmen a bit dour."

Peter Pye entered and announced Master Randolph. "He says it is important, Madam."

News of Elizabeth, Mary thought. She dismissed Lady Jean and smoothed her hair and skirts. As always, in spite of the many disappointments, she was hopeful and eager, but she hid her excitement as Randolph sat down. Stolidly handsome in claret velvet doublet and huge padded breeches, he murmured the usual opening compliments. Concealing her impatience, Mary waited for him to come to the point.

He stroked his full blond beard. "Bothwell has left Scotland."

She tensed, frowned in pretended fury. "What!"

"He stowed away in a merchant vessel a few days ago, bound for

France." He watched her, his hazel eyes limpid. "I am told he embarked from Leith."

"From under our very noses! I had men watching the ports, searching and guarding the Borders. Your mistress's spies are cleverer than mine."

"Spies? Surely you jest, Madam. I learned it only because Bothwell's vessel wrecked at Holy Island down the east coast. English soldiers recognized him and took him to Berwick where he is now, under guard."

"Ah," she said, feigning relief. "I am more than grateful. He must be returned to Edinburgh immediately."

Randolph shook his head. "I am sorry, Madam, Her Majesty intends to hold him. For years he has raided England, plundering our border, killing, pirating our shipping. You are aware that he intercepted a thousand pounds of gold bound for the lords of Scotland. Naturally my mistress regards him as England's mortal enemy."

"But Bothwell is my subject and a fugitive from my justice. I insist on his return."

He put his hand to his mustache and Mary wondered if he hid a smile. "I shall write Her Majesty to that effect, Madam. But you see, she is merely sparing you the expense and trouble of punishing him. She thought you would be pleased."

"Of course, I am delighted that he is captured. But it is I who must punish him. I also shall write Her Majesty and our letters will go by courier tonight." She struggled to sound casual. "What sort of punishment does Her Majesty have in mind? Imprisonment? Or—execution?"

"I do not know, Madam. She and Cecil may have discussed that, but I am not informed."

So Bothwell is done for, she thought—and through my own bungling. I should have pardoned him, summoned him to court and risked James's treachery. For all I know, James and Elizabeth are in this together, their spies conniving. There is not a chance in the world that I can free him.

Mary reached for her shawl, and Randolph rose to arrange it around her shoulders. "It is so cold," she said, hiding her worry in small talk, "that the water in my bathhouse was frozen solid this morning."

"I don't doubt it. Last night I had two warming pans in my bed and I awoke before dawn stiff as a corpse."

"Sometimes I sleep with my spaniels," Mary said. "They are better than warming pans."

"A husband," he smiled, "would be better still."

How many hundreds of times has he probed this subject, she thought wearily, and how many hundreds of times have I fenced?

He said, "I am surprised that Your Majesty has not considered Philip's son."

So Elizabeth was suspicious. "I did at one time," she said, assuming frankness. "But reports of the boy's depravity dissuade me. Of what use is power and wealth if one is in constant fear of one's husband?"

"How true, Madam. Indeed, the full extent of Don Carlos' depravity is too shocking to relate."

She knew he would say anything to discourage the Spanish marriage, but she was nevertheless curious. "I should like to know the truth."

"It is too vile, Madam. The least of his crimes is sodomy."

"Oh!" She was not sure what the word meant, but since punishment for the crime was branding she knew it must be horrible. "Isn't that the crime for which John Calvin bears a fiery fleur-de-lis on his shoulder?"

"That is a despicable slander, Madam, and most certainly untrue."

"Then why," she murmured, "does he not bare his shoulders and disprove it? Does some curious Huguenot modesty prevent him?"

"He probably would not dignify the lie, Madam."

Thus she led Randolph safely off the subject of the Spanish marriage, and after reminding him to write Elizabeth immediately, she dismissed him and sent a page in search of David Rizzio. If anyone can advise me, she thought, Davy can. In that wretched little body is a brain as shrewd as Lethington's—with the difference that it is loyal.

In the past months Rizzio had become far more than her favorite musician. He was her secret advisor, her most intimate confidant. They shared the same faith, the same interests. He gave her harp and cittern lessons, and she taught him the songs of France. Together they composed madrigals, read Livy and Ovid by the fire. Chastelard sulked jealously. Then, perceiving the innocence of the relationship, he joined them for evenings of poetry and music, reading his sonnets as Rizzio improvised lute accompaniment.

Mary knew that the lords regarded Rizzio as just another satin-cushioned lap dog, and she was careful not to enlighten them. Beneath the Italian embroidery of mode and manners was a mind dagger-sharp. He pulled her out of emotional quicksands, forced her to see matters as they were rather than as she wished them to be. Adaptable, objective, he steered her through the intricate courses of daily intrigue. He knew when she should conciliate, when to stand firm. It was he who advised her to grant James the Earldom of Moray. "Throw the dog a big bone, and while he is gnawing it strengthen your position with the people. You cannot fight both James and Knox—not with Bothwell immobilized."

She had told Rizzio the entire story of Bothwell, even to her infatuation, a confession she had kept from Father Black. There was nothing she could not entrust to Rizzio, no secret too private.

"Your Majesty . . ."

He stood in the doorway, and she said, "Shut the door, Davy."

He did so, removed his cloak and sat down by the fire. "Something is wrong, Madam?"

"Am I so obvious? Does my face show it?"

"No. But it is a bad omen when Randolph whistles down a corridor."

"He has reason to," she said, and told him of Bothwell's capture. All the fear, all the misery she had suppressed in Randolph's presence burst out as she spoke.

Rizzio said, "I think Lord James is behind this. You admitted to him that your search for Bothwell would be pretense, and he probably informed Elizabeth."

"What do you suggest, Davy?"

"Write her that you wish Bothwell returned to Edinburgh but make no issue of it. State your case mildly, almost half-heartedly, as though you really don't care one way or another. Then fill your letter with trivia. Be affectionate." He smiled. "She and Cecil will have the devil's own time figuring out your true motives."

She nodded. "Do you think there is any chance at all that she will free Bothwell?"

"To be truthful—no. Bothwell has been an embarrassment to England too long. His championship of your cause is too well known. Your letter at best will only confuse her; it will not persuade her."

Mary put her hands to her eyes. "She may execute him. It is a terrible thing to lose someone so—someone I—"

He said, "Of course it is. I have never met Bothwell but I feel that I know him as well as I know you. He is like a great mammoth who cannot adapt to this new world. He pits his strength against cunning, he fights in the open, while the Cecils and the Lethingtons connive from the shadows. The last chivalry on this earth dies with your Borderers. Bothwell was born a hundred years too late."

"And yet," she murmured, "he has a foot in the future. Science interests him, the new religion fascinates him."

"That is his tragedy. He is pulled between two eras and belongs to neither."

"And I?" she asked. "Where do I belong?"

"You are the past, Madam. With you the knights and troubadours fall to dust and the jesters' bells are silenced. For you the last romantics will polish their rusted armor and lift their spears. For you a final blooming before the fields of honor are stripped for the future."

"And the future?"

"Elizabeth."

My own future is bounded by her, Mary thought. It is she who holds my English crown, the fate of my unborn children and my only loyal lord. She said, "My only chance of escaping her domination is to marry Don Carlos. I am not only resigned to it—I am eager for it."

"This is a change! You had worried about his degeneracy."

"I think I could control one degenerate—I cannot control the dozens of rogues around me. James, Lethington, Argyll, Kerr, Ruthven, Lindsay—the list is endless. What depravity could be worse than Scotland's, a nation so morally obscene it reviles its one patriot and lifts its traitors to power? What more indecent than hypocrites led by a foul-minded old man in the name of God? I am sick of Scotland—its fanatics, its conspirators, its opportunists. I would leave it tomorrow without a backward glance."

"But even in Spain you would not be free of it. You need to hold Scotland against Elizabeth."

"As one holds a vulture off a festering corpse. I do not care what Philip does with Scotland; if he wishes to use it as a back door for the invasion of England, let him ravage it. I have ceased to care."

"I understand your disillusion, Madam. But sometimes as we fight for our property—be it a stony field—we come to love it."

"I will never love Scotland."

They were silent. Sleet beat on the window and logs shifted and sputtered in the fireplace. Mary's spaniels dozed on the hearth, spraddle-pawed, dream-quivered.

"I think," Rizzio said, "that your chance has come to fight Knox."

"With what?" she asked.

"Ridicule. I learned this afternoon that Knox is courting a thirteen-year-old girl."

"You are jesting!"

"No, Madam. The lass is Margaret Stewart, Lord Ochiltree's daughter. Ochiltree's harpist told me Knox visits her two evenings a week and is entertained as a suitor. Margaret is no sick child in need of prayer, but buxom and blooming."

Mary laughed. "So at last he trips on his own lust! But I can't believe he would be so stupid as to choose a lass nearly fifty years

[185]

younger than he. Doesn't he realize that even the most faithful of his congregation is apt to question the spirituality of his motives?"

"He is in senile love. I gather he wants to marry her."

Mary leaned forward. "We must spread this news, Davy, deliberately plant it where it will reach every ear in Edinburgh, spice the talk of the taverns and travel the country."

"Nothing spreads so swiftly as a simple bawdy song," Rizzio said. "I am sure Monsieur Chastelard will be happy to collaborate with me. When it is ready I will introduce it to the servants, it will sweep through brothels and barracks—and then there is no stopping it."

"You are a genius!"

"I am your most humble of servants."

"You live too humbly," she frowned. "I am going to move you from the servants' quarters to a guest house in the Canongate—"

"Please, Madam, not now. At the moment it would hamper my free movement between servants and nobles. And it would rouse your brother's suspicions. In the role of pet musician I can do far more for you than if you lifted me to obvious favor."

"Very well. But you shall not live in the shadows forever."

His smile was Francis'—shy, surprised, self-effacing. Impulsively, Mary went to him, put her arms around the hunched shoulders. "Some day," she said, "I will honor you as you deserve. Meanwhile you have my trust and my devotion."

"With such gifts," he said, "I join the gods."

III.

High on the rocks above Burntisland harbor, Rossend Castle grayed in the sea mists of February. Gulls screamed across the turrets, dipping down to the Firth of Forth, which stretched beyond Mary's window. She looked out on a watery world, dismal as all Scotland was dismal. Wherever she traveled there was the eternal damp, the murk, the gulls and curlews.

This night on the way to St. Andrews with James and Randolph and a small court she was the guest of Kirkcaldy of Grange. She had come to dread these stopovers in provincial castles, for they followed the same crude pattern. Her host's country neighbors would ride in to be presented to Mary in the Great Hall—gaping, incoherent men with their dowdy wives. There would be a banquet of greasy food clumsily served, interminable drunken toasts. Then when the floors had been swept of bones and bread and the dogs chased out, fiddles would screech for the Skip, the Fling, the Canary, and the lairds like clumsy dancing bears would stumble about the room with their ladies. By midnight the dourest matrons would be flushed and sweat-spattered, hair down their backs, caps askew. And then more food and more drink and the procession of men to the vomitorium at the side of the hall—a great stone basin with a hollow stem that connected with the moat below. Above on the gallery there was often a Leper's Lair, from which the unclean looked down through a tiny peephole, screaming above the squeal of the fiddles.

This evening, bored with the country capers, Mary and Chastelard traded clothes and danced the Purpose—he mocking her daintiness in velvet gown and frilled cap, she in his white brocade doublet and black hose. Long-legged and lovely, with a dagger at her waist, Mary swaggered through her role to rowdy applause, and the music was drowned in cheers. But she realized that this was fuel for Knox's fires, and at the end of the third measure she whispered to Chastelard to lead her off into the anteroom where Fleming waited to help her dress.

Resuming her bodice and petticoats she returned to the Great Hall and sat down beside James and Randolph. She said, "I hope this prank doesn't reach Edinburgh but I suppose it will."

James said, "A bit late for regrets, isn't it?"

"Your Majesty was beautiful," Randolph said. "The dance was charmingly satiric."

"Thank you, sir."

A stable boy brought a white dove to James and he held it in his hands. There was dried blood on its eyes, and Mary leaned forward to examine it.

"What ails it?" she asked.

"Her eyes have been sealed," James said, "the lids sewn together with thread. It is rather amusing. Watch . . ."

He tossed the dove into the air and she flew toward the oak ceiling beams, then spiraled down, blundering into the banners, the rock walls, the dancers. The crowd screamed with laughter, and James chuckled and said, "She may flounder about for hours."

Mary said, "She is in agony! She must be caught and killed."

James stared at her in surprise.

"Stop it," she said, turning her head, "It is horrible!"

"I am sorry," James said coldly, "if I have offended your delicate sensibilities. If you wish to spoil the sport, by all means end it."

"Sport!" she snapped, rising, "Senseless torture." She summoned a servant to catch the bird but it had already fallen, trampled by the dancers to pulp.

Chastelard came to her and suggested a walk in the garden, and she nodded mutely. Outside, he put his cloak about her and they walked through wet grass to the bluff that faced the sea. The moon had come out and the harbor was a glittering gold path bordered by darkness.

They sat down on a bench under the bare oaks. It was chilly, but Mary was grateful for the reviving air. She said, "That dove . . . I was sickened."

"I know, Madam."

"I wish I could get away from here, from the meanness and the ignorance and the insensitivity."

"And where would you like to go?"

"Anywhere." She did not mention Spain. The fewer people who knew of her marriage negotiations the better. In a year, she thought, I may shed this grubby kingdom for an empire.

"If only I could take you back to France with me," Chastelard said.

She turned to him quickly. "You are returning?"

"I see nothing else to do," he said. "I have failed to reach your heart. I was a fool to try."

"What could you expect of me?" she asked gently. "You know that I must marry for power."

He took her hand. "You could have love—for all of my life." His arm crept around her shoulder. "You are twenty, no longer a girl. This sterile friendship cannot go on. It is against nature."

"In my position I cannot be too careful. Even if it were not sinful, I—"

"Even if it were," he said, and drew her into his arms.

She welcomed his kiss as a sort of obliteration and met it eagerly, her head tipped back, her eyes closed. She brought to it all the imagery of their love verse, the cadence of beauty and passion. But with a terrible objectivity she could see herself in his arms, skirts gracefully spread, hand on his hair in the last act of a pretty pretense.

She felt nothing, neither desire nor revulsion.

Summoning all her gratitude, she tried to return his ardor. He had left fame in France to come to a country where poets were despised. He had borne the sneers of the lords and the discomforts of a wretched court. In the gloom of Holyrood his sonnets to her lit the hours like candles.

But she could not fool herself. The romantic structure of their relationship collapsed under his lips, too frail to bear the reality of a kiss. She drew away, sorry for herself, sorrier for him.

"Pierre," she said, "it is best you return to France."

"You are fighting yourself." He caught her to him, but again she pulled away.

"No, please . . ."

"You love someone else," he said sulkily.

She thought of Bothwell imprisoned at Tynemouth Castle on the North Sea. "No. There is no one else." And that was true. She had not seen Bothwell for a year, and time had cured her infatuation.

"But you do not love me?"

"Not as you wish me to. Forgive me if I hurt you."

He stared down at the grass. She wanted to comfort him, but it would be no kindness to encourage him and she said, "I must go in now."

Still he said nothing. She rose, removed his cloak from her shoulders and laid it on the bench beside him. He made no move to follow her as she walked through the dark garden toward the castle.

In the Great Hall she worried about Chastelard and watched the door but he did not return. Surely he would do nothing foolish. Probably he was still sitting there, dramatizing his despondency. Perhaps it would inspire a great poem. She could vision him a month from now reading it aloud in the pink, mirrored hall of Fontainebleau, the ladies hiding tears behind their fans.

Shortly after midnight the party dispersed and Mary retired to her bedchamber. Beaton removed her gown and petticoats and Livingstone drew the bed curtains. Mary slipped out of her shift and turned to take her nightgown from Beaton. Over Beaton's shoulder she saw a closet door suddenly open. She gasped, as Chastelard emerged. His face was white and strained, his teeth cut his underlip. Slowly he walked toward her.

Clutching the nightgown to her nakedness, she stared unbelieving, too stunned to move. Beaton turned, saw Chastelard and ran into the corridor screaming. At the same moment Livingstone rushed to Mary and tried to drag her toward the door, but Chastelard pushed her aside and caught Mary in his arms, throwing the nightgown to the floor.

Mary struggled furiously as he kissed her mouth, her shoulders and throat, his breath hot on her flesh. She tried to reach the dagger at his belt, but he twisted her arm behind her and with the other hand held off Livingstone. Mary heard shouting in the corridor, a rush of men through the doorway. James seized Chastelard, smashed his fist against the golden-bearded jaw and sent him reeling against a table that crashed to the floor with him.

As Chastelard tried to rise from wine-wet rushes and splintered glass James hit him again and he slumped, whimpered, lay still. Standing over him, James unsheathed his dagger.

"No!" Mary screamed and started forward, but Livingstone and Beaton caught her and wrapped a blanket around her.

"The Queen is right." Kirkcaldy of Grange stepped between James and Chastelard. "Blood spilled here can only stain Her Majesty's name."

James cursed. "That damage is already done."

Mary broke away from her ladies and ran to James, putting her hand on his shoulder. "Please, for my sake, let us settle this some other way."

Reluctantly, James replaced the dagger at his sash. He brushed Kirkcaldy aside and kicked Chastelard in the ribs.

Chastelard stirred, opened his eyes, crouched back against the table. James leaned over and jerked him to his feet. Chastelard stood swaying, rubbing his puffed face.

James slapped him. "Explain yourself. What were you doing in Her Majesty's chamber?"

Chastelard's eyes met Mary's. He was silent.

"Speak," Mary said. "I demand an explanation."

With his sleeve Chastelard wiped a trickle of blood from his lips. "Surely Your Majesty needs no explanation," he said.

She shook her head, bewildered. And then she was conscious for the first time of the watching eyes, of the many who had seen her naked. Guards filled the room behind her, holding back a corridor of lairds and ladies. Near the bed stood Randolph, and in sudden horror she turned and hid her face on Beaton's shoulder. What a tale for Elizabeth—for Philip. The Queen of Scotland naked with a man in her bedchamber . . .

Sick with humiliation, she lifted her head. "I have no idea why you were hiding here. I insist on the truth."

Chastelard shrugged. "I should prefer to protect you, Madam, but the circumstances leave me no choice. Do you deny that you asked me in the garden tonight to meet you here—to hide in the closet until your ladies had left you? Unfortunately I emerged too soon—this time."

"*This time?*"

"Your Majesty prefers to forget the other times?"

Incredulously she stared at him. "Have you lost your mind?"

"No." His smile was sardonic. "But I shall undoubtedly lose my life. One pays dearly for royal favors—"

His words were stopped by James's fist and he staggered but kept his feet. Blood dripped from his nose.

Mary said, "What reason have you for this monstrous lie? Why?"

Kirkcaldy said, "The thumbscrew will tell us."

"No," Mary said sharply, "I will not permit it. Besides, men will confess anything under torture, and I want the truth." She drew the blanket tight around her and went close to Chastelard. "Your story is incredible. A secret lover does not embrace his lady in view of her attendants. You deliberately sought to cause a scandal."

More gently she said, "Is it because I rejected your love? Are you so hurt that you seek to soil my name before the world so that no man will want me?"

"Be done with this, Madam," James said impatiently. "He'll tell us soon enough with the heat under his nails."

"No!" Mary turned back to Chastelard. "If you will confess the truth I will send you back to France unharmed."

He glared at her. "You know the truth."

This, she thought, is Chastelard's face—the lips I have kissed, the hair I have stroked. There is the little cleft in his chin to which I wrote a blithe sonnet and the dark blue eyes that looked on me with love. Those are his arms that guided me through years of dancing, that embraced me tonight. Yet this is not Chastelard. Another mind has possessed him and made him vile. What happened there in the garden—what demon sidled through the darkness and entered his body, turning out his soul?

She removed her chain and crucifix and held it out to him in the desperate hope that it might exorcise the evil. But Chastelard spat on it and said, "I am Huguenot."

Mary gasped and stepped back with the crucifix tight in her hand. "God help you," she said. "I cannot."

Kirkcaldy signaled to the guards. They escorted Chastelard out and dispersed the crowd in the corridor. Only James and Randolph remained.

Randolph said, "You have my deepest sympathy, Madam. And I know I speak for my mistress."

Mary tried to smile. "Must Queen Elizabeth know?"

James said, "Don't be childish, Madam. There were at least fifteen people in this room, to say nothing of those in the corridor. You cannot keep the story from spreading. The only thing to do is brazen it out, make it as public as possible—in fact, scream your innocence to the skies."

"To try to conceal this would be fatal," Randolph agreed. "Even if I so wished I could not keep it from my mistress. Knox will spread it throughout Britain."

Mary thought of the little song ridiculing Knox. What chance did it have now against this flamboyant scandal of her own?

"Of course," Randolph purred, "my mistress will support you, as best she can."

How she will love this, Mary thought. How she will gloat and gossip.

Randolph's eyes gleamed in the candlelight. "What do you intend to do with Chastelard?"

"Imprison him and hope for a confession."

Both men spoke simultaneously. "Imprison him!"

"His death will not absolve me. Only his confession can do that."

"He must be publicly executed," James said firmly. "To let him go unpunished would only fan the suspicion that you were lovers."

Confused, exhausted, she thought, I cannot trust James's advice. I must send a message to Rizzio at Holyrood.

"In a few days," she said, "I will decide whether Chastelard lives or dies."

IV.

A week later in the market place of St. Andrews a dense crowd jostled the high wooden scaffold. Chastelard, reciting Ronsard's "Hymn to Death," followed a Protestant minister up the black-draped steps.

Mary, on horseback, pressed close to the scaffold. She still hoped for a confession. In his cell at St. Andrews Castle Chastelard had stubbornly remained silent, but now, with death imminent, she felt he might speak the truth.

Beside her on a scarlet-caparisoned horse, James said, "He goes to hell in fashion."

Chastelard's white satin breeches, puffed and ruched, plumped out over long white netherhose. He removed his doublet and revealed a damask shirt shimmering with silver embroidery. The headsman took the ruff from his neck.

Mary said, "Chastelard has done me a ghastly wrong, yet I feel guilty."

"You were guilty of indiscretion," James said. "Perhaps this will teach you a lesson. To flirt and dance as you did is to leave yourself open to the worst suspicions."

"Spoken like Master Knox," she said sarcastically.

James ignored her and leaned back in the saddle to speak to Randolph on the other side of her. "The fellow may die rather well. I thought he'd weep and struggle like a woman."

"But how he dramatizes!" Randolph smiled. "See, he takes a last look at this world."

Chastelard, the minister beside him, was staring up past the gray gabled rooftops at the sky. He looked serene and very young, his sunlit hair curling in ringlets to the edge of his shirt.

A magistrate read the death warrant: ". . . against the honor, integrity and sacred person of our Sovereign Lady, Mary, Queen of Scotland and the Isles, Dowager Queen of France . . . and in payment for said crime to die by the axe on this twenty-second day of February 1563."

The minister prayed. "Now speak, and make peace with God and your enemies."

Mary's eyes begged, but Chastelard did not look at her. Head bowed, he said, "I have been impious and full of vanity and worldliness . . . May God forgive me as I forgive my enemies . . . I die cheerfully, a loyal subject, faithful even unto death to the wishes and commands of Queen—"

Mary leaned forward.

"—Catherine of France."

Seven years whipped back and Mary remembered a musk-scented bedchamber at St. Germain . . . a harsh voice: *I will discover that you are immoral and it will not be difficult to arrange proof. When that becomes apparent . . . no prince in Europe will want you for wife. Do not underestimate me, Maria.*

So Chastelard was Catherine's spy sent to Scotland to disgrace her.

Masked, Chastelard walked to the block. He paused and pointed in Mary's direction, his voice loud and clear.

"Cruel mistress," he said, and knelt.

The headsman raised the axe, swung. The head rolled into the ashes. Mary turned to face the narrow, speculating eyes of her people.

V.

*From the Palace of Holyrood
this 20th day of June 1564*

Madam, my dear sister Elizabeth:

Nothing so gratifies me as your interest in my matrimonial plans, and I am weighing your suggestion carefully. The more I ponder Sir Robert Dudley, the more I realize that you offer me the most precious jewel in your coronet of courtiers. How selfless, how good and generous you are, Madam!

Randolph tells me that if you cared to marry you would choose Dudley yourself, and that you plan to create him Earl of Leicester. Surely he would not leave the pinnacle of Your Majesty's favor to wed me? How could I take him from you and deprive you both so cruelly? Yet if it is your wish to give me your heart's favorite, I am humbly in your debt and will, of course, consider him . . .

She paused, put down her quill and looked across the library table at Rizzio. "Can you conceive of a worse insult than Elizabeth offering me her cast-off lover?"

"No, Madam. I am no match for her in conceiving insults. She

[193]

would have Dudley spy from your very bed. But she must be made to think you are interested in him until we hear definite news from Spain."

"I marvel," Mary said, "that the Chastelard scandal did not ruin my chances with Don Carlos. Lethington has achieved a miracle in keeping the negotiations open."

Rizzio nodded. "He has indeed, Madam. We must give the devil his due."

Mary smiled and returned to her letter.

. . . *Master Knox has the temerity to insist that he should be consulted regarding my marriage. I summoned him here and admonished him to tend his own business, reminding him that he did not consult me when he married Margaret Stewart in April—and she fifteen! They are the laughing stock of all Edinburgh—in privacy. Few dare to smile openly.*

Since Your Majesty released Lord Bothwell from the Tower of London on parole I hear he has been at your court hounding you for permission to travel to France. I ask that you let him go. It would be good riddance to us both, and if he chances to be killed in the Catholic-Huguenot uprisings who, Madam, is to care?

This week I heard Mass for the merry soul of my half-brother, Lord John, on the first anniversary of his death. He was stricken while hanging witches at Inverness. Witches, indeed, cause us great concern. Three were burned yesterday at the Market Cross.

Regarding Lord Matthew Lennox . . .

Mary sighed and reread the letter from Elizabeth. "Davy, she asks me to receive Lord Lennox and restore the lands and titles which he lost when my mother exiled him twenty years ago."

"Tell her you will, Madam. And I would receive Lord Lennox graciously. He heads the Catholic party in England. And his son, Lord Henry Darnley, might be a suitable husband for you should the Spanish marriage fall through."

"But Darnley is my first cousin. The Pope would not approve."

"He would approve any Catholic alliance for you, Madam. And remember, after yourself, Darnley is heir to the English throne. Marriage to him would double your claim to the succession."

Mary tapped the quill to her cheek. "So it would. Of course Darnley could not bring me foreign power, but it would be a solid triumph for Catholicism and a bitter blow to Knox. Darnley is about nineteen, isn't he?"

"I believe so."

Two years younger than I, she thought. "And handsome, from all reports," she said.

"A young Adonis, Madam. Why not summon Melville? He can supply the details."

Mary sent a page for Sir James Melville, her new envoy to Elizabeth's court. Small, debonair, he chuckled when she asked him about Darnley. "If I were a woman I would swoon at his very glance."

"He is so attractive?"

"Yes, and charming. Secretly, and under Elizabeth's very nose, the Lennoxes have raised him with an eye to sharing your throne. His dancing is superb, his verses acceptable, his musical talent unusual. He is high in Elizabeth's favor."

"I note Elizabeth does not suggest him for me," Mary said wryly. "He is too good a match. Does Elizabeth want Darnley herself? Has he replaced Dudley in her bed?"

"I do not know her current lust, Madam. I do know Darnley is one of her favorites."

"Very well, I shall tell Elizabeth his father may come here in September. Perhaps by then we will know about the Spanish marriage."

"Don Carlos could enrich you materially," Rizzio said, "But Lord Darnley probably could make you happier."

"But it would mean remaining in Scotland for the rest of my life—or Elizabeth's. I want to escape."

"When you see Lord Darnley," Melville smiled, "you may not wish to escape."

"That is why I shall not see him until all hope is gone for the Spanish marriage. I must not be tempted from a greater destiny."

"Sometimes," Melville said, "Your Majesty astonishes me. There was never a more womanly woman, yet your heart is set on an imbecile."

"Not my heart," she smiled. "For my heart I expect nothing."

VI.

That autumn of 1564 was so cold that Mary took to her bed for warmth. Covered by mink-bordered sheets and heavy fur robes, she conducted court business and received visitors. Fair-bearded Lord Lennox, eager and affable, kissed a mittened hand when he left her bedchamber after their first interview. He hoped, he said, to have his son join him in Scotland, but Mary put him off. There was still no word from Spain, and her heart lurched every time a courier arrived with mail.

In October Sir James Melville returned from Elizabeth's court.

"She knows you are negotiating with Spain, Madam, and she informed me she will declare war if you marry Don Carlos," he said.

"Poof!" Mary laughed, propped up on her pillows with the furs drawn to her chin. "Philip will invade England so fast that she'll never know what struck. She'll look around for her crown and find it on my head."

"Let us hope so, Madam. But she is tricky as a gypsy. She even tried to win me to her."

"With gold?"

"With gold-red curls, with lips and eyes. And though I am thirty years old in the ways of coquettes I never saw a six-penny bawd as bold as she. Madam, her gown was cut nigh to her navel."

"Were you tempted?" she asked.

"No, Madam—she is bony as a beef rib, but I was fascinated by her antics. She asks, 'Is Mary's skin as white as mine?' and thrusts her face an inch from me. 'Is Mary's hair as lustrous?' and tickles my chin with her curls. Then she says, 'I hear Mary danced the Purpose in netherhose—are her legs as fine as mine?' And by God if she doesn't raise her petticoats to her hips and stand there smirking, with her garters glittering diamonds. Naturally I was tactful but—"

"*Are* her legs as fine as mine?" Mary asked. "You have seen me in riding hose."

"Your legs are exquisite, Madam. Hers are shapeless stalks. Her hair is luxuriant but her lips are too thin and her eyes hold no dreams as yours do. Only her hands are lovely as your own."

"How did she react to your indifference?"

"She only peacocked the more, Madam. She danced for me, asking if you danced as high and handsome. She trotted out her skills at the lute and virginals and she sang for me. I admitted that she excelled Your Majesty as a musician though your needlework was superior. But when she backed me into a corner and asked me who was the fairest I said, 'You are the fairest in England and my mistress the fairest in Scotland.' Such a pouting you never beheld! She sulked a few moments and then said, 'Who is the taller, your mistress or I?' and I told her that you are taller, Madam. 'Then,' said she, 'She is too tall, for I am exactly the right height.' But in the next breath she was twittering how lovesome you are and kissing your miniature and your last letter."

"If I marry Don Carlos," Mary said, "my letter to her will begin: 'Madam, My Bastard Cousin . . .'"

"Bastard by birth but bitch by choice," Melville said. "I was present when she created Dudley Earl of Leicester, and during the ceremony she bent toward him and tickled his neck inside his ruff.

She said to me later, 'Is he not adorable? If your mistress will wed him I propose that she come here and the three of us share the same household.' "

"How could any woman be so revolting!"

"It's the coarse Tudor wit. Poor Dudley is betwixt and between. If he seems anxious to marry you, Elizabeth rages and if he objects she says he is disobedient . . . Lord Darnley awaits your bidding to come to Scotland. He said, 'When a goddess beckons, mortals go.' "

"A pretty sentiment!"

"Elizabeth, sharp as a knife, saw me talking to Darnley and asked me later if I liked him better than Dudley as a husband for you. I said, 'No woman of spirit would choose a beardless youth like Darnley.' I hope I misled her."

"What word of Bothwell?" Mary asked.

"Elizabeth granted your request and allowed him to go to France."

"Do you know how he fares?"

"He is penniless, Madam—a soldier of fortune selling his sword as he can. At least, so Elizabeth says. I believe he seeks the post of Captain of the Scottish Guard in the Cardinal's service."

After Melville left Mary realized that she had not even thought to inquire about Bothwell until the end of the interview. It was two years and seven months since she had seen him. The rust of time had dulled her interest in him. Yawning, she thought, I must send him money in care of the Cardinal. Some day I may need him . . .

By the library fire Mary broke the Great Seal of Spain and tried to slip Philip's letter from the envelope. But her hands were shaking, and she handed it to James. "Read it—but spare me the frills. Just tell me if it is yes or no."

James took the letter and carried it to a chair.

"It is more likely the usual maybe," Lethington said.

Mary fidgeted with her cap, her locket. She thought, If it is good news I shall celebrate my twenty-second birthday tomorrow with a party to rock Knox from his pulpit.

"Well?" she asked impatiently.

"A moment, Madam," James said. "He is still frilling—he makes no point as yet."

Lethington came over and stood by Mary. She put her hand to her plunging heart. Her throat was dry. She swallowed.

James looked up, and she saw the dream dead in his eyes. "The answer is no," he said.

No escape. No end to the farce with Elizabeth. No hope of a Catholic Britain.

Lethington swore. "What reason does he give?"

"He says, 'I understand, Madam, that your uncle the Cardinal of Lorraine has offered you in marriage to Archduke Charles of Austria. That being the case, and for other reasons, the negotiations to marry you to my son are at an end.'"

Mary jumped up. "How dare the Cardinal offer me in marriage without my permission!"

"The Cardinal will do anything Queen Catherine commands," Lethington said.

"Damn her!" James said. "Damn her soul!"

"Amen." Lethington slumped on the sofa. "Now we start anew."

"I'll not go through this again," Mary said. "Whatever move I make toward a good marriage either Catherine or Elizabeth will block. And my own uncle helps betray me."

"There *is* Archduke Charles," James said gloomily.

You want me out of Scotland, she thought, so you can resume sole power. Curtly she said, "I don't intend to leave here if I can't better my position. If I can't marry splendidly, at least I can marry solidly. I have in mind Lord Darnley."

Both men frowned, and she said, "I know what you are going to say—that Scotland will not stand for a Catholic King. I say Scotland be damned. It has brought me nothing but misery."

"Knox would insure your misery if you married Darnley," James said.

"Knox!" She spat the word.

"I beg you, Madam," Lethington said, "think long on this. Elizabeth will never acknowledge your claim to her throne if you marry a Catholic."

"She will not anyway, so what have I to lose? I have wasted four years of my life on her whims but I am through groveling. I shall ask Lord Darnley to come here as soon as the roads are passable."

They argued, pleaded, and finally James exploded, "Rizzio is at the bottom of this! He's a papal spy sent to persuade you to wed a Catholic."

"Are you daft, James? I would wed a Catholic in any case."

"I don't like Rizzio's influence on you, his pretensions. He has become entirely too conspicuous in your apartments."

Furiously she said, "If he is conspicuous it is by my command."

"The fellow is not a gentleman—"

"You tempt me to knight him," she said, "and if I hear more of this nonsense I shall." She went to the door. "I am dismissing my French secretary—I suspect he is in Catherine's pay. Rizzio will take his place. Further, I am giving Rizzio a house in the Canongate."

Lethington said, "This is dangerously foolish, Madam. How do you think your nobles feel to see a common varlet raised to such favor? To have to bow to him socially, meet him at table?"

"How does Rizzio feel to meet *them* at table, they with the manners of baboons? Do you call those dirty oafs aristocrats? What do they have but their titles?"

"Hot blood," James said, "and natural resentment against an upstart. There is beginning to be talk . . ."

"Rizzio is my friend." Mary's voice shook. "God help anyone who insinuates otherwise."

"Remember Chastelard," James said.

"And you," she snapped, "remember your place."

VII.

In February Mary journeyed to Wemyss Castle, James's country retreat on the north shore of the Firth of Forth. Perched on a cliff, it looked as bleak as other seaside fortresses. But inside there were golden wall hangings, gleaming with jeweled embroidery. Mary's slippers sank into thick carpets, and she supped at Italian marble tables. Elizabeth, she thought, had paid her hirelings well. An exquisite altar cloth that hung on a stair landing shook her with fury, but she said nothing. She was a guest and there was no point in further straining her relations with James.

In a short-skirted kirtle Mary played in the salt wind on the shore, gathered sea shells, fished in the rain. Livingstone, in guilty tears, asked to be relieved of her vow not to marry before Mary did, and presented her fiance, William Semple. Mary blessed the lovers and James gave a dance in their honor.

On the afternoon of February 17th a courier brought news that Lord Henry Darnley had arrived in Edinburgh and was on his way to Wemyss. In a flurry of excitement Mary's ladies dressed her in black velvet that glittered with gold embroidery, and a ruff of gold tissue. But she thought the gown too formidable and changed to ruffled black lace, a demure velvet bow in her hair. "Lord Darnley is only nineteen," she said, "so I will look as young as my mourning permits."

Lady Jean brought her a scented fan of frilled lace and said, "If he has been at Queen Elizabeth's court, you may be sure he looks a dissipated thirty."

Nervously Mary descended the staircase. As she entered the painted drawing room between tall gold candelabra, James rose from the fire.

"Lord Darnley has just arrived and is changing his muddy clothes," he said, "I trust you can contain your impatience."

Mary smiled. "Does he measure up to the reports of him?"

"You will like him. His parents have seen to that. Lady Lennox—as conniving a woman as struts the earth—has trained him from boyhood to please you. She has always had her eye on the Scottish throne for him, and nothing ever deterred her, not even your marriage. Her spies at Catherine's court knew Francis was sickly, knew your every mood and whim. Darnley conforms to those whims, as you will see."

"I am the last to object to that," Mary laughed.

And then her laughter died as she turned and saw a young man entering the room. He was a giant, she thought, at least six-feet-six, but superbly proportioned, broad-shouldered and flat-waisted. He wore a suit of pale primrose velvet the same shade as his hair and as he knelt before her, she saw that his hair waved luxuriantly, shining like gold in the candleglow.

She extended her hand. "You are welcome to Scotland, Lord Darnley."

He thanked her, kissed her hand, and rose. She looked up to a smile that caught her heart—the hopeful, eager smile of a boy.

"I regret I was not in Edinburgh to receive you, my lord."

"Your brother Lord Robert entertained me graciously," he said, and added impulsively, "but I couldn't wait to see you, Madam."

"And now?" she smiled.

"The legend and the dream fulfilled."

And you, she thought, are the most beautiful young man this side of myth. As they sat down and chatted of his journey she studied his face and could find no flaw. The skin had a smooth, golden fairness from fine brow to slightly pointed chin—a strong, stubborn chin that saved the face from effeminacy. The eyes were large, bright blue as robin's eggs, with long curly lashes. The lips were a firm, full pink. How jealous men must be, she thought, and women probably fall like ninepins at his feet.

"Tell me of Elizabeth's court," Mary said.

He knew what interested her, for he spoke of fads and fashions. "The breeches swell larger each month." He patted his own moderately puffed ones. "You should have seen Dudley last week at Whitehall. He waddled through the door—just clearing it—and when Her Majesty told him to sit down, he unfortunately chose a chair with a nail in the seat. It punctured his breeches and half a ton of bran rolled out."

She laughed, delighted. "Was the Queen amused?"

"No. She told him to go home and stuff his breeches with bedsheets."

"May I ask," she said, "what you use for stuffing?"

"My valet uses whatever is handy—hay, feathers, table linen—likely in Scotland he'll use heather!"

She led him to talk of Dudley, now Earl of Leicester. "What does he look like?"

"Portly, Madam, with a face flat as a sheep's. He squints. His teeth are rotten."

James spoke for the first time. "Dudley is completely fascinating to women in spite of these defects."

Mary said, "What fascinates Elizabeth would not fascinate me." James would prefer Dudley to Darnley, she thought, because he is Protestant. "I'd no more wed her cast-off lover than I'd wear her cast-off clothes."

Mary saw Darnley's relief and James's controlled fury. She thought, Now James will sulk and spoil our gaiety. Turning to Darnley she said, "Would you like to see the castle? There's time before supper."

"I would love to, Madam."

As she took Darnley's arm and left the room she whispered, "James is in a mood and I want to get away from him."

"He is upset because I am here. He dislikes me."

"No," she said, "he dislikes your religion. But he is susceptible to flattery. Praise his possessions and his snippety wife when we meet her at supper, and he will melt in spite of himself."

She led him into the portrait gallery and they sat down on a marble bench. He glanced at the pictures and said, "I have three of your miniatures. In one of them, you are fourteen with your curls down your back, a spaniel in your arms—a budding beauty. The second one was painted in your white mourning robes and you look like an exquisite nun. The third, in a black ball gown, is magnificent —a queen on a peak of loneliness."

He is perceptive, she thought. "I was lonely that first year here," she said. "I still am."

He was easy to talk to, and she was tempted to pour out all her thoughts and feelings as she did with Rizzio. But he must not think her too eager to push their friendship to intimacy. So she held herself in check, encouraging him to talk, studying him.

But it was difficult to be objective. At supper, at dancing afterward, she felt inordinate pride in him. He seemed to be all things to all people. With James he was deferential, his flattery almost feline in its subtlety. With Lady Agnes he was the entranced gallant. Her stiff little provincialisms cracked under his charm and she begged him to consider Wemyss as his second home. The Marys and Lady Jean were warmed at first glance, won at first dance.

As the evening ended, Lethington whispered, "It is unfortunate

that he's Catholic, Madam. Otherwise he seems more than acceptable."

"He is so adaptable," Mary said. "Everybody likes him. I vow he
could soften Knox to a jelly."

"No, Madam. God alone can crack Knox's shell. I beg you to be
cautious. Dally if you like but don't become serious."

"Do you think me a schoolgirl to love at first sight?" she laughed.

"I think you are a woman too long deprived of love. Dance, but
do not dream."

She danced through the February nights with Darnley at Holyrood. In March she gave a wedding banquet for Livingstone, pulled
the bride's bean from the cake herself and blushed to the roar of
applause. She walked the bleak gardens with Darnley and smelled
spring in every blast of wind. They went hawking. His hands on her
wrist binding the leather strip for the bird's talons fluttered her heart
and she thought, I begin to dream . . .

From the years of rigid discipline she summoned strength to resist
the dream. She realized that James and Lethington were right—
she could never unite Scotland under a Catholic king. Darnley's
graciousness in attending one of Knox's sermons to show the people
his tolerance only resulted in a blast from the pulpit about the
"Jezebel who seeks a Papist in bestial union." And Elizabeth, enraged, demanded the recall of both Darnley and his father, claiming
that Mary had tricked her, and hinting war.

"Very well," Mary told her nobles at a session of the Council in
Holyrood's Throne Room. "I shall send Darnley home. But I must
be the one to tell him, not you or Randolph."

She sent word for Darnley to meet her in the Royal Park. The
trees were beginning to bud and heather lay like a mauve quilt across
the meadows. While she waited for Darnley on a stone bench she
tried to stiffen her resistance to him . . . He is not brilliant or
erudite. (But clever and eager to learn.) He is too young. (But he
will mature to my own stature, he is adaptable and ambitious.) He
is Catholic. (Devout as I, and I would not have him otherwise!)

He came through the leaves in a flash of scarlet cloak and sat
down beside her, placing his plumed hat on the end of the seat.

"My lord, your Queen demands that you return to England," Mary
said. "She is furious—not at you, but at me."

"I refuse to return."

"You cannot refuse my command."

"Are you commanding me to go?"

Mary was silent, facing the fog of the future. Years of conspiracy with old men pulling her like a puppet on the strings of diplomacy. Years that would lead, perhaps, to a husband whom she would hate or tolerate or be mildly fond of. And as the years passed she would be less able to pick and choose, for as her beauty diminished so would her market value. Darnley might well be her last chance of happiness . . .

Darnley took her hand. "You love me," he said, "as I love you."

Miserably she said, "No, I . . ."

He bent and caught her in his arms, lifting her onto his lap. His lips did not have the practiced deftness of Chastelard's—he kissed her clumsily, hungrily, almost desperately. She drowned deep in the kiss, both arms around his neck, her body pressed to his, and she thought, This must last for the rest of my life. With this memory I can mock the winter nights, and age and death . . .

He drew back and looked at her wonderingly, touched her eyelids, traced her nose and bent again to her mouth. His hand slipped awkwardly to her breast and she let it lie there. She opened her eyes and said, "I love you," and tears dripped down, and she hid her face in his doublet because even the man she loved must not see her weep.

But this was folly, madness. She dried her tears, forced herself to rise and move away from him.

"You must leave," she said. "I command it."

He did not beg, save with his eyes. Mutely they walked toward the palace. As they entered the arcaded dimness of the inner courtyard a page brought Mary a note sent by Livingstone from her country estate.

Madam, Mary read. *I hear that Lord Bothwell has returned to Scotland and is somewhere in hiding . . .*

Mary slipped the note in her belt to finish later. She turned to Darnley, who stood waiting, his head bowed.

"Farewell, my dearest," she said.

He raised his head and looked at her with a wistfulness that tore her heart. Her chin trembled, she bit her lip. Then, heedless of a pacing sentry, she stumbled toward Darnley and he caught her tight in his arms.

Under his lips she said, "We will marry."

VIII.

Stealthily, on tiptoe, Mary descended the stairs, Fleming's yellow cloak hooding her eyes. As she approached the landing that adjoined the Great Hall, she heard the laughter of the lords, the rattle of dice. She moved down a step, fearful of being seen, but the noise came from the far end of the room. Turning her face from the doorway she plunged past it and safely reached the dark courtyard.

A guard saluted. "Good evening, Lady Fleming."

Mary nodded, keeping her face down, and strolled casually into the April-budded gardens and across the outer courtyard to the gate where Peter Pye awaited her. He was talking to the sentries, but as she approached he said, "Good evening, Lady Fleming. Your horse is saddled and ready."

The sentries unbolted the gate, and she and Peter walked across to Horse Wynd. A groom helped her mount Fleming's white mare. Peter followed her on a shaggy pony and they rode up the Canongate, were admitted through the Netherbow Port and galloped through Edinburgh's dark streets toward open country.

"You're a clever lad," Mary said, "and you deserve to know more than I've told you. We're riding to Crichton Castle to see Lord Bothwell."

"We are, Ma'am? I heard he was back but I thought he was on the Border."

"So did I until I received his message this morning. He said he had to see me urgently and dared not come to me."

"It's a queer kind of outlaw that hides at one of his own castles," Peter said, "and only twelve miles from Edinburgh."

"He's a queer kind of man," Mary said. "But as for hiding, he probably thinks that Crichton, being so near, is the last place his enemies would seek him."

As they galloped the dark moors under a moonless sky, Mary thought of all the things that could go wrong back at Holyrood. Suppose a courier arrived with an important message and James went to her apartments? Suppose Darnley, worried about her "headache," insisted on seeing her before he retired? Fleming had vowed to keep them out on the excuse that she had finally fallen asleep. But if they discover me gone, Mary thought, they will rouse the Town Watch and the troops, and Fleming may be forced to tell them where I am.

Avoiding villages, galloping peat bogs and low, brackened hills, they came to the slow-flowing Tyne, followed its dark gleam until Crichton Castle rose in the distance, black against the ash-gray sky. At last they clattered into the outer courtyard, and a lantern bobbed welcome. The drawbridge was lowered, and a servant with a torch came to help Mary off her horse.

"The Master awaits Your Ladyship in the Great Hall," he said. "I'll take the lad in the kitchen for refreshment."

He bowed and pointed toward the entrance, where another servant held the door open. Mary followed him through a dark stone corridor to a spacious firelit room. Dogs bounded to meet her, barking. Bothwell cursed them to silence and cuffed them down.

"Your Majesty." He bowed. "Crichton is honored. I don't deserve this visit but I'm damned glad you made it."

"You are my favorite fugitive," she said, "and you stirred my curiosity."

She glanced uneasily at the walls, which were hung with black. Folk said Bothwell communed with devils, practiced the dark arts. He followed her glance and laughed. "Those hangings shut in the light so that the castle looks deserted from outside. I am sorry the effect is so grim."

Reassured, she smiled, and he helped her out of her cloak, led her to a shabby chair by the oak fire and sat opposite her.

"You have changed, Madam."

"How?"

He examined her frankly. "Scotland has bloomed you—or love."

So he had heard about Darnley. Evading the subject she said, "You have not changed at all, my lord. You are brash as ever."

But he had changed. The eyes were warier, the full mouth harder. The years in prison had thinned him and his russet suit was loose at the waist. She noticed that the gold lacing at the slashed sleeves of his doublet was dulled and the white linen shirt frayed at the open collar.

He said, "Brashness is for youth, and I'm thirty—with a life to begin again. Except for the money Your Majesty so kindly sent I'd be penniless. My lands are mortgaged, my credit—" He grinned—"conceded at dagger-point. And my enemies on the Border have been stealing my lands and occupying my homes. When I arrived at Hermitage Castle last month I had to displace the Elliotts."

"A family?" she asked.

"Of three hundred."

She could not help but laugh at his casualness. "Did it take five minutes, or ten?"

"Five hours," he said, "and the help of all the rascals in the neighborhood. But I didn't ask you here to bore you with my misadventures. I'm on an unofficial mission for the Cardinal to nose out your marriage intentions. Queen Catherine is panting to know, so I thought I would ask you direct and feed them whatever lies you think best."

She said, "You are priceless!"

"On the contrary, I get a good price for the information—enough to buy me the horses and clothes I need and even lift a mortgage or two. Shall I tell them you plan to wed Robert Dudley?"

"No," she said. "I think for once they may know the truth—with

[205]

certain omissions. If Philip of Spain will publicly sanction my marriage—and he is certain to favor a Catholic alliance—I will marry Lord Henry Darnley."

"Good God!" he said.

"You needn't fear Elizabeth," she said. "If Philip sanctions the marriage she'd not dare attack Scotland for fear of war with Spain."

"You misunderstand me, Madam. I wasn't thinking of Elizabeth; I was thinking of you, wasting yourself on that lady-faced lad. Can you see him as king, leading your armies, defending your realm and your faith? What if the Protestants start civil war? Can you see him commanding the big guns at Edinburgh Castle—he who'd cower at sound of an abbot's belch?"

"How dare you speak of him so!"

"I have seen him in England. He's not a bad lad, Madam, but soft and vain, forever preening—Narcissus at the brook. And if he fell in he'd pull you with him."

She fought her temper. "Lord Darnley has been with me over two months—at Holyrood, Falkland and Stirling—under many and varied circumstances. And I've seen no indication of either vanity or weakness. Even James and Lethington have found no fault other than his Catholic faith."

"Darnley is on best behavior, Madam; he knows he is on trial. But do you really love him or does your body trick you?"

"You are insufferable!"

"I ask an adult question, Madam, with no intention of lewdness. You are young and romantic. Your husband was a sick child, Chastelard a fop, and now you are desperate for love. This is a sore time for you, a time to be honest with yourself, if not with me."

"I love him," she said. "That should be enough for you."

He groaned. "You're so strange a brew of worldliness and innocence that you may not understand this—but I am compelled to tell you. And then you can decide if you'll risk marriage."

"Well?" She lifted her chin.

"You were raised at Catherine's court. Surely you noted young boys strolling hand in hand in the gardens lisping verse to one another?"

"Yes," she said. "They were amusing—powderpuffs, we called them."

"There's another word," he said grimly, "not so dainty. Well, some of these puffs grow up and become fops, like Chastelard. Some even become men. And still others, though big in stature and deep of voice, never grow up. I'm afraid that's true of Darnley."

"No!" she said. "That I *know* to be untrue!"

He smiled. "You may be maturing him, Madam. I know only

that a year ago Darnley was surrounded by these puffs at court and paid no attention to women. To my knowledge he has never courted a girl until now."

"If he was a puff," she said, "it was a stage of youth. He is a man now, with a man's ardor. Certainly," she added, blushing, "I should know. He has kissed me."

"And blundered, I'd bet my soul!"

"He did not!"

"And how do you know? What is your comparison?" he asked scornfully. "Francis? Chastelard?"

As he came toward her, she shrank back in her chair, but her chin lifted haughtily and her eyes met his without flickering. With one hand he caught her wrists and pulled her roughly to her feet so that she stood pressed against him. As she raised her head to protest, he released her hands and let his arms fall to his sides. But their bodies still touched and she could feel the buttons of his doublet against her breast.

She was free to step back but she didn't. Against her conscious will she felt herself draw closer as though magnetized. Slowly her hands crept up his arms to his shoulders.

"You see?" he said. "Your body *can* trick you. You have no love for me."

She jerked back, gasping.

"Perhaps it was crude, Madam, but I wanted to show you yourself. Why be ashamed of what is natural?"

Furiously she whirled, picked up her cloak and started toward the door.

He reached it before her, closed it and stood with his back to it. "I deserve your contempt. But you and Scotland deserve something better than Darnley. Even if he's truly a man, he's a weak one. That I know, and swear on my honor."

Her lips curled. "Your honor!"

"You think I have none. Very well. But it is more important that you waken from this dream of lust. That's all it is, Madam, embroider it as you will—a healthy, natural lust. Bed it—but for God's sake don't wed it."

She was trembling with rage. "Open that door."

"If I had time I'd take you by force to Flanders—Norway—anywhere till you come to your senses." He turned and threw open the door. "I'm off to France in a week. And I'll not be back."

Mary swept past him into the corridor. "If you dare to come back," she said, "I'll have your head."

IX.

The fortress of Stirling, which guarded the Highlands, reminded Mary of Edinburgh Castle. It had the same sky-flung majesty crowning the summit of gigantic rocks and it overlooked a steep-pitched town. From a western lookout, she could see a moor broken with smoky hills, which towered away to Ben Lomond, the peaks of Ben More, Ben Vorlich and Stuc-a-Chroin. Walking around the battlements to the east she watched the sun-glittered Forth coiling to the sea through pink and white heatherbell bloom, and bluebells and flowering plum trees. Fey with Maytime, she stretched and stood on tiptoe as though to touch the low white clouds that frayed for an eagle's flight.

She could not be happier, she thought—except on her wedding day. The Spanish envoy was certain Philip would endorse her marriage, and Elizabeth, raging futilely, was outmaneuvered. Rizzio had written for the Pope's dispensation for first cousins to marry. Darnley, stricken with the measles, was recovering downstairs in a flower-filled bedchamber, and the physician said his skin would not be marred. Mary had nursed him night and day, oblivious to gossip. She knew what Knox was howling in Edinburgh—that her love was already consummated—but she was too happy to care. Even James, who had been sulking at St. Andrews, was back at Stirling apparently resigned to her decision.

If only I knew that God approved . . . but I still cannot reach him . . .

She left the lookout and walked down a steep flight of steps to an esplanade where the big-mouthed cannon pointed south. She would seek Father Black and ask advice. But before she reached the chapel a page summoned her to the Great Hall, and she knew as soon as she saw James and Lethington that they had news.

"Madam!" Never before had she seen Lethington excited, shaken. He smiled, spluttered, smiled again. "Randolph has just sent word from Edinburgh that the incredible has happened—Elizabeth will acknowledge you her successor if you will give up Darnley and marry Dudley."

She was stunned to speechlessness.

James came to her and put his arm around her. "Here is your dream, my dear—take it as a gift from God. Should Elizabeth die tomorrow, you are unquestionably Queen of England. Should she outlive you, your heirs are assured her throne."

Tears stung her eyes. She had waited so long, plotted and connived, hoped and prayed. And now it came too late.

"No," she said. "I am going to marry Darnley."

They stood aghast, and she waited calmly, determined to ride out the storm.

"Darnley brings us nothing!" James shouted. "I'll not tolerate him!"

"*You'll* not tolerate him? You are my subject—"

"But I control Scotland and I'll choose its king. You'll marry Robert Dudley!"

Lethington said, "My lord, take care—"

"Quiet, damn you!" James glared at Lethington, then turned to Mary. "You'll marry Dudley or you'll legitimize me—one or the other."

"Legitimize you! So you can wear the crown, call yourself king?" Her glance traveled contemptuously from his head to his boots and slowly up again. "You were born a bastard. You'll die a bastard."

Quietly he said, "You will pay a high price for that insult. It will cost you your kingdom."

"Indeed, my lord? Your threat of treason is something new, but you are old in treachery. You crawled on your belly for English gold five years ago—likely you still do. I'll have you brought to trial."

James laughed. "Do, by all means. I enjoy a farce. The jury of nobles is mine."

"The army is mine," Mary said, with more bravado than she felt.

"It takes more than smiles and a flutter of lashes to win an army. All you have is your bodyguard of halberdiers and a band of archers. I have six thousand armed men, Knox to stir recruits and—thanks to your gracious gift—the greater part of the Highlands under my thumb."

She thought quickly, desperately. If she released Huntley's son, Lord George Gordon, from prison, he would rally what remained of his clan and command a Highland army to win back his lands from James. But the Edinburgh area lay in Knox's fist. On the Border she could expect no help from the thousands who had never seen her, and she cursed herself for having postponed her visit there.

Bothwell. Only he could control the Border lords and the lawless rabble of southern Scotland. Only he had the experienced leadership, the audacity to win against odds. Time after time, with outmoded arms and a handful of men he had beaten back English armies . . .

As she hesitated she saw James relax. "You do well to reconsider," he said.

"Yes," she lied, "I am reconsidering." Bothwell was in France by now . . .

"I return to St. Andrews today," James said. "Within three months you must decide either to marry Dudley or legitimize me. Otherwise I will seize Scotland and establish absolute rule."

"And what of me?" she asked.

"The islands of the Hebrides are largely uninhabited. No rescuing knights would seek you there."

Her shiver was genuine.

James turned to Lethington. "Perhaps you can bring her back to her senses." Mockingly he bowed to Mary. "Your humble servant, Madam."

After the door closed behind him, Lethington said, "Madam, I implore you to marry Dudley. But if it comes to war between you and Lord James, I will not turn traitor. My regard for Your Majesty transcends politics."

She was surprised and touched. "Thank you, sir." Then she realized that this might be a trap. She dared not trust him.

Returning to her apartments, she hurried to her writing desk, pulled paper from the pigeonhole and drew a quill from its onyx holder.

My Lord Bothwell, she wrote. *I need you . . .*

As she wrote of James's treachery she thought of the last letter her mother had written her and took courage from it: *"You would never unite Scotland under Bothwell. But you may, with God's help, save it with his sword."*

CHAPTER SEVEN

I.

STRANGE OMENS WERE REPORTED in Scotland that summer of 1565. Shepherds saw shooting stars, and a sea monster sent Wigtown fishermen screaming to shore. From Moray Firth to Jura Sound spread tales of withering bay trees, trembling earth and croaking ravens. A black ship sailed in Bloody Bay and a coach drawn by headless horses clattered through Blairgowrie. Dogs were born with cloven hoofs, cats with horns. In the gardens of Holyrood Mary shuddered at a moon ringed with blood.

Pressing close to Darnley she said, "These portents frighten me. There are so many."

"Likely some of the tales are invented by Knox to discourage our marriage," he comforted.

They had been secretly betrothed in Rizzio's apartments at Stirling with only her priests and ladies as witnesses. Mary had created Darnley Earl of Ross and Duke of Albany and the banns had been published in the Canongate Kirk. In two hours—at dawn—they would be married in Holyrood Abbey.

Beyond the gardens, camped in the meadows, Mary could see the night fires of her hastily gathered army. From Fife, Teviotdale and Lothian men had rallied to her summons. Lord George Gordon, released from prison, had roused his clan, and Catholics in the Highlands pounded, a yelling avalanche, toward Edinburgh. Taverns and hostelries were crammed with soldiers, and in sunlight the High Street blazed with pikes and broadswords, battle axes and iron bonnets. Sir John Erskine, Commander of Edinburgh Castle, switched his allegiance from James to Mary. His cannon were trained on the town, silent, ready.

"It seems I worried needlessly," Mary said. "Did I tell you that during my Highland campaign three years ago an officer gave me a huge bunch of heather? I did not know then what it symbolized. Two thousand men had each gathered a sprig for me!"

"Two thousand in love with my sweetheart," Darnley said, "and thousands more a-dream. James will not dare to move against you—his threats were bluff. Even if they were not, we are growing stronger each day. And Bothwell must be on the way here; we know he has left France."

"So does James know," she said bitterly. "So does Elizabeth. They watch every move he makes, their spies are everywhere. Bothwell may not reach Scotland alive."

He lifted her chin with his hand. "What somber talk is this on our wedding day?"

She smiled for his sake. But it would not be the wedding she had dreamed. Her half-brother Lord Robert would be present, but only nine other nobles. The rest had shunned the ceremony as if it were obscene. Knox had called it so—"the carnal union of beasts fed on the filth of Rome."

"Perhaps," Mary said, "I would feel easier if the Pope's dispensation had arrived. But Harry, I dare not wait! I have a premonition that if I wait I may lose you. It is as if I were rushed toward happiness by terror." She looked up at the moon. "Blood on the moon means death . . ."

"Elizabeth's death," he said cheerfully. "Now that Philip has publicly sanctioned our marriage she is like to die of fury."

Mary shook her head. "She will live if only to spite me. Doubtless she curses me this very hour."

The brief July night was paling toward day and she said, "We must go in and dress."

Under his lips her mouth trembled and when she reached her bedchamber she was shivering uncontrollably. Her ladies dressed her in a silken chemise and petticoat. Fleming brought a damask and velvet mourning robe.

"Surely, Madam," Fleming said timidly, "you do not really mean to wed your new husband in the robes you wore at the interment of your last?"

"I wish to show Scotland that this is no frivolous ceremony. Besides, I vowed to wear mourning until I was wed."

Fleming helped Mary into the heavy robe with its sweeping sable sleeves and great hood. Her waist was girdled in gold, and a gold-and-diamond crucifix hung on a chain at her throat.

"Master Randolph was here but an hour ago," Beaton said. "He pleaded with me to try to change Your Majesty's mind."

"As well change the course of a star," Mary said. Suddenly she seized a handkerchief and brought it to her nose. Bright spots of blood flecked the linen.

Beaton stared in horror. No omen was more prescient of doom than a nosebleed. Mary sat down in a chair, crossing herself.

"I'll fetch a priest!" Beaton said, starting toward the door. "The evil must be exorcised—"

"No," Mary said. "The priests are at prayer in the abbey."

The bells rang out. Mutely, Mary rose and her ladies followed her down the staircase where the Catholic lords awaited her with Rizzio, Melville, Lord Robert and her half-sister, the Countess of Argyll. Soldiers, servants and townspeople lined the path toward the chapel. The sky was leaden, and far off to the south Mary heard the low mutter of thunder.

Between Lords Lennox and Atholl Mary walked to the altar, which was banked with pinks and carnations, green broom and heatherbell. There they left her with the Dean of Restalrig and two priests. Presently Darnley in jeweled white satin came to kneel beside her.

Most of Scotland is against this marriage, she thought, and I defy Protestant Europe. But it cannot be wrong to marry in my own faith, to snatch at the happiness that has evaded me so long. If it is wrong, then may God's will be done. May he strike me dead at this moment . . .

"In nomine Patris, et Filii, et Spiritus Sancti . . ."

Mary listened with her cold hand in Darnley's warm one. His strength seeped into her like new blood. She turned her head and glanced at his profile, the classic nose, the apricot skin, the gold-lashed eyes. His was perfect, sunny beauty. Remembering his kisses, she swayed toward him slightly. *Oh God, I have no words to thank you . . .*

Three rings symbolizing the Trinity were placed on Mary's finger. Prayers were said. After Mass, Darnley kissed her, bowed and preceded her out of the chapel. The Marys strewed musk roses in her path, and her lords escorted her to her audience chamber, where Darnley awaited her.

Blushing, Mary said, "The King and I shall not retire. We ask you to remain with us for feasting and dancing, for four days of revels. I shall change to bridal attire and join you presently."

Her ladies followed her into the bedchamber, removed the mourning robes and dressed her in ivory damask, the bodice, sleeves and train glittering with emeralds, a coif of emeralds on her hair. Mary said, "You are all so quiet. Are you not happy for me?"

"Indeed," Jean said, "Your Majesty's happiness is our constant prayer."

Fleming wiped away tears. "Weddings always sadden me, Madam."

"You may be a bride yourself," Mary smiled, "if you fall into the trap you set for Lethington."

"Your Majesty is perceptive. I did not mean to—I struggled against it—but I've fallen in love with Lethington. Would you object if we marry next year?"

"I would be delighted," Mary said, embracing her. "I want you all to marry." She saw Jean turn away and she thought, Poor lass, she still loves Alex of Boyne, who cares only for Beaton.

But she forgot her ladies' problems in the whirl of the day. At noon they banqueted in the Great Hall at a bridal table spread with fern and witchbell. Largesse was thrown to the people in the courtyard, given the servants. They feasted again at night. At nine o'clock at the Market Cross Darnley was proclaimed King-Consort of Scotland. As the trumpets blared out on the High Street, he and Mary danced the Royal Galliard under Holyrood's garlanded chandeliers. They shared a great gold loving cup rimmed with garnets.

Mary noticed that Darnley was drinking heavily, but she understood why. He had eaten little and was obviously under tension. It was no small strain to wed a queen in a country that abhorred him. No wonder he sought to relax with wine.

At midnight Mary retired to her bedchamber, and her ladies helped her into a filmy petal-pink nightdress girdled with silver. In a silver-tissue robe she watched Father Black and his acolytes bless her bed, swinging their lighted censors, perfuming the room with hallowed incense. Alone, she removed the robe and stood by the window, thinking of that other wedding night seven years ago when she had looked out on the fireworks of Paris. "Francis," she whispered, "forgive me that I love again . . ."

The door flew open, and Darnley lurched in from the audience chamber. The diamond chain she had given him belted his white nightrobe and her diamond rings, widened for him, flashed on his fingers. He held a goblet of wine.

Bowing, he swayed and stumbled into a chair, the wine spilling over the rim of the glass into his lap. His voice was furry. "My beautiful wife. Mos' beautiful woman in the world."

She went to him, gently took the glass, sipped from it and placed it on the mantel. He rose and retrieved it.

"I drink to you—my wife."

He emptied the glass and let it fall to the carpet. Swiftly he came to her, lifted her and carried her to the bed. She lay back against the piled pillows. He stood staring at her, frowned, then slowly backed away.

"Wine," he said.

"Harry . . . please . . ."

"Wine," he repeated on a sob. "Wine!"

She felt it was more than a whim—a desperate plea—and she realized he was frightened. Frightened of her rank, of his new life. She said, "You are my King. Whatever your wish it will be granted."

She slipped off the bed and went into the audience chamber, returning with a decanter of canary and two glasses. She would drink with him, ascertain his fear and remove it. She coaxed him to sit on the bed with her and clinked her glass with his.

"What troubles you, sweet?" she asked.

His eyes narrowed. "You do not really love me."

"But I do! How can you doubt me?"

"You've said nothing of the crown mat—matrimonial."

"I intend for you to have it. Later."

"I want my rights." His lower lip puffed out. "I want the king's apartments. Why should your ladies have them?"

"There are four ladies," she said, "and Holyrood is so small—"

"I insist on the suite below. I will not be slighted."

"You shall have the suite." He looked so young, so miserable that she forgave his mood. "I want only to make you happy. Have I failed, Harry, so soon?"

"You gave me a dukedom," he grudged. "Jewels and horses."

"I gave you my love."

Mary took his empty glass and placed it with hers on the bed table. She put her arms around him, pressed her body to his and kissed his lips. She felt him shiver, then tense. He pushed her away. His face, scarlet from wine, turned white. He looked about the room as though he sought escape.

"Are you ill?" she asked fearfully. "Has the wine made you ill?"

"Yes." He lay back on the bed. "Ill . . ."

Mary blew out the candle and lay down beside him, covering them with a silk sheet. Poor lad, she thought, he is young and sensitive, overwhelmed by his new responsibilities. He needs tenderness and understanding. In the darkness she touched his hair, a curly cap of silk. His breathing was deep and even. He slept.

Mary stared into darkness, hearing the night sounds—a tapping tree bough at the window, the scutter of rats in the wall. Bothwell's words invaded her mind against her will: *"He is soft and vain— even if he's truly a man he's a weak one."*

He is my love, she insisted, who needs my help.

She was still awake when Darnley stirred and stretched, and she drew him into her arms. Shyly she lured him, guided him with scant instinctive knowledge. She had thought men the aggressors in love, but evidently Darnley's respect for her restrained him. And he had something of Francis' awkward desperation. She thought, I am less a woman to be loved than a problem to be solved.

Then she ceased to think. She dug her heels in the bed, her body a rigid arc. Screaming in pain, she covered her mouth with her hands.

As the honeymoon weeks passed, Mary realized that Darnley drank for courage. Sober, he seemed incapable of lovemaking—tense, knotted with fright. With a few glasses of wine he was ardent, but too often he misjudged his capacity for drink. Many a night he snored while she tossed restlessly, loving him, wanting him.

Shamed by her roused passion, she confessed to Father Black. "Am I sinful?"

But he evaded her. It was not sinful to want children, he said, but lust was sinful. Bewildered, she confided in Rizzio, speaking in an embarrassed rush, her face turned from the candleglow.

"Madam!" Rizzio sounded so deeply shocked that she wanted to run from the room.

"The fool," he said, "should choke on wine!"

"I thought I had offended you."

"You know me better than that . . . I have seen him drunk but I had no idea he was barrel-mad. You even deceived me. I had thought you happy."

"I am," she said hastily. "It is my own wantonness that plagues me."

"You, wanton? Nonsense. God created women to be as you are—joyfully passionate, deeply loving. I beg you not to be shamed by what is only natural."

She flushed. "Bothwell said that."

"He knows you better than you know yourself, Madam. And I fear he was right about the King."

Quickly she defended Darnley. "He is so good, so gracious and amusing when sober. We like the same things, we are merry together. I am sure he loves me."

"Why should he not? You give him a priceless gift—yourself—which he hasn't the wit to take soberly. Your devotion borders on worship. As to material gifts, his every whim is gratified. What do you gain in return? With luck, a body not too wine-drugged to appreciate yours. A mind bounded by hunting, dancing and hackneyed verse." He grimaced. "And it was I who suggested him for your husband."

"You didn't know his wine habit," she said. "Perhaps I should give him more responsibility to steady him."

"I beg you not to! He pouts for power, but in his hands the crown would be a dangerous toy. Don't give it to him."

Coldly she said, "He is the King."

"In name only—thus far." Rizzio leaned forward. "Madam, I would save you from possible folly. If I talk against the King it is not to hurt you but to protect you. I swear by the Blessed Virgin that your happiness is my deepest prayer."

Mary studied the swarthy, thick-lipped face, the luminous black eyes soft with a love that asked nothing. "I am wrong," she said, "and you are right. Of late I am not myself. I jump at shadows and my nerves are frayed. James's threat is an axe above me. He has Scotland's best general, Kirkcaldy of Grange. I have no military strategist. Until Bothwell comes, my troops are leaderless."

They had not heard Darnley enter the room. He said, "What's this nonsense that the army is leaderless? I am King."

Rizzio rose and bowed deeply. "Naturally, Sire. But there is much boring detail you should leave to subordinates. We seek to relieve you of such matters."

Darnley shrugged, sank onto a cushion and adjusted his diamond garter. "Mary," he said, "has my corselet arrived from the goldsmith?"

"Not yet, Sire."

"I shall need it when we march." Petulantly, he added, "I can't appear in ordinary mail. I wish the corselet adorned with my crest in diamonds."

And I am pawning my jewels to pay my troops, Mary thought. "Sire—"

He sent her a charming smile. "Thank you, my love."

II.

Aware of her army's impatience, Mary sent a message to James at Stirling commanding him to appear in Edinburgh within six days. He did not come. At the Market Cross her herald blew the traditional horn proclaiming James Stuart, Earl of Moray, an outlaw.

On August 26th, pistols at her saddle bow, armor under her plaid, Mary led her troops toward Stirling. Diamonds flashed from Darnley's gold corselet, winked from a plumed hat. Behind them rode spearmen, halberdiers and pipers. James fled from Stirling to Glasgow, and by the time Mary reached Glasgow her army had swelled to five thousand. In a flanking movement, James circled back to Edinburgh and occupied the town with thirteen hundred horsemen. Proclaiming himself the champion of Protestantism, he felt safe in Knox's stronghold, certain of recruits.

But as his drums beat up the High Street, people barred their doors. The streets emptied. On the steps of St. Giles Knox pleaded, shouted for volunteers. But his voice was silenced by the big guns of Edinburgh Castle, as Lord Erskine fired Mary's defiance. Incredulous, enraged, James evacuated Edinburgh, withdrawing south to Dumfries.

Riding through violent storms, subduing rebels in St. Andrews and Dundee, Mary returned to Edinburgh. Her spies reported that Elizabeth was pouring gold to James and mobilizing an army at Carlisle in northern England. If they joined James's forces on the Border Mary could lose Scotland—not for lack of men but for lack of a strategist to direct them.

Confused, fearful, she turned to Lethington for advice, but he told her he was neutral; he would neither help nor hinder her. Catholic Sir James Balfour, whom she had put in charge of Scottish affairs, had a fine judicial mind but knew little of military matters. Rizzio, busy as Foreign Secretary, had neither time nor knowledge to spare. He was as ignorant as she of terrain, of mileage, of weather conditions and methods of adapting to them.

And so, virtually alone with her problem, she pored over maps and studied Caesar's *Commentaries*. But she could not coordinate cavalry and infantry and artillery, integrate Highlands and Lowlands into efficient alliance. Darnley, usually drunk, plagued her with demands for power. Sober, he went hawking.

Through the gray days of September, candles flickered in abbey and bedchamber flaring her plea toward God: *Send Bothwell . . .* But her agents reported three English warships prowling the east coast, four on the west. Elizabeth's army patrolled the Border. Bothwell must break a ring of fire and steel.

Day after day, Mary sat in the library conferring with her nobles, weighing a dozen different opinions. Her mind was a jumbled map pricked by doubts, her head ached from eyestrain and sleeplessness. Should she ride in a surprise attack on Dumfries—and perhaps be trapped between two armies? Scatter her forces? Wait?

She dared not take the advice of her Council lest they betray her into James's hands. Sleepless, she prowled Holyrood's corridors, paced the Great Hall after her household was abed. She found she could not sit still more than a few moments at a time and wandered from one chamber to another, stirring dying fires and warming herself briefly before she sought another place.

On the night of September 20th Mary sat alone in the library studying a map of northern England and the Border. Her hair was down her back, her lips unpainted, her ruff a limp ruin. For thirty hours she had worked without food or sleep and at last had reached a decision. The newest almanac predicted severe storms beginning in early October. If she was to move at all she must start before the roads became impassable. Luckily, the stars of her horoscope were in the ascendant during the next three weeks.

Peter Pye tapped at the open door. "Madam, there is a minister from Blinkbonny to see you. He says it is important—"

"I'll not be interrupted. Have him fed and bedded, and I'll see him tomorrow."

"He insists it is urgent, Madam, a matter of life and death."

She groaned. "Very well. Send him here."

A guard escorted him in. He was a big man in a black Geneva cloak that was muddied and torn. As he swaggered through the doorway she looked up from her desk, startled by his arrogant manner. Bowing, he pulled off his wide-brimmed hat and unloosed the muffler that hid his chin.

"Bothwell!" she rose, both hands outstretched. "Thank God!" She started toward him. The room seemed to tilt, darken, and she fainted.

When she regained consciousness she was lying on the library sofa, Bothwell and her ladies kneeling beside her. Sitting up, she said, "I am onto my old tricks. I swoon without cause."

Bothwell looked amused. "Perhaps there is cause, though your belly is flat as a board."

Her ladies turned shocked faces, but Mary smiled. "I believe I fainted from joy, my lord. I've awaited you so long . . . and almost despaired."

"I was collecting gunpowder and arms," he said, "in Brussels, Antwerp and the Netherlands. I shan't fight with sticks and stones, though I have in the past."

Mary dismissed her ladies. "How did you get through Elizabeth's net?"

"I sailed up the east coast in a pinnace through the little Border bays and outran the *Aid*. When I reached the mouth of the Tweed a privateer fired on me, but—" He shrugged—"I rowed out of range. It wasn't difficult. When I landed I knew James's spies would be on my scent, so I stopped at a moor kirk and relieved a Bible-thumper of his clothing. In short, an uneventful journey . . . How is the King?"

"Very well," she said, stiffening.

"You look a hag. Perhaps I misjudged the lad."

Instantly contrite, he said, "Forgive me—or slap me. You are worn to a nub. I think I know, Madam, what these weeks have meant with Scotland on your shoulders."

She turned from him. "If you speak another word I'll likely weep."

"Weep, then. It would do you good. Bottled tears brew poisons." He came up behind her and put his hands on her shoulders. "Weep. I am blind, deaf and dumb."

But she could not even if she would. For too many years she had hidden her tears. They would not come.

Bothwell turned her around and she drooped against him. "You are going to bed, Madam—and alone. There you shall stay until I permit you up. Meanwhile I'll be at work here with Erskine."

He swung her into his arms, carried her to the open door and kicked it wider. Past the astonished guard they went, up the stairs to her apartments. In the audience chamber Jean jumped up and followed them into the bedchamber.

Gently, Bothwell placed Mary on the bed and turned to Jean. "Her Majesty must not be disturbed. She's exhausted."

Jean curtsied. "Yes, my lord."

Eyes closed, Mary heard them discuss whether to call a physician and decide against it. As she sank toward sleep, she heard him say, "I have heard of you, Jean Gordon."

And Jean's voice, oddly husky. "Indeed, my lord? What do folk say?"

"Meet me one night and I'll tell you."

III.

On All Hallows' Eve north wind screamed down from the Highlands, bending bronzed wheat, tearing through hazel and prickly sloe thickets, whining across peat hags and stubbled moors. From Banff to the Border, folk saw elf fire redden the hills and heard the wail of witches on the wind. In kirkyards rowan berries were placed on tombstones and weighted with rocks so the dead would lie quiet. In Edinburgh, children with turnip lanterns shrieked past the graves of St. Giles, scuttering through the wynds and closes off the High Street.

Bonfires burned on Arthur's Seat, warning to vampires and hobgoblins. The straw-stacked meadows were pumpkin-lit, and fox whelps rolled in the moonlight. In the stables of Horse Close, mares and jennets neighed and whinnied, stamping their hoofs, restless in the leaf-whirled dark.

Holyrood's Great Hall blazed with lights for a victory ball. Mary and Bothwell, with Darnley for ornament, had ridden from Edinburgh with an army of ten thousand and chased James and his men from Dumfries into England. "A run-about raid," Bothwell grumbled, "All hunting and no fighting." The traitor lords were in exile at Newcastle. Elizabeth, cold to their failure, gave them scant welcome. They sulked, immobilized between her scorn and Mary's armed fury.

"They'll not plague Scotland again," Bothwell said at a pause in the dancing. "None can get past my Borderers, and our ships lock the coastlines. Forget the Bastard and his scum. Be happy, Madam."

"I am!" Mary pirouetted in a corn-colored gown laced with crimson, whirled in a froth of satin petticoats. "You have shed ten years from me. I feel like a lass again."

"Come, lass," he said, catching her hand. "Will you bob for apples? Play Hoodman Blind? Dance with me?"

They danced, and drank spiced sack, clinking mugs, laughing as Lord Robert, King of Misrule, pranced through the room with a scooped pumpkin on his head, waving a cattail scepter. Mary changed to shirt and breeches and called for a rapier. She and Bothwell fenced, skillfully, playfully, while the dancers squealed and scattered. He forced her up to a window seat and she tossed her rapier to him and jumped down, panting.

"Triumph becomes you," Bothwell said. "It's not my place to say it, but I'm damned proud of you. You headed your army like a man."

"It was dull," Mary pouted. "No thrill, save from storms. Rizzio says I'm at my best in danger. Perhaps I should seek it more often."

"You've not far to seek," he said, bending toward her.

She drew back and her lashes fell. "I—I must change to my gown and dance with the King."

Bothwell glanced toward Darnley at the wine buffet. "Dance—when he scarce can stand?"

"He is celebrating our victory." She shrugged.

"What did you give him for winning the war—a diamond for his navel?"

"Why must you be so lewd? Why spoil my peace?"

"Peaceful? I think you're wild as the night."

And he was right, as always. The battering wind, the gusted tapers, the music excited her. She was taut with expectation, ready for any prank. But she primmed her face and raised her eyebrows. "You are mistaken," she said, and turned as Beaton curtsied.

"May I interrupt, Madam?"

Mary smiled and Beaton blushed and stammered that Alexander Ogilvie of Boyne had just proposed marriage. "May I accept him?"

"If you are certain—"

"I am, Madam!"

"He is so dour—"

"Dour but darling. He will keep me from mischief, Madam."

"A pity," Bothwell said.

Ignoring him, Mary patted Beaton's cheek. "Marry with my blessing. We will discuss the wedding tomorrow."

Mary sighed as Beaton tripped away. "Poor Jean Gordon—she has loved Alex for years. This will tear her heart."

"Her heart pumps ice water," Bothwell said. "She's a prig."

"She is not! She is warm and loyal and wonderful, my favorite lady. I love my Marys, but none has Jean's character."

"She bristles with principles and reeks with integrity," he said. "Look at her, fit for a nunnery."

Jean sat alone near the fire, pale hair drawn back from pale face under a white velvet coif. A gray train lay like pooled rain at her feet, and a high white collar petaled her throat.

"Nun!" Mary scoffed. "She is Protestant. And though I deplore her religion, I find her true to it. She's no hypocrite."

"Oh?" He stared at Jean. "If she'd paint she'd be beautiful. A lovely bosom—"

"Doubtless she pads."

"I will inform you later." He smiled.

"My Lord, you are—"

"Lewd or insufferable? But you've roused my curiosity about Lady Jean. We have—incredibly—a virtuous woman among us, and barring Your Majesty, my mother and sister, I know none."

"You move in dubious company."

"But I move fast. Lest the lily wilt before our eyes, do I have your permission to pluck it?"

Mary pretended to yawn. "Jean is invulnerable. You waste your time."

"I have plenty of time," he laughed. "It is not yet midnight."

Bothwell bowed away from her, and she watched him cross the room to Jean and sit beside her. Then dancers obstructed her view. Groups of nobles collected to sing. Arms around each other, heads together, they bawled ballads:

> *Jock left his grave e'er the full moon rose*
> *And rode to his love at Ladykirk*
> *She swooned at sight of his winding clothes,*
> *Fell dead on her father's dirk.*

At midnight Mary watched Jean leave the hall with Bothwell, her gray gown drifting like ash past the tall candelabra at the door. He escorts her to her chamber, Mary thought. He will return presently. But he did not return. Mary changed her gown and danced with

Kerr of Fauldonside, George Douglas, Alex of Boyne. In astonishment, she welcomed Sir Nicholas Throckmorton, just arrived from London. His blond good looks were dulled by weariness, his face rutted with lines of strain. Perhaps it was true that Elizabeth wore her envoys to a frazzle by tantrums and vacillation. Throckmorton looked ten years older than when she had seen him last in Calais.

"My good friend!" Mary extended both hands for him to kiss. "I am delighted to see you." She led him to a quiet corner. "How is my dear Elizabeth?"

"Heartsick at Your Majesty's silence." He accepted a glass of madeira from a servant. "She begs to hear from you. Your last letter hinted that she conspired with Lord James and the rebels."

"She misinterpreted," Mary purred.

They fenced along the slippery subject of Elizabeth's attitude toward James. They discussed Scots piracy of English ships and Mary, straight-faced, assured him that Bothwell would never in any circumstance allow privateering. But it struck Throckmorton as curious that stolen shipments of English blue woolens coincided with a burst of blue wool raiment in Bothwell's area of Liddesdale. Curious indeed, Mary agreed blandly, for Bothwell's Borderers preferred leather. But she would investigate the coincidence . . .

"Will you be here long?" Mary asked.

"Only two days, Madam. I wish Her Majesty would appoint me here permanently, but she knows too well my admiration for you. I've made no secret of it." He hesitated. "Once, as your friend, I advised you. May I take that liberty again?"

"You may."

"Dismiss David Rizzio—and quickly."

"What!"

"Lord James has spread the tale that Rizzio is your lover. It is all over England and doubtless runs through Scotland like balefire. He says he found you in Rizzio's arms at Stirling and that in guilty retaliation you outlawed him."

"Exile is too soft for James!" she said. "He should hang like the lowest knave!"

"Madam, the harm is done. Even the ballad peddlers have the tale; I heard it in Berwick. Send Rizzio back to Italy. He cannot be more valuable than your reputation."

"But he is! My friends know the truth. Why should I care what my enemies think?"

"You must care. Knox—"

"Knox is impotent without James. The people have proven that they love me. Scotland is united, thanks to Lord Bothwell. And the King," she added hastily.

They turned to look at Darnley, red-faced and sodden, sprawled in a chair. A goblet lay on the floor beside him in a puddle of wine. He stared at nothing, grinning foolishly.

Throckmorton turned back to Mary, his embarrassment obvious.

"The King has been celebrating," she said, and she knew her laughter sounded false. "We all have."

"Madam, I am deeply sorry to tell you this. But the King visited Knox this week."

"Impossible!"

"Randolph told me tonight as soon as I arrived—he saw the King enter Knox's house at dusk on Monday. My own agent verifies this. I don't know what brews between them, but it is surely not to Your Majesty's favor. In loyalty to my mistress I should not be telling you this but I—" He paused—"fear for you."

You love me, Mary thought, and so you tell me the truth.

"Madam, I know you find it difficult to believe, for the King is a good Catholic. Knox could never convert him."

"No," she agreed. "Knox must have some other purpose. I must find out what it is."

"Tiptoe in this matter, Madam."

"I shall."

Mary saw Darnley bend forward in his chair and vomit on the floor.

"Excuse me," she said. "The King is ill. I must attend him."

Calmly, she walked the length of the hall, courtiers making a path for her. Smiling, she touched Darnley's shoulder.

"Come, Sire," she said gently. "Your gentlemen will help you to bed."

Darnley looked up, vomited again.

She motioned to his attendants. They helped him rise, and propelled him through the door. At the threshold Mary turned to Mistress McDoon, her words overloud in the listening room.

"Inform the chefs that His Majesty cannot eat shellfish. It sickens him."

IV.

Harry has found a new toy, Mary thought—myself. He now came to her bed boldly, eagerly and often. But though he whispered his devotion, caressed her to ardor, he left her unfulfilled. Perhaps, she thought, women are not meant to feel more than the preludes to pleasure.

Always he came to her fortified with drink. She reminded him that children conceived in wine-lust would be girls and pleaded that until she was pregnant he would not drink at all. He promised to drink only at meals. But inevitably, as she disrobed, she would hear the gurgle of wine poured in the audience chamber. If she chided him, he would storm at her for nagging.

His temperament was so erratic, his moods so changeable, that within a night he could twice break a promise and twice beg forgiveness. His repentant tears were scarcely dry before he reached again for the wine jug, his eyes defiant. But she loved him too much to revile him. Tenderly, she reasoned with him. Did he not know that stronger men than he had gone mad from the barrel-fevers? Could he not drink ale instead of wine? Darnley said he would drink neither. That night when she went to his bedchamber he was drinking whisky.

The hard-drinking lords had only contempt for him. It took a quart of whisky to stagger the weakest. Darnley was drunk on two goblets, asleep after four. His only sober hours were in the saddle when he rode to Hunter's Bog or hawked at Falkland and Linlithgow.

Mary framed two portraits of Darnley in her mind. In one, he was sprawled on his spine in a chair with his legs spread, chin sunk in stiffened lace, eyes shiny blue and glazed like Dutch tile. In his hand, which flashed jewels from every finger, a goblet tilted floorward.

The other picture—an overgrown hulk of a boy, self-driven and desperate, blundering along rushlit corridors, stumbling incoherent toward the peace of sleep.

V.

Late that autumn Bothwell returned to the Border as Lieutenant General of the Marches. Darnley had wanted that honor for his father, and when Mary told him of Bothwell's appointment he flung himself on her bed in a tantrum.

"You cannot always have your way," Mary said. More and more often she found herself treating him as a child. "Bothwell is the best man for the post."

He turned on her, face flaming. "Who says so—your boolie-backed Italian?"

His jealousy of Rizzio was becoming obsessive. Mary could not give Rizzio a coat or a bolt of suiting without an outburst from Darnley.

"Rizzio is your good friend, Harry." Or was before he met you, she thought. "It was he who suggested our marriage and furthered your suit. You should be grateful to him."

"For what?" He sat up and spat like a cat. "Am I never to have my rights? You gave the Crown Matrimonial to Francis—a blathering idiot—but not to me."

Do not kill my love, she begged him silently.

"Francis could not even give you a child, and by all signs I have."

So much was true. For the past ten days she had been ill in the mornings and her breasts were tender. "It is too soon to be sure," she said.

"I am sure of nothing," he whined. "For all I know the child is Rizzio's."

Mary closed her eyes and bit her lip, turning from him. She had taken his gibes before but none so brazenly indecent. "You are insulting."

"I too am insulted," he said. "The nobles are chattering like magpies. Sometimes you are closeted with the crouchie all day while we cool our heels in the anteroom. Sometimes you are with him half the night. I am damned tolerant but this goes too far. Knox says—"

He stopped abruptly.

"What does Knox say?" she asked quickly.

His eyes turned sly. "Oh—the usual sermons. He says Rizzio is a papal spy."

Mary thought, My own spies verify that Harry visited Knox secretly. If I can get Harry to confide in me . . .

She said, "I must persuade Parliament to agree to the crown for you. I've been so overburdened with matters of state that I've neglected you, haven't I?" She went to the bed and knelt beside him, her hands on his silken knees. "Forgive me, and let us drink together."

She brought whisky, drinking little herself, watching it turn him from arrogance to pettishness to sentimentality. She was his own true love, he said, beginning to weep. He would never love another. He did not for a moment believe Rizzio was her lover.

"Who would believe such a lie?" she asked carelessly, as though she expected no answer.

"Lord Morton . . ."

Greedy James Douglas, Earl of Morton, once James's friend but too cautious to join the rebels. Morton, Lord High Chancellor of Scotland, who feared she might give Rizzio his post.

"Lethington," Darnley babbled.

Jealous because Rizzio was usurping his position as Secretary of State.

"Lord Ruthven . . ."

Brutal, consumptive, said to be a sorcerer. Hating the world he was soon to leave, plotting from a sickbed.

"And I suppose," Mary sighed, "Knox believes it too."

"Knox wants me to spy on you," Darnley whimpered. "He sent

for me and hinted that Rizzio is your lover . . ." He continued the orgasm of confession. "Knox says you have treated me shamefully, that I must drive Rizzio from power, else I'll never have power myself . . ."

So Knox and the Protestant lords were rousing Darnley's jealousy to rid themselves of Rizzio. Mary stroked Darnley's hair, murmuring endearments. Presently, maudlin with whisky and emotion, he slept.

Later that night Mary told Rizzio what had happened. "If it were not for Harry's implication I would have Knox hanged! How can a man of God stoop to such vileness?"

"He cares not how he achieves results, Madam. If lies are expedient, then he will lie." Rizzio smiled ruefully. "I thought that my very ugliness protected Your Majesty from slander." He tapped his hunched shoulders. "Don't the fools know a woman could never look on me with love?"

"It is a shallow woman," Mary said, "who could know you and not love you."

"But Knox and your nobles misunderstand your love, Madam, or else deliberately brand it carnal. You cannot afford another scandal, and you no longer need me as you did. You have Bothwell to protect and advise you now."

"Meaning . . . ?"

"That for Your Majesty's honor I should leave Scotland."

"Oh no!" She rose and went to him, kneeling by his chair. "I can't lose you—I won't! If I am with child I shall need you even more to carry on the business of state. No one else is both loyal and capable."

"Think with your head, Madam, not with your heart."

"If you leave me," she said, "part of my heart will go with you."

"But if I remain, the slander will grow like an evil bloom rooted in the mud of Chastelard."

Wind stirred the tapestries of the audience chamber and the nymphs moved, fleeing forever the soundless hoofs of Pan. Mary shivered. "Don't leave me, Davy, I beg you."

A candle guttered out. Sand trickled from the hourglass on the table.

"I will stay," Rizzio said.

VI.

Mary announced her pregnancy at Linlithgow Palace on her twenty-third birthday. Blushing, radiant in a white velvet gown, she rose from her end of the banqueting table and smiled down the rows of nobles to Darnley.

"I ask you all to pray with me in thankfulness for God's grace . . ."
The small court rose, heads bent.

"Next June, if God wills, the King and I present an heir to Scotland."

Heads flung up, and there was a bedlam of congratulations, a roar of toasts. Darnley, his tongue whisky-thick, made an interminable and half-coherent speech while Mary stood in humiliated silence. He was dulling the glittering moment, prating of his prowess where Francis had failed, crowing and trumpeting. Randolph listened in sardonic amusement, Bothwell in hard-lipped scorn. Mary's ladies stared down at the table.

". . . and the son will be mine!" Darnley pounded the table, overset a pitcher of ale. He looked around belligerently. "I'll have the head of any man who says differently."

In an agony of embarrassment, Mary hurried down the table to Darnley and put her arm around him. "Come, Sire, we will go to our apartments and give further thanks to God—"

"God *knows* the child is mine," he mumbled, and allowed servants to lead him from the banqueting hall.

Mary started to follow him, then turned back. Too often of late Darnley had deadened her gaiety, and she was determined he should not tonight. She ordered the table trestles removed and shoved against the wall. She signaled the musicians in the gallery to play for dancing. But she had no heart for the revel. She could not bear Randolph's shrewd eyes, the pitying faces of her courtiers. To escape them, she fled into the adjoining chapel.

Above in the oaken loft, lepers stared down from a tiny sealed window, watching as Mary walked past the niched wooden saints to the high altar.

"God help me . . . I loved him so . . ."

She had loved Darnley almost at first sight, but she had seen only the bright façade and not the dark spirit. All the wealth of Spain— if she had it—would not suffice him. He would always want more jewels, more clothes, more perfumes, horses, land. At first, anxious to train him to power, she had discussed state matters with him, but he told her he knew more of government than she—was he not a man? If she said, "We will cease writing Elizabeth," he could find a dozen reasons why they should not. If she urged closer friendship with France, he urged coolness. Whatever Rizzio suggested was automatically rejected. Obsessed by his importance, Darnley insulted ambassadors, so that Mary was forced to receive them behind locked doors. Finally, to obviate the necessity of his signing state documents, Rizzio had an iron stamp affixed with Darnley's signature. They no longer endured his interference in government.

Mary had thought his arrogance a passing phase. Each morning she rose with new hope, sure that she could win him to stability and cooperation. It was futile. A dozen times a day his temper flared at some fancied slight. He drew a dagger on a messenger who delivered an unwelcome note. His valet had a broken jaw, his groom a bloody ear. Violence to servants was not uncommon at the Scottish court, but as Peter Pye said, "There's no knowing what the King may do. Saving Your Majesty's command, I'll not go near him. Gladly I'd die for your whim—but not for his."

"I am young," Darnley would plead when she admonished him. The eyes were so soft, the mouth so tender, the words so true. He was young. The heights of kingship were dizzying. Mary would forgive him.

But her pride could not forgive public disgrace. Tonight was the peak of humiliation, tonight was unforgivable. Randolph would write for posterity: "The King protests his child's legitimacy—a bit too shrilly."

"Is there anything I can do, Madam?"

Mary turned, surprised to see Bothwell beside her. "No, thank you. I'd best go to the King."

She started to move away but he caught her arm. "I've just seen the King. He's preparing to sleep."

"I will look in on him now before I retire," she said.

But Bothwell held her. "What is the matter?" she asked sharply. "Let me go!"

His grip on her arm tightened. "There's no need for you to nurse-maid a drunken boy. Come and dance with me."

He was too gravely insistent, and she said, "You do not fool me. Something is amiss."

She broke his grasp and ran from the chapel, hearing his footsteps behind her in the corridor and up the turnpike stairs. At the top, in the northwest tower, he caught her. "Madam, I implore you—he is mad-drunk."

But she flung off his arm and swept past the guard into the King's bedchamber. Candles burned in the oak-paneled oratory, dimly lighting lion tapestries of tawny saffron. Mary went to the bed and flung aside the curtains—and saw Darnley with a young page.

Strong arms caught her as she fell to the rushes. When she regained consciousness, she was on her bed in her own chamber. Jean was forcing brandywine between her lips, and Bothwell was standing beside the bed.

Mary closed her eyes, wanting to sink into darkness again. As long as she lived she would see Darnley on the tumbled velvet spread, naked save for his shirt, one arm under the boy's back, the other . . .

"Madam, speak to us!" Mary caught the fragrance of the gilly-flower scent Jean used, felt a cool hand on her forehead. She sat up and summoned a smile.

"Are you all right?" Bothwell asked.

"Yes. It is only my condition." She said to Jean, "I wish to speak to Lord Bothwell alone."

Jean left them, and Bothwell sat down in a chair by the bed. "I tried to spare you," he said.

"You tried to spare me the marriage." Mary turned her face, staring beyond him into the hooded stone fireplace. Heavily, dully, she said, "How did you know what was happening in his chamber?"

"The King's servants complained that he was fighting-angry at being put to bed, so I went up to help them. When I arrived, the scene had changed to romance—of a sort."

Sickened, she said, "I could not have believed it if I hadn't seen . . . " She hid her face in her sleeve.

"It was inevitable that you'd know sometime, Madam. And it is not only boys." Grimly he added, "Six-penny sluts at Jamie Sims's. Barmaids, serving wenches—cats, dogs, horses for all I know. The lad has catholic tastes—if you'll pardon the jest."

She could not look at him. "I suppose the whole court knows . . ."

"I've heard no talk among the nobles. But my page Paris tells me the servants are terrified by the King's demands for strange services."

"Oh, God," she said, "how can I ever face them? When I summon a page, how will I know whether he—if he—"

"Try not to think of that, Madam."

"How can I help it?" She leaned forward. "The King knows I saw him, I suppose?"

"Yes, he turned as I picked you up, and the page squealed and tried to cover himself."

"Then I shall have to talk to Harry tomorrow. And I've nothing to say. Nothing at all."

"Why say anything? Ignore him. He's served his purpose. You are with child."

Wonderingly she stared at him.

"Divorce him, Madam."

"Are you mad? I'd not have that sin on my soul."

"I wonder if you will feel the same way a year from now when he's held you up to ridicule before the world. Dragged your pride, exhausted your patience and frayed your nerves to flapping strings. You are no saint."

"No," she said hopelessly, "but neither will I sin."

There was no more to say, but she did not want Bothwell to go.

She could not bear to be alone in this chamber where twenty-three years ago tonight she had been born in this very bed. Alone she would wonder, Born for what? The deepest disgrace, the worst humiliation a woman can suffer.

Anxious to keep him beside her, she said, "Enough of my troubles. I am having a chamber prepared for you at Holyrood so you need not lodge in the Canongate. I want you near me."

"Thank you, Madam. A large chamber?"

"Yes, with a robing closet."

"Big enough for a wife?"

She gasped. "You plan to marry?"

"Lady Jean—with your permission."

The room spun for a moment. She had noticed Bothwell's attentions to Jean, seen them dancing and hunting together. But she had thought him merely amused by the novelty of Jean's primness. It had never occurred to her that he could be falling in love.

"You are jesting?" she asked.

"No."

"But I thought—I never thought—"

"Nor did I. But I'm getting old—thirty-one at Whitsuntide. It's time I stopped roving and found harbor."

Her voice strained for brightness. "There could be no safer harbor than Jean." She thought of Darnley, and the emotional safety she would never know. Over a lump in her throat she said, "I wish you all happiness."

Bothwell leaned toward her and his eyes locked with hers.

She repeated, dry-lipped, almost whispering, "All happiness . . ."

He was silent, searching her face, and she said, "You've said nothing of love."

"Jean loves Alex of Boyne and tells me she always will. I respect her honesty. Our marriage will ally my Borderers and her Highland clan. It will be profitable and peaceful. What more can one ask?"

"Love."

"I've seen too many flounder in love and drown. Not I, Madam."

"You are afraid."

He shrugged and smiled. "To each his own terror."

VII.

Mary spent that night in prayer, asking God's guidance. At dawn, exhausted but calm, she changed from a robe to a plaid gown and went to Darnley's apartments.

The bed hangings were drawn, and she stood hesitant. Then, taking courage, she pulled aside a curtain.

Darnley lay on his back beneath a fur coverlid, one hand under his head, the other curled at his side. Sleep-bloomed boyhood, she thought wryly, golden innocence. He opened his eyes and looked at her. He held out his arms.

Mary did not move. "If you have any possible excuse for your behavior last night, I should like to hear it."

He raised up on his elbow, ran his hand through tumbled curls. "I drank too much again. God, what a headache!"

She had meant to be calm, reasonable, but she lost her temper. "You've need to call on God," she snapped, "after last night—your humiliation of me at supper—" Her voice shrilled. "Do you remember what happened in this bed?"

He flinched, flushed, and she knew that he remembered but he said nothing.

"He-bawd! You were abed with a page!"

His eyes shifted from hers. "I was drunk," he said sullenly.

"Is that an excuse?"

"The lad forced me—"

"You lie!"

"—at dagger point."

"A lie," she spat. "I saw you as closely as I see you now."

His lower lip pouted out. "You spied on me. I don't sneak to your bed and watch you with Rizzio."

Mary bent and slapped him hard across the mouth. Tears trickled down his cheeks. He cowered back against the pillow, eyes round with fear. His voice was a croak. "What are you going to do?"

She could do nothing. She was tied to him, trapped. But she would not admit that. "What I do depends on you, Harry. You shall not have the Crown Matrimonial until you prove yourself worthy of it."

He sat up, brushing the tears from his eyes. "I don't want the crown. I want only your love."

"I cannot compete with your lovers."

"Mary . . ." Helplessly he spread his hands. "What can I say? You won't believe me. It is you I love. The others—drunken nightmares forgotten by morning."

"Forgotten by you, perhaps. Never by me. I saw you with that boy . . ." She held to the bedpost, dizzied, sickened by disgust. "What sort of creature are you? A changeling, a monster?"

"I don't know why I do these things," he said miserably. "You are all I want. But you are so busy, and I've nothing to do and sometimes I fill up with fear."

"And with drink. How well you hid your thirst until we were wed. How cleverly you tricked me!"

[232]

He shook his head. "I never drank until I came here, Mary. That is Christ's truth."

"Dare you say I drove you to it?"

"No, it is fear."

"Of what? You are guarded as I am, royally treated, pampered like a lap dog. What do you fear?"

"I don't know—and that is the horror. As soon as I entered Scotland, fear crawled my back and deadened my spirits. The very air, the fogs are evil. The land is unnatural. From Berwick to Edinburgh I kept my crucifix tight in my hand."

"And now you keep pages tight in your arms. Do you lose your fear in their kisses?"

He bent his head. "I never lose it," he said softly.

"You'll not ease your terror at my expense! Nor at Scotland's. I am told your ruttishness is scandal in the servants' quarters and God knows it will spread to the streets. You offer Knox the dung he needs to hurl at us and our church. You make Holyrood the brothel he always thought it!"

He looked up at her. "Never again will I betray you. Never again will I drink—"

"Too often you have mouthed promises only to break them. They are meaningless."

"Is my word as King meaningless?" he asked eagerly. "Could I betray a vow sworn on my word as King? Would I dare risk hellfire by breaking such a vow?" He leaned toward the bed table, picked up his crucifix and kissed it. "I swear on my Kingship never again to hurt you, nor to drink. I swear by God Himself and the blessed Virgin."

"Amen," she said on a sigh.

He swung out of bed, put on his robe. Then he knelt at her feet and kissed the tip of her slipper. She bade him rise and he said, "Can you possibly forgive me?"

"If God does, so must I. But I cannot forget last night. You revolt me so that I can scarce look at you. I am shamed by your very presence."

Humbly he said, "I do not wonder. But think of me as your lowest subject, begging nothing but to live in your shadow. Believe me," he said as she turned from him, "I ask only your mercy and a chance to prove my love."

"Love!" She laughed scornfully. "You could not love me and do what you have done."

"But I do. You taught me love such as I never knew." He flushed, met her eyes squarely. "There were boys before I met you. Never a woman."

"Yet now you've added a taste for sluts. I hear you go to Jamie Sims's."

"When I am drunk I reach for the nearest flesh, but not in love. Whatever you may think or say you cannot alter the truth of my love for you. Exile me, execute me, I would still love you, for I cannot help it."

Despite her disgust, she believed him. Men in love were different from women. Her father had bedded with others, yet he had loved her mother. King Henry had fathered Catherine's ten children, yet his love for Diane was steadfast until death. So could Darnley betray her with scum, yet hold her on the pinnacle of his heart.

With new dignity he faced her, his chin high. "I shall not plead for your love—you hate groveling. But I shall wait and pray and conquer my fear so as to be worthy of you should you ever want me."

Lest he see her tears, she went to the window. Above Loch Linlithgow bloomed a pink sunrise shafted with gold. God help me, she thought, I still love him. Not as I did, for the bright edge is tarnished; but my love is still there too deeply rooted to die of disillusion. I must help him to be what I thought he was . . .

When she turned from the window Darnley was kneeling in the oratory at the end of the room and she joined him, standing before the golden rail at the foot of the jeweled cross.

"I will summon Father Black," Mary said. "We will hear Mass."

That night in the King's Hall, Mary sat late with Rizzio discussing the forfeiture of James's lands and those of the other rebels. They decided to summon the exiles to appear in Edinburgh in March to be tried for their crimes before Parliament.

"James's position is comic," Rizzio chuckled. "He had expected Elizabeth to entertain him royally but, terrified of Spain, she holds him at arm's length and brands him a traitor to Your Majesty."

"Which he is," Mary said. "Yet, though it may seem strange to you, I miss him."

"Surely the blood tie is not stronger than your good judgment."

"My head tells me to destroy James utterly. My heart remembers his kindnesses, and my eyes vision my father in him."

"Your heart is too soft, Madam. Don't trust it. And I beg you don't submit to the King too soon. Let him prove himself. By denying him you may make a man of him."

"For all his debauchery," she said, "I think Harry loves me."

She had expected Rizzio to disagree but he surprised her. "I think so too, Madam. But his love is not simple—it is mixed with awe of you and fear of his own weaknesses and some inner terror I do not fathom."

"God is helping him," she smiled. "I am at peace tonight. I shall sleep well." She looked at the clock, surprised at the late hour. "It is nearly two!"

Rizzio, with a taper, led her up the spiral stairs and along the corridor to her bedchamber. As the guard saluted, her door flew open and Darnley stood there swaying. Glaze-eyed, he pointed to Mary.

"Whore." He hiccupped. "Judge not . . ."

VIII.

At noon on February 22nd the bells of the Canongate Protestant Kirk rang out for the marriage of Jean and Bothwell. Mary heard them, and pain tightened her throat. She had not dreamed the hurt would slash so deep.

But she smiled with practiced radiance as she awaited the bride and groom in Kinloch House on the High Street. Master Kinloch, a wealthy Edinburgh merchant, was giving the wedding reception, and she sat in his big parlor under white festoons of ribbons, surrounded by nobles and prominent citizens.

From the casement window at street level Rizzio said, "The Canongate is thronged! I've not seen such a crowd since Your Majesty's entry."

Darnley rose from his chair, wineglass in hand. "The people wish to see me."

"No, Sire," Mary said. He was already drunk, his face mottled red, his legs unsteady. "They await the newlyweds."

He stood belligerently, long legs spread. "They want to see me. And they shall."

Helpless, Mary watched him go to the open window. He pushed Rizzio aside and leaned from the casement, kissing his hand to the crowd. A cheer went up, then laughter. Hooting laughter without mirth or affection that sneered: He's drunk—as usual.

Darnley turned, smirking. "They love me," he announced to the room.

"Of course, Sire," Mary said, hands clenched in her lap.

Seven months of Darnley's drunkenness had not hardened her to humiliation. Each public appearance was fresh agony. She felt that her gains in popular favor were negated by Edinburgh's scorn of Darnley. The people had accepted her father's escapades as blithe, amusing. But they had not been these grimly reformed people. The hell-fire fed by Knox had burned tolerance to ash.

She could not keep Darnley in the shadows. He demanded the full light of public recognition. He could not be chained or put under guard. One could not hide a creature six-feet-six who was determined to strut and speak at public functions, to push and shove himself forward. She lived in constant anxiety at a time when she most needed tranquillity. Five months with child, she was frequently ill, her nerves raw as salted wounds. Since autumn she had been nagged by a pain in her side, and worried that her child might suffer in consequence.

The bells were tolling again. Was Bothwell kissing the bride at the altar or was that forbidden by the Protestant faith? Was rosemary scattered in their path as they left the church, were they pelted with wheat? Soon they would leave on their honeymoon and then would live at Crichton Castle twelve miles away. She would see less and less of Bothwell . . .

Rizzio, near the fire, sent her a smile and she translated it: It's best that Bothwell marries. It removes Your Majesty from temptation, puts him beyond your reach. For since your disillusionment with Darnley you are prone to compare the strong man with the weakling, to build dangerous fantasies.

That was true. She had told Rizzio, in a burst of self-revulsion, "I dream of Bothwell at night, then waken and toss in my bed like a creature in heat. Do I love him, or is the old attraction a sickness in my blood?"

"I don't think you love him," Rizzio said. "I think it a combination of hero worship and bodily need. Darnley roused that need but failed to satisfy it. He whetted your appetite for love, and now you starve."

Not since December, when she found Darnley with the page, had she allowed him to make love to her. Once in drunken frenzy he had tried to batter down her door. At Holyrood two halberdiers guarded her bedchamber, one in the corridor, one on the private stairs.

A roar went up in the street, and Darnley turned from the window. "The bride," he said sullenly, obviously irritated that the crowd's attention had been distracted from him.

At a signal from Master Kinloch, Mary and the guests hurried into the ballroom, which was hung with embroidered white satin. Gilded wheat twined in white ribbons adorned the chandeliers, and an arbor fashioned of evergreen boughs hid the musicians at the far end of the room. Trumpets sounded. The bridal party entered the garlanded doorway—Jean's mother, the widowed Lady Huntley, Jean's brother George, now Lord Huntley; her uncle the Bishop of Galloway, who had performed the ceremony. Behind them came the Gordons in their Highland kilts and the Hepburns, Bothwell's kinsmen. And then, surrounded by skirling pipers, the bride and groom

Jean's bridal dress was made from materials given her by Mary. The silver-cloth gown had a long train and the full, floor-sweeping sleeves were lined in white pearled taffeta. A coif of pearls framed Jean's face, hiding her hair, which fell in looped braids down her back. She seemed more like a nun than a bride, Mary thought, pale-lipped, her eyes cast down to the white satin prayer book she held.

But Bothwell had no churchly look. A pale blue cape swirled over one shoulder, a dress sword slapped his thigh, a sapphire-hilted dagger was tucked at his belt. Jean had pleaded that he leave his weapons with his henchmen before the ceremony, but he had growled that he'd not be caught helpless in church—reformed or otherwise.

Jean and Bothwell knelt at Mary's feet and she bade them rise, embraced Jean and offered her hand to Bothwell. But he did not kiss it—he had never kissed her hand and as always she thought it strange. He held her jeweled fingers for a moment and said, "We missed you, Madam."

"I could not attend a heret—a Protestant ceremony," Mary said. "But I am curious. Did all go smoothly?"

"By rote," he said drily.

Jean lifted her eyes. "It was beautiful, Madam."

The couple moved on to receive congratulations, and Mary watched Jean, noting her poise as she curtsied to Alex of Boyne and kissed Beaton, his bride of two months. Nothing in Jean's face revealed the tension she must have felt. In Bothwell's arms she will forget Alex, Mary thought painfully.

Jean cut the towering wedding cake, and Fleming found the bride's bean in her slice. When she married Lethington, all the Marys but Seton would be wed. But Seton seemed cheerful in her spinsterhood. Of late she had been preoccupied with religion and talked of ending her days in a convent.

Mary danced with Melville and Randolph, but uneasily, from the corner of her eye, she watched Darnley. Unless he was the center of attraction he was sulky, and to gain attention he would belittle or insult others. Now as the crowd danced or swirled about the bride and groom he sat on a couch at the wall, staring fixedly at Rizzio, who talked with Lady Huntley at the fireplace. Mary joined them, then maneuvered Rizzio into the card room.

"The King looks surly," she whispered, "and you know he always vents his wrath on you. Best stay in here or somewhere out of his sight."

"I told Your Majesty I should not have come here. The fewer public appearances I make the better."

"But I hate for you to miss the revels!"

"I'd sooner miss them than be glared at by the nobles—Bothwell and Lord Robert are the only ones who treat me civilly. I too have my pride, Madam. One slur too many and I'm apt to draw my dagger."

Mary nodded. "I know I ask too much of you, Davy. But I needed you here today to spark my courage."

"You look far from cowed," he smiled.

She wore a scarlet gown fringed with gold—a bit too flamboyant, perhaps, for a woman with child, but it lent bravado. Wearing it, wearing her smile, she felt certain that no one but Rizzio suspected her misery.

"Madam," Rizzio said, "don't linger with me. The King will note your absence."

She returned to the ballroom, where Darnley sat watching the door. If only he would fall asleep, she thought, the servants could remove him upstairs and I would be free of anxiety. But though his jaw was slack his eyes were open slits. From time to time a maid refilled his glass, but no one else approached him.

Bothwell intercepted her as she started toward the hearth. "May I bring you some refreshment?" he asked.

"Wine. I will drink to your happiness."

Bothwell beckoned a servant and Mary took a goblet from the silver tray. "To you, my lord, and to your lady—every joy."

He thanked her, then raised his own glass. "To Your Majesty. I know no man as gallant."

A compliment from him was so rare that her mouth made a little O, and he laughed. "Why so astonished?"

"Because you seldom flatter."

"I never flatter," he rasped. Abruptly he changed the subject. "Jean and I are grateful for your many gifts, Madam."

"There are more to come," she said, "a feast for you tonight at Holyrood, a tournament tomorrow at the castle, jousting, boar-baiting, Highland games, masques and dancing for four days and nights."

He tipped his tawny head to one side in mock horror. "Is it your intention to disable me before the honeymoon even begins?"

She laughed. "You will doubly appreciate the country quiet of Seton. I know of no lovelier honeymoon spot." She turned and watched Jean dancing with plump, bushy-bearded Lord Morton. "Poor lass, it's a heathen custom that the bride must dance with all who ask her."

"It's good for her," Bothwell said. "Jean needs people about her. She lacks confidence."

"I blame Alex for that. She was so sure of him for so many years, and then he rejected her."

"Proving his lack of imagination," Bothwell said. "Beaton's allure is all on the surface—she will fizzle out like a fireball. Jean—"

"Is a steady white taper."

He shook his head. "Steadiness implies dullness, Madam. Women cannot judge women. Jean's charms lie deep."

Uncomfortable, fearful of learning too much, she was grateful for the summons to the banqueting hall. A long table glittered with golden trenchers. Mary was seated at one end under a spangled blue canopy, Bothwell beside her and Jean seated next to him. At the other end Darnley sat beneath another canopy. Between them were the other guests, maypoles of ribbons streaming down from the oak chandeliers to their places.

Maids served venison, spitted chicken, geese, rabbit, lamb. Mary, mindful of Henry the Eighth's knighting a beef "Sir Loin," created a baron of a succulent cut. But throughout the feast she was watching Darnley.

He slouched in his chair, eating nothing. Slow of movement, unable or unwilling to rise, he drank each toast seated.

Lord Balfour proposed a toast to the unborn child. "To the future King of Scotland and England!"

All but Darnley stood and drank. There was a moment's reverent silence. Then, slurring his words but speaking them loudly, Darnley said, "I have thought of a suitable name for the child."

"James?" Mary asked, smiling nervously. "After my father?"

"No." He pointed to Rizzio, sneering. "Solomon—son of David."

Bothwell lunged forward, but Mary grabbed his hand under the table and held it tightly. To the stunned guests she said, "I wish you all to repair to Holyrood House tonight for further revels. But now," she smiled, "I must go."

She glanced warningly at Bothwell, released his hand and walked to the door, where Master Kinloch held her scarlet velvet cloak. She complimented him on the beautiful reception, then turned to wave good-by to the guests.

They were still standing by their places at the table. But it seemed as though a wind had bent them from Darnley, and even the two footmen behind him had moved far back as though he were leprous. His chin propped in a silver lace ruff was trembling.

In Holyrood at four o'clock that morning, Mary, her ladies and Lady Huntley led Jean to the bridal chamber. Mary had ordered the walls hung with white velvet. Sweet herbs perfumed the satin sheets and white fur coverlid. The bed curtains, of azure damask stitched in gold, matched the newly cushioned hearth chairs.

"Madam," Jean said, "never was a chamber so lovely."

"It is yours whenever you visit Holyrood," Mary said. She pointed to the robing room that adjoined it. "You will find a wedding gift in there. Wear it—if you like it."

Jean and her mother, carrying the bridal reticule, went into the robing room, shutting the door behind them. Fleming whispered, "Poor lass, I'd not be in her slippers."

"I would," Seton said. "I think Lord Bothwell the most exciting man I ever met."

"He'll not be faithful a week," Fleming said.

Beaton said, "Just last Tuesday in the sewing chamber he was flirting with Jean's seamstress, Bessie Crawford, while she stitched the bridal gown and telling her how handsome she was."

"She is handsome, in a coarse manner," Fleming said. "I'd not want Bessie Crawford in my household; the wench is too bold."

Mary half-listened. The past hours of anxiety and humiliation, the strain of entertaining and pretending gaiety, would culminate in this most painful duty—bedding Jean for the nuptial night. So far, she thought, I have not faltered. I can endure a few more minutes.

The door opened and Jean returned with her mother. "Your Majesty," she said, "this nightrobe is the most exquisite I've ever seen!"

The robe had wrestled Mary's conscience. To make Jean seductive, or fashion the lines to prim mediocrity? A clinging, transparent fabric or a stiff damask?

Jean blushed. "I cannot thank you, Madam; I am no poet."

For the robe was poetry. Grecian, flowing, cobweb-thin, it bared Jean's lovely shoulders and emphasized her breasts. Her hair fell, straight and shining, to meet the brighter gold of the girdle.

Lady Huntley brought a handkerchief to her eyes. "Madam, you are so kind. You have made my daughter beautiful."

"Nonsense," Mary said, "she was always so."

But she was not always so. This was both a disguise and a revelation.

Fleming blew out the rushlights by the window so that the room was dim, and turned back the coverlid. Jean embraced her mother, holding her for a long moment. She kissed Fleming, Beaton and Seton. Then she turned to Mary. "Madam, I ask a last favor—to see you alone."

When the others had left, Jean knelt by Mary's chair. "Your Majesty is only two years older than I, but so much wiser. May I ask your advice?"

"About what?" Mary asked fearfully.

"My marriage. I have not lied to Lord Bothwell. My husband," she added dazedly. "I told him I love Alex and that I always will. Tonight," she bent her head, "must I pretend a passion I do not feel?"

Damn you, Mary wanted to scream, why must you ask me this? Go to your mother, your Bishop uncle, bleat your questions to them! I will advise you wrongly, for I love your husband. I will lead you to ruin your marriage if you trust me . . .

"I shock you, Madam," Jean whispered.

"No." Truthfully, painfully, each word hurting her, Mary said, "I don't believe you could fool Bothwell with pretense. He is wise about women. Be natural. Do not feign an ardor you do not feel. In time—" She took a deep breath—"you may come to love him more than life."

"But I love Alex."

"Alex is a dullard. If ever he attains fame it will be in a footnote, as Mary Beaton's husband. But Bothwell's star is rising. He is the most favored and powerful noble in Scotland. When I forfeit James's lands he will be among the wealthiest. Be grateful to God that you have him to protect and cherish you."

"I am grateful, Madam, for I have little to offer of beauty or wit."

"He knows your value, never fear."

"He treasures honesty, Madam, above all things. And also," she smiled bleakly, "I think he weds me because he cannot have me otherwise."

Mary could bear no more. She rose hurriedly. "I must go. He will be waiting. Good-night, my dear."

Jean rose too. "Would you," she asked timidly, "bless the bed?"

Mary turned on her furiously. "I am no priest!" She was shaking with jealous rage, with exhaustion, her nerves strained to breaking. "You want no Catholic blessing!"

Jean gasped and stepped backward.

With a tremendous effort, Mary steadied herself, forced her voice to gentleness. "Forgive me, the King has upset me . . . I did not mean to hurt you. Of course I will bless your bed."

She went to it, touched the carved oak post and bent her head.

"God, sanctify this bed. Preserve and sustain this marriage against evil." She thought, Against me.

IX.

It was merciful, Mary felt, that she had little time to brood during the two weeks of Bothwell's honeymoon. At Holyrood in Council meeting Lethington accused Randolph of smuggling three thousand pounds to James and the rebels. Mary ordered Randolph from Scotland and wrote Elizabeth of his dismissal. She received in return a curt note from Elizabeth saying that she was taking James into favor.

But the threat did not worry Mary. The problems created by Darnley superseded all others. Day after day she sought ways to curb his drinking, his extravagance, but to no avail. He was insensitive to her pleas, or too whisky-sodden to hear them. He avoided her, shutting himself in his apartments and dictating mysterious dispatches. His secretary was discreet, and Mary was unable to learn whom he was writing or why. Early in March she surprised him in whispered conferences with Morton and his cousin, George Douglas. Once when she entered his presence chamber, he and Kerr broke off a conversation abruptly.

One thing relieved her tension. Darnley apologized to Rizzio for his suspicions of him, and actually courted his favor. "Doubtless he believes that my influence with Your Majesty will win him the Crown Matrimonial." Rizzio shrugged. "The lad is not subtle."

This ninth day of March, Mary worked in the library on her speech to Parliament. In three days James and his rebels would be in Edinburgh to appear before Parliament on charges of treason. The town was filling with curious nobles, with clansmen and Borderers. Morton's kinsmen, "The Black Douglases," crammed the taverns and hostels of the Canongate, and from the window Mary could see their banners whipping from spears, as a hundred rode by on their way to Hunter's Bog. Bothwell, too, was hunting in the Royal Park and would stay at Holyrood for the parliamentary session. Jean was at Crichton. Her mother, Lady Huntley, now lived at court and prattled to Mary of how happy the marriage seemed to be. After a visit to the newlyweds she said, "Your Majesty will be glad to know that Jean is gay as a linnet and Alex seems dead in her mind, though she is too stubborn to say so. When Lord Bothwell is hunting she stands in the watchtower pretending to see if he runs game, but the plain truth is she cannot bear him out of her sight."

"Doubtless Lord Bothwell is as happy as she," Mary prodded.

"I am sure of it, Madam, though he's not one to show his heart."

Nor must I, Mary thought. I must cut him out of my heart . . .

Wind battered the palace, and Mary could hear the two lions roaring from their pit in the rear garden. They had been one of Darnley's extravagances and he had insisted on having them close by beneath the walls of the south tower. They made her nervous. The wind roused them to fright or fury, and the wind was unceasing.

She continued writing, her quill scratching the crimes of James, Kirkcaldy, Argyll and the rest. But she wondered if James had not learned his lesson in exile. I shall discipline him, she decided, and forfeit much of his land. But I shall not ruin him.

Rizzio tapped at the open door and came in as Mary called a greeting. "Does Your Majesty need me? If not, I should like to accept the King's invitation to tennis."

"By all means do." She smiled at his eagerness. "But it is a windy day and a dubious honor."

"It's the sport I crave, not the King's company." Wistfully he said, "No one ever asks me to join in games. They think because my shoulders hump I am crippled, a weakling."

She had thought so too. It never occurred to her to ask him to hunt, to bowl or play tennis. But now she realized that these sports, trivial in themselves and taken for granted by her courtiers, symbolized manliness to Rizzio. She cursed herself for an insensitive fool not to have guessed his need for normality.

"I wouldn't prove too poor an opponent," he said, "if I had a chance to play with someone. Often I go to Leith sands and practice golf alone. I bowl when no one is on the green." He added shyly, "Each morning in my chamber I exercise my muscles."

How many times, she thought, he has waved from the courtyard when I set out for a day of sport, and I never knew his longing. He is barely thirty, yet I relegate him to the hearth like a gray-granny. It is no little offense I have committed in my ignorance. Rizzio's pride is involved, his self-respect.

"Hereafter," Mary said, "it is my wish that you join me whenever I golf or bowl or hunt. You shall choose six horses from my stables, and we will have riding clothes made for you."

"But I did not ask—"

"You never ask, my Davy. In truth, I wish you would, for I only guess your desires."

His eyes marveled. "You give so much for so little."

"You think you give me little? You are dearer to me than my own kin. I have nothing in life but you and Bothwell. I grope in a maze of rebels, weathercocks, dirty, illiterate oafs. But when I am most deep in disillusion I say to myself, 'There is decency in the world and loyalty and grace. There is Davy.'"

He knelt by her chair and kissed the hem of her skirt.

"Go to your tennis," she smiled, "and sup with me tonight at seven."

"Madam, you've honored me with supper invitations twice this week and the nobles are outraged."

"The nobles be damned! I will choose my guests as I see fit. Seven o'clock, Davy, in my apartments."

After he left she continued working on her speech, and two hours

[243]

later finished it. As she set her seal to the paper, Darnley came in timidly.

"We had to stop playing," he said. "The wind is too fierce." He placed his tennis racquet on the chair. "Mary . . . Mary . . ."

"Yes?" she asked sharply. "What is it?"

Like a hurt child reaching for its mother, he ran to her and knelt with his arms around her waist, nuzzling his face in the pleats of her dress. "I have been such a fool, such a besotted oaf! How could I doubt you or be jealous of a poor little crouchie? What in the name of God ails me?"

Her hand hovered above his hair, but she did not touch it. Longing to comfort him, she dared not. She must harden her heart lest he hurt it beyond repair.

"I saw Father Black just now in the chapel," he said, his voice muffled in the velvet of her gown. "He prayed with me and blessed me. He told me that God forgave me but that you—you might not."

His hair curling so brightly, so innocently under her hand . . . Poor lost lad, he had suffered these weeks and months even as he had sinned.

"You are ashamed of me and I am ashamed of myself," Darnley said. "Even in drink, when you think me blinded and stupified, I am most terribly aware. It is as if I look on upon myself, an observer powerless to stop the revel. But the revel is not blithe . . ."

His shoulders shook with sobs. "I promise that I will stop drinking, that I will not annoy you for love until you ask it. The same promise I made at Linlithgow—only this I shall keep."

"Why do you think you can keep the promise now?" she asked gently.

"Because I have lived in hell since. I want the heaven I am missing."

Mary touched a ringlet. "Harry, if for a week you keep your promise, come to me for another talk." She must encourage him to hope. "We may yet be happy. But it is up to you."

Darnley lifted a tear-shiny face. "You give me another chance?"

She thought of Christ's words: . . . *And if he trespass against thee seven times in a day, and seven times in a day turn again to thee, saying, I repent; thou shalt forgive him.*

"Yes," she smiled, "another chance."

The wind reached its peak at seven o'clock, screaming around the tiny turret supping room that adjoined Mary's bedchamber. Lord Robert, Rizzio and the Countess of Argyll sat at the table with Mary. She had not invited Darnley; he must earn the privilege of her company. And though she wanted Bothwell present, she resisted the temptation. It was best to see him only on Council or military matters. How many times, she wondered, have I closed my heart to him only to open it again? But if I work for a true marriage he has no place there.

With scant appetite Mary ate the first course—salted trout in Gaston's fine herb sauce. Winter vegetables, meat. It was Lent, but her physician insisted she needed red meat and red wine to build her baby's blood and bone. She was in the sixth month of her pregnancy, prey to apprehensions. The pain in her side, she noticed, attacked her when she was most worried, and she worried constantly that the baby might die, be monstrous or marked. Mistress McDoon said a drunkard's wife often gave birth to a harelipped child or an idiot, and always a girl.

From the window seat Arthur Erskine, Captain of the Guard, said, "I've never heard such a wind. It sounds like the wailing of lost souls."

It lifted the ruby velvet hangings at the small closed casement, and tapers in the silver candelabra on the table flamed high in the breeze. Though a fire burned in the blue-and-white-tiled hearth, Mary drew a wool shawl closer about her shoulders.

"Are you chilled?" Lord Robert asked her.

"No," she said. But she was depressed, unaccountably anxious. She realized that it was caused by her condition and aggravated by the wind. In the lulls she could hear the lions roaring.

As the candied fruits and cheeses and sweet wines were served, Erskine mentioned a white skeleton faun that had been seen by a groom in the Royal Park and by two hunters.

"Was it—"

Mary paused. Footsteps sounded on the private staircase that led to her bedchamber. Darnley had once been privileged to use those stairs, but no more. At night they were guarded, and she thought, He has wheedled the sentry or bribed him. Please God may he be sober . . .

Darnley appeared in the doorway, moving with slow, drunken dignity. As the guests rose, he bade them be seated and sat down on the bench by Mary, sliding an arm about her waist.

Heartsick, she moved away from him. He could not keep a promise four hours.

"Have you supped yet, Sire?" she asked, forcing herself to courtesy.

"I want nothing to eat."

But he drank. When he set down his empty goblet his hand was trembling. He would not meet her eyes.

There was a strained silence. As usual, Mary thought, Harry has ruined a cosy evening. If we talk he will interrupt, clamoring to express a half-coherent opinion. If we say nothing he will pout and turn hostile.

"Music," Darnley said, with a nod to Rizzio. "I should like to hear *The Shepherd's Lament*."

Rizzio, at the end of the table, took his lute from the floor and sang for them. Mary watched the flicker of his long white fingers on the strings, the shine of candlelight on the tortoise-shell and mother-of-pearl instrument. His face was in shadow. When he raised it, his eyes caught the glow of the candles. Eyes like black wells, limitlessly deep and almost articulate. They rested on Mary with such tenderness that her own eyes blurred.

The wind mourned around the turret, moody, dying down and then rising to a high, womanish scream. The song ended.

"Thank you," Darnley said. "Beautiful." He rose and went to Rizzio, patted his shoulder, complimented him on his fur-trimmed russet doublet, on the diamond that hung from his neck on a golden chain. It was obvious and heavy-handed flattery, but Mary found it preferable to his former belligerence. Rizzio, carefully humble, thanked Darnley and began another song.

It was a Border ballad of unrequited love, and against her will Mary's thoughts drifted to Bothwell. What harm could there be in asking him for an hour of music? She would summon him from his quarters, where he supped with Jean's brother and Lord Atholl . . .

As she started to speak to a servant, she heard the thump of boots on the staircase. The tapestry that hid the door to the bedroom was thrust aside, and she stifled a scream. Lord Ruthven stood in the doorway. Dim light from the bedchamber glinted on the dark armor he wore over his nightclothes. His tall body was emaciated, cadaverous from consumption. He had been abed three months and his face, framed by an iron cap, was death-touched. Staring from bony sockets, his eyes were livid, lit like black candles. He held a naked sword.

Mary jumped up, and so did her guests. Ruthven swayed, steadied himself with his legs apart.

"What do you want, my lord?" Mary asked. He was suspected of sorcery and she spoke fearfully. "By what right do you come here?"

His voice was a harsh croak. "I come for yonder poltroon, Rizzio. He has been here overlong."

"He is here by my command," she said sharply. "What do you want with him? What has he done?"

"Ask the King, Madam."

Mary turned to Darnley. Shifty-eyed he mumbled, "I know nothing of this."

To Ruthven she said, "You are a sick man—perhaps in high fever. Do you fancy that Rizzio has offended—"

"He has offended against Your Majesty's honor, your husband, your nobles and your realm." Ruthven stepped across the threshold, pointing his sword at Rizzio, and Mary ran to the head of the table and shielded Rizzio with her body.

"Lord Ruthven," she said, "I command you to leave this chamber under pain of death."

Erskine, Lord Robert and the two servants drew their daggers and started toward Ruthven, but he lunged his sword and shouted, "I'll not be handled!" Heavy footsteps pounded up the stairs, and Mary heard the clank of weapons against stone. George Douglas and two henchmen crowded the doorway behind Ruthven, swords and daggers drawn. Iron gauntlets hammered the bedchamber door, there was a loud crash of wood, and armed men poured through the bedchamber. Morton, Lindsay, Kerr and Patrick Bellenden pushed past Douglas and Ruthven and rushed toward Rizzio, overturning the table.

Mary sprang back from splintered glass and plates, and the Countess grabbed the candelabra and held it high, Rizzio, crouching behind Mary, held fast to the folds of her gown, but Kerr seized his hand and forced him to release his hold.

"For God's sake, spare him!" Mary cried. "He has done nothing!"

Ruthven pushed Mary into Darnley's arms. "Hold her, Sire!"

Kicking, raking Darnley's chin with her fingernails, Mary broke out of his grasp, but as she turned to shield Rizzio, Kerr pressed a cocked pistol at her womb and Bellenden held a dagger to her back. She felt it prick her shoulder blades and through her terror she thought, I dare not move . . . It is Rizzio's life or my child's . . .

"Save me, Madam!" Rizzio screamed. "For the love of God, save me!"

She shouted, "If Rizzio has harmed any of you, I swear I'll bring him to justice!"

George Douglas lunged a knife over her shoulder and it passed so near her throat she could feel the cold steel. There was a high, agonized shriek as he drove the knife into Rizzio's back. Darnley grabbed Mary, and she slumped against him, nearly fainting. Then, shaking the dark from her eyes, she lifted her head and saw Rizzio dragged to the door on his knees. The gold hilt protruded from his back and blood soaked through the russet doublet. As men pulled him through the doorway, Rizzio caught hold of Mary's bed curtains, clung to the fringe of the spread. Lindsay bent and hammered his knuckles with a dag butt, tore him away from the bed and out of her sight.

Hysterically Mary begged Rizzio's life. "I will pardon you all . . . I will give you gold and lands . . . titles. I will send him away. I will do anything you ask, *anything*, but for the love of Christ, spare him!"

Her pleas were drowned out by screams from the audience chamber that shrilled up and up, soaring to peaks of pain. Stunned by the screams, Darnley loosened his hold, and Mary broke free and ran through her bedroom. Darnley caught her as she reached the audience chamber and held her, binding her mouth with his hand to stifle her pleas for Rizzio's life.

She could not see Rizzio, for a dozen assassins surrounded him at the door near the staircase. Shoving, snarling, panting, they knifed one another in their frenzy to get at him. Rage-warped faces dripped blood and saliva. Daggers rose and fell, dug and slit and hacked until Rizzio's cries grew faint and died at last in a bubbling, gurgling spew.

The men stood back and Mary saw that the body was stripped of clothes—a smashed red pulp of flesh and bone-ends. The head, nearly severed, hung by a tendon. The mouth quivered, gushed blood. The eyelids flickered, the eyes opened wide, and she knew he was still alive.

"Kill him," she begged against Darnley's hand. "Kill . . . !" Again her view was obstructed as daggers plunged into Rizzio's heart.

"So perish vermin," Morton said, and spat on the bloody face.

They booted the carcass down the staircase, and she heard it bump from step to step. Kicking his clothes out the door, they left the room.

Darnley freed Mary, and she stumbled over to the hearth and vomited. Her ears rang as though a million bells clanged in her head, and the room seemed to rock. She clung to the mantel as the floor rose and the ceiling lowered. Darnley caught her as she fell.

On her bed, tended by the Countess, Mary regained consciousness. Heavy hoofbeats drummed over the drawbridge and she heard shouting in the courtyard below her window: "A-Douglas! A-Douglas!" The war cry of Morton's kinsmen.

Mary sprang up, saw Darnley and Ruthven in the supping room and ran to them, weeping hysterically. She lashed them with incoherent words that were drowned in shuddering sobs. The Countess held her close, trying to soothe her, and Lord Robert pushed her gently into the window seat.

"Wine!" Ruthven gasped. "For God's sake, wine!"

Darnley took a leather jug from the shambles on the floor, drank and passed it.

Mary rose, pointing at Ruthven. "You'll die for this!"

Backed against the wall Ruthven coughed, spat blood. "Sooner than you think, Madam."

"Then may God damn you and yours to eternal perdition!"

He lifted terrified eyes. "No, Madam—I beg you, do not curse me! This is your husband's doing."

She whirled on Darnley, saw the guilt plain in his face. "So *you* betray me! Traitor! Son of a traitor!"

"Rizzio deserved to die," Darnley said, but his voice wobbled uncertainly and he would not face her. "He turned you from me, body and soul—"

"Soul!" She flung back her head and her loosened hair tumbled down from its net. "You've killed my soul as you've killed my friend. Why didn't you kill my body, my child? Then you would have my crown and inherit Elizabeth's. But no, you are too craven, weak even in perfidy—"

There was a hammering at the door of the audience chamber and Mary ran from the room, Ruthven panting behind her. She reached the door ahead of him, but he jerked her hand off the latch.

"Get behind me, Madam!"

Mary stepped back and he opened the door. On the stair landing stood Bothwell, Huntley, Atholl and other loyal lords demanding to see her.

"Look at her, then," Ruthven said contemptuously.

"Bothwell!" Mary cried, stretching her arms toward him. "They have killed Davy, it's a bloodlust—"

"Quiet!" Ruthven took a paper from his belt, spread it out and held it up for them to see. "This is a bond signed by the King. What has been done is by his command. Go to your chambers; you are prisoners."

Standing on tiptoe, peering over Ruthven's shoulder, Mary saw Bothwell's hand jump to his sword. Then he turned. Morton's troops were crowding up the staircase behind him. Ruthven slammed the door, took Mary's arm as she stumbled and led her back to the supping room.

"Your Majesty," he said as she slumped in a chair, "you are confined to these apartments. Should you try to escape you will be shot. Eighty halberdiers guard you. The palace is surrounded by Morton's men. You may see no one but by the King's command, nor have your women with you." He turned to Darnley. "She is in your keeping, Sire."

The Countess, gray-faced, turned from the hearth. "She is with child, she must have care. For the love of heaven, allow her her ladies!"

"Go to your quarters." Ruthven nodded toward Lord Robert, Erskine and the two servants. "You also."

Alone with Ruthven and Darnley, Mary heard the ringing of the common bell in the Canongate. There was sudden clamor in the courtyard, and she rose and drew back the window hangings. Darnley thrust her aside. "If you show yourself at that window I'll slice you to collops! Stand back!"

Mutely, she obeyed.

Darnley opened the casement and leaned out, then turned slightly toward Ruthven. "The Provost and the Town Guard are at the gates . . . armed men are pushing through . . . demanding to know what is happening and if the Queen is safe."

"Tell them she is safe, that there was a brawl among the servants and Rizzio was killed."

Mary could hear the shouts now—her people demanding to see her. Bless them, she thought, God bless them . . . they cannot help me but they love me.

Darnley yelled from the window. "The Queen is safe and well. There was a quarrel between the Scots and French servants over the Mass and David Rizzio was killed in the fray."

He took a handkerchief from his sleeve and wiped his sweating forehead. "Go!" he shouted. "Go in peace. All is well here."

To Ruthven he said, "They go, but reluctantly. They are suspicious."

"What if they are? We outnumber them; we are heavily armed. And Lord James and his men are riding hard through the night and should be here tomorrow."

"Jesu!" Mary stared at him. "James—coming *here*?"

"I have pardoned him," Darnley said, "and the others."

So James was returning, not as a criminal facing trial, but in honor. Likely it was he who had conceived this plot, using Darnley to regain power. Using Darnley's jealousy to rid himself of Rizzio.

"But," Darnley added haughtily, "I am in command here."

"A marvel," she taunted. "A titmouse leads ravening wolves."

He reddened, thrust out his lip. "You'd best keep a civil tongue."

Ruthven mumbled, "I am going to bed," and lurched toward the stairs.

Darnley finished the wine in the jug, pawed for another in the rubble on the floor. His feet splintered glass, crunched the wreckage of silver and agate, sugar cakes, cheese and fruit. Rizzio's lute lay like a great smashed pear browned with rot.

Darnley found an unbroken bottle, unplugged it and drank, wiping his lips on his sleeve, leaving a reddish stain on the ice-blue velvet. He righted an overturned bench and sat down, staring at Mary defiantly.

"You brought this upon yourself," he said.

Rage was a tight knot in her stomach, but grief was flooding through, threatening her courage. Rizzio dead, forever gone; perhaps even now buried in haste by heretics.

She said, "For all your treachery you are Catholic. I beg you to have a priest say Mass for Rizzio's soul. Will you tell Father Roche or Father Black?"

"Father Black is dead."

She gasped. "Dead . . . murdered?"

He nodded, drank from the bottle. "Stabbed in his bed."

"But why?"

"The lords didn't trust him. They thought him a papal spy."

"My mother's confessor, and mine. Why did you not stop them?"

He shrugged. "What could I do?"

"I thought you were in command here," she sneered.

He glared at her and she said, contemptuously, "Drink; drown yourself," and went to the door, pausing on the threshold of her bedchamber.

Next to her bed the pale gray carpet was dark with spattered blood, and she followed its trail into the audience chamber as it zigzagged between overturned chairs to the door. The carpet was trampled to one side and a great red pool was widening across the stone.

Mary sank to the floor, reaching out to what was left of Rizzio, touching the still warm blood. Tears ran down her face, laughter bubbled from her lips and she sat shaken by gusts of mirth and weeping. She lifted wet hands, staring at them numbly, feeling neither horror nor grief. Her mind was emptied as though she were newly born.

"Mary!"

Looking up, she saw Darnley standing in the middle of the room. She rose, walked slowly toward him. He retreated to the fireplace, his hands outflung, his eyes bulging.

She whirled on him savagely. "Why fear this blood? You shed it."

His back was against the mantel. He could go no farther. She spread her wet hands hard against his palms. "There. His blood on your body as it is on your conscience. It will cost you dear."

He rubbed his hands on his breeches, cringing away from her. "You are mad!" He ran sideways to the door and she followed him. He flung the door open and grabbed a guard by the arm. "Come in here! Wipe the blood, wipe it up!"

"No!" Mary shouted as halberdiers jostled through the doorway.

"Listen to me." She spoke calmly and clearly. "I am your Queen and you will obey me. You may wipe the blood from the carpets, but never from the floor. There shall it stay—the mark of the King's treachery, the mark of murder. His child shall see it, God willing, and his grandchildren, and each generation to come, so long as Holyrood stands and this room endures."

The guards shuffled uneasily, glancing from her to Darnley.

"If you dare to remove the blood from that stone I swear by God and the Virgin and my crown that I will curse you all."

Several made the sign of the cross. Hastily, bumping into each other, they bowed backward and shut the door.

"I will order the maids to remove it," Darnley whimpered.

"Will they risk my curse for you?"

"I will do it myself then . . . No!" he cried as she started to speak, "Don't curse me, I beg you. I will leave the blood, I will do anything you say, only don't curse me!"

She glared at him, and he bent his head and shielded his eyes with his arm. "You are possessed!"

By hatred, she thought. Hatred so deep, so violent that it threatens the moorings of sanity and drowns the stream of love for my child. I cannot love Darnley's child, I will not. For my love brings death as it did with Francis, Rizzio, Father Black. It brings betrayal —the Cardinal, Chastelard, James, Darnley. So I will tear love out of me and fill with hate. God will not care. He never cared. To him I was a soft pleading thing, belly-crawling, and he spurned me. I will show him a change . . .

"Mary!" Darnley was sniveling, bent at her feet. "I never intended you harm . . ."

"The more fool you. You have your dagger." She smiled. "But my heart is flint. Run me through and you'll spark a fire that will consume you."

He lifted her skirt to his lips. "I cannot harm you . . . you are my wife."

I am no longer, she thought. I am your nemesis.

CHAPTER EIGHT

I.

FULLY DRESSED, Mary lay sleepless on her bed. The clock in the audience chamber struck the hours. As the room grayed she put on her shawl and went to the window seat. Below in the courtyard, torches lit a frigid dawn. Morton's troops paced back and forth, stamping their feet and blowing on their hands to warm themselves.

The child moved within her, and she trembled in panic. Doubtless the murderers' intention was to cause a miscarriage and clear the path to the throne. If I am to preserve my throne, my life, I must act quickly, she thought—before James comes.

She must drive a wedge between Darnley and the conspirators, win him back to her, bind him to her will. After her outburst last night it might be difficult, but it could be done. It must be done.

Lighting the rushlights between the long mirrors, she studied her reflection. Save for her thickened body, she was still beautiful. Her hair flowed in a shiny, luxuriant tangle. Her skin was luminously white, the moist texture of pearl. Her eyes, full of dark light, seemed fathomless. There was no trace of her ordeal, save the disorder of her hair and the rumpled, bloodied gown.

She thought, I can win Harry's body. But I must also regain his trust—use his terror to chain him to me. His cowardice is my strongest weapon.

After bathing, she sat down at her dressing chest in the tiny robing room. She rubbed dark kohl on her eyelids, underlined her eyes with gray salve. No paint. She must look pallid, tragic, ill. She left her hair as it was and changed into a long figure-concealing robe of violet velvet.

In the audience chamber she leaned against the wall, fighting nausea. The blood on the carpet had crusted in rusty streaks. Taking deep breaths, avoiding the dried pool on the floor, she rapped on the door, which was bolted from the outside. As the guards opened it she swayed, clutching her stomach. "Summon the King . . . hurry!"

Darnley came to her quickly, his hair touseled, his eyes cloudy with sleep. Moaning, she lay on the sofa surrounded by guards. Darnley dismissed them and asked coldly what ailed her.

"The baby," she gasped. "I fear I am losing our baby . . ."

Through half-closed eyes she saw him blanch, read his thought. If the child died, all Scotland, all Europe would hold him guilty. He had signed his name to a bond which Ruthven held.

"I'll summon the physician—"

"No!" she said, "I'll not have him blundering. He knows little of midwifery. I want Lady Huntley."

Darnley hesitated, and she bit her lips till the blood came. Then she heard his footsteps hurrying to the door.

At best, she thought, Lady Huntley can get a message to Bothwell. At worst her presence will be comforting, and I will not feel so isolated. My 'illness' may bring me other privileges—perhaps the midwife from town.

Puffing, her gray curls tucked in a nightcap, Lady Huntley sailed in like a great-prowed ship. But Darnley would not leave them alone. For more than an hour Mary was forced to play her role, writhing on the sofa. Finally Lady Huntley said, "Does Your Majesty feel able to walk into the privy?"

Mary met her wise blue eyes and thought, She knows I am pretending. She has something to tell me and the privy is an excuse.

"I will try," Mary said.

Leaning on Darnley, escorted by a guard, she reached the small stone chamber. Darnley would have entered with them, but Lady Huntley said, "This may be a bloody business, Sire. You'd best remain outside."

When they were alone Mary explained her ruse. "I want you to take a message to Bothwell—"

"He and my son escaped last night to Seton."

"Escaped! But how?"

"They were prisoned with me in the south wing chamber that overlooks the lions' den. That part of the palace wall was unguarded. Lord Bothwell lowered a rope into the den and they descended. The lions growled, and Madam, I near died of terror as I watched; but they climbed over the wall and signaled me that all was well. At Seton they will raise an army to rescue Your Majesty."

"Can you get a message to them?"

"I will find a way, Madam."

"Tell Bothwell I hope to join him at Seton tomorrow night." Hastily she explained her plan. "James arrives soon, perhaps with heavy forces. Bothwell must not come here, lest he be outnumbered and trapped . . ."

Darnley pounded on the door and Lady Huntley opened it. "You'd best carry Her Majesty to bed, Sire . . . The child is in God's hands."

Lady Huntley left them, promising to return later with the professional midwife, and Darnley carried Mary to her bedchamber. She knew he was thoroughly frightened. The scars from her nails where she had raked his chin last night burned red over his pallor. He asked her, over and over again, what he could do, and she told him to pray.

Mary refused food and drink and lay behind the closed bed curtains, moaning occasionally, hearing his pacing footsteps, the gurgle of poured whisky. She must prevent his drinking if she possibly could. Dull-witted he would be of no use to her. She called to him. "Harry . . ."

He drew back a curtain and sat gingerly on the edge of the bed as though fearful of joggling her.

"I feel a bit easier." She smiled wanly. "I think the child came near to death and so death touched me close. At such times we are given divine revelation. I saw that I had wronged you."

"You treated me despicably," he pouted.

"I was hysterical, mad with horror and fear. I did not mean the things I said, Harry." She looked up at him, allowing her eyes to plead for her. "I lack your strength."

"You are a woman." He shrugged.

She sighed. "I was willful and foolish, but not sinful. Rizzio was only my friend and secretary. You know that in your heart."

Softly she added, "Poor Davy, he was so thrilled when you asked him to play tennis. He came running to tell me, awed that you would condescend to invite him. He worshiped you, Harry. You are all he wished to be—handsome, charming, gifted." Her tears were genuine, and she wiped her eyes. "He died without the happiness of love. He said no woman would wed him because he was so repulsive, and he thought his very ugliness protected me from slander. He said, 'The world has only to look at the King and then look at me to know where a woman's heart would lie.' . . . Did the lords really think I was his mistress?"

"Yes. That was all I heard night and day. They pounded at me, calling me cuckold until my pride could bear it no longer."

"You were driven by mad dogs," she said. "Did you indeed sign a bond with them?"

"A bond?" He blinked.

"Ruthven claims he has a bond signed by you. I saw the paper in his hand."

"Oh—that." But he found bravado impossible and hung his head.

"I signed two bonds. One guaranteed impunity for the murderers."

May God damn him. "And what did the other provide?" she asked gently.

"That I pardon James and his rebels and restore their lands. Dissolve your Parliament and appoint another acceptable to the lords." His voice shook. "That I support the Protestant religion."

"Nom de Dieu! And what do the lords grant you in return?"

"The new Parliament will grant me the Crown Matrimonial, and the lords will recognize me as absolute ruler."

"Do you imagine for an instant that James will allow you to rule or give you the crown? Can you not see his plan—to destroy us both, proclaim himself Regent and stamp out Scots Catholicism forever? Harry, we are lost!"

"The bond protects me."

"It implicates you. It does not protect you, for men of honor did not sign it."

Darnley argued with her weakly, unable to refute the points she made.

"Is James the sort of man to change overnight?" she asked. "Was it not he who opposed my marriage to you? Do you begin to see the truth? They will kill us!"

He gulped, stammered. "What will I do?" He looked about the room as though seeking escape. Eying the whisky decanter he started to rise.

"No," she said, grasping his hand, "if ever you needed all your wits it is now. They are counting on you to be helpless with drink when James arrives." She tightened her hold on his hand. "It is easy to kill a man when he's sodden or deep in wine-sleep."

"What will I do?" he repeated. "You must think of something." He bent to her, rubbed his cheek against hers. "I will forgive you if you will help me. I was duped . . . but you are clever. You can save me if you put your mind to it. Your mind is trained to intrigue," he added magnanimously.

She concealed her disgust with a smile. "I am trying to think, but I have little strength. You must be strong for both of us, and for the child. I implore you not to drink—not a drop until we are safe."

He promised.

She asked, "Was Lethington a party to the conspiracy?"

"He signed the bond, then fled to Dunkeld in the Highlands."

A cautious traitor, she thought.

Darnley moistened parched lips. "Think of something," he whined. "Tell me what to do."

"You must not let the lords know we are reconciled. Speak of me with contempt. Try to find out what they intend to do with me."

"They await James's instructions," he blurted.

"You see?" she said triumphantly. "Not yours. Tell them I wish to see James as soon as he arrives . . . Go now, and for God's sake play your role carefully. We are doomed if you fail."

Mary raised her arms and he came into them. Revolted, she lifted her lips, forced them to cling to his. She pulled his hand to her breast, spoke languorously. "It has been so long, love . . . No," she said, as he started to lie beside her, "I am still too weak. For the sake of the child I dare not. But later . . ."

"I will bed with you tonight," he said.

An hour later Mary pretended excruciating pain and Darnley summoned the midwife. To Mary's relief he left them alone. She dared not try to fool a woman long experienced in such matters, so she said, "My pains are eased now that you have come. Your presence comforts me. I am prey to terrible fancies."

"And no wonder, Madam." The hard black eyes turned soft. "Try to sleep. I will be nearby."

At seven o'clock Mary heard the heavy drum of hoofs over the drawbridge, shouting and cheering in the courtyard. James has arrived, she thought, and went into the audience chamber to await him, bidding the midwife to remain in the bedchamber.

But James did not come for nearly two hours. Mary was half-asleep on the couch when the bolt on the door was unlatched and James, in a great black cloak, came through the doorway.

Mary rose to meet him, purposely tottering. He caught her in his arms and held her close, his frosty cheek against hers. She looked up and saw that his eyes were moist with hypocritical tears.

"Had you been here," she said, "they would not have treated me so!"

"I was appalled to hear of this," he said, helping her back to the sofa. "You, ill and confined—Rizzio dead—unbelievable!"

She encouraged his pretense of innocence, turned it to her own advantage. "Harry is the ringleader," she said, and poured out the story of Rizzio's death. "Harry *wants* me to lose the child. He'd have killed me, but he lacked the courage."

"I warned you about him," James said virtuously.

"If only I had listened to you!" She winced, her hand to her stomach.

His eyes were a green glitter in the rushlight. "I am told you have terrible cramps."

"Yes, they come and go. And each time I fear the baby is dead, but by some miracle it still lives."

From under his sleepy lids he was examining her carefully, and she thought, Likely he has little knowledge of women with child. I can fool him as I fool Harry . . .

"You must be very careful," James said. "Rest."

"How can I rest? The guards tramp back and forth and I cannot sleep. Why must they be here? I could not possibly escape in this condition. To ride a horse would shake me to pieces, doom the child to certain death."

He nodded. "And you hold Darnley responsible for all this?"

"Yes. And I am helpless. He commands the palace. He brags that he will command you too."

The thin black eyebrows raised. "He does, eh?"

"Indeed, you have never seen such peacocking. May God damn him!" she said in sudden fury. "He almost makes me hate his child!"

James was silent, playing with the velvet fringe of his cloak. The clock struck nine, a thin French tinkle with a music-box sweetness. He said, "You cannot be at the mercy of this fool. We must get rid of him."

"Yes," she said, "but not yet." *Not until I have used him against you.* "If my child lives Harry must acknowledge its legitimacy by being present at the christening when it is six months old. Otherwise there will be scandalous speculation."

"December." He made a little steeple of his fingers, then turned his lazy green stare upon her. "I think," he said, "that we understand each other at last."

"I think so too." She smiled.

At midnight Mary received Darnley in her bed, caressed him to passion but denied him fulfillment. "I dare not risk the child. But I shall rest and surely by tomorrow night I will be well enough—"

"But I want you now!"

"With the babe dead between us?"

She kissed his cheek, his throat. "We have years ahead, sweet, if we are careful." She would reveal her plan of escape gradually, a bit at a time, lest he drink and babble it. "Tomorrow, tell the lords that I'll pardon them, provided they remove their troops and guards from Holyrood. Give them your word that I will not escape—and speak of me grimly, resentfully."

"I'll complain that you refuse me your bed."

"Good. And when you leave me now, take the main staircase and appear sullen or angry as though we had quarreled. The guards will note it."

"James may see through this."

"He thinks I loathe you, that I blame you for everything, whereas —heaven help me—I rely on your strength as I do on God's."

[258]

He pulled her close and kissed her. "No," she said. "Tomorrow night . . ."

Reluctantly, he got up and put on his robe. When she heard the guards unbolt the door for him she rose, retching, to scrub herself clean.

Late the next afternoon Darnley brought James, Morton and Ruthven to Mary's apartments. The carpets had been washed of blood and pulled over to hide the stained floor. Workmen had repaired the door to the bedchamber, where Mary lay in bed under a fur robe.

She said, "As I have told the King, I wish to pardon both rebels and assassins. But he tells me you will not believe it save from my own lips."

"And lips may lie," Ruthven growled.

Controlling her rage, she said, "You need not trust my lips. You may draft a document of pardon and I will sign it, provided you withdraw all troops. To be constantly watched is humiliating, and God knows I could not travel if I wished to. If you doubt that ask the midwife or Lady Huntley."

"Why this sudden forgiveness?" Morton's fingers bushed his reddish beard. "It smacks of trickery."

"She won't trick me," Darnley said. "I'll vouch for her staying right here until the babe is born. You have my word on it."

"More binding than the King's word," James said insolently, "is the Queen's written pardon. If we draft the pardons and she signs them, how can there be trickery?"

The lords argued among themselves and finally agreed to draw up documents, which would be ready for Mary's signature that evening. Darnley brought them to her after she had supped.

"The troops are withdrawing, Mary!"

She was relieved, but there was difficulty ahead. "Where are the lords?"

"Supping at Morton's house. They thought it best to be out of the palace lest folk say you were forced to sign the pardons under duress."

Morton's house was on the other side of the abbey, too near for comfort, and she said, "Go there and tell them that I am asleep but that you will wake me to sign the documents if they wish. Encourage them to drink if you can do so without arousing suspicion."

"I'll rouse their suspicion if I don't drink."

"Tell them your stomach ails you."

He nodded. "What do you plan?"

"I'll tell you later," she said. "In an hour, when you return."

Obediently, he left. An hour passed and she cursed herself for a fool to think Darnley would remain sober in a celebrating group. Then she heard his footsteps on the private stairs and he came in, steady, clear-eyed, smiling.

"They drink heavily," he said. "You may sign the documents in the morning."

She laughed. "By morning you and I will be safe at Seton."

"Seton! But that is ten miles! You could not ride that far." Then his voice wheedled. "Could you, sweetheart? Could you not ride pillion?"

"Pillion or bareback, I will ride," she said, and began to prepare for the journey. She sent for Captain Erskine, asked him to choose a trustworthy soldier to accompany them, and have horses saddled and waiting in the abbey graveyard. At midnight they would take Darnley's equerry, Anthony Standen, and Margaret Carwood, one of her tirewomen.

Mary dressed in warm woolen plaids, laid out a fur cloak. She packed a small chest with her most valuable jewels, state papers, quill and ink. Darnley went to his apartments to arm himself. He would await her on the private stairs.

Gradually the palace quieted. The last troops rode off and the servants retired to their quarters. From her windows Mary could see the usual sentries at Holyrood Gate, and heard the changing of the guard at the drawbridge.

She took the writs of pardon and threw them in the fire, watching them burn to ash. Then she crept down the private stairs, joining Darnley as the Canongate clock bonged midnight.

They tiptoed down the cold stone steps past the butler's pantry and the cupbearers' room. These servants were French, and Mary felt sure they would not raise an alarm if they saw her. But no one was about. They entered the cellar, groping through pitch-blackness. Ahead flickered candles, and they came into the subterranean burial vaults, where deathlights burned through the centuries, revealing the carved stone effigies of Stuart kings and queens, the coffins and crypts of monks and nuns. It was cold, penetratingly damp. Darnley's hand tightened in Mary's and he murmured an Ave Maria.

Finally they felt fresh air and pushed open a broken door that led into the moonlit churchyard. As they ran toward the horses tethered by the abbey wall, Darnley stumbled and looked down in horror at a new grave.

"Rizzio!" he said.

Mary knelt on the mound. There was neither grass nor flower nor stone to mark his resting place. She made a cross in the earth with her gloved hand. "I swear another shall lie as low before a year has passed."

Darnley plucked at her shoulder. "James?"

She rose, dusting the earth from her gloves. "Who but him?"

They hurried to Erskine. He lifted Mary up to a pillion on his big gelding, then mounted in front of her. Margaret Carwood rode with the soldier. Darnley led the group, his equerry beside him.

As they cantered toward the palace gates, Mary lowered the hood of her cloak. Both arms around Erskine's waist, she hid her face in his leather-coated back.

"Who goes there?" shouted a sentry.

Darnley's voice was inaudible to Mary. There was a long moment of silence. She thought, We are trapped . . .

"Pass on, Sire."

II.

The horses raced through the windy moonlight over the moors toward Seton. Every lurch panicked Mary, for though Erskine moderated the gelding's pace there were treacherous moss hags, sudden plunges. Her body ached from constant tension against shock. But she thought, Only my mind is in pain . . .

She tried to shut out the horrors that crowded it, as she shut her eyes to the breathtaking, eye-blurring wind. Clutching Erskine, she listened to the sharp clop of hoofs on frosty ground, to the steady beat of her heart. Under her heart, did the child lie safe? Or was she shaking it toward oblivion?

As they neared Seton, a company of horsemen with flaming torches swept out from a wood to their rear, and Darnley, who was riding ahead, turned back and flogged Mary's horse with his whip.

"Come on!" he screamed. "For the love of God, come on! They will murder us!"

"I dare not go faster," Mary said, as Erskine checked the frantic gelding. "I'd rather be caught than lose the child."

"If this babe dies we can have another. Hurry!"

"Save yourself then," she shouted furiously. "Ride on!"

Darnley spurred his horse and galloped on with his equerry, disappearing over a hill. Mary turned. There must be two hundred pursuers—highwaymen, she thought, or a battle clan. Surely it was too soon for James's men or the Douglases to have caught up with her. She would throw herself on the mercy of the leader of this company, trusting that her condition and small retinue would rouse his pity.

"Halt," she ordered Erskine. He shouted her command, and the soldier ahead drew rein.

As the torches flamed close, showering sparks, Mary saw Bothwell on a great black stallion, his red cloak ballooning, his red hair tousled from wind. Lords Huntley and Seton rode behind him, followed by scar-faced, leather-jacked Borderers on their shaggy ponies.

"Thank God!" she said.

"Are you all right, Madam?" Bothwell asked anxiously.

"Yes," she said, limp with relief, "now that you are here."

"The King took fright, eh?" He grinned, snapped an order to his men. "You Hepburns follow the King and escort him to Dunbar."

"Dunbar?" Mary asked as the men rode off. "Why not Seton?"

"Seton House is too vulnerable. We'd not be safe. Can you manage another seventeen miles?"

Mary nodded. A mile ago she would have been unable, but Bothwell's vitality roused her own. She sat up straight, her panic shed. "Wherever you say, my lord."

They reached Dunbar at daybreak, clattering along the cobbled High Street that wound down a hill to the shore. Touched by sunrise, the red sandstone castle seemed afire on a chain of iron-black rocks that stretched into the sea. The cavalcade rode across a fortified passage from the mainland and Mary, supported by Erskine and Margaret Carwood, entered the tomb-cold hall.

The castle was unfurnished, rock-walled, floored with earth. Soldiers built a fire in the Great Hall and arranged a pallet of blankets for Mary by the hearth. But she lay down for only a few minutes. Sleep was a waste of time. She sat on the floor in the firelight and wrote dispatches summoning all loyal subjects to join her and ride against the rebels at Holyrood. By mid-morning, couriers were speeding her messages throughout Scotland.

Darnley arrived while Mary and her nobles were eating eggs at makeshift barrel tables by the fire. "Who is in charge here?" he demanded as the men rose.

"I am governor of the castle," Bothwell said. "Welcome, Sire."

"A fine welcome!" Darnley spread his jeweled hand, indicating the bare hall. "No chairs, no tapestries—is this your idea of entertaining Her Majesty and me?"

"Is this your gratitude for safe shelter?" Mary snapped. "We owe our lives to Lord Bothwell. Had he not escaped Holyrood—"

"I was not speaking to you, Madam, but to him."

"This is a fortress," Bothwell said, as though he addressed a child, "not a play-palace. But my men are preparing your suite as best they can."

"I shall go there and sleep. But first I wish madeira."

"Order a servant, then," Mary said sharply.

"Bothwell is my servant."

Slowly she shook her head. "He was. So was every noble, every

[262]

subject in the land. But no longer. You give no orders save to your own attendants."

Darnley's jaw fell. "What has come over you? Last night—"

"Last night I did what was expedient." She flushed. "Now I do as I wish."

"Are these the words of a loving wife?"

"No," she said, "they are not."

Crimson under the cold eyes of Bothwell and Huntley, he turned and started across the room. But midway he paused and turned, shivering.

"It's freezing," he pouted. "I shall go to my suite."

"One of the soldiers will take you there," Bothwell said carelessly.

After Darnley had left, Mary told them all that had happened. "If I had any mercy left for Harry he killed it in eight words: 'If this babe dies we can have another.'"

Bothwell swore. "If he signed bonds with the murderers and the rebels, you can have his head for treason."

"But I need him to acknowledge the child."

"Her Majesty is right," Huntley said. "Folk are likely to say the child is Rizzio's."

"God grant," Bothwell said wryly, "that it is light and lady-faced."

"And that it lives," Mary said. She was suddenly exhausted, so desperate for sleep that she stumbled as she rose. Bothwell caught her arm and she said, "Please take me to my chamber."

He swung her into his arms and carried her up a flight of stairs and along a corridor to a room where a turf fire burned. A pallet of horsehides lay near the hearth and he set her gently down on it, then bent to draw blankets over her.

"Shall I send for your woman?" he asked.

"No."

"You are not in pain?"

"No, just tired."

"Is there aught I can do?"

"Yes." She lay on her back, staring up at the shadows that moved on the ceiling. "Stay here until I sleep."

He sat down on the floor beside her, removed the little velvet coif that slipped sideways on her hair. Her lashes fluttered, and he said, "Sleep."

Eyes shut, she listened to the crackling fire, to the wind that pounded the fortress like a battering ram. She could hear the crash of the sea on the rocks, the roar of surf. I am safe, she thought. He is here and I am safe.

"You are all I have now," she said, opening her eyes. "All I have in the world."

"Ssh . . . you have the child."

"Harry's child, a loathsome, monstrous growth!"

"Is it fair to hate the child for its father's crimes?"

"Who prates of justice?" she scoffed. "Not I. I have reaped its rewards."

"Yet you protect the child."

"Yes, for it shall be—God willing—the first king to rule Scotland and England. It triply guarantees my succession to Elizabeth."

"So it does. But I think the babe will mean more to you than a political tool."

"Then you think sentimentally, my lord."

"You're still severely shocked. You've endured hell. In a few days you will feel different."

"Those who endure hell return bedeviled," she said. "My faith taught me to leave vengeance to God. But I shall not rest until Harry has suffered as Rizzio suffered. A slow stabbing, a day-by-day, hour-by-hour knifing of the mind."

"The wretch deserves it," Bothwell said, "but I remember what Rizzio said to me one night when I asked him how he bore the lords' insults: 'It's hard enough to be misshapen. Hate cripples the spirit.'"

"Then I'll be lamed for life, and gladly."

"You'd best not place all your hate in one basket," he said. "What of James?"

"It will be impossible to prove James's complicity, for I'm sure he was too shrewd to sign the bonds."

Bothwell nodded. "But James is more dangerous than Darnley. You must split James's alliance with Morton and the Douglases."

"How?"

"Proclaim Morton and his conspirators outlaws. Pardon James."

"Pardon him!"

"Yes. Continue to pretend that you believe him innocent of the murder plot. Forgive his rebellion against you. If you don't, he will likely flee to England with Morton. This time Elizabeth may join them to overthrow you when you are most helpless in child-sickness. I'd sooner have James at court where I can watch him than have him conspiring on the Border."

"Perhaps you are right," she said. "We have proven that James can do little alone. But with Morton's help, and Elizabeth's . . . I will think about this, my lord. I must ask Rizzio . . ."

She bit her lip, turned her wet eyes to the fire. There was only Bothwell now, a lion among hyenas.

"Madam," he said, "you *must* sleep."

"I've lost the need for it," she said, sitting up and throwing off the blankets. "And I must be alert—"

"For what? My men are ready. Others are rallying. You've sent your dispatches. Leave the rest to me—or don't you trust me?"

"Yes," she said, turning to face him, "I trust you."

And I love you. Desperately, shamelessly, and too late. I love you beyond my vows to God, my loyalty to Jean. Beyond fear of hell or hope of heaven.

"What are you thinking, Madam?"

That life is short as a dagger and as treacherous. I could die as Rizzio did, or in childbirth. But I shall not die without knowing your lips and your arms; whether your hair is soft to touch or crisp as October leaves. I shall not die without seizing what happiness I can.

"My thoughts?" She smiled and shrugged. "I was wishing I had brought another gown."

III.

Five days later, heading four thousand spearmen, Mary and Darnley left Dunbar for Edinburgh. Scorning a litter, she rode the big gelding, Bothwell behind her with his Borderers and four companies of infantry. On a road near Haddington they were met by Mary's ambassador to England, Sir James Melville.

"Madam, Morton and the conspirators have fled to England and Knox to Ayrshire!"

"Knox has fled?" she asked, astonished and delighted.

"He dubs it a 'call,' Madam. But note he is 'called' as your army advances and the conspirators flee. I'm told that he had a sermon prepared in advance of the murder, thanking God for Rizzio's death. He preached it last Sunday while you were prisoned at Holyrood."

"May he rot in Ayrshire!"

"Also, I bring you a message from Lord James. He states he has severed relations with all those who conspired in Rizzio's death and humbly awaits Your Majesty's orders from St. Andrews."

"Tell him I was outraged by his rebellion against me, but that I shall pardon him because—" She winced at the lie—"he had no part in the murder. However, he shall not come to court, nor Lethington either, until my temper cools."

Darnley's eyes were big with fright. "Surely you'd not pardon James!"

"Control your cowardice," she said coldly, and spurred her horse.

As Mary entered Edinburgh the guns on Castle Rock thundered welcome, and cheering crowds followed through the turreted West Port into the Grassmarket and the West Bow. Tinsmiths, goldsmiths, armorers and their leather-aproned apprentices left their shops and stalls to trail Mary into the Lawn Market and onto the High Street. The tall timbered houses, leaning together as though in gossip, were packed from galleries to gabled windows, and boys clung to the sloping eaves and chimney pots.

"A royal welcome," Darnley said, taking the adulation to himself. He bowed from the saddle and blew kisses to the crowd. Small boys pantomiming drunkenness reeled and stumbled, and Darnley beamed approval. He does not recognize a slur when he sees it, Mary thought. He finds no difference between a smile and a sneer.

At the Market Cross Mary halted the procession, and her heralds raised their trumpets in proclamation. Morton, his Douglases, Ruthven, Lindsay, Kerr, Bellenden and others were declared outlaws for conspiring in Rizzio's murder. Altogether there were seventy-three.

"A pointless gesture," Darnley yawned, "when they have already fled."

"It is Scottish law," Mary said, exasperated. "Your name would be among them were you not—God help us—my husband."

Darnley's angry retort was lost in the blare of trumpets as the heralds ended the ceremony. Mary signaled her guards to ride on.

"To Holyrood, Madam?" Erskine asked.

"No," she shuddered. "I shall stay in Lord Hume's house in Bell's Wynd until the castle is prepared for me."

She preferred Edinburgh Castle to the haunted Holyrood. Behind its bars, on its impregnable rock, she would bear her child. Not a pleasant place, but safe from memories too poignant, safe from the lost soul of Rizzio . . .

"I will have Rizzio interred in the Royal Crypt in the abbey," Mary said, her eyes cold on Darnley's. "Bishop Ross will say Solemn Requiem Mass."

Darnley nodded gravely. "I should like to be present."

In penitence? She was stirred by a tiny hope. One thing we share, Harry and I—our faith. It is the last link between us. For though he signed a bond against Catholicism, and I defied God, it is not too late to repent our sins and begin again.

They rode on toward Bell's Wynd, met by the white mists of the meadows.

Darnley said, "I wonder what happened to that big diamond Rizzio wore. Surely they did not bury it with him."

Sickened, she turned from him and rode on in silence.

IV.

The Clamshell Turnpike House, named for the shells that ornamented its staircase tower, became Mary's temporary court. Bothwell
set up field guns in the garden and placed a heavy guard around
Bell's Wynd to the High Street. Soldiers were sent to Holyrood to
bring Mary's ladies and favorite servants, her chests and wardrobes.
She had worn the same plaid gown for nearly a week, and now she
put on deep mourning and attended Mass for Rizzio and Father
Black at the abbey. A veil hid her tears from the crowd, but her
shoulders shook perceptibly as she rode back to the house. Darnley
admonished her, calling her shameless. "They think you weep for
a lover."

In Parliament House at a meeting of the Privy Council, Darnley
protested his innocence of the murder: "Upon my honor and word
as King I never knew, advised, ordered or approved the conspiracy
and violence offered Her Majesty. I only consented to the recall of
the rebels without the Queen's knowledge, and in that I admit I
did wrong."

"And your name on this murder bond, Sire?" Huntley asked
grimly, pointing to a copy Ruthven had sent from Newcastle. "Is
this signature forged?"

"It was signed under duress—a Douglas dag at my side. I could
not help—"

"We know the facts," Mary interrupted. "Let us on with the farce.
You will nail proclamation of your innocence at the Market Cross.
It will fool no one. But for the sake of the child we must protect your
honor."

Haughtily, Darnley asked, "Who questions my honor? I am King."

She thought, In love I lifted you to kingship. In loathing I can
fling you down to the shame you merit, degrade you before Europe.
And not a man here but will support me.

She looked about the great oak-paneled room at the rows of nobles
who sat grimly, slit-eyed and silent. Bothwell was the only one
Elizabeth could not buy nor circumstance change. The rest were
chameleons, altering color to English gold or James's persuasion. But
all were aligned against Darnley.

"I cannot be judged," Darnley said, taking their silence for awe.
"Only my peers may judge me, and none rank above me."

"I rank above you, Sire," Mary said, "and I shall strip you of
honor as you sought to strip me." She turned to her nobles. "My
lords, you see before you a master of treachery." *Surpassing even
yourselves.* "He betrayed me as Queen and wife, betrayed the church
he was sworn to defend, and then betrayed his bond of conspiracy."

She raised her hand as Darnley opened his mouth to protest. "Except by my command he attends no public functions, shares in no councils, signs no documents." She turned to face Huntley, whom she had appointed Chancellor in Morton's place. "All coins bearing his image shall be withdrawn from circulation."

Darnley spluttered with rage. "You dare to humiliate me—"

Ignoring him, she said, "As an example to the exiled murderers, we shall hang, draw and quarter their henchmen who held the gates and corridors of Holyrood." She read from a list. "Tom Scott, Henry Yair . . ."

And so that week bloody heads decorated the tower of Holyrood and the Netherbow Port. "Like old times," Mistress McDoon said cheerily. "In your father's day we could look up to a port or turret, see a death-grin and feel right lucky to be alive."

But I would be better dead, Mary thought. More and more often she considered death as a release. From Darnley, from her weathercock nobles, from the temptation of her love for Bothwell. For she knew that her love was no whim. It had smoldered for years, a banked fire. When the child was born and she regained her strength, she could be consumed by it. Unless she sent Bothwell away.

But who else could hold Scotland against Elizabeth, James and the exiled lords? Who else could govern while she was helpless in childbed? Her thoughts circled, returned always to the unalterable fact that she could not survive without Bothwell, neither as Queen nor as woman.

Bothwell sat in her councils throughout April. He rode to the Border, spread a net of his agents to watch the exiles in Newcastle, sent others into the Highlands to spy on James and Lethington. What little free time he had was spent with Jean at Crichton.

"I have ruined your honeymoon," Mary said one evening as he prepared to leave her house for a weekend at Crichton. "Poor Jean must be lonely."

"She is, Madam."

"Do you want her here?"

"If you need her. I'll be on the Border in June."

She hesitated. Jean's prattle of a happy marriage would hurt her, but her calm presence would be comforting during the confinement.

"Ask Jean to come to me when I move into the castle."

"She will be delighted. And I suggest you supervise James by inviting him and Lady Agnes to stay at the castle too."

Mary laughed. "A stroke of genius! There we can watch him!"

"And there," Bothwell grinned, "he can watch Darnley."

"Machiavelli! For that I shall give you Haddington Abbey."

"You jest."

"Not at all. Haddington was yours by hereditary right before Lethington maneuvered it to himself. Also, I'm giving you the lands around Dunbar. After all, you must support and feed the castle garrison."

"Thank you." Sardonically he added, "Now I will be better hated than ever. There's not one of your nobles who'd not cut my throat of a dark night."

"Was it not always so?"

"I was not always rich. I had less power."

"You govern the Border and command the fleet and the army. But I want more for you."

He shook his head. "Women with child are barmy."

"What do you know of women with child?" she teased.

"My women were *always* with child," he said gloomily. "My wife is the only one not caught."

"Anna Throndsen?" she asked.

"Our son died at birth."

"I understand that one of your children lives with your mother at Morham. Who is its mother?"

"Damned if I know," he said. "It was left in a basket on my mother's doorstep with a note claiming me as the father. A redheaded boy."

"How many children do you have?" she asked.

"Great God!" he roared. "How should I know? Can one believe every wench one tumbles? I gave them money when I had it, or stole them sheep from the English, or relieved a cottage from the Elliotts—why do you laugh, Madam?"

"Because," she said, tears in her eyes, "you are so—"

Outrageous, honest, lovable . . .

"—amusing."

"It's good to hear you laugh," he said, "even if I'm the butt . . . Well, I'd best be off." He picked up his cloak, paused. "Unless you need me?"

"I am well protected here." Mary indicated the iron bars he had set in the casements facing the High Street. "Each time I leave this room I trip on your troops." She lifted her chin. "I am not afraid, truly I'm not."

He stood hesitant and she said, "You must not deprive Jean, since she sees you so rarely. And you need a few days in the country."

"Every hour I'd worry, knowing you vulnerable here." He threw down his cloak. "I'm staying until you're safe in the castle."

Careful not to show her delight, she said, "I am happy to have you. But are you sure Jean will understand?"

"Why not?" He looked at her, startled. "You cannot think she'd be jealous?"

"Lonely women have strange fancies."

"Not Jean. She'd best not be jealous," he growled. "If there is any creature I abhor it's a suspicious woman, spying and prying, snooping and peering. If Jean were jealous I'd not live with her a day. But she is sensible. Besides," he laughed, eyes teasing, "she knows Your Majesty's child is your chastity belt."

"You are presumptuous!"

"You are smiling," he said.

V.

Edinburgh Castle, grim as a bared sword, was redecorated for Mary's confinement. The damp walls were tapestried in gilded leather, or hung with green velvet brocade embroidered with gold leaves and holly boughs. Sixteen Turkey carpets covered the floors, and carved oak furniture was brought from Holyrood.

Mary chose the pleasantest suite in the melancholy maze of rooms. She had a large antechamber with an oriel window overlooking the High Street and the town wall. There was room for her cabinets of gold-clasped, jewel-studded books, her writing desk and a chest containing state papers. The walls were hung with gold cloth, the chairs cushioned in purple velvet. Here she received visitors and ate most of her meals, which were prepared in an adjoining kitchen.

A tiny oak-paneled bedchamber completed the suite. It was eight feet square, just large enough to accommodate her gold-curtained bed and night table. From its mullioned window Mary could see St. Giles reaching above the red-roofed town that clustered on the backbone of the rock.

She was grateful for the massive safety of her fortress, but depressed by its darkness. Tapers in topaz holders and wall sconces burned day and night at her desk and bed, yet there was no cheer. When she walked about the ramparts on her way to or from St. Margaret's Chapel the height and dizzy vistas frightened her. As the wet spring passed, she spent more and more time on her bed, a book unread in her hands or her embroidery neglected beside her. Her body was heavy with child, her mind heavier with foreboding. The midwife said her labor might be difficult. The physician seemed falsely cheerful.

Darnley sulked or swaggered, depending on the amount he drank. At night he left the castle to wander Edinburgh's taverns and brothels, reeling home at dawn. Now he was visiting his father in

Glasgow, doubtless spreading the story of his ill-treatment at court and his outrage at James's return.

James and his wife had been with Mary for a month, watched by Bothwell's spies who, in the guise of servants, attended their suite in the east wing of the castle. Each day James came to Mary with fruit or flowers, a book or a new ballad. In the role of anxious and loving brother, he begged to be of service. Sir James Balfour handled Scottish internal affairs, but she allowed her brother James to shoulder some of the burdens of state. Under Bothwell's surveillance and without allies he was harmless.

On this warm May morning James sat at Mary's bedside, while Lady Agnes in the window seat embroidered a baby dress.

"When does Darnley return from Glasgow?" James asked.

Mary shrugged indifferently.

"God knows I share your distaste for him. But you treat him so arrogantly that you may force him to some desperate act."

"Doubtless he and his father are plotting against me. But the Lennoxes do not worry me." She did not add that Bothwell's agents watched Darnley as closely as they watched James.

"If you wish the world to think you are a reconciled couple, can you not pretend some regard for Darnley until the child is born?"

"No. For if I pretend affection he will plague me for power—and for his marital rights," she added bitterly.

Lady Agnes primmed her mouth. "Surely he doesn't try to share your bed in your eighth month?"

"He tried last week," Mary said. "My revulsion and the child's safety mean nothing to him. All I can do is ignore him."

"Is that Bothwell's advice?" James asked gently.

The gentleness, the apparent casualness of the question did not deceive her. Although, at Bothwell's suggestion, he and James had again sworn friendship, their hatred was raw under the bandage of expediency. James, she knew, hoped Bothwell could influence her to divorce Darnley after the child's christening. Once rid of Darnley, James could turn his wits to removing Bothwell and restoring his own power.

"Bothwell's advice has proved sound," Mary said. "For the first time I feel secure. He holds the Border against Morton and Elizabeth, and his ships patrol the coasts. The power of our army has frightened even Knox into flight. Or else his guilty conscience did so."

James stroked Mary's spaniel that dozed at her feet. "Poor Knox."

"Poor Knox indeed! I am told that in Ayrshire he asks his terrible God to deliver me stillborn."

"He is tormented by fear of failure, and he lacks your weapons.

You must remember he is an old man fighting a young, beautiful and almost legendary woman. You have caught the imagination of the people and won them from him. The lords of his congregation bow to your whims. He was unable to outlaw the Mass. He said to me once, 'God gave the Queen the power of enchantment wherein men are bewitched. He gave me only faith. Sometimes . . . my faith wavers and I am close to despair.' "

"I can scarce credit that."

"It's true. When news came that you were returning here with your army and he saw the people bannering their houses and laying tapestries over their galleries, he was close to tears. He walked along the High Street leaning on his staff, admonishing his congregation. 'The idolatress returns with the Romish Mass—yet you strew boughs in her path!' And from the pulpit that same day he asked, 'My God, My God—why hast thou forsaken me?' "

If I could believe James, she thought, I might be touched. For I share the pain of the God-forsaken, I know what it means to pray futilely. But James seeks to convert me at the edge of childbirth and insure a Protestant prince.

"Knox connived in Rizzio's murder," she said, "by rousing Harry's jealousy. He had preknowledge of the crime and did not warn me. That is treason I shall never forgive."

"But to understand is to forgive," Lady Agnes said piously.

"I understand Knox as a false prophet. And I do not forgive the slaughter of innocents."

"If only you could realize Knox's sincerity—" James began.

"I don't doubt his sincerity. But so was Herod sincere, so was Nero. Let us not prate of sincerity; it is no virtue of itself." Anger wearied her and James's arguments bored her. "I shall try to sleep."

After they left her, she summoned Jean to draw the hangings against the sun. But she could not sleep. She relived the moments with Bothwell, every word, every glance. Only once, last October, had he ever indicated any attraction to her. She remembered her words at the Victory Ball: "I should seek danger more often," and his retort as he bent toward her: "You've not far to seek." Had he been jesting? Was that enough to dream on?

He pities me now, she thought, because I am helpless. My condition arouses his gallantry. If I knew he loved Jean I might have the strength to resist my obsession. But I am not sure whether he loves her or merely respects her. Only she can tell me what I need to know . . .

Mary blew a little gold whistle, and Jean returned to the bedchamber, moving softly in her velvet slippers.

"Yes, Madam?"

"I cannot sleep," Mary said, "Sit down and talk to me. Tell me about Haddington Abbey. Your mother says you have made it lovely and livable."

Jean described the landscaping and furnishings. There was a lilt to her voice, an enthusiasm that bubbled over the calm surface of her words. How greatly she has changed in a scant three months, Mary thought. She seems far younger, quick to blush, her poise upset by happiness.

"You have forgotten Alex, haven't you?" Mary asked.

"Yes, Madam. I must have been daft to love Alex. Compared to my lord, he is a gaukie."

"I'm happy you've come to your senses. In truth, I was worried about your marriage. I feared that it was arranged for convenience."

"It was, Madam. But now I'm enthralled by my lord!"

"He too must be enthralled."

The gray eyes clouded. "He is not in love as I am, but I know he is content. He tells me he is no longer so restless nor so moody. He compliments my order of our estates. He says I am a perfect wife."

"Surely he admits love for you?"

"No, Madam, but oddly it does not matter. Just to be near him is all I ask. I think he has some stubborn fear of love."

"Perhaps his many affairs diffused his emotion so that he has none left."

"Perhaps. Yet in time I know he will soften." Jean took a note from her bodice. "He wrote me from Liddesdale. Here, Madam, read it."

My Lady, she read. *I am off to Jedburgh tomorrow and thence to Hawick. It is best I remain on the Border through Her Majesty's confinement, but I beg you will send a courier to Hermitage the moment the babe is born. I miss you and trust you are in good health.* B.

"He misses me!" Jean said. "Never before did he say that he missed me!"

"I am so happy for you," Mary murmured.

So Jean lives on crumbs, survives on hope. She has not his love. Smiling, Mary stretched and yawned. "I think I can sleep now."

VI.

Mary prepared for birth—and death. Her will was made, her confession heard. On June 18th, bishops, priests and physicians hovered in the antechamber with Du Croc, the French Ambassador, and Sir William Stanley, Elizabeth's envoy. Beaton's aunt, Lady Reres,

settled her great bulk in the chair by Mary's bed. She would supervise the midwife and wet-nurse the baby.

The gray afternoon slipped by. Half-dozing, Mary heard whispers,
the telling of beads. James tiptoed in and out. Lord Robert placed
an armful of roses on the bed table. She smelled whisky, as Darnley
bent over her.

"Mary," he said, "I love you . . . forgive me."

Eyes closed, she pretended to sleep. She would not forgive him
even on the rim of death, nor James. Ruthven was dead of consumption in Newcastle, a wandering spirit forever cursed . . .

She sank into sleep. Rizzio's hands clutched her skirt, his blood
spurted, soaking his russet coat. He caught at her bed fringe and was
dragged away, screaming through a cut throat . . .

"*Madam!*"

She was sobbing, and the room was full of people. Pain slashed
her stomach and she dug her fists into her mouth.

Arnault, the surgeon, ordered all but the midwives from the room.
He slipped a piece of barley bread under Mary's pillow to please the
fairies and protect her from their malice.

The pain subsided. The clock struck six. Rain thrashed the castle,
and Mary blinked as lightning flashed through the room. She lay
motionless, bracing herself against the next pain, rigid with fear.

Lady Reres said, "I mind the time I attended a poor lass in Doni-
bristle. She had neither bread, iron nor Bible for her bed, and the
fairies gave her no peace. Then when the babe was born—and a
cherub he was, like a hawthorne bud—the fairies stole him from the
cradle and left a kettle-black imp in his place."

"I've seen changelings too," the midwife said. "In Blairgowrie
there's a horrible harelipped babe—"

Mary's voice shrilled. "My child must be watched every moment,
do you hear? It must not be left alone an instant. You must swear—"

Pain shook her, sharper, deep-stabbing. Again she stifled her
screams, clutching the bedclothes. Pain and cessation, pain that
ground and tore and left her sweat-drenched and gasping. She spoke
God's name, knowing he would not help her. For she had not truly
confessed to Bishop Ross. If she died there was eternal hell, hell
worse than this . . .

She lost sense of time and place and identity. A lion paced its
chain in St. Germain, twining her in metal links that cut her flesh.
At Amboise, four white horses tore her apart and thundered across
a petal-strewn bridge. The Cardinal smiled and drew a lacy handkerchief to his lips as she walked into Ruthven's sword.

At midnight she was conscious, racked. They trickled brandywine
down her throat, toweled her face, clamped down her thrashing arms.

She screamed for Bishop Ross and when he came she whispered with her lips tight against his ear.

"I love sinfully . . ."

But her words were smashed back in her body by pain that raged and ravaged. She had tried to confess. Perhaps God would forgive her, perhaps in his mercy he would let her die.

Lady Reres' voice, tear-choked: "Holy Mary, help her!"

Dawn, and the draperies drawn back to a dull gold sunrise. The chanting of the priests, the last Mass. She clawed at her crucifix. Ten chimes of the clock. A shattering, bursting, rocking of the world and the smell of blood and incense . . .

An exultance of bells pealed from St. Giles, Holyrood Abbey, the Church of the Canongate and the tiny moor kirks across the North Loch. Then the castle-shaking cannon thudded through the silvery bells, reverberating like thunder from Arthur's Seat and the high crags of Holyrood. Mary opened her eyes. Arnault and Lady Reres stood by the bed and Bishop Ross knelt beside it.

"A beautiful prince, Madam," Arnault said, "lusty and fair."

Mary wanted to ask who guarded it from the fairies, but she had not the strength. Her lips moved soundlessly in thanks to God. She slept.

Two hours later Sir James Melville, booted and spurred, rushed from the antechamber to carry the news to England. Du Croc and Sir William Stanley, the French and English Ambassadors, were admitted to Mary's bedchamber where she lay propped against pillows of purple satin, the child wrapped in gold cloth beside her. Mary asked that Darnley be summoned, James and his wife and her ladies. The tiny room was packed full.

"Sire," she said to Darnley, "God has given us a son, begotten by none but you."

Darnley, color flooding his face, went to the bed and bent above the infant. Mary uncovered its face. "I protest to God, as I shall answer to him on the day of judgment, that this is your son. I wish all here to bear witness. For he is so much your son—" She touched the fluff of pale hair, the pointed chin, the long-lashed eyes—"that I fear it will be the worse for him hereafter."

Darnley kissed the child, then stood awkwardly, his long arms hanging at his sides, his chin half-hidden in his ruff.

Mary turned to Sir William Stanley. "This is the son I hope will be first to unite the kingdoms of Scotland and England."

"Shall he succeed before Your Majesty and his father?" Sir William asked.

"His father has betrayed me. We are broken."

Darnley raised his head, moved a step forward. "My sweet, is this your promise to forgive and forget?"

"I made no such promise. If Kerr's pistol had fired, what would have become of the Prince and me?"

"Madam, these things are all past."

Impatiently she said, "You may go."

Darnley glanced appealingly at Du Croc, at Stanley; met their accusing eyes. Stooping to avoid the low doorsill, he left the room. One by one the others came forward to kneel in obeisance to the child, to coo compliments on the plump perfection of his toes and dimpled elbows, to bow out.

Lady Reres placed the baby in an oaken cradle by the hearth, then sat down on a cushion beside it. She was a hulking woman, bloated and blowsy, rough-voiced and bawdy-spoken. But her competence with children was famed throughout the land, and she livened a confinement because she had more gossip than a ballad peddler.

Mary said, "You know Lord Bothwell, do you not?"

"Know him!" Lady Reres' laughter belched out. "Why, Madam, I was his mistress before my sister Janet. That was years ago when he was a lad in Elgin and I a sylph of thirty."

"Indeed? I want you to summon a courier to send him word of the birth."

"The Countess of Bothwell has already attended to that, Madam." Again she laughed, but mockingly. "God knows why he chose her for wife. He could have had livelier and handsomer women than she. Of course she is Highland-rich, but he's never been one to chase wealth."

"Perhaps he loves her," Mary said.

"Ho!" she scoffed. "A great love indeed when he beds her sewing wench so soon after marriage."

"Oh." Mary tried to keep her voice casual. "Would that be Bessie Crawford?"

"The same. The Countess sent Bessie from Crichton with other servants to open Haddington Abbey. She has been there ever since. And not a week ago Bothwell rode there and met Bessie in a ruined tower on the estate. I had it from Pat Wilson, who saw them enter and leave. But Bessie herself is not above bragging, the snisty slut. It's all over the servants' hall."

"How can he be so indiscreet?"

"He's never been one to hide his mischief. Broad daylight it was, too."

"Do you think Jean has heard of this?"

"Who would tell her, Madam?"

Mary remembered Bothwell's words: *"If there is any creature I abhor it is a suspicious woman . . . If Jean were jealous I'd not live with her a day."*

I can make her jealous, Mary thought, turn her into an abomination, and so subtly that Bothwell will never know it was I who changed his sweeting to a shrew.

"True it is that a wife is always the last to know," Lady Reres said.

And I know that I stand on the verge of betraying Jean, stabbing her as surely and as deviously as James and Harry stabbed Rizzio. They released a tide of evil which is drowning my conscience and poisoning my heart.

But what lies ahead for a virtuous heart? Nothing but misery with Harry, a struggle with Elizabeth for acknowledgment of my son's succession, a dangerous game of balancing precarious power. Why should I not snatch love if I can, a shaft of sunlight for the murky future?

She said, "I think Jean should know about Bessie, so that she can dismiss her before Bothwell returns from the Border. That bawd should not be in her service."

"Nor at his," Lady Reres snickered. "Is Your Majesty going to tell the Countess?"

"No. If she thought I knew, she would be doubly humiliated. She must not guess that I have any knowledge of this. I shall ask your niece, Beaton, to tell her. Beaton remarked Bessie's boldness even before the wedding. She will know how to break the tale gently and cushion Jean's shock."

"Shall I fetch Beaton now, Madam?"

Mary hesitated. Once begun there was no turning back. This would be only the start, the first destructive seed planted in darkness. There must be others scattered through weeks and months . . .

"Yes," Mary said.

That night bonfires reddened the hills of Edinburgh, and as the news spread to the surrounding villages five hundred fires blazed through moors and valleys celebrating the birth of the Prince. Below the castle, High Street houses were festooned with chains of daisies and fennel, pinks, St. John's Wort and bluebells. Mummers pranced in donkey caps with cattails pinned to their breeches. Over the din of kettle drums and cowbells, horns and screeching whistles, the iron-mouthed cannon boomed into the flaming skies.

Mary's heralds threw largesse and distributed ale and blithemeats. There was dancing at the stone skirts of St. Giles, for Knox was not there to forbid it. He had left Ayrshire for England. Bothwell's agents reported that he and his wife were living with the two sons of his former wife in a remote country town, and that he avoided public appearances. There was no indication that he conspired with Elizabeth. An old man in failing health, he puttered in his herb garden, read his Bible, wrote. It was doubtful that he would return to Scotland. If he did, Mary foresaw no threat to her.

She thought, Knox is done for. It is Bothwell's shadow that lengthens over Scotland now, and the world will feel his force. Force without fanaticism, power without tyranny. He is hated by the nobles who for years have maligned him to the people. But the people will learn, as the Border folk know, that his justice is merciful. I will make him so strong that no man can defy him. I will make him so happy that no woman can take him from me.

But there was Darnley blocking the dream. A leech who still clung to hope of her body and her throne. She sighed and burrowed deeper into the bed pillows. Divorce—a mortal sin. But if she wrote to the Pope explaining that Darnley had conspired not only against her but against the faith, he might annul the marriage. *I must ask Rizzio . . .*

Dear God, she thought, he is still alive to me, so much a habit of the heart that even now I turn to him for help. Somehow I must realize his death, lest I be freshly bereaved each hour. Others weep and relinquish the dead. I weep and hold them close.

From the window Lady Reres said, "A pity you cannot see the celebration, Madam." She leaned to the cradle, picked up the child and brought him to the bed. "Here, Madam. You'll want to kiss him good-night before I nurse him."

"No," Mary said, "take him away." She did not blame the child. She would protect him with her life if need be, guide him in the true faith and hope for his happiness. But she would kiss no spawn of Darnley's, now or ever.

VII.

On a night in mid-July Mary slipped out of the castle in a kitchen maid's cloak. Carrying a lantern she walked timidly, her hood pulled down, keeping to the east side of the High Street. Rain dripped from the eaves of the timbered houses, pooling the cobbles. Folk hurried by her without a glance and she relaxed, confident of anonymity.

With rest and exercise on the castle battlements she had regained her strength. The Royal Mile, sloping downhill, was not tiring, and she exulted in her freedom. How marvelous to walk the streets unburdened by train or ceremonial robes, unguarded, unheeded. No need for a fixed smile, no need to smile at all. This was a private pilgrimage.

She passed through the Netherbow unchallenged, seeing herself through the sentry's eyes—someone's shabby maid taking a message into the Canongate. Past the wynds and closes she went, thinking of her father, fancying his ghostly footsteps behind her. He would have tarried here at the Cock and Stag where men were singing a raucous ballad. She paused a moment, listening. It was a song her father had written—perhaps first improvised in this very tavern:

> And we'll gang nae mair a-roving,
> A-roving in the night
> We'll gang nae mair a-roving
> Let the moon shine e'er so bright.

Mary walked on past Horse Wynd and turned to the right. Opposite Holyrood Gate, facing the palace, Rizzio's house stood shuttered and dark, its galleries bare of tapestry, its tiny garden sprouting weeds among the roses. Mary tried the door and found it fast; took her duplicate key and opened it. The parlor, still faintly scented with India incense, bloomed wine-colored in the light of her lantern. It was tidy, save for ashes in the hearth and a tennis racquet on a marble table. She remembered that Darnley and Rizzio played tennis the afternoon of the murder. A tennis ball of wound cloth had rolled into a corner, and she thought it forlorn, pathetic.

Weeping, she moved up the spiral stairs to his bedchamber and stood shaken, unbelieving.

Time reverted to the ninth of March and the room awaited Rizzio's return from supper at Holyrood. The bed cover was turned down, pillows expectant. On the table lay a book of verse marked with a scarlet ribbon. The ivory-backed chair held his russet robe— one her seamstress had made him with extra width for the poor humped shoulders. The windows were shuttered against wind long passed to the sea.

She shivered, puzzled. Time was static in this room, and only Rizzio could set it in motion. Yet he lay in a cold crypt. How then had time been tricked, how had God blundered? Dazedly, she went into the study. There were his lutes on the stone window seat, scarfed from the sunlight that entered so rarely. The oak cabinets of books, the desk they had shared so often. The teakwood chest where he kept his personal papers.

He would want me to attend them, she thought, and found the chest unlatched. In the lantern light, sitting on the floor, she scanned paid bills, itemized expenditures. There were letters from friends in Italy, from churchmen, from beggars and favor-seekers. Music manuscripts and bits of balladry. Nothing here that an enemy might ridicule, yet she would destroy them. And then she opened a volume bound in Florentine leather, seemingly a scrapbook.

A dried oak leaf, powdering as she touched it. A button, a pressed heatherbell. A handkerchief—hers beyond doubt, with a scalloped crest; a bit of lace vaguely familiar; a falcon's feather.

And then she knew that all these things held memory of her. She had touched or discarded or lost them. But Rizzio had gathered them year by year, hoarding his treasures. Notes she had written, reminders, summons to conferences, invitations. So imperious they were, so curt, yet he had cherished them.

If I had known, she thought, if only I had known! But if I had, what could I have given him? Brighter leaves? Bigger feathers? Gentler notes? I could not have given the kind of love he dreamed of and deserved. And so, to spare me hurt, he did not ask it. His silence was his greatest gift to me.

She made a paper spill, caught it in lantern fire and burned the papers in the hearth. But the book she would take with her. She could not destroy what he had thought worth saving.

From the sofa she watched the brief blaze die. Shadows swallowed the desk. She rose, and said what she had said so often in this room.

"I must go, Davy. It is late."

VIII.

In the anteroom at Edinburgh Castle, Melville swirled off his rain-spattered cloak and drank the wine Mary offered him. He had ridden hard from England and apologized for his appearance as he sat down on the love seat with her, drawing his muddy boots away from her skirt.

"Elizabeth was dancing when I arrived in Greenwich, Madam. But the moment I appeared in the ballroom she left her partner and rushed to me. 'Is Her Majesty safe?' she asked me, hand to heart. I said, 'Yes, Madam; she has birthed a beautiful man-child.'"

"Did she swoon?"

"Nearly. She paled, staggered back a step and flopped on a bench. As her ladies hurried to her she turned to them and croaked, 'The Queen of Scots is mother of a fair son, and I am but barren stock.' Then abruptly she retired to her chamber. I think she was close to collapse."

"I could almost pity her!"

"You would if you saw her, Madam. For fifteen days she was ill of her kidneys and is so thin you can count her bones. And her teeth are raging her but she will not have them pulled, for she trusts no barber in England not to swell her jaws."

"She is aging."

"Indeed, thirty-three . . . Next day she managed with right good grace to send Your Majesty her felicitations and assured me she will be glad to be your child's godmother. She promises a golden font for him and will bring it to the christening herself if she is able."

"She will come to Scotland!"

"If her health permits. But in truth she is a sick woman."

They grimaced at one another in mock sorrow. Mary no longer wasted emotion on Elizabeth's vacillations. She had been disappointed too often. If Elizabeth acknowledged her and her son, well and good. If not, they would wait for her death and the slow but certain processes of English law which could not deny their claims.

"Elizabeth asked me if Your Majesty's labor had been difficult," Melville said. "I told her it was long and agonizing such as slender ladies are wont to have. I told her you cried out for death and wished you had never been wed." He chuckled. "I thought to give her pause lest she herself has hopes of marriage and motherhood—though I doubt she does."

"Did you tell her the child is the image of Harry?"

"Yes, Madam." He hesitated, frowning. "I have dreaded to tell you this, but I must. Elizabeth has daggered you."

"How?"

"I must preface this: As Your Majesty knows, Secretary of State Cecil rides high in England, and he wants no rivals, personal or political. He seeks to discredit Dudley, Earl of Leicester, and remove him from Elizabeth's favor. To some extent he has succeeded, and Dudley is bitter against them both. On my second night in Greenwich, Dudley and I had a private chat in his study and he poured out his troubles. He said, 'Elizabeth has used me as a stalking horse. She had no intention of wedding me to Mary. *Darnley was her choice for Mary's husband.*' "

Mary sprang to her feet. "She did not choose Darnley for me! She moved heaven and earth to prevent the match!"

"Think back, Madam. It was Elizabeth who wrote asking that you receive Darnley's father. That was her first step to maneuver the Lennoxes into Scotland. Did she ask this out of love for the Lennoxes, who head the English Catholics? Scarcely. She knew they were ambitious of your throne. She knew Darnley's charm, and depravity. It was her plan that you should meet and marry him."

"But she threatened war if I married him! She ordered him back to England!"

"Superb acting, so that you would not suspect she furthered the match. By appearing to oppose it, she whetted your appetite. God knows," he said in sudden brutal bitterness, "you had the hunger and fell to the bait."

Mary said, "She offered me Dudley and even the succession—"

"Knowing you would reject her lover as soiled goods. Thus she was safe in offering the succession if you'd wed him."

"But—"

"I fear there are no buts about it, Madam. We fell into her trap like mice to cheese. Dudley says she and Cecil laughed themselves weak at news of your wedding, slapping each other, and nudging and poking and rousing such gales of glee they near fell from their chairs."

Mary sat down, hiding her face in her hands. It was shame enough to be Darnley's wife. But to be Elizabeth's dupe, maneuvered puppet-like to a bastard's whim, was the supreme degradation. Not content with a nonentity, Elizabeth had chosen a creature vile as any in the gutters of London—a traitor, a coward, a drunkard, a he-bawd.

But, she wondered, was it Elizabeth who tricked me or my own body—as Bothwell warned? Was it her conniving, or my obsession for gold curls, apricot skin, a fine tall frame? I was guilty of the grossest folly.

Mary raised her head. "Do you think Elizabeth actually instructed Harry to come here and woo me?"

"No, Madam. She would not have risked his blabbing the scheme to you. She would not have trusted him."

"My lord," she said, "I ask that this be our secret. There's no need for James or Bothwell or Balfour or any of my nobles to know. For I feel such a fool—my pride slashed to ribbons . . ."

"My dear Madam, no one will hear it from me. I only wish I could have spared you, but had I not told you I would be remiss in my duty."

Wanly she smiled at him. "You are my good friend."

A small man, gold-whiskered, suavely charming and—most important—trustworthy.

"As your friend," he said, "may I say frankly that I find you far too fragile? You wrote me you had regained your strength but I fear you have not."

"I rose from childbed too soon."

Returning from her two-mile walk to Rizzio's house, she had fainted in her bedchamber. Since then she had felt weak and listless, with scant appetite and a persistent hollow cough.

"I'm as worn from my husband's pestering as I am from illness. He pleads to share my bed, gives me no peace noon or night. I treat him as the lowest varlet, but he has no pride."

"Then why do you not leave him? Slip off to some country castle without a court. Convalesce in quiet."

She thought of Alloa on the north coast of the Forth—rambler roses climbing the castle walls, the sea, salt winds to restore her bloom. The estate belonged to Sir John Erskine, now Earl of Mar. He had won her trust during these past months and she had made him the baby's guardian. "I might visit Lady Mar at Alloa," Mary said.

"An excellent idea, Madam."

She would go in one of Bothwell's sailing ships. Perhaps he would accompany her. Thrilled with the thought, she dismissed Melville and summoned Jean from the nursery.

"Your husband is due from the Border tonight, is he not?" *As if I did not know, had not counted the hours!*

"Yes, Madam."

Jean was very quiet these days, grave as she had been in spinsterhood, a slim, sad figure in pale silks moving between Mary's apartments and the nursery down the corridor. Beaton said she had received the scandal of Bothwell and Bessie in proud silence, thanked Beaton for telling her and turned away.

"I want Bothwell to prepare a ship for me," Mary said. "I am leaving for Alloa."

"Indeed, Madam? The sea air will do you good. I note you eat like a sparrow."

"And I note you seem depressed of late. I think you sorely miss Bothwell."

"I do not know what to think, Madam," Jean sighed. "But, I should not burden you with my troubles."

"Troubles?" Mary patted the love seat. "Sit down and tell me. Perhaps I can help you."

Hesitantly, eyes lowered, Jean recounted Beaton's story. "Bessie is a flaunty lass and half my menservants are mad for her. But I cannot believe my lord would stoop so low!"

"You do right to have faith in him."

"But there were witnesses to their tryst! And Beaton and Fleming warned me of his reputation before we wed. I thought he would change with marriage." Jean traced an embroidered thistle on a damask cushion, then moved her hand to trace another. The pale mouth was down-cornered and a muscle tensed in her cheek.

"Perhaps we cannot expect men to change overnight," Mary said gently.

The gray eyes lifted, lusterless as lead. "Madam, have you too heard gossip?"

Deliberately Mary floundered. "I—why—no."

"Please do not spare me!"

"There is always gossip about Bothwell. He has so many enemies."

"What do they gain by spreading his infidelities?"

"You are not certain that there are infidelities. But suppose there were. I'm sure the wenches mean nothing to him—the booty of Border brawls, a romp in the straw. It is you he—" Mary paused—"he married."

"You started to say 'he loves'—but perhaps he never will. If he can bed servants, Border bawds—"

"You do not know that he does!"

"But I lie awake at night and torture myself wondering—"

"Nonsense, you must not take gossip as gospel."

"What can I do, Madam?"

"Have you dismissed Bessie?"

"No, she is still at Haddington."

"That is well, for it would be unfair to convict her on such scant evidence. I would watch her, and Bothwell. I would keep my eyes and ears open and learn all I could by subtle questioning of his servants. That is the way of a clever wife. You must not confront him with your suspicions unless you are fairly sure of his guilt."

"And if I find him guilty?" Tears trickled down Jean's cheeks.

"That is up to you, my dear. Some women live a lifetime with a philanderer." Bitterly Mary added, "I will be one of them, unless the Pope is merciful."

"I weight you with my troubles when you have so many," Jean said. "I weep that one man may have betrayed me, and you are brave at the proven treachery of dozens." She dried her eyes. "Forgive me, Madam. But you have helped me. You are so good, so wise . . ."

Ashamed, self-sickened, Mary dismissed her.

Early the following morning Mary summoned Bothwell to the north outlook that faced the sparkling Loch. The sun-hazed city spread far beneath her, and dizzied by the height, she stepped back from the edge of the wall, one hand holding down her ballooning skirts, the other securing her coif.

As she waited for Bothwell she thought, He arrived at midnight and doubtless had little sleep . . . Painfully, she imagined his reunion with Jean. Likely Jean's suspicions had been drowned in love. In thrall of kisses a woman always believed what she wished to.

It was nearly three months since Mary had seen Bothwell, and she was dressed to display her newly slender figure. Motherhood had glorified it, swelling the pink satin bodice, and her tiny waist was girdled in pink roses, from which a skirt belled out in hundreds of pleats that glinted with silver embroidery. Ribbons from a coif of roses fluttered from her hair.

Bothwell came hurrying along the walk, apologizing for his tardiness. He swept her a deep bow. "Forgive me, Madam?"

"Of course." She smiled up at him. His hair was a wavy red turmoil, his dagger belt askew. Bare sun-browned skin peeped through the slashed sleeves where his shirt should have been. Evidently he had just awakened.

"Madam, you look worn."

Not beautiful, not glorious, but worn . . .

"Jean tells me you are ailing and wish to go to Alloa. I have a ship at Newhaven and can crew her by tomorrow if you wish."

"Please do. I want to escape from Harry."

"I hear he is still in barrel-fevers."

"Yes, either mizzled with drink or ill from it. If he would avoid me as I do him, I could endure living under the same roof. But he plagues me for love."

"Why, are the pages pocked and the brothels closed?" Bothwell groaned. "Damn me if I've not a genius for saying the wrong thing. What I meant was, how dare he woo you in face of your revulsion?"

"My revulsion whets his desire. I would be a novelty now, a perverted conquest."

"So you go to Alloa . . . But you can't flee him forever."

"No. After the christening in December, I shall write the Pope for an annulment. But until then I dare not break openly with Harry, lest folk say Rizzio is the child's father. I'll not spot the child's name nor endanger his rights."

"I hear he is bonny."

She shrugged. "He favors Harry."

"May I see him this morning?"

"If you wish," she said indifferently.

Bothwell frowned. "Surely you don't hold a grudge against him for his father's crimes?"

"No. I am a good mother."

"Dutiful and loveless. Reres nurses him, Jean tends him and you are a good mother."

"Is that your concern?" she asked, bored and angry.

"God knows I'm no baby-slobberer. It's not the child that worries me—it is you. I see a change that bodes no good. Hatred for Darnley has hardened you to iron."

"Scotland needs iron."

"An iron hand, yes. But not an iron heart."

"You are forever prating of my heartlessness. Yet the people love me now."

"They return in kind what you gave in the past. They remember your northern campaign and they appreciate your tolerance of the new faith, your justice and your mercy. But you must not so armor yourself that you lose these very qualities that make you great."

Scornfully she said, "Brute of the Borders, Scourge of the Seas, but you do not even begin to understand hatred, do you?"

"Mock me, Madam, and find out."

They glared at each other.

"If I wish to mock you," Mary said, "that is my privilege. You are my subject. I can banish you, forfeit your lands, execute you if I wish—"

"But you may not ridicule me."

He spoke softly, but his voice started a chill from her shoulder blades down to the base of her spine. His eyes turned dark, shiny and savage, and she stepped back fearfully, not realizing that she moved toward the precipice until she felt the stone wall at her back.

Tales she had heard of Bothwell flapped through her mind like ravens. If he wished to kill her he would not count the consequences to himself. She dared not move for fear he would seize her.

It seemed to her an eon that they stood there in the cloud-blown sunlight. Far below she heard the chimes of the Canongate Kirk, the deeper-throated bells of St. Giles. She was shaking inwardly and her hands were sweating. He is half-animal, she thought, and he senses my terror. Then he took a step toward her, and she ran sideways, sobbing. His hand clamped her arm and whirled her up against him. She put both arms around him, clinging lest he lift her off her feet and send her spinning down the chasm.

And then she began to laugh that this was their first embrace . . .

Bothwell broke her grip and held her off. "Stop it," he said. "You are hysterical. Must I slap you back to your senses?"

She drew a deep breath and steadied herself. "The height," she murmured. "Let me away from the wall—please!"

He followed her as she walked to a safe distance.

"My nerves are awry," she said. "I apologize."

"It is I who must apologize, Madam, and humbly. If I had endured the Rizzio ordeal, then childbirth—" He grinned—"I'd be in a highly unusual plight."

Her fear of him left as quickly as it had come, but she was still trembling.

"Forgive me for what I said, Madam. I'm a blathering blaitie-bum, and the less heed you pay me the better."

She wanted to put out her hand, touch him, be held in his arms like a tired child.

"You desperately need rest, Madam. But suppose Darnley follows you to Alloa?"

"If he does he won't stay long, for I am taking James. This fortress is so big that Harry can avoid my brother, but at Alloa it's a different matter."

"A pity James does not kill him for you."

"I prefer my way of killing," she said.

"Apparently you haven't killed his hope."

"That is last to go. After the christening, when Harry's usefulness is over, then I shall kill his hope."

"I'd not want your enmity," he smiled. "A quick, clean blow doesn't satisfy you."

"Harry did not order quick, clean blows at Holyrood. Rizzio was stabbed fifty-six times, Father Black fifteen."

"I understand your desire for vengeance but not your morbidness. That blood on the floor at Holyrood—"

"Is a record, a document of treachery. Should I ever falter, ever be tempted to mercy, I shall go to that chamber and pull back the carpet and regain strength from Rizzio's blood."

Perhaps he mourned the loss of her gentleness. But there was no way to retrace her steps through the blood and wine and vomit of her marriage. If only Bothwell had abducted her from Crichton that night last year—set sail for Norway, Flanders, anywhere. No Harry and no Jean. No heart forever haunted.

"Will you accompany me to Alloa?" she asked.

"Do you need me there?"

She had no excuse to demand his protection. Her own troops would guard her. James was helpless without his allies.

"Jean wishes to go to Haddington," he said, "but if you need us—"

"No." She forced a smile. "Resume your honeymoon. I will see you here in the fall."

The empty weeks between, the sea and the roses wasted. He would regain Jean's trust, kiss away her suspicions, fall in love . . .

"Come," she sighed. "I will show you the child."

IX.

That evening Mary gave a banquet for Bothwell and her lords in the Great Hall. The servants were bringing in trenchers of meat, when Darnley appeared in the doorway. As he walked to the head of the table and stood behind Mary's chair there was sudden silence, save for the hiss of brandy-flamed fowl and the footsteps of the maids.

"You wished something, Sire?" Mary asked frigidly.

"To bid you a good evening." Bending, Darnley caught her hand and kissed it.

She snatched away her hand and addressed the nearest servant. "Bring a basin of water that I may wash."

The basin brought, she washed the hand he had kissed and dried it with a napkin. Darnley gasped, shuffled back a step and, caught in the cross-fire of stares, turned to meet the measuring eyes of the servants at the buffet. Ignoring him, Mary sipped from her wineglass.

"Madam," he whined, "what have I done to deserve this?"

"You have discussed me in taverns." Bothwell had heard talk this very afternoon at a hostel on the road to Newhaven. "You have dared to reveal my most intimate behavior to the lowest scum. You babble your grievances to pimps and bawds. You debase me and yourself."

Darnley extended a pleading hand but she said, "You cannot deny it. So I shall repay you in kind, save that I address a fastidious company." She looked down the table at the Countess of Argyll. "A long lad, is he not? But if you imagine him a superb lover, you are wrong."

The Countess laughed uneasily. "His height is misleading, Madam?"

"Extremely." Mary stared contemptuously at Darnley, eying him from gold-sashed waist to brocaded slippers. "I urge him to take a mistress and leave me alone but none save bawds will have him."

Darnley, scarlet and shaking, swore and rushed from the room. Mary slumped back, her hands to her eyes. "I apologize to all of you. But he must share the depths of my humiliation. Knowing what he has said of me I dread to face my people."

James, sitting beside her, put his hand on hers. "You take a cruel vengeance, my dear."

She raised her head, glanced at him obliquely. "May it be a warning to traitors."

CHAPTER NINE

I.

LEAVING HER CHILD at Edinburgh Castle under the guardianship of Lord Mar, Mary visited Lady Mar at Alloa. She took long walks on the shore, danced and hawked and sat late at cards, welcomed all visitors save Darnley. Learning her whereabouts, he rode out from Edinburgh but stayed only a few hours. Mary's disdain and James's speculative silence shriveled his scant courage. He fled to Stirling.

No noble in Scotland would sit with Darnley at table or join in his revels. He had only his servants for companions, and Mistress McDoon told Mary that his bodyguards and valets treated him with insolent familiarity. But he needed them. Save for his father in Glasgow he had no one else.

Mary found her separation from him a dubious freedom. Under the surface of her thoughts he lay in ambush to spring out before she slept and upon awakening. If the Pope refused to annul her marriage, would she dare ask a divorce? How would it affect the status of her child?

Early in August she returned to Edinburgh on state business. But driven by restlessness she was off again in a few days, wandering from country castle to hunting lodge, pursuing game and in turn pursued by worry. Then, one afternoon in a forest in Glenarton as she waited for her falcon to return, Bothwell rode through a leafy thicket and she spurred toward him in delight.

"I had hoped you would join us," she said formally, for James's benefit. "How pleasant, my lord."

Bothwell nodded to James, who bowed from the saddle. "I'm not here for pleasure, Madam."

The hawk swooped down to her leather-gloved wrist, beak dripping, but she did not wait to see its kill. She ordered James and her attendants to continue the hunt, and rode back to the lodge with Bothwell, relieved to discover that Jean was not with him.

In Mary's oak-beamed parlor Bothwell took papers from a leather case and handed them to her.

"My agents intercepted these letters Darnley sent from Stirling yesterday."

They were addressed to the Pope, Charles IX of France and Philip of Spain. Mary read them in horror. They accused her of failing to uphold the Catholic faith in Scotland, and hinted that she conspired with Protestants to its ruin. Darnley stated that due to Mary's heresy and immorality he should be recognized as leader of the Catholic religion in Britain.

"You note he refers to previous correspondence," Bothwell said. "God knows how long he has been maligning you and trying to undermine our relations with Rome, Spain and France. It is obvious he suspects you intend annulment, so he seeks to discredit you with the Pope."

"Doubtless he has succeeded," she said bitterly.

Bothwell shook his head. "I'm not one to kiss the Pope's ring, but I admit he's shrewd and his spies must have informed him of Darnley's depravity. Charles and Catherine will lap slander like cream, but Darnley cannot lead them by the nose. I doubt he has done you serious damage—but not for want of trying. These letters are important only because they prove what we did not know before: Darnley is not a mere weakling. He is dangerous, vicious. You have been taunting a snake."

"And I shall continue."

"You may goad him toward murder."

"He lacks the courage, without allies," she scoffed. "Shall I tell James of this?"

"By all means. Darnley's meddling with foreign relations is one more grievance to add to James's list."

Mary nodded. "I am sure James plots Darnley's downfall. But what means he will take I do not know."

"It will be a means that does not implicate James. It's a curious coincidence that when James's enemies die violently he is always miles away, as he was when Rizzio was murdered. But he always reappears after the crime to bring about 'order' or collect the loot. Your mother used to say, 'When James Stuart goes on a journey, his enemies should beware.'"

"Ah, well, he'll cause us no trouble. For once we have him help-less."

Mary called for wine and they drank. "How is Jean?" she asked.

Bothwell hesitated, then burst out, "A changed woman and damned if I know why! Since I returned from the Border she's been cold as a corpse and so sullen you'd not know her. I ask what ails her, and she acts as if I'd whipped her and creeps off to weep. Or else she stares at me like a martyr and says nothing."

"How very strange. Perhaps she is with child."

"Not by me," he said grimly. "I'm not one to break locked doors more than once."

"You must have hurt her unwittingly."

"If I have she won't tell me how, and I'm through pleading. She can sulk at Haddington as long as she likes, but I'll not return there till she summons me."

It has happened sooner than I dared hope, Mary thought. But I must be cat-wary.

"I am grieved, my lord. Perhaps Jean is overtired. She worked long hours during my confinement."

"But she's had a month's rest. Madam, you would not know her for the bride she was. Even her face has altered. Her eyes are narrow, her lips tight and she walks on tiptoe."

Spying . . . listening . . .

"But I am sure Jean loves you," she said. "And whatever your reasons for marriage, surely you have come to love her too."

She paused, but Bothwell said nothing. "You must have patience, my lord. In time she will tell you what is amiss."

"Unless she enjoys being mysterious."

Are you innocent of infidelity, Mary wondered, or so casual in your affairs that Bessie sits feather-light on your conscience? But she dared not probe that aspect. It was enough that he had left Jean and was here.

"What are your plans?" she asked. "Are you returning to the Border?"

"Next month. I was hoping Your Majesty would invite me to hunt."

She concealed her exultance. "We would be happy to have you. Doubtless you are restless as I. But first let us remove the child from Edinburgh to Stirling. The climate is healthier, the nursery larger, and the Mars would prefer to care for him there."

"As you wish, Madam. Stirling is as fortified as Edinburgh Castle."

Humbly pleased to attend his comfort, Mary refilled his wine-glass and offered him pastries. Sun dappled the window hangings, but the low-beamed room was dusky, and she lit a staghorn candelabra and placed it on the table between them. Bothwell ate and drank, romped with a spaniel that nuzzled his boot, then clasped his hands at the back of his neck and stretched in the chair. His glance followed the flight of a fly on the ceiling. Presently his eyes closed, his hand fell to his dagger, and he slept.

Even in sleep he was wary, one hand on steel, ready to wake at a whisper. But there was no sound in the room save for a cricket chirping in the cold stone hearth. Sitting across from him Mary studied the sleeping face, loving each line and furrow. At his temples, silver streaked the burnished red waves and she thought it beautiful.

The hourglass trickled sand, the sun moved from the window. Still she sat watching him, tremulously happy in their privacy. He could hunt on any one of his estates but he wanted to be with her.

Hunting horns sounded in the forest. Bothwell sprang awake. "Great God!" he said, "I slept! Can you forgive my rudeness?"

She smiled. "You may tell your grandchildren that you slept in the Queen's presence."

"They won't be impressed," he grinned, "for my great-great-grandfather Patrick and my great-grandfather Adam slept in their Queens' beds."

"Jesu Maria! And your father proposed to my mother! You Hepburns aim high."

He nodded. "Queens fascinate us. 'The fair and fatal Stuart face' . . ."

"Surely not fatal," she laughed.

"Who knows?" he said.

II.

Mary hunted with Bothwell, James and a few attendants through August and into the early fall. Released from court formality, she behaved, as Bothwell said, like a filly in Maytime. They raced through moors and over mountains, fished and ran game, stopped in villages to join in tavern rollicks and country fairs. James seemed graver by the week, a young-faced old man watching the capers of children.

For Mary no hill was too high to climb, no stream too icy to swim, no hedgerow too broad to jump, if Bothwell was there. She lived completely in the moment. The future was tomorrow's cockfight or barn frolic. But as summer died the wind nipped cold through untapestried lodges and the Highland peaks were ermined with snow. Reluctantly, in early September, Mary ended her holiday with a visit to the child at Stirling. Darnley was there, but to her relief he avoided her and remained in his apartments until she left for Edinburgh.

There she lodged in the Exchequer House to study her funds. Every spare penny would be spent on the christening.

"It will be the most sumptuous event ever held in Scotland," she told Bothwell. "If Elizabeth comes, she must be impressed by our taste if not our wealth." She prattled of redecorating Stirling, where the ceremony would be held. "You shall be Master of Revels and host."

"Host, Madam? What of your husband?"

"I'll not have Harry ruin an elegant occasion. He will participate only as the child's father . . . But there is something more pressing to discuss. Lethington pleads to return to court this month. He writes me nearly every day."

"Surely you'd not pardon him?"

"Whatever his crimes, he did establish our alliance with Spain against Elizabeth. I need him to deal with her in the child's behalf."

"He and James are a dangerous combination."

"They will terrify Harry out of his wits!" She chuckled, tucking a curl into her cap. "Lethington is really no problem, my lord. True, he is slippery, but who is not?"

Bothwell sighed. "Another traitor returns to the fold."

"Fleming vouches for his good faith. She says she has given him such a tongue-lashing as he will remember on his deathbed. They will marry at the end of this month."

"So Lethington returns in Fleming's bond, shackled by love."

"Indeed, such shackles are often more effective than iron. I shall give them a wedding feast at Holyrood."

"Holyrood! Do you mean to live there again?"

Mary hesitated. "I shall force myself to. The castle chambers are too cramped, and so are these temporary lodgings. Holyrood is warmer in winter, fully tapestried. And if it is haunted as folk say, I've no reason to fear Rizzio's spirit."

"Spoken with sense, Madam."

"It is the conspirators who will find sleep difficult in Holyrood."

But Mary herself slept little the first few nights. When she dozed, the horror was re-enacted and she fancied she felt Rizzio's desperate fingers clutching the bed fringe. Once she awakened to the echo of a high scream in the audience chamber. But when she dared to enter it, her candle searched empty shadows. The guard on the stair landing had heard nothing.

She hoped that the wedding festivities for Fleming and Lethington would revive happy memories, but even as they feasted in the Great Hall she remembered Rizzio's love ballads and missed his music. The first time she supped in the tiny turret chamber she listened for footsteps on the private stairs. When Bothwell came to the door unexpectedly, she spilled wine, and shuddered as it trickled, blood-colored, down her dress.

On September 29th at ten in the evening she sat in her audience chamber conferring with French Ambassador Du Croc, Bothwell, James and Lord Glencairn. They were discussing christening arrangements, when a page brought word that Darnley had arrived from Stirling and was outside in the courtyard. Mary's first thought was that the child might be ill, and she said, "Summon him here at once."

"He will not come in, Your Majesty. He asks that you go down to him."

Mary threw on a cloak, and Bothwell accompanied her downstairs. Darnley's bodyguards remained on horseback while he paced the outer courtyard, his long furred cape pulled tight against the chill. Mary ran to him.

"Is the child ill?" she asked.

Darnley sneered. "Is that your greeting? No, Madam, the child is well." He drew her away from Bothwell. "I came to tell you that I am going abroad and shall live in France. It's plain I'm not appreciated here."

Mary gasped. She dared not let him leave Scotland before the christening. It would expose her to the vilest slander, and endanger her child's succession to the English throne. All Elizabeth wanted was the chance to say, "If Darnley will not acknowledge the child, why should I? It is Rizzio's bastard."

"Sire," Mary said, "this is no matter to discuss here in the cold. Come inside—"

"No!" He glanced nervously at Bothwell, then up to her lighted window. "You are not alone. You entertain guests."

"I am conferring with Du Croc and some of my lords, but they can wait."

"No. I shall wait here until they leave."

"But they are staying the night." She thought, He is fearful of the men he betrayed. "I shall dismiss them and we will talk in private."

"In your apartments?"

"Why not, Sire?"

He vacillated. Ten minutes passed before he agreed to come in.

Mary called Bothwell over. "The King and I wish privacy. Please tell my lords to leave the audience chamber."

She turned so that Darnley could not see her eyes. Slowly, emphatically, she winked at Bothwell.

"Yes, Madam," Bothwell said.

Darnley watched Bothwell walk away. "Swaggering swine! You have puffed him with power."

"He does seem a bit arrogant of late," Mary said. Agree to anything to get him inside . . .

"I hear you have pardoned Lethington." Darnley moistened his lips, glanced uneasily behind him. "Is he in the palace?"

"No, he and Fleming are honeymooning."

"You are mad to pardon him."

"Perhaps I have been mad, Harry. I am just recovering from shock that could have made me so."

"I knew it!" he said triumphantly. "Only madness could account for your malice to me."

Seton called from a window above them. "The gentlemen have left, Madam."

Darnley refused to take the main staircase for fear of encountering his enemies, so they climbed the private stairs. As they entered her bedchamber, Mary saw that the door to the adjoining room was shut.

"Whisky, Sire?" Mary asked.

He nodded and she said, "There is a decanter in the audience chamber."

Darnley opened the door, saw the lords and started to run back through the bedchamber, but Bothwell appeared from the supping room to block his way at the private stairs.

"Surely," Bothwell said, "you will not deny us the pleasure of your company, Sire?"

Glaring at Mary, Darnley walked into the audience chamber, Bothwell behind him. Du Croc and the lords rose, bowed and resumed their seats as Mary sat down.

"My husband tells me he is off to France," Mary said. "He plans to desert me and our child."

They turned shocked faces from her to Darnley. He stood with head bent, staring at the carpet, and Mary wondered if he saw the pale streaks made by the washing of Rizzio's blood. But at the far end of the room the bloodstains remained on the floor, never to be removed . . .

Finally James spoke. "Why do you wish to leave Scotland, Sire?"

Darnley said nothing.

"If you have grievances, surely Her Majesty deserves to hear them."

Darnley rubbed one boot against the other.

"These gentlemen are witnesses to whatever grievances you may state," Mary said. "We will be glad to hear them."

"Can it be," James asked in assumed horror, "that you have suffered some calamity of which we are unaware? Have you been ill-treated?"

Still Darnley was silent.

"I have raised you to the highest place in my realm," Mary said gently, "yet you wish to leave and expose your child to grievous slander."

"For your own honor, Sire," Du Croc said, "and the honor of Her Majesty, you must state your reasons. If you have none, such a flight would be a reprehensible whim. I believe I can speak for

France when I say you would be regarded as an ingrate, unworthy of the rank to which you have been exalted."

Glencairn said, "You would not be as welcome in other courts, Sire, as you are here."

"Here," James said, "you have all the luxuries you could wish. And to turn your back on a young and beautiful wife whom you have sworn to honor and defend, to desert your son, would be . . ." He paused. ". . . a dangerous error in judgment."

Darnley glanced up at James, his face twitching.

James smiled. "A fatal error, Sire."

Darnley opened his mouth and shut it. He wiped beads of sweat from his forehead.

"Surely it cannot be fear, Sire?" James asked incredulously. "Who has lifted a hand against you? Are you not guarded day and night?"

"Aye," Bothwell said, "Here you are safe. But once you are out of Scotland, Her Majesty cannot control your enemies. Morton and his Douglases, Kerr . . ." He let the sentence trail off.

"I—I—Her Majesty misunderstood me," Darnley stammered. "I thought perhaps a brief holiday in France—but I have reconsidered."

"Ah," Du Croc beamed. "That is better. The climate of France is not so pleasant this season. You do well to remain."

"Not here!" Darnley shrilled. "Stirling."

"Stirling, if you wish," Mary said, gracious and smiling. "You will find the hunting better." She caught Bothwell's eye, and smothered laughter.

Slowly, Darnley walked to the door that led to the main staircase. Mary followed him.

Scowling, he said, "Adieu, Madam. You'll not see me for a long time."

III.

That autumn Scotland's southeastern frontier was roused to anarchy with feuding and thievery. Bothwell rode to Liddesdale to subdue the quarreling Elliotts, Armstrongs and Johnstones and to round up offenders for trial. Mary agreed to meet him in Jedburgh October 8th and hold Justice Court. It was time she visited the Border, displayed her military might and her mercy. She sent her Marys ahead to rent and prepare a house for her in Jedburgh. It must be secluded, she told them, spacious but not pretentious. Big enough to accommodate her attendants—and Bothwell.

Eagerly, excitedly, she left Edinburgh, riding in a forest of tall spears. She wore an iron helmet plumed with yellow, a yellow velvet jerkin and breeches, a forest-green cloak buttoned in amber. Behind her rode James, Lethington, Huntley, and Bishop Ross, archers, halberdiers and pikemen.

Beyond the West Port, where the crowds thinned, Mary removed her helmet and placed it in the pannier of her crooksaddle, substituting a silk mask to protect her complexion from wind and dust. They rode through fire-colored woods and pine forests. Sheep grazed the summits of the humpy hills, and gulls swooped silver-winged over the harvested farms. Scarlet leaves drifted down and the air was blue with wood smoke and winey with fallen apples. Dalkeith . . . Dalhousie . . . Borthwick . . . crowds jamming the market squares to toast their Queen in ale and shatter their glasses on the cobbles.

A mile out of Borthwick, Bothwell's page Paris galloped toward them in a cloud of leaf-whirled dust. Spurring to Mary's side, he informed her that Bothwell had been wounded in Liddesdale.

Mary swayed in the saddle, steadied herself. "Gravely?"

"A smashed thigh and left hand . . . head injuries."

Paris told her that Bothwell had set out to catch Jock Elliott O'The Park, a famed highwayman. He found Jock on a moor and shot him off his horse. But Bothwell's own horse was about to bog, so he dismounted, tripped on a stump and fell. Jock, though wounded, attacked Bothwell with a sword, and when Bothwell fainted left him for dead.

"Where is your master now?" Mary asked.

"At Hermitage Castle. We took him there by cart, Madam. The physician thinks he may have a chance to recover."

"Return to your master and tell him I will come to Hermitage from Jedburgh. Bring me word of him there."

Panicky, Mary hurried her cavalcade into the Moorfoot Hills, through Galashiels, Melrose and Selkirk. When they reached her house in Jedburgh, Paris was awaiting her. Bothwell was out of danger, he said, and with rest his wounds would heal. But the physician had advised that Mary not come to Hermitage for at least a week.

In war-gutted Jedburgh Abbey, Mary gave thanks to God for Bothwell's life and heard Mass. Hoping Bothwell could be brought to her for convalescence, she made her house comfortable with tapestries and carpets brought from Edinburgh. The house was built of gray fieldstone and set in a formal park that sloped to the banks of the river. Rooks and swallows nested in the thatched roof, mice scampered in the walls. As in most Scottish homes, the rooms were small to hold the heat of the fireplaces.

Mary plunged into work, judging the criminal cases brought before her. She fined many prisoners, but executed none; granted the petitions of the poor and gave nearly as much money as she collected.

Anxious to stop profiteering, she fixed prices. A pound loaf of bread at fourpence; good ale fivepence a pint. For stabling a horse twenty-four hours, twopence. Innkeepers might charge a shilling a night for lodgings, or a shilling fourpence if a beef or mutton roast were provided the traveler.

Each day brought word of Bothwell's improvement and after a week Mary set out for Hermitage Castle with James and her troops. Sunrise stained the moors blood-red as they started the ride over thirty miles of steep hills. The country was rough and pathless, desolate save for a few peel towers and ruined keeps. Mist turned to heavy rains, and Mary cursed herself for wearing an elegant blue velvet cloak. Riding through flooded burns she was soaked through, splattered with black peat mud, the plumes on her hat limp as strings.

Just before noon they reached Ninestane Rig. A mile farther on, the fortress of Hermitage loomed through the mist. Square, massive, windowless, it hulked on the edge of a deep morass. The walls were fire-blackened, and years of battering rams had scarred the stone, but it stood like a savage watchdog, fangs bared to England, guarding the Eastern Border.

"It suits Bothwell," Mary said, a thrill in her voice. "It is as strong as he. Nothing on this earth can shake it. Doubtless it will stand when we lie dead a thousand years."

James lifted a thin black eyebrow. "By no drift of the imagination can I romanticize Hermitage, or its master. Both are crude, of sinister repute."

"Both have held against the English all their lives," Mary said angrily. "I warrant this castle is not furnished with Elizabeth's bribes, nor embellished with stolen altar cloths and abbey jewels."

"Your Majesty is quick to take offense when none is meant," James said hastily.

"I'll hear no slander of Bothwell," she said.

Spurring ahead of him, she rode to the tethering post. Bothwell's attendants helped her dismount and led her through the high arched entrance to a flagstone hall and down a stone corridor. James followed her into a room hung with bearskins, where Bothwell lay on a couch by the fire under fur robes.

His head was bandaged down to the eyebrows and his left hand hung in a linen sling. He smiled at Mary's obvious distress, and attempted an awkward little bow, asking her and James to be seated.

But Mary knelt by his couch. "My lord, I have been so worried. Your hip . . . I heard it was smashed so you may not walk for months."

"Then I'll ride." He grinned. "The hip is strapped and healing. Doubtless I'll be on my feet in two weeks."

James asked, "What happened to Jock? Did he die of his wound?"

"Yes, he managed to ride a mile but died in the saddle." Bothwell turned to Mary. "How goes Justice Court, Madam?"

Mary told him of the fines she had imposed.

"I've a pack of rascals in this area awaiting trial," he said. "With Your Majesty's authorization I'll judge them this week."

"From a sick bed?"

"Why not, Madam? It will take my mind off my body."

They discussed the business of the courts, and then Mary said, "Paris tells me Jean is not here. But surely she knows of your wounds."

"She does, but I ordered her not to come. There are no quarters here for women, and the journey is too difficult. You should not have made it."

"I had to see for myself that you are recovering," Mary said. "If I had—"

If I had lost you I would have wished to die.

"—If I had not come I would be fretting through the weeks."

Does he guess that I love him, she wondered? If James were not here I might tell him. No, it would take more courage than I have. I cannot face the possibility that he does not return my love. I am a coward.

"Your Majesty honors me more than I deserve," Bothwell said. She thought he sounded abrupt, impatient of her concern. Quickly she shifted the conversation back to the Assizes, and after food and drink had been served, she rose to leave.

"When you are well enough to travel by litter," Mary said, "you will convalesce at Jedburgh. I have comfortable quarters for you." Lest he object she added, "Perhaps I am too soft in my judgments. You must help me with the sentencing."

"As you wish, Madam."

He is not anxious to come, she thought as she began the return journey. Perhaps he misses Jean at Haddington and would prefer to convalesce there. Heavy-hearted, she jogged through the rainy afternoon, reaching Jedburgh in the early evening.

At dawn, Mary awakened with the familiar pain in her side. It was accompanied by a fever that climbed high in the afternoon, and she vomited blood. Returning from the privy to her bedchamber, she fainted, and was unconscious for two hours.

Alarmed, her physician Arnault lanced her veins and bled her; administered lily root and purges. A courier was sent to summon

Darnley from Stirling. Weak from nausea, Mary lay alternately sweating and freezing.

The second day, her vision blurred. Terrified, she held tight to Fleming's hand. "It is so dark . . . what time is it?"

Fleming hesitated, lied. "Midnight, Madam."

But the room was bright with sunlight.

On the fourth day Bishop Ross heard Mary's confession, and she stared at him sightlessly. She felt his crucifix touch her hand and drew back in horror at the cold metal. "Spare him!" she shrieked, "For God's sake spare him! He has done nothing."

Footsteps and sobs . . . hours of darkness . . . a whisper—James?

"Order the winding sheet from Edinburgh—gold cloth . . . woe weeds . . . black candles . . ."

Mary raised up on one elbow, heard her voice as though it echoed along a closed passage. "James?"

"I am here, Mary."

"Huntley? Lethington? Bishop Ross?"

"All here, Madam."

"Keep—keep unity and charity among yourselves . . . Commend my child to his godmother, Elizabeth . . . Do not let him suffer evil from his father, or anyone." Her voice seemed to slide away from her down the closed passage. "As to religion, press no man in his conscience. Now, I will see Bothwell alone."

"He is not here, Madam."

"Not here! But I need him! He *must* come!"

She could not die until Bothwell came. Not until she had entrusted him with Scotland, with her feeble heart. Pride counted for nothing now. She would ask him to hold her close. With his arms around her, she could face anything—even God's wrath.

With her last strength, she confessed to the Bishop her love of Bothwell, her sin against Jean, her vengeful hatred of Darnley. "I leave my enemies to God's judgment . . ."

The abbey bells tolled through the twilight, and Mary slipped back into delirium. Fleming's voice, choked with sobs: "Open the window to release her soul," and the creak of the casement unlatched and the wind driving the leaves across the park.

"Davy, it is too windy for tennis . . ."

At six in the morning of October 22nd, Mary's eyes were wide and unblinking. Her body twitched in convulsions. She lost the power of speech. Then her arms and feet stiffened. The Bishop prayed for her departing soul. The wind flapped the window hangings and flared the candles in the wall sconces.

Bothwell was carried through the door on a litter to Mary's bedside.

"Shut that window!" he ordered Fleming.

"It is open for her soul, my lord."

"And chilling her body to death," he said. As Fleming closed the window, he shouted at Arnault. "Don't stand there like a foggie; do something! Pour brandywine down her!"

Mary's jaws were rigid. Arnault pried her mouth open and forced brandy down her throat. She coughed brandy and blood.

James said, "Let her die in peace."

Bothwell glared at him, then stretched out his good arm and spun Arnault around. "Work on her; heat her body—by Christ if you don't, I'll cut off your manhood and throw it to the dogs!"

"Let her go in peace," James repeated.

But Arnault was bandaging Mary's rigid arms and legs, then jerking them frantically in an effort to restore circulation. When he wearied, Bothwell ordered his attendants to help, and they corded her toes and fingers and pulled on them, rubbed and kneaded her arms.

"Harder!" Bothwell shouted.

"This is barbarous!" James said.

"Stop it, my lord," Fleming pleaded. "They are thrashing her to death!"

Bothwell ignored them and called a burly henchman from the corridor. "Dalgleish!" Come here and grip Her Majesty's feet . . ."

For three hours they worked, sweat streaming down their faces. When one man tired, another took his place. The Marys huddled in a corner praying, weeping, unable to watch the tossed body on the bed. James paced the room, his mouth thinned to a line, his fingers twitching, a nerve jumping in his cheek. At the chest by the window he paused and examined the contents of Mary's jewel case.

At one o'clock in the morning, color crept into Mary's face. Her eyelids fluttered and her muscles relaxed. She moaned, and the men stepped back while Arnault removed the bandages and cords.

Slowly the room focused through blur. She turned her head on the pillow. "Bothwell!"

She tried to hold out her arms, but was too weak. "Bothwell," she whimpered. He leaned from the litter and stretched out his hand. She snuggled her cheek against it, and slept.

IV.

Six days later Darnley arrived. Lying in bed, propped up on pillows, Mary said, "I marvel you bothered to come at all. You were summoned nearly two weeks ago."

"I was hunting. The courier couldn't find me." Darnley shifted

[301]

uneasily in his chair. "At any rate you are recovering. But I hear your folly near cost you your life."

"Folly? What folly?"

"You rode sixty miles to Hermitage in foul weather. Romantic, but scarce sensible."

"What do you mean by 'romantic?'"

"A remote fortress; a wounded hero; his anxious Queen. Is that not romantic? I find it so. With the further poignancy that both hero and Queen are wed to others."

"So now you are jealous of Bothwell," she said furiously. "Spreading filth—"

"I, jealous of an oaf?" He laughed contemptuously. "As to filth, you reap what you sow, Madam."

"Get out of my sight!" Mary jumped out of bed, clutching the oaken post for support. Darnley sprang from his chair.

"Get out of here," she shouted, "lest I claw your eyes from their sockets!"

Holding to the bedpost with one hand, she lunged out the other to rake his eyes, and Darnley ran to the door, tripping over the cloak he held. She heard him curse as he caught his balance and pounded down the turnpike stairs calling his groom to bring his horse.

Fleming hurried in to help Mary back to bed. From his room below, Bothwell sent Paris to inquire if she was all right.

"Tell your master I chased out a rat," she said.

"Yes, Madam. We heard him go."

"How is your master feeling?"

"Better, Madam. He took some steps today, from bed to window."

"Tell him not to tire himself."

"He knows Your Majesty hopes to leave here in two weeks and is determined to escort you to Edinburgh."

"Not until we are both strong."

As Mary regained her strength, she spent much of her time in Bothwell's chamber. Chaperoned by Fleming or Seton they played Primero, sat late by the fire drinking spiced sack and eating coal-spitted apples. James rebuked Mary. "It is not seemly that you visit his bedchamber."

Bluntly, Mary said, "We are invalids, incapable of the exercise you hint."

"You borrow such talk from him!"

"It is a pity I can't borrow his fist to smash such insinuations back in your throat!"

"I am only trying to warn you. Twice slander has blackened your name. Twice men have died because of your willfulness."

"I promise you," Mary said, "that if there is a third, it will not be Bothwell."

V.

Lest she and Bothwell suffer a relapse, Mary journeyed slowly toward Edinburgh, resting at Kelso and Home Castle. Granted permission to ride through a strip of English territory, they followed the Tweed to Berwick, then proceeded up the east coast to Coldingham where they visited Bothwell's widowed sister Janet and her small redheaded son, Francis Stuart.

As they neared Craigmillar Castle, Bothwell said, "Your Majesty has seen enough of Scotland to make a judgment. Would you still trade it for France?"

Leaning toward him in the saddle, Mary spoke softly lest someone hear. "I would trade all of Scotland for one fair mile of Touraine."

"You baffle me, Madam. Touraine is flat as a plank."

"But it is gentle. Even in winter the snow falls like petals. Scotland is brutal."

In the north, storms were sweeping fishing boats to sea; men and animals froze in the ice-locked islands. And when winter pounded itself out in the March gales, there would be the dim-dripping spring that seemed to Mary a mockery of renewal. The rivers crawled through sodden moors and swamps, or overflowed their banks and spread terror in the lowlands. Summer brought thin sunlight, a brief flowering before it tarnished toward death. The wild, bright tartans of autumn woods presaged the murderous winter.

France had grace and balance. But here the cliffs were too sheer, the mountains too high, the caverns too deep, the coastline too ragged. She found no loveliness in the lonely wind-waved heather or the dark fingers of the lochs that pointed into miles of empty moorland. Even the soft quilts of the Lammermuirs held horror, for it was there in the sick-white mists that the Headless Men had wandered north from Flodden—a phantom army more terrible than the English.

Bothwell said, "I grant the brutal climate. But I warrant if you returned to France you'd find it insipid."

"Would I?" Mary pointed with her whip to Craigmillar Castle, a sprawled gray monster in the fog. "Would I not trade that pile of gargoyled stone for a white chateau on the banks of the Loire? Seaweed for water lilies? Mist for sun? Would I not exchange those dreary hay-strewn chambers for mirrored suites furnished in mother-of-pearl?" She smiled ruefully. "If you were a woman you would understand. Jean would."

It was the first time Mary had mentioned Jean in weeks, for

Bothwell had avoided the subject. But now she had to know if he planned to return to her.

"Speaking of Jean," she added casually, "are you going to Haddington?" She held her breath, looking straight ahead.

"No, Madam."

Still casually, she said, "Then why not complete your convalescence here at Craigmillar in the sea air?"

"Thank you. I shall."

If he loved Jean, Mary thought, he would not remain so long away from her. Yet neither by word nor glance does he indicate love for me. He is attentive to my comfort, amused by my company, fiercely loyal. Perhaps he even admires me, but his compliments are forthright, without a trace of tenderness. What keeps him so aloof? Surely not convention nor respect for my rank. A man who treats a queen as a woman would certainly dare a kiss. Perhaps here at Craigmillar I will discover his true feelings.

Edinburgh was only two miles away, and Mary sent for her most seductive gowns and scents. Several evenings she created opportunities to be alone with Bothwell. But when their hands touched at cards or billiards she knew it was merest chance. And no matter what she wore he seemed blind to her beauty.

I will make him want me. On a mid-November evening she dressed in her most daring gown, which she had worn only on her honeymoon in the privacy of her apartments. She remembered that its effect on Darnley had been remarkable. Of claret velvet, it bared her shoulders in a narrow drift of white fox, and the long full sleeves were cuffed with fox. A tiny velvet cap peaked at her hairline. Garnets flashed dark fire at her ears and wrists.

"Ask Lord Bothwell if he'd care for a game of chess," she told Seton.

Seton blinked at the gown, hurried off on her errand. Worriedly, Mary paced her little parlor. She had not commanded Bothwell's presence. He could send his excuses. He might prefer a book of astronomy, some military treatise or one of the Catholic tracts he was so fond of reading and refuting. Or perhaps he was in the village drinking and wenching . . .

"Lord Bothwell accepts with pleasure, Madam."

Usually one of the Marys remained nearby. Tonight she dismissed them. James could speculate as he wished.

Bothwell arrived, bowed, followed Mary to the chess table. He made no comment on her appearance, scarcely glanced at her bare shoulders. She poured him whisky, took wine for herself.

He seemed intent on the game, rarely looking up. While she

awaited his play she made no attempt to plan her moves ahead. She listened to the wind. "I closed the door because of the draft," she said.

Bothwell nodded, his hand hovering over a knight.

"I don't care what James thinks," she said. "I feel as safe with you as if you were my grandfather."

He looked up and she smiled, then let her lashes fall.

"But I am very glad you are not my grandfather," she said softly.

"So am I." He moved the knight.

"Why?" she asked.

"I've no liking for crypts."

He bent again to the chessboard. A pox on him, she thought; he always ignores my flirtation. But I will persist. Before this night is over I will know whether he loves me.

Mary refilled his whisky glass, pleased that he was drinking more than usual. Perhaps it would loosen his tongue. But he won the game in virtual silence, and sat back in his chair grinning.

"You were an easy conquest, Madam."

Blushing, she said, "My mind was not on the game."

"I know. You were thinking how magnificent you look in that gown and wondering if I would remark it."

"Why, I never—"

"You never looked more beautiful."

Ah, he comes round now . . . his eyes gleam . . . he leans forward . . .

"I have *always* liked that gown, Madam."

Crestfallen, she stared at him. Was he laughing at her, baiting her? His face was serious, but his eyes twinkled and she could not face them. Abruptly, she rose, picked up her lute and sat down on the bear rug by the fire. She had not played since Rizzio's death, nor sung since he gave her the last voice lesson. With music she would regain her dignity.

"What shall I sing?" she asked.

Bothwell considered. "The song we heard at the fair in Ladybank. Do you remember it?"

Mary nodded. An English country ballad, sad and strange as a long summer gloaming. Hesitantly she began it, gained confidence, sang in her soft soprano:

I gave thee garters fringed with gold, and silver aglets hanging by
Which made thee blithe for to behold, and yet thou wouldst not
*   love me*
Greensleeves was all my joy, Greensleeves was my delight,

*Greensleeves was my heart of gold, and who but my lady Green-
sleeves?*

Did he know a girl who wore green sleeves? Did Jean have such
a gown? Was he thinking of Anna Throndsen? Or was it just a
lovely song, stirring no wraiths?

There was a rap at the door, and Mary broke off in mid-note.
"Come in," she called impatiently.

James came in swiftly. "Your husband has arrived, Madam. He is
drunk. I thought it best—" He glanced pointedly at Bothwell—"if he
found you alone."

"I'll not receive him alone. I marvel he dares come here without
invitation."

"He has whisky-courage, Madam."

"I'll soon shatter it. But I want you both to remain with me, lest
he prove belligerent."

When Darnley appeared in the doorway, she saw no belligerence
but slyness, craft. He fawned toward her on legs that were steady
enough, but his eyes were bleary, his face slack.

"My beautiful sweeting," he said, and bent to kiss her shoulder.

Mary drew back in disgust. "Sit down, Sire, and state your business."

Again he reached for her, but she avoided his grasp. "What do
you wish?"

"My rights." He pointed a wavering finger at her. "You."

"Have you no pride?"

"Pride—whas that? I love you." He turned to James and Bothwell.
"Leave us."

"They remain," Mary said.

His loose lips tightened. "I say they shall go."

"I refuse to be alone with you."

"Then I refuse to ack—acknowledge your damned bastard."

"Sire," Bothwell said, moving toward him, "there is just time for
you to apologize to Her Majesty, if you make haste."

"I do not cross swords with inferiors," Darnley said, backing
toward the wall.

"I have in mind a horsewhip."

James stepped between them. "There will be no brawling. Sire,
for the moment we will ignore your insult, and ask your intentions."

"I intend to regain my rights," Darnley said, scowling at Mary.
"She will bed with me or explain her bastard to the world."

He is drunk, Mary thought, but his plan makes sober sense. If I
refuse him, my child will never wear the English crown.

"Our child resembles you," she said. "The world is not blind."

[306]

"But you are," Darnley sneered. "You have not seen him in two months. His hair is near as dark as yours and his complexion sallow as sand. To observant eyes—like Elizabeth's—he would pass for Italian."

It was true the baby's hair was darkening and possible that his skin had sallowed. The round blue eyes, the pointed chin, the long lashes would prove nothing if Darnley chose to ignore the christening.

The ceremony was planned for December 17th—nineteen days away. Somehow, Mary thought, I must bear his lovemaking until the child is safely baptized in his presence. Nothing he does thereafter can endanger its rights.

"Harry," she said, shuddering, "you may stay."

James nodded in satisfaction. She could not look at Bothwell.

"I'll lie with no log," Darnley said. "There are terms, my sweet. You will show proper ardor or I'll leave you before dawn."

Mary nodded, her head bent.

"I like a lively wench."

Bothwell said, "Surely Your Majesty is going to tell him?"

She looked up. "Tell him what?"

"Come, Madam," he said reproachfully, "you had best tell him."

Dazedly she said, "I don't know what you mean."

"Madam, I intend no disrespect, but it is not honorable of you to remain silent."

Dear God, she thought, perhaps I am going mad. I have no idea what he refers to.

"And you, Lord James," Bothwell said sternly. "Do you also remain silent?"

James shook his head impatiently. "I don't understand you."

"Very well." Bothwell turned to Darnley. "I think you should know that Her Majesty has pardoned your enemies—Morton, his Douglases, Kerr—the entire pack. A courier is on the way to Newcastle to summon them to court."

Darnley's face slowly blanched. He tried to speak, turned to Mary with a choked little cry and groped a hand toward her. His knees buckled and he gripped the back of a chair to steady himself.

"Is this true?" he croaked.

Mary hesitated. Bothwell had offered the solution to her problem if she dared take it. Or she could tell Darnley that she would send another courier to cancel the pardons.

From under her lashes she glanced at James, and he nodded almost imperceptibly. Naturally he wanted Morton back to unite the Douglases against Darnley and Bothwell.

Yet in nineteen days of Darnley's love she could lose her reason.

She thought of his wet lips on her body and tasted the salt of nausea.

"Yes," she said. "It is true. I am pardoning the exiles."

"You would have me murdered!" Darnley whimpered. "I'd not live two hours!"

Bothwell put his hand on Darnley's shoulder. "If you refuse to attend the christening, the lords of Scotland will boil you in oil."

"That I know," Darnley whined.

"Then let it be known that you will attend the christening, and none will molest you. Return to Stirling and remain secluded until next month. I personally guarantee your safety at the ceremony. You have my word."

"And mine," Mary said.

"Promise me a heavier guard," Darnley begged.

"Your guard will be doubled," Mary said.

Mutely, Darnley dragged to the door and left.

Mary closed the door and turned gratefully to Bothwell. "You may have saved my reason, but now I am forced to pardon men I loathe."

"I did not force you, Madam," he smiled. "The final decision was yours."

James chuckled. "The Douglases will control Darnley most effectively." He bowed to Bothwell, "My compliments—Lethington and I have long desired this, but saw no way to persuade Her Majesty. And now if Her Majesty will excuse me, I wish to tell him the good news."

James left and Mary sat down, at once relieved, bewildered and apprehensive.

"You vowed vengeance on the murderers," Bothwell said, "but they were James's puppets, Darnley's dupes. Don't diffuse your hate, Madam. Concentrate on the two who most merit it."

"My husband and my brother," she said bitterly.

She stirred the dying fire, and Bothwell put a log on it. As she watched the fire blaze to light, her mind lit too with sudden certainty. Bothwell loved her! It was when Darnley said, "I like a lively wench" that Bothwell had interfered—because he could not bear the thought of her bedding with her husband.

Happy tears crowded her eyes, and she turned her head lest he see. The murderers' return was as dangerous to him as to Darnley. Seventy-six enemies starved for power, their hunger sharpened by exile. Yet Bothwell preferred them back to her being in another man's arms. He loved her more than his life . . . But she wanted to hear him say so.

"Why did you do this, my lord?" she asked. "For months you have kept James and Morton apart. Yet now you are willing to throw them together, when you know they would dagger you."

Bothwell shrugged. "Perhaps I find the days too peaceful."

She went to his chair and knelt beside him. "That is not true. You are no young gilly-gawky who fights for thrill. Besides, your enemies do not fight; they sneak a knife in the back."

"True."

"Then why? Why did you do it?"

He was silent, his eyes deep in hers, and she leaned toward him, feeling the pound of her heartbeat.

"Because," he said slowly, "the damned lily-gutted arsecockled son of a bitch called me *inferior!*"

VI.

That night Mary suffered her deepest depression since Rizzio's death. She had agreed to pardon the murderers. It was obvious Bothwell did not love her. At best there was nothing ahead but conspiracy and frustration. I cannot even kill myself, she thought bitterly, lest my son suffer in consequence.

At dawn the pain in her side returned, and she sent for Arnault, who bled her. Melville came to her bedside with final word that Elizabeth was not well enough to attend the christening, but was sending as her representative the Earl of Bedford and eighty gentlemen. She asked that Mary's half-sister, the Countess of Argyll, serve as godmother in her proxy. Mary thought, If ever Elizabeth and I meet, it will be in some region of hell.

Despondently, she lay in bed, refusing to see visitors. Physicians came from Edinburgh to poke and purge. She heard Arnault in whispered consultation with another surgeon, "Her Majesty's spirit is sick as her body. She seems brokenhearted."

Wanly, on the third day, Mary rose and received James, Lethington and Argyll in her Council Chamber. Seated on a dais in an arched recess between two windows, she looked down at them coldly, thinking, They are contented as cream-filled cats. They cannot wait for the murderers to return and settle their scores with Darnley and Bothwell.

Huntley joined them, and Lethington went to Mary and knelt at her feet.

"We are extremely pleased by Your Majesty's decision to pardon the exiles."

She bade him rise. "You will not be so pleased," she snapped, "that I have changed my mind. I cannot bring myself to pardon the killers of a man I—" She flung up her head—"loved."

James said drily, "It seems that Elizabeth is not the only queen who vacillates. May I ask how you intend to deal with your husband?"

"I shall write him at Stirling and tell him I have reconsidered and am refusing to pardon his enemies. But he will not believe me, and fearing trickery, he will not dare come here to ascertain the truth. His terror will keep him at Stirling through the christening."

"I grant that is clever, Madam. But how do you propose to rid yourself of Darnley *after* the christening?"

"Through annulment."

Lethington and Argyll spoke in unison. "Impossible."

"I have explored that impossibility," Lethington explained. "Even if the Pope granted it on the grounds of consanguinity, the child would be declared illegitimate and lose his claim to both thrones."

"Then perhaps—" Mary winced at the word—"divorce."

The lords brightened. "That," Lethington said, "is wool of another color."

"We might be able to arrange it," James said, turning heavy-lidded eyes toward Mary, "provided Your Majesty pardons the exiles."

So they wished to bargain. Her first impulse was to refuse to discuss the matter. Then she thought, I am not shrewd enough to win a divorce by myself. Should I appeal to Rome without advice I might make grievous blunders. I need Lethington's brilliance, James's caution, Argyll's legal knowledge.

"If you do not divorce your husband," Lethington said, "he may do you further mischief."

"I know," Mary said. "Sometimes I think if I am not free of him I will do myself a mischief."

James appeared shocked. "You must not dream of such a thing, Madam. Let us help you. You need not even meddle in the negotiations. The sordid processes are beneath you."

How perceptive he is, Mary thought; how well he understands my cowardice. While they conspire I will shut my eyes and spare my conscience.

"I must make two conditions," Mary said. "That the divorce is negotiated lawfully. And that it does not prejudice my son."

From the doorway Bothwell said, "If a divorce is possible, I doubt it will prejudice your son. My parents were divorced, Madam, and I succeeded without difficulty to my father's titles and estates."

Surprised at Bothwell's presence, but relieved by his approval, Mary said, "Very well. But remember, my lords, you shall do nothing that may stain my name or my honor."

Lethington smiled. "Ease yourself, Madam. Let us tend this matter."

"Suppose the divorce is not granted?" Mary asked.

"Why then, nothing shall happen but what Parliament approves."

James cut in hastily. "Your Majesty will pardon the exiles?"

"Yes," she sighed. "Later." The divorce proceedings would take time. There was no hurry.

Bothwell remained after the others had left. "I have word from Jean, Madam. She wishes me to return to Haddington."

Mary took the blow in silence, groped for words. "Very well," she said finally. "But remember you must go to Stirling November 24th to supervise the christening preparations. Workmen and decorators will be awaiting you there."

"Yes, Madam. But I thought with your permission I'd bring Jean here to remain with you while I'm away." He smiled. "A change might sweeten her."

Or sour her so that you too will want a divorce. I will try once more, Mary thought. I have been too timid, too fearful. But this time I will stop at nothing.

"By all means," she said. "Jean shall come here."

That evening Bothwell went to Haddington, and returned with Jean the following afternoon. She was thinner and paler, Mary thought, a ghost of a girl. But she was obviously delighted to be reunited with Bothwell, and as obviously depressed when he left for Stirling.

"I am pleased," Mary said, "that you and Bothwell are reconciled. He never told me what happened, but I guessed that perhaps you had reason for jealousy."

"I never had proof," Jean said, "and I behaved despicably. I marvel that he returned to me."

"Did you confront him with your suspicions?"

"I told him I had been stupidly jealous after hearing gossip of him and Bessie Crawford, and I asked his forgiveness for doubting him."

"What did he say?"

"Nothing, Madam, at first. He seemed stunned. Then he roared out that jealousy was childish and unworthy of me, and warned me never to display it again."

"Did he deny the affair with Bessie?"

"Why, no." Jean seemed surprised. "Denial is beneath him."

You naïve fool . . .

"I would not dream of asking him to deny it," Jean said stiffly. Mary thought, Four months ago it was difficult for me to hurt

Jean because I liked her. But as my love for Bothwell grows, my liking for Jean diminishes, and I see her as she is—a cloddy Highland countrywoman without flair or wit. She is so smug that she will not even paint to emphasize good features, flaunting her plainness as though it implies virtue. She will cling to Bothwell like a burr, basking in his glory and contributing nothing but children dull and placid as she. Doubtless she orders her household efficiently, but I wager her cook is atrocious. Stewed beef, watery kale and—as exotic fare—a trifle of honeycakes, raisins and custard. She'd not have imagination to try new dishes such as I provide him—potato pie or a dessert of turnips embellished with cream and a dash of Spanish wine. Anything different intrigues him, but Jean is clamped to convention. Her vision is as narrow as his is broad. She will not adventure with him . . .

Mary said, "I am so relieved Bothwell is fully recovered, for I depend on his strength. When he was wounded I was frantic. I believe that worry over his illness caused my own."

"I longed to go to him at Hermitage, but he wouldn't let me."

"And quite rightly, my dear. He had a good physician and I made him quite comfortable at Jedburgh. Of course," Mary laughed, "there was gossip as there always is in a small town, but heaven knows we were invalids and my house was full of people."

"Who would dare gossip, Madam?"

"Harry said the whole town gossiped, but you know his evil mind. Though I must say James was little better. I heard nothing from August onward but 'What will folk think?' Just because your husband hunted and danced with me and frolicked at the fairs. To hear James, one would have thought us wanton."

"But of course," Jean said, "you were always chaperoned."

"Of course, except when we were lost in a forest or mired somewhere. But those things were unavoidable. Indeed, we were most discreet."

Jean's eyes opened wide. "Discreet . . ."

Mary smiled. "In my position I could scarcely afford another scandal."

Mary shifted to talk of Darnley and the hoped-for divorce, but Jean was quiet and questionless. Mary thought, she begins to wonder.

Lightly, brightly, Mary mentioned Bothwell frequently during the next two weeks. She talked of a new book they had read: "I vow it kept us up until cockcrow." And of his vigil by her bedside: "When I awakened after seven hours of sleep he was still there, his hand under my cheek. Imagine the strain he must have undergone, one hand in a sling, the other so cruelly cramped. But he said he'd not have roused me for the world."

Like a possessive wife, Mary remarked on more intimate matters: Bothwell liked his ruffles perked just so, with a touch of starch. What? Jean had not tried starch? Mon Dieu, it had been available for two years and no gentleman's linen should be without it.

On December 8th, Mary's twenty-fourth birthday, Bothwell gave her a parrot trained to say, "Pretty Mary," and she took more pleasure in the gift than in the furs and jewels and silk jersey hose that arrived from foreign lands. At night, her birthday ball honored the representative of King Charles of France, the Comte de Brienne. As Mary slipped into the claret velvet, the parrot squawked, "Pretty Mary," and she laughed, then turned to Jean.

"Do you think this gown is too revealing?"

"Not for a Frenchman," Jean said drily.

"But merchants and their ladies are coming from Edinburgh, and they are so pantingly respectable." Mary twisted and turned before the mirror. "However, I think I shall wear it. Bothwell says I am most beautiful in this—I mean, in this color." Humming, she scented her hair and trailed downstairs.

By such devices she roused Jean's jealousy. She took pains to beautify herself, bathing in cream and white wine, experimenting with new unguents from France. Violet salve deepened her eyes to mystery; gold and silver dust sparkled on her hair. She tried various wigs—auburn and taffy, and silvery white to complement a white robe she would wear at the christening.

Mary designed three new gowns to wear at Stirling which made the claret velvet seem decorous in contrast. Even her French seamstresses gasped at the low necklines, and Jean watched the final fittings in thin-lipped silence.

"Elizabeth's envoys will tell her I am far in advance of fashion," Mary said, "and that I most emphatically do *not* pad."

Fleming came in and stared admiringly. "Beautiful, Madam! But you will make us all look nunnish." She handed Mary a note. "By courier, from Stirling."

"From Lord Bothwell," Mary said, with a glance at Jean. She took the note to the window and read it. It stated that Darnley was visiting his father in Glasgow, but would return to Stirling December 16th, the day before the christening. All was in readiness for the ceremony. Bothwell trusted Her Majesty was well.

Dreamily, Mary looked up from the letter into Jean's expectant eyes. The eyes asked: "What does he say? Does he mention me? Does he miss me?"

Shivering in her bare-shouldered gown, Mary went to the hearth, grasped the poker to stir the fire and, as though by accident, let the letter fall into the flames.

"How stupid of me!" she said, smiling at Jean. "I meant to show it to you."

VII.

Stirling Castle rose like a giant cake in tiers of snow frosted with ice crystals. Candlelit from vaults to battlements, it sparkled against a violet sky, casting long shadows on the town below. Through the hilly streets billowed the banners of foreign horsemen. Hostels and barns were crammed with the retinues of ambassadors from Flanders, Savoy, Rome, Spain, France and England. Brawls broke out in the wynds, pledges were drunk in the taverns. Beggars, gypsies and peddlers swarmed everywhere. Village girls in berry-brown cloaks scuttered through the alleys, giggling or screeching as mailed arms pulled them into doorways. The Royal Guard clattered over the cobbles, their horses caparisoned in silver-fringed gold cloth and ear plumes. The Stuarts wore green damask suits, the Argylls scarlet, and Bothwell's Borderers swaggered in the color chosen for them by their Queen—blue, symbol of loyalty.

In sapphire-blue satin, Bothwell welcomed guests as they arrived in the Great Hall. The walls were hung with sequin-glittered white velvet, and the chandeliers were festooned with white jeweled ribbon to simulate icicles. The oak-beamed ceiling was hidden with star-spangled dark blue satin.

On ermine-covered tables lay gifts brought to Mary and her son. A diamond chain and pendant from Charles of France, who would be the child's godfather; a jewel-tipped feathered fan from the Duke of Savoy. Venetian goblets stemmed with rubies; elaborate baby caps and dresses; a coral teething chain; a miniature ruff embroidered in diamonds and seed pearls. From a dais between two oriel windows Mary received ambassadors and nobles under a white velvet canopy starred with silver. Her gown was white satin, its back-flaring ruff edged with emerald embroidery. Emeralds edged the square-necked bodice and clasped the points of her sleeves. Her white wig curled under an emerald-meshed snood.

As the last noble kissed her hand and bowed backward, Bothwell came to whisper that Darnley sulked in his apartments and refused to come down for the ceremony.

"Shall I force him at dirk-point, Madam?"

"No," Mary said. "The envoys know he is here in the castle, and that is sufficient. He has no part in the ceremony."

Relieved, Bothwell turned, then paused. "I trust you won't be offended, but Jean and I shall not enter the chapel. We'll watch the ceremony from the door with James and Bedford."

"You fear the Mass," she teased.

"As Your Majesty feared our Protestant marriage. You would not even witness it from a distance."

"Touché," she smiled. "We are quits."

At five that afternoon two lines of noblemen holding tapers formed a path of light from the nursery to the Chapel Royal. Charles's representative, the Comte de Brienne, carried the six-months-old child swathed in ten yards of silver cloth on an embroidered cushion. Priests followed, incense puffing from golden censers. Catholic lords bore the crimson-and-gold cloth of state, the salt vat, basin and ewer to the chapel altar where the Archbishop of St. Andrews waited with three bishops. The child stared fascinated at the great gold font sent by Elizabeth, blinking at the blaze of rubies and emeralds that encrusted it. Brienne lifted him across the font to the Countess of Argyll, who promised in Elizabeth's name to be godmother.

Mary bowed her head. *God have mercy on my child, who is innocent of his parents' sins. Grant that he may be the first to rule a united Britain under Thy guidance in the true faith . . .*

The holy water, the prayers, the deep voice of the Archbishop: "I christen thee Charles James Stuart . . ."

She had christened him Charles to honor the King of France—a diplomatic gesture. But she would call him by her father's name, James.

Heralds trumpeted, then repeated the child's name and titles three times. To the music of cithers, harps and lutes Prince James was returned to his nursery, and the guests were summoned to supper in the Great Hall.

Mary had placed the Comte de Brienne on her right, the Earl of Bedford on her left, Bothwell at the opposite end of the table in the place traditionally occupied by the King. Bedford said, "Your Majesty honors Lord Bothwell above all men. My mistress is amazed at his new power."

Mary laughed. "I am amazed at her amazement. She knows full well his value to me."

"She wishes to know what manner of wife he married."

"You may judge for yourself later. The Countess of Bothwell sups above us in the ladies' gallery."

The ladies' gallery was a convenient device for Mary. It prevented the overcrowding of the Great Hall, where forty servants were serving sixty guests from elaborate buffet tables. It gave gentlemen an opportunity to talk and drink freely without wifely interference. It removed Jean from Bothwell. But Mary had placed Jean at an outside table on the gallery. She wanted her to see all that went on below.

After the sweets and the toasts, Mary left Bothwell with the gentlemen and changed from her white gown to a taffeta ball dress. Long identified with bawds, taffeta had recently been accepted by Spanish court ladies, and Mary had chosen the material for its rich, shifting colors that shaded from deep pink to violet to purple. It made her skin seem whiter, her eyes glowingly dark. She wore no necklace to break the beauty of her shoulders, but amethyst earrings and a coronet of amethysts in her hair.

Her return to the Great Hall was honored by utter silence, save for scraped benches as the men rose to bow. Pausing near Bothwell, she ordered the hall cleared for dancing. As the guests went to seats by the window she said, "Lord Bothwell, you shall dance the Royal Galliard with me."

"But Madam, that is the King's privilege."

"Who knows that better than I? I'll show the world in what esteem I hold you."

Bothwell looked down at her with an odd, deep light in his eyes and she thought, For once I have touched him.

He led her reverently through the dance—a stately pacing, a floor-deep curtsy, a solemn bow. So had the Stuart kings and queens gravely circled the great halls of the past, under heavy crowns, purple and ermine catching the glow of the wind-flared tapers and the firelight stirring shadows on the ceiling.

The dance ended. The foreign guests, unsure whether it was proper to applaud, beamed and bowed. The Scots maintained a sullen silence. Mary signaled Lord Robert to summon the ladies from the gallery.

Bothwell said, "I thank Your Majesty for the honor of the dance, but I fear it was unwise to usurp your husband's privilege."

"He is drunk or asleep in his chamber."

"He is alive," Bothwell said drily. "It is he who should have danced the Royal Galliard with you, sat opposite you at table and greeted your guests. This will cause gossip, Madam."

Mary tilted back her head. "And if it does?"

"Can gossip serve any good purpose?"

"Yes. That dance served notice that you are the foremost noble of Scotland. I will teach folk respect for you."

"A high-minded purpose. But the only respect I win will be with these." He pointed to the sword and dag held by his bearer.

"They will learn respect as well as fear," Mary said stubbornly. From the corner of her eye she saw Jean shyly approaching, and she beckoned to her. Jean curtsied, her stiff white damask skirts spreading to reveal an underpetticoat of blue lace. "How lovely you look, my dear."

"Thank you, Madam," Jean said, chin high.

"My lord," Mary turned to Bothwell. "She has been neglected all day. You must dance with her."

"No," Jean said. "With Your Majesty's permission, I shall retire. I have a migraine."

"Oh, I am so sorry."

Bothwell said, "If Your Majesty will excuse me a few moments, I'll escort her to our quarters."

Solicitously, Mary bade them go. When Bothwell reappeared, she made no move to summon him but danced and chatted with her guests. It was not her strategy to flirt with Bothwell unless Jean was present.

The next afternoon at the bull-baiting in the snowy park, Mary kept Bothwell and Jean beside her. The bull was chained and as mastiffs tried to creep beneath his belly, he stamped and tossed them, Mary clutched Bothwell's arm in assumed terror; warmed his wound-healed hand in her white fox muff; stood pressed in front of him to shield her back from the wind-driven snow. Jean's face was pinched with cold and misery. Under a squirrel hood, she stood forlorn, unnoticed, until Lord Robert brought her a covered mug of hot spiced wine.

Throughout the revels Darnley remained secluded in his mulberry-tapestried apartments. He summoned the Catholic ambassadors, but they refused to go to him. Their rulers had instructed them not to intrigue with him or heed his complaints. Except for servants, no one went near him. But Mary learned how he fared from Bothwell's page Paris.

"Madam," Paris said, "William Taylor, your husband's valet, tells me your husband sleeps and wakes in nightmare."

Darnley would awaken and call for whisky to still his twitching muscles and calm his heartbeat. Then he would rise and pull back the window hangings to see if it was day or night. Hour after hour, he sat in the window seat hoping someone would pass in the courtyard—someone, anyone—to look at. One dusk he had seen pipers and thought in his drunkenness that they were serenading him. But when he leaned out to thank them, town urchins threw snowballs through the casement, and he drew back, cursing and sobbing, to throw himself on his bed. Often he awakened screaming that James and the Douglases were behind the arras, and Taylor would draw back the tapestry to show him the stone wall. Fearing poison and trusting no taster, he refused to eat, and when Taylor proved that the food was harmless, he accused him of trickery and being in James's pay. He would allow no one to shave him lest his throat be cut, and his hands shook so that he could not shave himself. Taylor persuaded him to stop drinking for a day and a night, but when he was sober, the devil taunted him with voices, and he sat in his chair replying to imps Taylor could neither see nor hear. The voices told Darnley to kill or be killed, and he would draw his sword and start to the door threatening James's life, but Taylor would pull him back or call the guard to help subdue him.

Paris said, "Your husband is haunted by apparitions visible to no one but himself."

A ghost hound padded through Darnley's chambers, gaunt, white, with long blood-dripping eyes. Eyes were everywhere, staring from the walls, from the ceiling, through the windows. To evade them, Darnley covered himself with sheets or cowered behind the arras drenched in sweat. But when he drank, the apparitions fled, the voices were silenced. Then he would sit with bared sword or cocked dag listening for human enemies, for the creak or the footfall or the rattled casement that would presage his death.

Mary spared no pity for him. He had created his own hell, and she had problems of her own. In a gathering of foreign diplomats there was bound to be both political and religious tension. Soothing, wheedling, she walked a high, nervous tightrope, distributing her favor as evenly as possible, sowing seeds of intrigue for future blossoming. It was not too early to work for her son's empire and she needed the full force and financial power of Catholic Europe behind her. Lest Darnley's letters damage her, she set to repair political bridges to France, Spain and Rome.

She was successful. But the Scots Protestants branded the christening revels expensive, flamboyant and "reeking of the Pope's hand." The papal dignitaries were disturbed because she had not allowed the Archbishop to put his holy spittle in the child's mouth.

Bothwell roared with laughter when she told him. "Why didn't you?" he asked.

"I'd let no pocky priest spit in *my* child's mouth! It is a filthy apish trick, rather in scorn of Christ than in imitation of him."

"So at last you question Catholicism!"

"I do not question Catholicism, I question the Archbishop's mouth. He is just over the pox, I tell you, and could likely disease the Prince."

"But you said the rite scorned Christ."

"So it does. But do you embrace all Protestant rites? No, you'd not even enter one of your own churches save to marry."

"Again we are quits. What news of your divorce, Madam?"

Mary frowned. "James and Lethington are vague."

"Because they contrive no divorce."

"But you were at the conference; you heard—"

"I heard them grope your mind, Madam, and gain from you an

admission that you wish to be rid of your husband. But they know as well as I that the Pope would be stark mad to grant your petition. You have no grounds acceptable to your church."

"Treason, murder, adultery, drunkenness, conspiracy—what more do I need?"

"You need to turn Protestant," he chuckled. "As for annulment, your only grounds are consanguinity, and that would render Prince James illegitimate."

"Then what shall I do?"

"You'd best frighten off Darnley by pardoning the murderers as soon as possible. You know that the moment your guests are gone and his fears are lulled, Darnley will be harassing you again. I see no end to it unless fear drives him from the country."

Mary sighed. "I long to be free of him legally!"

"Why? Do you plan to wed again?" he mocked.

She was in no mood for banter. Unwilling to accept Bothwell's certainty that divorce was impossible, she spoke in confidence to the high papal emissaries. Without exception they advised her not to broach the matter to the Pope. Divorce was hopeless. To ask it would jeopardize her standing in Rome, and gain her nothing.

Still she hesitated to sign pardons for the murderers. There were banquets and masques to take her mind off the matter; there was Jean to make desperate. How long, Mary wondered, will she bear my flirtation with Bothwell? How long before she turns on him in a shrewish rage and screams out her suspicions? Another hour? A day? A week?

The fêtes ended with a mock battle staged near the churchyard on the evening of December 19th. A sham fortress was assaulted by demons, centaurs and Moors as the defenders shot fireballs and firespears. Wrapped in sables, Mary stood between Bothwell and Jean, her hands covering her ears as the fireworks shrieked up to blaze against the night sky in streamers of gold and crimson. It was magnificent and horrifying, and she wished Bothwell had never thought of it.

"An abominable masculine idea," she said to Jean above the tumult, "to play at war."

Jean nodded stiffly. It is all she can do to be civil, Mary thought. To speak to me is more than her pride can bear.

"You've heard nothing yet, Madam," Bothwell laughed. "Wait until the fort blows up."

Fires caught on the wooden portcullis, tongued inward. As the defenders raced to safety, the fort exploded in a tremendous upheaval of wood, stone and upflung earth, leaving a great cavern in the snow.

It was not by design that Mary turned and buried her face in Bothwell's shoulder. She was trembling, terrified. He laughed at her, held her off; then as she swayed, he yelled for brandywine, which she gulped gratefully, apologizing for her childishness.

"Was it not dangerous?" she asked him.

"No, Madam, but it took a yim of doing. Gunpowder is tricky."

He turned to where Jean had stood. "She's gone—likely ran like a rabbit!"

"If she was as frightened as I, you'd best go to her," Mary said. "Please, my lord, she may need you."

He left—reluctantly, Mary thought. Surrounded by her guests, she went to the Great Hall. Many were leaving at dawn the next morning to spend Christmas or Twelfth Night in their respective countries. Since she would not rise early, she bade them farewell and final toasts were drunk.

By midnight she was alone. She was about to retire to her apartments, when Bothwell joined her by the fire.

She knew what his words would be before he spoke them.

"Jean wishes to return to Haddington. She is ill from constant migraines."

So she wants to escape . . .

"I'm sorry, my lord. She does look peaked. But I need you with me, and I would not want her to be alone at Haddington with only a country physician. Arnault must attend her here."

"That is what I told her, but she insists she needs the quiet at Haddington."

"In a few days there will be all the quiet here she could desire. James takes Lord Bedford to St. Andrews for the holidays; Lethington and the others go to their country homes. We will have a serene Christmas here and then journey to Drummond Castle, where the hunting is said to be excellent."

"Very well, Madam. Jean shall stay."

On the afternoon before Christmas Darnley begged to see Mary, and she went to his apartments. The change in his appearance shocked her. His half-grown beard was snarled and shaggy, his eyes bloodshot. A black ermine-trimmed doublet hung on his scarecrow frame.

"Why have you refused to allow the ambassadors to see me?" His voice was drink-slurred. "Am I leprous?"

"Yes," she said. "Politically and morally. But I did not forbid them to see you; their rulers did. No one wishes to become embroiled in your problems. Problems," she added, eying the whisky decanter, "created by your own weakness and treachery."

He changed from belligerence to petulance. "For eight days I've seen no one but my servants."

Mary shrugged. "You are prisoned in your own cowardice. You could have joined us at any time."

"Is James still here?"

"He leaves for St. Andrews in an hour."

Darnley asked about the other lords, and she told him that only Bothwell, Lord Mar and her half-brother Robert were remaining through Christmas.

"Bothwell is my friend," Darnley said. "He guarantees my safety here. I shall come down and join the festivities."

And spoil them, Mary knew. She had looked forward to a carefree Yule gathering. Her few nobles, jesters and story tellers and musicians. At Christmas she lifted social barriers; all of her servants joined in the frolics. Inevitably, Darnley would be the one unmanageable element, the profound embarrassment. He would demand attention, strut and slobber, ogle the young maids. Any hope of serenity would be impossible.

"It is Christmas Eve," he said. The bloodshot eyes in the raddled face were soft and shining, and Mary thought, I too see an apparition: Darnley in childhood, eager for the sight of Yule greens and holly-wreathed candles.

"It is a time for charity, Mary." He pushed back a curl that drooped low on his forehead. "Can we not begin anew? I know I am disheveled, but Taylor will shave me and I will wear my crimson damask—"

Mary turned away. "I am speeding some English guests to Newcastle with pardons for your fellow assassins."

He gasped, staggered back a step.

"As you have remarked," she said, "it is Christmas Eve. I must be charitable."

Two hours later, without farewells, Darnley and his retinue galloped down Stirling's rocky height through a blinding snowstorm. Mary believed he was bound for Glasgow, where in his father's house he would feel comparatively safe.

With Mistress McDoon and Peter Pye, Mary stripped the Great Hall of velvet and satin, and decorated it with snow-powdered greens. Oak beams were festooned with ivy and bay, the mantel and casements with holly and laurel leaves. Foresters trundled in the huge Yule log, and Mary summoned everyone in the castle to sit upon it, sing a song and drink a toast. Then it was pushed into the hearth and lit with the brand saved from last year's fire.

The wassail bowl was set up on a long table, dressed with mistletoe and rowan and filled with brandywine and spiced fruits. Mary waited on her servants, passed them platters of marchpane, candied flowers, tiny mince pies baked in the shape of Christ's crib. The fiddlers began "Tom Tyler" and she danced with her grooms and pages, butlers and chimney sweeps, woodcutters and kitchen lads, while Bothwell, Lord Mar and Lord Robert danced with the serving women. Jean, sitting aloof by the fire, watched a boisterous game of Shoe the Mare. The longest straw was chosen by Gaston, the fat French cook. As a wild mare who had to be shod, he puffed and snorted about the great room, eluding capture until Lord Robert tripped him and dove for his feet, pulled off his shoes and shod him in honey and feathers.

They played Blind Man's Buff and Hot Cockles. At midnight Mary distributed gifts and led the caroling. Then with her chefs she went to the kitchen to inspect the fine peacocks which would be served for dinner next day. They would be baked whole in dough, tails projecting through the crust in feathery splendor, bills gilded and brandied to flame at the table. There were apple-mouthed boars, geese, plover, roe, moorfowls, herons, swans, partridges and cranes. Mary nodded approval and returned to the Great Hall to end the frolic with a final toast.

At the door she extended her hand for the serving men to kiss, embraced the serving women and wished them all a Merry Christmas. Lord and Lady Mar bade her good-night and Lord Robert and his wife retired soon after. Only Jean and Bothwell remained talking quietly by the fire. Jean's face was lifted to his—trusting, worshiping. They smiled, clinked goblets, drank.

She is touched with radiance, Mary thought, she has come alive. What has he said to sparkle her eyes and smooth the strain from her face? Does she mistake Christmas sentiment for love, brandyglow for true passion? He is sorry for her. He believes the migraine myth and is tender with her as a father to a babe. That is all—that *must* be all.

Slowly Mary extinguished the tapers on the table. She was reluctant to leave Bothwell and Jean, yet she felt an intruder.

"Madam." Bothwell turned. "Jean is much better. I've persuaded her to journey to Drummond with us for the hunting."

"Wonderful," Mary said, joining them. "We will take only a few servants, dispense with formality and do as we like. You shall have a second honeymoon."

"Thank you, Madam," Jean said coolly.

She hates and fears me, Mary thought. But she is not ready to break. Something he said or did has given her new courage. I must find a way to shatter it, and quickly.

The dawn after Christmas they rode twenty miles through hard-frosted moors to Drummond Castle in Perthshire. It stood square-towered on a rocky summit that terraced down in wastes of snowy heather and overlooked the Vale of Strathearn and the frozen estuary of the Tay. They rode through an avenue of cypresses and cedars to the castle entrance, where Mary's grooms, sent ahead with other servants, came out to tether their horses at the courtyard wall.

As she entered the wide stone hall, Mary noticed a motto carved on the gallery above crossed spears: *Gang Warily*. But she was in no mood for wariness. She would trust her impulses.

They hunted all the next day, bringing in three bucks, a doe and rabbits. At dusk Mary changed from riding clothes to her new yellow velvet gown, the deep-necked bodice laced at the waist with gold-threaded amber. At supper with Jean and Bothwell she had gay gossip of the French and Spanish courts. Much of it was at Elizabeth's expense, and Bothwell roared appreciatively.

"Did you hear whether Elizabeth still loves Dudley—I mean, Lord Leicester," Bothwell said, using Dudley's new title.

"Apparently the affair continues, though she has eyes for others. There's a jest about that." Mary glanced at Jean, hesitated. "But I'd best not repeat it."

"Come, Madam. Jean has likely heard worse."

"Well, then . . ."

The story involved a lover ignorant of Elizabeth's anatomical deficiencies, and Bothwell bellowed delightedly. Jean stared down at her napkin, two bright spots of color in her cheeks.

"You see, my lord?" Mary spread her amethyst-ringed hands. "I have shocked your wife."

"Eh?" Bothwell turned to look at Jean. "Shocked, are you? I have told you jests as frank."

Jean said nothing, twisting the napkin in her lap.

Bothwell glared at her. "When a jest is made," he said, "you will have the grace to laugh."

"My lord," Jean stammered, "I—"

"I know your brand of humor, my lady. The prattle of your servants' children is not the beginning and end of wit. But I laugh at such wit out of courtesy to you. You shall return that courtesy to others or, by Christ, sit in your chamber alone."

"Perhaps," Jean said, her voice trembling, "you wish me to go to my chamber now."

"If Her Majesty can forgive your damned priggishness, stay."

[323]

Mary said, "She meant no offense. Of course she may stay."

"No." Jean rose, pushed back her chair. "I am sure Your Majesty will be happier without me."

Before they could speak, Jean ran from the room. Bothwell stared after her, swore softly. "I apologize for her, Madam. I'll pack her off to Haddington tomorrow."

"She is ill."

"That is no excuse." He rose abruptly. "I'll stop this moodiness if I have to beat it out of her. You will excuse me, Madam."

It was an order, not a request. After he left and the servants removed the table, Mary took her embroidery to the fire. He might be an hour or more.

But the hours passed and Bothwell did not reappear. Bare branches slapped the window, rattling like bones, and she heard the pelting of sleet and the rise of the wind. Smiling, she imagined the furor upstairs. Jean is telling him of my wanton behavior, and Bothwell is branding her a jealous, lying termagant . . .

At midnight, Mary went upstairs. Bothwell's suite was far down the corridor and she heard no sound. In the hall outside her apartments the guard had fallen asleep on the floor. She caught a whiff of whisky and smiled tolerantly. After all, it was the Christmas season and no enemies lurked here.

As Mary entered her bedchamber, Seton sprang up guiltily from the hearthrug. "I am so sorry, Madam, I must have dozed."

"Go to your chamber and sleep. I'll not need you."

Alone, Mary slipped into a white damask nightrobe. At her dressing table she sat down and unbound her hair. It was brushed three hundred strokes every night, and now she began the task herself. Her arm ached after a few minutes but she kept on.

"Two hundred and sixty-six . . ."

She had not heard such a wind since the night of Rizzio's death. There was a crash in the garden as a tree uprooted and struck the cobbled courtyard, but when she ran to the window the sleet was a solid, slanting sheet and she could see nothing. The tapestries shivered and ballooned, rushlights flickered wildly. She went to the bed and slid the long-handled warming pan from the foot toward the icy pillows.

There was a rap on the door—Seton, she thought—but when she opened it, Bothwell stood there in a belted green robe.

"I must speak to you, Madam," he said.

"But my lord, it is late."

"Now." He pushed past her, closed the door and stood with his back to it.

"What do you wish?" Mary asked nervously. He was white with

anger and the scar of his head wound made a red contrast to his pallor. "Is something amiss?"

"Very much amiss. Jean tells me you have tormented her for weeks, insinuating that we are lovers."

Mary gasped, appeared to grope for words. Finally she said, "But this is astonishing! What on earth could cause such fancies? Is she feverish, delirious?"

"No, Madam. Quite in her wits."

"But I don't understand. What did she say?"

Coldly he recited Mary's recent machinations, and she listened in pretended incredulity, shaking her head sadly. "Jean has built fancies on facts, my lord. I did speak of you often; after all, you are the subject dearest her heart. I did remark you liked my claret gown, and I did drop your letter in the fireplace. But evidently her jealousy has distorted my every word and act."

Bothwell's lips tightened. He said nothing.

"I have been patient with your presumption in coming here," she said sharply, "but now you must go. We will discuss this tomorrow."

"We will discuss this now."

"You do not order me! This is not Justice Court and I am not on trial. I need not defend myself against a jealous woman!"

"In years of judgment, Madam, I am not without some insight into character. Even if Jean had motive, she could not invent this tale. She lacks the imagination and guile. She is incapable of lying."

"Do you think I am lying?" Mary asked furiously.

"And do you think me a fool?" Bothwell left the door and came close to her, his mouth drawn down in an ugly line. "Do you suppose I have forgotten our conversation in Edinburgh last spring when I told you that beyond all things I abhorred a jealous woman? Is it coincidence that soon afterward Beaton came to Jean with gossip of me and Bessie Crawford—and that *you* advised Jean to watch and spy upon me?" His scorn was flaying. "I puzzled over your flirtation with me at Stirling; now I understand it."

"You understand nothing! You take the word of a jealous fool against mine!"

He smiled, and she shivered. "Very well, Madam. Give me your word that you did no harm to Jean—that her story is untrue—and I will believe you."

Mary stared at him. Her word was her queenship, made sacred by God. To betray it was unthinkable.

"This is no trick," Bothwell said. "On *my* word I will believe you."

He would never give his oath falsely—not if he were racked. She had only to say, "On my word, Jean lies," and he would accept that unquestioningly, beyond any vow Jean could make.

"Well, Madam?"

Mary lifted her head. "I will *not* give my word."

She saw admiration in his eyes before they darkened ominously.

"So you admit you tortured an innocent who could not retaliate, who was helpless against your rank. Why?"

She would never admit her love now. For she saw it as a spirit sickness, a body lust. Haughtily she said, "What I do requires no explanation. I will not be questioned by an inferior."

"You have so lowered yourself that I may question—and punish."

Mary stepped back, feeling a deeper terror of him than she had on the heights of Edinburgh Castle. She saw in one moment what others had seen for years: the cruelty, the animal cunning. His head was lowered, his lips drawn back from his teeth. In prideless panic she retreated toward the window. She was shaking violently and her voice quavered. "Get out!"

Bothwell moved slowly toward her. Her scream emerged as a shrill squeak.

"Who is to hear you above this wind?" He laughed soundlessly. "And if you are heard, it is a lovers' brawl."

In her fright she had moved backward against the wind-blustered hangings. There was nothing near for her to clutch as a weapon, not even a chair to put between them. She edged sideways, in line with the fireplace. If she dared run ten feet forward and seize the iron tongs . . .

But he too had changed direction, blocking her way to the hearth. There was no escape but the window and she dared not risk a two-story fall.

He was an arm's length from her. She pressed against the wall, spoke through jerking lips. "Coward! I am defenseless!"

"So was Jean."

"I did not try to kill her!"

"You tried to kill her trust in me, her marriage. Why?"

Not under torture would she tell him. She clenched her teeth and waited.

He struck her hard on the mouth. "That is for Jean."

Tears sprang to her eyes, and she raised both hands and clawed at his face but he seized her wrists, spun her around and pinned her arms behind her. Viciously she kicked backward and he threw her forward. She sprawled on the floor, her face in the rushes. Panting, cursing him, she turned over on her back. As she started to rise he bent down and, grasping the high collar of the nightrobe, tore the damask from throat to hem. Futilely she tried to cover herself with the split robe. He knelt, pinning her body between his knees. Grasping her flailing arms he spread them wide.

"This," he mocked, "is for me."

Mary squirmed and struggled, her breath coming in gasps. Through tears of shame and rage she saw his hard, down-curved lips, his dilated eyes. She spat as his face came closer and her saliva dripped down his cheek. Trying to scream, she found she had no breath for it. As his mouth clamped on her breast, she strained violently. Her sight blurred and she fainted.

When consciousness returned, her body was locked tight in his. Her hands were free, and she raked his neck with her fingernails until she drew blood, but he would not release her. She fought with all her strength, cursing, sobbing, pleading.

Finally he rose. She lay limp, sickened and shamed, her cheek ground into the rushes. He had treated her like a drab, a creature too low to kiss. He had placed her on an animal level from which she could never rise. For days at a time she had been able to forget other horrors—Amboise, Chastelard, Rizzio. But the memory of this would beat forever in her own body. Though Bothwell died for it, she would live with it.

Bothwell glanced down at her contemptuously. "Why so stricken, Madam? That was what you wanted, was it not? Why did you take such a devious means, tormenting Jean and trying to wreck our marriage? You had only to ask me, as Bessie did."

"Carrion! Swine!" Mary sat up, jerking the robe about her. "You are so vile, so—" Tears choked back her words and she dug at her eyes, bit her lips and tasted blood—"loathsome . . ."

"Indeed," he said, "I was only accommodating. Perhaps a bit rough, but your coyness made that necessary." He poked the fire, added a log to it. "A pity you swooned. Like your husband, I prefer a lively wench."

She rose, stumbled on the hem of her gown and ran to the door, but he reached it before her.

"The morning is young, Madam—not yet two. Surely you would not end this idyll?" He dragged her to the table, poured a goblet of wine and offered it to her.

Mary slapped the glass away. "You'll pay for this with the axe!"

"A high price. I grant your beauty, but you contributed nothing else."

Again she tried to get past him to the door, but he picked her up, carried her to the bed and tossed her onto it. The nightrobe fell open and she clutched it together, but he tore it off her. "Rags ill become you."

Mary reached for the sable coverlid on the end of the bed. He

[327]

threw it to the floor. She tried to burrow under the covers, but he pulled them off. Sitting beside her he observed her critically from tumbled hair to polished toe nails. There were bruises on her shoulders and he said, "They look like a sculptor's thumbprints on marble."

His slow scrutiny of her body enraged her, but she knew she would gain nothing by screaming. Even if the guard heard her, Bothwell could easily overpower him, might kill him to prevent his talking. The guard's death would not help her. Only her wits . . .

But her mind was a blurred red haze of fury. Huddled on the bed, shrinking to its far corner by the wall, she crossed her arms over her breasts; watched as he went to the table and brought back a flagon and glass. Setting them on the bed table, he poured wine and this time she accepted it. Perhaps it would lend her strength, stir her brain.

As she handed him the empty goblet she said, "May I go to my clothes press?"

"Is that where you keep your dagger?" He laughed. "I thought you had an axe in mind."

He sat down beside her and she pleaded hopelessly, "You must go. Jean will be expecting you back."

"I left her sleeping, exhausted from tears."

"She will waken and wonder where you are. Surely you would not let her find you here?"

"Your concern for Jean is something new."

"You have avenged her. For God's sake, go!"

"Go? I like it here." His glance idled about the room—the topaz hangings brought from Stirling, the marble-topped dressing table with its filigree chests and bottles, the mirror that reflected firelight. "A warm chamber, good wine—and you are still a novelty." He turned again to look at her. "I marvel you are not deformed from corseting."

"And I marvel you can sit here knowing you die this very day!"

He chuckled. "On what charge—rape?"

"I will charge you attempted my life."

"Come now, Madam. My worst enemies could not believe I'd fail at a simple killing. You must conceive a more convincing tale." He removed his robe and tossed it on the floor. "Meanwhile . . ."

Desperate, hysterical, she screamed, but he flung her flat on the bed and smothered her lips with his mouth. Not a kiss, she thought, but a gag. She scratched and kicked and he lifted his mouth and laughed as she struck wildly, missing his eyes. He crumpled her arms behind her and pulled her face up to his. Slowly, deeply, he kissed her lips.

Her captured arms ached unbearably and she went limp, whimpering against his mouth. He released her arms and she let them fall to
her sides. His hand traced the line of her throat, stroked her breast.
She grabbed at his hand, but again he jerked her arm behind her. His
fingers teased a path from chin to thigh. His lips opened hers.

Shuddering, she felt the slow start of fire through her body and
struggled to resist it. But it built under his lips and burned along
the path of his hand. He moved his mouth to her wet eyelids, down
her throat and breasts. She felt a deeper degradation, for he be-
guiled her participation and was amused by his power to stir her.
For a few moments she fought savagely, biting and clawing. But her
fury enhanced his pleasure, and she cursed him and lay rigid until
his lips lured her again to weakness and self-betrayal.

Slowly her shame turned to wonder, then to awe, and finally to
rapture. She lost all consciousness of self, sinking and surfacing in
the tide of his desire as if there were no barriers of skin and bone
between them. The high-crying wind, the metallic rattle of sleet
seemed distant, and she had no thought of time. Pinned under him,
her body grasped a truth her mind had never suspected: She was
not set apart but boweled in the universe. If she died in this moment,
a tiny upheaval would shift or slacken the wind, stir the frost-blue
reeds in hill pools and tremor the heather. And half a world away
some star remote as heaven would flicker for her passing.

The fire fell into ash. The candles died in dripping wax. Bothwell
released her, turned on his side. Propped on one elbow, he looked
down at her snarled hair, her tear-stiff lashes and bruised shoulders.
He sat up, bent his head and slowly, reverently raised her hand to
his lips.

He treasured her hand against his cheek, then bent and kissed
her cold little feet, covering them with the sable robe. Wordlessly,
he tidied the bed, brought her pink-pearled comb from the dressing
table and sitting beside her, smoothed the tangles from her hair. He
took her torn nightdress to the clothes press, chose a white furred
robe, and slipped it about her shoulders.

Propped against the pillows she watched him rebuild the fire at
the hearth. Firelight rosied the round full throat that hardened to
magnificent shoulders, shadowed the deep lightly-haired chest and
long legs. His skin shaded from pale amber to burnished gold, and
she wished for a sculptor to make imperishable the hard-gleaming
sheen of bone and muscle, to cast him in fiery bronze as he stood
before the blaze stretching like a cat. He had the insolent grace of
an animal; she thought of Darnley's soft pink body and shuddered.
She would forget Darnley, Jean. The course of her life had changed
and flooded beyond them.

Bothwell put on his robe and poured fresh wine. He returned to the bed, drew her into his arms and tipped back her head. Lips on hers, he trickled madeira down her throat, and she opened her eyes in astonished delight.

"Have you never drunk from lips before?" he asked, smiling at her surprise.

She shook her head. There was so much of love she had never suspected. He had bloomed the world for her, and happy, humble tears dripped down her nose onto the fur at her throat. In her gratitude she was incoherent. She knew only the cliches of love, and she needed words like new-mined diamonds.

"It is true that you practice magic," she said. "Two hours ago I wanted you dead. But now . . ." She bent her head in sudden shyness. "You work sorcery."

"A shoddy sorcery," he said bitterly, "learned in too many beds. You mistake base metal for gold."

"You cannot spoil my happiness," she smiled. "You have lifted me too high to fling me down." She put her hand in a deep, wavy ridge of his hair, caressed the cheek he turned from her. "What did I ever know of love? Pity, friendship and lust—Francis, Rizzio, Harry. I knew love's counterpoint but not its theme. The little streams but not the sea. I was never swept far from shore—until now."

Impatiently he said, "You wish to be lost, drowned, obliterated. You move to your own destruction."

"If this be destruction, I am grateful to you for it."

He swore. "What a gift you have for embroidering rags!" Abruptly he went to the window, jerking aside the hangings. He rubbed his hand on the frosty casement and looked out on a snow-swirled dawn.

She could not fathom his change of mood, but it seemed to be guilt. Was he regretting his betrayal of Jean? Did he wish himself back in the cool, safe haven of Jean's arms? But how do I know Jean is cool? A year ago he said, "Women cannot judge women . . . Jean's charms go deep." Deeper than mine? He has taught her, trained her to his will. Perhaps he compares us and finds her more passionate, more artful.

Her voice was small, shriveled. "Obviously you regret this. We will pretend it never occurred. You and Jean—" She swallowed painfully—"may return to your estates today."

He did not turn from the window.

"I ask nothing of you beyond continuing your military duties. You will remain my counsellor." She strove desperately to sound casual. "My little outburst was a stratagem, my lord. I dignified my wantonness with talk of love."

Swiftly he came to her, glaring. "You lie, and I'll have no more

[330]

f it. We had a truth bond once; we will again. Yes, I regret this. I took you like a bawd, first in hate of you, then for amusement. In your innocence you are grateful for timeworn tricks. It's your gratitude I cannot bear—to be thanked for spurious love."

He sat beside her and she drew back, chilled and miserable.

"Do you know how many women have sighed to the same strategy? Dozens. They are countless, forgotten. I meant you to be one of them. I thought only to humble you, and I find I have humbled myself."

She caught his hand in both of hers. "You would not feel humble if you did not love me. For years you have fought loving me; you would not even kiss my hand. Your heart wore armor. But now there is no need for it."

"There is more need than ever. You do not know me, Madam." She winced at his coldness, let his hand fall.

"I am no fop," he said. "No lover to be bedded at your pleasure. If I lost myself in you, you too would be lost."

"I am already."

"You are not! You are still capable of making your own decisions, ordering your life and your realm as you see fit. You can resist me now, for I have only played with you. You belong to yourself. But be warned—once I took you in love you would have neither conscience nor will nor judgment of your own. The tide would sweep you too far for returning. And there would be no spars to grasp, no Chastelards or Rizzios. I'd not share the smallest part of you."

She held out her arms, the white fur frothing back from her wrists, but he shook his head. "Think well on this. All of your life you have ruled others, dominated your husbands and your friends. You are accustomed to supreme authority. With me you would not have it."

"I would not care." She swayed toward him. "I love you."

He caught back her hair and held her face close in his hands. "Men will fight and die and lust for you. Men will dream of you when you are moordust and witchbells. But none will ever possess you, brain and body, as I do."

His hands on her face were painfully hard. Her cheek muscles were taut and she spoke through stiff lips. "If you love me I want no other."

Pulling her into his arms, he kissed her lips, tore the fur from her shoulders. She heard the changing of the guard in the courtyard, footsteps in the corridor.

"It is dawn," she whispered fearfully. "Come back tonight."

"The dawn be damned," he said, "and the world."

CHAPTER TEN

I.

MARY SLEPT ALL OF that day. At dusk she arose and went to the window. Winter on tiptoe, she thought, a tired day's silence before sleep. No breath of wind stirred snow from the cedars or troubled the ivy on the wall. Cypresses branched violet shadows on white gardens, and yew hedges were crystalled like Venice glass. Never, she thought, had the world been so exquisite nor her perception of it so acute. She wept, hugging the twilight to her, watching the sky change from turquoise to opal to gray.

She had heard that one did not recognize happiness save in retrospect. But I am happy now, she thought, in this moment, happier than ever in my life. Every part of me, body and brain, is taut, quivering, receptive. I could write a sonnet to match Ronsard's, a song to haunt the centuries. I believe I can even reach God, for God is love.

But she did not pray. Far off a black dot bobbed down the snowy road, dipping out of sight in hill cuts, reappearing. As it came close she saw a horseman who bore Darnley's banner high on an iron spear.

Reluctantly she left the window, dressed, and received the courier in her antechamber.

"The King is ill of the smallpox," he said, snowy boots dripping on the hearthrug. "His father has summoned the best physicians in Glasgow and they are hopeful of saving him."

"Have they fumigated him?"

"Aye, Madam, they placed him in a meat-pickling vat and fumigated him with cinnabar. He is being sweated. His chamber is hung with red cloth to absorb the fever."

Mary nodded approvingly. "I shall send my own physician from Edinburgh for consultation."

"His Majesty moans, and weeps your name, Madam."

"Delirious," she said coldly. "It is to be expected with a fever. Keep me informed of his condition. Tell him that when he is better uggest he convalesce in a more salubrious climate, France or Italy."

"Yes, Madam." The courier waited.

"That is all," she said.

Mary joined Bothwell for supper in the Great Hall. Mindful of he listening servants, she asked, "Is Jean ill again?"

He nodded. They chatted formally until supper was over. Alone by the fire, she told him of Darnley's illness.

"Smallpox?" He laughed. "It's likely the yaws caught from some lut."

Mary shuddered. "Or leprosy. Sometimes it is difficult to tell hem apart. But his illness does not concern me now. I wish to hear bout Jean."

He stiffened and she said, "Did you tell her about us?"

"I told her I loved you."

"What did she say?"

He pounded his fist with his hand. "What could she say? She vas gallant. No tears, no taunts. She told me she would go to Crichton tomorrow."

"She said nothing else?"

"Nothing."

"Was she not shocked at the idea of divorce?"

"Divorce?" He seemed incredulous. "I didn't ask it. I still have espect and affection for her, and I'll not hurt her more than I have. What a wretched fate you suggest for her—a deserted wife, protected only by her servants, scorned, slandered, the prey of fortune hunters. Even if I wished a divorce I've no grounds. She has kept her marriage vows."

"You love her!"

"Perhaps in the way you loved Rizzio."

"It is not the same at all!" she said furiously.

"No, but there are elements in common—pity and tenderness and admiration. Unless she wishes to wed someone else, she remains my wife."

"So I am lowered to the position of mistress while she remains on pinnacle, proudly presented as your wife—"

"But, my sweet," he interrupted gently, "you persist in forgetting hat you too are married. Why should I divorce Jean when you remain Darnley's wife?"

"You know I loathe him!"

"That is beside the point. He is your husband. If I divorced Jean ou would still be no more than my mistress."

"I would know you were mine alone."

Impatiently he said, "What is it you fear? That I'll bed with her? Can you imagine her submitting to me now I have told her of you? It would take more than rape to win her back, if I wanted her."

"She is not easy as I am," Mary gibed. "She is a *virtuous* woman."

"Save your malice," he said softly, and as always when he spoke in that tone, fear iced her back. "Your jealousy is obsessive." He rose. "Good-night."

"Where are you going?" she asked in panic.

"To my quarters."

"Will you come to me later?"

"I don't know."

She rose, standing beside him, longing to touch him but not daring to. "Can you not understand that I love you too much to share you? Last night you said you'd not share me with anyone, yet you ask me to share you."

"I ask only that we both show some measure of honor even in our dishonor. I have betrayed Jean's love, but at least I can continue to give her my protection—legally and with my sword."

Mary tried to understand his position. His principal trait was loyalty, and so he was ridden by guilt. Always champion of the underdog, he was stirred and saddened by Jean's helplessness. *Jean plays on his pity*, she thought, *simulating a gallantry she does not possess. How well she knew what would impress him—a proud, tearless dignity, impeccable self-control. I thought her stupid, but I find her formidable.*

She borrowed Jean's dignity. "Very well. But fidelity is a cornerstone of honor. I ask your word that you'll not bed with her."

"Your jealousy may tempt me to try," he said, "but you have my word that as long as our love endures I'll not touch Jean, nor any other."

He took her in his arms. She pressed her body to his, lifted her lips, sank deep in his kiss.

Bothwell escorted Jean to Crichton the next morning, and three days later met Mary at Callander Castle, where they were entertained by the Livingstone family over New Year's. But by Twelfth Night they were back in Edinburgh merrymaking at Holyrood with James, Lethington, and the highest nobles of the land.

Early in January, Mary received Rizzio's murderers in the Throne of State room. She greeted them frigidly, not offering her hand as they knelt and bowed backward from the throne. Bothwell and James stood near her on the dais under a purple velvet canopy.

Mary said, "My lords, none of you is welcome at court. I cannot forget that I saw you last in blood frenzy. Suffice it to say you are pardoned—all save George Douglas, who struck the first blow, and Kerr, who threatened me with a pistol."

[334]

Red-bearded Morton was their spokesman. "We humbly thank Your Majesty. We wish to make clear that your husband instigated Rizzio's death. We only followed the King's orders as loyal subjects."

"I like hypocrisy no better than treachery," she said. "You know full well that your loyalty was to me, your anointed Queen, not to my consort. I pardon you only because I hope your presence will frighten my husband out of Scotland."

Morton met her glance, blinked at the loathing in her face. "I understand his illness is severe. Perhaps it will solve Your Majesty's problem."

"Do not count upon it," Mary said drily. "God cannot want him."

"He'd plague the younger angels," Bothwell added softly.

She turned and smiled at Bothwell, holding his glance a moment too long. Bothwell's eyes warned her and she thought, I must be cautious. . .

As she started to speak of Darnley, she saw Morton slyly nudge young Ruthven and she was suddenly, shatteringly angry. These were her subjects, not her masters. She did not love at their command. In a horrified flash, she saw that their jealousy could do to Bothwell what it had done to Rizzio. Some evening at Holyrood the nightmare might be re-enacted.

"My lords," she said, "next time you set upon one of my friends I vow you will die. Not by the sword with dignity, but at the Market Cross as common criminals. You will hang until weak, then be revived. While still alive you will be quartered, your manhood and bowels knifed from your bodies and flung to the dogs." She touched her crucifix. "This I swear by God, the Virgin and my word as Queen."

Taking Bothwell's arm, she stepped down from the dais and left the room.

Alone with Bothwell in her audience chamber Mary said, "Did you note the way they drew back as I passed them, fearful of my very skirts? At last I have taught them terror."

"At least you have taught them caution." He grinned. "You shivered my spine. Now I shall shiver yours. Our agents from Glasgow report that an English ship lies at anchor in the Clyde. It's elegantly outfitted with scarlet satin hangings, the bunks curtained with gold cloth."

"Harry plans to sail!" she said delightedly. "When he is recovered he will flee!"

"With your child."

She clutched his arm and he said, "Never fear, he'll not get within the shadow of Stirling. My troops are on the way there now. There are conflicting rumors. Some say Darnley plans to kidnap the Prince and take him to kinsmen in England. I've also heard the tale that Darnley will seize the child, crown him and proclaim himself Regent. By God, it's even bruited that Darnley will voyage to the Scilly Islands and become a pirate! But of this we can be certain—he is trying to frighten you into reinstating him, or at least noticing him. To be ignored frets him to a frenzy. He had hoped his illness would arouse your sympathy, but since it didn't he snares your attention with plots and rumors."

"Rumor or not, I'll go to Stirling at once, bring the Prince back here and place him under guard."

"Your horse is saddled and your escort waiting."

Mary smiled and sighed. "What a king you would make! Decisive, venturesome—"

"And popular," he mocked. "How Scotland loves me!"

She said, "I am Scotland."

II.

Mary brought Prince James to Holyrood and installed him in a barred and heavily guarded nursery. She found him greatly altered. The fine fair hair had coarsened and darkened, and the skin was sand-colored. The ears had grown out of proportion to the thin, pointed face. He resembled no Stuart or Lennox, no one she had ever seen. A queer babe indeed, and oddly quiet. Lady Reres said he was shy with Mary because she was a stranger to him. With folk he knew well, he bounced and gurgled, as bright a baby as she had ever tended.

Through her Glasgow spies, Mary kept close watch on Darnley. His fever was diminishing. His father's house was at once a convalescence home and headquarters for conspirators. Here Darnley's disgruntled Scots and English kinsmen plotted means of dethroning Mary and lifting Darnley to power. Here by night came fanatic Catholics who hated Mary for her tolerance and regarded Darnley as champion of their faith. She learned that Darnley had spies at Holyrood, and dismissed suspect servants.

Almost daily, warnings came to Mary from friends in France and Spain, Flanders and Savoy. "Watch Darnley . . ." She learned that he continued to write Charles and Philip, accusing her of Protestant sympathies and of misconduct with Bothwell. James brought word of a plot to imprison her, and so did a servant of Beaton's.

Grimly amused, she said to Bothwell, "My husband fails even as a traitor. He blurts his plans to everyone."

"It's an obsession for attention, love. He would quit his plots if you wrote him a single kind word."

[336]

"He will never get it! To feign even kindness would sicken me. I am so deep in love with you I cannot waste thought on him."

Though Bothwell now lived at Holyrood, Mary dared not let him visit her chamber at night. The palace was too small, too heavily staffed for secrecy. They met at the darkened Exchequer House in the Cowgate. Each midnight she slipped out of Holyrood, a long cloak over her nightrobe, a taffy wig hiding her hair. Bothwell's henchman, George Dalgleish, met her beyond the palace gates and escorted her to the house. The hours in Bothwell's arms were made poignant by brevity and secrecy. Such snatched happiness whetted her desire and sharpened her excitement.

But each morning was a little death, as Dalgleish conducted her back to the palace in the icy, slate-colored dawn. Only her love, like poppy-drug, dulled her humiliation as she crept past knowing sentries across Holyrood courtyard to her private staircase. She assured herself that Bothwell was worth any risk, any sacrifice of pride. But when she reached her bed she lay sleepless, remembering a sentry's blankly correct face and avid eyes.

She was certain the Marys knew of her absences at night, though they never hinted it. No longer did they come to her chamber and pull back the hangings at sunrise. They awaited her summons, and she slept until noon. She spent hours beautifying herself. New attire was expensive and the christening had depleted her funds, but Fleming was clever at making over old gowns and nightrobes. Nightrobes fit for a trousseau, transparent and jewel-gleaming. What matter, she thought, that the trains swept stone floors or dusty hay? Bothwell must be dazzled. Her beauty must blind him to visions of Jean.

But she did not depend on it to hold him. She knew she could lose him without self-discipline, and so she assumed a new dignity. She spoke of Jean rarely, but with respect. When Bothwell visited Crichton one weekend to go over yearly accounts, she neither objected nor questioned him, though she was sick with jealousy. His love rewarded her. At their reunion he gave her the Hepburn ring, a diamond horsehead, the neck bridled in emeralds. She wore it on a chain around her throat, hidden between her breasts. It was inscribed with his motto—"Keep Trust."

She did keep trust in him. She was certain of his fidelity. But Jean's very existence degraded her. When courtiers mentioned the Countess of Bothwell she raged to think that Jean bore his name and belonged to him in the eyes of the world. Resentment simmered hotly under her pretended tolerance. She thought, Even in love I cannot be wholly myself. I must play the part he assigns me.

From midnight to dawn, the Exchequer House became her secret home. From the street it appeared deserted, the front garden an unkempt snarl of dried bushes and thistles. They lit candles only in the rear chambers which overlooked the kitchen garden, and heavy hangings obscured the glow. The bedchamber was small and bleak, the bed uncurtained, the one chair uncushioned. Scarcely a romantic trysting place, but she felt safe there. Dalgleish kept watch outside, a shadow in the wynd.

On a mid-January morning she lay in bed while Bothwell stirred the fire to new light. The Canongate clock boomed two and she mourned the vanishing hours. How they speed in this room, she thought, how they loiter at Holyrood! I would trade a year of my life for one full night with him.

She wondered about Jean. Bothwell had not mentioned her since his visit to Crichton a week ago. Did he write her? Did Jean write him? Impulsively she asked him.

"Yes," he said, "we write each week." He glanced toward the pouch belt that lay with his doublet on the chair. "I had a letter from her today."

"Does she—" Mary forced a smile—"ask you to return to her?"

"Surprisingly she does. She thinks I am witched, infatuated." He went to the bed and kissed the top of Mary's head. "As indeed I am."

"But it is more than that!"

"Far more. I love you."

In his arms she thought, I am content with the depth and fierceness of his love. I shall not think of Jean. And yet, I wonder what wiles she employs to try to pull him back? If a love letter lies in that pouch I must read it. I must know what she plots.

Bothwell rose, put on his cloak for warmth, and lit his pipe. The tobacco weed was fragrant and Mary sniffed it appreciatively. He said it was an Indian herb introduced into England by Sir John Hawkins and this led him into speculation about the New World. He did not believe the trees were gold-bearing. Elizabeth's sailors were celebrated liars.

Mary listened with half-attention. She must find some excuse to get him out of the room, and read Jean's letter.

"I am hungry," she said finally. "Would you slice some bread and cheese and pour some ale?"

"Avec plaisir, Madame." He bowed, puffing out his stomach in imitation of Gaston, and waddled toward the kitchen.

Mary leaned from the bed, grabbed the pouch and opened it. There were two letters from Jean and she scanned the first one hurriedly.

Infuriated she read: *I think this a passing passion. The luster of her position sheds a false radiance. She is a will-o'-the-wisp whom you follow, enthralled, through the swamps of love. Please God she does not mire you as she has mired others. She draws evil as a honey-pot draws flies. I tremble that your happiness is in her hands . . .*

Mary unfolded the second letter. . . . *Whatever happens and however long your infatuation persists, I shall be waiting. You may come day or night for an hour or a lifetime as it pleases you. Your chamber is daily strewn with cedar, all is in readiness . . . I must be honest with you—I am not brave. I weep away the nights, and to eat is torture. But be not remorseful for my sake. I do not hold you guilty, love. She is a fever you cannot help and I pray that God will guide you safely through it . . .*

Bothwell spoke contemptuously from the doorway. "So you spy."

Startled, she turned, her throat tight with fear. "I did not mean to spy! But I had to know what she—"

"You could have asked me." He put the tray of food down on the table and came to her. "I would have shown you the letters. I have no secrets from you."

Ashamed, she said, "Forgive me."

He jerked the letters from her hand and replaced them in the pouch. "Very well. But your prying is disgusting."

"Disgusting? I find her insolence disgusting. How dare she call your love for me a fever? Who is she to judge this as infatuation? What does that pallid creature know of passion?"

"I'm damned if I'll tell you," he said.

"Doubtless you compare us!"

"You force me to, and to your detriment."

"Are you blind?" she scoffed. "Can you not see these letters are artful contrivances designed to nag your guilt? And do you think *she* composed them? They smack of a writer's hired eloquence. They have the spurious sincerity of a cheap ballad. I don't believe she really loves you or ever did. She married you because of your rank and growing power and to gratify her need for self-importance. She prefers to be the Countess of Bothwell to plain Lady Gordon. Yet in her secret heart she still loves Alex of Boyne—"

"Quiet! You are mad with jealousy. And I thought you had changed."

"Why should I change? Why not you? Am I to make myself over to your whim, live my love as a lie?" She rose, her pink gauze night-robe spilling lace to the floor.

Defiantly she faced him. "Am I never to be myself? Long ago I escaped the dominance of Madame Diane and the Cardinal, but I never escaped the necessity of pretense. I had to pretend to the world that Francis was normal, Darnley decent. I had to lie to Elizabeth and my nobles, maneuver, dissimulate, scheme. But when I won you

I thought in private I could be truly myself. I believed you wanted a bond of truth as much as I. But no! You do not want a woman in love—you want a diplomat. When I wish to speak of Jean, as is only natural, I must first compose my face to sweetness. Then, after cautious consideration, in a gentle voice, I dare to phrase my question. Jesu Maria! Can you not see how constraint brews poisons in love? If I must hold you by hiding my feelings, my heart will turn crafty and false. Is that what you want?"

He started to speak, but her eyes blazed him to silence. "There is enough deceit in my public life without your compelling it in private. For three weeks I have crept to you at midnight like a slut. How do you think I feel to sneak past my sentries at dawn in a disguise that fools no one? To see James sneer when I leave a masque early, to come upon my courtiers whispering? Yet I would count the humiliation as nothing if when I entered here you accepted me as I am. Instead, you force me to exchange my physical disguise for an emotional one. You seek to mold me in Jean's image—"

"God, no!" he said, his hands hard on her shoulders. "I want you only as you are, shrew or vixen, I care not, for your very jealousy honors me." He crushed her close. "Do you think me insensitive to your feelings? Each dawn when you leave me I vow our meetings must stop and curse myself for risking your good name. But then as the day dies and the night comes on I know I must have you at any cost, and I send for you."

He ran his hand through the long, shining waves of her hair. "Forgive me, love. I too am jealous, but of your thoughts. Don't hide them ever again."

"If I become a shrew," she smiled, tilting her head to one side and teasing his nose with a finger, "you may order me to the ducking stool and immerse me in the North Loch."

"I'd far prefer to spank you."

She nuzzled her head on his shoulder, sighed contentedly. "Do you ever daydream about us?"

"Dreams are futile. Why?"

"I have a favorite daydream," she said wistfully. "To waken with you in my bed at Holyrood and find in the dawn not panic but peace. To hear the clock strike five, to see the sky lose its stars—and to sink back in your arms and slumber on. To chatter with the Marys when they bring our breakfast tray. To eat with you by the fire and dress with you and descend the stairs on your arm. To enter the Throne of State chamber and say to my nobles, 'Good morning my lords . . . we overslept.'" She lifted her head. "To be your wife."

The candlelight shadowed his face, highlighted the hard planes of his cheeks and deepened his eyes to fathomless blackness. "A sweet dream. But impossible."

"Unless she would divorce you. Unless Morton and James rid me of Harry."

"They are rabbits. I have sat in their councils."

"You did not tell me—"

"Because the councils came to naught. Morton requires what you dare not give—a warrant of consent, signed and set with your seal."

"Consent . . ." She stepped back from him slowly, her body rigid. A candle hissed and died in smoking wax.

His smile was grim. "I know your nature, love. You do not ask 'Consent to *what?*' lest you learn too much and burden your conscience. So it was with the proposed divorce. So it is now."

Hastily she said, "I know they want my consent to forcing Harry out of the country. I gave it verbally." Her words tumbled faster. "Indeed, any means they take—of frightening him—will suit me so long as I am not involved. You may tell them that."

She turned from him, but Bothwell caught her face between his hands and forced her to look up at him.

"I will spare you all I can," he said. "But this you must know: For once, James, Morton, Lethington and the rest fully support me. However, being men of excessive tenderness—" His voice was heavy with sarcasm—"they delegate to me the honor of the act. They will look through their fingers and say nothing."

"Cowards!"

"Though we treat him like filth Darnley *is* the King and they shudder at involvement in regicide."

"Please!" she begged. "Please say no more."

"I must. For you are going to help me."

"*No!*"

"You will go to Glasgow and persuade Darnley to return here."

"No! I cannot, I will not!" Her eyes stretched wide and she tried to break away from him, but he held her tightly. "For the love of God—"

His lips stilled hers. He picked her up and carried her to the bed.

At dawn, he said, "Lethington, Morton, Balfour and I will perfect a plan. You will go to Glasgow—"

"*I beg you*—"

"—this week."

III.

At sunrise on January 21st, Holyrood courtyard was thronged with the Royal Guard and troops waiting to escort Mary to Glasgow. They had prepared a canopied horse litter for Darnley's return journey, and its gold-cloth curtains ballooned in the fierce wind. Bothwell, in a great fur-collared cloak, paced to and fro, rubbing his gloved hands, looking up at Mary's window. He would accompany her as far as Callander Castle.

Mary stood in her bedchamber, pale and taut-faced before the long mirror. She wore a tight white leather jerkin that flared out from her hips, black breeches and boots of pearl-embroidered white Florentine kid. White ruffles foamed at her throat, white plumes curled from the brim of her black velvet hat. Slowly she turned from the mirror, took her pearl-handled riding whip from Fleming.

Beaton fastened the last clothes chest. "There, Madam, everything is packed."

Darnley's favorite gowns. The claret velvet . . .

Mary sat down and buried her face in her hands. The Marys clustered around her asking if she felt faint but she shook her head. Bothwell was inflexible. She could not move him to mercy or postponement. For the past five days she had argued with him, cajoled, quarreled, pleaded. She told him frankly that she wanted Darnley dead, but that she could not bear his death on her conscience. She wished the end without knowing the means. Bothwell understood her need for self-trickery and did not blame her for it. But he reminded her that Darnley was vicious. To wait could be dangerous. She must consider the child's safety as well as her own happiness.

She thought, It is shockingly simple. I must choose between Darnley's life and Bothwell's love. Bothwell did not threaten her, but she felt that if they could not look forward to marriage she would lose him to Jean. Ultimately he would tire of secret love and chafe at its limitations. Skulking was not natural to him. He would miss the freedom of his country estates, the peace there. Jean's letters would set him a-dream. Most men in their hearts wanted normality and ease. Bothwell, despite his venturesome nature, was no exception.

She was learning him like a book slowly unfolded. For all his rough masculinity, he was fastidious, with a touch of the sybarite. He cursed the lack of a bathing tub in the Exchequer House, the dusty flea-bitten rushes, the timbered ceilings too low for a man so tall. Like herself he wanted his dressing gowns, his slippers, a change of linen. Trivial things in themselves, but the lack of them was discomforting.

She thought, We are accustomed to comfort, beauty, grace. For all the savagery of our love, we are not beasts to cohabit in a den. But we dare not furnish the house, nor leave clothing there. I am hampered by the absence of luxury, not for myself but for him. My body alone cannot hold him. I must create an aura of exquisiteness, of gaiety. A woman must be forever inventive. Love can die for lack of imagination, and I cannot begin to express mine fully. We should have friends to spice our relationship, we should gossip and chuckle abed as well as make love. Within our reach should be globes and maps and the dozens of books that interest him. Music. But I cannot sing or play for him lest someone hear from the street. It is a house of silence and shadows, whispers and smothered laughter. And if we cannot look forward to marriage, there will be less laughter as the months pass. Bothwell will grow bored and restless. I cannot bear to watch the death of love. Better that Harry dies now.

"He is better dead," Bothwell had said. "He will never learn to live with you, nor others, nor himself. His presence on this earth mocks God."

"God must decide that, not we."

"You didn't wait for God's wrath to execute Chastelard nor young Gordon in the Highlands nor the wretches whose heads you had for Rizzio's murder. This too is justice, and long overdue."

"There is a difference between execution and . . ." She could not speak the word.

"One is public, one private," he said. "One is legal, the other illegal. But you've broken the law before."

"Never! I abide by Scots law."

"Four years ago, my love, you passed a law making adultery punishable by death."

And now she was taking the law into her hands and leading Darnley toward death.

She glanced at the Marys, desperately envying their innocence. Fleming's problems? None. She loved Lethington and Mary, and asked nothing of life but to serve them. Beaton thought her dullard husband profound, and butterflied happily in his shadow. Seton was calm, radiant in her dream of becoming a nun. Livingstone, retired from court, raised a family in the country.

Not one would ever feel the burn of murder on her conscience.

I cannot do it, Mary thought. I cannot go to that sick boy, seduce him back here with promises of passion and power, and deliver him to his death. Even for Bothwell I cannot do it. I will go down to the courtyard now where the troops are gathered and I will say, loudly and decisively, "I have changed my mind. I am not going to Glasgow." Bothwell cannot kiss away my will with five hundred men looking on.

She said, "I have decided not to go to Glasgow."

Beaton came to kneel at her boot. "Madam, I am bold to say this, but we wish you would go. If you and your husband are reconciled —even if only outwardly—the terrible gossip will stop."

"What gossip?"

"Forgive me, but they say—" She turned her head—"that Your Majesty is Bothwell's mistress."

"And if I am?" Mary said coldly.

They stared at her in horror.

"Who are you to judge others? You, Fleming—your chameleon husband is not fit to tie my lord's boots. I love Bothwell, and I count myself honored by his love."

Even as she spoke her anger died. Poor lasses, they stood like broken stalks, heads bent, shoulders slumped. Impulsively, she gathered them in a clumsy embrace. "I know you seek only my good. Forgive me. I am so tired, so tossed by love and hate."

They soothed and petted her. Beaton said, "We only thought that if Your Majesty went to Glasgow it would stop the talk."

"But I *cannot* go. If you realized what . . ."

Suddenly she began to laugh hysterically. Beaton's round face, aghast at what she had precipitated, seemed to Mary inexpressibly comic. She laughed until her throat ached, until her eyes flooded tears. She ran into the audience chamber and fell sobbing on the couch.

Finally she quieted, dried her eyes, went to the table near the door and poured wine. But her hand was unsteady and claret brimmed over the rim of the glass and trickled onto the pale gray rug. Red stains on the floor . . .

She put down the glass. Like a sleepwalker she moved haltingly to the corner and pulled aside the carpet. Rizzio's blood spread darkly to the staircase.

For a long time she stood looking down at it. She was half-conscious of the impatient clamor in the courtyard, of the Marys whispering in the bedchamber doorway. She saw herself rise from a pool of warm blood and walk toward Darnley. *I am your nemesis.* She felt her gloved hand make the sign of the cross on Rizzio's grave. *I swear another shall lie as low before a year has passed.*

It lacked seven weeks of being a year.

Seton spoke timidly from the doorway. "Madam, you are white as a spookie. Please, may we help you to bed?"

"Bed?" Mary strode to the table, gulped the wine and snatched her whip from the sofa. "I am going to Glasgow."

IV.

Mary stayed overnight at Callander Castle. At sunrise, while the troops saddled the horses, she met Bothwell on the gallery that overlooked a fog-drifted garden.

"Can you not go all the way to Glasgow with me?" she pleaded.

"No. The Elliotts are rising in Liddesdale, and I must gather moss-troopers for an attack. Then I return to Edinburgh to perfect plans with my gentle friends."

"Trust none of them! They will use you to do the deed and then betray you. Who sanctions this plot besides James, Morton and Lethington?"

"All sanction it. Those actively concerned are Balfour, Archibald Douglas, Huntley, Argyll, Cassilis and some of my servants. Protestants and Catholics for once united."

"Promise me this—his death must seem an accident."

"We are considering various accidents. Lethington favors poison administered in his physic or draught—"

Hastily, she interrupted. "I shan't bring him to Holyrood lest he infect the child. But I know he will want to convalesce in luxurious surroundings."

"Agree to any place he chooses so long as you get him to Edinburgh. Then Lethington and I will decide where to lodge him. It should be isolated. Perhaps Craigmillar."

Mary was aware of a curious trembling. Outwardly she was composed. But inwardly every organ of her body seemed to be shaking.

Bothwell said, "Paris is a clever and dependable lad. I'm placing him in your service and he will accompany you to Glasgow and bring your messages to me. Tell Paris all that Darnley says to you. I want to know his fears, his suspicions, his ambitions—everything."

She nodded. "I will try to learn all I can. But it will be difficult."

"Darnley is clay in your hands."

"He was at one time. But his father has turned him against me. Perhaps the Lennoxes will even attempt my life."

"Do you think I'd send you there if there were the smallest danger? Would the Lennoxes dare attempt your life in their own house? Do you not have Huntley with you, a heavy guard, troops?"

"Yes, but my blood runs water when I am not with you. Only your love sustains me."

"Your hate will sustain you when you see Darnley again."

"But suppose it does not? Suppose I change my mind?"

"Your mind is no longer yours, love."

Swiftly he drew her behind the arras into his arms. Hidden by the tapestry, enfolded by his cloak, she burrowed her head in the hollow of his shoulder. Gradually she stopped trembling.

She said, "How can I bear to leave you? I may be there a week or more."

He pulled down her collar and pressed his lips to the fluttering pulse of her throat. "You'll bear it for the sake of your future."

And Scotland's, she thought. My mother warned me against giving

Bothwell political power, but he was only a wild lad in her time. Now he has matured, is capable of wise rule. He has proven it on the Border time and again. But I will not force him on the people until they know him well. After Harry's death and a decent year of mourning, he will divorce Jean. Then he will accompany me to public functions, we will hold circuit courts throughout the country, travel to remote areas. In two years we will marry. With marriage to look forward to, a hidden love affair will not seem constraining. We will find a charming cottage close to Edinburgh and furnish it for our secret use.

She said, "You shall be King. You shall wear the crown and have joint powers of rule."

Bothwell drew back and looked down at her, his face a conflict of astonishment and anger.

"Are you mad?" he asked. "Has love unhinged your reason?"

"You know I plan for us to wed! I told you my dream of being your wife."

"And I told you it was impossible. We are not removing Darnley as an obstacle to your marriage, but as a disgrace to Scotland and a danger to you and the child."

"But I want to marry you!"

"What could I bring you but trouble? Europe regards me as a pirate, a scurvy adventurer. I am Protestant. You'd be excommunicated by Rome, lose the friendship of France and Spain. For such an affront Philip would break his alliance with you against Elizabeth. Among your nobles—anarchy."

"So you warn me against yourself! What are you—counselor or lover?"

"Both, and shall always be. I'll not have you lose your realm and the world's respect for my sake."

"Don't you *want* to marry me?"

"Yes! I want you by every law the church and state can devise— ten thousand witnesses, seals on a mile-long parchment and every cannon in Scotland booming through the bells. But it's a traitor's dream and I'm damned if you'll snare me into it."

But I will, she thought.

V.

My Lord:

Being gone from the place where I left my heart you may easily imagine what sort of countenance I have, considering what the body is without a heart. That is why, until dinner time, I scarcely spoke to anyone and why nobody ventured to present himself, thinking it would not be tactful to do so . . .

The bearer of these letters will tell you of my arrival. He [Darnley] . . . said he was so glad to see me that he thought he should die . . . He told me of his illness and that he would make no Last Will but leave all to me; adding that I was the cause of his sickness for the sorrow he had of my strangeness toward him. And then he said, "You will not accept my repentance or my promises. I admit that I have greatly offended, but not in the matter which I have always denied. So have many other of your subjects and you have pardoned them.

"I am young. You will say that you have often forgiven me and that I repeat my offenses. May not a man of my age, lacking good counsel, fall twice or thrice and fail in his promises, and afterwards repent and rebuke himself by his experience? If I can win forgiveness I protest I will not fail you again. I ask nothing but that we may be at bed and table together as husband and wife. And if you will not I shall never rise from this bed."

Mary set down her quill on the writing desk and glanced toward the bed. The heavy red damask curtains were open, and Darnley lay on his side facing her, breathing deeply in sleep. A yellow taffeta mask with a slit for his mouth covered his pitted skin from forehead to chin. Squirrel robes were piled on him, tucked tightly into the mattress so he could not push them off.

The windows were closed. In the hot firelight the room was unbearably fetid. It smelled of Darnley's unwashed body, of pock-rot, cinnabar and rancid oils. On the bed table stood jars of skin unguents mixed of stag's blood, chopped mice, lynx claws and butter. Mary lifted a camphored handkerchief to her nose, and continued her letter to Bothwell, quoting what Darnley had said to her:

". . . God knows that I am punished to have made you my God and to have no other thought but of you . . ."
I asked him whether he would go in the English ship. This he denied on oath but admitted that he had talked with the English . . . In the end he desired that I would lodge here with him. I refused and told him that he must be disinfected and that this could not be done here. I told him I would bring him to Craigmillar where the physicians and I would cure him without my being far from my son. He said he was ready to go wherever I wished provided I would assure him of what he required of me.
You have never heard him speak better or more humbly. And if I had not proof that his heart is as wax, and were mine not as diamond, no stroke but coming from your hand would make me but to pity him. But fear not for the plan shall continue to death . . .

[347]

*I write you everything no matter how unimportant so that you may
form your judgment. I do here a work that I hate much . . . Trimly
I lie, dissemble, and mingle truth therewith . . . By flattering him
I wheedle information.*

*. . . Forgive my bad writing—you must guess at half of it. I am ill
at ease and glad to write you while others are asleep, since for my
part I cannot sleep as they do, nor as I wish I could—between your
arms, my dear life, whom I beseech God to preserve from all ill and
send you good rest . . .*

*I am weary and sleepy and yet I cannot forbear scribbling so long
as there is any paper. Cursed be this pocky lad who troubles me so
much. But for him I should have pleasanter matters to discuss. He
almost killed me with his breath, which is worse than your uncle's.
And yet I sat no nearer to him than in a chair by his bolster, and
he lay at the further side of the bed . . .*

*You make me dissemble so much that I am affrayed with horror;
you make me almost play the part of a traitor. Remember that if it
were not for obeying you I had rather be dead. My heart bleeds for
it. In short, he will not come with me unless I promise him bed and
board and forsake him no more. He will do whatever I wish and will
come, but he begged me to tarry until after tomorrow.*

*I submit myself wholly to your will. Send me word what I shall do
and whatever happens to me I will obey you . . .*

She paused and glanced again at Darnley. He was moaning in his
sleep. Then he turned over with his back to her, the great mound
of robes like a shaggy hill.

His eager welcome had astonished her. Bothwell was right—his
plots had been nothing more than bids for attention. She had not
seen his father. The craven Lennox, with an ill-auguring nosebleed,
had shut himself in his chamber, where he remained throughout her
visits. She had taken lodgings across the square, but spent most of
her days and nights in Darnley's bedroom.

Darnley was anxious to go to Craigmillar for sea baths, which he
hoped would draw the inflammation from his skin. His physicians
would accompany him. With nurses also in attendance, it would be
dangerous to contrive poison and so she warned Bothwell:

*Consider if you might not find some way more secret than a
draught, for he will take physic at Craigmillar and the baths also.
To be short, he is very suspicious yet trusts my word . . . I shall
never willingly beguile one that puts his trust in me. Nevertheless,
you may do all . . . For my own revenge I would not do it . . . He
is furious when I mention Lethington or you or my brother . . .*

[348]

*So that I may cut this short, the bearer will tell you the rest . . .
If I learn anything more I will make a note of it each night. Burn
this letter for it is too dangerous, neither is it well phrased for I
think of nothing but grief if you be at Edinburgh.*

*To please you, my dear life, I spare neither honor, conscience, nor
hazard nor greatness . . . See not her whose feigned tears you ought
not to regard more than the genuine sufferings which I endure to
deserve her place. To win it, against my own nature, I betray him
who would hinder me. May God forgive me and give you, my only
friend, the good luck and prosperity that your humble and faithful
lover wishes you . . .*

*It is very late. Although I am never weary of writing to you, yet
will I end, after kissing your hands. Excuse my poor writing and read
it over twice. Excuse also that I scribbled . . .*

Love me always as I shall love you.

Mary sanded the ink, and reread the letter. She saw that it was
replete with repetitions and inconsistencies, but she was too weary
to edit it. Writing him was a necessary purge. To keep her thoughts
pent was impossible.

With Bothwell she felt herself in thrall, an extension of his brain
and body. But when she was away from him for two days, the drug
of his domination wore off and she grew weak and vacillating. At
once she loathed and pitied Darnley, worked for his death and
prayed for his life. She asked God to intervene and spare him, even
as she fed his vanity and purred promises of love.

Now, the letter folded in her belt, she lay her head on the desk,
too weary to leave the house for her lodgings. What matter, she
thought, whether I sleep tonight or perish of exhaustion? I should
have died at Jedburgh; God meant me to. But for Bothwell, I would
have.

She had the strange fancy that God and Bothwell struggled for
her soul, that it was bruised and scarred from being tossed between
them. But in this tired moment, God was closer than he had been
for years. She knew that in spite of the sin she meditated—perhaps,
indeed, because of it—she could pray and be heard.

Slowly she lifted her head. It was true—He waited to hear her.
In this ghastly red-hung chamber was the presence she had lost. In
flooding tears, she slipped to her knees, her face in the cushioned
chair.

She begged forgiveness. In an ecstasy of gratitude she thanked
God for returning to her. She knew it was not by chance that he had
chosen this moment to lift her back to him. Though at the very
point of murder, she had not done it.

Swiftly she rose and walked to Darnley. The very shadows seemed fraught with white incandescence, which she sensed rather than saw. Her body was feather-light, as though in shedding her guilt she was weightless. As she reached the bed, Darnley turned over. The mask caught on the corner of his pillow and slipped from his face. She had not seen it uncovered, and she gasped. The closed eyelids were glutted with sand. The pox had dug deep pits in the fair skin and mottled it with a red scabrous crust, bloating the nose and cheeks. The lips were dry and fever-cracked. A stubble of golden beard pushed through the postuled chin.

She was shocked. He might never be handsome again. But with the loss of his beauty, so might he lose his vanity. Perhaps it would be his salvation. God sent afflictions so that men might gain wisdom.

She bent, smoothed a fair curl. Poor lad, no one had untangled his hair nor trimmed it, and it fell to his shoulders in snarled ringlets. But even in her compassion the stench was too great to bear and she buried her face in her handkerchief.

I cannot warn him and reveal the plot. But I can tell him that I have changed my mind and will return to Edinburgh alone. For a time he will be safe here, and then I will send him to France.

"Harry," she said, and touched his shoulder.

He opened his eyes, saw her, and grabbed his face. Finding no mask there he cried out and turned on his stomach, hiding his face in the pillow.

"My mask . . ." He groped about, patting the sheet, found the mask and put it on. Then he turned to her, propping himself on one elbow.

"Harry, I must talk to you."

"You saw me uncovered," he said peevishly. "I wonder you did not run."

"The physicians will heal you. Harry, I have changed my—"

"Is it not the grossest irony that I, of all men, should suffer this blemishing? They say with care and prayer the scars may vanish, and God knows I have prayed. But I must have a new unguent, a mix of diamond dust, oil of Spanish olives and lily essence. It is very expensive." His voice honeyed. "Will you obtain it for me, love?"

She nodded mutely.

"Thank you, sweet. My apothecary will tell you the cost. And when I go to Craigmillar the litter must be fully curtained so none shall see me. What are the curtains made of?"

"Gold cloth."

"Laced or furred?"

"Plain."

"Then order them edged with ermine . . . Why do you look so

tragic? Does it martyr you that I should travel properly? Taylor tells me you have a new ivory saddle and your horse is dressed in China brocade. Am I to be a pauper in your train?"

"No."

He stretched and yawned. "Why did you waken me?"

"No matter," she said on a sob. "Go back to sleep."

During her five-day visit in Glasgow Mary wrote Bothwell four letters. She knitted him a bracelet of silk fashioned with a lock and key tied by two golden cords. And she wrote him a sonnet.

> For you what bitter brew of tears I wept
> When you ordained yourself my body's master
> Before you had my heart. For you I kept
> Sad vigil on a previous disaster.
> You nearly died before our love had birth
> And terror seized upon my heart and head
> Both for the love I bore you and the dread
> Of losing my sole rampart on this earth.
> For you I turned my honor to disgrace
> Though honor is our one sure joy and pride,
> For you bade Conscience seek a humbler place,
> Chilled my most faithful friends and set aside
> Virtue for shame. But what would I not do
> Love of my heart, love of my life, for you?

Paris rode to Bothwell with Mary's letters and gifts, and returned with messages and an exquisite sapphire ring.

"Lord Bothwell presents this jewel in token of his love for Your Majesty. He says that were his heart in his own possession he would send it willingly."

Mary blushed, pleased but embarrassed. She was not sure she liked this wiry, beak-nosed young man. True, he had an accurate nose for plots. The flappy ears missed little and the long, sardonic mouth was discreet. But his manner was slyly impudent. As he bowed and gave her the ring he looked as though he was about to wink.

"Thank you, Paris. Tell your master I shall wear this in love and pride." The ring fitted her finger perfectly and she held it toward the candleglow, enchanted by its sparkle. "What messages do you bring?"

"My master and Sir James Balfour spent an entire night discussing where the King should lodge. They decided against Craigmillar as too public. Balfour suggests a house in Edinburgh owned by his brother. It has been empty for years and is extremely isolated, surrounded by fields and the ruins of old churches."

"Jesu, it sounds dismal! Harry would never agree to it."

"Balfour insists it is very pleasantly situated on high ground, with gardens. He suggests you tell the King that the climate is healthy." Paris smothered a grin behind a grimy hand. "There are no marshes or fog-traps as there are at Holyrood."

"Have they prepared this house for his arrival?"

"They are doing so now, Madam. Furniture and tapestries are being brought from your palace."

Mary sighed. "Very well. I will do my utmost to persuade him, but I'd best let him think he is going to Craigmillar until we reach the outskirts of the city. I must say Balfour's ruins offer little inducement to a luxury-loving invalid. Is the place near Holyrood?"

"A ten-minute ride. It is on the southern slope of Edinburgh. The region is known as 'Kirk O'Field.' "

VI.

Mary left Glasgow on January 26th, riding at the head of her troops with Lord Huntley. Behind them, Darnley lay in the horse litter on a purple velvet traveling couch, shielded from the wind by gold-cloth curtains bordered in ermine and lined with squirrel. He was piled with blankets and furs, his face wrapped in a linen mask.

They journeyed toward Edinburgh by easy stages, resting at castles on the way. It was brutally cold. A piercing north wind drove snow along the black-briared moors and gusted it from the hills. Streams were frozen solid, the cattails bent in grotesque crystals. Mary looked up at the sky. It was cloudless, ice-white, save for the black raven that had hovered above the cavalcade for three days.

Huntley's protuberant blue eyes followed Mary's glance. "The devil take it!" he said. "I wonder if Darnley knows that raven trails us?"

"He cannot see it. And surely his servants would not trouble him with so ill an omen."

Revolted yet fascinated, Mary stared at the bird. At dusk it flew off to scavenge for food but always returned to join them at sunrise as they continued their journey.

"It is certain that the bird knows," Huntley said.

Mary crossed herself, glanced at Huntley warningly. He was stupid as a sheep, she thought, and he looked like one, long-nosed and short-chinned with a loose, wide mouth. A blond spade beard swept back toward his cold-reddened ears. Like his sister Jean, he was tall and slender. Bothwell said Jean had poured out her troubles to Huntley, who had been shocked and saddened. Mary thought, For all his seeming respect Huntley considers me a wanton, a marriage-corrupter. He wants Bothwell to return to Jean, and so he is my enemy.

It was well to know an enemy's heart. She asked, "Have you heard from your sister since your stay in Glasgow?"

"No, Madam."

"I know she is unhappy," Mary said, forcing the issue. She motioned him to ride aside with her out of earshot of the troops. "But she and Lord Bothwell are ill-matched."

"They were once happy, Madam," Huntley said stiffly.

"Come now! You know that Jean loved Alex of Boyne when she married."

"True. But she came to love Bothwell instead."

"Doubtless she will change again. She seems capable of turning from one love to another."

"That is not her nature, Madam. She could never love Alex again. And of course he is married."

"Does Jean ever see him?"

"He rode by Crichton two weeks ago to pay his respects. After all, they are old friends."

Mary wondered if Bothwell knew of Alex' visit. If he thought his madonna was faithless he would not be so tender.

"Madam," Huntley said, "in all humility, as your loyal subject, I beg you be prudent in this matter. Not for my sister's sake, but for your own. Bothwell can bring you only harm."

"I thought you were his friend," she said scornfully.

"I am. In many ways I admire him. But not as your—your—" He floundered, reddening. "He should be only Your Majesty's protector, as he was your mother's."

"He loves me and I love him," she said. "Nothing, no one, will ever break us." Let him tell *that* to Jean . . . "I shall ride back to see how the invalid fares."

Mary turned her horse and trotted back to Darnley. As she approached, she saw that Darnley's guards had halted with lifted spears. The raven, wings spread wide, was hovering above the litter. It swooped down and settled on a stave of the gold-cloth canopy.

The captain of the guard raised his pike and struck at the bird, but missed. It rose croaking, and with a thrash of wings soared and flew eastward.

Sir James Balfour and his men met them on the outskirts of Edinburgh. Mary halted the cavalcade and rode a few yards with him for a private talk. She asked hopelessly, "Is Bothwell still determined to proceed with this?"

"Yes, Madam. The house at Kirk O'Field is in readiness."

"We will never get Harry to go there!"

He smiled. "Your Majesty minimizes your charm."

Balfour's smile showed broken teeth stained with coltsfoot and tobacco weed. He was stocky, black-bearded—some said black-hearted. But for two years he had proven an efficient Privy Councilor. He had a cool jurist's mind, a passion for detail and thoroughness. Mary understood why Bothwell relied on him. No plot would be haphazard in his hands.

"We must appeal to Harry's vanity," Mary said. "He is frantic for fear the people will see him before his pox heal. Come with me and we will try to persuade him."

They rode to Darnley and pulled back the curtains of the litter. He sat up on velvet cushions, greeting Balfour with a haughty nod.

"Sir James suggests that you convalesce in his brother's house at Kirk O'Field," Mary said. "No one will see you there, whereas at Craigmillar, I am told, a great crowd awaits you." It was a lie, but she knew he would believe it."I'd not be happy with a thousand star-eyed women jostling for a glimpse of you."

Darnley fingered his mask. Through the slits his eyes darted from Mary to Balfour.

"The house is not large," Balfour said, "but comfortable, and healthily situated on high ground among gardens. You'd not have the fierce sea winds of Craigmillar but gentle breezes. Your salt-water baths could be arranged."

"Are there quarters there for my wife?" Darnley asked.

"Indeed," Balfour said. "Her Majesty could have the chamber beneath you."

Darnley turned to Mary. "Do you promise to lodge with me?"

"Of course, love."

"Then we shall go there."

Astonished at the ease of it, Mary said, "As you wish. We should be there by late afternoon."

Riding with Balfour and Huntley, Mary said, "He is vainer than any coquette. I gave him a little mirror to wear at his belt, and I vow he keeps count of each pock as it fades and vanishes."

"He'll not count them long," Balfour said softly. "We plan—"

"I don't wish to hear your plans," Mary interrupted quickly. "I thought Bothwell had told you that I'll hear no details—none."

"I beg forgiveness, Madam."

They rode on in silence. The wind died, the white sky grayed, and fog drifted in from the Forth. Pushing through the crowded, narrow

streets of Edinburgh down Blackfriar's Wynd, they passed Archbishop Hamilton's house and came to Kirk O'Field.

Mary looked about her with deepening depression. In the mauve-
gray twilight she saw desolate untilled fields surrounding a
quadrangle of ruined church buildings. St. Mary's Kirk loomed
roofless in falling walls. There were empty arcaded cloisters emerald-
green with mold, the flagstone walks broken to rubble. What had
been almshouses for the poor were now stone shells along a wretched
lane called Thieves Row. On the south side of the quadrangle, its
gallery abutting on the City Wall, stood the only habitable dwelling
—the old provost's house, where Darnley would lodge.

From a distance she saw that it was a small two-story house built
of stone and sheltered by gaunt oaks. Birch trees leveled by an ice
storm strewed the ground like long silver splinters. In the fog-laden
dusk the gardens gloomed in a dark tangle of dead rose bushes,
honeysuckle and lilac.

The house was lit with candles and as they drew near, servants
appeared in the doorway. Light from their torches streamed upward
in a great gold glow. Above the dormer windows and crow-stepped
gables Mary saw a dark object silhouetted against the sky. She told
herself it was a strangely placed weathervane or a trick of light and
shadow—or a terrible fantasy of her mind.

But her men saw it too. There were sudden curses, prayers, a
splutter of Ave Marias. Beak down, hunched in its glossy feathers,
a raven perched on the peak of the red-tiled roof.

VII.

The old provost's house was built over an arched crypt. At the
cellar level were a kitchen, servants' quarters and storage vaults.
Above this on the ground floor were Mary's two rooms.

The front door opened into her long, narrow reception hall, which
had a raised dais and fringed canopy for the Chair of State. There
was a tiny bedchamber. As Paris unpacked her chests, she looked
around in shuddering amusement. Bothwell had brought furnishings
from Holyrood which, though elegant separately, clashed in color.
How like a man to choose orange-cushioned chairs, mauve tapestries,
the green-and-gold Bed of State. He could not know how she loathed
the sight of that bed. She and Darnley had shared it occasionally
when she had slept in his suite at Holyrood. The sable coverlid was
lined with satin and embellished with the Stuart and Lennox crests
embroidered with love knots.

Paris hung her gowns and cloaks in the high oak clothes press,
moving in soundless velvet slippers. Since she dared not have the

Marys here, he served as gentleman of the bedchamber. His versatility astonished her. He was spy, conspirator, courier and butler. But he was also deft at starching a ruff, lacing a petticoat, mending and pressing.

"Will Your Majesty sleep here tonight?" Paris asked. "Shall I lay out your night attire?"

"Yes," she sighed. "I must stay here often enough to forestall my husband's suspicions." But she was determined not to stay here every night. Only in Bothwell's arms could she find the courage to play her role. Some evenings she would escape by pleading pressing business at Holyrood, midnight conferences regarding the Border unrest. Then she would slip out to the Exchequer House and meet Bothwell.

Paris left her, and she changed her travel-soiled gown and climbed the spiral stairs to Darnley's suite above. His anteroom was hung with rabbit-catcher tapestries. On the dais was a large and majestic commode fitted with twin pans. It was upholstered in black velvet and canopied in yellow satin with red-and-yellow fringe. Above was a sleeping gallery for his valets.

Mary entered his bedchamber, which corresponded to hers. It was tapestried and carpeted in violet. Red-cushioned chairs surrounded a small table covered with green velvet. Near the fireplace was a big bathing tub with an unhinged door for a lid.

Darnley lay in a great bed curtained in violet velvet. As she entered he grabbed his mask and bade Taylor fasten it securely. Then he dismissed his servants.

"How do you feel, love?" Mary asked, sitting in the high-backed bedside chair. "Have they made you comfortable?"

"Fairly so." He glanced about the room. "But I need a proper bath cover and another table for my unguents, a big mirror—"

"Have patience." She smiled. "They will be brought. And I shall have exquisite food sent from Holyrood to tempt your appetite."

"You know what tempts me most," he said.

He moved to the edge of the bed and, leaning toward her, unclasped a garnet button on her bodice. Quickly, she caught his hand to her lips and kissed it.

"You must not, Harry—not until all your pox have healed. Would you infect me?"

"Yes, with my passion."

"That you did long ago." Disgusted by his desire, her lies came easily. "My ardor never died, though I sought to kill it. Even when I most mistrusted you, I wanted you."

"Not Bothwell?" he asked, withdrawing his hand from hers.

"Mon Dieu! First you are jealous of Rizzio, now of Bothwell. I marvel you do not revile me with the harelipped porter at the Netherbow. Credit me at least with some taste."

"Most women find Bothwell attractive," Darnley persisted.

"Indeed, the primitive male appeals to some. But probably his reputation as a lover is established upon his own boasting. Lady Reres was once his mistress, and she says he was no paragon—rough and bumbling."

"Did you ask her?"

"Fie on you! You know how she trumpets her past, and none can stop her. Be reasonable, Harry. I have known Bothwell seven years. If I had wanted him would I not have taken him long ago and prevented his marriage?"

He shrugged. "I hear he has left his wife."

"Do you blame him? She'd bore any man." Mary yawned. "I am sleepy, weary from the long ride. Forgive me if I sup in my bed?"

"If you wish," he said coldly.

Someone has roused his jealousy anew, she thought. Old Lennox must have heard gossip that last day in Glasgow. "I will breakfast with you," she said. Rising, she leaned toward him and kissed his throat between the mask and the velvet dressing jacket. "Sleep in peace, love."

Surely he is safe tonight. They would not dare the deed so soon, nor while I am in the house . . .

But she could not sleep. The old house creaked and stirred. At midnight, wind raved through the fields, banging the shutters to and fro and beating bare branches against the casements. Was someone taking advantage of the wind's clamor, placing a ladder against the wall or climbing a rope to Darnley's window? The only other entrance to his chamber was through her anteroom and up the spiral stairs.

Sweat covered her, and she threw off her blankets and the sable robe, then shivered with cold. She could not endure this another night. She must know what to expect and when to expect it. Yet to know was to share too great a burden of guilt.

I am a coward, she thought, worse than my nobles. And if I do not warn Harry, I am a murderess in the eyes of God as surely as if I plunged the knife . . . Will it be a knife or poison? Strangulation, or a thin, hot iron thrust up the rectum to burn out life and leave no mark?

Gradually the wind died. On the roof the raven croaked. The men had tried to kill it, but half-heartedly. None dared the wrath of the Devil.

At dawn she looked out the window. In the garden her guard was being changed. Archers and halberdiers commanded by Captain

Erskine swung onto their horses and rode off into the mist. Moss-troopers took their posts, shaggy-bearded, leather-coated Borderers —Bothwell's men.

A week later in the Exchequer House, Mary slipped out of bed while Bothwell slept, and groped to the clock on the mantel. In the faint firelight she saw that it was nearly four. At five she must meet Dalgleish outside and return to Holyrood. Darnley thought she had attended a midnight conference there with Lethington and Huntley.

Shivering, she put on her nightrobe, her shoes and cloak. She lit a candle from the fire and went into the stone kitchen, where she tipped the ale jug and poured two mugs. With the candle, she carried them into the bedchamber on a tray.

Bothwell was up, replenishing the fire. As it blazed high, his shadow in the great cavalry cloak sprawled across the timbered ceiling. She said, "I wish the people could see you now."

"Great God!" He ran his hand through the heavy, tangled waves of his hair. "Why?"

"Because they say you cast no shadow."

He chortled. "Satan, am I?"

"It's been rumored for years that you learned the black arts from Janet Beaton."

"Among other things." He grinned.

"It is not a jesting matter. When you killed the raven yesterday it proved you do not fear the Devil."

"Why should I?" He took the mug she offered, and they sat down on the bear rug by the fire. "If a man regards God as supreme he fears no lesser deity."

"If you feared God you would not kill. Tell the conspirators that you have reconsidered. Let them risk *their* souls."

"I'll not break my pledged word."

"They would break theirs in a second."

"Association with swine does not make me one. I'll not stoop to their level."

"Then," she burst out, "do the deed soon! For the past week I've clutched my sanity like a slipping rope and I cannot hold much longer. Why do you wait?"

"Because each day emphasizes your innocence. The people must believe in this reconciliation. They see you come and go between Holyrood and Kirk O'Field bearing food and gifts for Darnley. They presume you are nursing him. The delay is essential to strengthen your position as loving wife."

"And each hour strengthens his lust."

Bothwell swore. "Does he dare to handle you?"

"No, but I loathe the way he looks at me. His eyes feast through that mask. He watches my every move. And there is no end to his pleadings that I forsake 'state business' at night and devote more time to him. I promised to spend next Sunday evening with him. He has ordered some special wines for the occasion and a new dressing jacket. His skin has almost healed, and he hopes to remove his mask."

"But not your petticoats, by God! I'll drop by Sunday night and we will drink his health together."

"His health is so much improved that the physicians say he may move to Holyrood next week. He wishes to go on Monday. What can I do but agree?"

"Agree, by all means. Cart some of his furniture back to Holyrood so that he feels the move is imminent."

"Better that I cart some of my own furniture," she said. "This afternoon I'll make a spectacle of returning my State Bed to Holyrood. I will tell Harry that I am having it regilded to use as a renewed bridal bed."

Bothwell nodded. "I'll send a humbler bed to replace it. We must keep him at Kirk O'Field through Tuesday night."

"Tuesday . . ." She shivered. "On what pretext can we keep him?"

"On Monday morning you will waken with an agonizing pain in your side. You will remain abed until late Tuesday afternoon, when you will feel well enough to go to Holyrood and supervise final preparations for Darnley's arrival. Most of his servants will accompany you, bearing chests and furniture."

Her lips moved stiffly. "And then . . . ?"

"Darnley will expect you back after supper. While he awaits you, his remaining servants will be dispatched." He looked at her and smiled. "Do you wish me to tell you the rest?"

"No!" The curious trembling had come over her. "You've told me all I need to know."

"Let's trust his father doesn't come from Glasgow to nose around."

"He won't," Mary said. "He is kitten-spined. Besides, when I left last night Harry was writing a letter to him commending my goodness and the comforts lavished on him. Paris will contrive to scan the completed letter before it is sent."

"Good. Proof to the world—in writing—that you are an affectionate wife. Whatever happens you will not be involved."

"Please," she said wearily. "Must we talk of it further? Is there no way to forget this horror?"

He took her mug from her hand. "One way," he said, and pulled her into his arms.

VIII.

February 9th was Carnival Sunday. Edinburgh's houses were bannered, their galleries tapestried, the streets strewn with green boughs, tinted straw and gilded wheat. Gaunt John Craig, who had replaced Knox as minister of St. Giles, stood on the church steps and denounced the masqueraders who turned the Sabbath morn into a pagan revel. But he lacked Knox's fire and fury. His voice was drowned out in the collieshangie of bells, horns, trumpets and kettle drums.

Festivities began at Holyrood at ten in the morning, when Mary attended the wedding of two servants, Sebastian Paget and Christina Hogg. Later she presided at a midday feast for them. In the afternoon she rode to Kirk O'Field and spent an hour with Darnley.

"Remember your promise," he said. "You remain here tonight."

"Yes, love. I must attend a farewell supper for the Savoyard Ambassador at Balfour's house, but I shall be here at nine."

"And we move to Holyrood tomorrow?"

"Yes," she lied. "What time do you wish to leave?"

"At eight in the morning. And I want an escort of nobles— Lethington, Bothwell, Cassilis, Morton, Huntley, Argyll and your brother James."

"They shall be here—all but James. He left for St. Andrews this morning. His wife is ill with child."

She remembered Bothwell's words: "It is a curious coincidence that when James's enemies die he is always miles away." The stench of blood was growing too strong for him.

"Damnation!" Darnley said. "I particularly wanted James here tomorrow. It is time my nobles and I were reconciled. I wish to assure them that I hold no grudges."

Mary hid a smile. So he was willing to forgive the men he had betrayed. More likely, she thought, that he wishes a great display of pomp as he travels by open litter to Holyrood. He visions himself a golden Adonis surrounded by the highest nobles of the land. He wants to impress the people.

"I admire your tolerance," she said drily.

"You have pardoned them, and so shall I. Now mind, they are to be here precisely at eight in the morning."

"Yes, love." She rose. "I'll return tonight."

Wearing a gown of willow-green velvet, Mary supped at Balfour's house in the Canongate under a canopy of silvered oak leaves. Ambassador Moretta, Bothwell, Huntley, Argyll and Cassilis were in carnival costume, their dark satin suits glittering with jewels, masks swinging from their belts. At nine o'clock Mary rose from the table, bade farewell to Moretta and thanked Balfour for the feast.

On the High Street her guards stood warming themselves at braziers, while grooms scurried to bring horses from the tethering post. There was snow on the ground, and her slippers were thin. Bothwell carried her to her horse and lifted her into the saddle.

She whispered, "I'd best visit Darnley alone. If you come, it may rouse further jealousy."

"I'll not have you alone with him. We'll take Huntley, Cassilis and Argyll along."

With her nobles, preceded by guards and torchbearers, Mary rode up Blackfriar's Wynd, past the sentries at the gate and two hundred yards on, to the snowy meadows of Kirk O'Field. Bats rose from the ruins of St. Mary's Church and flapped toward the broken spire. Wind from the sea was sharp with salt.

Darnley, wearing a short sable-trimmed dressing jacket, received them in bed; graciously bade them be seated. He showed no resentment that Mary was not alone. Evidently he was delighted by the attention, and removed his mask for a moment to show them his healing skin. It had coarsened considerably and lost its apricot bloom, but they complimented his appearance.

"I vow you are handsomer than ever," Mary said, slipping off her cloak and sitting in the chair beside him. "You must have a new portrait painted."

"Then I shall need a new suit." Darnley glanced at Bothwell's black satin doublet with its slashed silver sleeves and passementerie. "That is striking, my lord. Who made it?"

"George Dalgleish, Sire. He was a tailor before he became my henchman. May I offer his services, and whatever fabric and furs you choose?"

"Thank you," Darnley said. He turned to the other three lords. "I wish to forget our former differences. We will drink to renewed friendship."

He sent Taylor for wine and whisky, which Mary declined, saying she had been troubled by a pain in her side and feared it might recur if she drank. The lords rose and toasted Darnley.

"To Your Majesty." Bothwell bowed to Darnley. "Health and long life."

Mary pulled her chair closer to Darnley, talking softly to him while the lords drew chairs to the table and played at dice. The clock struck ten-thirty.

Darnley whispered, "In twenty-four hours I will bed with you at Holyrood."

"Yes, sweet. And you will find your suite more beautiful. The bed is regilded and recurtained in your favorite shade of violet."

His eyes believed her, and further lies stuck in her throat. She turned from him, pretending to adjust her headdress, swallowing over a lump in her throat. Then, impulsively, she blurted a remembrance that had haunted her for hours.

"It was exactly eleven months ago tonight that Rizzio was murdered."

Darnley gasped. The lords turned from the table, their hands rigid above the dice. Helpless to recall the words, Mary stared at Bothwell in horrified silence, twisting her handkerchief to a knot.

"Why must you remind me?" Darnley asked shrilly. "Is it not over and done with?"

"Yes, yes, of course," she said. "I would not have thought of it, but Moretta mentioned it at supper. You recall it was he who brought Rizzio here from Italy." To cover her confusion, she reached for the psalm book that lay on the bed table.

"That is a Protestant book," Darnley said apologetically, "but I cannot read Latin as well as you."

"Shall I read to you?"

He lay back on the pillows. "If you like."

Mary ruffled through the pages. Passing St. Giles, she had noticed that the 55th psalm was posted for the evening service. She turned to it, reading aloud:

Give ear to my prayer O God; and hide not thyself from my supplication. My heart is sore pained within me and the terrors of death are fallen upon me.

Fearfulness and trembling are come upon me, and horror hath overwhelmed me.

Mary glanced up. The lords sat staring at the dice. She dared not look at Darnley. Hoping for a less sinister passage, she skipped a few lines down.

Day and night they go about it upon the walls thereof; mischief also and sorrow are in the midst of it. Wickedness is in the midst thereof; deceit and guile.

For it was not an open enemy that hath done me this dishonor, for then I could have borne it. Neither was it he that hated me that did magnify himself against me for then I would have hid myself from him.

But it was even thou, my companion, my guide, and my own familiar friend—

Bothwell interrupted. "Madam, forgive me, but it is nearly eleven o'clock. Have you forgotten that you promised the newlyweds to attend their masque at Holyrood?"

"Mon Dieu!" she said. "I completely forgot!"

Darnley jerked upright. "But you promised me! You said you would spend the night here."

"I said I would spend the evening, and so I have," Mary said lightly. "Now I must keep my other promise. You will have years of my company, but never again will my servants have their Queen at their wedding masque. I cannot disappoint them."

"God damn it, you must!"

"I cannot," she said coldly. "But I will come for you in the morning."

Darnley brightened. Eagerly, he caught her hand. "Eight o'clock. Mind you do not oversleep. And be sure all your nobles are with you."

"Yes, sweet."

Huntley helped Mary into her cloak. She bent and kissed Darnley on the forehead above his mask.

He clung to her arm. "You will be dancing late. How do I know you will not oversleep and keep me waiting?"

Mary smiled and removed one of her rings. "Here—a pledge of my return at eight. Sleep well."

With her nobles, she descended the spiral stairs and walked out to the front garden. As Bothwell helped her onto her horse, Paris came running up to them. His hands and face were black, and Mary laughed.

"Jesu, Paris, how begrimed you are!"

Paris bowed to her, whispered something to Bothwell and scampered into the house.

As the cavalcade moved off, Mary asked Bothwell what Paris had said to him.

"He thinks he may have some urgent information for us. If so, he will be at Holyrood within the hour."

"What kind of information?"

"I don't know."

Preceded by torchbearers, they rode past green-brown hedgerows through the Netherbow and down a mob-packed Canongate to Holyrood. The palace was lit from cellar to towers, and as Mary entered the inner courtyard she heard the blare of pipes.

In the Great Hall she danced with the bridegroom, with Lethington and Bothwell. At midnight Bothwell whispered that Paris had arrived, and Mary retired to her audience chamber, where Bothwell and Paris joined her.

"Tell Her Majesty what you just told me," Bothwell ordered.

Paris said, "Madam, at Kirk O'Field you noted I was begrimed. It was from poking about the vaults in the cellar. There's enough gunpowder stored there to blow the house to kingdom come—and three feet of fuse ready for firing."

Stunned, she looked from him to Bothwell. "But why? Who put it there?"

"I don't know, Madam. But assuredly the King's servants know. It would be impossible to introduce barrels of gunpowder into the house and completely undermine it without the knowledge of the servants. There are eight, and four sleep in the cellar."

"Harry's servants would not dare murder—someone orders them," Mary said. "When did you learn of this, Paris?"

"Tonight about nine-thirty, when Your Majesty was upstairs with the King, I took a notion for some brandywine but found the cellar door locked, which struck me as strange. Still, I've a neat way with locks, and that one proved simple. I made my way in, and then I smelled gunpowder. A few yards down the corridor I noted a break in the cellar wall, which someone had tried to cover with an ale keg. Then I heard footsteps on the stairs and fled out the back way. I dared not explore the vaults until the cellar servants retired after you left."

"Enough," Bothwell said. "I'll change clothing, gather my men and go see for myself. Come, Paris."

"No!" Mary begged. "It may be some trick to kill you—to kill us all. James ordered this! Why else did he leave this morning instead of Tuesday? With Harry and me dead, he would be Regent."

"James has more sense than to risk a fiasco with gunpowder," Bothwell said. "It's a fine means for spreading panic, but a clumsy and unpredictable killer. I've seen houses leveled and folk sitting among the ruins with no more than bruises."

Bothwell started to the door and she ran after him, clung to him and kissed his lips. "For God's sake be careful. You are all I have."

Alone, Mary paced the audience chamber, unable to sew or read or write. She should write Elizabeth about her reconciliation with Darnley and her plans for a second honeymoon, but she was too tense to put her wits to it. At quarter to one Fleming brought word that a courier urgently desired audience, and Mary received one of her Glasgow spies. He told her that Lord Lennox, Darnley's father, had left Glasgow and was at Linlithgow twenty miles away. Lennox had a large retinue but it did not look like a battle clan.

"Does he plan to come here?" Mary asked.

"I doubt it, Madam, for he has taken over the inns and hostels and looks to be settled for a time."

Another puzzle, she thought. Why should the ailing Lennox leave his comfortable Glasgow mansion for a dismal village? To hunt? It was possible but unlikely.

Mary dismissed the spy. The pipers were silenced, the palace grew quiet. She lay on the couch.

The clock struck two.

A shattering explosion shook the window casements, shivered the Venetian glass ornaments, shuddered the portrait above the fireplace. Mary sprang up. It was the world's end, the rending of earth and sky. No, a thousand thundering cannon.

Gunpowder.

The reverberation still echoed. Teeth chattering, heart plunging, sweat pouring from her, she stood in the middle of the room clawing at nothing, gasping for breath. There was clamor in the corridor, shouting in the courtyard, the ringing of the common bell in the Canongate. Presently church bells joined in tolling the city alarm: Three bells, silence. Three bells, silence. Death bells.

Bothwell was dead. She felt it deep in her heart's fiber. Bothwell and Darnley lay in the rubble of Kirk O'Field.

Mary moved to the window on unsteady legs. She flung open the casement and the wind caught her breath. In the courtyard, torchbearers ran to and fro like headless chickens. Dogs howled under kicking boots, horses neighed and whinnied. The drawbridge lowered in a great creaking whine of rusty iron. Mary looked up at a sky pitch-black, moonless and starless.

Candles flared throughout Edinburgh and half-naked people spilled into the streets. A panic-stricken mob choked the High Street, and those nearest the palace swarmed flap-cloaked down the Canongate to Holyrood. The bells tolled. *Bong, bong, bong.* Hollowly, drearily, endlessly.

Mary closed the window and walked to the table. With infinite care she removed green leaves from an ivy plant and let them fall to the carpet. She watched a candle die in smoking wax. Then she turned and looked about the room at the live tapestries and the dully gleaming altar.

The door burst open.

"*Bothwell!*" she cried, and ran into his arms.

Close, close she clung to him, smothered in his plaid cloak, her face against his chest. Wonderingly, she drew back. The spread cloak revealed a velvet dressing gown. She looked down. His feet were slippered.

Behind him, Huntley coughed embarrassedly. Mary turned and saw that he too wore night attire under his cloak.

Bothwell held her tightly. "Darnley is dead. The house is blown to pebbles."

"You are safe," she said. "Safe . . . safe."

"Come, steady yourself. We must go to Kirk O'Field."

"No!"

"As Sheriff of Edinburgh it's my duty. And you are coming with me."

"I cannot!"

"You must. Does a wife sit in her bower at a time like this? The people expect you to go to him."

"I won't!"

"Get your cloak."

Under the lash of his voice she went obediently to her bedchamber and brought her cape to Bothwell. He drew it around her, fastened the golden clasps and hooded her hair.

"Listen to me," Bothwell said, raising her chin. "I've not time to tell you what happened tonight, but you have my word for this: I did not kill Darnley, though God knows I meant to. Should anyone ask, I was in my bedchamber before the explosion."

Mary looked at the clock. It was ten minutes past two.

Bothwell gathered his men in the courtyard. Followed by a crowd, they rode to Kirk O'Field, where another crowd awaited them. The house was leveled, a scattered heap of rocks, wood, tile, tapestries, bone and pulped flesh. The four servants who slept in the cellar had been blown to fragments. The three who had slept on the second floor were alive, for the sleeping gallery, resting on the city wall, remained intact.

The crowd moved back respectfully, as Mary, supported by Bothwell and Huntley, stumbled along the snowy ground. Skirting jagged rocks and splintered furniture, they went to the back of the house. In the south garden the crowd was dense, orderly, silent. Town watchmen held lanterns, and Mary's torchbearers intensified the glare. There was an acrid stench of gunpowder.

Darnley lay straight on his back under a pear tree in the snow. One arm was tight at his side, the other curved toward his groin, and his legs were close together. He wore only a nightshirt, which was raised above his naval.

Bothwell said, "Has anyone touched the body?"

"No, my lord." An old man spoke, crept close and crossed himself. "I was the first here, but not for God himself would I touch him, nor has anyone."

The man, apparently a harmless dull-wit, said he was a beggar who lived in the ruined cloister. Bothwell questioned him closely and dismissed him. Then he knelt to examine Darnley.

There was not a bruise on the body, not a powder burn nor even a bit of ash. No blemish save pox scars. The eyes were closed, the face expressionless.

Mary stood silent, dry-eyed. Huntley brought torn cushions for her, and she murmured thanks and sat down, arms clasping her knees. She watched Bothwell intently. He alone seemed real.

A few feet from Darnley lay his valet, William Taylor. He was crumpled face down in an awkward kneeling position, and wore a nightshirt, a nightcap and one slipper. Bothwell turned him over. His body bore no mark. Close by lay his dagger on a belt. Bothwell examined the steel and found it clean.

Near the bodies, neatly folded on the snow, was Darnley's sable-trimmed violet dressing jacket. His slippers lay side by side as though carefully placed. There was a folded bed quilt. A small oak chair stood upright.

Bothwell examined each object minutely. None was torn, singed nor ashed. He frowned in puzzlement, walked to the edge of the gutted house and back again, estimating the distance as eighty paces. He ordered the guard to search the rubble for human remains and to bury them in the field. He bade them look for weapons and powder barrels.

Then he turned to the crowd. "If any among you heard or saw anything which may be helpful in the apprehension of the murderer, it is your duty to come forward and testify."

A servant who lived at Hamilton House near Blackfriar's Gate said she had hurried into the wynd after the explosion and seen a number of armed men running toward her from the direction of the house.

"How many?"

"It was so dark, my lord, I could not tell for certain—perhaps a dozen. I caught a man by the arm and felt velvet. It was no commoner who killed the King," she added triumphantly. "Poor folk wear honest wool."

"Did the man speak to you?"

"No, my lord. He broke from my grasp and ran."

A second woman, tall and shawled, spoke with quiet authority. "I lodge in the house nearest this garden, my lord, with my sister and my two young babes. The babes are sickly, and at one o'clock I was tending them. Sometime thereafter I heard screams, and my sister and I ran out into our field. We could see nothing in the dark, but we heard a man's voice pleading, and he said the same thing over and over, for perhaps five minutes: *'Pity me, kinsmen, for the love of God!'*"

"Kinsmen? You are sure he said that?"

"Positive, my lord. My sister will tell you the same."

"Have you ever heard the King's voice?"

"No, my lord."

The three valets who had survived the blast—Nelson, Taylor's son and Symonds—were being treated for minor bruises at Hamilton House and came at Bothwell's summons. They said the cellar servants had retired about eleven, but they had remained up to tend the King. At midnight Darnley had sung a psalm and had a cup of wine in bed. They banked his fire, while Taylor pulled out the trestle cot, preparing to sleep at the foot of the royal bed. Darnley bade them blow out the candles, which they did, saving one to light themselves into the adjoining anteroom and up to the sleeping gallery.

"What was the King wearing when you saw him last?" Bothwell asked.

"That nightshirt, my lord." Nelson's voice quavered. "His dressing jacket lay over that very chair, and his slippers on the floor."

"And you three went to sleep in the gallery?"

"Yes, my lord. None of us heard anything until we wakened to a terrible roar and spew, and found the house fallen about us."

"Did you know there was gunpowder in the vaults?"

They swore they knew nothing of gunpowder, had seen no strangers enter or leave the house during the week.

"But come to think of it," Symonds said, "when you and Her Majesty were leaving for Holyrood at eleven I saw Paris run out to you with his hands and face soot-black—"

"Aye," Bothwell said contemptuously, "so he did. He'd blacked for the masque at Holyrood, but I told him if he had no cleaner disguise none would dance with him. I forbade him to come with us . . . Is there anything else you recall?"

"No, my lord. Nothing."

There were no other witnesses. An artist in the crowd volunteered to make a sketch of the death scene, and Bothwell urged him to do so. It was a poor drawing, without perspective, but showed most of the scene clearly enough. Bothwell placed it in his belt to study at leisure.

An empty powder barrel was found in the ruins and trundled into the garden. Bothwell estimated it had contained sixty pounds of gunpowder, and ordered it kept as evidence. Then he turned to Mary.

"Madam, we have here a ghastly puzzle. But one fact is clear. You announced your intention of remaining here tonight and the murderer, or murderers, expected that you would be in the house. The blast was intended for you as well as the King."

The crowd murmured, a long dreary sigh of horror.

Mary blinked. His words slid off the surface of her mind. The queer gnarled pear tree, the corpses, the neatly folded garments all seemed remote, unreal.

Bothwell said, "I believe Your Majesty will agree that someone set this scene to mislead justice. Two corpses hurled by the force of an explosion through a shattered wall or roof could not land unmarked some eighty paces away. Nor could these garments alight, neatly folded, by an upright chair and paired slippers." He bent over Darnley. "I wager the King was frightened, perhaps by the smell of smoke as a slow-burning fuse was lit. He ran from his bedchamber, and Taylor followed with his clothes and a quilt to protect him from the cold. The chair I cannot explain—men seize strange things in panic. Or perhaps the murderer placed it here to confound us . . . Do you follow me, Madam?" he asked sharply.

Mary moistened her lips. "Yes."

"The King, followed by Taylor with the clothing, fled down the stairs through the postern gate and into this garden. He ran into the arms of the murderers who had lit, or were waiting to light, the fuse. They smothered him, perhaps with his own nightshirt, and killed Taylor in the same manner. They folded the garments and quilt to mystify investigators. Then they fled."

Mary nodded. "Just as you say, my lord."

Bothwell's frown was a warning. It stabbed sharply through her daze. Now she was fully conscious that a vast crowd watched her. In the blue-white glare of the torchlight she felt naked and bewildered. Obviously something was expected of her. But what?

"God knows we respect Your Majesty's sorrow." Bothwell paused for a long moment. She stared at him, shaking her head helplessly, grinding her hands together. "But though you are numb with horror, can you possibly recall anything said by the King tonight that would cast light on this?"

Light, she thought—I cannot bear the light! The torches and those women's eyes probe me like hot lances.

She hid her face in her hands.

Huntley said, "Her Majesty is too shocked to recall anything. Perhaps tomorrow—"

"Tomorrow the killers will likely be over the Border or at sea! Her Majesty must think, and we must act, and quickly."

"Her Majesty is too grieved," Huntley insisted.

Grief . . . Mary lifted her head. She must display grief. The people thirsted for her tears. If she gave them, the sharp eyes would soften to pity, and Bothwell would not frown at her.

"Harry," she moaned. "My love, my husband."

Like a spectator of her own drama, she saw herself rise and run to the corpse. She knelt by Darnley, hiding her face on his breast. His skin was cold, and she fought nausea. Her shoulders shook in dry retching. They would think she was sobbing.

But there must be real sobs, sounds for them to hear. She made the sounds, lifting herself from the corpse and rocking to and fro. Her voice wailed up, wavered as a hand came down on her shoulder, clamping it cruelly.

"Madam," Bothwell said, and though his voice was soft she recognized its cold rage, "come away."

Mary rose obediently, hands to her eyes. She heard Bothwell order his men to carry the bodies to the stable and stand guard there until a litter came from Holyrood. Peering through her fingers, she saw them lift Darnley, and she resumed her loud sobbing. Everyone must hear her. Soon she would see pity in those faces.

But through her fingers she saw that the faces were coldly appalled. No one approached her to kneel and murmur sympathy. None blessed her. In the merciless blaze of the torches they looked from her to Bothwell and back again.

Bothwell announced that all loyal citizens should watch for men whose clothing bore powder burns. He warned the Town Watch to halt any who sought to leave the city by West Port, Netherbow or other gates. "I will set a guard on all ports, order search of all outgoing ships, alert the Border patrols . . . Fear not, the King shall be avenged!"

There was no response. No sounds save the crunch of horses' hoofs in the snow, the wind in the charred bushes, and Mary's dry-eyed weeping.

IX.

Mary and Bothwell returned to Holyrood at four o'clock that morning. Edinburgh was wide-awake. Nightcaps poked from gabled windows, galleries and forestairs were thronged. The crowd was so dense that it split the seams of the Canongate and spilled into the lantern-lit wynds. Tall spears of the soldiers slid monstrous shadows up to the high-peaked roofs.

There was no clamor, no shouting, but a long sustained murmur of fear, incredulity and horror. It followed Mary to the outer courtyard, worried and confused her. Could they be mourning Darnley, a king they had detested? Were they making a lout into a martyr?

Bothwell helped her dismount and escorted her to her apartments. At the door he said, "You will do three things this morning." He spoke slowly, distinctly, as though she were a dullard child. "First, you will order the palace dressed in woe-cloth. Then you will sleep. Then you will eat. I will come to you at ten o'clock."

She pleaded a hand toward him. "Don't leave me!"

"I must. I'll be in my chamber."

He summoned her ladies and left her.

Mistress McDoon and the maids trembled down to the abbey crypts and brought up vast damask mourning cloths to cover the carpets. The walls were hung with black velvet; black candles replaced the rushlights. The French servants heard Mass at sunrise and the Protestants slipped out at dawn for prayers at the Canongate Kirk and St. Giles. Couriers raced through the foggy moors with word of the King's death.

Mary slept, a heavy dreamless stupor. Obediently, she ate the egg and drank the ale Fleming brought to her bed. Seton and Beaton dressed her in a mourning gown she had not worn since her marriage and swathed her hair in a black lace veil.

Bothwell came to her audience chamber at ten o'clock. She sat with him on the couch, her skirts spread stiffly between them, her throat taut in a high ruff that framed her face like the petals of a black tulip.

"I hated to waken you," he said, "God knows you need rest. But you must break your trance and listen to me."

She reached for his hand. "I am listening."

He studied her, frowning. Her eyes were like black glass. The hand he held was icy. He raised it to his lips, then warmed it between his own.

"Part of your shock is fear for the state of my soul," he said. "For your heart's ease I want you to remember that I did not kill Darnley."

"I knew you couldn't."

"Don't glorify me—it's the Devil's jest that I didn't. This is what happened after Paris and I left you last night . . ."

Bothwell had changed from carnival costume to rough clothes. With Paris and George Dalgleish he set out for Kirk O'Field at twelve-thirty. They were challenged by sentries at Holyrood and Netherbow gates. Rather than create suspicion, Bothwell gave his name boldly and made no attempt at disguise. In the Canongate he collected his henchmen from their lodgings—John Hay, John Hepburn, Black Ormiston and two servants, Wilson and Powrie. In the Cowgate he roused Archibald and George Douglas and their men. They went on foot to Kirk O'Field. The house was dark and silent and they crept around to the back, surprising Sir James Balfour and his kinsmen in the garden.

"None of us dared make noise so we spoke in whispers. I asked Balfour what he was doing there and he evaded me guiltily. I caught him by the throat and forced a confession from him. He admitted he was playing a double game. We thought he plotted with us for Darnley's death, but actually he was plotting *your* death."

Mary shook her head in an effort to clear it. "That is impossible. It was Balfour who suggested we take Harry to Kirk O'Field."

"Because there you would be isolated, vulnerable to his plans. It was Balfour who undermined the house, who planted the fuse. *Because Darnley commanded him to.*"

"No! You are mad!"

"I was mad with rage, but I let Balfour talk. He said there is a Catholic plot against you in Paris. It is led by Bishop Laureo, who brands you a Protestant dupe. The plan was to kill you and your Protestant lords and place Darnley in power as Regent. Details were arranged by Lennox and Darnley in Glasgow, conspiring with Balfour in Edinburgh. When Darnley agreed to lodge at Kirk O'Field it was because Balfour had written him that it was the ideal place for your murder."

"I can't believe it!"

"Your dear sister Elizabeth knew of the plot and so did Queen Catherine. There was one difficulty: the house could not be mined until Darnley was certain you would be in it. Your whimsical behavior—coming and going without advance notice—drove him nearly frantic. That is why he pinned you to a promise of spending Sunday night there. But your death was not sufficient to satisfy Bishop Laureo; if possible the explosion must also kill your Protestant lords —James, Lethington, Argyll, Huntley, Morton, Cassilis and myself. Hence Darnley's insistence that we all be there promptly at eight o'clock Monday morning.

"On Sunday morning while you were at Holyrood, Balfour and Darnley's servants mined the house, sent Paris on an errand and locked the cellar door. There was a final conference in Darnley's chamber. Upon our arrival at eight o'clock on Monday, Balfour and the servants would be in the cellar ready to light a slow-burning fuse. Darnley would make some excuse to go to the stables and run through the postern gate where saddled horses would be waiting to take him to his father at Linlithgow."

"Jesu! His father is in Linlithgow now."

"So I heard, with a thousand men and two thousand on the way. Well, love, you need not mourn your golden lad, nor trouble your conscience. Likely he prinks in hell at this moment and commands the devil to provide cooler apartments."

Mary shuddered. "But how was he killed?"

"I am coming to that. When Balfour saw my superior force and realized his plot had failed, he begged to join me against Darnley. I itched to kill him but dared not cause an uproar between his men and mine. To be short, I reinstated him in our cause, and while our men remained quiet in the garden he led me into the vaults. I saw the gunpowder laid ready, every nook and cranny stuffed full. I thought of that treacherous fool upstairs pimping for foreign fanatics and plotting to raise himself on your corpse—and I lit the fuse."

"But you said you didn't—"

"I thought, if he wants an explosion, by Christ he'll get it, and if the blast fails to kill him I'll return and strangle him as I'd first planned. Perhaps in my fury I made noise, or perhaps he smelled smoke. At any rate Darnley fled down the stairs. His valet followed, carrying his garments and, for some strange reason, the chair which you saw. They ran out into the garden and the Douglases caught them. When I came up from the cellar, I saw Darnley lying under the tree. Archibald Douglas had smothered him with a cloak and sat on his face. George Douglas killed the valet in the same manner."

Mary shuddered. For a moment she sat in silence, her cold hands pressed to her eyes. Then she said, "That woman testified she heard someone plead, 'Pity me, kinsmen.' "

"She heard Darnley appealing to the Douglases to spare his life. They are kin, you know."

"Why, so they are."

"Let me continue . . . Darnley's garments were scattered on the snow, and my fool man Wilson, out of mawkish respect for dead majesty, folded them reverently and set the chair upright. I estimated it would be fifteen minutes before the powder fired and hoped to be in Holyrood by then. We raced down Blackfriar's Wynd, where that woman from Hamilton House pulled at Balfour's cloak. He shook free and we all ran on, slowing our pace at the Netherbow, where once again the sentry challenged, and again I gave my name. Then we split in different directions. When the house exploded, Paris, Dalgleish and I were just inside Holyrood courtyard, and I ran upstairs and put on my nightclothes."

"But the Holyrood sentry saw you return?"

"Aye, but none will dare testify to it, as you'll see."

"I see chiefly that God was with you. He did not let you kill Harry."

"No," he said in supreme disgust. "God reserved that honor for Archie Douglas, and let me explode four wretched little sons of bitches."

"They too were traitors."

"Yes, and so were the three who survived, but we can't prosecute them. We can't reveal Darnley's plot without implicating ourselves. All we can do is pretend a search for 'unknown assassins.' "

"Must Balfour go unpunished?"

"Yes. At least for the time being. Murder makes odd alliances—though temporary."

[373]

She was silent for a moment. "You were angry with me at Kirk O'Field. Why?"

"Your act of grief was so false that it was embarrassing. And I could not stop you or warn you. But it was my fault for taking you there—I should have realized your addlement." He added gently, "You are still addled, and no wonder. But since you can't pretend sorrow, remain silent. We dare not risk another such exhibition."

"Tell me what to do and I will do it."

"You must call a meeting of your Privy Council immediately to satisfy the people that we are trying to avenge the King. I grant you it will be a farce, since every member present either counseled the murder or participated in it. But farce or not, such a meeting is imperative lest the people say we are remiss in our duty."

So Mary met with her nobles at noon in the Tolbooth on the High Street. The doors were locked and neither pages nor guards admitted. Argyll, Lord Justice of Scotland, presided from the dais. Mary sat above him, alone in the oaken gallery.

In the middle of the timber-paneled room, black-clad nobles sat at a long table, their heavy gold neck chains gleaming in the light of a dozen tapers. Balfour, Bothwell, Huntley, Morton and Lethington bowed their heads, while the Bishop of Orkney led them in prayer that God would help them avenge the murder. Argyll solemnly denounced the unknown persons who had assassinated their beloved King.

Then Argyll asked if anyone present had information or evidence. Bothwell rose with a man's velvet slipper in his hand.

"This, my lords, was found today in Blackfriar's Wynd. It may have been lost in the murderers' flight from the ruins."

Argyll examined the slipper and passed it down the table. When it reached Morton, he exclaimed in surprise.

"This is not evidence," he said. "Indeed, it looks to be the slipper my cousin Archibald has been missing for two days. He was running a stag near Hamilton House and lost it then. I mind he valued the gold rosette."

Argyll said, "That being the case, you may keep the slipper to return to your cousin."

Morton bowed from his chair. "Thank you."

"A pleasure," Argyll said. "Is there other evidence?"

"There was," Bothwell said. "My men found a powder barrel in the ruins of Kirk O'Field, and I ordered it preserved. Unfortunately a half-wit stable boy burned it for firewood."

"A pity," Argyll sighed. "Now we will never know where and by whom the gunpowder was purchased." He paused at a rapping on the door, and Bothwell went to the door and unbolted it.

"A courier with a letter for Her Majesty from our French Ambassador," Bothwell said. "Does Her Majesty wish it brought to her?"

"No," Mary said. Her apathy had returned. "Give it to Lord Lethington."

The Council recessed for five minutes while Lethington read the letter. Then he rose.

"Your Majesty, my lords," he said. "This letter, dated January 27th, is from Archbishop Beaton in Paris. It is alarming because of its very vagueness. He warns of a plot against Queen Mary, but was unable to learn details of it, though he questioned Queen Catherine and the Spanish Ambassador. I quote: '*I advise Your Majesty to take heed to yourself, for there be some surprise trafficked to your disfavor. Order the captains of your guard to be diligent in their office . . .*'"

Bothwell said, "But for God's grace, Her Majesty would be dead. Of what value is such a warning now?"

"Of great value," Lethington said blandly. "The letter comes most opportunely, serving as proof that the murderers designed to kill the Queen as well as the King."

The lords murmured approvingly.

Lethington continued sadly, "Some skeptics will question that the Queen's life was intended. They will say, 'She left Kirk O'Field at eleven o'clock to attend the Holyrood masque in a torchlight procession so conspicuous that half the town saw her. Why, then, were the murderers ignorant of the fact? Why did they blow up the house at two o'clock when they knew she was safe at Holyrood?'"

"That *is* a difficult point," Balfour agreed. "We can only suppose that the assassins were stupid peasants."

"I don't believe the people will care for that interpretation," Bothwell said drily. "Let us leave it at this—the assassins were stupid."

"It is unfortunate," Morton said, "that we cannot reveal the King's treachery. But for various reasons . . ." He let the sentence trail off.

Huntley said, "Lord Lennox will doubtless seize on the point of the Queen's return journey to Holyrood, and insist that the blast could not have been meant for her. Her Majesty should write him a conciliatory letter promising to avenge his son and inviting him here to see justice done."

"I have written such a letter," Lethington said. "It awaits her Majesty's signature. I have also—" He brought a paper from his leather case—"a statement which, with appropriate variations, I propose Her Majesty send to the rulers of Europe."

"Let us hear it," Argyll said.

Lethington read: *This night past, the 10th of February, two hours after midnight, the house wherein the King was lodged was, in one instant, blown into the air with such vehemence that there is nothing remaining . . . It was done by the force of gunpowder and appears to have been a mine. By whom it was done or in what manner appears not yet . . . We hope to punish the same with such rigor as shall serve as an example . . . for all ages to come . . . The matter is so horrible and strange we believe the like was never heard of in any country.*

Whoever has taken this wicked enterprise in hand, we assure ourselves it was intended as well for ourself as for the King (for we lay for the most part of all last week in that same lodging) and that same midnight of very chance tarried not all night, by reason of some masques at Holyrood. But we believe it was not chance but God . . .

Lethington looked up at Mary. "Will that serve, Madam?"

She glanced at Bothwell. He nodded and she said, "Yes, my lord."

"Now," Argyll said briskly, "we must offer a reward for the apprehension of the assassins. I suggest two thousand pounds and free pardon to anyone, conspirator or not, who will give information."

The Council agreed.

"Citizens should give such information to Lord Bothwell. As Sheriff of Edinburgh, he can best judge its value."

Bothwell nodded. "Should a citizen come to me with information I deem false, he will be arrested for obstructing justice."

"Naturally," Morton said. "It would be wise to publish that fact. In this way you will be spared the blather of fools who imagine they saw sights they did not see."

Mary half-listened. The scene held the same dream quality she had felt at Kirk O'Field. The oak-paneled walls, the high sunless windows barred with iron, the men at the long table—all were illusion. The tapers imitated tapers and their light was phantom. She extended her hand and touched the gallery rail, surprised to find it solid.

The Council adjourned in mid-afternoon. Mary rode toward Holyrood in an open litter between Bothwell and Lethington. She was conscious of the same appalled silence which the crowd had demonstrated the night before. After her triumph over Knox, the people had showered blessings on her. It was not unusual for them to shout praise of her beauty, cheer a new hat or cloak, reach out to caress the trappings of her horse. Now she heard a muttered curse, and crossed herself.

The cavalcade paused at the Market Cross. Heralds proclaimed national mourning, denounced the assassins and announced that a reward for information leading to their apprehension would be posted within twenty-four hours.

Trumpets sounded, and the horses moved forward. Rain pattered the cobbles, splashed from the peaked eaves of the houses, dripped from the fringe of Mary's black canopy. The crowd, like a vast shawled shadow, followed close and pressed at the gates of Holyrood. There was a stench of steamy bodies, wet wool, horse, and the musk of Mary's perfume.

As she stepped from the litter, a whisper began, flowing backward up the Canongate through the Netherbow to the High Street:

"The bed."

Along the gray wynds and closes the word traveled, through the Cowgate and Candlemaker's Row, the markets and the West Bow. By dusk, all Edinburgh recalled that the Queen had ordered her costly Bed of State carted from Kirk O'Field the day before the explosion.

"Aye, she saved her bed—but not her husband . . ."

CHAPTER ELEVEN

I.

DARNLEY'S BODY was carried to Holyrood on a board and embalmed by Arnault and an apothecary. Mary's lethargy had so delayed burial that there was not time to fashion a casket sufficiently long. The six-feet-six corpse was wound in a silk sheet and crammed into a six-foot oak box, without cloth of state or banners. The interment was late at night in Holyrood Abbey. In the dark vaults that smelled of centuries, Mary held tightly to Bothwell's hand and listened, dry-eyed, to the Mass for the Dead.

When she was alone with Bothwell her mind was lucid. Away from him, it moved torpidly. She embroidered endless pink roses on a white satin altar cloth. She kept her Council waiting two hours while she stitched a green vine.

For days she smelled gunpowder, insisting that it blew in on the wind from Kirk O'Field. Juniper was burned throughout the palace. In her chamber she wore a camphor mask or sniffed a cloved orange.

Bothwell was with her as often as discretion permitted. He begged her cooperation, wheedled, and finally shocked her out of her inertia. Alone in her audience chamber he said, "I am going to Crichton."

She sprang up from the couch. "Why?"

"Jean is ill."

Mary scoffed, "She is ill with jealousy and uses any excuse to bring you back to her."

He thrust Jean's letter at her. "Read this."

Mary read it and shrugged. "It is most artfully contrived—even to the tear-splattered parchment—but if it is true that she is cramping and vomiting, there's doubtless an excellent reason. The sly wench is probably with child by Alex of Boyne."

Without a word Bothwell grabbed his cloak and started for the door.

"Wait!" Mary ran to him, clung to his arm. "I did not mean that,

[378]

love. But you must not leave me now—you are my strength, my brain."

"You've a brain of your own. Exercise it or it will rot."

"I can't."

"You don't try. You crawl about like a shelled tortoise. I've been patient, God knows. Now I must be brutal. You made a guilty spectacle at Kirk O'Field. Since then you've done nothing to remedy it. Lethington is shouldering all of your responsibilities, trying desperately to hold your lifeline to France and Spain. Your Council works without you, sitting in session all night. And do you care? No, you embroider rosebuds. The people crave assurance from you, standing like dogs at your gates. They are pathetic, weighted with love and suspicion. You could remove the suspicion even now. You could address them informally, as you used to do. Because they love you, they would contrive to believe in you. They *want* to believe in you."

"I am not as I used to be."

"To them you are romance—the most beautiful woman on earth, the most generous, the most fascinating. Do you know what I saw in a Jedburgh hovel? A three-legged stool covered with linsey-woolsey and raised on four bricks like a throne. 'The Queen sat here,' they said. You had hallowed a common stool."

Tears flooded her face. "They think of me as I was, not as I am. How can I face them? I am a murderess."

"You're a sniveling coward."

Her head flung up, and she slapped him hard on the mouth. "Not even you may dare that!"

Bothwell laughed exultantly and pulled her into his arms. For a long while she trembled there, and then she drew back. "I must send letters in my own hand to Elizabeth, Catherine, Philip and the Pope. I must study all the notes of councils I have missed. I must recall my ambassadors for conferences. There is Lennox to wile . . . Dear God, so much to do and I begin so late!"

"But you begin. That is the marvel."

"You are the marvel. I almost lost my life—and you saved it by remembering the masque at Holyrood. I almost lost my reason—you saved that too. I think you were born to protect me."

"And to love you."

"Dare we meet at the Exchequer House tonight?" she asked eagerly. "We have not been together for a whole week, not as we want to be."

He kissed her hungrily. His hands slid down her body, and she went limp in his arms.

"Tonight," she whispered.

"Tonight," he said, "I must go to Jean."

II.

A haar shrouded Edinburgh. Town watchmen groped through the streets with lanterns, but the light failed to penetrate the murk and they blundered, cursing, into walls and stiles. Their broad-brimmed hats dripped moisture, and cold knifed through their heavy cloaks. "*All's well* . . . " their voices echoed dismally down the wynds. "*All's well* . . ." But they knew better. It was a night for thieves, for prowling cats—for the restless dead.

Sometime during the night pictures of Bothwell were nailed to the door of the Tolbooth, posted at the Salt Tron, the Market Cross and Holyrood Gate. Sketches of a red-haired man with blood-dripping hands, labeled "Here is the King's murderer." Placards appeared on church doors denouncing "Bloody Bothwell," Balfour, Dalgleish, Powrie and Wilson.

Each morning the Town Watch tore them down. Each night they reappeared. Balfour left hastily for his country home, and handbills announced he had killed a servant who had talked too much.

Mary sent Paris to Bothwell, warning him not to return from Crichton without an armed guard. The following day Bothwell rode into Edinburgh with fifty burly Borderers. Sullen crowds muttered from windows and forestairs. Women hooded their children's faces against his Evil Eye.

In her apartments at Holyrood, Mary told him what had happened within the past few days. "They are even hawking your portrait in the streets as 'The King's murderer.' Someone may assassinate you!"

Bothwell laughed. "Is not Satan invulnerable? But I've sent to Liddesdale for more men. A show of force will stop the bill-stickers."

"I've posted the death penalty for anyone found distributing those placards. If I knew who started them—"

"Likely the sentries who saw me the night of the explosion, or friends they told. Don't worry, love; it's a nuisance, not a tragedy."

"But you don't know how shiversome it is! I rode to Council yesterday and folk shouted, 'God preserve Your Majesty—if you be innocent.'"

"If I had been there, I'd have washed my hands in their blood."

"But you were with Jean. *She* needed you more than I. *She* has a queasy stomach."

"She has, and the physicians are baffled. She cramps horribly and cannot eat."

"She'd not eat with you present," Mary scoffed. "She starves to impress you."

He seemed too deep in worry to heed her malice. "There is nothing I can do," he said, "nothing. Except be with her as often as possible."

"I suppose you will ride twelve miles and back to see her each day. You might as well live at Crichton."

"I would, but for the damned placards. If I left Edinburgh, folk would take it as proof of my guilt. They'd say I was a skulking coward."

Abstractedly, he went to the window. Armed guards paced the courtyard, their ranks swelled to a hundred. At the gates the people stood, surly as barred animals.

"It's a broody atmosphere," he said, turning to her. "You should leave it. Go to Seton. It's only ten miles, and you can ride into Edinburgh whenever necessary."

"If I can't be with you, I care not where I am."

"I'll come to you often," he promised, "but you'd best leave."

"I'll leave tomorrow," she said. "But let us spend this night together."

"I can't. I must return to Jean."

"Jean, Jean, always she comes first!" Miserably, she added, "I think she always will."

But for all her jealousy and gibes she now believed Jean's illness was genuine. Guiltily, she thought, If only she would die and spare me the shame of wedding a divorced man . . .

Leaving the Prince at Holyrood, Mary rode to Seton, where Mary Seton's family made her welcome. Their house was pleasantly situated on the Firth of Forth, surrounded by open fields. Though she wore black, Mary made no other pretense of mourning. For forty days after Francis' death she had remained in strict seclusion. But six days after Darnley's murder she and Bothwell played golf on Seton Links and won an archery match against Lords Huntley and Seton, who paid off the wager with a dinner party at Tranent.

News reached Edinburgh of "ghastly frivolities." John Craig's Sunday sermon excoriated those who "wear mourning on their backs but not in their hearts."

Lethington rode to Seton to remonstrate. "If Your Majesty must amuse yourself, pray do so in private. To sport publicly is bad enough, but to sport with Bothwell—a man suspected of your husband's murder—is an affront to Scotland, and, indeed, to the entire world. You should not even receive him."

"You were glad enough to receive Bothwell into a certain scheme," she said. "Now you and your conspirators would turn on him and outlaw him."

"No, Madam. I would bring him to trial."

"So!" she said, outraged. "That is why you urged him to do the deed—so you could use him to rid yourselves of the King and then accuse him of murder!"

"My dear Madam, if he is innocent—" Lethington's fox-face was impassive—"then give him a chance to prove it."

"I'll give him more than that, my friend."

She gave Bothwell governorship of the fortresses of Dunbar and Blackness, the command of Edinburgh Castle, control of the Port of Leith. She placed all key fortresses in his hands. She gave him a diamond-and-onyx ring, a silver casket overlaid with gold. She tried to give him Darnley's jewels, which he flatly refused.

"If you've no thought of your own reputation, consider mine," he roared. "I'll not be seen dead prinked out in ruby rosebuds and pink pearl flowerets. Sell them!"

She sighed. "I wish you would. You are always in need of cash. You cannot maintain your estates, your troops, on pride."

"I have for more than thirty years," he said grimly. "I'll take nothing of Darnley's."

But she wheedled him into accepting one horse, a glossy, prancing mare from Ireland, the swiftest in the royal stables. She suspected that he took it mainly because James had coveted it for months.

Lennox replied cautiously to Mary's invitation to come to Edinburgh and see justice done. Obviously he was fearful of a trap, though he did not know how much Mary suspected of the gunpowder plot. He urged an immediate parliamentary inquiry into Darnley's death, and the arrest of the men named on the placards. Mary replied that Parliament was convened for April, and that she could not assemble her nobles before then.

Within two weeks all Europe had heard of the tragedy, and horrified messages came by courier from Rome and France. The Pope and the papal legate denounced Mary's failure to bring "the Protestant murderers" to trial. Catherine warned that Darnley's death must be avenged if Mary was to clear herself of complicity, and strongly hinted that if this was not done France would regard her as an enemy. From Paris, Archbishop Beaton wrote bluntly: "You yourself have become the object of calumny here, being regarded as having planned and commanded the crime. If it is not avenged it would be better had you lost your life."

Elizabeth's secretary wrote that Her Majesty was sending a special envoy on a visit of condolence. Philip of Spain was contemptuously silent.

Meanwhile Jean's illness grew worse. Bothwell rode frantically between Crichton, Edinburgh and Seton. Late in February the physicians despaired of Jean's life, and Bothwell wrote Mary to excuse him from court. The day she received the letter, James arrived at Seton.

Mary welcomed him coolly. While the other conspirators sweated through the aftermath of murder, James had leisured at St. Andrews, ostensibly attending his pregnant wife. Mary said, "I marvel you are back so soon. There is still unrest in Edinburgh."

"Dreadful," he said, ignoring her sarcasm. "Shocking!" He sat down beside her on the love seat, suavely handsome in gold-stamped black satin. "Have you any clues as to the assassins?"

She laughed hysterically, then forced herself to calmness. "Yes, my dear brother. We know for a certainty that one of the plotters fled to St. Andrews seventeen hours before the murder to escape involvement."

His mouth curled tight. "I can only attribute such a jest to your state of shock."

"What brings you here?" she asked bluntly.

"I came to tell you that the Countess of Bothwell is dangerously ill."

"I am aware of that."

"But are you aware of her ailment?"

"No one is. The physicians are puzzled."

"The physicians are bribed." His long white lids folded, hooding his eyes. "She is dying in slow agony—of poison."

Mary sprang up from the love seat. "Preposterous! Who would poison her?"

James shrugged. "Need you ask?"

"You insinuate that Bothwell—"

"You see?" he asked lazily. "You jump to the inevitable conclusion. No one but Bothwell would profit by her death. He will wed you over her corpse—and the King's."

"Who but you would believe such filth?" She caught a flicker of amusement in his eyes, and her voice soared to shrillness. "What proof have you?"

"What the courts call 'the evidence of circumstance.' A month ago Bothwell asked her for a divorce."

"You lie! He has not asked her!"

"My agents say differently. One of them overheard a terrible scene at Crichton. Jean cried out that she was his wife for life. Bothwell cursed her and said life is short, and subject to surprises."

"I don't believe one word of it!"

"Shortly thereafter," James continued calmly, "Jean complained of a curious taste in her mouth after drinking wine. She fell ill of cramps and vomiting. Bothwell came often to see her, and solicitously served her wine and food himself. Huntley could verify this, if he wished."

"So you think Huntley—her own brother—stands by while Bothwell poisons her!"

"Why not? Bothwell has promised him considerable land for his cooperation."

"How dare you come to me with this shoddy tale?" She longed to rake and scratch the sneering face. "Your gullibility astounds me! Did you really think I'd believe such drivel?"

"I hoped the truth would penetrate your madness. You behave like a woman deranged."

"It is not for you to dictate my behavior. I'm no longer a chit cowering in your shadow."

"But you are lost so deep in Bothwell's that you may never emerge."

"I don't wish to emerge."

"Then you are ruined."

"Hypocrite! How many times have *you* plotted my ruin?"

James's eyes turned cold and hard as the jade chains on his breast.

She said, "You schemed the first murder plot not only to kill Darnley but to rid Scotland of Bothwell by pinning the guilt on him. But the gunpowder plot—Darnley's plot—upset your plans and exploded your ambitions. Now you pick up the shreds and come slinking to me with tales of poisoning. Perhaps you authorize those placards to rouse the people against Bothwell. But each day he grows stronger. I am placing every fortress in Scotland at his command. It will take more than lies to topple him."

"And I suppose you intend to marry him? A man regarded as your husband's murderer?"

"Yes, if I can persuade him. Thus far he refuses to wed me."

James laughed harshly. "He is cleverer than I supposed."

"What do you mean?"

"He knows you dare not marry for at least a year and fears you may tire of his lovemaking. So lest you take him for granted, he evades talk of marriage and thereby whets your appetite for it. Thus he reduces you to a drab panting for respectability."

"Get out!"

James bowed, an ironic tilt of the head, rose and went to the door, pausing with his hand on the latch.

"Well?" Mary asked.

"When what might be termed your 'indecent interval' of mourning is over, you may recall it was I who warned you against wedding

Darnley. If you had heeded me then, you'd have spared yourself hell."

"If ever I heed you," she said, "may I burn in hell."

III.

Rumor thrived in the wet mists of Edinburgh. The Queen had danced to a tune called *Well is me Since I am Free* . . . The King's suits were being altered to fit Lord Bothwell . . . Lord Bothwell was poisoning his wife so that he could wed the Queen . . .

At Seton, Mary prayed for Jean's recovery. For if Jean died, Bothwell's name, now blackened, would be forever infamous. She thought, Should the world indict him for double murder I dare not marry him. Such a scandal would never die.

Early in March she hurried back to Edinburgh to receive a visit of condolence from Elizabeth's envoy, Sir Henry Killigrew. At Holyrood, her audience chamber was a gloom of black velvet and onyx lit by black candles. Killigrew kissed a hand stripped of all jewels save the wedding band.

"Your Majesty," he said, and lifted his eyes to her face.

Her face was a tragic mask pallored with French wax, the eyes shadowed by deep gray kohl. She wore no lip paste. Her hair was hidden by a severe black coif and a crepe veil flowed to the hem of her skirt, which swept into a four-yard train lined with sable.

"Queen Elizabeth is with Your Majesty in spirit."

"Thank you. I have longed for her presence." Mary bade him be seated. To display the full effect of her mourning, she stood at the fireplace, one sable-sleeved arm on the mantel. "I trust Her Majesty is well?"

"No, Madam, for she shares your grief." Killigrew opened his dispatch case and brought out a sealed letter. "This is for your eyes alone. Her Majesty wrote it in her own hand. No one has seen it."

Mary thought, No one but Cecil, Leicester, Walsingham and a dozen secretaries.

"Before you read this, Madam, I am charged to say that it was written in heart's blood, for you are Her Majesty's cousin and so was the late King." He paused, and his eyes met hers frankly. "In the past there have been petty rivalries between you, as may occur when queens are shunted among diplomats. But that phase must pass. The explosion at Kirk O'Field reverberated to your mutual hazard. If regicide rides the world, so must anarchy."

This man is clever, she thought. Would that I had an envoy whose guile is skillfully cloaked in passionate sincerity. A homely man, thin as a string, square-jowled and bunchy-chinned—but eloquent.

"Her Majesty perceives that you are tossed by emotion and troubled by vicious gossip. Once she too was the victim of slander—"

When her lover's wife, Amy Robsart Dudley, was found at the foot of a staircase with a broken neck . . .

"—and so, better than others, she understands Your Majesty's plight."

Killigrew rose and gave her the letter. Mary took it to the taper-light and broke the Great Seal. She set her face in respectful antici-pation. Killigrew would report every flicker of expression, every tension of muscle.

But as she read, she forgot him. The words beat down her cyni-cism. It was as if Elizabeth of England put a skinny arm around her and held her close—warning, scolding, pleading.

Madam:

My ears have been so astonished and my mind so grieved and my heart so terrified at hearing of the abominable murder of your late husband and my deceased cousin, that I have even now no spirit to write about it; and although my natural feelings constrain me greatly to deplore his death, as he was so near a relation to me, nevertheless, boldly to tell you what I think, I cannot conceal from myself that I am more full of grief on your account than on his. O Madam! I should not perform the part of a faithful cousin or an affectionate friend if I studied rather to please your ears than to endeavor to preserve your honor; therefore I will not conceal from you what most persons say about the matter, namely, that you will look through your fingers at taking vengeance for this deed and have no intention to touch those who have done you this kindness, as if the act would not have been perpetrated unless the murderers had received as-surance of their impunity.

Think of me, I beg you, who would not entertain such a thought in my heart for all the gold in the world. I exhort you, I advise and beseech you to take this thing so much to heart, as not to fear to bring to judgment the nearest relation you have, and to let no per-suasion hinder you from manifesting to the world that you are a noble princess, and also a loyal wife.

Tears blurred Mary's eyes. She put down the letter and turned away. Not for years had she believed Elizabeth sincere, but she did now. I need her, she thought. Perhaps she needs me. We are islands surrounded by men. James, Cecil, Lethington have pushed us apart on the tides of their own ambition.

Her back to Killigrew, she said, "Tell your mistress that . . . I wept."

"Yes, Madam," he said gently.

"She says, 'Do not fear to bring to judgment the nearest relation you have.' That would be my brother James. Nothing would please me more than to put him on trial for murder."

"Yes, Madam." His voice was amused. "Quite so."

She turned to face him. "However, I believe Her Majesty uses a figure of speech. And unfortunately James was miles away at the time of the crime. It is customary for him to be absent during crises."

"That has often been remarked, Madam."

"Lord Lennox plagues me to bring Lord Bothwell to trial. Yet I am sure he is innocent."

"Then he can clear himself, Madam."

She was silent, knowing all too well what the verdict of James, Morton, Lethington and their friends would be.

Killigrew said, "Nothing short of Lord Bothwell's trial will satisfy Europe, Madam."

"And if I do not try him? Come, be frank."

"Your Majesty will lose the friendship and respect of all nations. Folk will say that Bothwell is your lover, that you conspired in the crime and now seek to shield him. Down through the centuries his name and yours will be synonymous with the vilest of murders—regicide."

Fleming tapped at the door, opened it, curtsied. "Excuse me, Madam—a letter."

All letters from Bothwell were to be delivered immediately . . .

Mary's fingers trembled on his seal. She thought, A year ago I would have welcomed Jean's death, but now if she dies so will my hopes. Fearfully, she opened the letter.

Madam: This morning Jean seemed so greatly improved that we believe she will recover . . .

IV.

"You must try me," Bothwell said, swinging a long leg over the arm of a rosewood chair. "I demand trial."

"You are jesting!" Mary said.

"Not at all."

"But you know as well as I that the lords will delight to convict you now that they have used you in getting rid of Darnley."

"I'll gamble on that."

"It is no gamble, but certain death!"

"Come, love, I'm a loyal subject demanding trial. Shall we say the twelfth of April?"

"But they will convict you."

"If they do I'll escape."

"How blithely you talk of escaping!"

"But I always escape," he said.

"Then what of me? While you escape somewhere, I am left with mad dogs."

"But I always come back."

Exasperated, she said, "Have your trial. It will cost me my kingdom in bribes but if you insist—"

"Bribes?" He swung his feet to the floor with a clump of boots. "Do you honestly think you have enough gold or lands or titles to bribe that pack of hyenas? They want my blood. They fear I'll wed you and strip them of all they've stolen for the past twenty years."

"I'll not allow the trial unless I command the jurors," she said.

He laughed. "Love, you are barmy. Don't you know I am able to care for myself? Need I hide behind your petticoats?" He stared solemnly at the frills of black lace that puffed from her spread skirts. "Charming. If you will lift them slightly—"

"Stop it!" she said. "You've pestered me enough. You shall have your trial."

"Then write old Lennox. Order him to appear at the Tolbooth on the twelfth of April, with witnesses and evidence against me."

"No!" she said. "I've changed my mind. I cannot do it. If they fought openly and honestly you'd have a chance, but they dagger in the dark. You have only a handful of friends—Cockburn of Skirling, Huntley, Langton—and they may change overnight. The jurors will be selected by Justice Argyll, and he'll appoint your enemies."

"You underestimate my persuasiveness," Bothwell smiled. "By the twelfth of April I'll not have an enemy bold enough to belch."

V.

Through the wild, wind-clawed hills of Liddesdale rang Bothwell's war-cry, "A-*Hepburn!* A-*Hepburn!*" In lonely, chasm-hung castles men grabbed pikes, hackbuts, dags, knives and broadswords and flung onto shaggy horses. They raced from barns and peeltowers, tolbooths and hovels, and galloped north, hundreds rousing hundreds. In a pewter sky, balefires glared red from the Cheviot Hills through Hawick to Peebles and hissed to death in torrential rain. "A-*Hepburn!*" Men and horses tossed northward through March gales, mired in swamps, pulled out, rushed on. Two thousand steel-capped leather-jacked Borderers, cutting scarfs flapping from their throats, axes slung at their saddlebows, black with peat-mud and bog-muck. "A-*Hepburn!*" Three thousand, shouting, braying on slug-horns, their torches showering sparks through the storm-torn sky. Four thousand, riding belly-to-saddle, beard-to-mane through spike-branched forests, eyes crusted with salt from the sea-tanged wind. "*A-Hepburn!*" Five thousand, an avalanche hurdling the Moorfoots, the Pentlands, the Lammermuirs, splashing waist-deep through flooded burns and meeting at last with a great hill-shaking shout at the gates of Edinburgh.

From the battlements of Edinburgh Castle, Mary looked down through morning sunlight. The army crawled from the hazed hills, twisting and turning up the steep-pitched streets like an endless serpent of molten iron.

"Mon Dieu!" Mary teased as Bothwell joined her. "Your kin are monstrous prolific!"

"They're not all Hepburns," he said gravely. "They're Johnstones and Armstrongs and Elliotts and Sinclairs. More than five hundred broke jail to come here, bless their black hearts."

"*Broke jail?* By whose order?"

"By mine."

She gasped. "But it was you who jailed them!"

"So I did. They know I gave them fair trial. Now they come to insure a fair trial for me."

She began to laugh. "Do you mean to tell me that rabble down there will return to jail when you order them to?"

"Of course," he said with the tired patience of an adult explaining to a feeble-witted child. "They'll return to jail because I have their word for it."

"You trust the word of criminals?"

Bothwell glared down at her so fiercely that she drew back a step. "I trust the word of Borderers," he said.

Bothwell's Borderers enveloped Edinburgh like a vast steel cloak. The High Street became a solid mass of men from Castle Rock to Holyrood. Inns and hostels accommodated only a few hundred. The rest camped, in the Royal Park, the Lang Gait, on the shore of the Loch, raising great fires against the bitter nights.

They were orderly, but inquisitive. Moor-born, many had never dreamed of a town so vast, and they poked frost-reddened noses into every nook and cranny of Edinburgh, climbing onto burghers' galleries and staring in awe at chimneys and commodes. But they stole no more than kisses, and tradesmen welcomed them. The brothels did a lively business. Whoremaster Jamie Sims marveled to Bothwell, "They're men, by God! I've not sold one aphrodisiac, nary an egg nor a prune. They find sixpence high for a wench, but they don't quibble the price nor cheat on their hour. A pack of gentlemen they are."

"Gentlemen in their fashion," Bothwell told Mary, "but curious as cats. The guard caught one this morning shinnying up the palace wall—he wanted to see the Prince. You'd best take the child to Stirling."

So Mary took the Prince to Lord and Lady Mar. When she returned to Holyrood a letter from Lennox awaited her. He asked postponement of the trial in order to formulate charges against Bothwell, Balfour and minor suspects. Mary refused. It was he who had demanded haste, and he had had sufficient time—nearly two months. She sent a courier to remind him that by Scots law the accusing party might bring only six attendants to the Court of Justice.

Fearful of Bothwell's Borderers, Lennox remained in Linlithgow with his three thousand men. He sent word that he was ill and that a servant, Robert Cunningham, would appear for him by proxy.

As the day of the trial approached, Mary waited tensely for the appointment of the jurors. To her relief, neither Lethington nor Morton was selected. But of the fifteen jurors chosen, eight were Bothwell's old and bitter enemies, four unpredictable, three friendly.

On April 8th, four days before the trial, Mary received James at Holyrood.

"Madam," he said, "you may be interested to know that there's rumor of a bribed jury."

"I do not doubt it."

"Last night I supped with Master George Buchanan. He said that in future ages folk will say, 'There sat the judges, not chosen to judge but picked out to acquit.' As a scholar and historian, Master Buchanan is not one to speak lightly."

"Buchanan speaks lies. He writes history to suit his own prejudices. Why, even the four assessors thirst for Bothwell's blood—including Lindsay. And Argyll himself—Lord Justice—what justice will *he* dispense?"

James shrugged. "A pity I'll not be here to attend. But lately I have had a longing for foreign travel. I leave tomorrow for Paris and Rome."

She caught her breath. He had hatched some new plot or he'd not be leaving Scotland . . .

"Thank you," she said, "for the warning."

VI.

On the morning of the trial, Mary leaned from her bedchamber window and waved to Bothwell in Holyrood courtyard. He wore a magnificent black velvet cloak sleeved in sable, and the wind streamed it back to reveal onyx-and-silver-hilted weapons at his belt. He was mounted on Darnley's black mare, caparisoned in black with silver fringe. As he waved back at Mary, diamond-embroidered black gauntlets caught the fire of the sun.

She longed to warn him that he looked insolent. Defendants came to trial soberly, piously, not with faintly amused arrogance. His very manner would infuriate the jury. Next time she saw him he might be celled in the Tolbooth and marked for death.

Preceded by his Borderers, Bothwell rode off between Morton and Lethington, followed by two hundred hackbuteers. A thousand of his men raised a jagged forest of spears around the Tolbooth, shouting encouragement as he entered its grim stone walls.

At noon Justice Argyll called the court to order. The jury was sworn. Caithness, the foreman, was James's best friend. Lords Boyd, Rothes, Sempill, Herries, Hamilton and Forbes were Bothwell's old enemies, long in league with Elizabeth. Alex of Boyne had reason to resent Bothwell's infidelity to Jean. Four of the jurymen were indifferent. Three were Bothwell's friends.

A clerk read the charge: . . . *against James Hepburn, Earl of Bothwell, for art and part of the cruel, odious, treasonable and abominable slaughter of the late and right excellent, right high and mighty prince The King's Grace, dearest spouse to our sovereign lady The Queen's Majesty, under silence of night in his own lodging, he taking the night's rest . . .*

At the bar Bothwell denied the charge.

Robert Cunningham, serving as Lennox' proxy, read from a paper: *My lords, I am sent by my master to declare the cause of his absence—the shortness of time and the fact that he is denied his friends who should have accompanied him. He desires a postponement of forty days to collect evidence. If this is not granted, and if the trial proceeds to the acquittal of the Earl of Bothwell, the jury shall have done so in willful error and not in ignorance.*

Cunningham presented copies of the correspondence between Lennox and Mary. Bothwell's counsel pounced on the fact that Lennox had first pressed for haste and had had two months to collect evidence. The court ruled that the trial should proceed.

"Has Lord Lennox sent any witnesses?" Argyll asked. "Any evidence however small?"

"No, my lord," Cunningham said.

"Does anyone in this court wish to present evidence against Lord Bothwell?"

Silence.

"Does any witness wish to testify against him?"

No one came forward.

Bothwell's counsel addressed the jury. "You cannot convict a man merely on the accusation of his enemy. To do so would be to convict yourselves of the grossest injustice before Scotland and at the bar of God."

The jury retired. At dusk, after five hours' deliberation, the foreman announced a unanimous verdict: Not guilty.

That night, Mary and Bothwell celebrated secretly in the Exchequer House. Paris smuggled in a feast of cold game, pastries and Spanish wine. Mary shed her mourning for a robe of emerald green satin.

"We must find a house more isolated than this," Bothwell said.

"It won't be necessary," she said, leaving the table to sit on his lap. "For I shall make an honest man of you. We will marry much sooner than—"

"No." He scowled, wrinkling red eyebrows. "I've told you I won't wed you."

"But Jean is well and you are acquitted."

"For lack of proof, but not for lack of will. All that prevented the lords from presenting false evidence was fear of my Borderers and a certain paper I hold which implicates Lethington and the Douglases. The people haven't changed. As I rode back to the palace they were glum, stubbornly sure of my guilt. Until Archie Douglas comes forward and confesses—which he'll never do—I'll bear the stigma of regicide."

"But you say you have a paper implicating the Douglases."

"It implicates me too," he grinned.

"Nevertheless, you are acquitted, and Europe will recognize you as guiltless."

"With Master Buchanan endlessly blathering about a bribed jury?"

"I care not," she said happily. "We will marry."

"You'll not lose your crown for my sake. I'll keep it on your head if I have to nail it there. I'll not marry you, ever."

She pressed her face in the crisp waves of his hair, ran a path of kisses from his temple to his throat.

"And you'll not wheedle me into it," he said.

She retraced the path upward and he caught her tightly and kissed her lips.

"Suppose I were not Queen," she said. "Would you divorce Jean and wed me?"

"Faster than lightning."

"Then you must arrange a lightning divorce. We will wed next month."

"Why?" He smiled. "Do you plan to abdicate?"

"No, but you have admitted you love me enough to wed me. That is all the assurance I need to go ahead with marriage plans."

"Damnation!" he roared, thrusting her off his lap. "How many times must I tell you—"

"Let me tell *you*," she said, slowly and delightedly. "I think I am with child . . ."

VII.

By mid-April, Mary was certain that she was two months with child, and she prayed for a girl. At Holyrood, she explored her store-rooms, fingering bolts of cloth she had brought from France. The pale green gauze would make charming robes for a copper-curled little Princess. The butterfly damask, the white embroidered satin . . . She found tiny coifs her mother had saved from her own childhood, and little stockings and dolls. The Princess Mary would be the most beautiful, the best educated, the wisest royal lady in Europe.

Bothwell grumbled that Mary had tricked him, but after his first hock he began strategy for the future. Parliament ratified the jury's decision, and prohibited Bothwell's defamation by placard or bill. But he told Mary that he must win the lords' approval before they married.

"You will never win their approval," Mary said. "We will wed without it."

"Do you want our wedding celebrated with civil war? The people supporting your nobles against you?"

"But how can you possibly win the lords' approval?"

"Persuasion," he smiled.

After the final session of Parliament, Bothwell invited twenty nobles, including Privy Councilors, and eight bishops, to a banquet at Ainslie's Tavern. There he dispensed mountains of food, and barrels of whisky. By midnight, few guests could stand up for the toasts.

Bothwell rose, banged his mug on the pine table and called for silence. From his belt pouch he took a long white paper.

"My lords," he said, "I have prepared this bond which awaits your signatures. It asserts your belief in my innocence of the King's murder—"

Someone vomited in the rushes, and Bothwell smiled and continued.

"—and it stipulates that you defend me against defamation and slander."

Lindsay belched. The sound reverberated up to the smoke-hazed rafters, and Bothwell bowed to him. "My compliments, sir. This bond provides further that should Her Majesty consider wedding a native-born Scot instead of a foreign prince, you will support my suit, promising to further the marriage by vote, counsel or other assistance."

The men stared at him dazedly, loose-lipped and bleary-eyed.

Morton stumbled to his feet. "You said—" His voice was thickly slurred—"You said you would wed the *Queen?*"

"If she will so humble herself."

"Have you asked her?"

"How can I? I am not yet divorced. Even if I were free, Her Majesty is sure to refuse me on the grounds of my religion—unless by some miracle this bond persuades her."

Morton's eyes narrowed, then widened in an attempt to focus. "I thought Her Majesty enam—enamored of you."

Bothwell laughed harshly. "If she were, I'd not need your help."

He moved plates and goblets from his end of the table, unrolled the document and set it down, weighting it at both ends. A servant brought ink and quill.

"Well, my lords? Who shall be the first to sign?"

The lords mumbled to one another.

"It's hellish hot in here," Bothwell said. He went to the door and opened it wide.

Outside stood halberdiers. Beyond them, bright moonlight glinted on steel helmets and bristling pikes. Five thousand voices thundered in song:

> *Ho for the Sinclairs, the Armstrongs, the Elliotts,*
> *Ho for the Hepburns, and ho for the world . . .*

The lords looked through the door; at the pike-barred windows; at one another. Morton walked slowly forward, weaving his way through the littered rushes. He read the document and signed it. One by one, the other nobles staggered to the table and wobbled their names down the long white page.

"I thank you, my lords," Bothwell said. "There is only one chance in a million that Her Majesty will accept me, but if she does, you will be rewarded as you deserve."

VIII.

Spring came to Edinburgh in long lilac hazes, primrose-yellow sun showers that stippled the North Loch in dancing ripples. The Royal Park purpled with heather, the outlying fields daisied and bluebelled. But Mary saw the memory of winter bleak in the faces of the people. They could not forgive what they did not understand. The murder at Kirk O'Field was a mystery thickening with time.

Darnley's ghost stalked Holyrood. The maids saw him and ran shrieking from his audience chamber. Mary felt him in her bones. Once in her bedchamber on a humid night, the hangings at the closed window streamed frantically forward and a clammy, death-smelling wind passed through the room. The Bishop of Ross exorcised the palace, but Mary was not at ease there. On the day of Bothwell's banquet she returned to Seton.

Late that night, Bothwell rode to her, arriving at dawn. Incredulously, delightedly, she read the bond.

"Thank God for your Borderers," she said. "Somehow I shall reward them all."

"I have paid them and dismissed all but eight hundred," Bothwell said. "Such a force is staggeringly expensive. Now, love, Morton or Argyll will doubtless ride to you as soon as they are sober. Tell them I have been here and proposed marriage, and that you rejected my suit as the grossest impudence. Tell them that I mock your mourning, and that for such irreverence you contemplate my head. Use the strongest possible language and excoriate them for putting their names to the document."

"But how will I justify my change of mind when I wed you next month?"

He grinned. "Leave that to me. I am going to abduct you, ravish you, and force you to wed me for your honor's sake."

She thought the plan audaciously in character. No one in Scotland would doubt Bothwell's ability to conceive and execute it.

"But love," she said, "such a crime will further blacken your reputation."

"It is your reputation that matters. None can blame you for wedding me if you are forced to it. And it will explain the child, born prematurely of your terrible shock."

"When," she asked lightly, "am I to be abducted?"

"The sooner the better. Leave for Stirling tomorrow and visit the Prince. As you return to Edinburgh on April 24th, I'll intercept you at Almond Bridge and abduct you to Dunbar."

"I shall take care to have a small retinue."

"Not so small as to appear unnatural. Bloodshed is unnecessary, so choose attendants who won't be likely to offer resistance. I suggest Lethington, Sir James Melville and Huntley. Huntley knows what I intend."

"You trust Huntley? Why should he help you wed me? He is loyal to Jean."

"He is most loyal to his Queen. The Gordons," he added wryly, "are old-fashioned. Next to God, they worship the crown."

"Very well," she said dubiously. "Does Jean know of this?"

"Certainly not," he snapped.

"When will you ask her for the divorce?"

"After the abduction."

"I think you find excuses for delaying. She should be prepared. Not that she will care greatly—Alex of Boyne will comfort her."

"Damnation! Are you at that again? He's visited Crichton only twice since our marriage."

"So *you* think."

"He is devoted to Beaton. And Jean—God help her—is devoted to me."

"I trust her devotion is selfless enough to relinquish you. If she refuses a divorce, I shall be the laughing stock of Europe—a queen ravished and with child, but unable to marry."

"Fear not. Jean's pride would not let her hold me against my will."

"I wonder," Mary said.

Early that morning, after Bothwell returned to Edinburgh, Morton visited Mary. She pretended rage at Bothwell's presumption in proposing marriage, and warned Morton that he and the other nobles who had signed the bond were not to appear at court for a week, lest she lose her temper and punish them severely.

At nine o'clock Morton slunk away. At ten, Mary, accompanied by Peter Pye, slipped out of the house and rode to Crichton. She had to know Jean's intentions regarding divorce. If she refused, then the abduction would be both useless and dangerous.

Mary dreaded the visit. As she rode through the blossoming moor she shivered, feeling already the cold gray judgment of Jean's eyes. A formidable enemy, armored in righteousness. The Bible mentioned her: *Who can find a virtuous woman? For her price is far above rubies.* Jean had no price. She could not be bribed with lands or jewels. What could one offer in exchange for a husband?

The gray walls of Crichton rose from newly landscaped gardens that sloped to the banks of the Tyne, and Mary looked about with grudging admiration at the changes Jean had made. Rambler roses climbed the walled courtyard. The orchard, once neglected, was a tidy mass of pink-and-white bloom, and grape arbors were trellised with roses. *With the fruit of her hands she planteth a vineyard.*

Servants rushed out to gasp welcome and help Mary from her horse. As she walked into the cool stone hall her slippers rustled flower-strewn rushes, and the fragrance of crushed petals mingled with the rosemary that burned in braziers. The summer tapestries were up—pale blue and lilac woven with gold.

A butler conducted Mary to a small, white-paneled parlor. A

tapestry frame stood in one corner, and a table bright with skeins of silk and wool. *She layeth her hands to the spindle and her hands hold the distaff.* There was a pale blue carpet, chairs upholstered in azure and violet silks. An intimate, feminine chamber, with rows of potatoes growing in pots on the window seat and green vines climbing up the casement.

Jean hurried in and knelt at Mary's feet, then took her cloak and offered her a chair. At Mary's request, Jean sat opposite her across a small white table.

She has changed, Mary thought uneasily. She has learned to beautify herself. A tiny white linen coif revealed a coronet of blond braids. The planes of her face had hollowed so that cheeks and nose and chin seemed chiseled of marble. Faint rose paste accentuated the generously curved mouth, and a touch of gray shadow mysteried the eyes. She is not above paint now, Mary thought, nor any trick that will hold her husband.

"Please forgive my appearance," Jean said. "I have been in the woods searching for plants."

She wore a peasant's kirtle, the blue skirts bunched to the back over a short white petticoat, the bodice laced tight at the waist with crimson silk. A perky, provocative costume that revealed slender ankles in red-heeled slippers.

"Would you care for refreshment, Madam? I've an excellent French chef."

"No, thank you. But perhaps a glass of wine."

Jean poured Spanish wine from a rose glass decanter and offered Banberrie tartlets. *She bringeth her food from afar . . .*

"A fine wine," Mary said.

"It is my husband's favorite."

Jean said it so smugly, so possessively, that Mary trembled with anger. But her voice was controlled. "Your husband does not know I am here. I prefer that you not tell him."

"As you wish, Madam. I shall instruct my servants to say nothing."

Mary hesitated. There was no subtle way to approach a gross request. She said, "You are aware of the relationship between your husband and myself?"

"I am."

Damn her, Mary thought. She looks at me as honest burgher women look at bawds on the High Street—a cool, superior stare.

"You think him merely infatuated," Mary said, "but he loves me. We are going to wed."

Jean said, "He is wed to me and will be always."

It was a flat statement, without inflection. Her eyes met Mary's calmly.

"Soon he will ask you to divorce him," Mary said.

"I will refuse."

"I command that you agree."

Jean's chin lifted. "Master Knox said long ago that when the commandments of our princes cross God's will, we may resist them. My marriage was made in the sight of God. Only he may dissolve it."

"You subscribe to treason!"

"Then exile or execute me." Jean raised her wineglass with a steady hand, sipped and replaced it on the table. "But you shall not wed him."

"Once you said you'd not hold a man against his will."

"I do not hold my husband against his will, for he loves me."

Mary laughed scornfully. "He has proved it by deserting you."

"His body may be yours, Madam, but his heart and his soul are mine."

"Is it not obvious to you that a man who scorns your body cares little for your heart?"

"No." Jean appraised Mary, a long glance that held neither envy nor malice. "Your body is indeed lovely. It may be long before he tires of it, but tire he will, for he cannot trust you. What he has sought all his life—and never found until he wed me—was a woman he could fully trust."

"Do you imagine yourself the only woman so endowed?"

Jean ignored her sarcasm. "He was raised by a procurer bishop. From the time he was a lad, he knew only coarse women, and he heard them hold marriage to ridicule and revile love as a fool's fancy. Thus he thought all women bawds, revering none but your mother and yourself. Then he met me. I had no enchantments, but he seemed to know at once that for all my lack of wit and beauty, I would never hurt him, never betray him."

The heart of her husband may safely trust in her.

"That may well be true," Mary said impatiently, "but I too have his trust."

Jean shook her head. "No, Madam. After the stratagems you employed against me, he will never trust you, much as he may wish to. You are too full of guile, too devious."

"Not because I wish to be," Mary said. "Circumstance has made me so. God knows I am forthright as you in my heart."

"Perhaps so, Madam. But your position will always force you to betray your true nature."

We are stalemated, Mary thought. *There is nothing left but to*

[398]

shatter my pride and throw myself on her mercy. I have wronged her, victimized her, and now I must crawl to her to save my crown.

Mary said, "I am with child."

Jean gasped. Her eyes turned hard and hostile.

"You suspect a trick," Mary said, "but it is true. That is why I must wed, and quickly."

Jean's voice trembled. "Does my lord know this?"

"Yes." She told Jean about the bond, the proposed abduction. "Now only you stand between us."

"So you come begging," Jean said contemptuously.

"What else can I do?" Mary asked desperately. "Shall I bear a child out of wedlock? Shame Scotland before the world? Bothwell is the only Scot I can wed; there is no unmarried noble of sufficient rank or wit. Negotiations for a foreign husband would take months."

Jean was silent. She sat in the chair like a propped corpse, her eyes dead on Mary's, her face drained of color.

Mary said, "Elizabeth has long sought an excuse to deny my son's legitimacy. If she discovers I am with child, she will seize on my wantonness, and say that the Prince was also conceived out of wedlock. He would never inherit England. I would be forced to abdicate. The Regency would go to James, and so, ultimately, Scotland would fall to Elizabeth's gold."

Mary rose and went to kneel by Jean's chair. "Yes, I am begging, and humbly. If it gives you pleasure to see me thus—"

"Rise, Madam." Jean's voice was like splintered glass. "I will divorce him."

Strength and honor are her clothing, and she shall rejoice in time to come . . .

IX.

The next day Mary journeyed from Seton to Stirling with Lethington, Melville and Huntley. She found the Prince well, but again was struck by the oddness of his appearance. Had he not been guarded from birth, she would have suspected that the fairies had stolen her golden child and substituted this darkling stranger in his place.

For two days Mary wandered the gardens of Stirling, wrote Bothwell, argued with Huntley. He regretted promising Bothwell help in the abduction, which he felt was a mad enterprise. He suggested that instead of marrying Bothwell she retire to a French nunnery and bear the child there. She said the idea was preposterous. She dared not leave Scotland for fear James would return and seize power. She dared not leave Bothwell—Jean had become too attractive.

On April 23rd she wrote to Bothwell:

My Lord, since my last letter your brother-in-law Huntley has asked my advice as to what he should do after tomorrow because there are many people here, including the Earl of Sutherland . . . who would sooner die than suffer me to be carried away while they were acting as my bodyguard. On the other hand, he is afraid that if there is trouble it will be said that he was ungrateful in having betrayed me. I told him that he ought to have arranged for all that with you, and that he should get rid of all those whom he most mistrusts.

. . . I am astonished to see how irresolute he is in the hour of need. I say to myself he will play the part of an honest man; but I thought it well to let you know of his fear that he may be charged and accused of treason, so that, without distrusting him, you may be the more careful and be the better equipped. Yesterday we had more than three hundred horsemen—his and Livingstone's. For the love of God see that you are accompanied by more rather than by less; that indeed is my chief anxiety.

I must go to write my dispatches, and I pray God that we may soon have a happy meeting. I write in haste so that you may be warned in good time.

Later that day Mary left Stirling with her lords and three hundred horsemen. They spent the night in Linlithgow and resumed their journey at dawn on April 24th.

As she rode toward Edinburgh, she realized that it was the ninth anniversary of her marriage to Francis. For a moment the wild moor vanished, and she saw the vast blue-and-gold carpet spread before Notre Dame, visioned herself bent under jewel-massed wedding robes and head-throbbing crown. She had been so sure of happiness then. It had seemed her right, like the crowns of France and Scotland. But in nine years she had learned differently. Happiness was seized at the expense of others. You trapped it greedily in darkened beds, held it briefly, lost it to daylight. You intrigued for happiness, plotted and murdered for it. And now on this hazy moss-colored moor, you gambled your honor for it.

She was nervous, and fearful that Lethington sensed it. Riding on her left with Sutherland, he looked at her often, and, she thought, speculatively. She tried to appear natural, hummed a song, chatted of trivia. Several times she thought she heard pursuing hoofbeats and turned in the saddle, but there were only her own horsemen riding behind Huntley and Melville.

Six miles from Edinburgh the cavalcade approached Gogar Burn where it joined the Almond River. Ahead the horizon blackened as a dark cloud took shape. Beneath it a vast force of horsemen—perhaps eight hundred, Mary thought—thundered toward them. As Mary's men bared their swords and lifted their spears, she ordered a halt. "Drop your weapons!" she shouted. "We are outnumbered!"

As Bothwell's horsemen surrounded the cavalcade, he spurred up and seized Mary's horse by the bridle. "Madam," he said loudly, "you cannot go to Edinburgh. Grave danger awaits you there."

"What danger?" she asked.

"A rising. The people are demonstrating against Your Majesty's failure to bring the assassins to justice, and their mood is ugly. I'm taking you to Dunbar."

"I'll be the judge of that," she said, pretending anger. "Who are you to order me?"

"Your humblest subject, who seeks to protect you, Madam. Lethington, Huntley and Melville will accompany us. Livingstone and Sutherland will proceed to Edinburgh with your troops."

Mary said, "I'll ride to Edinburgh myself and put down the rising."

"You'll not ride another furlong toward Edinburgh, Madam."

Mary saw Lethington's hand slide to his sword. "No," she said to him, "this smacks of treason, but there will be no bloodshed." She summoned one of her captains and ordered him to escort her troops to Edinburgh and call all loyal citizens to arms.

When her troops were out of sight, Bothwell said, "There's no rising in Edinburgh, Madam. You are my prisoner. And—" He bowed to Huntley, Melville and Lethington—"these gentlemen are scarcely in a position to defend you. But lest they try, they'll be disarmed."

Mary railed at Bothwell as his henchmen took the lords' swords and daggers. "Traitor! What do you hope to gain by this?"

"Your heart. Your hand in marriage."

"I vow I'll have your head."

Huntley glared at Bothwell. "Are you clean mad? Her Majesty's troops will gather an army and ride against Dunbar."

Bothwell shrugged, signaled his men forward. Cursing him, refusing to ride by his side, Mary began the long journey.

They arrived in Dunbar at midnight. Wind churned the North Sea as they reached the shore and drummed across the drawbridge. Mary was hungry, weary, but light-hearted. All had gone remarkably well. She felt that Melville and Lethington were convinced by her rage, but she was careful not to overplay it and retired into frigid silence.

Since her last visit to Dunbar, Bothwell had furnished the fortress crudely but comfortably. The Great Hall, where supper was laid, was hung with wool and bearskins. There were massive oak benches and a long table. Though she could have eaten an entire chicken, she nibbled at her food and dulled her appetite with ale.

Lethington tried to reason with Bothwell. "You stand to lose all you have gained," he said. "How can you hope to succeed? The Queen will not wed you, even should you force her signature to a marriage vow, for what is signed under duress is valueless."

Melville warned, "You are committing treason. But perhaps the Queen will pardon you if she is freed at once."

"I will," Mary said. "A full pardon."

"I want no pardon," Bothwell said. "I want Your Majesty's hand in marriage. For seven years I have loved you."

Mary rose. "Such talk revolts me. Where are my apartments?"

A servant escorted her to the second floor. She saw with delight that Bothwell had furnished her bedchamber elegantly, even to golden candlesticks, a Turkey carpet, tapestries of green and crimson. A lute lay on a brocaded chest and she reached for it, then shook her head ruefully. Though the walls were ten feet thick, she dared not play.

A manservant helped her unpack and brought an iron bathing tub, warm water and wool cloths. She poured French musk in the water and soaked luxuriously, listening to the rock-pounding surf. Dunbar was one of the strongest fortresses in Europe, the arsenal for the entire kingdom, holding most of Scotland's gunpowder. If rescuers come, she thought, they will not get past the inland fortifications.

But rescuers would not come. She smiled, chasing the soap that slipped from her hand. Her troops were deliberately scattered, while Bothwell's Borderers were a tight unit. By the time an army was ready to move on Dunbar, she would proclaim her capitulation.

She rose and dried herself, put on a heavy wool robe, for the room was chilly despite the crackling fire. She was fastening feathered slippers, when Bothwell came in, closing the door behind him.

Mary ran to him and he held her close, tipped up her chin and kissed her mouth.

"I'm so happy!" she said. "I feel so wonderfully free!"

He chuckled. "You must needs keep that feeling to yourself."

"Do you think Lethington suspects?" she asked.

"Perhaps, but no matter. He'll not emerge from this a hero." He unbuttoned his doublet and tossed it on a chair, standing by the fire in white, full-sleeved shirt and crimson breeches. "Damned if I didn't pick the right escort for you. Melville and Lethington are men in a council chamber, but mice on a moor. They'll pose no problem."

"What are they doing now?"

"Drinking in the Great Hall . . . How are your lungs, love?"

"What do you mean?"

"Can you scream loud enough to be heard downstairs?"

"Perhaps, if you open the door."

"Come," he said, drawing her to the door and opening it.

She began to laugh. "No!"

He held her tightly. "You've needed to scream all of your life. You wanted to scream at Amboise, but discipline clamped your lips. You wanted to scream at the Cardinal, at Catherine, at James. Now is your chance."

"I cannot," she said, her laughter gone. "It would sound false. I am too content. Perhaps tomorrow . . ."

"Now," he said.

"I am not a maid to be ordered."

"You heard me."

"And you heard *me*," she said angrily.

He slapped her hard. She struck at him, missed as he drew back. She lunged at him, and he put out his boot and tripped her to the floor. Bewildered, furious, half-hysterical, she screamed. He pulled her to her feet, slapped her again and dragged her back to the door, tearing the sleeve from her robe. She screamed, her voice echoing down the vaulted stone corridor, screamed and screamed and screamed. He slammed the door and lifted her to the bed, soothed and petted her like a kitten. She wept, and he cradled her in his arms, rocking her gently, murmuring his love for her. Finally she quieted. Her arms went about his neck, her breasts thrust upward, pressing against his chest.

"We have the whole night together," she said. "No creeping away at dawn. I can lie in your arms as late as I wish."

"For a week," he said.

"Please, ten days!"

"As Your Majesty wishes." He kissed her hand. "But confine your love to the nights, dearest. By day you must appear to loathe me."

"That," she smiled, "will be the only difficulty."

"There is one other," he said. "Jean. I'd prefer to ride to Crichton and ask the divorce, but I dare not leave here. I'll have to send Paris with a letter." He released Mary and walked restlessly about the room. "To write her seems a coward's trick."

"But it's best not to see her," Mary said.

"To divorce her," he said bleakly, "is like cutting out part of my heart."

"She'll soon find another heart."

"God knows I hope she does! Some man who will care for her

[403]

as she deserves." He turned and faced Mary, almost accusingly. "For all her poise, she has no judgment of men. As a wealthy divorcee she'll attract the scum of Europe, and I'll be powerless to protect her."

Damn her, Mary thought, I may never be rid of her. Likely she will haunt his thoughts for months, even years. If she does not wed, he will worry about her loneliness. If she does, he will worry about her happiness. There seems no end to her dominance.

Mutely she blew out the wall tapers, slipped off her robe and climbed into the high oak bed. Bothwell stood by the hearth looking into the fire, one elbow on the mantelpiece, his head bent.

He has forgotten me, she thought. Jean's hold on him is stronger than mine. She will cloud our wedding, our honeymoon, perhaps our very marriage. Perhaps she is right, that I have only his body.

"You do love me, don't you?" she asked. "It is more than mere passion you feel?"

He did not turn. "I must write her. Likely her reply will take time."

"Write her *now?*"

He picked up his doublet, put it on and went to the door. "Why postpone surgery?"

"Come to me later," she said coldly, "if you survive."

As the hours passed and Bothwell did not return, Mary chided herself for her anger. I must put myself in his place, she thought, and try to understand what this divorce means to him. Jean is his gentle Rizzio, his helpless Francis. In a sense she represents his own integrity. Not only has he broken his marriage vow, but he is inflicting emotional torture. Somehow I must conquer my jealousy, for it burdens us both.

When he came to her just before dawn, she apologized, drew his tired face to her breast and held him close. The letter, he said, was on its way. Jean would receive it in the afternoon.

Mary said, "I want you to be honest, as always. It is not too late to change your mind. I would not hold you." Her face in the gray light from the window was composed and tearless. "I believe I love you enough to want your happiness more than my own. You would have to leave Scotland, take Jean away. And I—"

"You'll not wed some scoundrel to give my child a name." He pulled her to him fiercely. "Jean is my deep affection—but you are my love."

"There must be many kinds of love, as there are pebbles on the shore," she said. "Each shaped and colored differently, hewn rough or smooth by time and the tides. It is the sum of our loves that makes us what we are. Had I not loved Francis—in my way—I would not be the person you love now. Had you not this feeling for Jean, you would lack the honor and compassion that make you the person I love."

His lips silenced her. Heedless of time, she slept until noon. Awakening in his arms was the ultimate luxury of love, far sweeter than her dream of it. A servant brought their breakfast, which they ate by the fire, and she said, "Whatever betides, this is truly our honeymoon."

"Before you see your lords," he said, "you must wipe your face of contentment. You look like a flounder-filled cat."

She stretched and smiled. "My contentment goes deeper than you know. In loving you I seem to love all things . . ."

The child within her; the warm, glowing room. Even the look of the breakfast table, firelight silvering the dumpy pewter ale pitcher, the crusty gold of grilled flounder, and ivory cream surrounding a porridge island. Ronsard once said that poems could be written to a thousand humble objects—a skein of flax, a needle, a butterball. Seen with perception, they could be beautiful. She had not agreed; her sonnets had praised sunsets and roses. But now she thought, I was only partially alive.

She went to the window. Surf frilled the jagged black rocks. Heaving, limitless, as far as the eye could reach, the desolate dark green grandeur of the North Sea.

She said, "I think God must have conceived Scotland in passion. Perhaps he made it first, crudely tossing sky and earth and sea together in a very rage of creation."

"England," Bothwell said, "was an afterthought. What gloom and damp and small hills he had left over he shoved south, together with some inferior humans whose coldness and conceit disappointed him. No, come to think of it, the English aren't human. I wonder what he intended when he made them—land fish?"

"You are absurd," she said, coming to him and bending to kiss his cheek. "You don't hate the English as much as you pretend. You liked Throckmorton and Bedford."

"The only two Englishmen I've ever known who weren't awed by their own omniscience . . . But let's not chatter. You've a role to play, and you'd best dress for it."

Mary chose a smoke-gray gown, a gray velvet coif for her hair. She wore no paint, but the mirror reflected sparkling eyes and an upturned mouth. She said, "I am too happy to look ravaged. I wish we were alone here so I could be myself. Could you not free the lords and send them back to Edinburgh?"

"I might at that. They will make your plight public and thus prepare the way for your capitulation." He glanced at her worriedly. "Now mind you don't overplay. Say as little as possible. Appear too crushed for words. I'll join you shortly."

So when she descended to the Great Hall she met her nobles in virtual silence. Lethington, Huntley and Melville seemed tongue-tied with embarrassment. Finally Lethington asked, "Was that Your Majesty who screamed last night?"

Mary nodded mutely.

"We ran to the staircase, but the guards would not let us pass. Madam, what in God's name can we do?"

She shook her head.

"Has Bothwell asked you to sign a promise of marriage?" Melville asked.

"Yes. But I refuse. I'd sooner die, if I had the means."

They begged her to take courage. "It is only a matter of time until help comes," Lethington said with false cheerfulness.

"It is already too late," she said hopelessly. "My shame cannot be cleansed in blood."

Huntley said, "Sign the marriage promise, Madam. Then when you are safe in Edinburgh, repudiate it. We will swear it was signed under duress."

"I sign nothing that I will not honor," she said haughtily.

Bothwell entered. "Good afternoon, Madam; gentlemen."

The men stared at him. Mary turned her back.

"I am releasing you," Bothwell said.

"Thank God!" Mary said.

"Not you, Madam. You remain here until your heart softens. But the others may go." He turned to Lethington. "Go to Edinburgh and inform the lords that my intentions toward Her Majesty are entirely honorable. I believe the Privy Council will agree that nothing must stand in the way of a speedy wedding."

"What of my sister, your wife?" Huntley asked in assumed anger.

"Under the circumstances I expect she will divorce me."

"Clever," sneered Lethington. "You rape your way to the crown."

"What pleasanter method?" Bothwell smiled.

Melville swore. "Have you no shred of honor?"

"Indeed, I honor the Queen with a name as proud as any in Scotland. And how many rapists are willing to wed their victims?"

Lethington glared at him, then went to kneel at Mary's feet. "Madam, it may take ten days or more. But we'll raise the whole of Scotland to batter down this fortress."

Bothwell gave him a long, steady look. "I've nine hundred men here and more on the way. Sooner than relinquish the Queen," he said softly, "I will kill her."

Jean wrote to Bothwell agreeing to the divorce. She would apply immediately to the Protestant Court of Edinburgh on grounds of Bothwell's adultery with Bessie Crawford.

"And I," Bothwell said to Mary, "have sent evidence to the Catholic Court that Jean and I are fourth cousins, so that our marriage can be annulled."

"If your marriage is annulled I'll not be wedding a divorced man!" Mary said delightedly.

He smiled. "You enjoy self-trickery."

"It is not trickery!"

"It is Catholic collusion—what else?"

"Ah, sweet, let us not quarrel. We have only a week together. Perhaps never again in our lives will we know such freedom."

Freedom to love through long, delirious hours, the draperies drawn at the wind-beaten casement, the fire and the rushlights dying unheeded. There was no clock, no hourglass. Mary's little French watch lay silent in its golden case.

Yet, though time was banished, she felt its rhythms in the sea that pounded three sides of the fortress, in the ebb and flow of the harbor tides. She saw the bleak garden bloom with wild hyacinth, and on a soft gray morning the pear trees budded, and forget-me-nots blued the rock clefts. On warm days she stripped to her shift and swam with Bothwell, played in the surf, fished in the coves. They walked inland to gather hawthorne boughs for her chamber, lay and loved in the tall wild grasses. When storms kept her indoors, she sat by the fire in her bedchamber embroidering pale satins for baby coifs and dresses. She planned the little Princess's wardrobe down to the last ruffle and bow.

Mary came to cherish Dunbar. It was old and ugly, floored in mud and oxblood, its halls carpeted in eelgrass and cattails, but like Hermitage it had the savage majesty, the fierce, rock-hewn character of its master. The French chateaux she had thought so lovely seemed effete in contrast. She was falling in love with Scotland.

On the night of April 30th, the Witches' Sabbath, Mary and Bothwell walked on the shore after supper. The sea was so still that reflected stars scarcely moved on its surface. The moon was a red-rimmed scythe.

"Look!" Mary said. "Blood—again!"

She turned and buried her head in his shoulder. "I dread our return to Edinburgh. You know they'll not honor their bond. They wait for the chance to kill you. It will be a ghastly game of hunters and hunted, with you the prey. At best, we will live surrounded by guards, our marriage ringed with steel."

"How else can it be?"

She drew back, looking up at him. "It is ironic that as I come to love Scotland, I also consider leaving it."

"Leaving it?" His voice was incredulous. "What do you mean?"

"Your safety means more to me than my crown. We could run away. You have boats in this very harbor. We could take a small crew and sail to France, live on my lands in Touraine—"

"Christ's blood!" he said. "Have you no courage? Would you relinquish your throne to James without a battle? And even if you would, do you think I'd let you? Have I fought for your crown all of my life only to see it end in a traitor's keeping?"

"James would crown my son King and rule for him until he was of age."

"Aye, James and Elizabeth would rule your son. He'd be a captive king, toadying to England." She started to speak, but he burst out violently, "I'll wed no quivering coward!"

"I am not a coward! But I see what we face."

"Then we'll face it, not run from it."

She laughed on a little sob. "Please don't chide me if I am giddied by such freedom as I never knew. For the first time in my life, I am unhampered by duties, by visitors, by protocol. Is it any wonder I am reluctant to resume my burdens?"

"No wonder," he said, kissing her unbound hair. "My Queen would be a kailwife if she could." He saw tears gather like tiny diamonds in her eyes. "Come now, no tears. We shall visit here often after our marriage and draw the bridge to friends and enemies alike. You shall spin and sew and stir soufflés to your heart's content."

She smiled at him. "A promise?"

"My bond."

Hand in hand, they walked back through the black-and-gold glitter of sea and stars, over the drawbridge into the sleeping lilac-fragrant gardens.

X.

The lords of Scotland gathered like eagles on the heights of Stirling Castle. Mary's spies reported locked-door conferences, rumors of a newly signed bond that pledged Bothwell's destruction. Two plays were produced with boy actors—"The Murder of Darnley" and "The Death of Bothwell." In the latter, the actor who portrayed Bothwell was hanged and cut down barely alive.

Heavily armed, Bothwell and Mary rode to Edinburgh, arriving on the evening of May 6th. At the West Port, Bothwell ordered his men to drop their spears to their saddlebows, signifying that the Queen was no longer captive. He dismounted, bared his head and humbly led Mary's horse through the Grassmarket up the steep rock to Edinburgh Castle.

Mary saw her people's bewilderment, and learned that they were divided. Some thought she had acquiesced willingly to captivity, others believed her Bothwell's victim. Because he had brought her to the iron-barred fortress, many insisted she was still his prisoner. To quiet such talk, Mary returned to Holyrood, riding the Royal Mile with her own archer guard and halberdiers.

Jean's divorce and Bothwell's annulment were granted with record speed—eleven days from start to finish. Thus Mary was able to proclaim her intention to wed on the day after her return.

Her nobles, most of whom were at Stirling, heard her in tight-lipped silence. After they left her audience chamber, she summoned Bothwell.

"Love, they were meek as mice!" she said. "Even the Douglases made no argument."

"They know their forces are outnumbered. But we must keep them outnumbered. I've barely enough to pay my troops, and I've had to let some go."

"I'll ask a loan from Philip," Mary said.

"He'll not send a doubloon if you wed me."

"Then," she said gaily, "I'll melt down Elizabeth's christening font. It's a cumbersome monstrosity anyway."

He laughed. "She'll be livid when she hears she has supplied gold to keep me in power."

"But the power is essential. We must have a standing army of at least four thousand troops . . . Now, we must see to the banns. We will hold the ceremony in the abbey—"

"The abbey? Great God, you're not presuming I'll wed you in Catholic rites?"

She stared at him blankly, her jaw slack.

"I'm a damned peculiar Protestant, I grant you," he said, "but a Protestant nonetheless. My love for you has not lost me my wits."

"Do you mean—" She gulped—"you'll not wed me in my faith?"

"Whatever led you to think I would?"

"Your annulment."

"That was only to soften Catholic shock and make it easier for you."

"Jesu!" she cried. "You cannot do this to me! I not only would lose my self-respect, but the Catholic world would turn hostile. I'd not have a friend in Europe."

"I told you that months ago. That is why I refused to wed you."

"But I didn't understand. I thought . . ." She slumped against the wall.

"You thought I would convert. I won't. A man who would change faith like a cloak is capable of any expedient."

"But for my sake—for our child's sake—surely you will turn Catholic."

He shook his head. "What of *my* self-respect? When I wed you, I'll hear honest Scots spoken, not a gabble of Latin mouthed to mock God."

"Then," she said coldly, "go to Jean. Reconcile. Remarry."

"I'll do no such thing. I'll be at the Border until you send for me."

"I'll never send for you!"

He caught her roughly by the shoulder. "You have always needed me. You always will. You can reach me at Hermitage."

Abruptly he crossed the room, opened the door.

"Wait!" she said.

He paused.

"You cannot leave me! Folk will say you ravished me and refused to wed."

"Tell them *you* refused. All women change their minds. Your lords will rejoice, your people will dance in the streets. And none will blame you for bearing a bastard conceived in rape."

"I'll bear no bastard!" she said furiously.

He was with her in four long strides. His kiss spun her down like an unreeled spool to deep, languorous darkness. Her arms went round him. Dimly, from the vault of consciousness, she thought, He cannot leave me though he tries, for we are indivisible, complete, one. She lifted her head, caught her breath, met his eyes.

Slowly he bent his mouth toward hers and said, "We will marry—"

"Yes!"

"—in the Protestant faith."

XI.

Bothwell sent the Parson of Oldhamstocks to St. Giles to arrange proclamation of the marriage banns. But John Craig, Knox's successor, refused to publish them unless Mary sent a statement in her own writing assuring him that she had not been abducted against her will. Such assurance refuted her previous statement to her lords, but she gave it anyway. Craig hesitated, asked to attend a meeting of the Privy Council at Holyrood.

Mary received him graciously in the Great Hall. She dared not antagonize him at so crucial a time. As he kissed her hand, bowed backward from her dais and stood with her assembled lords, she studied him carefully. A hard, bleak face, but his eyes were kindly under bushy gray brows. Unlike Knox's, his manner was humble. She thought, I warrant he is truly a man of God, worthy of my respect.

Mary called the meeting to order and bade the assembly be seated. "My lords, Master Craig has asked to address us concerning my marriage—" She smiled across the room at Bothwell—"which I hope will take place next week."

Craig rose, bowed to Mary and the lords. He moved toward Bothwell's chair, spoke with a depth of sadness in his voice. "Lord Bothwell, I charge you with adultery, ravishing, breaking the ordinance of the Kirk, the suspicion of collusion between you and your wife, the sudden divorce and proclamation—and last—the suspicion of the King's death which your marriage would confirm."

Bothwell rose. "I admit to no such charges, sir." To Mary's relief he was calm, even gentle. "Can you prove them?"

"No, my lord. But I feel their truth in my heart."

"If you have evidence, do not hesitate to present it."

"I have none." Craig's voice shook. "Thus I am forced to proclaim the banns at St. Giles and Holyrood Chapel. But I am here to call heaven and earth to witness that I abhor and detest this marriage as odious and slanderous to the world, and I exhort the faithful to pray earnestly that a union against all reason and good conscience may yet be overruled by God."

Mary intervened hastily lest Bothwell lose his temper. "We regret we shall not have your blessing, Master Craig, but if God wills we shall wed next Thursday. Is there anything else you wish to say?"

"No, Madam."

"Then you may go."

Craig's words haunted her. If he preached as he spoke, the people would be dangerously stirred. On Sunday she learned what she had feared—that his sermon at St. Giles was an expansion of his statement in Council. That afternoon she sought to repair the damage.

In a simple black gown she rode her white palfrey up the High Street to the Tolbooth. There, before hastily assembled Lords of Session, Bishops, Archbishops and other high dignitaries, she made a formal statement. It was true, she said, that Bothwell had abducted her against her will. But because of his kindly behavior and his long record of service to her mother and herself, she was pardoning him unconditionally.

"Of rape?" snapped the Bishop of Ross.

"By Scots law," Mary said demurely, "the crime of rape is not punishable if the woman later acquiesces."

Ross threw up his hands and raised his eyes to heaven. "Madam, you are lost! Henceforth the Catholic world will regard you as heretic!"

"Scotland is largely Protestant," she said. "In wedding a Protestant, I bow to the will of my people."

She smiled, trailed to the door. Outside a mob awaited her, and she thought of what Bothwell had said: *"They want to believe in you . . . to them you are romance . . ."*

He was wrong, she thought, looking into the hostile faces. I have become what Knox labeled me—a scarlet Jezebel. The women frightened her, their eyes steady, merciless, cold with contempt. I cannot appeal to them, she thought, for these stolid souls shawled in self-righteousness know nothing of passion. To them love is a duty or a snickering shame. Only the young folk might understand, if I could reach them through the barriers set up by the old.

But she dared not address them. She could only hope that in time Bothwell's magnetism would win them. Surely they would compare him favorably with the drunken weakling who had been their king.

As she rode through the Netherbow and into the Canongate, a debtor in a piebald suit, clutching his yellow bonnet, fled ahead of her, pursued by a bailiff. By law, the debtor was safe from the bailiff and his creditors for the whole of Sunday if he could reach the Girth Cross within the sanctuary of the abbey lands. Mary hoped he would succeed, but when she reached the Cross, a crowd was arguing violently.

The debtor lay astride the line of the Cross, flat on his stomach, face in the dust—half in sanctuary, half out. The bailiff tugged at his legs, but angry citizens, determined on fair play, dragged the bailiff aside and appealed to Mary to settle the dispute. She saw Bothwell riding toward her and seized the opportunity to display his justice to the people.

"As Sheriff of Edinburgh, Lord Bothwell shall judge this case," she said. "What say you, my lord? Is the debtor safe?"

Bothwell dismounted and examined the debtor. "By Christ, Madam, he's plopped precisely midway on the line. From the waist up he's in sanctuary—but arse down the bailiff gets him."

The crowd whooped with laughter. "Slice him! Cut him in half!"

Bothwell asked the debtor his name.

"Robin McWimpy," he squeaked. "My lord, my bonnet has rolled and I dare not move to grasp it."

Bothwell retrieved the bonnet, shook lice from it, tossed some coins in it and placed it in the grubby hand.

"Robin," he said, "since your nobler parts are in sanctuary, I pronounce you free."

The crowd cheered. Bothwell mounted his horse and spurred to Mary. "Balfour awaits you at Holyrood," he said softly. "The bastard brews trouble."

Mary received Balfour in her audience chamber. He had asked to see her alone, but she insisted that Bothwell be present.

"What is it you wish, my lord?" she asked uneasily.

Balfour smiled, stroked his curly black beard. "I understand Your Majesty plans to wed Lord Bothwell."

"I believe it is common knowledge," she said drily.

"Are you aware, Madam, that it was he who lit the fuse and exploded the house at Kirk O'Field?"

She felt the downslide of her heart.

"I was witness to it," he said. "But naturally I would not dream of making this fact public."

"Considering that it was you who mined the vaults," she said coldly, "I can readily understand your reluctance."

"My guilt will be difficult to prove, Madam. But if I wished to reopen the case against Lord Bothwell and appear as witness against him . . ." He paused. "I should dislike embarrassing him on the eve of his wedding to you."

Dear heaven, she thought—even though he could not prove Bothwell's complicity it would be fatal to our marriage plans.

Bothwell said, "The court would find it strange that you did not testify previously."

"I would tell them you threatened my life. You recall that I left town . . ."

Bothwell swore. "What is your price?"

"The command of Edinburgh Castle."

"I'll see you in hell first!"

"Wait!" Mary said, as Bothwell moved toward Balfour. "I'd sooner pay him the price than postpone our wedding." Her eyes pleaded, and she willed Bothwell to read her mind: Once we are safely married we will wrest the fortress from him by fraud or force. But now we have no choice.

To her relief, Bothwell winked at her. He turned to Balfour. "You understand that should you act contrary to Her Majesty's interests, she will remove your command?"

"Naturally. But I am Her Majesty's most humble servant."

Aware that her temper was rising, Mary dismissed Balfour and ran into Bothwell's arms. "I am certain James orders Balfour! In this way he controls the defense of Edinburgh. We must raise more troops, and quickly!"

He held her close. "Don't worry, love. Leave Balfour to me."

XII.

In the Great Hall of Holyrood Mary created Bothwell Lord of Shetland and Duke of Orkney, placed the heavy gold coronet on his head. She signed the marriage contract, witnessed by Huntley, Lethington, Lindsay and others.

On the eve of her wedding, her priests came to beg that she refuse a Protestant ceremony, but she shook her head mutely.

Tears in his eyes, Father Roche said, "You place lust of this man above your love for the faith." He echoed the Bishop of Ross. "Madam, you are lost."

Lost, lost . . . She stood at her altar in the gray dusk and looked up at the white marble face of the Virgin. The eyes seemed reproachful, the mouth ineffably sad. Through a blur of tears, Mary groped for the holy beads that lay on the altar cloth. Her hand moved clumsily, and an image of Christ shattered on the floor in splinters of agate and blood-red glass.

Dazedly, she picked up the fragments and placed them on the jeweled cloth. She knelt to pray. A proverb burned her mind:

"Her feet go down to death; her steps take hold on hell."

I am two selves at war in one body, she thought. One self is God's, the other Bothwell's. I cannot be true to both.

Mary supped in her apartments that night, received a few visitors. French Ambassador Du Croc warned that she would lose the friendship of France if she wed Bothwell, and refused to attend the ceremony. Lord Herries arrived from the Border in a mud-splattered cloak, threw himself at Mary's feet and begged her to change her mind. Melville made a final plea, to no avail.

At three in the morning the Marys brought her bath and wedding attire. They dressed her in a black crepe gown with a jet bodice and jet-banded sleeves. A jet coif, a black lace ruff. They made no pretense of gaiety, but moved silently between robing closet and bedchamber.

"If you command—" Beaton's chin trembled—"We will attend the ceremony."

"I command no one's conscience."

Mary embraced them. Slowly she descended the stairs, their tears wet on her cheeks, a crucifix tight in her hand. As she reached the Great Hall, the clock struck four.

She paused in the doorway. At the end of the room, near the altar borrowed from the Canongate Kirk, stood Bothwell, the Bishop of Orkney and the wedding guests. Aghast, she counted thirteen guests.

Huntley and Melville led her past the night-black windows to the oak altar, which stood between tall candelabra. It was banked with mayflowers, but the marsh marigolds were already fading, the roses losing their petals. At a signal from the Bishop, Bothwell moved from the shadows into the taperlight and stood beside her. She did not look at him but bent her head in prayer.

The Bishop took his text from the second chapter of Genesis. Mary closed her ears to his sermon, but she heard sudden rain settle into a steady downpour. A dreary omen for a bride, and the month of May was unlucky.

. . . but of the tree of the knowledge of good and evil, thou shalt not eat, for in the day that thou eatest thereof thou shalt surely die . . .

Good and evil . . . She raised her head and saw the browning edges of the mayflowers, the monstrous overripe rose petals staining the oak like new blood. No image of Christ, no compassionate Virgin, none of the holy symbols to warm her heart. Only this crow-voiced preacher admonishing them to cleave to one another in the Eden of their kingdom.

Aye, she thought bitterly, an Eden flourishing with serpents. We cleave together or perish. And when I perish, I lose my immortal soul.

Panicky, she visioned hell, the lapping tongues of eternal fire, the cindery subterranean agony of the damned. She who had thought of death as birthing the perfect life must fear it to the end of her days.

I must escape—run . . .

Bothwell gripped her hand. She turned and looked up at him. His eyes, flecked with tawny lights, held hers with such intensity that she felt immobilized, powerless to move. In the candleglow, his hair was red-gold as a new-minted coin, his skin bronze. His doublet of dark amber was laced in gold and his sword hilted with topaz. No portrait of a Stuart king had ever looked so royal. Through her terror blazed pride in him, love, desire, an aching tenderness. *He is all I shall know of heaven—but enough.*

Calmly, she made her vows, gave Bothwell her ring and accepted his. They kissed, lips lingering, then turned from the altar hand in hand and faced the tiny group of guests.

"My friends," Mary said, "be the first to greet my husband—His

Grace the Duke of Orkney." She glanced up at Bothwell. "King-Consort of Scotland."

The rain stopped at dawn. After toasts were drunk, Mary and Bothwell descended to the courtyard with largesse for the people. But only a few beggars whined along the arcaded walk with a trio of pipers.

Mary gave them money, took Bothwell's arm and walked into the damp gardens. "The people are probably at the gates," she said. But only the sentries stood at the palace wall, pacing the puddled cobbles.

She gave the sentries gold. One of them was removing a placard from the gate and she asked to see it.

"It appeared during the night, Madam, and looks to be written in a foreign language." He handed her the paper. "Is it French?"

"Latin," she said. "*Mense malas maio nubere vulgus ait.*" She flushed. It was a line from Ovid:

> *The people say*
> *That wantons marry*
> *In the month of May.*

She crumpled the paper and put it in her bodice. Walking back to the palace, she repeated the verse to Bothwell. "Who could be so cruel on my wedding day?"

"An educated man. No commoner conceived that."

As they reached the courtyard, mist rose from the meadows, blown on an east wind. She saw the slow, sullen gathering of a haar.

"Would you like to ride to Seton before we're shrouded?" Bothwell asked.

"No." The absence of the people, the placard, the evil fog depressed her. The terror she had felt at the ceremony returned to stalk her thoughts. "I don't know what I want to do."

She had planned no wedding breakfast, no ball, no evening feast. Most of her nobles were at Stirling. She could not hope to fill one supping table. Lifting her eyes to Bothwell's, she forced a smile. "Let us go to my apartments."

The Marys had laid out a gold satin bridal gown, but she did not put it on. She poured wine for Bothwell, lit extra tapers in the audience chamber. Then she sat beside him on the sofa, mute with misery.

"You are oversensitive," he said. "Why allow a bill-sticker to ruin your wedding day?"

"It is more than that."

"The ceremony?"

She nodded.

"You need never again participate in Protestant rites."

"That is scant comfort," she said, "I have lost hope of heaven."

"Great Zeus! Do you actually believe such gobbledycock?"

She jumped up. "You have had your way—your dreary, chilling, meaningless, heretic wedding! Must you also mock my faith?"

"I mock any bloated conceit. Catholicism has fattened on ignorance and superstition until it is gouty."

"Who are you to judge, who know nothing of it, who shun it like poison?"

"It is poison, to the mind."

She tried to retort, but he raised his voice, pounding, pounding his heresies until finally she fled to the door. But he followed her, slapped her hand from the latch, held her in the vise of his arms.

She laughed wildly, hysterically. "You can't hold me! I'll kill myself! Give me your dagger, let me die! Oh, God, let me die!"

Contemptuously, he released her and she slumped to the floor. "When you have spent this childish tantrum," he said, "you will find me in the Great Hall."

He left her, slamming the door. She heard him talking to someone in the corridor, then footsteps descending the stairs. For a long time she wept until, exhausted, she dragged into the bedchamber and sobbed herself to sleep.

She awakened late in the afternoon. The room was a brown haze of shadow. She lit tapers, stood before the mirror in her crumpled black gown. Her hair snarled to her hips, and her eyes were puffed and darkly circled. She bowed, spoke ironically to her image. "The bride."

Fleming tiptoed in from the audience chamber. "Ah, Madam, you are finally awake. Sir John Hamilton has been awaiting audience for several hours. Will you see him?"

"Yes." Perhaps he would lift her spirits. He was a handsome black-bearded young scamp, a comrade-in-mischief of Lord Robert. "Ask him to wait in the audience chamber."

She joined him there, wearing the gold satin bridal gown, a gold wig, a half-ruff of gold lace that bared her throat. He murmured the usual compliments, but his face was unnaturally grave.

"Well, Johnny?" she said affectionately. "What brings you to court?"

"I heard Your Majesty was to be wed," he said. "I arrived too late to prevent it."

"Surely you did not think you could prevent my marriage?"

"I felt it my duty to try, Madam."

[417]

"I thought you came to cheer me," she smiled, "but you come to scold."

"I come now to see that you are safe. All afternoon there have been terrible rumors. Melville swears that he heard you call for a dagger to kill yourself."

"Jesu!" she said. Melville must have been just outside the chamber.

"If Bothwell has harmed you, by Christ I'll kill him!"

"Nonsense," she said. "We quarreled over religion. Melville has invented a drama."

"Naturally I take your word, Madam. But there's not one but knows you were wed in fear of your life and not of your own free will."

"That is not true! Because the lords hate my husband they presume that everyone does. They refuse to face the truth—that I love him."

For I do . . . though he taunts my faith, deserts me on my wedding day . . .

"Again I bow to your word, Madam," he said bleakly.

"Ah, Johnny, must you too be dismal? One would think I'd held a wake, not a wedding."

"Forgive me, Madam, but I can't pretend merriment. I have loved you too long."

She laughed. "It is fashionable to love the Queen, and safe. Many young men use love of me as an excuse to escape marriage."

"Not I!"

He swept her so suddenly into his arms that her astonished gasp was lost under his lips. She smelled brandywine, and realized he had probably been drinking excessively. For a few moments she remained deceptively passive, then moved suddenly and with all her strength, breaking his grasp.

"Get out!" she said, moving backward to the door.

The door opened. Bothwell came in.

Mary turned. Her voice trembled. "Good evening, dearest."

Bothwell bowed, nodded to Johnny.

"I was just leaving," Johnny said, pawing at his ruff. "I—I came to offer my felicitations."

"It was kind of you," Mary said. "I regret you cannot stay."

Hastily, he left them. Mary sat down in the nearest chair, pretended to adjust her shoe buckle. *Surely Bothwell saw nothing.*

She raised her head, asked casually, "What did you do today? I suppose the haar was too thick to hunt."

"What happened?" Slowly he walked to her. "What happened with Johnny Hamilton?"

"I don't know what you mean." Her eyes opened wide.

"You would know if you looked in the mirror, Madam."

Fearfully, she went to her bedchamber. Her gold wig was askew and coils of dark hair rippled down her back. Lip paint smeared her chin and cheeks.

He came up behind her. "I gave you a chance to tell me what happened. You preferred to evade. So I must conclude that you accepted more than felicitations from him."

"I did not! He kissed me against my will!"

"If that is true, then why your guilty evasion?"

"It was not guilt!"

"Then why did you lie to me?"

"I dreaded another scene!"

"What did you do to encourage such a liberty?"

"Nothing! He had been drinking."

"Are you handled by every cock o'fool who seeks audience?"

"Oh, God," she said, hands to her ears. "Is this to be the pattern of our marriage?"

"You set the pattern, not I. If you'd lie to protect Johnny Hamilton he means more to you than your honor."

She turned on him furiously. "You abhor jealousy, yet now you rave like a maniac!"

"And how would you act if you found me with Fleming in like condition and I evaded an honest question? You'd shrill and yowl to the turrets." He caught her arm roughly. "Wouldn't you?"

"Yes, but I would believe your word if you gave it. And I give you my word Johnny Hamilton is less than my dog to me."

His eyes softened. "Don't ever lie to me again. Don't ever evade. I find it difficult enough to believe in your love."

Hurt, she said, "You find it difficult when I risk a kingdom for you?"

"I find it almost incredible," he said softly, "because you—are you."

Touched, she went to him, put her arms around his neck. "You must never doubt my love. And we must not quarrel as we did this morning."

He held her close. "I should not mock your religion. But I think you suffer needlessly. Pride has sustained you these dark years, not faith. Remove the prop of religion, and you'd still stand square to the wind."

"I cannot be happy without it."

"Then be absolved."

"The Pope will not absolve me."

"The Pope is a flunkey with the pompous pretensions of his kind. But God will absolve you."

[419]

"That is *your* faith," she snapped, drawing back from him.

"It is common sense to seek the source of mercy. In Jedburgh the debtor's wife could not get past your sentry but she had the wit to throw a stone to your window and you looked out and heard her petition. So with Protestants—"

She said, "Oh, *puke* Protestants!"

Bothwell laughed, a great, delighted bellow, swung her into his arms and kissed her lips. Her wig fell off and her hair cascaded down, gold pins showering the carpet. He carried her past the bed to the private stairs.

"Where are you going?" she said. "I cannot be seen like this!"

"The haar will hide you, love. We're riding to Arthur's Seat."

"Are you mad?" She glanced at the fog-swept window. "On such a night—"

"Our wedding night," he said. "I want you above the world."

CHAPTER TWELVE

I.

ALONE WITH BOTHWELL in their heavily guarded apartments, Mary was passionately happy. But once outside those dim, fragrant chambers she was fearful. Though most of Bothwell's enemies were at Stirling she worried that they might use a servant to kill him—a groom or a page. She wondered why Lethington remained at Holyrood. Was it to spy? Or because he delighted in a most difficult diplomatic game?

"Madam," he told her, "you challenge me to the most preposterous task of my career. I must explain to the Pope, Charles and Philip why they should accept a heretic rapist and suspected murderer as King-Consort of Scotland."

"Since you so hate my husband, I marvel you try."

Lethington seemed genuinely astonished. "A secretary of state neither hates nor loves, Madam. He manipulates the emotions of others."

But Lethington's efforts availed her nothing. His letters met contemptuous silence. Mary received no wedding gifts, no congratulations, no messages from Rome, France or Spain. Through her ambassadors she learned that the Pope considered her heretic. She had lost the support and friendship of the Catholic world.

Late in May she called a meeting of the Privy Council in the Great Hall and addressed the few members present:

"I hope that the Pope will forgive me, for the Bishop of Ross has written him that I repent the Protestant ceremony with all my heart. I have sworn never again to betray my faith."

Lethington said, "I fear Your Majesty's repentance comes too late. The only person pleased is Elizabeth. I hear she crows that your marriage deals the death blow to English Catholicism."

Bothwell said, "Perhaps she crows too soon. I believe we could regain Catholic support if we sent the Prince to the court of France for a Catholic education."

[421]

Mary beamed at Bothwell. "Why did I not think of that? It is a brilliant scheme." From the dais she looked down at her nobles. "Do you agree?"

They were silent, exchanging glances.

"Well?" she asked Lethington impatiently. "What say you?"

"The lords at Stirling would never agree, Madam."

"The Prince is my son and I shall educate him as I see fit!"

Lethington said, "Forgive my bluntness, Madam." He turned to Bothwell. "But the lords so mistrust Your Grace that they are keeping the Prince in their guardianship. Should you wish to visit him at Stirling you are welcome, but should you try to remove him you will be refused."

Bothwell sprang up from his chair. "This is treason!"

"They do not so regard it," Lord Oliphant said. "They believe Your Grace has designs on the child's life."

"They believe no such thing!" Bothwell said furiously. "They fabricate this tale as an excuse for rising against me. They failed to prove me a murderer, they could not condemn me for rape, so now they charge I conspire against the Prince's life!"

Mary turned to Lethington. "Why did you not tell us this before?"

"We just learned of it this morning," he said.

"I warrant my brother directs this infamy!"

"Aye," Bothwell said, "Lord James will reappear as a hero to save the Prince from my villainy."

Lethington said quickly, "I am sure Lord James knows nothing of this."

Mary glanced at him sideways with a bitter little smile. Though appearing to maintain neutrality, Lethington was undoubtedly in league with the rebels. He was telling her only as much as they wished her to know.

"Are you commissioned to hint that if I will give up my husband —divorce or exile him—I may rule in peace with my son by my side?" she asked.

"I am not commissioned at all, Madam." Lethington shifted uneasily under Bothwell's stare. "However, if you were free—if the Duke retired to some other country—I am sure they would return your son to you."

"So they offer a choice between my son and my husband?"

The lords were silent.

Bothwell said, "Should you choose me, Madam, it means civil war."

She read his thought: We are ill-equipped. It will take time to raise money, to gather the disbanded Borderers. We have few faithful nobles—the Setons, the Flemings, the Borthwicks, the Gordons and the Hamiltons. Balfour commands Edinburgh Castle, and his loyalty is dubious.

It infuriated her that her son should be held as hostage, used so cynically as the tool of traitors. She felt for the first time a fierce rush of tenderness for the child. She would fight to the death for him.

Mary rose and flung her head high. "Then it is civil war."

Lethington gasped. "You hazard your crown and the crown of England!"

"Yes! I shall not only force my nobles to submission, but demand Parliamentary grant of the Crown Matrimonial for my husband. He shall be King of Scotland."

"But Madam, were you to lose—"

"I will not lose my husband," she said. "If need be, I shall follow him in a white petticoat to the world's end."

II.

While Bothwell conferred with loyal nobles, Mary took Elizabeth's gold and jeweled font to the mint for melting. French Ambassador Du Croc pleaded with her to let him negotiate with the rebels, but she was scornful of compromise.

"Madam," he said, "never have I known you so headstrong. I marvel that you risk your crown for a man with whom you are miserable."

"What!" They were sitting on a bench in the garden, and she moved closer to him, thinking she had not heard him correctly.

"We all know how gallantly you hide your heartbreak, that in these two weeks of marriage you have virtually been a prisoner in your chamber."

"Mon Dieu!" she laughed. "For a Frenchman you are strangely obtuse. Is there a bride who does not love such imprisonment?"

"Lady Lethington says your husband is fiercely jealous."

"I boasted to her rather than complained," Mary said. "The Duke and I quarreled about Johnny Hamilton, but that is past."

"Can Your Majesty deny that Melville heard you cry out for a dagger to kill yourself?"

Exasperated, she said, "That tale has doubtless spread clear to the New World. Why this distortion of truth? Is it so that the rebels will have further excuse to 'rescue' me?"

Du Croc was evasive, and she asked angrily, "Have you written King Charles this gossip?"

"It is my duty to inform my master of my impressions."

"Then you shall correct that impression," she said coldly, and dismissed him.

It outraged her that no one—not even the Marys—were convinced of her love for Bothwell. And perhaps even now he believed Jean's love was deeper than her own. My protests are in vain, she thought, but I will leave proof, written in my own hand. That night she completed a sonnet:

> Unto his hands, wholly unto his power
> I place my life, my son, my honor, all
> My country and my subjects. In his thrall
> I am bound closer with each passing hour.
> My self-surrender has but one intent:
> To show, despite the gathering clouds of strife
> My love for him is deep and permanent,
> Blood of my bone, the very breath of life.
>
> Let come fair weather or the rage of rain!
> I care not, for my soul is in his keeping,
> In harbor of his heart I shall remain
> Constant in happiness, faithful in weeping,
> Her tears are but a false and feignèd brew;
> I risk the ravening world. My love is true.

She showed it to Bothwell, and he read it, smiled and shook his head. "You do me too much honor, love. And I haven't the skill to reciprocate. May I keep this?"

"Of course."

He locked it in his silver casket, where he kept important papers. Then he turned to her. "Our friend Lethington has just slipped out of the palace. Paris saw him laden with luggage riding north. Fleming is with him."

She could not blame Fleming for following her husband, but she sighed at thought of losing her. And Lethington's treachery hurt.

"A rat deserts the ship of state," Bothwell said. "Be glad."

III.

Each day brought reports from Bothwell's spies at Stirling. Morton was mobilizing the rebels in command of Kirkcaldy of Grange, and sending couriers throughout Scotland urging the people to rise against "Bloody Bothwell" and deliver the Queen and the Prince from his monstrous tyranny. Lords Atholl and Glencairn were rousing the Highlands, and Lord Argyll the west. It was believed the rebels intended to ride to Edinburgh and attack Holyrood.

Balfour suggested that Mary and Bothwell move to Edinburgh

Castle for safety but, suspecting a trap, they refused. Instead they ordered Huntley and his Gordons to watch Balfour and net him with spies. Dalgleish would guard the jewels and state papers which Mary and Bothwell locked in the castle vaults.

At Holyrood, Mary called to arms all loyal nobles, freeholders and yeomen. On the pretext of a rising on the Border, she asked them to meet her at Melrose on June 15th with arms and provisions for fifteen days. Hastily, on June 6th, she and Bothwell, with hackbuteers and artillery, rode on the first lap of their journey south to the massive moor-wild safety of Borthwick Castle on the River Gore, fourteen miles from Edinburgh.

They arrived at noon, and Lord and Lady Borthwick made them comfortable in the state apartments on the south side of the castle. Servants unpacked Mary's few gowns, her armor and helmets, her silver bathing basin and portable altar. Messengers were dispatched to rally neighboring nobles and their forces, to help defend Borthwick in case of attack.

As the hours passed, Mary grew increasingly uneasy. From her window above the courtyard she watched small detachments ride in— gloomy-faced, silent. Not the hundreds she had expected, but groups of three and four. By evening only sixty had answered her summons. She and Lord Borthwick together had fewer than five hundred men.

But Bothwell was confident. "We have the Border behind us. We'll lure the rebels to Melrose and smash them clear into England."

Mary tried to shrug off her apprehension. But that night as they heard music and ballad peddlers in Lady Borthwick's bower, she found herself listening for hoofbeats, for the curdling war cry of the Douglases. Pleading a headache, she retired early, and Bothwell joined her in her bedchamber at nine o'clock.

"I am nervous," she confessed. "Restless as a cat." She sat down at the dressing table, unbound her hair and began to brush it. "Perhaps a game of cards would relax me. Shall we play Primero?"

"I'm sorry, but I'd best ride to Crichton while I have the chance."

The hairbrush clattered to the floor. "You'd go to Jean *tonight?*"

"There's no need for you to worry. This castle could withstand an indefinite siege."

"You'd leave me and go to Jean!"

"Crichton is only a mile. She has some estate business to discuss and requires my signature on a deed."

"So that is why you chose this place—to be near Jean!"

"Oh God, you begin this again."

"Yes, because I am never rid of her! Now you pretend business with her."

"You have my word on that," he snapped.

[425]

She was aware of his fraying patience, but was too angry to care. "I have your word but *she* has your love."

He turned on her savagely. "You alone can force me to infidelity and, by Christ, that seems your intention." He jerked on his gauntlets and picked up his riding whip.

"So you admit you will bed with her!"

"I admit nothing. Feed your imagination as you like."

He started to the door, and she ran after him and caught his arm. "Tell me the truth!"

"Never again. You have broken our bond with mistrust." He pulled free of her. "Stew in your own brew, Madam."

He left, slamming the door.

Sick with jealousy, she paced her apartments. Undoubtedly, Bothwell would be back but not as her husband—as Jean's lover. When the rebels were whipped and she was firmly enthroned, he would leave her.

As I deserve, she thought. Bothwell could have sneaked to Crichton, and I'd have been none the wiser. But he honored me with the truth as few wives are ever honored, and I threw his gift in his face.

At three o'clock she heard him return, and waited vainly for him to come to her. Finally she went down the corridor to his bedchamber, knocked timidly and opened the door.

He stood by the window putting on his breast armor.

"Where are you going?" she asked.

"To Melrose. I want to see early arrivals and rally more. I'll be back in two days."

"May I go with you?"

"No. You're safer here."

He fastened the hooks of his armor, reached for his helmet.

"Did you—" She spoke gently, hesitantly—"go to Crichton?"

"Yes."

She ran to him, put both hands on his steel shoulders. "Forgive me, please forgive me! I'd welcome the cruelest truth about Jean in preference to lies."

"You've had the truth and doubted it. You'll not have it again."

Her hands dropped from his shoulders. His manner was cold and impenetrable as his armor.

"I'll not grovel," she said. "Even for your love."

She turned and walked back to her chamber.

Each hour recruits straggled into Borthwick and sought the cool stone shade of the inner courtyard. The weather turned humid. Hot rains washed the moors but did not break the sultriness. Mary roamed the damp, steamy rooms, ill with child, with loneliness and worry. From the tower turret she scanned the moor for enemies and watched for Bothwell's return.

He returned to her as coldly as he had left. She followed him to his apartments hoping he would take her into his arms, but he called a servant for water and towels and, ignoring her, pulled off his armor and dusty clothes and bathed.

"How many men do we have at Melrose?" she asked.

"Fewer than a hundred of my Borderers."

She gasped. "But even this soon there should be far more than that! Did you ride to rally them?"

"Aye," he said bitterly, "but Morton's agents were there before me. For weeks they've been rousing the Border against me—ever since I abducted you. Word has swept from coast to coast that you and the Prince are my prisoners and that I threaten his life."

"But how could your Borderers believe such lies?"

"They are simple, credulous folk, men of brawn, not brains. They are told that your proclamation summoning them to arms was made under duress, and that their duty is to rescue you. Many have already joined the rebels at Stirling. Others who will not ride against me hug their huts."

"Jesu! We cannot fight the whole of Scotland with a few hundred men."

"But we will," he said.

She sat in silence, while his servant helped him into a thin white robe. He was deeply sun-coppered and she thought he had never looked so handsome. She longed to go to him but dared not.

"How many men can we count on?" she asked.

"I count on nothing," he said savagely. "But with luck, and all the men our friends can muster—perhaps two thousand."

"Will they come here?"

"No, we'll join them at Melrose in five days." He turned to the servant. "Draw the draperies." To Mary he said, "You will excuse me. I've had no sleep."

Her voice matched the chill of his own. "Nor have I," she said, and left him.

Bothwell joined her at supper with the Borthwicks in the Great Hall. They had just finished, when an outrider reported a company of horsemen approaching from the north. Bothwell ordered the drawbridge raised and, followed by Mary, rushed up to the watchtower.

In the lingering daylight, they could see about a hundred horsemen racing toward the castle gates.

Bothwell plunged down the spiral stairs and she ran after him. Lord Borthwick joined them in the main hallway, and they went out to the guardhouse overlooking the narrow moat and drawbridge.

Bothwell's soldiers made way for them as they hurried to the iron-barred window. Massed at the gates were a hundred hackbuteers. Their leader dismounted and shouted across the moat.

"We come from Lord Huntley in Edinburgh. A thousand rebels are pursuing us. For God's sake lower the drawbridge and let us in!"

"Show me Huntley's message or his token," Bothwell called.

"I am instructed to give the message only to His Grace the Duke of Orkney."

"I am he," Bothwell said.

The man bowed. "There was no time to bring a letter or a pledge, Your Grace." He glanced fearfully behind him. "For God's sake, shelter us!"

Bothwell laughed. "Return to Lord Morton, or whoever commands you, and tell him this trick was old in Caesar's time. I'll wait here to parley with him."

Cursing him, the man mounted and rode off with his troops. Bothwell summoned his officers, snapped commands, and they went to their posts at drawbridge and battlements. Lord Borthwick and a dozen soldiers remained with Mary and Bothwell.

A volley of musket fire thudded the east wall, and Mary gasped. Bothwell stared down at her contemptuously. "I've told you these walls are impregnable—they waste their ammunition. But if you are afraid you'd best go to the deepest dungeons."

"I am not afraid!" she blazed. "I was startled."

Outside the gates there was sudden shouting, the drum of a thousand hoofs on the cobbles. The screams she had dreaded shrilled up through musketfire: "A-Douglas!" She peered through the grating with Bothwell. In the bright torchlight she saw Lord Morton dismount.

Her voice rang out to meet him. "What is the meaning of this, my lord?"

He turned to the window, bowed, removed his helmet. "We mean Your Majesty no harm. We come to deliver you from the murderer of your late husband, who now would murder your son."

"My husband was acquitted of murder. You yourself signed a bond pledging him your friendship and approving my marriage."

"That was under duress. We come to deliver you."

"As Judas delivered Christ," she said.

"Nay, Madam, it is for your own good and the good of your realm. Send out Bothwell, and we will leave peacefully."

Bothwell shouted, "She'll send you to hell first, you sanctimonious slobberhead!"

Morton peered at him and cursed. "Lord Home and I have a

thousand men surrounding you, and this is only an advance force. Will you come out like a man, or doom the Queen to slow starvation?"

"By that question," Bothwell said, "you admit you cannot take Borthwick by force. Here we stay."

Morton appealed to Mary. "My men have cut you off from all help. We have formed an iron ring that none can pass."

Bothwell turned to Mary in mock astonishment. "Can it be he has discovered Sextus Julius' *Stratagems and Subtleties of War?*"

"Butcher! Murderer!" Morton yelled in a frenzy of fury. "Traitor! Coward!"

Morton's men joined him, hurling insults at Bothwell, taunting him to come out and fight. Bothwell laughed. But when they reviled Mary, calling her a whore, he whitened with rage and drew his sword.

"Morton!" he shouted. "You'll fight me in single combat. I'm coming out."

Lord Borthwick and four of his soldiers seized Bothwell. He struggled savagely, then quieted as suddenly as he had flared. He said, "Unhand me. I'll not go out."

But they held him.

"Do we have your word you will not go out?" Mary asked.

Bothwell said, "My word."

They released him. He sheathed his sword, caught Mary's arm, nodded toward Borthwick. "Quick, come to the Queen's apartments."

In her bedchamber Bothwell said, "I think Morton speaks the truth, that this is only an advance force. I must get out while there's still a chance, and gather my troops."

"You'd be shot the moment you stepped outside!" Mary said.

Bothwell went to Mary's wardrobe, pawed through her gowns, pulled out the simplest—a dark russet silk. "Give me a petticoat," he ordered.

She hesitated and he said, "You heard me, Madam." He pulled off his doublet and breeches.

Reluctantly, she gave him the petticoat. He put it on, tearing the waistband to make it larger and securing it with his sash. He took the gown, slashed the side seam of the bodice with a knife and squirmed into it, girdling his waist with a sword and dagger belt. Then he looked down in dismay. The hem of the gown came well above his ankles, exposing big feet in leather boots.

"My cloak will hide you," Mary said, "if I rip out the hem."

While she worked on the cloak, Bothwell outlined his plan. "When they discover I have fled they probably will seek me in Melrose, so I'll ride to Haddington and rally our men from there. Madam, send two messengers to Huntley in Edinburgh—one may get

[429]

through—and tell him what has happened. I don't think Morton will linger here once I'm gone. Likely by tomorrow night you'll be free to join me. Slip out to the woods at ten o'clock. Starting near the line of birches is a rough path. Follow it north for a mile to the first clearing, and I'll meet you with horses. I'll be there from ten to midnight."

"And if I cannot come?"

"I'll be there the next night or one of my men will."

Mary pulled the last threads from the cloak and Bothwell grabbed it but she said, "Wait, you need a better disguise." She outlined his lips with red paint. Then she fitted her taffy wig to his head, and he put on the cloak and drew up the hood.

Mary sighed. "At least your boots are hidden."

Bothwell went to the mirror. "Great God!"

Lord Borthwick laughed. "No man who sees you will ever forget you."

His height was startling and his face grotesque—the full mouth crimson in the hard sun-browned face, the coquettish taffy curls perking from under the pink, ruffled lining of the hood.

He said in mock horror, "If Morton's men see me, I'll be lost in the nearest haystack."

"It is not comic," Mary said. "You may be killed."

"Not if I don't struggle," he said coyly.

"Please don't jest!" She went to him and drew him close. "Love, my dear love . . ."

He was rigid in her arms. Slowly she released him and turned toward the window to hide her tears.

Lord Borthwick said, "Your Grace, you'd best take someone with you."

"I'll take the young laird of Crookston." Bothwell went to his chamber and returned with a pistol, which he held under his cloak. He bowed to Mary. "Until tomorrow night, Madam."

But for Lord Borthwick's presence, she would have begged his love on her knees. Instead she said, "God go with you."

He left her without a backward glance.

Alone in her bedchamber, Mary looked at the clock. It was nine-twenty. If Bothwell was not captured within the hour she could believe him safe.

Thankful for a task to pass the time, she wrote messages to Huntley and dispatched two couriers to Edinburgh. The golden hands of the clock crept to nine-forty.

She sat in the window seat cursing the strange northern climate where summer daylight lingered until midnight. Bothwell could not fail to be seen, and the absurd disguise would fool no one. Once long ago before she had come to Scotland, he had made legend by escaping the English in a woman's clothes, and his enemies would expect some such trick. She should never have allowed him to go in such attire.

Leaning out the window she listened intently, agonized by each shout. Far off in the woods she heard a shot, and stiffened in terror. Perhaps the soldiers were hunting game—or had caught Bothwell and killed him. Morton would take no chances on his captive escaping.

The clock struck ten. A guard rapped on the door and announced Lord Borthwick. Mary walked slowly forward, her heart pounding.

"Madam," Borthwick said, "they have captured Crookston."

Her tongue was thick with panic. "And my husband?"

"Escaped by a bowshot. Two of my men saw it. Lord Home's troops bore down on them and the Duke fled one way, Crookston another. Apparently they think the Duke rides toward Edinburgh to join Huntley and are preparing to give chase."

Her body sagged with relief. "Will Morton lift the siege here?"

"I think so. Unless he admits that the rebellion is against Your Majesty, he has no excuse to stay."

Even as he spoke they heard the shouting, clanging, neighing din of departure. Mary ran to the window. Long lines of horsemen spread slowly into the moor, moving north like a black stormcloud.

Borthwick left her. She stood at the window until the sky turned gold and deepened to darkness. Then she knelt at the altar and thanked God for Bothwell's life.

As she rose she felt the first stir of her child and stood awed, shaken by love and longing. And then in terror she thought, Until I am safe on my throne no one must suspect my pregnancy. I must start to lace tightly. For if the rebels discover I bear Bothwell's child, they will find a means to kill it.

IV.

The following night at ten o'clock Mary prepared to join Bothwell. For fear that Morton had left patrols in the area, she dressed in a page's jerkin and breeches, slipped into her own riding boots and caught her hair into a cap. Lord Borthwick strapped a sword and dagger to a belt at her waist and supplied a short cape. He led her to the same postern door whence Bothwell had escaped, knelt and kissed her hand.

"May God protect you, Madam."

"And may he reward you and your lady for protecting me."

She opened the door, looked out into the garden, grateful for the soft rain-gray light. Borthwick's hackbuteers paced on their rounds, and she waited until they had passed, then dashed for the birch trees that bordered an oak thicket. The castle dogs set up a clamor, but none followed, and she entered the dripping green twilight of the woods and took the path north.

For twenty minutes she walked through gently slipping rain, her boots sagging into moss. Never before had she been totally alone, and realization of her freedom struck her with the fire and force of brandywine. She capered, jumping to touch a high bough, skipping along the path like a child. How could folk take such ecstasy for granted? Yet she had never heard anyone say, in excitement, in awe, "I was alone . . ."

Bothwell loved solitude, she knew. He had spent weeks on the desolate Border Marches seeing no one, hearing nothing but curlew cries and the sigh of the wind-pushed heather. Miles of sad-colored moors, stretching free and far as the heart could reach. But he took such freedom for granted. She thought, He has not been prisoned with people for twenty-four years as I have.

She rounded a bend in the path, and her heart plunged. Ahead was a wide clearing—surely the one he had mentioned. And he was not there.

I must not panic.

She took the Rouen watch from her belt. It was nearly eleven o'clock. He had said he would be there from ten to midnight. Nothing could have kept him away but force.

She sat down on the wet grass and leaned against a tree trunk. As the daylight faded, the forest seemed spectral, unreal. Flowers were white as the parchment death-blooms she had seen on French graves. High-arching tree boughs rose like Gothic vaults shutting out the sky.

Solitude, she thought bitterly. Ten minutes ago I was drunk with it, but now it presses me like a rack. Freedom . . . what does it avail me if he is not here to share it? He may lie in some filthy cell in Haddington, or ride in chains to Edinburgh.

But he is not dead. When he dies I shall know it, not with the mind but with the heart. We are too close, that he could die and I not know.

Slowly the forest darkened. Far off, she heard the grumble of thunder. Then it came closer, and lightning blazed through the clearing. Rain poured through the canopy of oaks, and she huddled back against the tree trunk, pulling up the collar of her cape and hiding her face on her drawn-up knees. Storm or not, she would stay until midnight and then grope her way back to Borthwick—if she could.

But now it was too dark to see her watch. She began counting the minutes.

Rain drenched her thin velvet cape, poured down her shoulders. Through cracking thunder she heard another sound—faint at first, but unmistakable—hoofbeats. She rose, and as she ran forward she heard Bothwell's voice, the jangle of spurs, the snort of horses.

"Mary!"

She was in Bothwell's arms, cradled like a baby. She lifted her face to his, her eyes blurred with rain and tears. "Thank God you are safe!"

"I'm sorry I was delayed; I spied a patrol and circled to avoid it."

"Where do we go?" she asked.

"Dunbar," he said.

He wore men's clothes now—wool breeches and a Borderer's leatherjack—and he took a plaid cloak from his saddlebow and wrapped her in it. Then he carried her to the cob he had brought and lifted her into the saddle.

"Morton left a hundred men in this area to patrol in groups of ten. You keep watch to our rear, and I'll ride ahead. Our only hope is to outrun them."

She touched his shoulder. "Dearest, am I forgiven?"

He caught her hand and kissed it. "Damned if I'm not a doltish fool!"

He swung to his horse and they left the forest. Thunder rolled and crashed, and when she turned to look behind her, the moors for an instant were fired bright as day. As far as she could see there were only the woods, the brackened hills, and stubby trees starkly outlined by the lightning.

She laughed in sudden exultation, spurred her horse, and set her face to the storm.

V.

Safe at Dunbar, Mary summoned all loyal subjects between the ages of sixteen and sixty to join her immediately. Balfour sent word by Bothwell's lawyer, Edmund Hay, that unless they marched on Edinburgh at once, he would be forced to come to terms with the rebels and surrender the castle.

"This may be a trick to trap us," Bothwell growled. "I'd not trust Balfour in chains."

"Surely if Edinburgh is dangerous, Huntley would have warned us not to come," Mary said. "Don't you think the Gordons can manage Balfour?"

"I don't know. I don't like it. Nor do I like to loiter here." He smashed his fist on his hand in sudden decision. "When we have two thousand men we'll march."

Two days later they left Dunbar with hackbuteers, cavalry, moss-troopers and three portable field guns. Lord Fleming and the Hamiltons would meet them at Musselburgh with reinforcements, and Bothwell was confident they would draw recruits on the way.

It was hot. Not a breath of wind stirred the baking moors, and the troops suffered from thirst, for few had brought water jugs. Sweat poured from under their sizzling iron helmets and those in armor were tortured. Occasionally a foot soldier fainted and was lifted into a wagon litter that followed the cavalcade.

Mary had borrowed clothes from a woman of the garrison—a white linen bodice, the full sleeves caught in points; a short red kilted skirt that came just below her knees and a wide-brimmed red velvet hat. She fanned herself with the hat, looking hopefully at the sky for a sign of rain. But the yellow glare was cloudless. For fear her skin would burn, she borrowed a cutting scarf from a soldier and wrapped it about her face as best she could, preferring the heat of the wool to the shame of a reddened complexion.

Evidently the rebels' lies had not yet reached this area, and to Mary's delight she was cheered in every village. Loyal contingents joined them. Women brought buckets of drinking water and tended the sick. At Haddington six hundred horsemen and infantry lengthened the lines. Two miles farther, at Gladsmuir, they were met by Lords Borthwick and Seton with their troops.

Bothwell took a rough count. "I'd say we have nearly thirty-five hundred men."

Mary smiled. "We only begin!"

In Gladsmuir's market square her heralds trumpeted, and Mary addressed the people: "A number of conspirators . . . after they failed to apprehend us at Borthwick have made seditious proclamation that they seek to revenge the murder of the late King and relieve me of bondage and captivity. They pretend that the Duke, my husband, is minded to kidnap my son, whereas it is they who hold him prisoner. As an excuse for their treason they now make a buckler of my son, but their real intention is to overthrow me and my heir that they may rule Scotland at their pleasure. Thus I am forced to arms, and I ask that all faithful subjects join me. You will be rewarded with the lands and goods of the conspirators, each according to his merit."

The crowd cheered and more men joined the ranks. Slowly, the cavalcade moved on toward Edinburgh. At nine o'clock that night, they reached Seton House.

After supper, Mary and Bothwell retired to their apartments. In a thin blue robe borrowed from Lady Seton, Mary sat at the window fanning herself, looking down at the troops who camped beyond the gardens.

"With the Gordons and Hamiltons we'll number five thousand or more," she said.

"Never count on 'or more.'" Bothwell smiled. He lay stretched out on cushions at her feet. In his wide-sleeved white shirt, barelegged and brown, he looked like a tall lad, his autumn-colored hair a bright tousle on the cushion.

She said, "I count on you. No matter how few men I had, I'd not be afraid if you led us."

He nuzzled her foot with his lips.

"Lord Seton says you are the best forest and hill fighter in Europe."

"Best or not, that's why I'm loath to march on Edinburgh. If we can lure the rebels into the hills . . ."

They talked until after midnight. Then a guard called through the door and said Bothwell's agent from Edinburgh desired audience. Mary threw on a cloak, and they received him in the anteroom.

"Your Majesty—Your Grace." He knelt to them, rose. "The rebels, reinforced by Highlanders under Atholl and Glencairn, are moving out of Edinburgh toward Musselburgh with three thousand men."

"Did Balfour fire on them?"

"Not a shot, Your Grace."

Bothwell swore. "So Balfour is in league with them. What of Huntley?"

"Huntley and his men are in Edinburgh Castle, but whether as Balfour's prisoners I know not."

"Have the rebels roused my people to arms?" Mary asked.

"They tried, Madam, but without success. The people are apathetic. They have no artillery and few munitions. If I may be blunt —they may not support Your Majesty, but they're damned if they'll join the rebels. Had Balfour fired the castle guns yesterday, I've no doubt the rebels would have fled headlong. But now their reinforcements have come, and they march to engage you."

Bothwell roared happily. "The damned fools! If they'd stayed in Edinburgh and holed up in the castle they could have held the city indefinitely—and blasted us to hell if we stuck our noses near. But now they quit the best strategic position in Scotland to fight me on terrain of my choosing."

"Balfour will hold the castle, Your Grace."

"Not after I smash the field army. We'll maneuver them south to the hills."

Bothwell gave the agent gold, dismissed him. Back in the bedchamber he said, "This is June 15th. In two days, I warrant, we'll be in Edinburgh watching the traitors hang."

"June 15th!" she said, pulling off the heavy cloak. "Why, this day is our first anniversary! We have been married exactly a month."

"By God, so we have!" He went to her and drew her into his arms. "You don't regret it?"

"How can you ask that?"

"Because I've brought you little but trouble."

She burrowed closer to him. "I regret only my jealousy, my distrust of you. I shall never again harass you about Jean. That I swear."

He tipped back her head and looked into her eyes. "I shall never again see Jean alone—that *I* swear."

"I don't require that vow."

"But I require it of myself. Should Jean need my help we will go to her together. But," he smiled, "I believe a fine gentleman will assume her protection, in time."

"Who?" she asked.

"Lord Sutherland."

Courtly, educated, exceedingly wealthy . . . Mary said, thoughtfully and truthfully, "He is charming, but too old for her. His hair is silvering."

"But his heart is pure gold. She told me that he is courting her, but she said, 'I feel no attachment to him whatever—yet.' "

Mary's laugh rippled. Then she sobered. "There is something I must tell you."

She told him of her visit to Jean at Crichton. "It was a terrible thing to do, but I was beside myself. I asked her to promise not to tell you."

Bothwell turned from her, his voice flat and sad. "She kept her vow, naturally."

"You are angry with me and I don't blame you. But at least the truth is between us."

He asked, "Do you realize the depth of Jean's loyalty to you? It goes deeper than her resentment of you, or even her love for me. It is such loyalty that keeps rulers enthroned. And it is fast dying in this world."

"I know. I owe Jean more than I can ever repay."

He turned quickly. "Do you really feel that? Or are you trying to please me?"

"I mean it. Now that I know you don't love her, my jealousy departs and my reason returns. You were Jean's very life. What can I give in return?"

"She would accept nothing."

[436]

"By giving me you, she gave me the right to bear our child in pride. If the child is a girl, I shall christen her Mary Jean."

"A royal gift that Jean will treasure her life long. But I marvel at your change of mind."

"My mind was torn with fear and jealousy," she said. "But now it is healing. I have endured such evil as befouled my very soul. But the good was there too, sunk deep. It was as though I were two persons housed in one body: a virtuous woman—a vengeful vixen. An innocent—and a sly, conspiring bitch. I was God's servant and Satan's slut, and the two were always at war—hence my wounds."

"They will heal quickly when you are safe on your throne. But you are not unique—we are all mixtures of good and evil."

"But I know no one so sharply defined as I. Most folk are gray, but I am black or white."

He chuckled. "Come to bed, my lily. We must be up at sunrise."

Bothwell slept, but Mary lay awake tormented by the heat, vainly seeking a cool spot on the moist satin sheet. She thought of the day ahead. Likely they would meet the rebels in battle, and she knew Bothwell too well to hope he would command from the sidelines. Ghastly pictures invaded her mind—Bothwell slain by musket fire, arrowed or axed.

She tried to pray, but prayer only emphasized her fear and she sought reassurance, cuddling against his back, one arm around his waist and her head on his shoulder. He stirred, and mumbled that it was too hot to sleep entwined. He tried to move away, but she held him.

"Love," she whispered, "I am afraid."

He turned over and gathered her close. "You said you'd never be afraid with me."

"But I am afraid *for* you. If anything happens to you I would kill myself."

Swiftly he sat up, glaring down at her through the lifting darkness. "What blasphemy is this? Were you not born to rule? Do you take God's gift so lightly that you'd smash it on my account? By Christ, you'll live and fight for Scotland as your mother did, and you'll not rest until James and his swine are blood in the Market Square." He added more gently, "You have the battle-boogies. They will flee by morning."

She raised from her pillow, put her arms around his neck and drew his mouth down to hers. Love for him ached through her body, her tears slipped down between their lips.

"Close as we are," she said, "I long to be closer. It is a need so powerful that I wonder if it is not a hint of what will come hereafter when God removes the barriers of flesh and allows us to be one."

[437]

They lay back on the pillows and she sighed, settled her head on his shoulder, her mouth against his throat. Her long hair rippled like a warm silk shawl over his chest and sweat trickled from him, but he held her close, stroking her forehead until she slept. The brief night died and the sun rose violently in a blood-red blaze, spreading the sky with a sheet of fire.

All morning in the dusty sun-sizzled hills, the two armies maneuvered for favorable ground. Six miles from Edinburgh, Bothwell's outriders spotted the rebels at Musselburgh, and he and Mary led their men to Carberry Hill, which overlooked the town.

It was an excellent strategic position, for enemy cavalry would have to ford the stream below and scale the slope which Bothwell guarded with field guns. Scattered old entrenchments made the hill even more formidable. Just before noon, Bothwell's troops dismounted and prepared their defenses, removing ammunition from the carts, loading the great brass cannons, bringing up water from the stream.

Mary watched pityingly as the men toiled in the sun, their faces fiery, sweat streaming from foreheads to whiskered chins. She sat on the ground above them in the sparse shade afforded by the royal banner held by her standard bearer. Its red, rearing lion scarcely moved in the yellow folds, for the heat was windless and held a heavy breathless quality that presaged storm. But the sky was a cloudless glare.

Across the stream a mile away on the opposite hill, she could see the sun-silvered spears of the rebel army. Morton had more cavalry than Mary, and it was better trained and equipped—the horsemen of Kirkcaldy of Grange and Tullibardine. She saw blobs of color—plaids of the fierce Highland infantry gathered by Lindsay, Mar, Glencairn, Atholl and young Ruthven. Bothwell estimated the rebel army to be about the size of their own—thirty-five hundred men. They were a massed blaze of steel broken by piked banners and the dark mahogany shine of horseflesh.

Shading her eyes with her hand, she watched Bothwell sauntering among his troops, laughing and joking as though this were nothing more than sport. Because of the heat, he had removed his armor and wore an open-necked shirt and breeches of the new English sad-color, which he thought made him inconspicuous. But she smiled, for his hair flamed red like a beacon light in the sun and as he came to her, she said, "You'd best hide your head, love. None can miss that target."

Bothwell laughed, and bent down to her with a cup of water, which she drank thankfully. He said, "One thing we have in plenty

[438]

—water. Barrels and barrels of it, for if the rebels ford the stream we'll not have another chance at it."

As she handed him the empty cup, he looked at her worriedly. "We must build you some sort of shelter lest the heat sicken you."

She had ridden for six hours in the sun and was beginning to feel faint but she said, "Nonsense! Our men have enough to do—poor broiling wretches. They had yesterday's miserable march and now this incredible heat."

"I'm hoping for a quick engagement lest they be prostrated. Save for our mosstroopers and hackbuteers, the army is civilian. They're not in condition to endure this heat."

"Huntley and his men and the Hamiltons should come soon," she said, scanning the horizon.

"They should have been here an hour ago, unless our messages were intercepted by the rebels."

"Dare we attack until they come?"

"It would be foolhardy. But we can repel attack, never fear."

"Fear?" She opened her eyes wide. "My battle-boogies are fled."

"Good." He squinted across the valley to the opposite hill. "Look, we have visitors."

Mary saw fifty horsemen trotting down the hill toward the stream, a white banner held high on a pike.

"A peace parley," Bothwell said, and left her, shouting for troopers to meet the peacemakers and escort them up Carberry Hill.

The mediator proved to be French Ambassador Du Croc. He came puffing up to Mary, knelt beside her and kissed her hand. Then he sat down, wiping his face with a silk scented handkerchief and smoothing his pointed gray beard.

"Are you well, Madame?" he asked.

"Aside from the heat, yes," she said, wondering if his sharp little eyes noticed that her nineteen-inch waist had expanded to twenty-three. But she had borrowed a corset from Lady Seton's tirewoman and laced it as tightly as she dared. If Du Croc perceived her condition, he would assuredly inform the rebels, if only to spread fascinating gossip about a premature pregnancy.

"Please," she said lightly, "don't tell Queen Catherine how disheveled I look."

"I shall tell Her Majesty the truth—that you resemble a beautiful little girl on a picnic."

"Would that I were!"

She had lost most of her hairpins, and her hair, framing her face in damp spirals, threatened to tumble. Her short red skirt was torn at the hem and the white linen bodice grayed with dust. But she had refused Lady Seton's rigid velvets. This was practical battle dress, and she was as comfortable as her corset and the hellish sun permitted. *If only I can fight off illness . . .*

"In the name of my master, King Charles, I seek to avert this battle, Madame, and do all in my humble power to prevent bloodshed."

He prattled the platitudes of diplomacy, the words tripping daintily from parched lips. Civil war, a ghastly business. Surely she valued the lives of her devoted subjects and would not shed their blood for love of one man?

"My devoted subjects—" She nodded toward the opposite hillside —"started this. They show their devotion by treason. For the third time in my reign they make war on me."

"They give three reasons, Madame: To deliver you from the Duke's power, to avenge the King's murder, and to save the Prince."

"Tell them these three reasons I refuse their benevolence: I love the Duke and glory in his power. They themselves acquitted him of murder and signed a bond recommending that I marry him. As to the Prince, it is clear to any fool that the lords hold him as hostage."

"But it is for the child's safety."

"It is also clear," she said, "which side *you* are on."

His hands flew up. "No, Madame. I merely quote the lords! They commission me to state that if Your Majesty will abandon your husband, they will serve you faithfully on bended knee."

"Tell them I will never abandon him so long as I draw breath. But if they retire and disband their forces and pay my husband the honor due him, I will pardon their treason."

"Yes, Madame."

Bothwell came up and greeted Du Croc. Bluntly he asked, "Am I the sole cause of the rebels' wrath?"

"The lords are the Queen's humble subjects, but Your Grace's mortal enemies."

Bothwell grinned. "A straight answer, for a diplomat. They've been my enemies for years, but now envy has them tight by the throat. What in the name of God have I done to offend them since my marriage? I've not threatened the lives or lands of any. Don't they know that fortune is free to any man who can grasp it? There's not one among them but wishes himself in my place."

He looked down at Mary with such pride that happy tears blurred her eyes. She felt gowned in roses and crowned with stars. The faintness that threatened her eased, and she turned to Du Croc and said, her pride matching Bothwell's, "We are wed just one month today."

"Then may I offer felicitations," Du Croc said with a wry smile. "I doubly regret my need to speak frankly. But surely—" He turned to Bothwell—"Your Grace is aware that you place Her Majesty in a dangerous and distressing position. I appeal to you in the name of France to depart Scotland and leave your Queen to a peaceful reign."

Mary said, "Peaceful? With Morton and my brother exploiting my weakness to their own greed? You know as well as I, Monsieur, that my husband is my only protection."

Bothwell said, "There's a way to settle this without undue bloodshed. I'll fight any man of my rank in single combat."

"You'll do no such thing!" Mary snapped.

Du Croc mopped his brow. "The lords did have such a proposition in mind, if the Duke were amenable."

"I am more than amenable," Bothwell said eagerly. "I'll gladly meet any Earl—Dukes being old and few."

Du Croc squirmed uncomfortably. "The lords did not have one man in mind, Your Grace, but a series of champions for you to fight—perhaps ten or more."

"Jesu!" Mary sprang to her feet. "Do they call that chivalry, to so weaken a man that after the tenth duel he falls dead from exhaustion? To use the sacred field of honor for such treachery is blasphemous!"

"I agree," Du Croc said, and added hastily, "I mean that His Grace would inevitably be vanquished."

Bothwell bowed sardonically. "Eventually, perhaps. But how I'd love to challenge the top ten traitors of my rank! To kill Morton, Glencairn, Atholl, Lindsay . . ." He smiled at Mary. "That surely would justify my death. You'd have none but your brother to contend with then."

She turned on him fiercely. "You'll not fight one of them! That is my command and you'll obey, for I am first your sovereign and second your wife!"

"If Her Majesty forbids it," Du Croc sighed, "there is nothing more to be said." He kissed Mary's hand and left.

"You are first my wife," Bothwell said, "But I'd not show you disrespect in his presence."

"You will not fight in single combat," she warned. "If you do—"

A wave of nausea overcame her and she struggled to smile. He must not be worried on her account and she said lightly, "Please have someone bring me more water. I perish of thirst."

He left her, and she sat down and bent her head, taking deep breaths. *I will not faint. I will show no sign of weakness before these armies.*

The standard bearer said, "Is Your Majesty ill?"

"No," she said, her head still bent. She sharpened her voice. "How dare you address me? I am in prayer."

A soldier brought her water and she drank a little, dipped her scarf in the cup and cooled her face and throat. She longed to lie down, but she sat stiffly, staring straight ahead, swallowing, willing down the sickness.

An hour crawled. Heat waves shimmered in the valley between the two armies. Slowly, almost imperceptibly, the rebels moved down their hill, and as slowly Bothwell's forces moved down theirs. Two hours, three. The sun lingered and the air grew so heavy that Mary could scarcely breathe. Clumsily, she tried to ease the corset, but it was wooden and there was no way to grasp the leather laces under her bodice. Beside her, the standard bearer stood silent, rigid.

The rebels forded the stream, then halted, and Bothwell moved his men forward to force the issue. But the rebels waited, refusing to join battle. Like suspicious sniffing hounds, the men circled and shifted, glaring across the strip of bracken that separated them.

Mary signaled a soldier to bring her horse, and she rode down the hill to sit on a grassy mound at its foot. Presently the standard bearer came to take up his position beside her.

She said, "Does it seem to you—or is it my fancy—that our army is smaller?"

"I have seen men leave the ranks to get water, Madam."

But they had not returned . . . Men swayed, crumpled. The leatherjacked Borderers stood, feet apart, propped on their spears, the sun shining directly in their eyes. It is not a battle, Mary thought, but a contest of endurance—of theirs and mine.

Bothwell rode up to her. "Damned if I know what's happened to the Gordons and the Hamiltons."

"They will come," she said. Each word was agony, spending her scant breath. "I worry about the deserters."

"Deserters? I ordered the sick men off the field and out of the way."

You lie for my sake, she thought. We both play the game of pretending all is well.

"The rebels keel over too," he smiled. "Heat-sickness knows no politics."

He left her, whistling, and she watched him ride to the field and mingle among the men. Spines stiffened, smiles flashed, hands saluted. Water boys passed jugs. But the desertions continued. The sun is stronger than Bothwell, she thought. The rebels are better trained than our civilians.

She prayed for a miracle—for Bothwell's Borderers to come whooping across the hills. For the Gordons and the Hamiltons. For a storm to break the terrible relentless heat. For the sun to shift. If the enemy attacked now, her troops would be sun-blinded.

Mary saw a hundred of her men swim across the stream, now rebel territory.

Swiftly she rose, straightened painfully, ordered her horse. A soldier helped her mount, and she galloped to the field. Moors and sky reeled, she blinked against darkness, willed herself to keep the saddle. Somehow she must prevent others from the tempting coolness of that stream. *God show me how . . .*

She rode to the water barrels and dismounted. Her men crowded around her in a mixture of awe, curiosity and delight. She filled jugs with water and went among them, urging them to drink. She dampened her lace handkerchief and cooled their faces. She told them how proud she was that such men defended her, that she knew what they suffered, and that they would be rewarded beyond their pay.

For an hour, tortured and trembling, she moved up and down the lines—and the lines held. But her strength was fading, and she knew that at any moment she might disgrace herself and them. She clenched her teeth, hurried to her horse and galloped back to the grassy mound where the standard bearer still stood, eyes ahead, unblinking.

"Don't follow me," she gasped. Dismounting, she ran beyond him. She knelt with her back to the armies, folded her hands as if in prayer, and was violently sick in the short sheep-nibbled grass.

Weak, with throbbing head and corset-stabbed body, she returned to her place by the standard bearer. Hopelessly, she saw more men deserting, deaf to Bothwell's pleas, his threats. The tedious inaction had routed them as surely as the heat, and she realized that the long delay was General Kirkcaldy's deliberate plan. He would wear her army to faintness, then attack.

She could not blame her men. They were not defending their homes and loved ones, they had no inspiring cause. Told by the rebels that they were fighting only for Bothwell, they shrugged and walked away.

The sun declined slowly, but its heat lingered like a furnace that refused to cool. Bothwell galloped up to her and this time he made no attempt at pretense.

"The heat is likely to last till midnight when the light goes. We can expect more desertions unless I can restore morale. There's only one course—single combat."

"It is your murder!"

"I have a chance. Our men don't. Kirkcaldy may wait five or ten hours, and then attack—and massacre."

"I'll not have you fight to your death!"

She pleaded with him for five minutes, but vainly.

"I can outfight any yellow dogs they send me. I ask your permission humbly, but if you don't grant it, by God I'll disobey you and so turn traitor myself."

She forced a smile. "I'll not have you a traitor. Challenge if you must. God is with you."

He kissed her hand, and they rode down to the front lines. Bothwell sent a herald to convey the challenge: "To any noble of equal degree, in armor or doublet, with whatever weapon he chooses, to fight to the death."

The herald returned with word that Bothwell must fight twelve champions. His Borderers shouted angrily, shook their fists at the rebels in outrage. They begged Bothwell not to fight; they would stand by him all night, all week if need be, and they gathered around his horse like great shaggy watchdogs, whispering to him, putting their hands on his boots. But Bothwell shook them off.

"Who is first to challenge?" he asked, swinging off his horse.

"James Murray of Purdovis," said the herald.

Bothwell roared, "Refused! I demanded a man of equal birth. Why that arsecockled little bonnet laird wouldn't even limber me!"

His men laughed and cheered.

Bothwell shouted, "The Duke of Orkney rejects Murray and challenges the Earl of Morton to be first."

Morton accepted, and chose to wear armor and fight with the broadsword. Mary dismounted and helped Bothwell into his armor. Her hands shook as she fastened the iron hooks, but she smiled composedly. No one must suspect that she was terrified as she had never been in her life.

"A favor, my lady," Bothwell said. "Something of yours to take into battle."

As she looked up at him, Rizzio's words haunted her: *"The last chivalry on this earth dies with your Borderers . . . With you the knights and troubadours fall to dust and the jester's bells are silenced. For you the last romantics will polish their rusted armor and lift their spears. For you a final blooming before the fields of honor are stripped for the future."*

None here but she and his Borderers understood how dear to Bothwell's heart was this grace of a world forgotten, when vows were sacred and bonds inviolate. Oh God, she begged, spare him! But if he must die, touch his last hour with glory. Blind him to this shabby treachery and sound the trumpets of his imagination. Show him a great green field circled with gold-cloth banners and jeweled pavilions. Toss roses from a thousand fair white hands. And when the Queen of Beauty offers her favor may she not weep . . .

Mary slipped from her hand the ring Bothwell had given her—the Hepburn ring marked with his motto. Made small for her, it slid only part way down his little finger, but she saw his eyes light as he looked at it.

"Well?" Morton shouted. "Do you fight or make love?"

Bothwell knelt and kissed the tip of Mary's dusty little boot. Then he strode over to Morton and bowed formally.

Morton said, "I call these thousands to witness that I am killing you to avenge the King."

How contemptible, Mary thought. Gentlemen did not boast or revile one another on the field of honor.

Bothwell said courteously, "God's judgment be manifested."

"But should I lose," Morton said, "God does not judge you innocent. He merely gives you another chance to fight."

Bothwell's soldiers roared "Shame!" and Morton rumpled his brick-colored beard, glared from under tufty brows. "The Duke of Orkney deserves no better. He should be flattered that we condescend to cross swords with him."

Morton began a speech so venomous Mary marveled that Bothwell kept his temper. But he stood in silence, proudly, his great shoulders erect, his hand caressing the blade of his bared sword. Finally Morton paused for breath and Bothwell said, "Are you ready, my lord?"

Morton turned aside and conferred with his seconds. Then he said, "Your Grace, I have decided to delegate this combat to the Earl of Lindsay."

There was a moment's stunned silence. Then Mary laughed, peal after peal, nearly hysterical. As the crowd turned to look, she shouted, "Is Master Buchanan present?" Into the silence she added, "If so, I command him to record for posterity that James Douglas, the brave and honorable Earl of Morton, rejected combat with his peer on the battlefield of Carberry Hill."

"Your husband will fight whom I choose," Morton said furiously, and stalked back among his troops.

Big, black-bearded, scar-faced Lindsay swaggered up to Bothwell. "I will fight Your Grace however you please—on horse or on foot, doublet or armor, man for man, or six for six, or twelve for twelve."

Bothwell said, "As I am, armor and broadsword, man for man.".

Lindsay knelt on the ground and prayed long and dramatically. ". . . and I beg God's mercy to preserve the innocent and in his justice to overthrow the vicious murderer of the King."

Slowly he put on his armor, and Morton came forward and handed him a huge two-handed sword.

"Are you ready, my lord?" Bothwell asked.

"Aye, but we'll not fight here," Lindsay said. "A mile east is a fine level moor."

He described its precise location, and Bothwell consented to go there immediately.

"We will take with us an equal number of men," Lindsay said. "A hundred each."

"Agreed," Bothwell said.

Before Mary could protest, Bothwell galloped off with his Borderers. Presently Lindsay and his men rode in the same direction. Mary was tempted to follow them, but she dared not leave her army leaderless. She remained on the front lines with her soldiers, moving about lightheadedly as though in high fever or deep dream.

But her mind was alert. She realized why Lindsay had urged combat elsewhere. He wanted to remove Bothwell as a magnetic force, as a potential hero; but he also wanted to leave her troops to boredom and inertia. The excitement that had sustained them for the past forty minutes had died. They were fraternizing with the enemy at the stream, slipping off into the hills.

She summoned all her strength in an effort to stop them, pleading with them, promising rewards. But though they protested their loyalty to her face, they disappeared when her back was turned. Less than a quarter of her army was left.

Even now, she thought, we would have a chance if Huntley and the Hamiltons arrive. The instant they appeared she would halt this preposterous single combat and fight in the field. But though she strained her eyes, she saw no sign of them—only her soldiers creeping off in groups of ten and twenty.

Mary turned at the sound of hoofbeats. Lindsay's men galloped back into their ranks and she sent a herald hurrying to them. Was the Duke alive? Where was Lindsay? What had happened?

But the herald said, "They do not speak, Madam. They seem to know nothing."

Some terrible trick, she thought. She ran to her horse, and men lifted her into the saddle. But as she started to ride east she realized she could not desert the field even if Bothwell lay dying. Her place was here with her few faithful troops.

So she waited, riding the lines. Finally she heard pounding hoofs, saw whirled dust, and stared eastward with her hand to her throat. Bothwell was leading his men, and she drew a great shuddering sigh of relief and spurred to him. But he ignored her. His face was livid with rage, the scar on his forehead glowing red as a new burn.

"Where's Lindsay?" he shouted across to the rebels. His voice turned to a snarl. "Where's the filthy yellow coward?"

The rebels said nothing.

Bothwell rode slowly along his front line peering at the massed rebels. Then he said, loudly and contemptuously, "You heard Lindsay challenge me, but he never came to the appointed place—nor did his men. He has lost the right to honorable combat. When I find him I will horsewhip him—that I swear."

Mary rode up to him. Softly she said, "None of them intended to duel with you, love, only to cause such long and deadening delay as to exhaust our men."

Bothwell surveyed his thinned forces. Men straggled from the field as though lead weighted their boots. Others stumbled running for the cool stream. The first glow of sunset streaked above Carberry Hill staining the moors with rose-colored light.

Bothwell threw back his head and laughed harshly. "The field of honor! When will I learn that the world has rotted?"

Quickly he turned to face the rebels. Mary gasped. Slowly, inch by inch, they were advancing with a huge painted banner stretched between two pikes. It portrayed Darnley lying dead under a tree and the baby Prince kneeling beside him. In red letters near the child's mouth: "Avenge my cause, oh Lord!"

Bothwell spurred forward, shouting to his men to follow him. But they scrambled back confusedly, scattering. Two hundred of Kirkcaldy's horsemen broke from the mass and swept around in a flanking movement to cut off retreat. In vain Bothwell begged his men to advance—cursed, threatened. But they pressed back toward Carberry Hill in panicked disorder.

Mary rode to Bothwell. "They'll be slaughtered!"

She stared at him in alarm, for he looked as if he were about to charge the enemy alone, his face so fury-wracked that it was scarcely human. Then, as though with tremendous effort, his hands fell limp to his sides. He drew a deep breath and expelled it on a sigh. "It would be massacre. We'd best make what terms we can."

Mary sent a herald across the stream with a flag of truce and asked that Kirkcaldy come to her in ten minutes and discuss peace terms.

Bothwell said, "Tell him you will give me up. Nothing less will satisfy them."

She said in horror, "I'll never give you up!"

"You must, so that I can gather more men at Dunbar." He smiled, the ghost of his old grin. "Pretend to abandon me on condition of my freedom and right to travel. Go with them to Edinburgh and toady to them for a few days—no longer than a week—for James may be on the way to Scotland. Slip out of Holyrood when you can and meet me at Dunbar."

He leaned from his horse, touching her arm with the great iron paw of his gauntlet. "Everything depends on your ability to trick them; you have before, you can again. Tell them you love me but that you love your crown and your son more. Sigh and be sorrowful. Kiss me good-by as though you relinquished me utterly—and don't spare your tears."

She tried to smile. "In truth, I cannot spare them."

"Try to come to me this week, and send me messages by Paris. Meanwhile, I'll gather my Borderers if I have to choke sense into them with my bare hands. If Huntley is in Edinburgh, have him join me with his men and the Hamiltons. This time I'll stay barricaded at Dunbar until my army is invincible."

He pulled a paper from his belt pouch and gave it to her. "Here is a dag to hold a few traitors in line."

Mary glanced at it. "Jesu Maria!"

It was the bond of Darnley's murder signed by Bothwell, Balfour, Lethington and Morton's cousins.

"A dag indeed!" she said, thrusting it in her bodice. "But I cannot fire it without harming you."

"Should anything befall me, use it. Post it at the Market Cross for all to see. Send copies throughout Europe."

"Should anything befall you . . ." She turned to him in an agony of fear. "I dare not leave you! Let us flee together, quickly! They'll not fire on us, they'll be glad enough to be rid of us. We will—"

"We will not! You'll fight for your crown."

"It has brought me only evil and dishonor! Let James have it to blacken as he pleases. God knows he cannot make it bloodier!"

He swore savagely. "How many times have I told you that you and your crown are indivisible, divinely one? If God meant James to rule Scotland he'd not have made him a bastard."

"You love Scotland more than me!"

"You said once that you are Scotland, and truer word you never spoke. You are more than a woman—you are this sky, this moor, those hills, that stream. And by Christ I'll keep you so if I have to leave you forever."

"No!" she said in panic. "Forget what I said; I will fight for my crown to the death. Only promise to await me at Dunbar."

"I promise." He took the Hepburn ring from his finger and slipped it on hers. "My pledge. Not hell itself can keep us apart for long." He lowered his voice. "Here comes Kirkcaldy; I'll leave you to talk in private."

Bothwell rejoined his men. Mary dismounted, and Kirkcaldy came to kneel humbly at her feet. As he rose she said, using the blunt language he best understood, "Of all the rebels, sir, I consider you most honest. Do you pledge on your honor the loyalty of my nobles?"

"I do, Madam."

She studied him—a grizzled, square-set old warhorse—a rebel but not a traitor. He had had no part in Rizzio's murder nor in Darnley's. His blue eyes were direct and unflinching.

"What terms will you make should I surrender?"

"None for your husband," he said curtly. "But we will submit to Your Majesty if you will leave him."

She pretended to vacillate. Then she looked at the dark massed hordes of his men and said, "If I give up my husband and return to Edinburgh, how am I to know I will not come as prisoner rather than ruler?"

"Because you have my word," he said simply. "We are your humble subjects."

"I love my husband," she said. "And yet—never to see my child again . . ." Tears stood in her eyes, and Kirkcaldy's face softened.

Finally she said, "I will leave my husband but only on this condition—that you sign a safe-conduct paper permitting him freedom of travel. He will go to France as soon as he outfits a ship."

Kirkcaldy frowned. "We have a blood bond against him, Madam."

"The lords have long experience in breaking bonds. This will be easy. If they refuse, then I will assume that I have neither their devotion nor their trust."

"I will tell them, Madam."

He left, and she turned to face Carberry Hill, watching the pink sky streak with primrose. She bent her head and prayed for Bothwell, begging his life, his freedom.

Presently Kirkcaldy returned, accompanied by Bothwell on foot.

"Madam," Kirkcaldy said, "you are never to see your husband again, nor will he make any attempt to see you. Is it agreed?"

"On condition of his freedom," she said.

Kirkcaldy handed Bothwell a paper. "Safe-conduct for twenty-four hours, Your Grace. Thereafter you will be a hunted outlaw."

Bothwell examined the paper, slipped it in his pouch.

Kirkcaldy put out his hand. "Your Grace—" His voice was rough, but his eyes paid tribute—"you do a brave thing in surrendering both your wife and your army. Had it not been for the heat—who knows?"

Bothwell clasped the big red hand. "The most grueling battle never fought." He grimaced. "Deliver me hereafter from civilians in heat."

Kirkcaldy smiled. "If you wish, you may take a dozen of your men."

Bothwell thanked him. "I surrender my sword." He unsheathed it and placed it in Kirkcaldy's hands. "But by God I want it back."

"You'll likely need it." Kirkcaldy chuckled and returned it to him. He bowed to Mary. "I'll leave you to make your farewells, but be brief. I can't restrain my men much longer."

Kirkcaldy walked away. Bothwell removed his gauntlets, opened his arms and Mary went into them, her body pressed to the armored strength of his. He felt her tears and whispered, "It won't be long, love. You may even find it possible to come to me tomorrow night. But use the utmost caution, take no risks."

They kissed lingeringly and tried to part. But as Bothwell released her, she swayed to him again and his arms went about her; and as she gained courage to leave him, he pulled her back to him. Finally, he broke away from her, ran to his horse and shouted for a dozen Hepburns to follow him.

She stood with her arms outstretched, heedless of her pouring tears. Then she dug the tears from her eyes and ran after him, stumbling on legs suddenly weak, crying out for him to wait. He was about to mount his horse, but he turned and rushed to her, gathering her and crushing her so tightly that she gasped.

She drew back for a moment and touched his eyes, gently traced his reddish brows, caressed the hard, high planes of his cheeks.

"Be careful, love! If I lost you . . ."

We cannot lose one another after enduring so much. For love, we betrayed the innocent, piled treachery on treachery and, forced to the ultimate wall, opened the door to murder. We have traveled so swiftly that the dust of our deeds is hot in our faces. But it cannot obscure the truth—that despite our frenzy to be one, we are here divided, torn apart by the very crime we thought would unite us forever . . .

Lips on his cheek, she said, "You are my world."

And beyond the safe boundaries of your arms, beyond your shielding sword lie ambushes, the swamps and mires of the unknown.

His arm tightened about her. "Swear you'll do nothing rash?"

She buried both hands in his hair and drew his head down.

"This is my pledge," she said, and raised her mouth.

The kiss was deep, desperate with pain and passion and prayer. For a long while they clung, heedless of time, of watching eyes. Then abruptly Bothwell left her and swung on his horse. Followed by his men, he rode up the slope of Carberry Hill.

Mary saw him turn and check his horse. He raised his sword and she waved. Between them in the valley crept the first long shadows of twilight. But behind him the sky was afire with molten yellow light. Silhouetted between two cannon, he seemed rooted as rock, black iron against gold.

Then he was gone. His kiss still bruised her mouth and her body felt the press of his armor. She stared at the slowly tarnishing sky, the bracken-budded hill, the empty world.

VI.

Kirkcaldy knelt reverently to Mary, then lifted her to her horse and led it by the bridle into the rebel camp.

As she passed through the ranks of the common soldiers, she heard low muttering like the growl of dogs, but it scarcely touched her. She was too hot, too weary, too desolate to care. Her hair had fallen below her waist, she had lost the red hat and one sleeve was ripped, exposing a shoulder fiery with sunburn. Slowly she rode toward her nobles, gathered under a wide straw-colored canopy held by brass staves.

"My lords," she said, flinging up her head, "I am come to you not out of fear for my life, but to save Christian blood. I yield, but I come to you trusting in your promises of respect and obedience due me as your lawful sovereign."

They were silent, brows raised, faces blank, as though she spoke a foreign language. Only their eyes, like bared swords, glittered in sweat-running faces. Morton, Lethington, Glencairn, Mar . . . standing in armor and staring at her like strangers. And behind her the low growling deep in the throats of the soldiers.

Suddenly the soldiers broke out of line and surrounded her on three sides. They made obscene jests about her short kilted skirt, sneered bawdy compliments on her long, beautiful legs, her bared shoulder. They taunted her with the loss of a lusty husband and offered themselves as substitutes.

Then Kirkcaldy's voice like a rawhide lash: "Back, swine!"

Kirkcaldy thrust about him with the flat of his sword, while Mary sat stunned, incredulous, sustained in the saddle by disbelief that such a thing could be happening. The soldiers dispersed quickly, and Kirkcaldy apologized to Mary with tears in his eyes, saying that his men were nerve-worn and heat-wracked, out of their minds with exhaustion.

"And those men—" She pointed contemptuously to her nobles. "Are they too exhausted to come to my aid? Too exhausted to fall on their knees and pay me the respect due me?"

Still they stood and stared in silence, and her anger flared in a great surge as she saw Lindsay behind them. "So, Lindsay! You

[451]

sneak back now that my husband is gone. You shame your rank!"

"Perhaps," he said insolently, moving forward, "Your Majesty has done the same by your choice of husband."

Mary slipped off her horse, walked to him and seized his hand, raising it high. "By the hand which now is yours, I swear I'll have your head!"

She let his hand fall and turned the blaze of her eyes on Morton. "Is humiliation and insult the price I pay for surrender?"

"The loser always pays a price, Madam," he said grimly.

"So," she snarled, her throat tight with rage. "You duped me with false pledges." She glared at Kirkcaldy who stood beside her. "And you betrayed me to them!"

"Nay, Madam!" he said. "It is not I who betrayed you. On my oath I had their pledges. May God strike me dead if I had not!" He strode toward Morton. "Can you deny it?"

Morton, taller by a foot, looked haughtily down. "Who are you— a laird—to use this tone with me? Get on your horse and order your men to make ready to march."

"Who are you—a dishonorable lout—to order this army's general?" Mary shouted. "May God damn you, Morton! You hide behind that hypocritical banner, you prate of avenging the King; but you yourself counseled his death and ordered your cousin Archie to smother him!"

Her voice soared above Morton's furious retort. "You were too much a coward to sign the bond but you made your cousins sign it, and I'll testify to your guilt and so will others." She threw back her head and laughed in high hysteria. "Lethington signed that bond; do you think he will go to the gallows without putting the noose on your neck?"

"Bond!" Lethington's lips were white against his sunburn. "What bond? Where is such a bond?"

"Ah," she said slyly, "would you not give all your gold to know? I will tell you this much: it is the hangman's rope swinging above you both. If I am molested, the bond will go instantly to the Provost of Edinburgh for posting at the Market Square."

She saw Morton and Lethington exchange quick glances and surmised their thought—that Bothwell held the bond. Let them believe that, let them sweat in their armor.

"Your husband killed the King," Morton said loudly. "If there were such a bond his name would be on it."

"Even if his name were on it," Mary said, "what matter now? He goes into exile, he has nothing to lose. But you—you lose your greedy life."

"Your Majesty presumes that we intend you harm," Lethington

said hastily, "but nothing could be less true. We seek to protect you against the people's wrath and win them back to you. Your marriage has done you vast harm, but it is not irreparable."

"Now that your husband has deserted you," Lindsay said, "the people will be pacified."

"He did not desert me! He left me at my command!"

"He hid behind your petticoats," Morton rasped. He fastened Mary with angry, red-rimmed eyes. "This too is for history, Madam. Scholars will write 'At Carberry Hill the assassin Duke of Orkney deserted his wife and his army. *There went a coward.*'"

"There but for your perfidy," she said, "went the greatest king Scotland would ever know."

She would not relinquish the dream, not ever. She would smash these traitors, appoint a new Parliament, crown Bothwell King.

She said, "I am ready to ride to Edinburgh."

The corset that stabbed so cruelly would be agony on a galloping horse. Her stomach was weak with hunger, yet the thought of food was nauseating. Most torturing of all were her thoughts: her fear for Bothwell, and the child within her; fear that despite Lethington's soft words she was a prisoner.

The standard-bearer brought her the wool scarf she had left on the hillside, and she covered her bare arm as best she could. She tried vainly to twist up her hair. It fell below her waist in a stifling silky cascade.

"Does Your Majesty wish to ride in a cart?" Lethington asked.

To curl on a bed of soft plaids . . . to ease her aching body, perhaps to sleep . . .

"No!" she snapped. "The Queen of Scotland is not hay to be carted to her capital. I shall lead my army."

They moved in the endless gray-gold twilight through oven-valleys into the windless hills. Mary heard the soft, cushioned thunder of thousands of hoofs, the creak of leather, jingle of spurs, once in a while a curlew crying or a gull screaming in from the sea.

The light was saffron and changeless, and they needed no torches. Ahead of her, guards held aloft the terrible banner, painted on both sides. She could not avoid Darnley's uncanny likeness, the anguished face of her son.

She had looked forward to the first village—to rest for a few moments, to drink a cup of ale. But from Musselburgh onward the villages were thronged with furious people reviling her, cursing her for a whore and a murderess, pressing close to gloat at her dishevelment. Kirkcaldy's sword beat off clawing hands, but he could not silence the obscenities.

[453]

The moors gave peaceful respite. Each time they reached a town it was the same—a slow press through angry crowds. Deantown . . . Newton . . . Square Town . . . Hilltown . . . Cauldcoat. So slow was their progress that the six-mile ride took four hours.

Ahead she saw the lights of Edinburgh, the towering battlements of the castle black against a deepening dark brass sky, the ragged outline of rooftops straggling down the spine of the rock. She visioned Holyrood as heaven—her golden bathing tub filled with warm water and drifting rose petals; her soft silk-sheeted bed and the mercy of sleep.

They entered by the Cowgate Port, and she braced herself for the onslaught of the crowd. Torches bobbed toward her like giant fireflies bursting out of the shadowed fields. The mob roared forward like a sea and all about her was blinding light—and Kirk O'Field.

The house lay like a stone monster squashed among blood-red roses. Roses flaunted in the garden, blooming between pulped oak chairs and splintered tables. The sleeping gallery tilted grotesquely on the city wall, and bats, startled by the light, flapped up from it and sought the spectral shells of the cloisters.

"Justice!" The people swarmed about her. "Drown the murderess and avenge the King! Drown her in the loch!"

The cavalcade circled back through Candlemaker's Row and the West Bow up a steep wynd to the High Street. It was packed so densely that the guards had to pierce their way with long spears through a ravening, snarling, shoving, howling rabble. Men threatened Mary with swords, which Kirkcaldy and the soldiers beat back. Women leaned from low-hanging galleries to spit on her as she passed.

"Harlot! Doxy! Jade!"

She was frantic with fear, with humiliation and nausea, with the heat-heightening torch-glare. Her face was wet with spittle and tears and sweat. Market women hurled rotten fruit and she put up one arm to protect her face.

From her stall a fishwife held up a great iron pot. "Boil her! Boil the whore!"

The mob roared approval, moving tight-packed around the street vendors' booths. They raged at Mary for deserting her son.

"You'll not kill the Prince as you killed the King!"

The cavalcade passed St. Giles and inched toward the Market Cross. In her path men held up a huge painted placard that showed her reclining with Bothwell on a bloody bed.

"You saved your bed but not the King!" they shouted. "You saved your bed to bawd with Bothwell!"

At sound of Bothwell's name, Mary flung up her head and straightened in the saddle, railing at them for traitorous knaves, screaming that she would have vengeance on them all.

One of Morton's soldiers rode up to taunt her. "Do you see why your husband fled? But I'll protect you—for a price."

She seized her whip and struck him full in his sneering mouth. He reeled in the saddle, caught his balance, cursed her and fell back into the ranks.

Blood pounded in her head, and her voice shrilled high in hysteria. She snarled and spat at the shrews, flaying them for hypocritical bitches, threatening them with the breast-screw.

"Burn her!" A magistrate shouted from his window. "The penalty for husband-murder is the stake. Give her the law—burn her alive!"

"Burn her!" The mob took up the cry and began to chant it. A woman lifted an armful of faggots. "Gather your wood! Burn her at the Market Cross!"

The chanting drowned Mary's voice and panicked her. She stretched out her arms to silent bystanders and begged them to save her. "I am the blood of Bruce, your anointed Queen! Help me, in the name of God!"

Babbling incoherently, she appealed to a group of young men. "Rescue me and I'll knight you. I will do anything, anything . . ."

"Burn her! Burn her! Burn her!"

Kirkcaldy rode up to her as she slumped half-fainting in the saddle. "We're taking you to the Provost's house." He shook her shoulder and she roused. "Do you hear me, Madam?"

In her hysteria she thought he meant the old provost's house at Kirk O'Field and she screamed that it was haunted rubble full of bloody flowers.

"Nay, I mean Sir Simon Preston's house—the Black Turnpike facing the Cross." Grimly he added, "I think we'll reach it none too soon."

"Burn her!" The mob was stoning the guard. Kirkcaldy jumped on Mary's horse, shielded her with his body and shouted for the guard to press to the west side of the High Street. As they did, people were trampled under the horses' hoofs and screams soared through the chanting.

Mary went limp, her head and arms hanging. She was vaguely aware of Kirckcaldy's grasp, of being lifted from her horse and carried up a garden walk. She heard the mob's furious, frustrated roar as an iron door clanged shut behind her, and then she lost consciousness.

When she revived, she lay on a hard cot by a barred window that faced the High Street and the Market Cross. She turned her head. Eight armed soldiers stood between her and the bolted door.

She looked down in horror. Her bodice was slit, gaping from throat to waist. Desperately she sought the murder bond. It was gone.

VII.

Covering her torn bodice with her scarf, Mary pleaded with the soldiers to leave the room so that she might remove her corset. They refused. She begged for a woman to be sent her. They refused, saying their orders were to guard her and feed her, nothing more.

But she would not eat. The thought of food was revolting. She would not drink the wine they brought for fear of poison. Turning her back on them, she knelt on the high cot and looked out through the barred window.

A few feet below her the mob still raged the High Street, and at sight of her their chant broke out with renewed fury. "Burn her!" They carried wood to the Market Cross and lit a huge bonfire that turned the night to brilliant day. They lit another fire in the garden below her window. In its glare she was mercilessly exposed and sank down on the cot with her hands to her eyes, trembling with fear and fury and nerve-twitching exhaustion.

The room reddened with fireglow, and the walls and ceiling spun with shifting shadows. All night they kept the fires alight, and an endless roar in her ears, "Burn her, burn her, burn her . . ."

She pleaded with the guards for writing materials, and slipped from her finger the sapphire ring Bothwell had given her.

"If you will do as I ask and deliver my letter to a trustworthy courier, you may sell this and split a fortune among you."

As they hesitated she said, "On my word, no one need ever know."

The guards agreed, brought ink, quill and paper, and she gave them the ring. She wrote Bothwell and told him all that had happened.

. . . Dear Heart, I will never forget or abandon you, though I need be absent from you for a time. Be comforted and on your guard. For your safety did I send you away and I plead with you to do nothing foolhardy for I am prisoned not alone by my nobles but by my people . . .

A guard took her letter away and returned a few minutes later to say that it was safely dispatched to Dunbar.

At dawn she sought the window and pleaded with her people, crying out that she was betrayed by Morton and the very nobles who had counseled the King's murder and her marriage to Bothwell. But their chant had hypnotized them so that they could not or would not hear her. Her voice was a brook's babble against the pounding of a sea.

The banner depicting Darnley's death was planted on a staff in the garden, inciting farmers and fishermen who surged in from the Lang Gait, Duddingston and Leith. They shook their fists at her and varied the chant. "Burn her! Burn the husband-murdering whore!"

She saw Lethington pushing through the mob toward Holyrood and she called to him to come to her, but he jammed his hat over his eyes and walked on as fast as the crush permitted. She stretched both hands through the bars and called his name repeatedly as the crowd stopped shouting to listen.

"You fear to face a defenseless woman!" she cried. "Come to me, or be shamed before these people!"

Lethington hesitated, and the mob turned to stare at him curiously.

"Coward!" she mocked. "I am guarded by eight halberdiers, yet you tremble to approach me!"

Lethington turned back, and the crowd made way for him as he scuttled up the garden walk past the bonfire. Presently the guards admitted him to Mary's chamber. He removed his hat and bowed to her, beads of sweat dripping down his narrow, sunburned face.

"By whose order was my bodice torn when I swooned?" she demanded.

His eyes flickered over the scarf that shawled her. He said he had no idea what she meant.

"The murder bond, with your signature, was seized from me when I was unconscious," she said.

He shook his head. "I fear you are delirious, Madam. There was never such a bond—at least none signed by me."

She saw it was hopeless to pursue the matter and she said, "Why am I here? I demand to go to Holyrood."

"Had we not brought Your Majesty here, the mob would have dragged you from your horse to the Market Cross. When they quiet, we will remove you."

"I see no soldiers below forcing them homeward," she said angrily. "I hear no guns fired from the castle to disperse them."

He stroked his black, pointed beard. "We are doing the best we can, Madam."

She laughed shrilly. "If this is your best, how do you and Morton expect to govern—when you cannot even control a mob? Or is it James you are waiting for?"

[457]

"Madam, we protect you from the people's wrath and your own folly."

"I have given up my husband, what more can I do?"

"We do not think you have abandoned him, Madam. In fact—" He pulled from his belt pouch her letter to Bothwell—"this proves you have not."

She glared at the shamefaced guards, then turned back to Lethington. "Very well, you know the truth. I will never abandon my husband, nor he me. Put us on a ship to drift at the wind's will."

"You do not mean that."

"I mean it with all my heart. Send us to Leith and outfit the smallest boat, and we will leave Scotland forever."

"No, Madam. Wherever you were you would be the rallying point for Catholics the world over, seeking to re-establish you on your throne."

"In other words I am too dangerous to free."

"You are not prisoned," he said, his voice shocked. "You are secluded, until such time as you come to your senses. When you are willing to divorce Bothwell and wed a man chosen by your Council, then you will be at liberty."

"I see. I am to wed a man so weak that James and Elizabeth can dominate him to the ruin of Scotland and the doom of Catholicism."

"Madam—" He spread his long fingers in a pleading gesture. "Heed me and I will advise you rightly. The sooner you forget Bothwell, the sooner you will return to Holyrood in safety and honor. The people will not endure him even as Duke, and you seem determined to force him on Scotland as King."

She said, "Many are forced to circumstances they do not relish— for their own good."

"You speak as a woman bewitched. You still do not realize what brand of man you married."

"A man of any breed is rare in this land of skulking beasts," she said bitterly.

He shrugged. "And you think this paragon among men is at Dunbar?"

"I know he is. And invulnerable."

"He is not at Dunbar," Lethington said. "He is at Crichton, with his wife."

"He is at Dunbar! And I am his wife!"

"He does not refer to you so. From the very day he wed you, he spoke of Jean as his wife and of Your Majesty as his wench—and the whole court knew. That is why we sorrowed for you—to see our Queen reduced to a wife betrayed."

She said, sadly and quietly, "I never thought to see a Lethington turned shabby."

He flushed, and ordered the guards to wait outside. When they had left she said, "Once you were subtle; now you are transparent. Once you played a lone hand; now you run with rabble. I think a fine brain sickens."

She moved toward him and spoke gently. "Politics was once a game to you—a sport, no more. You were dispassionate, while others lusted for power. You were the cool one, disdaining greed. But now you are fevered as a bitch in heat—and for what? To be James's pawn, Morton's servant? They will draw a little Scottish map in which you may intrigue, whereas I gave you the world. And I would again."

"Madam, you have tossed away your world."

"Not yet! News of my plight will rally thousands who had no cause until now. Perhaps my imprisonment here is providential." She moved yet closer. "Use your wits for Scotland's glory, and your own. While appearing to work with Morton and James, inform Europe's rulers of my betrayal and beg me Catholic armies. Write to Philip and Charles, and they will pour us gold to fend off Elizabeth. There is a magnificent game for you—and immortality. You have the power to halt the Reformation, aye, even to build a Catholic Britain from the treachery of Protestant Scots."

"You ask the impossible."

"Nothing is impossible to you. Only you can juggle so many elements simultaneously, weave so intricate a web. Suppose you remain on James's side—what can you gain? He and Morton are so greedy of power and gold that they will grant you nothing. But I have been generous to you—"

"Please, Madam!" He backed away from her.

"Is not your first loyalty to your Queen?" She looked up at him, her eyes pleading. The crafty fox-face flinched under her glance as though it might crumple.

Her voice was tender, almost a caress. "I know that you wish to be on the victorious side, for to you failure is vulgar. You think of me as lost, but you are wrong. Those Catholics who were offended by my marriage will move heaven and earth to put me back in authority. For this insurrection has no precedent in history. This threat to me threatens the divine rights of all rulers, and well they know it. Even Elizabeth may rise in wrath and brand this plot perfidious."

She put her hand on his shoulder. "You have no ties to any faith, no duty to any but me. You are free to assume your proudest task —if only you will."

"I am not free." His voice shook. "I am blood-bonded against Bothwell, and so long as you cling to him I can do nothing for you —nothing." He turned away from her, spoke with a slight stammer. "Believe me, Madam, when your heart relinquishes your husband your troubles will end."

"And my life," she said.

Slowly he went to the door, a tall spear-thin figure moving through rose-colored shadows. He is in sunset, she thought, and he knows it. Likely Morton holds him hostage with the murder bond.

Impulsively, she ran to him and pressed her cheek against his beard. For a moment he held her tightly, then with a choked little curse he released her.

"Lethington, Lethington," she cried, "how great you could have been!"

The sun rose red and searing, but the mob kept the bonfires flaming. On her cot Mary lay sweating and sleepless. Despite her fear of the people she felt they were her only salvation. Their emotions conceivably could be swayed.

Summoning the dregs of her strength, she appeared at the window again. Their fury beat on her in a long, savage roar, but she waited until it expired in catcalls and scattered taunts.

"Hear me!" she shouted. "For the love of God—"

"If you had love for God you'd not have wed your husband's murderer and deserted your bairn!" screamed a woman.

"I will explain! I will tell you all that happened."

"Aye, tell us why you saved your bed instead of your husband!"

The heckling was constant, merciless. For an hour Mary begged to be heard. Then her scant control splintered. In a delirium of rage and weeping, she cursed, pleaded, threatened. She clawed off the hot wool scarf and stood bare-breasted, her hair in witchlike snarls, her eyes bright with hysteria.

"Shame!" they yelled. "Wanton, cover yourself!"

But a great uneasiness was on them, their hostility dulled by horror. Mary screamed for a dagger to kill herself, for mercy, for rescue, for revenge. She tore at the rusty iron bars, bloodying her hands, and rocked at the window, crooning soundlessly to the baby that moved within her.

The crowd was split between pity and revulsion. Fist fights broke out as some yelled for mercy and others for burning. Half-fainting, Mary clung to the window bars. Then she released them, and with the sensation of plunging down a dark chasm, sank to the cot.

Guards forced brandywine through her lips and she opened her eyes. Her mind was clear, but she was too weak to sit up, and lay back on the cot, her muscles constricted to numbness. Again she refused food and turned her face to the stone wall, praying for sleep.

But she was too tense and the mob too clamorous. The death chant had stopped, but they now demanded her trial. Some shouted that she was mad, bewitched by Bothwell; others insisted she was fevered. They called for her physician, and she heard the cry travel down the street, borne toward Holyrood on a thousand voices.

She hoped Arnault or her apothecary might come to her, but the afternoon passed without visitors. At seven o'clock the people demanded to see her, and a guard went to the window and said that she was asleep.

"Asleep—or murdered?" someone shouted. "Let us see her!"

She marveled. A scant few hours ago they would have fed her to the fire, but now they feared for her life. The terrible, lovable mob she would never understand . . .

Painfully she rose, adjusted the scarf at her bosom and appeared at the window. The crowd hailed her—not in affection, she thought, but with relief. They seemed returned to sanity—the cautious, slow-to-judge people she had first seen when she entered her kingdom six years before.

"Good people," she said, "either satisfy your cruelty and hatred by taking my miserable life, or release me from inhuman tyrants . . ."

They let her speak. When she had finished a few hurled insults, but the burghers—the freemen of the trade guilds of Edinburgh—lifted their ancient standard, "The Blue Blanket," and shouting that they would rescue her, ran to arm themselves.

Smiling, waving, Mary blessed them, and gaining courage she addressed the hostile people who remained. But as she spoke, trumpets sounded from the direction of Holyrood. The mob lurched to the east side of the High Street, scuttering from the path of three hundred hackbuteers. Morton and Atholl galloped up and tethered their horses at the garden gate.

Morton looked up at Mary's window and bowed deeply. "Madam, we come to escort you to Holyrood, if such is your desire."

They had brought her white palfrey, saddled in ivory and caparisoned in green velvet; her pipers and archer guard. Seton, with Mary's cloak over her arm, waved a great bunch of roses.

"Is this a trick?" Mary shouted. "Why is it that you come now when my people arm to defend me?"

"It is no trick," Morton assured her. "If Your Majesty wishes to remain here we will bring your effects from the palace."

Anxious for witnesses, she said, "Do you swear before these people that if I go to Holyrood it is not as prisoner but as Queen?"

"I swear, Madam. But you were never prisoned, only guarded."

Lethington has effected my release, she thought. He has pointed out the dangers of holding me captive. Doubtless my nobles have been conferring all day and are nervous as cats now that the people have shifted . . .

She addressed the crowd. "You have heard Lord Morton vow that I am not prisoned. Should he break his vow—"

Her voice was drowned by the mob's threats to Morton.

"—should he break his vow and I do not appear here at the Cross tomorrow noon, storm Holyrood."

She left the window. The guards held the door open, bowing low as she passed them. Down a short flight of stone steps she went, past halberdiers, and out into the garden.

Seton placed the cloak about her and gave her the roses. As Atholl lifted her to her palfrey, the freemen, armed with swords and dags, came running toward the cavalcade, and Mary lifted her hand for silence and told them what had happened.

"Once again I accept the sworn oath of Lord Morton," she said. But she repeated her order to storm the palace if she did not appear by noon the next day. "I thank you for your loyalty and your courage. Bless you—all of you."

Many in the crowd cheered her and yelled warning to Morton and Atholl. An old burgher held the blue banner toward them. "My lords," he said, "the Queen is in your trust. Should ill befall her you will reckon with us." He glanced at Mary through shrewd gray eyes. "If Her Majesty has aught to say to us of sin and repentance, it must be when she is less weary."

"Tomorrow," she promised.

The cavalcade moved off toward Holyrood. Riding between Morton and Atholl, Mary was tortured by the slow progress, but her spirits lifted. There were scattered threats, but for the most part the people were silent and watchful, reserving judgment. She did not know what she could tell them tomorrow that would spare her the shame of a public trial, but she would not fret about that now. It was enough that she was returning to Holyrood.

At the gate her sentries cheered her. Her favorite servants awaited her in the inner courtyard, petting her as though she were a tired child. In her bedchamber, for the first time in three years, all of her Marys attended her, for Fleming had returned with Lethington, and Livingstone had ridden in from the country at news of Mary's imprisonment.

As they removed her gown, Mary said, "My battle of Carberry Hill was with the most vicious corset ever worn by woman."

They stripped her of the cumbersome wood casing. As she sank into the great golden bathing tub by the hearth she said proudly, "You see I am with child."

"Yes, Madam," Fleming said gently. "God grant that it be safe." She poured rose leaves into the bath from an agate vial. "Have you told anyone?"

"No! If my nobles knew, they might seek means to miscarry me. No one must know until it is too obvious to hide." She grasped Fleming's hand. "I want your oath that you'll not tell Lethington."

Fleming kissed the wet, scented hand. "Madam, you have my oath."

For a long time Mary soaked in the warm tub. Then Arnault came to oil her scratched palms and treat the welts made by the corset. She swore him to secrecy when he remarked her pregnancy. He insisted that she go to bed at once, but though she longed for sleep she knew it would be impossible until she had determined her nobles' attitude. She would seek Lethington and find out if she was unconditionally free.

The Marys dressed her in thin black silk and accompanied her to the Great Hall, where a table was laid for supper. Her nobles bowed and smiled as Lethington led her to her place beneath the royal canopy. Morton stood humbly behind her chair assisting the servants as they brought her meat and vegetables.

The sight and smell of food was repugnant, but for the sake of the child Mary asked for milk. Morton himself served as taster. The nobles ate slowly and she waited impatiently, anxious to talk with Lethington before she collapsed from exhaustion.

Morton addressed the Master of the Stable, who sat below the salt. "Are the horses saddled?"

"Aye, my lord."

Morton came from behind Mary's chair. "Madam, prepare to leave at once. We are sending you on a journey."

She gasped and wobbled to her feet, pushing back her chair. "What new treachery?"

"You must go immediately lest the people rise against you," he said.

She stared at him with such blaze-eyed contempt that he flushed from forehead to throat—a sun-scorched, bushy-bearded redhead, grim-lipped and shifty-eyed.

"If the people rise," she said furiously, "it will be against you, and well you know it. Tomorrow if I do not appear they will march on Holyrood—"

Lethington interrupted. "The principal peril to you is your husband, Madam. So long as he is free, you and the Prince are in the gravest danger."

[463]

Mary whirled on him. "May God damn you for a black traitor!" She turned back to Morton. "And you, whose oaths are shameless blasphemy! May the people tear you both to bloody bones!"

Morton took her roughly by the arm, and Atholl rose to hold her other arm. She knew they feared she would try to escape, but she lacked the strength. Hopelessly, she appealed to Mar and Glencairn, but they remained seated and silent. She asked repeatedly where they were taking her.

"Soldiers will take you as far as Leith," Morton said. "Lindsay and young Ruthven are your escort from there on."

A long journey, she thought—perhaps to some empty island in the Hebrides where even Bothwell can never find me.

"You may choose two tiring women to go with you, but not your Marys. You may have your physician. You will take nothing but a nightrobe." Morton nodded toward Seton. "Bring it here, and a cloak."

As Seton left the room, Fleming ran to Lethington and pleaded to accompany Mary, but he ignored her and reached for a pear, peeling it delicately lest the juice spot his wrist ruffles. Livingstone and Beaton in tears entreated Morton to let them go with Mary, but he cursed them and told them to be quiet or leave the room.

Mary chose two of her tiring women to accompany her, Jane Kennedy and Maria Courcelles. They had been with her for years and were devoted and resourceful. Presently they joined her with Arnault. Morton warned them that should they call for help on the journey or try to escape, they would be shot.

Arnault said, "I trust it is not a long journey, for Her Majesty has not eaten since yesterday dawn. She is—exhausted."

Morton glanced at the clock, which pointed to midnight. "It is a thirty-mile ride. You should be there by daybreak."

At least, Mary thought gratefully, it is not the Hebrides.

"Such a ride may kill Her Majesty," Arnault said, lapsing into furious French. "I cannot allow—"

Mary said, "Never mind, my friend." She was fearful that if Arnault angered them they would forbid him to go. "I will ride slowly, never fear."

Seton brought Mary's cloak and riding boots, and gave her nightrobe to Jane. Mary thought of her jewel chest, remembered that it was in Edinburgh Castle, probably wrested from Dalgleish and now in Balfour's greedy hands.

Morton and Atholl accompanied the little group out to the courtyard, where fifty halberdiers waited to escort them to Leith. Arnault lifted Mary to her horse—a wretched cob—and she looked down at Morton contemptuously.

"You make no secret of your treachery," she said. "Why so mysterious about this trip?"

"Because some of your servants are Bothwell's spies. I will tell you now. You journey to Kinross-shire to be the guest of Lady Margaret Douglas."

So James's mother was to be her jailer, and the loneliest keep in Scotland her prison. She knew it well from hawking expeditions—a desolate island fortress surrounded by a deep lake. Lochleven . . .

VIII.

Riding into Leith, Mary saw that the town was massed with Morton's men, evidently sent to prevent her rescue. But the night-capped people, cloaks covering their undress, made no effort to help her, though some cheered her. One young man leaning from a window yelled, "Take courage, the Hamiltons are roused! Tarry on the road as long as you can!" Others chimed in, "Ride slow!"

At Queensferry, Lindsay and young Ruthven joined her and dismissed the troops. A boatman rowed the little party of six across the moonlit Forth.

Then they began the long ride through rolling moors and camel-backed hills. For a while the thought of rescue sustained Mary. If the Hamiltons knew of her plight, then perhaps Bothwell did too. But when two hours passed she lost hope. They were alone in the interminable night, their horses' hoofs the only sound in a darkened, sleeping world.

She tried to ride slowly, in hope of rescue and fear for the child, but each time she lagged Ruthven or Lindsay whipped her horse. At times, exhausted and close to fainting, she slumped in the saddle, and the dark countryside swirled about her in a wheel of moon and trees and June-scented earth. She begged to halt, but despite Arnault's frantic protests, Lindsay or Ruthven lashed her cob and it plunged on.

Three hours, four . . . She screamed for rest, to stop even for a few moments, but they flogged the miserable horse on, and on. Jolting over rough roads, she prayed for the child's life, caught her breath in terror as they whipped her horse down steep hills treacherous with rocks and peat hags. In villages she shouted for help and, looking back, saw candles wink on. But no one pursued them.

"I am riding to my death!" she gasped. "You are killing me."

Lindsay's reply was to whip her horse.

The sky paled to pewter. They rode past tidy, dew-spangled fields and sheep bells tinkled on the far slopes. They rounded Benarty Hill and clattered through Kinross so fast that Mary could not beg help of the few folk who came to their windows that faced the Old Back Causeway. Lindsay flogged her horse toward the shore, where she halted it at the water's edge and slumped in the saddle.

Red ripples beat against her eyelids and she swayed. Ruthven lifted her from her horse and half-dragged, half-carried her to a boat. She was eased onto a narrow wooden plank and would have pitched forward had not Ruthven caught her close in his arms.

She heard grinding against sand as the boat was pushed into the lake, the creak of oarlocks, felt the rise and fall of breeze-rippled water. Ruthven's arms tightened about her, and she opened her eyes and raised her head.

At first in her exhaustion and confusion she thought that Ruthven was his dead father, who had helped murder Rizzio. He had the same bony face and deep-set black eyes, the same cruel, thin mouth. But, oddly, the eyes were soft and the mouth smiling. He whispered, "Fear not, Madam."

Too weak to wonder at the change in him, she sank back, resting her head on his shoulder. She stared dully at Lindsay and the oarsman, at Arnault and her ladies, who huddled at the other end of the boat. Then she looked back at the vanishing shore. Through the trees she could see a few dumpy stone houses, a church and a graveyard. The steel-colored lake was surrounded by low hills that crouched bleakly and blackly against the gray dawn.

Ahead rose Lochleven Castle Island—two acres of fortified stone dominated by a massive square keep. From high walls on the southeast corner protruded the round, dunce-capped Glassin Tower. There was a bakehouse, a laundry, a garden that fared poorly from years of battering wind. Even on this June day the trees were nearly leafless, and the ivy on the walls a gaunt green webbing.

Here she had come for hawking parties, bringing a gay court. But never had she lingered for more than a day or two. The castle was too grim, too cramped. And its chatelaine, Lady Douglas, too formidably polite.

"I must see you alone," Ruthven said, caressing Mary's hand under cover of her cloak.

She snatched away her hand, angry, bewildered, but too ill and dazed to chide him or question his action. The boat bobbed past Glassin Tower, and she could see soldiers on the battlements, and great-mouthed cannon. Slowly the sun rose, cutting a red gash across the hills, shining on the water so that it lapped blood-red against the fortress's high gray walls.

Castle servants pulled the boat up to the landing and secured it with chains. Ruthven lifted Mary and handed her to a soldier, who set her gently down on the shore. She swayed, clutching the soldier's arm, and Ruthven came up to steady her.

A few stone steps above her stood small, blond-bearded Sir William Douglas, Laird of Lochleven, half-brother to James; and beside him his mother, Lady Margaret Douglas, tall and slender in dark brocade, rigid as though corseted in iron.

"Welcome, Your Majesty." Sir William came down the steps to kneel at Mary's feet. "We are honored."

Mary tried to speak, but the ground, the castle walls spun in circles of grass and stone.

"Her Majesty is ill," Ruthven said.

Lady Margaret's sharp green eyes flicked over Mary's cloaked figure. "In that case," she said, "Her Majesty will wish to go to her apartments immediately."

Supported by Sir William, followed by Lady Margaret, Mary walked to the Glassin Tower. Entering a small anteroom, they climbed stone steps to a dreary rock-walled bedchamber furnished with a few oak chairs and a table. Sir William removed Mary's cloak, and she sank gratefully onto a blue-curtained bed by a barred window.

"You may leave us, William," said his mother.

Obediently, Sir William bowed to Mary and trotted away.

Lady Margaret said, "Presently I will send for your women to make you comfortable." She studied Mary from unbound hair to dusty riding boots. "What ails you, Madam—besides exhaustion?"

Mary hesitated. She could not trust this woman who had been her father's mistress and her mother's bitter rival. For Lady Margaret had always considered her son James, bastard though he was, the rightful King of Scotland, and she resented Mary accordingly. She would undoubtedly write to France and tell James that Mary was carrying Bothwell's child.

"You are with child," Lady Margaret said.

Mary tried to smile. "I have gained a little weight. Perhaps it looks as if—"

"It does." The green eyes narrowed. "I should know. I have borne twelve children."

Six bastards by Mary's father, James V, and six legitimate children by Sir Robert Douglas, who died twenty years ago at the Battle of Pinkie.

"When does Your Majesty expect the child?" Lady Margaret asked.

It was useless to lie. "In October."

"It is well that your physician is with you. I will help him as midwife."

"You are kind," Mary said gratefully. "Pray be kinder still and tell no one."

"It is becoming obvious."

"If I am artful none need know for a while. If my nobles find out, I fear for the child's life."

"Nonsense. Your Majesty is overwrought."

"They tried to cause a miscarriage when I was with child by Harry. But they hate my new husband far more than they hated Harry. They would take no chances that Bothwell might have a son second in line to the throne. James must not know. Please do not write him of this."

"James would never harm you. You have always misunderstood him, Madam."

Dear heaven, Mary thought, mother love knows no evil. She wondered if this woman had a vulnerable point, save in her love for her children. Probably not; she seemed hard as rock. Her steel-gray hair was half-hidden by a severe black brocade coif banded in gold. Her face was a proud and beautiful ruin slashed with deep wrinkles, but the eyes were huge, darkly green and heavily lashed, the mouth a full crimson flower in a havoc of sagging cheeks. Though she was about fifty-two years old, her figure was slender and graceful and she held herself magnificently—like the queen she had hoped to be.

"Madam," Mary said wearily, "you are right to love your son. But you would be wrong to betray the confidence of your Queen, prisoner though I am."

"You are not prisoned." Lady Margaret echoed Mary's nobles. "You are secluded." She bent and touched Mary's forehead. "And fevered. I shall send Monsieur Arnault."

She curtsied stiffly, as though it was an effort to humble herself before this daughter of Mary of Guise; then, her brocade gown rustling over taffeta petticoats, she swept to the door.

Hopelessly, Mary watched her go. Through the barred window she saw her cross the courtyard past armed sentries—beyond them, the lake and the empty sky and the far free shore of Kinross.

IX.

For two weeks Mary was gravely ill, and unconscious for hours at a time. Over and over she called Bothwell's name, hugging her pillow as if it were his body, and covering the linen case with tear-salty kisses. No one was admitted to her suite except Arnault and her ladies, though Sir William called formally each morning to ascertain her condition.

He and his wife, Lady Agnes, and his younger brother George lived

[468]

in the big square keep across the courtyard. There was a small garrison of sixteen men, and quarters for servants. Lady Margaret and her two unmarried daughters slept in the New House on an island less than a mile away, but spent most of their time on Castle Island.

Starved from her two-week fast, Mary recovered slowly, and gradually regained her strength. On the first day that she was able to receive Sir William she pleaded for news of Bothwell, but he told her firmly and politely that he would not discuss happenings outside the island.

Mary's worry over Bothwell's fate lengthened her convalescence. Hour after hour, she considered means of approaching Lady Margaret but hesitated, fearing rebuff. Finally she sent for her and, shedding her pride, crawled out of bed and begged news of Bothwell on her knees.

"Rise, Madam," Lady Margaret said coldly. She helped Mary back to bed. "Your husband is not worth your suffering."

"He is worth my kingdom to me!"

"It would seem he has already cost you that."

She is so frigid, so remote, Mary thought—yet of all women capable of understanding my passion. For love she bore six children out of wedlock, disgraced the proud name of Erskine and shamed her family. And for what? To be my father's mistress, sharing him not only with my mother but a dozen other women as well.

"Be seated," Mary said.

Lady Margaret sat down on a rough oak bench as if it were a chair of state.

"You have loved deeply," Mary said, "Surely you cannot be untouched by love in others."

"You throw away your realm."

"You threw away your honor."

The green eyes, so like James's, turned hard and narrow. "Does Your Majesty taunt me with what is past?"

"Indeed not. I do not judge you, nor shall you presume to judge me. If I remind you of the past, it is to point out that you were not always unfeeling."

"The years change us, Madam."

Mary shook her head. "I think you have fortified your heart as you have fortified your island. Have you forgotten that you loved as I do?"

Lady Margaret smiled bitterly. "Your father left me reminders."

"But for chance," Mary said, "you might be Queen of Scotland— not I. I am told that after my mother's sons died in infancy my father despaired of a male heir and wished to legitimize James and wed you. He asked my mother for a divorce, and for the sake of

Scotland she agreed—but your husband refused to relinquish you."

"That is true." Lady Margaret's voice was stiff to the point of cracking. "I am surprised you were told the tale."

"I heard it in France as I grew up, and I thought, despite my loyalty to my mother, that you must be a remarkable woman if your husband loved you so much that rather than lose you he took your lover's children and raised them here at Lochleven."

"Say rather that my husband was a remarkable man."

"Tell me about him."

Lady Margaret began haltingly, her words as rigid as her body. Then gradually she eased. The words poured out as though for thirty years she had locked them tight and now in sudden release could not stem the flow.

". . . Sir Robert was so good to James and my other natural children. He treated them as his own, yet never allowed anyone to forget their royal blood. When a stranger referred to James as 'James Douglas,' my husband would correct the error, saying, 'That is James *Stuart*, my wife's son by the King.' He was proud of me, Madam, and he taught me pride. Because of him I can lift my head and face the world."

"A remarkable man indeed."

"But I did not appreciate his goodness, Madam. I thought him soft, spineless, unmanly. God forgive me, I despised him."

"So you wished to leave Sir Robert and marry my father?"

"Yes. I wanted the throne for James, and of course I loved your father—but who did not? He was dazzling, fearless, a red-gold glory of a man. When he died I thought the sun had set forever. But a month later, here on the battlements, I found myself frantic because my husband was half an hour late at hawking . . . I realized he was not soft, but steadfast, saintly." She turned her head. "When he died at Pinkie Cleugh—but I cannot speak of it."

Mary thought, I killed him. Even as a babe I was fatal to my defenders. At Pinkie Cleugh thousands of Scots perished to protect me from Henry Tudor's bloody wooing when he wished me to wed his son. And God knows how many thousands died in the path of the Butcher Hertford.

Embarrassed by Lady Margaret's silence, Mary looked out the window. Near the courtyard wall was a tall oak, deep-rooted in grass and surrounded by stone. It was leafless but magnificently branched, a massive skeleton.

"God grant I stand so firm to the winds," Mary said.

"God grant Your Majesty respite—and wisdom."

Mary knew that Lady Margaret wished to be dismissed, and she bade her go. Tearless, her face composed, Lady Margaret moved toward the door.

Mary lay back on the pillows, exhausted by her futile effort. It would take years, if ever, to win Lady Margaret's friendship. Such a woman did not bend to flattery, however subtle. Most certainly she did not break a trust. James could not have chosen a jailer with fiercer integrity.

Lady Margaret turned at the door. "Bothwell left Dunbar by ship and has sailed past the Forth, probably to meet the Hamiltons and Gordons somewhere in the north. There's a price of a thousand crowns on his head."

She was gone before Mary could speak.

X.

While she was still abed, the lords plagued Mary to abdicate. Lindsay and Ruthven, obviously representing James, pleaded that she yield the throne to her son and appoint James as Regent during the Prince's minority. Sir Robert Melville, brother of Sir James, begged that she agree, for her own safety, hinting that physical force might be employed if she refused. All of them insisted that she divorce Bothwell.

"Never," Mary told them flatly. "I'll not divorce him and I'll not abdicate. It is easy for traitors to imprison a queen, but not so easy to dethrone her."

During these interviews she sensed that Ruthven was on her side. Vaguely, she remembered his tenderness in the boat. He might be the weak link in the chains that were drawn about her, and one afternoon when she rose for exercise she contrived to see him in the garden—alone save for watching sentries who paced a few yards away.

"My lord," she whispered, "is there something you would say to me privately?"

He looked down at her. She was wearing a long figure-concealing lace cloak borrowed from Lady Margaret, and unconsciously she pulled it closer. His narrow black eyes were too knowing, too bold.

"I think it shameful that Your Majesty is held here."

She smiled at him. "At last we agree. What would you recommend?"

"I have considered various means, Madam. Fifty armed men could easily overpower the garrison and take you away. But the problem is gathering an army to defend you once you are free."

That is Bothwell's problem now, she thought. Storming Lochleven would be child's play for him, but raising an invincible army another matter.

"Surely the difficulty is not too great, for you?" She knew the power of her eyes. She had only to glance at a man obliquely and let her lashes fall, feathering her cheeks. Odd eyes, as her mirror told her—strangely long, fascinating in their change of color. Now, in her dark lace cloak, she knew that they were black and brilliant, and that Ruthven, looking into them, was sinking deep in dreams.

"You are fearless," she said, "one of the few I know who does not whine and cower at thought of danger."

But Ruthven was dangerous, she thought. Often faces belied men's characters, but Ruthven was as cruel as his thin-slit mouth and greedy as his eyes.

"You want power," she said softly, "and why not? You are young. I admire ambition. I will give you whatever you wish."

"In writing, Madam?"

"Aye, if I had paper and ink. They allow me nothing to write with."

"If I meet you here tomorrow with an artist's pad, paint and brush, and you pretend to sketch the shore . . ."

"Indeed," she said, "paints are as binding as ink. What is it you wish, my lord?"

"The price is high, Madam—yourself."

She stared at him in dismay.

"Wed or unwed; with or without child; crowned or naked . . ."

Enraged, she turned away, and heedless of the staring soldiers ran toward her quarters, bumping into a fair young man who was walking toward the landing with fishing rod and tackle. He bowed and stammered apology, and she would have hurried on but for his expression. He stood in obvious awe, transfixed as if she were a vision. Then he knelt on the cobbles and kissed the hem of her gown.

Mary bade him rise, and he blinked as if in radiance.

"Are you not George Douglas, Sir William's younger brother?" she asked.

"Aye, Your Majesty."

"Why have I not met you?"

"I warrant my mother and my brother think me beneath Your Majesty's notice."

She smiled. "So handsome a young man is beneath no woman's notice."

She flattered him, for his face was too square and his body too stocky. He was about eighteen, she thought, but his hair was so fair that it was nearly white. Evidently he wore Sir William's cast-off clothing, for the quilted black coat, heavy with padding, was too tight and the sleeves exposed his sun-red wrists.

He was scarlet with embarrassment, stammering thanks for her compliment.

"Please escort me to my quarters," Mary said. "I am distraught—one of my nobles affronted me."

George glowered across the courtyard. "Who, Madam?"

"No matter, he has gone." Mary gave him her arm and he guided her toward the tower as if she were made of glass. "They would not dare such insolence if I were free," she said.

"None will dare it again, Madam! Not while I am near!"

"You are kind, sir. But I'll not burden you with my battles."

"You must. I want you to." He flushed. "I'd protect Your Majesty to the death!"

"I am certain of it," she said. "I have been wondering why you looked familiar, and now I realize the reason. In Fontainebleau there was a portrait of young St. George—shining and armored. You resemble him. I'd fear no dragons in your company."

George gulped, and Mary controlled the impulse to laugh. He was shy and sweet, and she was touched by his admiration. At the tower doorway she gave him her hand to kiss, and he lingered, seeking an excuse to remain.

"Have you met the girls of the family, Madam?" he asked.

"No, but I have seen some attractive young ladies from my window."

"There are my two maiden sisters, Janet and Catherine; William's seven daughters, the eldest fourteen, and his niece. Probably my mother will set them to spy on Your Majesty, now that you are well enough to be up. Be warned, they are snoops. If you've anything to hide they will find it, be it only a grassblade under your mattress."

"Thank you for the warning, but I've nothing to hide. I've no possessions but the clothes I wear and a single nightdress."

"Have you asked my brother to send to Holyrood for your clothes?"

"Yes, but nothing has come. I warrant my nobles are fighting over every scrap of lace and velvet in my wardrobes. And God knows I'll never see my jewel chest if Balfour has it."

"Is it a silver casket overlaid with gold?"

"No, a red brocaded one, extremely large. Why?"

"Because I heard William say that a silver casket was captured from one of your husband's servants."

Mary clutched his arm. "Was the servant's name Dalgleish?"

"I think so, Madam. Lord Morton's men caught him and tortured him for information regarding the King's murder; and they took the casket from his lodgings, where he had removed it from the castle for safekeeping. It contained your husband's papers."

"What papers?" Mary asked frantically. "Letters? Poems?"

"I don't know." He stared at her white face. "Madam, are you ill?"

"Yes." She turned from him. "I must go now."

In her bedchamber she sat down and thought about the silver casket which she had given Bothwell before their marriage. She was not sure what he kept in it, for it was always locked, but probably there were letters from Jean, marriage contracts, deeds to property. She had seen him place her last sonnet there, and it worried her to think that others, proving her guilty love before Darnley's death, might be there too.

Dear heaven, she thought—the letters I wrote from Glasgow! There was the long incriminating one advising against poison for Darnley and suggesting a more secret means. *"Burn this,"* she had written, *"for it is too dangerous . . ."*

But had Bothwell burned it? Had he burned the one from Stirling proving that her abduction was collusive?

All that night she was sleepless. If the letters were in Morton's hands he could execute her for conspiracy in murder. The sonnets alone could send her to the stake as proof of adultery.

At dawn, bidding her women stay in the anteroom, she started down the tower steps, caught her foot in her long skirt and fell. It was merely a stumble down three steps, but pain slashed her stomach and she fainted.

She was in bed when she regained consciousness, and Arnault stood over her, his eyes full of tears. Then he told her, gently, both his hands on hers, his tears falling on her face.

"You have lost twins, Madam . . ."

At midnight in bed, Mary murmured as many prayers as she could remember from the Mass for the Dead. She knew that at that moment, by her order, Arnault and Lady Margaret had rowed out into the moonlight. A prayer, the slide of gold cloth into water, her children consigned forever to God's care.

XI.

Two days later, on July 24th, Jane Kennedy told Mary that Sir Robert Melville had arrived from Edinburgh and desired audience.

Mary shook her head. "Tell him I cannot see him. I am too weak."

Too weak, too despondent to rouse her wits. Abed for forty-eight hours, she had stared at rock walls, at timbered ceiling, out the window—seeing only a lost prince and princess. The two children wandered her imagination hand in hand, more vivid unborn than the living who passed to and fro in the courtyard.

[474]

"Lords Ruthven and Lindsay are also in the antechamber, Madam, but Sir Robert wishes to see you first. He is so insistent that I fear he may force his way in if I refuse."

"Very well," Mary sighed. "They know I am helpless."

Melville came in swiftly and without ceremony. Though usually mild-mannered, he dismissed her ladies brusquely, telling them not to return until he summoned them.

"Such highhandedness ill becomes you," Mary said. "You see I am abed."

"I'm sorry, Madam, but I must act quickly. It was difficult to persuade Lindsay and Ruthven to give me a few minutes alone with you, and they may come in at any moment."

From the scabbard of his sword he drew some tightly rolled papers. "I brought these at the risk of my life, Madam. Messages from Lethington, Atholl and Tullibardine. Most important, a letter from Ambassador Throckmorton which is fully authorized by Queen Elizabeth." He gave them to her. "Scan Throckmorton's letter quickly, then hide all of them under your pillow."

Mary read Throckmorton's letter. He begged that for her physical safety she sign abdication papers. Later, he said, when she was free, she could legally repudiate them on the grounds of having signed them under duress.

"Throckmorton is in Edinburgh now, Madam, working day and night to persuade Morton to release you."

"Bless him," Mary said. "I trust him, but not his mistress. He writes this at Elizabeth's command."

"The messages from Lethington and the others all urge the same procedure."

"Naturally. They are traitors."

"Even traitors—as you term them—may offer wise counsel."

Mary placed the letters under her pillow, and shook her head. "I will not abdicate."

Melville fell on his knees by her bed. "I implore you, for the sake of your life . . . your son . . . your realm . . ."

"Never. Never again will I do anything my conscience forbids."

Melville rose. "I have done all I can, Madam. If you refuse to abdicate, there will be a public trial. John Knox is back in Edinburgh reviling you, inflaming the people to insurrection. At best you will lose your crown and your name will be forever defamed. If—"

The door burst open. Lindsay and Ruthven, both in armor, entered, followed by two notaries carrying writing materials.

"Madam," Lindsay said curtly, "we have wasted enough time." He opened a leather case. "Here are the abdication papers and Letters of Regency. Read them."

"Why? I refuse to sign them."

He glared at her. "Then the notary will read them to you."

She was to renounce all powers of government, authorize the immediate coronation of Prince James and confer the Regency on Lord James Stuart during the minority of the young King. Morton, Lennox, Argyll, Atholl, Glencairn and Mar were to govern until James returned from France.

"Preposterous!" Mary said. She was trembling violently, and lest they notice she pulled the sheet up to her chin. "I'll sign nothing."

"Then hear the alternative, Madam." Lindsay snatched one of the papers from the notary. "*Mary Stuart, Queen of Scotland and the Isles, is to be prosecuted and condemned for these crimes: for breach and violation of Scottish law —*"

Adultery, she thought . . .

"*— incontinency with the Earl of Bothwell and others —*"

Chastelard . . . Rizzio . . .

"*— and for the murder of her husband, whereof the assembled lords have proof against her by the testimony of her own handwriting.*"

So Bothwell had not burned the letters!

Ruthven handed her the papers and the inked quill. "Sign, Madam."

"I will not!" She pushed away the papers and quill. "Try me before my people. Tell Lord Morton that my testimony will hang him and his murdering kinsmen—George and Archibald Douglas. Tell Lethington and Balfour I will have their lives too. If my royal word is not believed in a Scottish court, it will be believed by Elizabeth, and none of you can survive without English gold."

Lindsay was white with rage. "You'll not live to see a court!" he shouted. Suddenly he leaned over the bed and grabbed her shoulder viciously with his iron-gauntleted hand.

Mary screamed as the iron bit into her flesh.

"Sign!"

She chewed her lip. Sweat trickled down her forehead.

"Sign, damn you!"

She shook her head, tears flooding her cheeks.

Lindsay released her shoulder and his hand went to his dagger. "Get out of bed! If you don't sign, my orders are to take you to your death."

She cowered back, rubbing her shoulder. Behind Lindsay, Ruthven and Melville stood grimly waiting. Scream or struggle as she would Sir William would not help her. Lindsay could drag her from the island, drown her or dagger her at his pleasure.

He seemed to read her thought. "In transporting you to the mainland, an accident will befall you as you try to escape." He grabbed the quill from Ruthven, forced it into her hand, leaning so close that his black beard touched her cheek and she could smell stale sweat and sour ale.

"Sign, you bitch!"

She spat at him. "Move back—your stench sickens me!"

Surprised at her sudden fury, he stepped back. Swiftly, she signed the papers, and threw them at him. She would repudiate them the moment she was free.

Lindsay picked up the papers, handed them to the notaries, who witnessed them and affixed the Great Seal of Scotland. Then he turned to Mary. "I am told you are with child."

She glared at him. "Doubtless you hoped your threats would cause my miscarriage, but you arrived two days late. My twins are already dead."

Lindsay jerked down the sheet that covered her, revealing her slender body in a white linen nightdress.

"You see?" she said, her voice choked with rage. "You've been denied the murder of Bothwell's children."

She pulled up the sheet, shifted her aching body. "Likely you would have enjoyed the deed."

Lindsay shrugged. "I'll enjoy more seeing your outlaw husband brought to justice. It is only a matter of time. Our men are scouring the north."

So Bothwell had safely reached the Highlands, perhaps even now had joined the Hamiltons and Gordons.

"He'll hang for murder," Lindsay said. "George Dalgleish has confessed that Bothwell killed the King."

Mary said, "Under torture, Dalgleish naturally admitted what you wished to hear." She faced Lindsay defiantly, her glance traveling contemptuously from tousled black hair to the spurs on his dusty boots. "It seems you have courage after all, my lord. Though too fearful to fight my husband at Carberry, you are brave enough to torment a helpless woman. May God damn you! If there is justice in heaven you will die as you have lived—hideously and cravenly—a creature too rotten for vultures!"

She turned on Ruthven. "And you, my lord—do I still attract you without a crown? Do you still wish to help me escape? If so, meet me in the garden as we planned, bring me the sketch pad and paint brush for bond-signing and I will consider the matter, again."

Ruthven spluttered, asking what she meant, but she smiled in silence, watching Lindsay's speculative eyes.

The notaries gave Lindsay the papers and he replaced them in his case. Turning his back on Mary, he started toward the door.

"Oaf!" she said. "I have not dismissed you."

"You forget," he sneered, "that you are no longer Queen."

Outrage, grief at the loss of her babies, the horror of abdication and threatened death, fear and longing for Bothwell all converged on her in an overwhelming tide. But she dragged her exhausted body straight up against the pillows.

"My lords," she said, "though you strip me of my kingdom, my lands and my jewels I am still your superior. You will address me as 'Your Majesty,' and you will bow backward when dismissed. I am Dowager Queen of France and Duchess of Orkney." She raised her chin. "I bear the proudest name in this land—Mary Stuart, Countess of Bothwell."

Three hours later Jane brought Mary a note concealed in her bodice. "From Master George Douglas, Madam."

Mary opened it apathetically, but after she read it she turned to Jane excitedly. "He asks me to exercise on the shore at supper time. A boat will be left unguarded. I am to row to Kinross, and he will meet me at the kirkyard with horses!"

"But you dare not rise, Madam! Master Douglas doesn't know the nature of your illness or he'd not suggest such a thing. To row a half-mile could mean your death. You must not—"

"It is certain death if I stay here—at best a slow rotting. Go tell Master Douglas I will do it."

At six-thirty, fully dressed save for her coif, Mary lay in bed, the sheet drawn high lest anyone look in on her. Through the window she watched the activity in the courtyard. At a quarter to seven Lindsay, Ruthven and Melville strolled into the keep for supper. Presently she saw Lady Margaret and her daughters, dressed for the evening, follow them. She guessed that Sir William was in the Great Hall, and that most of the servants would be there serving the meal until eight o'clock.

At seven, supported by Jane and Maria, Mary walked slowly outside. The evening was warm and the sky streaked with sunset above the Lomond Hills. She wished she could wait until midnight when it was dark, but evidently George was taking advantage of some special situation, and she was thankful for any chance of escape.

She had walked only a few feet, when the captain of the sentries, William Drysdale, came up and took her arm, bidding her ladies fall behind.

"You are better this evening, Madam?" he asked.

She tried to smile. "Still very weak, sir." She leaned on his arm. "But a prisoner goes mad within four walls. I thought I'd sit in the garden for a while."

"Allow me to take you there."

There was nothing to do but thank him graciously. She knew he was suspicious, not necessarily of her present actions, but through knowledge of her past escapes. Drysdale was Sir William's garrison commander and Lindsay's friend. And thus, implacably, her enemy.

Despite Drysdale's courtesy, she knew instinctively that he was hostile toward her—a grizzled, heavy-set man whose Protestant fanaticism was well known. She had sensed on first meeting that neither her charm nor her beauty would win him. Probably he subscribed to Knox's evaluation of her—the Romish harlot, the subtle, slippery seductress . . .

Followed by her ladies, they crossed the inner courtyard, went through the gate and outer court into the garden. Mary's slippers trod pink and red rose petals stripped from their bushes by the wind. But there was no wind now. The lake was glassy, unrippled.

Mary sank down on a bench. She dared not walk needlessly for fear of hemorrhage, and evidently her genuine terror of her condition showed in her face, for Drysdale said, "Rest, Madam. With your permission, I'll go make ready for supper."

Languidly, she nodded permission. As soon as he was out of sight, she rose and turned to her ladies.

"We will loiter along the shore, and when we pass sentries, for God's sake be not tongue-tied but chatter naturally."

They retraced their steps as rapidly as Mary dared, passed the gate sentries and those that guarded the big boats at the landing. They sauntered on the grassy shore, rounding the curve at Glassin Tower.

"Look, Madam!" Maria pointed ahead. Bobbing on its chain was a small boat, oars laid across the middle seat.

No sentries were in sight.

"Help me in, quickly!" Mary said.

They helped her into the boat, pleading to accompany her, but she refused. "I doubt that Master Douglas has horses for you. Stroll on around to the other landing and walk through the courtyard to my apartments. If anyone asks where I am, say that I am in the garden waiting for you to bring me cushions and wine. Take cushions and wine to the garden, and remain there until you are questioned. Then appear surprised, but not alarmed, by my absence."

"God go with you, Madam."

They unchained the boat and pushed it out. Mary picked up the oars and settled them in the locks. Clumsily, she tried to maneuver the boat toward Kinross Kirk. But she had never rowed before, never troubled to notice how boatmen handled their oars. It had looked simple, but now she found it was not.

Dear heaven, she thought, I have no time to practice; my very life depends on speed. Painfully, she struggled with the oars, but she was scarcely two hundred yards from the castle shore when her arms began to ache unbearably, and she trembled in fear of more serious symptoms. Arnault had sternly warned against exerting too soon.

She slumped in the seat to rest, her head down, hands limp on the oars, letting the boat drift.

Then from the castle she heard the loud warning bell and looked up in terror. Sentries on the battlements were pointing to her and shouting. Already boats were being launched, and she could not hope to outdistance them or escape musketfire.

She waited, helpless, hopeless. Building in her was a vast indifference to life, death, prison, freedom. Beyond a certain point, suffering turned to apathy.

Three boatloads of angry soldiers surrounded her. Drysdale stepped into her boat, and she rose and tottered back to the rear seat to let him row. "A grave error," he snapped. "You have forfeited your privileges."

She said nothing, staring at the grim old castle that rose from the water like a scaly gray monster. On shore she could see Sir William and his family, Lindsay, Ruthven, servants and soldiers crowded at the water's edge.

As she stepped ashore, Sir William took her arm. His mild, myopic blue eyes were dark with anger, but apparently he resented the soldiers' negligence as much as her attempt to escape. Evidently he had been told of her miscarriage, because he reproached her for risking her life.

"You are in my keeping, Madam," he said, "and if harm befalls you I am held responsible. I regret that we must confine you to grimmer quarters."

Still she said nothing.

Lindsay took her other arm as they walked toward the courtyard. "Tricky jade," he said softly between his teeth. Then, more loudly, "Who helped you?"

"No one," Mary said. "I saw the boat unguarded and seized my chance."

"There'll not be another."

They led her to the massive keep where Sir William lived with his wife, niece, and young daughters. Preceded by Lady Margaret holding a lantern, Sir William carried Mary up three flights of dark spiral stairs so narrow that she feared they could not get past the bends, and her hand brushed tomb-cold walls molded green with age. Lady Margaret unbolted a heavy iron gate and they entered a rock-walled sitting room meanly furnished with a few oak chairs and a table.

Beyond was a bedchamber partitioned by a long oak screen. Sir William placed her on a bed curtained in shabby brown velvet.

Lady Margaret's lantern cast trembling shadows on the crude fieldstone walls. There was a bench, a small table with tapers in pewter holders. Nothing else save a fireplace, barred windows, a closet.

Lady Margaret said, "At night my daughters or William's wife or niece will sleep beyond the screen. During the day you may have Jane or Maria with you. You may not go outside unless accompanied by a guard or a member of my family."

Mary leaned back against the hard bolster. "May Monsieur Arnault be near me?"

"He will have the suite above you," Sir William said. "When you are able to descend the stairs you may take your meals with us in the Great Hall on the floor below."

Mary's voice was strained with weariness. "You have been far kinder than my nobles. I know you have a thankless task."

"Thankless indeed," Sir William said. "By attempting escape you endangered us as well as yourself."

Mary thought, Morton and James would likely have his head if I broke free. Gently she said, "I regret I am such a burden to you."

"Your Majesty is not a burden, but a trust. And you will be wise to come to an understanding with us. We will allow you embroidery materials, a dog or a bird if you wish. I myself will take you hawking and fishing. We may even permit you to receive certain letters if you give us your royal word that you'll not attempt escape."

Letters! To hear news of Bothwell, however deviously . . . to know what was happening in the world outside . . .

"In that manner you could ease our worry," Lady Margaret said, "and we in turn could ease your captivity."

Mary sighed and shook her head. "I cannot give my word, Madam. So long as I draw breath, I'll seek to escape and regain my rights."

Lady Margaret and Sir William exchanged glances. Then silently, sadly, they bowed backward out of the room. Mary heard the iron door clang shut and the bolts drawn fast.

CHAPTER THIRTEEN

I.

THE DOUGLAS WOMEN alternated in sleeping in Mary's bedchamber. Sir William's wife, niece or eldest daughter were always in attendance. Though not unkind they took their duties seriously. Every dish that arrived from the kitchens was uncovered and peered at. Flowers picked by Jane and Maria were carefully examined lest they hide letters. Mary was allowed no writing materials, no sewing, lest she try to stitch a message to someone outside.

Three days after Mary's abdication, Lady Agnes, Sir William's wife, came to spend the night. She was about thirty, with black curls and rosy, dimpled cheeks. Despite Lady Margaret's instructions, she could not repress a tendency to gossip and now as she embroidered a pair of sleeves for Sir William, she said, "I convinced my husband that with so many of us guarding Your Majesty, it would be impossible for you to smuggle out an embroidered message. So you are to have a sewing box and tapestry frame."

"Thank you so much," Mary said, staring at her idle hands. "I welcome anything to pass the time, for I cannot concentrate sufficiently to read. I—"

The sudden rolling, booming thunder of castle cannon interrupted her and she ran to the barred window. The shoreline of Kinross seemed aflame, the sky and lake blood-red for miles around. Below in the courtyard, men ran and shouted and she smelled the acrid stench of gunpowder.

Bothwell! she thought exultantly. Bothwell has come with the Gordons and Hamiltons, artillery, firespears and fireballs. He is burning Kinross in his path.

Again the castle cannon roared over the din in the courtyard. Lady Agnes, looking over Mary's shoulder, put her hands to her ears. "Pesk take it, I begged William not to fire the cannon, but he's so damnably stubborn. Besides, he should show more deference to Your Majesty."

Mary whirled to face her. "What do you mean? Is it not an attack?"

"No, Madam, it's a celebration." She looked pityingly at Mary. "None of us wished to tell you, but your son was crowned today at Stirling."

"Oh, God . . ." Mary left the window and sat down. She had hoped that her few loyal lords would prevent the coronation until she had repudiated the abdication. But now James VI—thirteen months old— was King of Scotland. Even if she won her freedom, she would be only Dowager Queen or Regent.

"Lord Lindsay sent us a courier at suppertime," Lady Agnes said in her frilly-lace-paper voice. "Master Knox preached the coronation sermon—they've abolished the Mass forever—and the King was sworn to defend Protestantism. They lifted his little hand, and held the heavy crown above his head . . ."

And I not there to see . . . But perhaps it is merciful that I was spared the sight of traitors forcing the new religion on a child too young to know the faith of his fathers and binding him to defend heresy . . .

"Has James arrived from Paris?" Mary asked.

Lady Agnes hesitated. "I should not tell you any news, Madam, but if you won't betray my confidence . . ."

"Never."

"Lord James is on the way to Scotland, expected any day."

He will lose no time in proclaiming himself Regent, in renewing the old Knox-Elizabeth alliance, in weighting my shackles. Likely he will move me to a stronger fortress.

The cannon thudded, shivering the walls, reverberating in the Lomond Hills. Sprays of fireworks burst against the deep red sky and hissed toward the lake, dying against the water in rosettes of flame. In the courtyard men drank the health of the new King. Throughout Scotland, Mary knew, mugs would be clinked by bonfires from the Border to Banff and beyond.

Lady Agnes went to the table, poured two goblets of madeira and brought one to Mary.

"Your Majesty will wish to drink the King's health," she said.

"I do not recognize my son as King, and never shall." Mary took the glass, lifted it. "If God wills after my death—to King James VI of Scotland and James I of England."

They drained the goblets and crashed them into the fireplace.

II.

Maneuvering cautiously through the days that followed, Mary contrived to charm her many jailers. Sir William's eldest daughter and niece were easy conquests, so awed by a queen's attention that they followed her about more as slaves than spies. What valueless trinkets were sent her from Holyrood Mary distributed among them and Lady Margaret's daughters, and listened intently by the hour to tales of insufficient dowries, unrequited love and dreaded spinsterhood. She comforted, advised, flattered. By mid-August, they were vying with each other in making her more comfortable.

They tapestried her bedchamber, curtained her bed in moss-green velvet, stitched a counterpane of green taffeta and fringed it with gold silk. They hung her sitting room with hawking tapestries, canopied a chair of state with crimson satin and curtained a window in the same material. In the south window recess they created an oratory with a small altar and portrait of Christ. The ugly oak furniture was replaced by ebony.

Lady Margaret sighed, and smiled ruefully when the redecoration was complete. "I chided my daughters, Madam. I warned them they were dupes to Stuart fascination. And what do you think Janet said to me, the snisty baggage? 'You too were a dupe, Mama!'"

Mary laughed.

"And the men!" Lady Margaret spread her hands helplessly. "Dear heaven, the men are worse!"

Sir William gave Mary a spaniel, books, a chess set. He and his wife took her fishing and boating on the three-and-a-half-mile loch, and she went ashore and explored the ruined monastery of St. Serf's Island. The castle soldiers, all but the doggedly hostile Drysdale, fought to escort Mary on her walks. George Douglas stripped Kinross of flowers, and brought her plants to make table gardens.

George visited Mary in the daytime, when his family was at dinner and Jane and Maria her only attendants. Every day or so he had new plans for her escape, all of which she rejected as too rash.

"I think you are anxious to be rid of me," she teased.

"Rid of you! I will go wherever Your Majesty goes, and forever."

He was too transparently infatuated, and she said, "If you are to help me escape, you must conceal your affection for me. So many flowers, so many walks in the garden—your brother will grow suspicious."

"He thinks I am dazzled," George said glumly. "He even dares to jest about it. But someday he'll discover I'm not a moonstruck lad, but a man in love."

"Ah, now, you must not say such things! I am nearly six years older than you, a wedded wife."

"What matter? I ask only to be part of your household, to spend my life in your service."

His gallantry touched her, but his impulsiveness worried her. This stolid-appearing boy, square-set and slow-moving, was the very antithesis of his looks. Reckless, highly emotional, he was ready to hazard his family's honor for her freedom.

One miracle he accomplished—the receipt and delivery of letters. He made contact with John Beaton, brother of Mary's French Ambassador Archbishop Beaton, who was hiding in the neighborhood of Kinross. Beaton informed Mary that he was at her service for the dispatching of messages, and named the loyal lords to whom she should write. At Dumbarton, Huntley, Arbroath, Ross, Fleming, Boyd, Herries, Galloway and Argyll—the last to her surprise—had signed a bond to liberate her. At Niddry, Lord Seton and Mary Livingstone's husband, William Semple, were dedicated to her cause.

Pen, ink and paper were locked in Sir William's study, but Mary learned to write laboriously on torn white petticoats and handkerchiefs with ink made from chimney soot and water. While her jailers were in the Great Hall at dinner or supper, she wrote messages to her nobles, to Elizabeth, Catherine and Philip. Jane and Maria guarded the gate, ready to signal her at sound of steps on the staircase. She kept the letters in her bodice until George came to smuggle them to Beaton. Received letters were burned immediately—all but one.

> *August 1, 1567*
> *From the Palace of the Bishop,*
> *Spynie*

My love:

Being hunted as a wolf and harried through the Highlands for weeks I have here taken refuge with my great-uncle Patrick. He welcomed me hospitably, but three of his bastards, knowing the price on my head, sought to collect the reward. I was forced to kill one and turn the others out of the palace, occupying it with my fourteen men.

Relations with my uncle now being somewhat precarious, I am leaving here and sailing my little fleet of four ships to the Orkneys, where I will find safe harbors. I cannot raise men on shore. Everyone, including Huntley and the Hamiltons, is rabbity at thought of alliance with an outlaw. But in the Orkneys and Shetlands, thanks to your grant and my title of Lord Admiral, I should have no difficulty in recruiting merchant seamen, fishermen and pirates to your cause.

To these northern folk, an Edinburgh edict means nothing and Morton and his swine less.

My dear love, take courage and be of good cheer. No matter what your jailers tell you, half the world is with you. I hear of good source that Elizabeth works relentlessly for your liberation, for she knows full well that what happened to you can befall her too. She will not recognize your son as King, for to her you are still the supreme ruler. Nor will she accept James as Regent, lest her Cecil be infected with similar ideas. I am told she forbade Throckmorton to attend the coronation. Fear for herself makes her your most powerful friend. Write to her.

Love me, my dearest, as I love you. Keep trust in me no matter what you hear of me. Nothing will prevent my coming to you, but I must bring sufficient men to take you from Lochleven back to your throne.

Your husband and faithful lover,
James, Duke of Orkney.

That letter she read until she knew it by heart. Then she burned it.

On August 15th her brother James arrived at Lochleven with Morton and Atholl. They came to Mary's apartments as she was sitting down to supper, and she rose from the table and ran to James with both hands outstretched. At any cost she was determined to be gracious. To rouse his anger might cost her life.

"My dear brother," she said, "how I have longed to see you!"

He was impeccable in a French quilted velvet doublet of dark crimson, the sleeves slashed to reveal gold brocade. He held her hand lightly in his long, elegantly tapered fingers, then released it. Evading her glance, he looked about the sitting room.

"I see they have made you quite comfortable," he said.

"Aye," Morton said sullenly. "A veritable bower, Your Highness."

Mary turned on Morton. "You do not address my brother as 'Your Highness.' Now, leave us."

But Morton and Atholl made no move, and James did not dismiss them. The three, obviously ill at ease, looked everywhere but at Mary. They stared at the ceiling, the floor, walked over to the oratory, glanced out the window.

Mary linked her arm in James's. "Come, sup with me."

"No. Please continue your supper, Madam."

Mary sighed and obeyed. They watched her nibble at her food, but they never met her eyes. Standing by the fireplace, they shifted their feet, cleared their throats, rumpled their beards. Finally Mary rose and went to James.

"Do you need a bodyguard in my presence?" she asked. "What is it you fear?"

"Nothing," he said stiffly. "Why should I?"

"Then walk with me in the garden—alone."

"If you wish," he said, and escorted her downstairs.

As they strolled in the long, soft twilight, James remarked on the trout fishing, the weather. Mary begged for news of Edinburgh and the courts of Europe. James told her about his new falcon training in France.

"For the love of God!" she said. "Did you come here to talk trivia? Tell me your plans for me."

He stared just beyond her shoulder. "I am protecting your interests."

She bit back angry words. "When do you take the oath of Regency?"

"Next week." He sighed. "I do so only out of duty. The lords constituted me Regent without my knowledge. Naturally I am reluctant . . ."

Do you imagine you fool me, she wondered, or is this a statement you made so often that you parrot it unthinkingly?

"I marvel," she said, "that my lords do not take my life and be done with it. They have stripped me of everything else."

She glanced at James sideways, saw his faint, hastily erased smile. He plays cat and mouse with me, she thought, the most ghastly game he could invent.

She asked, "What will you do with me?"

Evasively, he said, "We require three promises: That you will not interfere in government nor try to rally supporters; that you will divorce Bothwell and marry a man of our choice; that you will not ask help of King Charles or Philip."

"Since Charles is dominated by Catherine, he is not likely to send me troops," Mary said. "Philip is miserly of money and soldiers, and so slow of decision that I'd be a gray-granny before he moved." She did not mention Elizabeth, for James must not know what she had heard from Bothwell. "It is impossible for me to rouse supporters, since I cannot send or receive letters."

"And Bothwell?" James asked. "Have you reconsidered? Why clutch wildfire when you need rock?"

"The rock you would choose for me would be so small a pebble you could hurl it from Scotland," she said bitterly. "You would have me wed a weakling, or one of your henchmen."

"Will you relinquish Bothwell?"

She looked off toward the faint, far lights of Kinross. "No. I will die his wife."

"You will soon be his widow."

"Then I will die so." She glanced at him appealingly, put her hand on his arm. "I have no army. I am no threat to you. What do you gain by my captivity?"

"It is you who gain, not I," he said impatiently. "Every preacher in Edinburgh is excoriating you as Clytemnestra, Delilah, Jezebel. The people would drag you to the stake and burn you alive, for Knox warns that unless you are punished, a plague will fall from heaven. So you see, I favor you by secluding you here."

"I demand to appear at court in my defense," she said.

For just as I softened the mob's fury after Carberry Hill, I can soften it now, win them from Knox as I did before . . .

James seemed to read her thought. "This time, Madam, your charm will not suffice. There is proof of your complicity in murder and adultery. Bothwell kept your letters to incriminate you should you ever wish to be rid of him."

"You lie!"

He shrugged. "If you appeared in court, those letters would set afire the faggots of the stake."

He was right. With the letters in Morton's keeping, she was helpless to defend herself.

"In time you will thank me for keeping you here," James said.

He guided her back to the keep, while she struggled to control her rage. His effort to make himself appear her champion against the people infuriated her. She thought, He keeps me alive to use me as a pawn in some plan of his own.

"I return to Edinburgh tomorrow," James said. "Good-night, Madam."

"James," she said, her eyes so insistent that for the first time he returned her glance, "you have managed to evade guilt for Rizzio's murder, for Darnley's, for my imprisonment and abdication and for the coronation of my son in heretic rites. All these crimes occurred while you were absent, so the people presume you are clean."

"I am," he said. "Do not blame me for your follies. You precipitated your troubles by persistently ignoring my advice. You forged your own shackles—with Bothwell's help."

"You will forge yours," she said quietly, "greed by greed. Some day you will arrange a crime and fail to depart on schedule."

"Leave prophecies to Master Knox."

"And what does he prophesy?" she asked scornfully.

James shrugged. "He is an old man now, and ill. We pay little heed to his visions."

"But what does he vision?"

"A strange thing—that Edinburgh Castle will run like a sandglass and that its commander will be seized and hanged against the western sun."

"Is Balfour still its commander?"

James smoothed his hair. "Why, no. As a matter of fact . . . at the moment . . . I am."

III.

From her window Mary watched the summer die. Kinross, half a mile away, was a cluster of straggling rooftops blurred by the blue smoke of burning leaves. The hills were brassy with autumn, oaks aflame along the horizon. Then wild geese honked southward and mists rose, obscuring village and hills and lake. On still evenings she could hear owls, and the thin, strange barking of foxes in the woods. Boats moved from the mainland bearing the winter's supply of firewood, root vegetables, game, salted fish. For four months the island would be locked in winter, enveloped in bone-chilling, heart-freezing damp.

Mary lived for letters. Though she heard no more from Bothwell, George Douglas brought news of him, and Lord Seton wrote disparagingly of his "craven flight to safety." She learned that immediately after becoming Regent, James sent Kirkcaldy of Grange to hunt down Bothwell with eight ships and four hundred hackbuteers. The fleet nearly cornered Bothwell's four ships on Bressay Sound in the Shetlands, but Bothwell ran north up the channel and lured Kirkcaldy's *Unicorn* over a submerged rock which sank her. One of Bothwell's ships was badly crippled, but he sped farther north through dangerous currents that crashed and boiled against the wildest coast in Britain. At Unst, the northernmost end of the Shetlands, Bothwell anchored and awaited the enemy. When they arrived, he battled them for three hours at sea, lost two ships, but fought on from the *Pelican*, though its mainmast was shot away and his men begging to surrender. A sudden squall blew up, and Bothwell ran his ships before the wind and escaped. Then a storm drove him to the Norwegian coast, and he was detained in Bergen on suspicion of piracy.

Lady Margaret added to Mary's information. "Bothwell is no hero to the Norwegians, Madam, but a dirty, penniless adventurer suspected of regicide. The authorities in Bergen demanded his passport, and he had the presumption to say that since he was King of Scotland, no one could authorize him a passport."

"God bless him! I can hear him now . . . but he is in trouble?"

"He was—and with a woman."

Mary closed her eyes and bit her lip. She would not believe such slander, yet she dreaded hearing it.

"This woman, Bothwell's former mistress, lives in Bergen, and when she learned of his arrival, she filed a claim against him in court accusing him of seduction on the promise of marriage."

"Was it Anna Throndsen?"

"Yes—some such name. She also asked for the return of money lent Bothwell seven years ago."

"Jesu!" Mary said. "Imagine him humiliated in an alien court! Mark you, he has supported that bitch all these years, though I doubt he has means to prove it. What did the court decide?"

"Bothwell volunteered to pay her an annuity and give her his smaller ship, so she was satisfied."

Mary smiled. "She'll be less satisfied when she discovers that an outlaw can own no property; she will never get a Scots penny. But did he get his passport?"

"No. To rid themselves of an unsavory and politically dangerous guest, the Norwegians put him on a warship and sent him to Denmark. By now he has probably arrived in Copenhagen. I tell you this for a purpose, Madam. It is obvious that he has deserted you. To pin your hopes on him is to feed yourself fantasy. If you renounce him, James will likely release you. James works for your own good. He loves you."

"That is a fantasy on which *you* feed," Mary said gently.

"I know my own son. But if you will not divorce Bothwell, James's hands are tied."

"His hands seem remarkably agile," Mary said. "He grasps all I own."

Jewels, lands, horses, silver plate, tapestries, even clothes. Mary had written Robert Melville begging attire from the Keeper of the Wardrobe at Holyrood, and James had grudgingly sent three gowns —black, white and crimson, simple ones without jewels or fur. He sent her an ugly black wool cloak she had never seen before, shoes, two changes of linen and a nightrobe. She thought of her sable-sleeved brocaded dresses, her mink and ermine capes and muffs, the earrings, necklaces and coronets that now furnished gold for James or glory for his wife. The least of her losses, but humiliating, infuriating. The only jewels she now possessed were a crucifix, pearl earrings, her wedding band and Bothwell's motto ring. Her only money was what Lord Seton smuggled to her through George. But in one respect James was generous. He permitted Melville to send her gold and silver thread for sewing and tapesty work.

It was the dreariest winter of her life. Despite continuous fires, she was never warm. The damp seeped through the tapestries, dripped from the cracks in the timbered ceilings, filmed the casements. When she left the hearth, even to walk the length of the sitting room, she wore her cape. Gales lashed the castle, and for days it was impossible to venture outside.

On December 8th the Douglases celebrated Mary's twenty-fifth birthday with a banquet in the Great Hall. Lady Agnes conducted her back to her apartments and handed her a small package containing quill, ink and parchment.

"Madam, I tremble to give you this. William would divorce me if he knew. But I cannot bear for you to be cut off from your friends."

Mary thanked her, touched to tears. Past birthday gifts—the treasures of Catholic Europe—had never seemed so precious. Lady Agnes kept the writing materials in her chamber and gave Mary only what she needed for each letter, then took the letters to Beaton in Kinross or gave them to George to deliver.

Mary did not doubt that if James discovered their conspiracy, their punishment would be swift and severe. Week by week her hatred of him mounted. He had forced his gentle family into the position of common turnkeys, had likely threatened them with death or ruin if they refused to act as her jailers. Yet despite it all, they loved him with the proud blood-love she once had felt.

Late in December James returned to Lochleven, this time with Morton and Balfour. Mary received them in a spacious hall in the outer courtyard that she used on occasion as a presence chamber. As they entered the room, a fierce gust of wind blustered open the latticed casements, and when Balfour hastened to close them, Mary said, "Such violence heralds an arch-traitor."

Balfour, seeing the rage in her face, retreated behind James.

"How dare you bring this creature to my presence?" Mary asked.

"You have kept worse company," James said coldly.

"I know not who is worse—you, Morton or Balfour. But assuredly Balfour has your taste for greed. In order to get command of Edinburgh Castle, which I placed in his trust, you gave him five thousand pounds cash, a priory, a pension for his son and a full pardon for his infamy at Kirk O'Field."

"Who told you these lies?" James asked.

She was angered to recklessness. "What I know, the world knows. You pose so sanctimoniously as the savior of Protestantism, the Good Regent, benevolently secluding a scarlet woman from the righteous wrath of the people. But the rulers of Europe sneer at you for a low, presumptuous bastard. Even Elizabeth, who shares your stigma, considers you an insolent upstart and refuses to recognize you. Charles and Catherine regard you as little better than a turnspit tending the fires of insurrection. Aye," she said, as his hands shook and his cheek muscles tensed, "you've cause to be uneasy. Your Catholic lords are

against you, your chameleon Lethington wavers, and this filth—"
She pointed to Balfour and Morton—"will cut your throat as they
cut mine, signing bonds with one hand and drawing daggers with
the other."

James started to speak, but she shouted him down. "Many times
I have forgiven your treachery, kept you at court, honored you. But
now if you offered me my freedom on your knees, I'd rot here
rather than accept it. Whatever comes from your hand would stink."

She went to him, caught his hand, flung it violently high. "I too
can prophesy," she snarled. "These swine shall bear witness to my
prophecy that one day you will burn in the hell you made for me—
and may God grant me the privilege of seeing it!"

James's eyes were green fire in a twisting, pallid face. Balfour was
backed to the wall as though pinned there. Morton quavered that
he would do all in his power to help her, that he was her loyal
friend.

"You say that because you fear I will escape and hunt you down,"
she said scornfully. "And so I will, God willing."

James said, "You have drunk shame to the dregs. You can hope
for nothing but God's mercy."

"And his vengeance," she said. "I will never receive you again.
Burn me—hang me—but spare me the nausea of your presence."

She swept past them out the door into the gray rainlight of the
morning.

An hour later while his family was at dinner, George Douglas
hurried to Mary's apartments.

"Madam, I know not what you have told James, but he is insane
with fury. He accused me of telling you outside news, called me a
treacherous informer and ordered me off the island on peril of hanging. My mother and brother pleaded for me, but James is determined
I shall leave Lochleven today."

Shocked, Mary stared at him. Her tantrum had cost her the one
man who could help her escape.

George flushed. "James says I am enchanted, that Your Majesty
will wile me to my death." He spread his stubby hands. "So—I
must leave you."

"Where will you go?" she asked, fearful for his safety.

"James cares not where I go, so long as I am off Lochleven. I shall
live at Kinross Inn and there keep contact with John Beaton and
your loyal nobles. Their headquarters are now at Hamilton Palace,
eight miles from Glasgow. The old Duke de Chatelherault has
massed his clan to your rescue."

She knew that her enemies were shifting to her cause not through love but for expediency. Chatelherault, heir to the throne after the young King, would not trust James to protect his claim.

"I will work constantly for Your Majesty's escape," George said. "I will think of nothing else. You will not see me, but often I shall lie concealed in the reeds watching your window, hoping for a glimpse of your shadow moving against the candlelight."

"May God keep you and reward you."

"My reward will be your freedom. Madam, try to cultivate the friendship of young Willie Douglas, who has charge of the boats. If you can win him, your escape is assured."

Mary frowned. "Your large family confuses me. Is Willie a cousin?"

"Nay, Madam, no blood relation but a foundling who was left at Lochleven in a basket. My brother William gave Willie our name and a good education. He cares for the boats and serves as page. Likely you've seen him about—a sandy-haired boy of fourteen."

She nodded. "I have seen him serving in the Great Hall."

"He is William's pet and has the run of the island and the shire. A pleasant lad, but shy of girls. He is interested only in hunting, fishing and gambling with the soldiers."

"Send him to me this afternoon," Mary said. "Tell him I wish his advice on my hunting tapestry."

George nodded. "Proceed cautiously. He loves William as a father, and might betray you."

He came to her and knelt. "Good-by, Madam."

"My dear friend . . ." Mary bent and stroked his straight blond hair. "I wish I had some token to give you." Impulsively, she removed one of her pear-shaped pearl earrings. "Here, take this. Should you need money, sell it."

"I have money, Madam—William gave me a-plenty. When I've perfected a plan for your escape, I shall find means to return this pearl to you as a signal. When you receive it, make ready to flee."

He took the pearl, kissed her hand, went to the door. For a long moment he stared at her, as though memorizing her from lace-veiled hair to velvet slippers.

"I love you, Madam."

He turned and left her.

Willie Douglas knelt to Mary on knobby knees. As he rose, she repressed a chuckle. He was tall, stalk-thin, all arms and skinny legs. Sandy curls roofed a long, narrow face dominated by a big nose. As he swallowed, his Adam's-apple bobbed nervously.

Mary said, "I want advice on my hunting tapestry, and Master

George assured me you were an expert. But—is there another Willie Douglas on the island?"

"No, Madam." His voice cracked and he reddened. "Why?"

"Master George said you were a boy." Her eyes widened incredulously. "But I see you are a man . . ."

During the next few weeks Mary consulted with Willie on various pretexts. She asked his opinion on training hawks, on baiting trout, on casting. She gave him gold for his advice. He took it reluctantly, but she insisted that a man needed gambling money and listened as though entranced to his tales of gains and losses. In mid-January he suggested that he could be of service if she wished to escape.

Young as he was, Willie appeared to have the caution and judgment that George lacked. He realized that another failure would mean the dungeon for Mary, perhaps death. In the spring, he said, he would find means to release her. Meanwhile he smuggled her letters to George, and rejected George's harebrained schemes for her escape.

He brought news from her loyal nobles. They said that Elizabeth, through the efforts of Ambassador Throckmorton, had saved Mary's life. James had determined to take Mary from Lochleven and cast her to the people's wrath, but Throckmorton had warned James that if Mary suffered "accident" or execution, England would invade Scotland and depose him as Regent.

Mary knew that Elizabeth acted from self-interest, abhorring insurrection above all things. Yet she could not help but be touched, and she wrote Elizabeth gratefully, receiving in turn deeply affectionate notes and assurances of help. "You can at any time count on the Queen of England as a true friend." Some day, Mary thought, I will repay her for my life.

Through Hepburn of Riccarton, Mary learned news of Bothwell. In Copenhagen he had appealed to King Frederick of Denmark for troops and ships to rescue Mary. Frederick refused. He would not aid a man suspected of regicide. But he was delighted by Bothwell's arrival, for now he had a political pawn. Detaining Bothwell at elegant Malmoe Castle in the province of Scania, Frederick sat back to await offers from James, Elizabeth, Charles and Philip. He would release Bothwell to the highest bidder.

James demanded Bothwell's extradition, but Frederick refused on the grounds that Bothwell's guilt of murder was unproven and that his accusers were rebels to the crown.

You need not grieve too deeply about your husband, Hepburn of Riccarton wrote Mary. *Frederick likes Bothwell, treats him as a king and provides entertainment, fine garments and pleasant quarters be-*

low his own suite. His servant Paris is with him. Fear not, Madam, Bothwell will find means to escape, though Malmoe is heavily guarded. Be thankful that for a time he is safe and unharried . . .

Mary was thankful, but apprehensive. Charles and Philip, regarding Bothwell as the Protestant murderer of a Catholic King, would be eager for his death, but she did not believe either of them would pay Frederick's price, which she guessed to be high. James or Elizabeth might do so, for both had personal as well as political grudges. Mary wrote Frederick begging Bothwell's release, and promising him anything he desired when she was free. She wrote Bothwell ardent love letters which Hepburn carried to Denmark.

Time did not dull her longing for Bothwell. Often she wakened in tears, his name on her lips. Music was nearly unbearable. At supper when the musicians played love songs, she sat rigidly, willing herself not to weep.

Bothwell's henchmen—Dalgleish, John Hay, John Hepburn and William Powrie—confessed under torture that Mary was guilty of "art and part" in Darnley's murder. But on the scaffold, Hay publicly denounced Balfour, Lethington, Argyll and Huntley as the contrivers of the plot. The people were so inflamed that the four nobles fled Edinburgh. James ordered the drawn and quartered remnants of the executed men placed in baskets and displayed throughout the market towns of Scotland.

In mid-March, Willie Douglas joined Mary as she walked on the windy shore. "Madam," he whispered, "I've a plan for your escape. Next week the laundress who comes from Kinross to bring fresh linens and to pick up soiled ones will go to your chamber and change clothes with you. Then the boatmen will row you to Kinross, where Master George will await you with horses."

Mary hesitated. "Do the boatmen know of the plot?"

"No, Madam, I dare not tell them. Your disguise will deceive them."

The plan appealed to her, but she worried about the fate of the laundress.

"God love you, Madam, she'll come to no harm. Sir William is no woman-beater. Give her a bit of gold, and she'll be miles from here by the time Lord James hears of it."

So it was arranged for the afternoon of March twenty-fifth.

Maria Courcelles guarded the staircase, while Mary and the tall brown-haired laundress switched clothes. Fingers shaking, Mary fastened the buttons of the bodice, and Jane Kennedy laced it at the waist. The short blue skirts bunched to the back under a white apron that came just above Mary's ankles.

"A good fit, Madam," Jane said. "Now muffle your head in this scarf and draw it high above your chin."

The laundress, in Mary's black gown, spoke timidly. "I would offer Her Majesty my shoes, but they are far too large."

"These slippers are old and shabby," Mary said. "None will note them." She removed her rings and crucifix and hid them in her bosom. "I am ready."

Jane, Maria and the laundress kissed her hand and wished her Godspeed. Mary picked up a large bundle of soiled linen. Holding it high to shield her face, she crept down the spiral staircase and reached the courtyard.

Her heart was beating furiously. Her feet and spine icy, her forehead sweating, she walked slowly toward the sentries who stood at the gate. Captain Drysdale was on duty there, and she buried her face in the linen and prayed.

"A heavy fardel, eh?" he asked.

"Aye, sir." *God grant I have lost my French accent and sound like a Scot!*

Drysdale motioned to a sentry to open the gate for her. Willing herself not to run to the shore, she maintained an even pace. At the landing, two boatmen awaited her—bearded young men in rough linsey-woolsey jerkins.

One of them took the linen and helped her into the boat. The other pushed it off the sand, jumped in. Mary sat at the far end staring down at the watery planks in the bottom.

She dared not look up at the men and turned sideways, pretending to watch the wind-rippled water, her hands tucked in the voluminous folds of the apron. She heard the creak of the oarlocks, the men's comment on the weather. The boat seemed to crawl.

They were nearly in mid-lake, when the oarsman said, "You've a pretty ankle—let's see your face."

"Please, sir," she said desperately, "I'm pocked."

"The Laird has ordered us to examine the faces of all women who leave the island," the other man said. "Unscarf yourself."

"Please sir!"

The oarsman rested his oars and leaned forward to pluck at her scarf. She raised both hands to protect her face.

"Blood of Jesus!" he shouted. "This is no washermaid! Look at her hands!"

The hands that Ronsard had made immortal in verse. The hands that were legend—long, slender-fingered, white and smooth as new snow.

The oarsman tore off her scarf. "The Queen!"

Tears flooded her face. "Have mercy!" she cried. "Take me to

Kinross, and I'll give you jewelry. You can live royally for the rest of your lives . . ."

The other boatman cursed. "And how long would we live with Lord James hunting us down for treason? No, Madam—we go back."

The oarsman turned the boat.

"Wait!" Mary said. "If I go back it may mean my death. At best, I'd be celled in dark solitude. I beg you—I entreat you—say nothing to Sir William!"

They shook their heads. The Laird had been kind to them. It was their duty to tell him.

"What of your duty to me, your anointed Queen? In the eyes of God I am still supreme ruler. I command you to say nothing of this."

They were grimly silent. The boat moved closer to shore.

She said nothing more. But she begged them with her eyes. The men stared at her, their own eyes bleak, their faces closed. The boat ground onto the sand.

Hopelessly, she stood up, drawing her scarf across her chin. The oarsman helped her to shore. The other took her bundle of linen.

Sir William sauntered down the steps, his hounds bounding ahead of him.

"What's amiss?" he asked.

The oarsman hesitated, looking at the boatman. Then he said, "The washermaid has forgotten Her Majesty's linen. She must go back for it."

IV.

Three days later, Sir William came to Mary and told her he had dismissed Willie Douglas from his service.

"Indeed?" Striving to seem casual, Mary looked up from her embroidery. "Why, sir?"

"Because of you, Madam," he said sadly. "This is your doing. In the courtyard, my daughter and niece saw Willie drop a packet of letters, retrieve it, and hurry here to you. Further, Drysdale reports that Willie flings gold about the barracks—a suspicious amount. I confronted Willie, and he admitted that he smuggled you letters through George. I have warned George that if he values his life he must leave Kinross."

"I'd not have him risk his life on my account," Mary said, "nor Willie either. But where has the lad gone?"

"He loiters at Kinross." He sighed. "I trusted him as a son, and he betrayed me. What happens to him does not concern me."

But she knew that it did. His gray eyes were clouded with pain, his words heavy with hurt.

"Willie loves you," Mary said. "But he also loves adventure. Smuggling my letters was a bit of mischief that you surely will forgive."

"I fear there's more to it than smuggling. I believe he is plotting with George for Your Majesty's escape. Between them they could send my family to the gallows."

Wearily, he rose, ran his hand through his thin lint-blond beard. "Your Majesty will never cease to victimize your friends."

His own wife, she thought guiltily. Lady Agnes was in her ninth month of child-sickness, but insisted on being rowed to Kinross with messages for John Beaton.

"Will you tell James of this?" Mary asked.

"No, Madam. None of us would survive his wrath. He would probably hang George . . . I suppose it is futile to ask Your Majesty to cease your intrigues?"

"Futile." She smiled. "But I promise you this. When I escape and regain power, I'll see to it that James cannot harm you. After Morton's death, you inherit the Earldom of Douglas—but I shall first reward you in some other manner, as soon as I am free."

"I thank Your Majesty . . ." He looked uneasily about the room as though fearful of being overheard. "James is anxious that you wed Morton."

"Jesu!"

"He may send Lindsay with divorce papers for you to sign."

Under torture . . .

On April 30th, Lady Agnes persuaded her husband to forgive Willie Douglas, and to Mary's delight he returned to the island.

The following day Lady Margaret came to Mary in tears. "I have just been to Kinross," she said, "where I bade farewell to George. He wished to leave Scotland and seek his fortune at the French court, but I persuaded him to go to Edinburgh instead and make peace with his brother James."

Mary turned her head lest Lady Margaret see the shock in her face. So George had deserted her for James. She could depend on Lady Agnes and the faithful John Beaton as letter bearers. But Willie might well be frightened and cured of intriguing, and with George gone, the firebrand of the escape conspiracy was ash.

"George is ambitious," Lady Margaret said, dabbing at her eyes. "He will make his way to a high post once he and James are reconciled."

"I am sure of it," Mary said bitterly. She feared her depression showed in her face, and she went to the window, staring down at the courtyard. Willie was working on a boat. Behind him stood

[498]

Captain Drysdale, and she wondered whether Drysdale had taken it upon himself to watch Willie's every move, or if Sir William had ordered it.

"Oh!" Lady Margaret said. "I nearly forgot." As Mary turned, she reached into her belt pouch. "George said for me to give this to Your Majesty. One of the boatmen found it on the shore and offered to sell it to George, but he said it belonged to you."

Lady Margaret extended the pearl earring.

Mary spent that afternoon in an agony of suspense. Her escape was imminent, but how or when she could not imagine.

At dusk while the Douglas family was at supper, Jane Kennedy admitted Willie to Mary's sitting room. He told her the escape was planned for the following evening. "If you approve the plan, Madam—"

"I will approve any plan!" she said. "Tell me quickly."

"Tomorrow morning, Lord Seton and a bodyguard of fifty men are crossing the Forth to await you in the woods near Kinross and carry you to Niddry where troops will join you. Supposedly, they are attending an assize. There is one great risk—that Seton's men may be seen from here. Your Majesty knows how any activity ashore intrigues Sir William."

Because he feared a rescue party, Sir William was eternally at one of the windows or pacing the shore. For lack of entertainment, the Douglas ladies scanned the horizon, hopeful of visitors. A single horseman could cause an hour's speculation, particularly if he did not take a boat to the island.

"I've devised a means of keeping the Douglases and soldiers and servants indoors," Willie said. "In the morning about eleven, I shall play host to the entire island with a feast and entertainment to celebrate my homecoming." He grinned. "The Laird asked me how I could afford it, and I told him I had Your Majesty's gold, was penitent of taking it and wished to spend it on food and wine for my benefactors. He has approved. We shall hold the feast in the hall farthest from the castle gate. From there one cannot see the shore."

Mary said, "In courtesy, none may leave the hall before I do, and I shall prolong the feast until late afternoon."

"Please do, Madam, for as long as bright sun lingers we are in danger."

"What of the sentries on the battlements?"

"They too are invited."

"And when the feast is over?"

"I trust that wine-sleep will overtake everyone. Your Majesty had best have supper here. While I serve Sir William in the Great Hall, I will contrive to get his key to the outer gate leading to the boats. A sentry always locks the gate at night and brings the key to Sir William at the supper table."

"But the key always rests beside his plate in full view of everyone. You take an impossible risk."

Willie said, "While pouring his wine, I shall accidentally drop my napkin on the key, and in lifting the napkin I shall also lift the key. Your physician, Monsieur Arnault, will distract Sir William's attention while I do this. I shall leave the hall immediately, and as I pass through the courtyard to unlock the gate I'll signal to this window." He turned to Jane Kennedy. "You be stationed there."

"Shall I accompany Her Majesty?" Jane asked.

"Yes. As soon as I wave to you, bring Her Majesty downstairs and walk to the outer gate. You should both wear scarfs and hooded cloaks. Has Your Majesty one that is inconspicuous?"

"Yes," Mary said. "James gave me a plain black wool that likely belonged to some kitchen wench at Holyrood. I've never worn it."

"That is well. But—" Willie frowned— "Captain Drysdale is the wasp in the pudding. He watches us both too closely, and he's far too dour to linger at my feast or drink himself dull. I leave him to your wits, Madam."

"Does Lady Agnes know of this plan?" Mary asked.

"No, Madam. Master George dares not tell anyone else."

As footsteps sounded on the stairs, Willie said loudly, ". . . so if it pleases Your Majesty to attend my little feast I shall be honored."

Mary yawned, as Lady Margaret came in. "Indeed, it will relieve the tedium. You may count upon me."

That evening Mary walked in the garden, and as usual Captain Drysdale paced at her side.

"There are several things I need in Edinburgh," she said wistfully. "Now I am clean out of sewing materials, and I wanted a length of satin to make a christening gown for Lady Agnes' child. Could you go to Edinburgh for me?"

The gray-bearded chin thrust forward belligerently, but before he could speak she took from her reticule a list of what she wanted. "And for your trouble, sir, this token of my appreciation."

She handed him a draft on the state treasurer.

Drysdale gaped. His eyes widened, glittered. "I will leave in the morning, Madam."

But in the morning he might meet her rescuers on the road. "Please go now," she said. "Otherwise I'll not have the christening dress ready in time."

An hour later, in the soft, pale moonlight, she saw Drysdale row away.

Willie's feast was attended by the entire castle staff. Serving a buffet of food and wine, Willie acted the Abbot of Unreason, clowning and capering so drolly that the Douglas ladies laughed themselves to tears and vowed he must go to London to train as a player. Mary sang, accompanying herself on the lute, then involved Sir William and the soldiers in a drinking game which she prolonged until after three o'clock, when the company dispersed to their apartments and Mary pretended to nap.

At five o'clock she joined Lady Margaret in the garden. The sun lingered, warm on her back. Glancing across the lake, she saw horsemen galloping toward the woods and the glitter of helmets and lifted pikes.

"Look!" Lady Margaret exclaimed. "I wonder who they are. We must send a messenger to find out."

"Gentlemen returning from an assize," Mary said calmly. "Have you forgotten that the spring Law Days have begun?" Quickly she added, "God knows what justice my poor subjects will get under James's regime."

The diversion was successful. Lady Margaret turned from the lake and faced Mary defiantly. "Madam, you persist in slandering my son. There is no fairer man on earth than James."

"My plight scarcely proves that," Mary said. "I can tell you other cases . . ."

She continued arguing with Lady Margaret until the horsemen were out of sight, until the first long shadows fell along the grass and Sir William came and escorted her to her apartments. The little clock on her table pointed to seven.

"A pleasant evening," Sir William said. He went to the window, leaned out the casement.

"What are you doing, you young fool?" he shouted to someone below.

Mary ran to the window and peered over Sir William's shoulder. She saw Willie Douglas bending over one of the boats. Quickly, she put her hand on Sir William's arm. "Wine!" she gasped, swaying toward the wall. "I am faint . . ."

There was no wine in her chamber, and he rushed downstairs to the Great Hall. Mary looked out the window. Willie was driving wood pegs into the boat chains to delay pursuit. She heard Sir William's returning footsteps and sank into a chair.

He hovered over her as she drank the wine, and she realized he had forgotten about Willie. Jane and Maria brought her supper, and Sir William served it himself, fretting that she was unable to eat.

"It is my old complaint," Mary said. "The pesky pain in my side."

"I shall send for Monsieur Arnault," he said.

"No! Please, sir. His medicines sicken me."

"Then I shall send my daughter and niece to attend you."

She assured him that Jane and Maria would care for her, but stubbornly he summoned his niece and daughter. Behind them, carrying her purchases, came Captain Drysdale.

Drysdale said, "In Kinross they told me that Lord Seton and a large troop of horsemen passed through the village today."

Sir William's voice was panicked. "For what reason?"

"They said they were attending an assize."

"Ah, yes." Sir William relaxed.

"Master George is still at the inn," Drysdale said. "I asked him why he lingered, and he said he was waiting to determine whether Lord James was in Edinburgh or Glasgow. I told him Lord James was in Glasgow, and he said he would go there at once. But his manner seemed strange. Shall I row over and see if he departs?"

Sir William was silent, considering. Mary bit her lip, forcing back nervous tears, grinding her hands together.

"Wait until morning," Sir William said finally. "If he is not gone by noon, he will have to reckon with me." He took Drysdale's arm. "Come, let us go down to sup."

With Drysdale at table, Mary thought, Willie can never steal that key.

When the men had left, she turned to the Douglas girls. "I don't need you. Go down and sup with your family."

"We have supped, Madam."

There was no way to be rid of them. They began a game of chess. Jane and Maria looked helplessly at Mary. She paced the room; then, noting the girls' curious stares, sat down and pretended to read. She heard the jumping of her heartbeat, the girls' idle talk as they called a play, the ticking of the clock.

Seven-thirty, eight o'clock . . . Surely by now, unless Drysdale had interfered, Willie had served sweets and fruit and taken the key. Perhaps he lingered in the courtyard, exasperated because Jane had not appeared at the window. But she could not yet motion Jane to her post.

Mary said, "I am chilly. Jane, fetch my cloak."

Jane brought the humble black cloak, a silk scarf tucked in the sleeve.

Mary rose, stretched. It was her custom to pray after meals, and she said, "I shall go up to Monsieur Arnault's chamber for my evening devotions. Light me up the stairs, Jane."

"Yes, Madam." Jane cloaked herself. "The stairs are so drafty." She sniffled as she picked up a taper. "I vow I am taking the New Acquaintance—my throat is sore as a boil."

Young Margaret Douglas rose from the table. "Papa would want us to come with you."

"I wish to pray in solitude," Mary said. "You will hear my footsteps overhead, so there's no need to watch me."

The girls smiled, resumed their game. Mary sent Maria a warning glance. "Keep the young ladies wined and amused. Take my lute and sing for them."

"Yes, Madam."

Mary and Jane hurried upstairs to Arnault's sitting room, which was directly above Mary's. They leaned from the window. In the courtyard, soldiers and blue-kirtled maids flirted in the shadows. The boats rocked in the gentle breeze. In the soft spring twilight, the shore was a green straggle of woods peaked by stone roofs, the hills low gray cushions resting against a dark gold bed of sky.

"Willie may have signaled us and despaired," Mary whispered. "Let us pray he is still in the Great Hall."

Pray . . .

She went to Arnault's little altar and knelt. First, as always, she asked Bothwell's safety, then her own. Once out of prison and enthroned, she could buy Bothwell's freedom from Frederick, no matter what the cost in jewels and lands. If need be she would give her lifetime dowries from France.

"Madam! Willie signals us! He motions us to come down!"

Quickly they tiptoed to the steps, inched down to the landing that led to Mary's apartments. Maria's lute song muffled their footsteps. Twisting down the spiral staircase, they approached the landing of the Great Hall.

Mary paused, holding her breath. She heard Arnault's voice in mid-jest, Sir William's encouraging chuckle, a ripple of feminine laughter. They crept on down the stairs.

At the bottom they paused, stiffening themselves against the rock wall. Servants were lighting flambeaux at the entrance, and they had hoped for darkness.

"Look!" Jane whispered.

Captain Drysdale had emerged from the shadows, a heavy-set figure in dark green velvet with chain-mail sleeves. The sentries came to attention, the flirtatious maids hurried off to their quarters. Drysdale paced back and forth, hands at his back, head swiveling.

By now, Mary thought, Willie has reached the great gate that leads to the landing. How long will he dare to wait there? Two minutes? Five? At any moment Sir William may miss the key, yell for Willie, rouse the garrison.

Mary stepped forward, pulling her hood down over her eyes and her scarf to her chin.

Jane clutched her arm. "No, Madam! We dare not!"

"We must." Mary swept boldly into the light.

Slowly, they started across the courtyard. "Drysdale stares," Mary whispered, locking her arm in Jane's. "Tip your head to mine—we are deep in gossip. Laugh!"

Jane threw back her head and laughed, holding her hood so that it would not slip down.

"Chatter!" Mary ordered. "He follows us!"

"Silly wench," Jane said, "he has no more than a sheep to his name. You'd do far better to snare the blacksmith's son . . ." She continued scolding, her voice shaking, breathless. Mary ached to know if Drysdale still followed them, but she dared not turn.

Then she saw Willie at the gate, beckoning them to hurry. They ran the last few feet, as Willie unlocked the gate. When they were safely through it, he relocked it and threw the key into the mouth of a cannon.

They followed him down to the pier and he helped them into a boat and pushed off.

"Both of you lie on the bottom," he said. "Should they fire on us you'll be protected."

They flung themselves down on the hard wet planks. Willie pulled strongly on the oars. He had muffled the locks with rags, and they sped almost silently across the tranquil water.

Looking up, Mary saw the slow-rising moon, a thin spray of stars in a darkening sky. She said, "Is there any activity on the island?"

"No, Madam. The battlement sentry must see me, but I warrant he thinks nothing amiss. All went well at supper. To my amazement, the Laird closed the window in the Great Hall, which he has never done before. Usually he watches the lake while he eats."

They were more than halfway across the lake, when Willie asked Mary to stand up and wave in signal to George. She did so, fluttering her white scarf fringed with red. The shore seemed dark and deserted. Then she saw two figures rise from the scrub and race to the water's edge.

As the boat approached them, she recognized George and John Beaton. They pulled the boat to the rough wooden pier and helped her out, kneeling to kiss her hand.

Laughing, weeping, she embraced them both. "Where is Lord Seton?"

"On Benarty Hill, Madam. He watched for your signal, and will join us on the road to Queensferry."

Quickly the little group plunged into the woods, where Beaton's men were waiting with horses. George lifted Mary into a sidesaddle. Willie came up and bowed deeply.

"Farewell, Madam," he said, "and Godspeed."

Mary gasped. "Surely you are coming with us?"

"Your Majesty did not ask me to."

"I've been a scatterbrained fool! Of course you must come. You and Master George shall be in my service for life. I'll not ride without you."

"You must, Madam," Willie said. "There's no horse for me."

"Take Jane's. She shall ride with John Beaton."

Heading the little cavalcade between Willie and George, Mary clattered through Kinross. Despite her hood, she was recognized by villagers. To her delight, they cheered her on, blessing her and wishing her well. Exultantly she waved to them, threw back her hood and let her hair stream in the breeze.

Lord Seton and fifty horsemen swept down Benarty Hill and joined them. They galloped south to the seacoast and were ferried across the Firth of Forth. There, up the high bank, Lord Claude Hamilton awaited them with fifty clansmen, and they rushed on toward Niddry Castle, sixty miles from Lochleven.

They plunged down hills, through streams, jumped hedgerows. Mary's body was one with her horse, and the speed enraptured her. She turned in the saddle to smile at her men. Moonlight turned them to shining knights, sparkling their pikes and helmets, their mailed sleeves. Green and scarlet plaids whirled in the rising wind, cutting scarfs streamed backwards. The creaking bridles and plopping hoofbeats formed a rhythm in her mind: *Free-dom, Free-dom* . . . Far and free the moors stretched in moon-gilded heather and bright gold gorse. She sniffed deeply of earth and horse and dew-damp mayflowers.

But her rapture turned to pain at thought of Bothwell. He should be riding with her, his arms roping her waist, his chest a leather-jacked cushion for her head. She had a wild impulse to turn the cavalcade to the seacoast and take ship for Denmark, throwing herself on Frederick's mercy, asking nothing but to share Bothwell's captivity. But that was a coward's plan. She must rally men, smash James's army, win back the means to buy Bothwell's freedom.

God forgive me, she thought—if all else fails I will give Scotland to Frederick.

V.

At two o'clock in the morning they reached Niddry Castle in West Lothian, where Lady Emily Seton welcomed Mary and brought her food. She ate, but she would not sleep. Until dawn she wrote dispatches. Loyal citizens were summoned to arm, and meet her at Hamilton Palace in Lanarkshire. She sent John Beaton to France to plead troops and ships from Charles. Couriers set off for England and Spain. Mary begged funds from Philip, reminding him that her cause was the last hope of Catholicism against the Reformation. She informed Elizabeth of her escape.

Below in the courtyard there was the clang and clatter of armed men, the drumming of hoofs across the drawbridge, the war cries of arriving clansmen. When the sky paled, Mary went to the casement and was greeted by a great shout. Two hundred fighting men raised their broadswords, then knelt in the dust. Lord Herries galloped in with thirty Borderers, and she saw Bothwell's kinsman, Hepburn of Riccarton, and hurried down to meet him in the Great Hall.

"Tell me of Bothwell!" she said.

"I saw him last month, Madam, and he was well as a caged eagle can be. He gave me letters for you."

He opened a dispatch pouch and handed Mary the letters. She would wait to read them in private.

"So Frederick allows him visitors?" she said.

"Aye, and even dispatches. He is royally accommodated . . . Elizabeth has asked Frederick to send Bothwell to England to stand trial for regicide. Since she seems unwilling to pay for this favor, Frederick refuses."

"Thank God!"

"But Cecil has so worked on Elizabeth's fear of assassination that she is asking Frederick to execute Bothwell. She believes that as long as he is alive no ruler is safe."

"Has James yet offered a price?"

"Evidently not. He wants Frederick to execute Bothwell and send the head to Scotland to be stuck on a pike at Kirk O'Field."

Mary shuddered. "We must speed my enthronement so that I can negotiate with Frederick. This week I want you to rally a force of men and demand the surrender of Dunbar, for we need the great store of ammunition there. Then journey to Denmark as my ambassador and promise Frederick anything he asks if he will release Bothwell and allow him to return with you."

"I'll do all in my power, Madam."

Hungrily, hastily, she read Bothwell's letters, assuring her of his love, and his good health. At sunrise she and her men resumed their journey to join the clansmen massing at Hamilton Palace eight miles from Glasgow.

At the palace, seat of the Duke de Chatelherault, armed men poured into the courtyard. During that week, more than a hundred lairds brought their troops. Loyal lords rode in daily—Rothes, Fleming, Livingstone, Cassilis, Argyll. Nine bishops came with their attendants. Huntley sent word that he was rousing the Gordons in the north.

Before her lords, Mary formally repudiated the deeds of abdication and issued a proclamation excoriating James—"a spurious bastard"— and his supporters. Gently, smilingly, she asked the Protestant Argyll why he had deserted James to join her.

"Because all of us, Protestants and Catholics alike, are victims of his greed," he said. "He strips us of all we possess." From his belt he took a tiny velvet box. "Lady Lethington was able to save this for Your Majesty, and asked me to give it to you."

It was the heart-shaped diamond ring Elizabeth had sent five years before, pledging her assistance in time of trouble.

"Thank you." Mary slipped the ring on her finger. "If need be, I will send it to remind Elizabeth of her pledge. We may need English troops."

Argyll was the most experienced soldier Mary had, and she placed him in command of her forces. He advised that she march to Lord Fleming's nearly impregnable fortress of Dumbarton on the coast north of Glasgow.

"But James is in Glasgow, directly in our line of march," Mary said. "Doubtless he has sent for the big guns at Stirling. We have little artillery and many of our weapons are outmoded. We'd best avoid battle until our forces are larger. If only Charles will send troops—"

"His troops can land most easily at Dumbarton, Madam. But if Scots continue to join us, you'll not need them."

Scots clogged the roads to Hamilton—brutish, undisciplined Westerners, Borderers, men from Fife and Lothian. They came armed with broadswords, axes, bows, pikes, hackbuts. Within a week, six thousand were camped about the palace.

Spies reported that James had only thirty-five hundred men, and insisted he would not dare attack on the road to Dumbarton. "Even at worst," Lord Herries said, "Your Majesty could flee to France from Dumbarton. Here you are vulnerable."

Finally, on May 13th Mary, mounted on a Spanish jennet, gave the signal to march to Dumbarton. She had no royal standard, no jeweled corselet. In the rumpled black gown in which she had escaped Lochleven and a helmet borrowed from a mosstrooper, pistols at her belt, she headed her army north along the Clyde under a sky gashed red with sunrise.

Leading an advance guard of two thousand men, Mary approached Glasgow. In her path above Govan Moor, the village of Langside snuggled on a hilltop. She rode toward it, shielding her eyes from the sun, then caught her breath in panic as Lord Claude Hamilton yelled an order.

"Halt! *Ambush!*"

Above her the hill was crisscrossed with bushes, cottages and kail-yards. The sun struck the spears and helmets of kneeling men half-hidden by hedgerows. Quickly, shouting for George and Willie Douglas, Lords Fleming, Livingstone and Herries to follow her, Mary turned and raced half a mile to Cathcart Knowe, which commanded a view of village, hill and moor.

She was certain that her forces could take the hill. Proudly she watched while two thousand Hamiltons, banners aloft, rode up the narrow defile. James's hackbuteers sprang up on both sides with sudden, savage fire. Swept by a rain of bullets, her clansmen fell back, dead and wounded men and horses plunging down on the troops behind them. Kirkcaldy opened cannon fire from a nearby ridge on Mary's spearmen who struggled up the hill, trampling their fallen comrades. Panting, gasping at its summit, they were met by James's pikemen—fresh, cool, professional butchers.

While Mary's troops flung their long spears against a wall of massed steel, swaying backward and forward, James's bowmen were engaging her cavalry to the rear. Argyll's men and horses screamed through a crossfire of arrows and fell, choking the path of her foot soldiers who pressed forward to scale the corpse-littered, blood-slippery hill.

Through sun, smoke, incredulous tears, Mary watched forty minutes of carnage. Kirkcaldy, Balfour, Lindsay and their troops charged into her pikemen on the moor and sent them reeling back with hackbut fire. At the same time, James and his men charged Argyll's cavalry. She saw Argyll half-rise in his saddle, lift his broadsword, shout a command to advance—and suddenly tumble from his horse.

Her troops, now leaderless, fell back in complete disorder. A few of her Borderers, dripping blood and gripping broken pikes, tried to rally. James's Highlanders howled down on them with axes and broadswords, and those who survived threw down their weapons and ran for their lives.

Mary stared at her fleeing troops, the staggering, screaming wounded, the open-bellied horses writhing on the moor. At least three hundred dead, five hundred wounded, thousands scattering in panic before James's pursuing horsemen. She saw a wounded Borderer knife himself, and hid her face in her hands. But she could not drown out the tortured screams of men and horses.

"Madam, you must flee!" Herries' voice was sharp with fear. "You dare not linger—they will trap you!"

She turned a white, nerve-twitching face. The agony of the men on the hill and on the moor seemed her own. Their screams went through her like fire.

"Madam, look!" Willie Douglas shouted. "Look at Lord James!"

James was pointing to her, evidently ordering his men to take her captive. As they started toward her, Herries said, "We'll make for the Border!"

She spurred down the far side of the hill after Herries, Lords Fleming and Livingstone pounding behind her with George and Willie. Her mind was a red blank of horror. Where Herries led she would follow, but beyond obedience she had no thought.

They thundered through moors, past the Black Loch. Evading the town of Kilmarnock, they hurtled the Muirkirk Hills to Sanquhar, then on to the Valley of the Nith. For ten minutes they stopped at a charcoal-burner's hut for buttermilk and oatcakes, then fled on through sunset, twilight, night.

Finally, sixty miles from Langside, they were in terrain that Herries knew like his own heartbeat—Bothwell's Border country, desolate and wild. Skirting Dumfries, they took a path that led past a peel tower to a barn.

"My barn," Lord Herries said. "You can sleep here safely, Madam."

She dismounted. Lord Fleming carried her into sweet, hay-smelling darkness. She was asleep before she touched the bed of straw.

But two hours later, before dawn, they were off again in chill darkness that turned gray, wet, windy. A storm met them head-on, and they clenched their teeth and bowed their heads as the west wind howled in from the Solway Firth and the Irish Sea. In midafternoon the sun pushed through racing clouds, and fearful of being seen, they took refuge in a ruined and deserted convent. Willie gathered berries for them, and Mary slept on the hard cloister walk until Lord Herries roused her at nightfall.

"We go to Dundrennan," he said.

Dazed, trembling, questionless, she stumbled after him to her horse. She had the vague idea that Dundrennan was one of his castles, some last outpost of her kingdom. Oh God, she thought, if Bothwell were here and we were riding toward Hermitage! A strong man, a strong fortress—and sleep.

On and on through a calm, starry night, down deep ravines, skirting treacherous bogs, jumping, plunging, climbing. The district of Galloway, shepherds watching their white-faced sheep and foxes running the moonlit hills. The tiny, gable-roofed village of Kirkcudbright, its candles snuffed, its gardens a-dream. A mirage of peace where folk slept safely and roused from featherbeds to wonder at hoofbeats at this ungodly hour of midnight. Kirkcudbright . . . Mary found that her eyes were wet. To be a ruffle-capped kailwife asleep in her husband's arms while the cat dozed by the turf fire . . . to have the certainty of tomorrow.

Salt wind dried her tears and crusted her lashes. She sniffed the sea. Ahead in a secluded glen, white Gothic arches rose from orchards and gardens emerald-green in the moonlight. Another mirage, she thought—a holy sanctuary standing against the fury of the Reformation.

"Dundrennan Abbey." Lord Herries said.

They checked their horses at the outer court. Startled, sleepy-eyed lay brothers with lanterns lit their way up the east walk to the chapter house.

Monks roused Abbot Maxwell. Softly on sandaled feet, he entered the great vaulted chamber, an old man in a dark robe that whispered along the stone floor.

"Welcome, wayfarers," he said.

"Fugitives," Mary said. "I am your Queen."

She stood in her muddy, thorn-torn gown, her briared hair tangling down her back, her face grayed with dust. Meeting his incredulous eyes, she pulled from her bosom the ruby crucifix, kissed it, extended it that he might see Francis' initials in diamonds on the back.

"Father, we are hunted! Shelter us, give us food. We have ridden more than ninety miles . . ."

"Ride no more, Madam. Fear no more." The abbot knelt, kissed Mary's grimy little hand. "God has brought you to haven."

Monks led Mary up a staircase to a bare rock-walled room with a stone floor. They lit a fire in the hearth and brought her cold mutton, fruit, honey, oatbread, wine. But she had no appetite. On a hard pallet she stretched her stiff body and prayed for sleep.

But she could not sleep. There was no peace for her in Scotland, no refuge. She would not place Dundrennan and its monks in James's plundering path. Tomorrow she must go.

Where? France? Doubtless her brother-in-law King Charles would welcome her. But she remembered his unnatural lust as a child and shuddered. Catherine loathed her. The Cardinal would have no interest in her, since she was not a marriageable pawn. And it would be shaming to return, a ragged beggar, to a country where she had once ruled supreme. A Stuart could not live on crumbs flung by Valois, De Medici and De Guise. Life at court would be degrading, and she would not retire to a convent as long as Bothwell lived.

Spain? Difficult to reach, a perilous, pirate-threatened voyage. She would need a ship and trustworthy sailors who would not deliver her to James. And if she reached Spain, what could she expect of Philip? A strange dark spider of a man to whom she had no tie of kinship, only that of religion. He had never forgiven her heretic marriage to Bothwell. And like the Cardinal he would have no use for her if he could not marry her off to his advantage.

Italy—hopeless. The Pope considered that she had betrayed Scotland to the Reformation.

But there was England. Elizabeth had saved her life from James, and would save it again. Shrewd, vain, touchy, vacillating, once treacherous but now her friend. Had not Elizabeth reviled James and refused to recognize him as Regent? Did she not regard the little King as a mere pretender? And beyond all, did she not have an almost fanatic reverence for the divine right of queenship and a consequent loathing for insurrection?

Mary thought back to the note Elizabeth had written her in 1562, sent with the diamond ring. At the time it had seemed just another diplomatic gesture, a graceful insincerity. But now Mary seized upon it and tried to recall its wording. *"I send Your Majesty this diamond in pledge of friendship. Should you ever find yourself in extremity you have only to return it and I will come to your assistance."*

Elizabeth would not break her royal vow. Her word—and Bothwell's—were the last integrities left in a world turned treacherous.

At dawn Mary wrote Elizabeth, pleading for her help. She enclosed the diamond in the message, and a monk dispatched it to a fisherman who would carry it to Cumberland. Then Mary summoned her lords.

"We are going to England," she said.

"Blood of Jesus!" Fleming stared at her. "We dare not, Madam!"

"I know what you fear," she said calmly. "You are a good Catholic and mistrust heretics. But Queen Elizabeth has pledged me her friendship. Her recent letters have professed her desire to help me."

Herries' lean, weather-harshed face was shocked, his gray eyes dark with anxiety. "Would Your Majesty flee one trap only to enter another?"

"England is no trap, but a refuge. Elizabeth will defend my right of rule as she defends her own, welcome my supporters, lend me troops and gold."

"Your Majesty reckons without her advisors," Livingstone said.

"Cecil will not allow her to be swayed by sentiment. His only concern with divine rights of rule are *her* rights. To him, Your Majesty is a troublemaker to whom disgruntled English subjects will rally, whom English Catholics will seek to enthrone as Queen. From his view he has every reason to fear and abhor you."

"But I do not seek the English throne," she said, "at the moment."

Livingstone smiled wearily. "You see, Madam? You admit it is a dream close to your heart. You consider yourself Queen of England and Elizabeth an upstart bastard. Cecil is aware of that, even if Elizabeth is not. He has the guile and ruthlessness of the Cardinal, the dark, scheming patience of Philip, the Puritanism of Knox. Put yourself in his power and you are lost."

"Elizabeth is ruler, not Cecil!"

They argued for an hour. Finally, exasperated, she said, "I command you to take me to England."

Reluctantly, they sent George and Willie Douglas a mile to the coast to arrange for a boat. At noon, escorted by monks, she and her little company rode across the hill to the Abbey Burnfoot. A fishing smack rocked at anchor, sails full in the wind. Far across the Solway, Mary could see the vague, rocky outline of Cumberland.

George Douglas knelt in the sand. "Madam, Willie and I do not presume to advise you. But we beg that you go anywhere but to England."

Mary turned to the boatman. "How long a voyage?"

"Four hours with a fair wind, Madam." He squinted at the sky. "The weather could not be better."

"Then let us go."

The Abbot and his monks knelt to pray as Mary and her men embarked. Beyond the hill the abbey bells rang out farewell.

Her hair scarfed against the breeze, Mary watched the receding shore. There spread the western Borderlands, flowery and fair on this May day, a vast lilac-and-azure garden. Beyond to the east lay Bothwell's fierce hills and Hermitage Castle forever guarding southern Scotland. Her thoughts, like balefire, swept northward through her kingdom. She blessed the moors, the sky-thrusting mountains, the valley-cuddled villages. People she had never known, places she had never seen. The Hebrides, islands scattered like dark sea-polished rocks . . . she stretched her heart to every one.

She flung back her head and shouted in the teeth of the wind, Bothwell's rage in her voice. "By God, I'll return and take what is mine!"

CHAPTER FOURTEEN

I.

THE VILLAGE OF WORKINGTON, Cumberland, welcomed Mary with astonished enthusiasm, for northern England was strongly Catholic. As she walked through the town she was cheered and flowers were strewn in her path. In her ragged black gown, her torn Jersey hose, her muddy shoes, she swept regally erect past kneeling people who spoke her name like a prayer.

Lodged in the Town Hall, she wrote immediately to Elizabeth detailing her troubles . . . *I entreat you to fetch me as soon as you can for I am in piteous condition not only for a Queen but for a gentlewoman, for I have nothing in the world but what I had on when I made my escape . . . Have pity . . . upon my extreme misfortune . . .*

Crowds of Catholic gentlemen rode in from the surrounding countryside to welcome Mary, to marvel at her white, exhausted beauty, to pledge their devotion. They told her that they respected Elizabeth, but loathed her Protestant advisors—Cecil, Leicester and the Earl of Bedford. They felt that Mary's presence in England would give Catholics new hope, new impetus to fight the Reformation.

Elizabeth's High Sheriff Richard Lowther thundered into Workington heading an armed escort. With enormous pomp and pageantry he conducted Mary and her men to Carlisle Castle to await Elizabeth's envoy.

The castle was beautifully situated among gardens, blossoming orchards and glossy, landscaped playing greens. Mary made allowances for her gloomy bedroom and presence chamber, for Elizabeth had not expected a royal visitor. *She is more than kind,* Mary thought —*her tact is boundless. Rather than embarrass me by bringing me to Hampton Court in rags, she secludes me here. Doubtless at this very moment she is sending me seamstresses, jewelers, wigmakers.*

Lord Scrope was her host, and his plump lady lent Mary a violet lace mantle to hide her tattered gown. Her hair bound in violet ribbons, she wandered the gardens, the spacious oak-paneled halls, impressed by the many servants in splendid uniforms. Poor Scotland, she thought—my finest palace was not so staffed as this country castle, where even soldiers wear ruffs and velvet hats and neck chains of gold . . .

A week passed. Mary's lords grumbled that Elizabeth's silence was at once sinister and insulting, but she upbraided them for impatience. Elizabeth must arrange special quarters for her at Hampton Court, engage servants, attend to the thousand details of welcoming pageants. She was obviously too busy to write.

On May 28th, twelve days after Mary's arrival in England, Elizabeth's vice-chamberlain, Sir Francis Knollys, arrived at Carlisle. Concealing her excitement, Mary received him in her presence chamber.

"Her Majesty bids Your Majesty welcome. She returns your diamond and sends you this letter."

Mary broke the Great Seal of England, took the letter to the faint light from the leaded window and read it. Slowly she turned, her shoulders slumped, color drained from her face.

"I cannot—I simply cannot believe it," she said.

"Ah, Madam, you must understand my mistress's position," Knollys said, fawning toward her. "She is sick at heart over your misfortunes—they tear at her very soul—but she cannot receive you until you are cleared of complicity in your late husband's murder. It is — " He reddened under her accusing eyes — "a most delicate situation. Her Majesty is the Virgin Queen, untouched by scandal, and Your Majesty has — " He floundered, mopped his face with a bit of lace. "Your Majesty is—eh — "

"Tarnished?"

"Indeed not! But some folk think so, and until you are cleared, and Her Majesty has every faith that you will be, it is impossible for her to see you."

"But I *must* see her!" Mary said desperately. "I must tell her all that has happened."

"She knows what has happened, Madam, and her sympathy is profound. But until you are cleared—"

"Jesu, I am not on trial!"

"Some sort of inquiry must be set up, whereby both Your Majesty and your brother may present evidence, a meeting of conciliation—"

He stopped, open-mouthed at the fury in her face.

"Tell your mistress that I will leave for France at once!"

"Ah, no! Her Majesty is adamant that you not seek French aid."

For she dreads a French invasion of Scotland, should Charles decide to smash James from power and enthrone me. She fears France might attack England. She knows my presence would rally the Catholics . . .

"*She* is adamant!" Mary exclaimed. "So am I! I do not need her permission to travel. But I had hoped—I had believed that she—"

In sudden tearful rage she threw off the lace mantle. "Look at me, ragged, dirty—all but barefoot! She returns the diamond she gave me, but dishonors the pledge it represents!"

"Madam!"

"Aye, tell her that! But likely you'll not for fear of a slapping, slipper-hurling tantrum!"

"Your Majesty misjudges her gentle heart. She will do all in her power to help you. She has sent you attire." He summoned a page, who brought in an oak chest and opened it.

Mary removed the contents piece by piece—two small strips of worn velvet, two pairs of shoes and two torn linen shifts.

Straightening, she turned to Sir Francis and smiled bitterly. "Tell Her Majesty I am overwhelmed by her generosity."

"I—eh—the maidservant must have packed the wrong . . . Surely, a mistake—"

"No," Mary said. "The mistake is mine. You may go."

He bowed out. For a long time she wept. Then she sent for Lord Herries, told him what had happened and showed him Elizabeth's letter. "We go to France."

Gently he took her arm and led her to the window.

"What do you see, Madam?"

"Scotland," she said, her eyes on the far green hills.

"And below in the yard?"

"Soldiers."

"Placed here to prevent Your Majesty's escape. We tried to warn you. Carlisle is no guest house, Madam! It is your prison."

II.

Throughout northern England, Catholic nobles and gentry gathered to hatch plots for Mary's escape. They met in meadows, in taverns behind locked doors. In July, Elizabeth, nervous of Mary's proximity to the roused Border, moved her to the stronger castle of Bolton in Yorkshire. Sir Francis Knollys and Lord and Lady Scrope were her warders. Armed guards patrolled the halls, the courtyard. When Mary exercised, a hundred troops watched her.

After her initial shock, Mary resumed the strategy so successful at Lochleven—charming her jailers. The men allowed her to bowl and run hares. Lady Scrope became her fast friend and smuggled mail for her. Mary Seton and Jane Kennedy came from Scotland, bringing what they could wrest from Mary's wardrobe at Holyrood —one taffeta gown, a cloak, sleeves, slippers, face paints and saddle covers. Her little household was supplemented by tiring women, pages, an apothecary, a French and a Scots secretary.

Mary sent Lord Herries to Elizabeth to plead her freedom, but Elizabeth refused to receive him. Mary tried to send Lord Fleming to France to enlist Charles's aid, but he was forbidden to leave England. Elizabeth's envoys repeatedly begged Mary to effect her release by clearing herself of murder.

"I'll not appear in any court," she told them. "Elizabeth is not my sovereign and I'll not be judged by her. There will be no trial."

Not a trial, they insisted—a friendly conference at which Mary could air her grievances. James would be asked to justify his rebellion. He and Mary would each present commissioners, and Elizabeth's Council would arbitrate. They swore that nothing would be disclosed which could damage Mary's honor. If Mary was cleared, Elizabeth would restore her to the Scottish throne, provided she relinquished her claims to the English throne.

Knollys said, "Her Majesty wishes above all to prove your innocence."

"Aye," Mary said bitterly. "So that the Virgin Queen may not be soiled by kinship with a murderous harlot."

Gradually they dulled her resistance. She agreed at last to an October conference at York.

"But I'll not appear," she said haughtily. "I'll not acknowledge your Queen's jurisdiction."

"We ask only that you appoint commissioners to represent you."

She appointed Lords Herries, Livingstone and Boyd, Cockburn of Skirling, the Bishop of Ross and the Abbot of Kilwinning. James would appear personally, along with Morton, Lindsay, Lethington, Buchanan and Lennox. Elizabeth would be represented by three arbitrators—Sir Ralph Sadler, the Earl of Sussex and Thomas Howard, the Duke of Norfolk.

"I am pleased that Norfolk is to arbitrate," Lady Scrope said, seated with Mary in the fading light of a September afternoon. "He is a fair and generous man." Demurely she added, "He is my brother."

"Indeed?" Mary put down her embroidery. "I hear that he is the highest and wealthiest peer in England."

"What you will not hear publicly is that he admires Your Majesty beyond all women."

"Surely not beyond Queen Elizabeth?"

Lady Scrope lowered her voice, glanced about uneasily to make certain they were alone in the presence chamber. "He is in love with you."

"Impossible! We have never met. He has never seen me."

"Many men love you who have never seen you. And Thomas has collected your portraits for years." She dimpled. "You have survived three wives in his heart. He is thrice a widower, yet only thirty-three." She took from her belt a folded parchment. "He asked me to give you this."

Mary lit a taper and read a timorous love letter. She knew that Norfolk, born wealthy, had further enriched himself by his marriages, choosing his wives to gain land and manors. And now, she thought, he is insatiate. He wants more power. Perhaps he even considers wedding me, enforcing my claims to the English throne and proclaiming himself King. If he has such a dream, I will encourage it to effect my escape.

Dreamily, Mary looked up from the letter. "Beautiful, eloquent. But—"

"But of course," Lady Scrope said hastily, "Your Majesty is married."

"When one has not seen one's husband in more than a year he becomes a blur," Mary lied. "My memory of Bothwell is fast fading."

So she would tell the world, for diplomacy's sake. But even now Bothwell's Danish courier and her page Horsey carried messages across the moors, across the autumn-dark sea. She belonged to Bothwell too wholly, too fiercely, to forget him. The bruising beauty of their love could not be erased by time. His memory brought her alternately pain and hope, despair and courage. Horsey said Bothwell was heavily guarded at Malmoe, for Frederick was awed almost superstitiously by his strength and resourcefulness. Armed men served his food, while halberdiers watched from the doorway. When he walked in the gardens a small army followed. Yet Bothwell wrote confidently: *Fear not, love, we will be together ere the year has died.*

While Lady Scrope prattled about Norfolk, Mary stood at the window. Sunset bathed the Yorkshire moors in clear gold light. Does Bothwell stand at his window, she wondered, marking the death of summer, seeing my face with the eyes of his heart? Does my thought meet his at this moment?

"It is well that Your Majesty forgets your husband," Lady Scrope said. "Shocking man! Vile reputation! I am told King Frederick allows him wenches . . ."

Mary looked down at his ring. *Keep Trust.*

Always, she vowed. Forever.

III.

The Conference of York began on October 4th. Through her commissioners, Mary accused James of treason, insurrection, forcing her abdication on threat of death and usurping the Regency. James justified his imprisonment of her on the grounds that she had married her husband's murderer. He said she had voluntarily resigned her crown and constituted him Regent without his knowledge—he being in France at the time.

To Mary's wry amusement, he did not charge her with complicity in Darnley's murder. Apparently he realized that the subject of Darnley's death was a two-edged sword and feared she might conceivably have a second copy of the murder bond involving two of his commissioners, Lethington and Morton.

Herries wrote Mary: *If Elizabeth expected a show of firespears, she is sore disappointed, for the conference thus far is almost genial, neither side willing to produce evidence or say much. However I like it not that Lethington is engaging in private talks with the English arbitrators. I fear he trafficks treachery . . .*

She found that he did. Lethington wrote her, enclosing copies of the letters found in Bothwell's silver casket. *Would you, Madam, not prefer to withdraw charges against your brother, lest these documents bring you shame?*

Appalled, but not intimidated, Mary decided that her only recourse was to disclaim the letters. She wrote her commissioners: *In case they allege they have writings of mine . . . they are false and feigned, forged and invented by themselves to my dishonor and slander, and there are many in Scotland that can counterfeit my handwriting.*

Elizabeth, anxious that the conference be conducted under her surveillance, ordered it moved to London, and appointed Cecil and Leicester as additional arbitrators. The inquiry resumed at Westminster in the Painted Chamber.

Mary, following the testimony through Herries' letters, realized that her commissioners were more devoted than shrewd, children in the cool, unscrupulous hands of James and Lethington. Then suddenly James released a thunderbolt. He stated that Mary had plotted and commanded Darnley's death and that Bothwell was merely her tool.

Infuriated, Mary wrote to Elizabeth demanding to appear in her own defense. She would name Darnley's murderers, two of whom sat at the council table. But Elizabeth played for time and evaded the issue.

Mary spent her twenty-sixth birthday in prayer. But she learned that on that very day James placed the silver casket on the council table. He produced eight letters that Mary had written to Bothwell and several of her sonnets. Cecil and the other English commissioners read and examined, their fingers winking jewels in the light of oaken candelabra. They conferred, exclaimed, shuddered. Cecil, blue eyes frosty, mouth tight, studied the long letter written from Darnley's bedchamber in Glasgow.

Mary's commissioners protested that these were flagrant forgeries, and were silenced by knowing smiles. Then, on Mary's instructions, they retired from the conference, branding it an unlawful trial in which the defendant was not allowed to appear.

A week later the conference ended. Summing up, Elizabeth announced that nothing had been proved to the discredit of James and his supporters, nor had they in turn produced anything "whereby the Queen of England should conceive any evil opinion of the Queen her good sister." Nevertheless Elizabeth's Privy Council informed Mary that because of the foul charges against her, the Queen could not receive her without blemishing Elizabeth's own honor.

Completely confused at the inconclusive verdict, Mary asked Herries what it meant. "How can it be that I am neither cleared nor condemned?"

"Elizabeth walks a slippery ledge," he said. "Had she condemned you, your punishment would have posed a terrible problem. If she executed you, every Catholic in Christendom would demand vengeance. Philip would assuredly attack England—perhaps with Charles's aid—and smash Protestantism in Europe forever. Further, Your Majesty would be a martyr—and that her jealous heart could not abide."

"Nor could her jealous heart abide to clear me!"

"Had she cleared you, she would be forced to invade Scotland and re-establish you on your throne, to spend blood and gold. But this way she has achieved her aim at no expense—damaging your reputation while maintaining the pretension of objective arbitrator. Now she can detain you in 'honorable custody.'"

"On what grounds?"

"Legally on none, but you are in her power. Nor is she compelled to receive you."

"She is afraid to receive me."

"True, because you would outshine her at court and set every man a-dream. All she has heard from her envoys is talk of your beauty, your grace, your allure. She knows that in your poorest gown, unpainted, you are more dazzling than she in her state robes."

"Always that savage jealousy," Mary said. "Yet if I could see her, talk to her, I know I could win her to me."

"And precisely for that reason Cecil will make certain you never meet. Perhaps Elizabeth too is fearful of your charm."

Mary walked the length of her presence chamber, dry-eyed, shoulders erect, her taffeta skirt scuffling sweet hay. Back and forth she walked, tiger-lithe, her eyes black in a marble-white face.

"Do not despair," Herries said, his own voice despairing. "Philip and Charles will protest."

"Aye, but that's all they will do. Were I dead at her hands, they would take vengeance. But alive they will let me rot."

"Madam, cease your intrigues, at least for a time. Rest, pray. There is God—"

"There is Norfolk," she said.

"Do you think he will press suit to a woman so blackened? Elizabeth has wind of his interest in you, for he tried to hush Lord James's murder charge. I'm told she confronted him—archly, as is her way when she has no proof: 'A little bird tells me you would a-wooing go to the Queen of Scots.' And Norfolk said, 'Madam, would I seek to wed a notorious adulteress, a murderess? I love to sleep on a safe pillow. What would I gain? In my bowling green at Norwich I account myself as good a prince as the Queen of Scots, and the revenues of Scotland are not comparable to my own.' Madam, forget Norfolk. He is Protestant."

She smiled, her eyes cynical. "Norfolk is a man—and ambitious."

IV.

Lady Scrope assured Mary that Norfolk had tricked Elizabeth. He still loved Mary ardently. If he felt there was hope for his suit, he would propose marriage.

"Write to him that there is indeed hope," Mary said. "But I am amazed that the casket letters did not dissuade him."

"Lethington hinted to him that they were forged."

"*Lethington* hinted that?" Mary asked unbelievingly.

"Aye. He told my brother Your Majesty is not black as painted. He encourages the idea of marriage."

So Lethington has switched to my cause, she thought. Perhaps he resents James's power, finds his hypocrisy too distasteful even for his strong stomach. Perhaps in his strange twisted heart he loves me and seeks my freedom.

"My brother Norfolk loves you more than ever, Madam, for now he considers you a martyr."

Now he considers the throne of England . . .

"He would turn Catholic for Your Majesty, and he has allied

himself with the Northern Catholics who plot your escape. The leaders are the Earls of Northumberland and Westmoreland."

"I wonder how I should establish contact with them."

"Simple, Madam. Westmoreland is my brother. You may write to him."

Mary laughed. "I am indeed fortunate in your brothers—and in your friendship."

But Lady Scrope's usefulness came to a sudden end. Elizabeth, evidently suspicious of the Scropes, ordered Mary to Tutbury Castle in Staffordshire.

It was a vile, sunless place, more a dilapidated hunting lodge than a castle. Mary's apartments were crack-walled and the thin, rotting tapestries could not prevent drafts. The roof leaked so that she and her ladies had to raise woolen tents and canopies to keep dry in rainy weather. There were no drains to the privies and a constant stench pervaded the castle. Mary complained to Elizabeth of cesspools beneath her window, of having to exercise in a potato patch. Mold wiped from the furniture reappeared in four days. Mary suffered from damp, from cold. Her bones ached and cramped, and her apothecary diagnosed rheumatism.

The Earl of Shrewsbury and his wife, Countess Bess of Hardwick, were Mary's new jailers. The Earl was gentle and kindly, but terrified of Elizabeth. He and his wife demanded to see all of Mary's outgoing letters and warned her against secret correspondence.

With George and Willie Douglas, Mary worked out elaborate stratagems to send messages. Letters were slipped between the sole and lining of Jane Kennedy's slipper, hidden in hollowed fire logs, smuggled in outgoing laundry. Seton went to the village with "alms for the poor," and paid carters and traveling peddlers to act as couriers. Mary studied cipher passionately. With her Scots and French secretaries, she worked out a code and dispatched its key to her correspondents, who learned it and burned it. She doubted that even Cecil with all his wit could decipher her code.

Thus she kept contact with the rulers of Europe and Catholics in the north. The Bishop of Ross became her secret agent, his headquarters in London. Lethington pledged himself to her cause, and urged her to accept Norfolk's proposal of marriage. *He is your chief hope, popular with Catholics and Protestants alike. If any man can rally England to your cause, he can.*

And so she accepted Norfolk's diamond engagement ring. To Bothwell she wrote: *I have naught but scorn for this opportunist duke. Believe me, our affection is entirely political. Our love letters would amuse you, so pallid they are. But I must use Norfolk to gain my freedom. He frets that I will not divorce you, so to display my good faith I shall have to make a gesture toward seeking a divorce. I feel sure James will not permit it, for fear I will wed profitably. But if by miracle he should, and papers are sent to you, for God's sake refuse to sign them. I would rather rot here than divorce you . . .*

Bothwell replied that if a divorce would win her freedom he would sign the papers . . . *for I know you will not wed Norfolk nor any other until we are free to marry again.*

The winter passed dismally. Mary's rheumatism grew worse, and she had a constant cold. But though she stayed abed huddled under rabbitskin robes, she was never idle. Her messages spread throughout Europe—feelers to Rome, to Spain, to France. Cautiously, deviously, through agents who moved shadow-like through England, Philip sanctioned the Catholic plot. He sent the conspirators six thousand crowns, and promised that when the northern lords were strong he would invade England, depose Elizabeth and place Mary on the throne under Spanish protection.

This was her dream through the long, dripping days of February. With Seton, she wove new tapestries for the damp, mold-covered walls, embroidered a cloth of state to canopy a chair that served as throne. Needle threaded with gold, she stitched French phrases between thistles and fleurs-de-lis. Countess Bess Shrewsbury gushed that Her Majesty's needlework was exquisite, but she did not understand the words that glittered on the satin canopy.

"What do they mean?" she asked.

"They are merely pieties," Mary smiled.

She had no intention of discussing religion, for she sensed hostility under Bess's assumed deference. She resents me as an interloper in her household, Mary thought. At the same time she is careful not to offend me lest some day I become her queen.

Bess was about fifty. Elaborate headdresses adorned her crimped red-gray curls, and her brows were fashionably thin above small, shrewd brown eyes. Her figure was full and handsome and she frequently remarked that she herself looked far more regal than Elizabeth, a poor stalk of a woman for all her padding.

She astonished Mary with the vilest slander of Elizabeth. At first Mary thought Bess was Elizabeth's spy seeking to trap her into confidences. But soon she realized the venom was genuine. Bess evidently hated all women who had more power or prestige than herself. Her urge to dominate was manifest in her bullying of servants, her children and her patient, meek-mannered husband. Mary treated her cordially, trusted her not at all.

In March, Mary sent Lord Herries to Scotland to inform her friends of the English Catholic plot and bid them to stand ready

to aid in the Spanish invasion. Herries and the Duke de Chatelherault were seized by James and flung into Edinburgh Castle, now
commanded by Kirkcaldy of Grange. Then riding with armed troops,
James sought out Mary's adherents and ravaged their lands, plundering and burning their castles and leaving a smoking waste from
Dumfries to Inverness, from Dunbar to Glasgow.

Mary was ill with fury, and the old pain in her side returned,
digging and thrusting. She felt that a curse lay on all who befriended
her. When Charles sent installments of her dowry from Touraine,
she dispatched much of it to the men James had victimized, asking
them not to use it in her interest but for themselves and their
families. One comfort—the Douglases of Lochleven had not been
harmed.

Her rheumatism grew worse. Late in April the Shrewsburys took
pity on her condition and moved her, with Elizabeth's permission,
to stately Wingfield Manor in Derbyshire. In warmth and sunlight
she improved, and sent George Douglas to France as her unofficial
ambassador to plead help from Charles.

That summer Elizabeth grew so pale and thin that Leicester and
other members of her Privy Council feared she might die, and they
met in secret to determine her successor. Mary's claims as heiress to
the crown were invulnerable. Unknown to Elizabeth and Cecil, they
petitioned Mary to start divorce proceedings, with a view to wedding
Norfolk and mounting the throne in case of Elizabeth's death.

Dismayed by the thought of divorce but delighted by the Council's
acknowledgement of her claims, Mary wrote to Lethington asking
him to act in her behalf and explore the possibilities of divorce. But
the Scottish Parliament pointed out that if Mary was in earnest,
she had only to ask Frederick to execute Bothwell. It forbade her
divorce by a vote of forty to nine.

Mary was relieved. After all, she did not need Norfolk to effect
either her enthronement or her escape. In the autumn Philip's
troops would land on the east coast, join her supporters and liberate
her.

On a gray August morning a courier from Scotland brought word
that James had charged Lethington with conspiring in the murder
of Darnley and imprisoned him in Edinburgh Castle. For an obvious
reason, Mary thought. James knows Lethington is on my side.

She also learned that Bothwell's page Paris had been extradited
from Denmark to Scotland. At St. Andrews under torture he
screamed that Bothwell had mined the house at Kirk O'Field and
stored gunpowder in Mary's bedchamber. On the scaffold a few days
later he recanted his "confession" before he was hanged.

In early autumn, Bess came to Mary's apartments and told her to prepare to leave. "Your Majesty is to pack at once. We return to Tutbury."

"Jesu!" Mary said. "That drafty place will be my death! Why does Queen Elizabeth—"

"She is howling angry." Bess plumped down uninvited in a chair. "She learned that Norfolk proposed to you, and she summoned him to London and tongue-whipped him to a whimpering babe."

Worried lest he had disclosed the Catholic plot, Mary asked, "She is angry merely because he proposed to me?"

"Aye—and because you encouraged His Grace. And now as punishment for all the trouble you have caused, we must return to that bedpot of a castle!"

"How dare you speak to me thus? Tutbury is your castle. It is you who have failed to cleanse it, install drains, repair the roof and walls. Yet you are rich on the corpses of three husbands."

"And you are poor on the corpses of two!"

"You impudent slut! You have come here unannounced. You have dared sit in my presence without my permission. These things I have overlooked because we are doomed to live together and I prefer harmony. But you have arrogantly abused your privileges. Unless you can give me good reason, I shall write the Queen and have you removed from my service."

Bess rose, her head bowed, her chin puckered.

"Why do you dislike me?" Mary asked gently. "Come, tell me frankly."

"Because—" The words came out roughly, unevenly—"my husband is enamored of you."

"Nonsense!"

"He does not look upon me or other women as he looks upon Your Majesty—as though dazzled. If ever I saw a man in love—"

"But that is not true!" Lord Shrewsbury had never been more than courteous, a courtly, graying man in poor health. A troubled man serving three women—Elizabeth, his wife and his captive.

Bess said, "Your Majesty is beautiful and, what appeals even more to a man, helpless."

"I do nothing to wile your husband," Mary said coldly. "If you find the situation so insufferable, appeal to Her Majesty to relieve you of your duty."

"I dare not! She honors us by this trust."

"Then do not speak to me of this again," Mary said. "And dare not presume you are my equal."

Bess knelt in a flurry of black brocaded skirts. "Ah, Madam, forgive me. I am an old fool."

"Rise," Mary said. "You have nothing to fear."

But *I* have, she thought. Bess is primitive, generous one moment, savage the next. A vastly dangerous woman.

"Then we may be friends, Madam?"

"Of course," Mary said.

V.

Three days after Mary's return to Tutbury, soldiers with drawn dags burst into her apartments and ransacked her wardrobe and chests. Outraged, she watched them strip her bed, tear the canopy off her "throne," search her desk for correspondence. Fortunately she had destroyed all letters from the Catholic plotters. Bothwell's were safe in her memory. By mutual agreement, she and Norfolk had returned each other's messages as soon as they were read, and she had burned hers.

The troopers stood sullenly in the debris, evading Mary's glance, whispering among themselves. They ordered Bess to search her and left the room. Humiliated, furious, Mary stripped to her shift and shivered by the fire while Bess pawed over skirt, bodice, petticoats, shoes and hose.

"Dress, Madam."

Bess went to the door and yelled to the troopers that no letters were concealed in Mary's attire.

"I am sorry, Madam, but from now on your restrictions will be more severe," she said. "We are taking the lock from your door. Soldiers may raid your apartments at any time. The Queen is certain that you brew trouble—and God help us all if she's right."

On October 8th Elizabeth flung Norfolk into the Tower of London.

Mary was frantic. How much did Elizabeth know? Did she suspect the Catholic plot? Would Norfolk be tortured and betray the plans?

On a dark dawn in early November, she prayed at her makeshift altar. There *must* be a rising before Norfolk babbled the plot. Surely by now Philip's ships were inching through the mists of the North Sea. Surely her Scots were racing across the Border to join Northumberland, Westmoreland and their factions. Please God . . .

Two evenings later Mary was eating supper by the fire, when Lord Shrewsbury hurried into her presence chamber almost running on gouty legs.

"The north has risen to Your Majesty's cause! Northumberland and Westmoreland have entered Durham with six thousand men!"

Mary sprang from the table. "God be praised!"

"God is mocked, Madam. They heard Mass in Durham Cathedral,

burned the Protestant Bible and Book of Common Prayer, demolished the holy communion table, smashed the pulpit. They are riding toward Ripon and meeting no resistance. Obviously they are on the way here." He mopped his face, took a deep breath. "Please understand why I must place armed men in your apartments. It is not meant to humiliate you . . ."

He is a sick man, she thought, and a terrified one. Gently she said, "I understand. Do what you must." She was anxious to know whether Spaniards had landed but dared not ask. "Are there any foreign troops—I mean, Scots?"

"Aye, Scots. They gathered fast as a squall." He dragged to the door. "I have sent for reinforcements. Tutbury is poorly defended . . ." The sentence trailed out with him as he left the room.

Tutbury is ramshackle, Mary thought exultantly. Westmoreland could take it easily with a thousand men.

The next day one hundred soldiers rode in to supplement Shrewsbury's. The castle's defenses were strengthened with embankments, a rusty field gun rolled into the potato patch. Ten days passed without news, and Mary paced her chambers, prayed, alternately sang and shivered. Then she learned that Westmoreland had entered Ripon, marched bloodlessly through Tadcaster. She estimated that by now her rescuers must be less than sixty miles away.

Her old dream of empire was close as it had never been before. She visioned herself heading the army toward London, Catholics rallying through village after village. The struggle for the capital, victory bells pealing from Westminster to Land's End, echoing from cathedral to cathedral—Canterbury, Salisbury, Exeter—and north to the broken abbeys, where monks would dare light candles for the Mass.

A Catholic Britain—and she its rightful queen! She would be generous to Elizabeth, perhaps pension her to Ireland . . .

"Why do you laugh, Madam?" Seton asked.

"I was thinking of Bothwell as King of England," she said. "God help the pompous of this realm!"

That night, November 24th, Mary lay awake listening for hoofbeats. They could not be far now . . . thirty miles . . . twenty . . .

She dozed. Suddenly her bed curtains were jerked aside and she jolted awake. Bess Shrewsbury leaned above her with a taper.

"Rise quickly, Madam, and dress. We ride to Coventry . . ."

In Coventry, Mary was lodged at the Bull Inn and surrounded by armed men. Confined to two upper chambers, she endured another week of suspense. The Shrewsburys would tell her nothing.

By Lord George's nervousness and his wife's fawning manner, she guessed that her rescue was imminent. But to be without news was agonizing. Mary's servants were not allowed belowstairs. When Willie Douglas tried to approach the public room to eavesdrop as the soldiers talked, Bess boxed his ears and locked him in a vacant chamber.

At her barred window Mary watched the first snow fall, like lazy white feathers from an open pillowslip. Then she leaned forward excitedly. A courier galloped into the yard. Soldiers gathered about him, and a cheer went up. They tossed their helmets in the air and shouted to the innkeeper for wine. She heard the bells of Coventry ring out the doom of her hopes.

For Westmoreland's men had panicked. Deep in England without Spanish help, they scattered from the path of Elizabeth's advancing army. Her twelve thousand troops, led by Earls Warwick and Sussex, chased the rebels toward Scotland. Not a dag was fired, not a pike bloodied. Northumberland and Westmoreland escaped across the Border, but hundreds of their men were taken prisoner. In market towns eight hundred corpses swung on gibbets until the sun rotted them.

On the journey back to Tutbury Mary saw those corpses, grin-faced or faceless in wind-flapped garments. These are my victims, she thought, as surely as though hanged by my own hand. Farm boys, shepherds, coopers, crofters—lured to their deaths less by Catholic zeal than by the romance of my cause . . .

I shall cease my intrigues, she decided, resign myself to prison. I have shed enough blood on this earth.

That evening at Tutbury she told Seton her resolve. "I am finished with conspiring. Save for my letters to Bothwell, the Shrewsburys may see my correspondence, for it will be innocent. My webs will be woven only at the tapestry frame."

"Resignation is wise, Madam. When God intends your freedom, he will release you."

That was true. Mary sat down by the hearth, her hands idle in her lap. Wind whistled through the chinks in the roof, banged a broken shutter. Her spaniel put his paws on her skirt and jumped into her chair. Cheek snuggled against his coat, she stared at the crackling fire.

The future? Prayers. Embroidery. Books. A gray-granny's life. The masques over, the ballrooms forever darkened, the hunts ended. Never again a wild wet night on Arthur's Seat and her heart reeling under Bothwell's lips . . .

"I cannot resign myself!" she cried. "I *will* not!"

[527]

She rose, tumbling the dog from her lap, strode to the desk and sat down to write Norfolk.

Your Grace: Circumstances have delayed my writing to you, but think not that my devotion has altered or my faith wavered. Be of good cheer, for His Majesty of Spain, as Defender of the Faith, cannot forever procrastinate. I shall petition the Pope . . .

VI.

That January of 1570 news reached Mary of James's vengeance on rebel Scots. Those who escaped Elizabeth's army were cornered across the Border, ambushed in hill pockets, tortured and hanged. The gates and tolbooths of southern Scotland were piled with human arms and legs. There were tales of gruesome sport on the frozen moors—James's troops playing catchball with severed heads. Northumberland was seized and imprisoned in Lochleven.

From prison in Edinburgh Castle, Lethington wrote Mary of James's ravenous appetite for gold. He had sold to Elizabeth six ropes of Mary's pearls, a lacing of large pearls and twenty-five loose ones for three thousand pounds.

Nor is he content to steal from the wealthy—he also thieves from humble folk. In December he ordered his henchman Bellenden to confiscate the small estate of Hamilton of Bothwellhaugh near Roslin. Knowing that Hamilton was away at the time and his home undefended, Bellenden raided it by night. He found Mistress Hamilton abed and turned her out naked in the snow. She wandered the Pentland hills all night. Next day when Hamilton returned, he found her in the forest insane. Hamilton and his clan have sworn vengeance against Lord James for having ordered the crime.

On January 25th a hard-riding courier arrived from Scotland, and Lord Shrewsbury brought him to Mary. As the courier poured out his story, she visioned the gray little town of Linlithgow in wan morning sunlight and a cavalcade passing down the High Street on the way to Edinburgh . . .

James rode behind his guard. Mounted on a black horse caparisoned in green and scarlet, he waved diamond-heavy fingers at the crowd that pressed close on both sides. Slowly, acknowledging cheers from the balconies, he approached the dark, shuttered house of the Archbishop of Hamilton.

Below the lattice window, a hackbut barrel inched through a hole in the wood. Hamilton of Bothwellhaugh waited until James was opposite him. He took careful aim and fired.

James clutched his stomach and reeled from his horse, trampled by the panicked horses behind him. Some of his men ran to Hamilton House and battered down the doors to search for the assassin. Others carried James through the surging, yelling mob to Drummond's Lodging four doors west.

James was placed on a pallet by the fire. A surgeon drew back blood-wet velvet and crimsoned linen. The bullet had passed through the stomach. From noon until eleven at night James screamed in agony . . .

"Did he have aught to say?" Mary asked the courier. "Did he repent his sins?"

"Nay, Madam—he died screaming."

Died in the little village where I was born, she thought.

"Did Hamilton escape?" Shrewsbury asked.

"Aye, my lord. It is believed he has escaped on a ship—probably to France."

Mary said, "Tell my lords that though I did not order this deed, I could not be more pleased. I shall pension Hamilton of Bothwellhaugh and bless him every day of my life."

Now, she thought, James's friends will fight one another for the prize of the Regency, and when the slaughter is done, Lethington may rise to power in my name.

"It is too early to be certain," the courier said, "but it is believed the nobles will agree on Lord Lennox as Regent."

VII.

Mary benefited little from James's death, save that Kirkcaldy of Grange was emboldened to rescue Lethington from prison. As Regent, Lennox maintained cordial relations with Elizabeth, who hurled her army across the Border to punish rebel subjects hidden in the hills. Day after day Mary heard of atrocities in southern Scotland, and suffered with the victims. She was seized with prolonged fits of fainting and the strange malady which she called "the Jedburgh illness"—fever, vomiting, muscle rigidity. Elizabeth sent her personal physician from Greenwich and affectionate letters.

Mary could not fathom Elizabeth's gusts of tenderness. During the spring she courted Mary with hints of possible release. She permitted the Shrewsburys to move Mary to Chatsworth in Derbyshire, the most beautiful mansion in England. There Mary was allowed to receive occasional visitors. The Bishop of Ross came to her in August.

"Elizabeth has released Norfolk from the Tower," he said. "The

plague is raging there, and she has given him the comparative freedom of a private residence."

Mary was jubilant. "Then we can plan anew."

"Perhaps. But Norfolk gave Elizabeth a written promise to renounce Your Majesty."

"Was he in earnest?"

"At the time. Whoever stands nearest Norfolk draws him like a
lodestone. He is a weak fool, torn between ambition and terror of
Elizabeth."

"Am I still his ambition?"

"Aye, Madam. But your letters must be more persuasive. He must
truly believe you intend to appeal to the Pope for an annulment."

"I will indeed appeal." She knew it would be futile, but while
the appeal dragged through Rome, Norfolk would be convinced of
her good faith. "He surely would not wait until I am divorced to
help me escape?"

"No, but he would be a fool to risk his life if you made no move
toward divorce. To be blunt, Madam—he wants the throne, not
you."

"And I too want the throne—not him." She laughed. "You shall
see how neatly I inveigle His Grace into another plot."

Within two weeks of his release, Mary's love letters plunged
Norfolk deep into a second attempt at her freedom. This time he
was joined by Robert Rudolfi, a Florentine banker and secret agent
of the Pope. The Bishop came to Mary with their completed plan.

"Philip has half-approved this scheme," he began.

"He must fully approve it. The reason he failed us before was
that he lacked sufficient time. He must not be rushed. If need be,
take a year."

"Yes, Madam. As before, the Catholics will rise, Philip will invade. But simultaneously Elizabeth will be assassinated. We have
hired the killer, one James Graffs. When she passes through a village
on one of her travels he will—"

"No! I'll not hear of it!"

"But Madam, we must obliterate the very symbol of the Reformation. With Elizabeth dead, your claim is supreme."

"I will not hear one word of regicide."

"But she is your mortal enemy."

"I fear God's wrath more than I fear Elizabeth."

"The assassination will likely be attempted whether Your Majesty
approves or not."

She glanced at him obliquely. "Tell the conspirators that should
they persist in this murder plot, I shall warn Elizabeth."

He smiled. "I shall tell them."

VIII.

The year passed slowly for Mary, in apprehension, boredom, illness. She was moved by the Shrewsburys to the old Norman castle of Sheffield in Yorkshire. Again she fell sick of the pain in her side, which physicians believed to be an inflammation of the womb or the spleen. The winter of 1570-1571 was unusually severe and she was perpetually cold.

But by spring she was warmed by news from Edinburgh. Kirkcaldy of Grange revolted against Lennox and commanded Edinburgh Castle in her name. Lethington joined him there with a garrison of Hamiltons and other supporters. John Knox was assailed anonymously. On kirks and gates appeared placards accusing him of betraying Scotland to the English. He suffered a paralytic stroke, and though he still preached at St. Giles, his speech was affected and only his eyes held the old fire.

There was little to relieve the monotony of Mary's life. Bothwell's letters were the only gleam in a drab pattern. He would find means of escape. It was only a matter of time . . .

Mary gave Philip ample time, yet he hesitated to commit himself on an invasion. The Pope was more helpful. To smooth the way for an English Catholic rising, he excommunicated Elizabeth and proclaimed her a bastard.

In April, Norfolk sent Rudolfi to Flanders, where he enlisted approval of the plot from Philip's Governor of the Netherlands, the Duke of Alba. From there he went to Madrid and prodded Philip with letters from the Pope. Philip finally agreed to mobilize a force of six thousand men in Flanders. Alba would invade England—but not until after Elizabeth's assassination.

Thus the plot was stalemated. Norfolk would not rally the English nobles unless protected by Philip's invaders. Philip would not move a ship until Elizabeth was dead and Norfolk's nobles were in armed rebellion. Mary, exasperated by the impasse, tried vainly to budge the conspirators to action. She feared that Philip's blighting caution and Norfolk's timidity would doom her to prison the rest of her life.

On a September afternoon, Lord Shrewsbury asked urgent audience. As he appeared in the doorway, Mary ran to him, thinking him ill. His forehead dripped with sweat and he trembled as he knelt to kiss her hand.

"Her Majesty knows everything, Madam," he said. "Your traffic with Norfolk and King Philip, the plans for assassination and invasion—the entire plot."

Mary forced an astonished smile. "What babble is this, my lord?"

"The babble comes from Norfolk's servants on the rack, from the Bishop of Ross, who is threatened with death. Cecil has known of this plot since April, but bided his time, gathering evidence. The Queen will have you for treason."

"I am not her subject," Mary said haughtily. "She has no evidence against me." Unless, she thought fearfully, the key to my cipher has been surrendered to my enemies under torture. "I never plotted her death, and none can blame me for trying to escape illegal confinement."

"She is mad with rage. Heads will fall, Madam."

"Not mine!"

"I fear you are overly confident."

"I am confident of one thing. Elizabeth's greatest dread on this earth is that I will die at her hands."

Shrewsbury stared at her curiously.

"She fears Philip," Mary said. "She fears a world-wide Catholic uprising. But most of all she fears the judgment of posterity."

IX.

Elizabeth orders not my death, Mary thought, but my humiliation . . . Her household at Sheffield was suddenly reduced from thirty to sixteen. French and Scots servants, including Willie Douglas, were dismissed abruptly. The Bishop of Ross, screaming in the shadow of the gallows, made a statement which Elizabeth permitted to be proclaimed throughout Britain:

The Queen of Scots is unfit for any husband. She poisoned her first, the King of France; consented to the murder of Darnley; brought Bothwell to Carberry Hill to be murdered; and last of all pretended to consider marriage with the Duke of Norfolk with whom she would not have kept faith . . .

Angrily Mary wrote to Elizabeth, accusing her of again breaking her royal pledge that public slander of Mary would not be allowed. Elizabeth in turn accused Mary of gross ingratitude, of ungoverned passions, of Norfolk's ruin.

Norfolk awaited trial in the Tower. A *silly Maypole of a man*, Mary wrote Lethington. A *Darnley motivated not by religious zeal but self-glorification. I cannot waste pity on him.*

Her pity was all for her gallant, ragged Scots who carried on an uneven struggle against Lennox' army. In September they had raided Stirling Castle in an attempt to carry off the little King and place him in Lethington's charge. They failed—but killed Lennox.

Kirkcaldy's men shot and stabbed him, Lethington wrote. *It promises to be a bloody year* . . .

Bloody in Scotland, bloody in England. On January 14th Norfolk was tried for high treason in Westminster Hall before a jury of twenty-seven peers. Mary learned to her surprise that he faced his accusers with dignity. Calmly he admitted knowledge of the conspiracy, but futilely insisted he had committed no treasonable act.

The court found him guilty. Both houses of Parliament petitioned that he and Mary die on the block. But Elizabeth stated, "I cannot put to death the bird that fled to me for succor from the hawk."

Norfolk must die alone. Shortly before he was led to the gallows at Tower Hill, he repented his treatment of Elizabeth.

"As for the Queen of Scots," he said, "Nothing that was begun by her or for her has ever turned out well."

X.

Sheffield lay parched in early September heat. In the garden Mary and Seton sat under the shade of a great oak. Bees droned in the crisped rose bushes. Dahlias spewed wine-black petals on dead grass.

The atmosphere was heavy, stifling. Mary pushed damp hair under her satin coif. "It is difficult to breathe."

"It is, Madam." Seton stared at the sky—a cloudless saffron, glaring toward sunset. "And no sign of rain."

Mary sighed and picked up her embroidery—a little velvet hat for her son. She hoped the new Regent, Lord Mar, would allow James to wear it.

"At least I can be grateful that Lord Mar is still James's guardian," Mary said. "He is a kindly man. But I resent his allowing Master Buchanan to tutor him. He is poisoning his mind with heretic doctrine and lies about me."

"At five," Seton said, "your son is too young to form judgment."

"Not too young to learn to hate me and love Elizabeth. If only I could find means of sending him to France to be educated. They say he is a clever pupil."

She looked up. A cloud of dust rose at the castle gates and as it lifted, she saw horsemen bearing Elizabeth's banner. She hurried into the manor.

In the hall a servant asked Mary to join Lord Shrewsbury in his study. As she entered the room, he abruptly broke off his conversation with Sir Francis Knollys, bowed to Mary and offered her a chair.

"Madam . . ." His voice was heavy with shock. "The most de-

praved act since the crucifixion of Christ. I can scarcely credit . . ."
He turned to Sir Francis. "Tell Her Majesty."

"Madam, on August 24th, St. Bartholemew's Day . . ."

Paris, two hours past midnight. The old gray palaces dreaming among dew-wet gardens, the spires of Notre Dame and the Palais Royal silvered by moonlight. No sounds but early fallen leaves scudding along the cobbles and the slide of the Seine against stone banks.

Across the square from the Louvre, in the belfry of the Church of Saint-Germain-l'Auxerrois, Catherine de Medici looking out on the sleeping city. The black-hooded face of an old flabby animal, the loose lips wet, the eyes pricked hot with excitement.

"Mother . . ." King Charles's words lapping softly in the darkness, his timid hand on her shoulder. "Must we?"

Catherine lifting her arm, her cape swirling back in the wind, her voice snarling out to the bellringer. *"Now!"*

The bells signaling the massacre to begin. Catherine holding her trembling son and far below, like the sharp barking of wolves, the guns opening fire.

Knollys said the Royal Guard broke into Huguenot homes and butchered families in their beds. People poured into the streets and were mowed down by hackbut fire, speared, beaten to pulp. Babies were tossed into bonfires of Protestant pamphlets. Protestant leader Admiral Gaspard de Coligny was shot and his headless trunk dragged through the streets by children who knifed off the hands and genitals and offered them for sale. A pregnant woman was disemboweled and her embryo smashed in the gutter. By morning three thousand corpses littered the streets and choked the Seine.

The slaughter spread to the provinces. At first systematic, it became a frenzy of indiscriminate killing. Such a stench of blood and charred flesh hung over Paris that priests burned incense in the streets and hawkers did a lively trade in camphor and cloves. Looters stripped the bodies, even to the women's hair, which was sold to wigmakers.

At dusk the second day, a black-caped woman hooded to the eyes was seen wandering among the corpses outside the Louvre, bending to smile at the headless, the faceless, spitting out a lifetime of bottled venom, gloating that seventy thousand Protestants lay dead . . .

"At supper that night," Knollys said, "diplomats remarked that Queen Catherine looked fully ten years younger."

Sickened, Mary said nothing. A terrible disaster for Catholicism, she thought, far more horrible than the slaughter of Protestants at Amboise. And it can have fearful repercussions for me, for I am the figurehead of the faith in Britain and I may be sacrificed to Protestant vengeance.

Bitterly Mary said, "Catholics will not dare to show their faces for months . . . What does the Pope say?"

"He and the Cardinal of Lorraine, who is visiting in Rome, were delighted. His Holiness has ordered a Jubilee and medals will be struck commemorating the 'blessed occurrence.' *Te Deum* was sung in the chapel of San Marco. An artist is painting the massacre on the walls of the Vatican, and Rome is illuminated for three nights of celebration."

Blood-blinded fools, she thought. For seventy thousand martyred Protestants we will reap the world's loathing. Catherine has made Catholicism synonymous with barbarism.

"And King Philip?" she asked. "Surely he retains his sanity?"

"Madam, when the news was announced to him—for the first time in his reign he was seen to smile in public."

"Revolting!" Shrewsbury said. He faced Mary almost accusingly. "How can Your Majesty defend this infamy?"

She asked, "How did you defend English atrocities against Catholics? The priest-baiting and abbey-wrecking?" Without awaiting an answer, she turned to Knollys. "Does Queen Elizabeth have any message for me?"

"I am to tell Your Majesty that she does not hold you personally responsible for the massacre."

"Indeed!" Mary said. "How very generous of her! But I've no doubt Cecil will do his utmost to spread the belief that I conspired with Queen Catherine in this. He and Knox will stir Britain to fury against me and my faith."

She moved to the door. "I know what Cecil tells Her Majesty—that I am a viper curled on England's hearthstone. But unlike other vipers—" She turned and faced them—"I am most dangerous dead."

XI.

In mid-October, Bothwell's Danish page, Einer, met Seton secretly in Sheffield's wooded park, gave her a letter and repeated other messages for Mary.

"Your husband learned of a terrible plot against you," Seton told Mary. "A few weeks ago Queen Elizabeth dispatched Sir William Killigrew to Edinburgh. He was instructed to offer Your Majesty to Regent Mar and Lord Chancellor Morton, with the stipulation that you be executed four hours after your arrival in Scotland. Thus Queen Elizabeth would avoid blame for your death."

"Jesu! What did Mar say?"

"He refused even to consider the proposition."

"But I suppose Morton was eager to accept?"

"Yes, Lord Morton urged Lord Mar to accept—with the proviso that Queen Elizabeth send men and money to subdue your forces holding Edinburgh Castle. This she refused to do. Thus, by God's grace, the plot failed."

"Likely it is not the first such plot—nor the last," Mary said grimly. Shivering, she added, "How eerie to learn weeks later that one almost died . . . How is Bothwell faring?"

"Einer says His Grace is still well treated. But . . ."

"But what?"

"He is lean with pacing and never still. He goes to the window constantly and batters the iron bars, bruising his hands. They are brutally scarred, and he never lets them heal but tries again—and again—to break the bars. He is forever plotting . . . and forever disappointed."

Tears slipped down Mary's cheeks. "Give me his letter."

My love:

The bearer will tell you of Elizabeth's treachery. Whatever her present attitude, remember that she will dagger you at first chance —provided another hand plunges the knife.

A time may come when I am unable to write, but you will know it is not lack of love. You have sunned a dark life and the radiance lingers. But I do not see you plainly—you are shimmer and fragrance. Often I awake and the fragrance is close in this chamber, and I reach out and grasp a handful of shadows and curse the dream.

I curse myself. You think Elizabeth your jailer but it is I, for I forged your shackles in the heat of passion and now they are cold on your wrists. Often I wonder how our lives might have shaped had I not come to you that night at Drummond—had I taken Jean to France or retired to Hermitage. Yet I am convinced we would have met again one day at Stirling or Holyrood, in a wood or on a moor, and our destinies would be unchanged.

I should never have left Carberry Hill without you. Over and over in my mind I toss you upon my saddle and gallop for Dunbar on a road that never ends—for I know not the ending.

Love me always, as I love you, ~~no matter what you hear.~~
> *Your husband,*
> *James, Duke of Orkney.*

No matter what you hear . . . He had crossed that out, but she could read it and it troubled her. The letter was unlike him, mystic, strangely introspective.

Mary turned to Seton. "When you take my reply to Einer, inquire if my husband seems despondent. Lest he conceals illness from me, insist that Einer tell you the truth. I *must* know."

But when Seton returned from the woods she assured Mary that Bothwell was not ill. "He is only restless, Madam, as you are."

"Prison is far worse for him," Mary said. "He is moor-bred, he needs great spaces. Is he allowed to hunt?"

"Oh no, Madam. But he is permitted to exercise occasionally in a walled garden."

The walls black with big-snouted cannon, sentries watching with aimed halberds.

"Does King Frederick still seek to ransom him?"

"Your husband believes so, Madam. But the price is said to be one million crowns."

"Thank God," Mary said, "that Elizabeth is penurious!"

XII.

Lethington's predicted bloody year was not yet over. Undeclared warfare continued in Scotland. Elizabeth bought the fugitive Northumberland from Mar and Morton for two thousand pounds and executed him at York. On October 28th Mar died so suddenly after dining with Morton at Stirling that poison was presumed. On November 24th Morton succeeded Mar as Regent.

That same night in Edinburgh, in his little gabled house on the High Street, John Knox fell back on his pillows and gasped his last words: "It is come!"

Lethington wrote Mary that he was ill, *Thin as a wynd-cat and diseased in every bone*, but still able to climb the ramparts of Edinburgh Castle, and determined to hold it in Mary's name. She could never vision Lethington as a warrior, armed and helmeted. Always in her imagination he sat in cushioned chairs, his elegant fingers holding wineglass or chess piece. Again she wondered why, of all men, he had come to her aid. He was no champion of lost causes. He abhorred failure, because it implied stupidity. Yet with the grizzled old Kirkcaldy he now commanded her last outpost. By defying the Regents he was denied what crumbs of power they might otherwise have thrown him. What, then, did he gain? Why did he do it? Surely, not at Fleming's persuasion. Her influence was not as strong as his will.

Perhaps, Mary thought, Lethington had never been so much an opportunist as an individualist. And now he will not be herded or intimidated by such men as Morton. Aging, ill, he stands foursquare against both Elizabeth and the lords of Sotland, contemptuous of Catholic and Protestant alike.

Mary's fourth English winter was dreary and troubled. She had verbal messages from Bothwell, but no letters. Einer and her courier Horsey said that Bothwell's bruised hands were too swollen to hold a quill. Otherwise he was well.

In April, Elizabeth's ships sailed into Leith with cannon and five hundred hackbuteers. Day and night five artillery batteries bombarded Edinburgh Castle from points across the North Loch, from Castle Hill, Grayfriar's and St. Cuthbert's. Morton's men joined in the relentless hammering. Kirkcaldy and Lethington fought magnificently, but their two wells were inaccessible. The thirsty garrison held out until the English captured the eastern approach to the fortress. On May 29th, refusing to deal with Morton, Kirkcaldy surrendered command of the castle to Sir William Drury.

When the news reached Mary, she argued with Shrewsbury that it could not be true. She would not believe that her last defense was gone.

But it was, and with it—Lethington. Imprisoned by Morton, he died mysteriously a few days later. Some said of a stroke. Others vowed that rather than face the humiliation of public execution he swallowed poison.

Mary learned that on August 3rd Kirkcaldy was hanged at the Market Cross and John Knox's prophecy was fulfilled. As Kirkcaldy died on the gibbet, a heavy slide of sand sifted from the battered castle. The corpse slowly turned and faced the western sun.

XIII.

When Einer arrived at Sheffield in July, Mary determined that she herself would question him about Bothwell. But she was not permitted beyond the courtyard and was allowed no visitors save Elizabeth's representatives. Somehow she had to smuggle Einer to her apartments.

"What does Einer look like?" Mary asked Seton.

"Small, fair-haired, beardless. About twenty-four, Madam."

"Small . . . could he hide in the large laundry basket?"

"Perhaps."

Mary took gold from her reticule. "Then see if you can arrange it."

By now Mary had several friends among the Shrewsburys' servants in the laundry, bakehouse and kitchen. Late that afternoon pages carried the laundry basket, topped with clean linen into Mary's presence chamber. While Seton stood guard in the corridor, Einer clambered out, a grave, blue-eyed young man in wrinkled, travel-worn brown.

Mary bade him be seated. "Did you bring letters from my husband?"

"No, Your Majesty. His Grace's hands are still unhealed and he cannot write. But I bring news. He has been moved from Malmoe to Dragsholm Castle in North Zealand."

"But why?"

Einer hesitated. "We know not, Madam. Perhaps King Frederick grew weary of his guest."

"What manner of place is Dragsholm?"

Again he hesitated.

"Come," she said sharply. "If you do not tell me I can easily find out."

"Madam, Dragsholm is a state prison, the strictest in the land, and loathsome. The meat is rotten, the pallets filthy. His Grace's cell is underground and windowless."

"Jesu!"

"He is not even allowed exercise, though other prisoners walk inside the moat."

"Why did Frederick suddenly send him to this dungeon? Did he try to escape Malmoe? Is this his punishment? Tell me the truth."

His eyes evaded her. "I do not know, Madam."

She went to Einer and knelt by his chair. "I think you do know. Perhaps your master has pledged you to silence and you are trying to spare me. But for the love of God tell me the worst! I can endure anything but my imagination."

She saw the pain in his eyes, the tightened mouth.

"Please, Einer . . ." She was on her knees, weeping, imploring. "You love him—I love him—I have every right to know."

He bent toward her as though to touch her, drew back and turned his eyes from hers. "He—he felt it coming, Madam. He anticipated it—but you were not to know. Months ago I swore not to tell you."

"Not to tell me what?"

"Madam . . . he is green-mad."

Mad. The word rocked her to the floor, slapped her silent. She groped for Einer's hand and clutched it tight.

"It is true, Madam. I noted it first last year. He grew too quiet. For hours he would stand at the window and stare at the sky, or pace his chamber. Though allowed visitors, he would see no one but his servants. He ceased to write, he ceased to plot. Instead of using his brain to try to escape, he struggled with the bars, ripping his hands.

"As the weeks passed he grew fiercer, stranger in manner. One day

[539]

he smashed the furniture to bits, pulled down the hangings and shredded them. The guards came running and it took four to subdue him. I was there, I saw it all . . . Then suddenly he was calm, so lucid you would marvel. That night he wrote the last letter I delivered to you. He himself said it might be his last. I think he knew the attack would come again—and again. He told me in the future to read all that he wrote, lest it be strange. He said, 'The Queen must receive nothing to trouble her. Swear you will tell her always that I am well and cheerful. She must never lose hope lest she lose the will to live.'

"After that he wrote Your Majesty again, many times. Forgive me, but I did not deliver the letters, for you would have known. They were ravings, cursing and tales of Border forays mingled with words of love for you. I burned them."

She huddled on the floor, still holding his hand, too shocked to speak.

"King Frederick was patient, at first. But again His Grace was plagued by devils in the brain, and again he tore his chamber to shreds and splinters. His Majesty declared him a madman and sent him to Dragsholm."

Mary slipped her hand from Einer's and looked up at him. Her voice was broken, almost incoherent. "There is no hope?"

"What can one do, Madam? A surgeon cannot probe the devils. To lance the brain means death."

"Has he had a priest or a minister?"

"Yes, Madam, a priest asked to see him, and exorcised the evil spirit but it was of no use. The violence continued and now he is chained—"

"Chained?"

"Aye. When he first was placed in the cell, he smashed his face against the wall and broke his nose. Fearing he would kill himself, they chained him to an oaken pillar in the middle of the room. The chain is about eighteen inches long. He is able to walk only part way round his pillar, the chain being too short to permit a full circle. Fortunately the shackle is close enough to the earth floor so that he can sink down and rest or sleep. But he sinks into filth."

"Does he—" She spoke over a great lump in her throat. "Does he realize where he is?"

"Sometimes he does, Madam—and that is the horror. It would be merciful if he were always deviled, but often he looks at me with sane eyes and speaks with a sane tongue, and that I cannot—I cannot—"

"I know," she said. "You cannot bear it, nor could I. But *he* does."

"Sometimes he is a growling, snarling fury, pulling on that chain until the veins stand out in his neck like ropes. Other times he paces as far as it will reach, back and forth, padding like a beast . . ."

She gasped, wondering if she too was mad. For she could almost smell rhododendron and hear the lazy bees on a day long ago in the garden of St. Germain . . . She was a child again, and the young lion paced its chain, back and forth, to and fro, wearing away the grass.

Dear God, she thought, was I being given a glimpse into the future that day? Was I seeing Bothwell at Dragsholm? Was that why I wept?

Now she wept with her head on Einer's knee, racking sobs that tore her throat and shuddered her body. Einer put a timid hand on her shoulder.

At sound of hunting horns in the distance, Seton opened the door. "Madam, Einer had best leave; he can take the side stairs before Lord Shrewsbury returns from the forest."

Mary nodded, dried her eyes, and Einer helped her to her feet.

"I shall write King Frederick demanding better quarters," Mary said. "Meanwhile, please stay with my husband." She gave Einer gold. "Bribe him such comforts as you can."

"That I cannot do, Madam. I have tried, but the guards take the gold and do nothing."

"Then keep the gold for yourself." She followed Einer to the door. "Dear friend, you must do what I would do were I there. In moments when he seems himself, when you can reach his mind, tell him that I love him more than my life. Tell him how proud I am to be wed to a man so brave, that I would not trade places with any woman on earth. Make him feel my need of him and my trust in him—forever. I shall pray."

"The merciful prayer, Madam, would be for his death. But the strange thing about madmen is that as the mind rots the body often flourishes. He seems stronger now than he was two years ago."

"But he cannot live on like this! Wretches on the rack are not so tortured! They suffer for a day or two but not for months."

"He does not suffer continuously, Madam. When last I saw him he sat smiling at the foot of his pillar, and he held the chain as though it were a rein. He thought he was riding up a great height, and he said rose petals were blowing in his face . . ."

XIV.

That year of 1573 drew to an end, and Twelfth Night tapers were pools of hardened wax. At her polished metal mirror Mary saw a face smooth and white as the tapers had been, but without glow, its flame extinguished. She was beautiful still, but grave as a death mask. Bronze lights were muted in her hair, a wraith of a wrinkle haunted her mouth. She was thirty, and she knew that she looked every year of it.

Sometimes she was sensitive of her appearance, sending for unguents from France and trying new wigs. But often she went for days without a glance in the mirror, leaving her hair and her face to Seton's pins and paints. Always she wore stiff black gowns of brocade or velvet, the long skirts hiding legs swollen from rheumatism. On damp days she leaned on a polished rosewood cane, hobbling painfully between her chambers. Unable to kneel at her prie-dieu, she stood for hours in prayer, begging Bothwell's recovery —or his death. Frederick evaded her pleas that he be moved to pleasant quarters, indicating politely that a madman was unaware of his surroundings and better left in darkness.

Because she mourned the death of Bothwell's mind, other deaths touched her remotely. King Charles died and was succeeded by his brother Henry III—another weakling for Catherine to dominate. The Cardinal of Lorraine passed away at Avignon, and though Mary feigned grief, she felt only nostalgia for the god of her childhood.

Fleming wrote that Lady Jean had married the Earl of Sutherland. *I saw her in Edinburgh, radiant and big with child. Her husband treats her like a queen, and indeed she resembled one, magnificently jeweled, her train so heavy with pearls it required two little black-moors to lift it from the dust of the High Street. She said she was shocked by news of your husband's madness. So are all who knew him, friend and enemy alike . . .*

Mary lavished her love on Bothwell, sending him gifts she embroidered—belts and sleeves, a doublet stitched with golden vines. She wrote to him each week, hoping that in moments of sanity he would realize she had not failed him. But he could not respond, and she desperately needed response. Without affection she felt that she too would lose her reason. As the months passed she became more and more dependent on her servants—Seton, Jane Kennedy, Elizabeth Curle and her husband Gilbert, who served as Mary's Scots secretary. Other favorites were her French secretary Claude Nau, and Dominique Bourgoing, her physician.

Inevitably, she spent much of her time with the Shrewsburys at cards and for evenings of music. Always she was careful not to rouse Bess's jealousy, and when Lord Shrewsbury suggested a walk or a ride in the park, Mary insisted that Bess accompany them. But Bess was stormswept, undisciplined. She would rage at her husband for spending too much money on Mary's household, pout and sulk.

Then as suddenly she would confide in Mary as her "dearest friend," and reveal ambitious plans for marrying off her children.

One of these plans developed secretly. Without Queen Elizabeth's permission, Bess married her daughter Elizabeth to Charles Stuart, Darnley's younger brother, who had a claim to the English throne. Infuriated, Queen Elizabeth sent Bess to the Tower of London for three months. Far from chastened, she returned to Sheffield to spread gossip that the Queen had inherited the yaws from her father, causing a sore on her leg.

Bess oozed malice from every pore. "She is shrewish, vulgar, treats her ladies abominably . . ."

Somewhat as you do, Mary thought. God help you if there comes a time when you must depend on servants for affection.

Most of the servants at Sheffield were Mary's staunch friends. Pages and scullery wenches came to her with their troubles, and she made their problems her own. The Shrewsburys' most trusted retainers were her secret allies. Even the Earl's ward, twelve-year-old Anthony Babington, intrigued for her surreptitiously. Through him she learned Elizabeth's instructions days before they were put into effect. When he traveled to London he carried her letters.

Plots continued in Mary's behalf: Ardent young men hid in the woods near Sheffield or found pretexts for visiting the village. They sent her poems and love letters, measured by eye the space between her window and the ground and suggested escape schemes. Scarcely a firewood basket or shipment of cloth or box of sewing silks came to her that did not contain a message. Would Her Majesty consider changing clothes with the Countess of Shrewsbury's female fool? Or introducing a barrel of drugged wine to the guards, climbing the courtyard wall, feigning death and escaping in a coffin? Eagerly Mary considered every plan, reluctantly rejected each. But it cheered her that so many folk were working for her liberation. George Douglas wrote from Paris that Willie had joined him there and both were conspiring for French aid.

And so she had loyalty, even worship. She had comforts, subject to Elizabeth's whims, and small luxuries which she bought with her own dowry installments. But never the precious privilege of walking unguarded past yew hedges, beyond gates into the woods or the village.

When Elizabeth relaxed restrictions and allowed her to hunt if she felt well enough, Mary in turn wooed her with affectionate letters and gifts. She created royal headdresses of gold lace and silver spangles, gauze and net. She embroidered sleeves and ruffles for her, and had sweetmeats delivered by the French Ambassador. Elizabeth sent thanks and a wry message by her envoy: "As people grow old they accept with two hands and give with one finger."

Time was measured by small events—the long wait for a shipment of Barbary pigeons; the birth of a maid's baby; the death of a beloved dog. Mary collected little animals—strays or aristocrats, it made no difference so long as they could be cuddled. She had poodles and spaniels and terriers. Doves perched on her wrists, kittens climbed her skirts. She even loved a muskrat, but freed it because she could not bear to see it chained.

Einer wrote that Bothwell's arms and legs were swollen with dropsy, that he was overgrown with hair and filth. "I pray that he cannot long survive. Yet, though ill and three years mad, he still is stronger than most men. Forever he fights his chain or paces it. He has worn a little path in the earth halfway round his pillar. He screams Your Majesty's name a hundred times a day and lunges an imaginary sword . . ."

In Scotland, Morton pronounced pious judgment on Bothwell: "He who deals with the Devil ends his days in the Devil's claws."

Of the Regents since James, Morton was the cruelest and greediest. Mary heard that his sober Puritan clothes concealed a corselet fashioned of a solid mass of her jewels. By death-threat and torture, he forced men who had inherited priories and vast abbey lands to transfer their deeds of property to him. His henchman Lord Cassilis stretched the commendator of an Ayrshire abbey on iron bars above an open fire and basted him with oil, until he agreed to turn over his leases, which he signed with a half-roasted hand.

"Scotland needs an iron hand but not an iron heart," Bothwell had said. In Morton it had both. Though he stamped out all resistance, Mary waited hopefully for the inevitable rebellion of his own lords. The pattern of the Regency was violent death, and she felt that Morton could not long escape it.

In May 1576 came strange news of Lord Huntley. On his Highland estate after a day of hunting and football, he sat down to feast. Suddenly he glanced up, pointed to the ceiling, screamed in horror: "Look—look—*look!*"

His guests saw nothing but the hooded falcon on the oak rafter. Huntley tumbled from his chair to the floor, dead. Mary thought, He died at sight of a terrible vision—Darnley.

Mary herself had terrible dreams of Darnley. Religion became increasingly important to her as an antidote to fear, loneliness and illness. She was not allowed a Catholic chaplain in her household, but a devoted priest disguised himself as a gardener and persuaded the Shrewsburys to hire him. He met Mary in the garden every day from spring to late fall, ostensibly tending her flowers, actually tending her soul. But lest she suddenly be deprived of him, she wrote to the Pope and received the extraordinary privilege of administering the holy elements to herself.

She tried desperately to win her ten-year-old son from heresy. Vainly she wrote to him begging that he disregard the teachings of Buchanan and the Protestant lords. She wooed him with gifts of toy cannon and golden arrows. They were never acknowledged, because Mary never acknowledged him as King. Always she addressed him as Prince of Scotland.

Fleming wrote: *Your son is pathetic, Madam, torn between what his guardians say of you and what he wishes to believe.*

Poor little James, Mary thought. Poor awkward lad, brilliant and sensitive, nervous and fearful. Fearful of dogs, of knives, of the dark; of the huge transparent figure said to haunt Darnley's apartments at Stirling. Fearful that Europe scorns him as Rizzio's bastard. Fearful that I helped murder his father. Every preacher in Edinburgh pounds at him to believe me a criminal, a harlot bloated with Romish iniquity. A penitent woman, her legs bloated with rheumatism, plagued by a liver ailment . . .

In the wan autumn sunshine of Sheffield garden, Mary hobbled through falling leaves and eased down on a bench to rest. I am too old to fight, she thought, too young to die; a sluggish River Styx that runs between two worlds.

The gardener-priest walked toward her, looked cautiously about, then slipped a letter from his belt.

"From His Holiness, Madam. The Thames waterman just brought it from London."

Mary read it and sprang to her feet, her cane clattering to the ground.

"Father!" she said as the priest bent to retrieve her cane. "You have heard of Don John of Austria?"

"Indeed, Madam. King Philip's natural brother . . . the hero of Lepanto . . . the first knight of Christendom."

"The last knight of Christendom!" She held the Pope's letter like a banner. "Don John wishes to rescue me!"

He smiled. "And then? A Catholic Britain?"

She jerked off her somber coif and tossed it in the air, laughing as leaves fluttered in her face and caught in her tumbled hair. "A Catholic world!"

XV.

Slowly and secretly, the plot progressed. Philip appeared to approve it. As his new Governor of the Netherlands, Don John would prepare Spanish ships and troops for the invasion of England. English exiles in Rome promised funds to finance a rebellion of English Catholics. Loyal Scots would pour across the Border on signal.

Don John proposed marriage and sent Mary his portrait. Since her disillusion with Darnley she mistrusted perfect handsomeness, but this dark young face was also superbly royal. There was defiance in the chin, honesty in the deep black eyes. Her ladies sighed at his beauty. She was stirred by his strength.

The Pope's envoy wrote: *If Your Majesty could search the centuries through, you could not find a prince more truly your match in piety, bravery and beauty. Like yourself he is utterly devoted to the true faith.*

Don John's bravery was known afar. He had beaten the murderous Moors in Andalusia, captured Tunis. He dreamed of forming a vast Christian empire in Africa and the East mightier than Alexander's. As Admiral of the Holy League of Rome, Venice and Spain, he had whipped the Turks in the decisive naval battle of Lepanto. A hero indeed, Mary thought, and her one hope of deliverance.

Graciously she ignored the fact that Don John was the bastard son of the late Spanish Emperor Charles V and a serving wench, and she accepted his proposal. Once she was free of prison, she would find a way to avoid marriage. She would never relinquish Bothwell.

Months of waiting followed, but faith sustained her. Surely the Pope was divinely inspired to propose this scheme. In the hands of God, the Pope and Catholicism's greatest warrior it could not fail. But she reckoned without Philip's obsessive caution and equally obsessive jealousy of his brother. Don John was too ambitious for Philip's comfort, too popular with the people, too compelling a personality. In a sudden turnabout, Philip denounced the plot to rescue Mary as preposterously dangerous. Despite the Pope's pleas and Don John's frenzied appeals, he refused to permit an invasion of England.

But to Mary's delight, Don John defied Philip and massed his army in the Netherlands. He had no money, no credit, few ships and poorly equipped soldiers. But this was a crusade. He would wait, and God would provide.

To hide her excitement from the Shrewsburys, Mary feigned deep depression. One evening as she joined them at supper, Lord Shrewsbury remarked on her pallor. She had accentuated it with French wax.

"I am pale with hopelessness, sir," she said.

Ashed in her fireplace was an optimistic letter from the Pope's agent. Catholics in Rome would help finance invasion.

"To brighten your mood, Madam," Shrewsbury said, "there is

news from Scotland. The Council has deposed the Regent Morton and taken command of Holyrood and Edinburgh Castle."

"In my name?" Mary asked.

"Well—no, Madam. In the King's name."

Nevertheless she was delighted at Morton's fall from power, and raised her wineglass in a silent little toast to the Fates who dogged the Regents—especially Atropos . . .

Bess Shrewsbury helped herself from a platter of duckling. "There's also news from the Netherlands." She salted the duckling and slit it in two with a dagger. "A terrible epidemic of camp fever. Don John of Austria is dead . . ."

XVI.

Seton pulled the bed curtains against the April moonlight. "Good-night, Madam."

Mary slid between the sheets and lay back on the pillows. "Good-night, my dear."

The door closed softly.

In the garden a nightingale sang. A mouse scuttled in the wainscoting. On its cushion Mary's Persian cat opened wide green eyes, stretched and prowled the sweet hay.

The little clock chimed one . . . two . . . Mary lay awake, fighting the deepest depression she had ever known. Bleakly, she thought, Why struggle further? There can be but one ending.

Rising, she thrust aside the bed curtains and shivered through the moonlight to the window. Nothing moved in the garden below. Trees, bushes, hedges were fixed as a portrait, the roses waxen on their trellises. No wing-flutter, no quiver of leaf or fall of petals. A death in life, she thought—and so it is with me.

Spiritless, she dragged through the flowering days. Then on a bright May morning Lord Shrewsbury asked audience.

He said gently, "Your husband is dead, Madam. On April fourteenth . . ."

So the world had stopped. Hands limp in her lap, she said, "My heart knew."

"Think of it as release, Madam. He was ten years imprisoned, five years a-dying. Now he is free."

Balefire, swampfire, lightning in the hills. Hoofbeats in the galloping wind and gorse-dust on the moors.

"They buried him near Dragsholm, Madam, in the church of Faarevejle. He lies in an oaken coffin."

So they think . . .

XVII.

The clock ticked and the sandglass sifted, and the slow years budded, withered, died . . . 1579 . . . 1580 . . . 1581. Mary was thirty-eight, her hair fading to gray under blond or chestnut wigs. Plagued by illness, she could not exercise often, and the tiny waist thickened. But though her body grew flabby, her shoulders were erect. Magnificent in her stiff black gowns, trailing jeweled trains, she still inspired love. And a new generation was stirred to gallantry in her behalf.

She snatched hope from a dozen plots involving invasion or escape. But Cecil and Walsingham, like wise hounds, sniffed out each one. Brave men died for her on the rack, swung from gibbets, knelt at the block. Yet for each who died another sprang to her aid. Catholics swarmed to her like moths drawn to altar light, and Cecil was helpless to extinguish her glow.

And enemies also perished. In Edinburgh, Morton was tried for complicity in Darnley's murder. He confessed knowledge of the crime, but said he dared not prevent it because Mary had approved it. Found guilty of "art and part," he was led to the Market Cross and decapitated by The Maiden, a beheading device which he himself had brought from Halifax. His head was exhibited on the highest gable of the Tolbooth.

Mary wrote to George Douglas who had returned to Scotland. *Make my commendation to the lords. I give them most hearty thanks for the execution of Lord Morton who was my greatest enemy.*

But she knew that her greatest enemy romped at Whitehall and Greenwich. Elizabeth was nearing fifty in a wild resurgence of youth. Her laughter cackled more shrilly, her stick-legs flung higher in the ballroom. She was avid for compliments, snatching them greedily to store against the years. Her lips and hair had never been brighter, nor her attire more flamboyant. In monstrous-skirted gowns, her waist a rigid V of jewels, she coquetted with Catherine's youngest son, the Duke of Alençon, and was even betrothed to him. But as Mary's ambassador wrote from Paris: *She plays cat and mouse. With one paw she dangles the English crown before Queen Catherine's eyes. With the other she claws Your Majesty's hopes of the succession. Fear not, she will never wed.*

The threat of Elizabeth's marriage passed, but her malice persisted. When Mary's rheumatism became unbearable and she asked permission to return to Buxton's hot springs, Elizabeth refused until Mary groveled. Then, grumbling at the expense entailed, she allowed her to go. There were petty, humiliating battles over expenditures for Mary's household. Elizabeth begrudged her fifty attendants and Mary fiercely defended her need of them. She asked no luxuries of Elizabeth. With her own dowry money she bought Turkey carpets, silver services and furniture. If she must rot in prison she would rot in elegance.

There were little heart-clutching changes. Seton left Mary and entered a convent in France. News came of Beaton's death. The Earl of Sutherland died, leaving Jean the mother of fine children, the mistress of vast estates. Fleming wrote: *An old romance is blooming in mid-age, Alexander Ogilvie of Boyne is courting Jean again. Both are in mourning but they will marry someday.*

Mary felt like a spectator of a morality play. She saw the wicked die violently and the good rewarded. Jean would wed her childhood sweetheart and live in honor among children and grandchildren. Sir William Douglas had inherited Morton's earldom, and his family dwelt in peace at Lochleven. George Douglas was young King James's Ambassador to France. Willie Douglas had vanished mysteriously and Mary's inquiries in France and Scotland proved futile. But she did not worry about him; in the pattern of events he was likely safe and happy, surviving the havoc she had brought to others.

But the havoc she had brought on herself was spiritual torment. In the dark nights kneeling at her altar or lying restless abed, she panicked at thought of death. She did not fear the act of dying; she dreaded the aftermath, the fires of hell.

God might forgive her for her part in Darnley's murder, for she repented daily, nightly. But he could not forgive her adulterous love for Bothwell or her heretic marriage—because she could not truly repent them.

"Have patience," her priest said. "In time you will forget your husband, and then you can repent."

Yet though Bothwell's image blurred in her conscious mind, he came alive in her sleep—sometimes so vividly that she awoke reaching for him, her lips warm from the dream of his kiss. God and Bothwell still struggle for my soul, she thought. But God must win at the edge of death.

XVIII.

On New Year's night 1584 Lord Shrewsbury entertained at Sheffield, and guests came from as far as London to drink from the wassail bowl and dance in the Great Hall. Crippled by rheumatism, Mary held court at the fireside surrounded by high nobles. It amused her that several members of Elizabeth's Privy Council had come to pay their respects—men who realized that Elizabeth was mortal and

Mary her rightful successor. They ogled and flattered her, complimenting the elegance of her simple black gown sleeved with ermine, praising her soft voice, her pale, subtly painted face. Wine-loosened tongues whispered that Elizabeth might not survive a kidney ailment. Her teeth were infected, she was thinner than ever. Perhaps the new year would see a new queen.

Mary reflected that the new year could not be worse than the old. Another Catholic plot had failed after a brilliant start. Hundreds of young French and Spanish priests disguised as peddlers and artisans had invaded every corner of England and said Mass secretly in huts and ruined abbeys, castles and manor houses. Among them were Jesuit missionaries skilled in conversion. They were so persuasive that nobles close to Elizabeth rededicated themselves to the old faith, and pledged their support to Mary.

Such undermining tactics rocked the Reformation to its foundations, and stirred the sluggish Philip to reconsider the conquest of England. But while Philip procrastinated, Cecil and Walsingham swooped suddenly and ruthlessly. Priests were sent to the Tower and tortured for information. In London priests were publicly disemboweled. Others were hunted down and prisoned.

Once again Mary wept for her victims, and once again Elizabeth imposed severe restrictions on her. For a while it was impossible to send or receive letters, because her servants were searched before and after leaving her apartments. She was not allowed visitors and only recently had she been permitted belowstairs.

Tonight, wistful for happier new years, Mary watched the dancers and envied the humblest. At forty-one, her bones were old. Like a gray-granny she must hug the inglenook where the fire warmed her joints, and count it a blessing that she was alive. But oh, to caper to those viols and cithers, to flaunt and whirl! Not a woman present was as graceful as she had been. They moved stiffly, hampered by the huge projecting farthingales under their petticoats. A passionless Puritan lot, for all their bright raiment and tossing curls. Or am I jealous, she wondered, cursed with a young heart in an aging body, reluctant to admit that my noon is past and my twilight deepening?

The great stone hall was warm from the press of bodies, the fatty smoking candles, the torches burning in iron brackets, the blazing hearth. Mary pressed a pomander ball to her nose and sniffed the cloves. Sheffield needed cleansing. The rushes that trenched the sides of the hall had not been replaced since August, and smelled of old bones, sour pork pies, the rancid droppings of harvest and Yule feasts. Braziers of burning musk and ambergris could not offset the stench. The painted canvas strips and tapestries had hung for months without airing, and to pull aside a window curtain disturbed swarms of lice. Yet Sheffield was considered elegant, and Elizabeth hinted that Mary was fortunate to live in such luxury. Perhaps I am, she thought. The filth of a castle is preferable to the filth of a cell in the Tower.

Final toasts were drunk and the guests, with Mary's permission, dispersed to their chambers. She lingered by the fire, dreading the long, painful climb up spiral stairs to her apartments.

Lord Shrewsbury joined her by the hearth, and she bade him sit down. He winced into a chair, stretching his gouty leg across a hassock. A servant brought sack still hot from the poker, aromatic with spices and roasted apples.

"A lovely revel," Mary said politely. "But I warrant you missed your wife. When does she return from Chatsworth?"

He hesitated, tipped his chin into his silver lace ruff. In the firelight his hair held the sheen of old pewter.

"Bess will not return, Madam," he said. "We have quarreled violently."

"Ah, but you have done so before," she said, smiling. Mainly about money, she knew. Bess thought that he mismanaged their estates, and considered herself shrewder in business than he. She was constantly building manor houses, partly to enhance the value of her property, partly because a soothsayer had predicted that she would never die so long as she was building.

"We never quarreled like this before, Madam. She has left me —and I hope forever." He paused in obvious embarrassment. "I grieve to tell you this, Madam, but in her fury to hurt me she also has grossly slandered Your Majesty."

"In what manner?"

"She has spread the lie that Your Majesty and I have been lovers for fourteen years."

"Jesu!"

"Worse, that Your Majesty had a secret pregnancy nine years ago, and that the child was born here while she was in the Tower and sent to France before she returned. I feel certain she does not actually believe this tale, but contrived it to our mutual ruin. Should it reach the Queen, I most certainly will be relieved of your charge and Your Majesty's name blackened throughout England."

Throughout the world, she thought. Elizabeth would spread the scandal to best advantage. The Pope and Philip, whether they believed it or not, would find me too soiled to defend.

"I fear you are right," she said. "Though we both are ill and you are nearly seventy, folk will believe the worst. Damn Bess for a vile bitch!"

"She has always been jealous of Your Majesty. And now she visions her grandchild, Arabella Stuart, as possible heiress to the English throne. Thus she will do all in her power to discredit Your Majesty."

Mary said, "Perhaps I did well to take precautions against poison."

"The poison she spreads with her tongue is deadly. I would have spared you this, but I felt you should know the reason if you are suddenly removed from my charge."

"I dread a change," she said. "A harsh warden, perhaps a cruel one . . . Is there nothing we can do to stop the gossip?"

"We can pray that by some miracle it does not reach the Queen. I do not worry for myself; my life nears its end. But I fear lest this new lie convince folk that past charges against Your Majesty were true."

Chastelard, Rizzio, Bothwell . . .

Mary hid her face in her hands, took a deep, sob-choked breath. "This may mean my ruin."

Gently he said, "You have built from ruins before, Madam."

"But I am weary," she said, her voice muffled in the white fur of her sleeves. "So weary . . ."

XIX.

In April Mary was horrified to learn that her latest "adultery" was the talk of London. Elizabeth rocked with laughter, and spread the tale gleefully to foreign ambassadors.

Mary wrote to Elizabeth, hotly denying the slander and insisting that Bess be forced to admit she had lied. But Elizabeth was in no hurry to vindicate Mary. During that spring and summer she left her in Shrewsbury's care—a refinement of cruelty, Mary thought. Folk presume that we live in sin.

Shrewsbury went to London and begged Elizabeth to relieve him of his duty. But it was not until late August that Mary and her household were removed from Sheffield to Wingfield Manor in Derbyshire, where Sir Ralph Sadler became her jailer.

To Mary's relief Sadler was not a tyrant. But he kept her heavily guarded and insisted upon reading all outgoing letters. Her secretaries were searched upon leaving her apartments, her ladies permitted no farther than the courtyard. He made it clear that he would not be tricked.

Yet Mary tricked him. Years of intrigue had trained her to patience and perception. She knew instinctively which of Sadler's servants to flatter, which to bribe, which to mistrust. Within six weeks she was directing a new system of letter delivery and espionage.

The danger stimulated her. In September she felt able to cope with Elizabeth, and again demanded that Bess Shrewsbury prove the charge of adultery. Could there not be a quiet, dignified hearing behind closed doors?

Elizabeth's reply was to throw Bess into the Tower, trumpeting loudly that her "dear sister's honor" was again in jeopardy. In November Bess was called before the Privy Council. She went on her knees to Elizabeth and confessed that she had spread groundless slander, and that there was no evidence of adultery between Mary and her husband.

That week Mary received a note from a Catholic agent in London. *I fear Your Majesty's exoneration is a farce, for the Countess of Shrewsbury is not being punished. Has it not occurred to you that the Queen herself commanded the Countess to start the slander? Her hatred of you is maniacal.*

And so, at last, is my hatred of her, Mary thought. Elizabeth has been my enemy for twenty years, yet until now I considered her less a woman than an element—an ill wind, a haar, evil but impersonal. I have felt contempt for her, disillusion, bitter resentment. But now I loathe her.

Mary went to her desk. In a small golden chest lay copies made by her secretaries of letters she had written to Elizabeth since her captivity—letters alternately affectionate and defiant, pleading and disdainfully chill. But never had she written maliciously, never had she wounded Elizabeth's pride. A vulnerable pride, Mary thought, tormented by the stigmas of bastardy and ill-breeding. Now I shall claw it to shreds.

She sat down, dipped her quill in ink:

Madam:

I am constrained to inform you of what the Countess of Shrews-bury has told me. I reproved the lady for saying licentious things about you which of course I do not believe, namely . . . that you repeatedly shared a bedchamber with Leicester. She said that indubitably you are not like other women and it was folly to advance the notion of your marriage with the Duke de Alençon since such a marriage could never be consummated. She said it was shameful that you were not content to bed with Leicester, Christopher Hatton and other Englishmen but must compromise yourself with the foreigner Alençon and his servant Simier.

The Countess, in fits of laughter, advised me to place my son among the ranks of your lovers, saying it would help me. I replied that such an act would be interpreted as sheer mockery. She answered that you were so vain and had such vast opinion of your beauty—as if you were the Queen of Heaven—that she wagered she could easily force you to take the matter seriously. She said you were so fond of exaggerated adulation that no one dared look you full in the face since it was supposed to shine as radiant as the sun; that

she and the Countess of Lennox scarcely ventured to exchange
glances for fear of bursting into laughter over the way in which they
were openly ridiculing you . . . You see you are made game of and
mimicked by your ladies. She even mimicked you for the amusement
of my women, though I swear to you when I perceived it I forbade
them to sneer at you . . .

Mary paused, recollecting what else Bess had said, then wrote in
detail. Elizabeth mishandled her gentlewomen, had broken the
finger of one and slashed another's hand with a knife because a meal
had been served clumsily. She repeated the old gossip that Elizabeth
had a running sore on her leg (a hint of the yaws supposedly inherited from her father), and was likely to die of spreading rot.

If I may have an hour's speech with you I will give more particulars
of the names, times, dates, places and other circumstances to prove
to you the truth of this. You will find no relative, friend, nor even
subject more loyal and affectionate than myself.

Mary sanded the ink, perfumed the four pages with essence of
white rose and summoned her French secretary, Claude Nau.

"Read this," she said.

He read it, lifted a shocked face. "Madame," he said, "you hammer
your own scaffold! For the love of God destroy this. As it is, Her
Majesty can scarce abide you in the same country. Should she read
this she will not abide you in the same world."

Nau argued so passionately that Mary agreed not to send it, but
locked it in her desk for future consideration.

"I would feel easier if Your Majesty burned it," Nau said.

"No," she smiled. "I like to think that I hold a sword above her,
though I may never let it fall."

XX.

Two months later in a howling January snowstorm, Sir Ralph
Sadler removed Mary to the frigid, ramshackle castle of Tutbury.
It had stood vacant since her previous visit sixteen years before. Rats
slithered through the fallen plaster, bats clung to the rotting rafters.
The holes and chinks had widened with the years, so that the few
tapestries blew uselessly against the wind.

In her gloomy little presence chamber, Mary's ladies removed her
snowy cloak, wrapped her in mildewed blankets from the bed and
seated her by the fireplace. It smoked, drawing poorly from holes in
the falling roof. She looked in horror at the bare flagstone floor, the
cracked and peeling walls, the furniture green with mold.

"It will be warmer with Your Majesty's carpets and hangings,"
Elizabeth Curle said, her voice falsely cheerful. She went to the

bed, plumped the sagging mattress. Plaster sifted down from the ceiling and a fall of snow drenched the bed. Elizabeth jumped back, cursing under her breath.

"We must raise a canopy as we did before," Jane Kennedy said. She turned to Mary. "Remember our tents, Madam?"

"Aye—too well."

"Has Sir Ralph explained why we were brought here?" Elizabeth asked.

"No. But I think it obvious." Painfully, Mary shifted her swollen legs. "I am meant to die here. The damp will kill me."

"But it is murder, Madam!"

"Indeed—and Queen Elizabeth knows it full well. Her own physician told her years ago I could not endure this place in winter. So she returns me here, sixteen years frailer, to perish slowly." Mary smiled grimly. "It spares her the onus and expense of my execution."

Something has prodded Elizabeth to this, Mary thought. Perhaps the discovery of a new plot in my behalf. Young hotheads hatch them without my knowledge, yet I am blamed when they come to light.

Her ladies made up the bed with her silk sheets and fur robes, and helped her into it. There she remained through much of the winter, unable to keep warm in any other manner. Her carpets and tapestries proved useless against the drafts, and her servants suffered despite the warm clothing she provided them. In March, all of Mary's ladies were ill from chills and fever, and Bourgoing, her overworked physician, fell sick of the New Acquaintance and was unable to tend them.

Mary sent Claude Nau to London with messages to Elizabeth begging her removal, but he returned with only the vaguest promises.

"I have at least discovered why Your Majesty is so cruelly neglected," he said. "It is your son's doing."

"My son's!" She sat up on the bed pillows. "What do you mean?"

"While there was a possibility that he would ally with your friends in France and Spain, Queen Elizabeth maintained you in fair condition. But now he has abandoned Your Majesty and made a bond with Elizabeth, promising to betray all the plots against her."

"I cannot believe it! Whatever our political differences, James is my son, my own blood. Now that he is of age he must help me—"

"No, Madame," he said. "Queen Elizabeth has bought him for five thousand pounds a year, vague assurances of the succession—and six pairs of bloodhounds." Wryly, he added, "He has outgrown his fear of dogs, and made such an issue of the bloodhounds that delay in their shipment nearly terminated the negotiations. Above all else he loves hunting."

"He is truly his father's son," she said. Arrogant, pleasure-mad, swayed easily as a willow in the wind. Yet, unlike Darnley, a brilliant theologian, passionately spreading heretic doctrine and encouraging the printing of Protestant literature.

"He is clever, Madame, and fast becoming Queen Elizabeth's equal in duplicity. He plays Your Majesty and Queen Elizabeth against one another to achieve her crown." Nau paused, seeing her stricken face. "Surely," he added gently, "this is no surprise to you?"

"Perhaps I am naïve," she said. "But I thought that when he came of age he would shed his advisors and work for my freedom. He is eighteen, with a mind of his own—"

"But Madame, his mind was turned against you years ago. Face the truth."

The truth is that I was an indifferent mother, she thought, so deep in hate of Darnley that I scarce could look at his son.

"I am glad I never loved James," she sighed. "For if I had a mother's true devotion I could not have borne these years of estrangement."

"Then you feel nothing for the King—the Prince," Nau corrected hastily as she frowned.

"Nothing but contempt that he sells himself and my country to Elizabeth. But are you sure of your information?"

Nau named his informants, sources she had always found reliable. "Doubtless Your Majesty will hear from the Prince yourself in reply to your proposal for an Act of Association."

James replied a few days later, stating that since Mary was a prisoner in a foreign land he was in no position to form any association to share the crown with her. However, he added bluntly, he would recognize her as Queen Mother.

Queen Mother! Infuriated, Mary instructed her faithful French Ambassador, the old Archbishop of Glasgow, to withhold the title of King from James.

A mother's curse shall light upon him, she wrote. If he persists in this perfidy you can assure him I will invoke the malediction of God. I will deprive him of all the greatness to which he can pretend. He shall have nothing but what he inherits from his father. No punishment human or divine will be adequate . . .

Words, she thought hopelessly. How many millions of words have I written—and all futile. She flung down her quill, lay back against the bed pillows. The struggle was too cruelly uneven. She might as well give up.

Her gentleman of the chamber spoke from the shadows. "Are you finished writing, Madam?"

"Quite finished," Mary sighed.

He removed the writing board, the ink and parchment. "There is a sailorman in the village, Madam. He was at the tavern tonight."

"Indeed," Mary said listlessly.

"He told Sir Ralph's cook—who told me—that King Philip has ordered vast amounts of wood sent to a Spanish port."

Wood . . .

"Workmen are being hired by the thousands—metal-smiths, sail-makers, ship-fitters."

Mary sat upright. "This could mean my liberation! At last, by God's grace, King Philip is building an armada!"

CHAPTER FIFTEEN

I.

FROM MANY QUARTERS Mary heard of Philip's projected invasion of England, but she was not so credulous as to believe that his sole aim was her rescue. He wanted vengeance for English raids on his shipping, for the new law proclaiming it treason for Catholic priests to set foot on English soil. Principally, he wanted Elizabeth's crown for himself.

But Mary would not begrudge his ambition, if he deposed James and replaced her on the Scottish throne. Together in peace, she and Philip could rule a Catholic Britain. To please him and to spite her son, she informed Philip that she was making a will leaving him her Scots crown and her inherited English rights.

It would take him more than a year to prepare the huge fleet—one hundred and thirty ships and thirty thousand men. But the dream was in the making, and Mary was content to wait. With freedom in sight she could bear the gloomy castle and the gloomier weather.

In April Mary's health improved and she sought the sunlight, which never reached her apartments. There was no garden, only a quarter-acre of fenced ground near the stables. But it was all she had of springtime, and she cherished the hours there. The trellises were rotting, the arbors broken and bare of vines, but out on the heath were slopes of pale primroses and she caught the scent of wild strawberries.

Seated on cushions under an oak on a warm afternoon, she brushed her poodles and collared them with ribbons.

Sir Ralph Sadler approached with another gentleman and introduced him. "May I present to Your Majesty Sir Amyas Paulet?"

She smiled. "I have heard of you, Sir Amyas. You were English Ambassador to France, were you not?"

"Yes, Your Majesty." A flat, toneless voice. A thin solemn face.

She thought he resembled the caricatured Puritans one saw in Catholic pamphlets—his long nose wrinkled in fixed disapproval, his mouth puckered as though tasting vinegar. Above his gray, forked beard were eyes hard and sheenless as gravel.

"Sir Amyas is to have charge of Your Majesty henceforth," Sadler said. "I have told Her Majesty that I am too old for the responsibility."

Mary forced herself to composure, but she dreaded this change. Sir Amyas was known to be a fanatic Protestant, and his taciturn manner was not reassuring.

"The Queen commands more severe restrictions," Sir Amyas said. "Your Majesty's household must be isolated completely from the castle staff."

"For what reason?"

He ignored her question. "You are aware of the new law—the Bond of Association?"

"I am." A law aimed at me . . . binding all Englishmen to prosecute to the death those who conspire against Elizabeth . . . depriving of all rights as claimants any pretenders to the throne in whose favor such men conspire . . .

"It is a law which we trust will deter Your Majesty from further intrigue."

"But how can I prevent others from plotting against Her Majesty?" she asked angrily. "I cannot control the world."

"But I," Sir Amyas said, "can control you."

II.

Sir Amyas' control was so rigid that Mary's secret correspondence was halted completely. If she wished to write, she had to go to his study, beg paper and write in his presence. She assumed that he gave her letters to Cecil or spy-master Walsingham to forward or hold at their pleasure. Since her servants were forbidden to mingle with the castle staff, she had no means of smuggling out messages nor receiving any. The summer and autumn passed without news of any sort.

Her dislike of Sir Amyas deepened to violent hatred. She could have borne harshness, but he was also mean, petty, with an almost feminine venom. On his second day at Tutbury, he had ordered her canopy of state torn down from the chair in the dining hall. "Such royal insignia is unnecessary and unsuitable."

"*Unsuitable!*"

"Particularly as Your Majesty is so often confined to your chamber."

[559]

He considered her apartments needlessly luxurious, and held his nose against the incense that burned in her presence chamber. In October he announced that he was reducing expenditures.

"Her Majesty shall not pay one penny for wax candles burned to Romish idols," he said, pointing to Mary's altar. "Rushlights are good enough. Hereafter your fires shall be of turf or sea coal. The number of logs you consume in a single month would heat my chambers for a year."

"But I need heat. I could die without it. The damp—"

"It is scarce October, and you have both fireplaces ablaze . . . Now, as to food. Your French cuisine is fantastically expensive. Artichokes . . . oranges . . . almonds . . . fowl boiled in Madeira! And how in the name of heaven does your household consume two hogsheads of French wine a month?"

"I bathe in it," she said.

He snorted. "I asked you a serious question, Madam."

"I answered you seriously."

"But Her Majesty herself does not bathe in wine!"

"Her lack of refinement is not my concern."

"In your position such flummery is ridiculous!"

"In my position it is imperative." She thought, Such things are all I have left of grace. A bath of wine restores my bloom and nourishes my pride.

"Your Majesty shall bathe in water and eat plain English fare."

"I am not dependent upon Her Majesty's charity," Mary said haughtily. "My Master of the Household, Andrew Melville, will see that you are paid for whatever expenses I incur. I shall bathe in wine and burn wax tapers and applewood. I'll not live like a pig because I inhabit a sty."

"You are improvident, Madam. A woman in your position—"

"Precisely. I never forget my position, as you do. My bed is rotting, but I spread it with satin. These walls are crumbling, but I hang them with damask. My husband is dead, but I still perfume my nightrobes and bind my hair with corals."

"Preposterous!" He stared at her, sneering. "You'd best save your gold for your woe-wraps. You are forty-two—an old woman."

Stricken, she took a step backward. An old woman . . . The thought had entered her mind before, but softly, on tiptoe, unsure of itself. To hear it stated made it suddenly, brutally true. It was no less a fact because he spoke in hate. Her hair waved white under the auburn wig. A high ruff hid her wrinkling throat. The fine skin of her hands was branched with veins of violet.

Her chin trembled. Her shoulders slumped. Mutely she turned and crept into her bedchamber, shutting the door.

III.

Terrified at thought of another winter at Tutbury, Mary shed her pride and repeatedly begged Elizabeth to lodge her in warmer quarters. Finally on Christmas Eve Sir Amyas moved her to Chartley in Staffordshire.

The house was strongly fortified and heavily guarded. But Mary's rooms were dry and snug, and for a while she was content with negatives—she was not cold, her bones were not tortured, she would not die of the damp.

Yet she felt she might as well be dead as buried here behind these moated walls. News was the breath of life, but Sir Amyas told her nothing. The days passed, one like another. For hours she stood at her barred window staring at the ice-white sky. Once in sudden violence she tried the bars and looked in horror at her bloody hand. Thus had Bothwell started the path to madness.

At midnight on January 16th, Nau came to Mary's presence chamber greatly excited.

"Sir Amyas' butler crept to my room just now, Madame, and told me of a marvel. This afternoon the village brewer delivered beer as he does each week, trundling the casks into the wine cellar. As the butler paid him, the brewer whispered, 'You will be rewarded handsomely if you will aid the Queen of Scots.' Since the butler is underpaid and hates Sir Amyas, he listened to the brewer's proposal. Each week in the village a corked tube containing letters will be inserted in the bunghole of a beer barrel. Each week Your Majesty may fill the tube with letters and the butler will replace it in an empty cask to be taken away." Nau brought the tube from his belt. "Here is the first message, Madame."

Thrilled, she removed two letters from the tube and deciphered the first. It was from Thomas Morgan, a trusted agent in Paris, recommending to her Gilbert Gifford, an honest youth willing to die in her cause. Then she read Gifford's letter. He explained that he was a resident of the neighborhood, and offered to renew her correspondence through the brewer's deliveries. He and his Catholic friends would pay butler, brewer and carefully selected couriers.

With writing materials provided by the butler, Mary wrote to Gifford and accepted his service. Thereafter she sent and received letters each week and by May was in full communication with Rome, Spain, Scotland and France. From Paris, Morgan reminded her that Anthony Babington, once her secret friend at Sheffield, was still her devoted supporter. He was living in London now and might prove useful.

Useful indeed, she thought—young, adventurous, wealthy, ardently

Catholic. She wrote Babington a gracious note, and on July 10th received his reply, which her secretaries deciphered in her study.

Most mighty, most excellent, my dread sovereign lady and Queen:

It may please your gracious Majesty to excuse my long silence . . . In May there came to me one Ballard, a priest of virtue and learning and singular zeal to the Catholic cause and Your Majesty's service. This man informed me of great preparations by the Christian Princes (Your Majesty's allies) for the deliverance of our country from its miserable state . . . As delay is extremely dangerous it may please Your Majesty to direct us and so advance the affair . . .

Myself with ten gentlemen and a hundred followers will undertake your deliverance from the hands of your enemies. As to getting rid of the usurper, there are six noble gentlemen, all my intimate friends, who for the love they bear to the Catholic cause and Your Majesty's service will undertake the tragic execution . . .

Upon the 12th of this month I shall be at Litchfield expecting Your Majesty's answer . . .

Your most faithful subject and sworn servant,

Anthony Babington.

Mary put down the letter and stared into the fire. The old familiar plot—a rising of British Catholics with simultaneous Spanish invasion—Elizabeth's assassination. Her death will not be on my conscience, she thought, for I have not ordered it and could not prevent it. These are hot young fanatics, dedicated as much to her murder as they are to my liberation. Had I never lived, they would still want her blood.

She rose and carried the letter to her desk, rereading it in the light of the candelabra.

Nau's voice was sharp. "Madame, you must not answer that!"

"Not answer it?" she asked incredulously. "I would clutch at the merest straw—and this is far more."

"Or a trap."

"I know Anthony Babington better than you do," she said indignantly. "For more than a year he helped me under Lord Shrewsbury's very nose. I would trust him with my life."

"I do not question his loyalty, but his letter is reckless. To answer it would be folly. How can you be sure that these 'ten gentlemen' are trustworthy?"

"They are his intimate friends."

Gilbert Curle, her Scots secretary, said, "Monsieur Nau is right, Madam. To write him in your own cipher you must send him the key. If it falls into enemy hands—"

"Why should it? Master Gifford is extremely careful of his

couriers, but to be doubly safe I shall ask him to deliver this to Babington himself."

They argued far into the night and again the next morning. But she was determined to write.

It was a long letter and she asked detailed information. How many troops could be raised in England, what military leaders would they appoint, where would the chief force assemble, from what ports would foreign help arrive, what arms were needed and how much money was required? How did they plan her escape?

. . . Beware that your messengers carry no letters upon them . . . take heed of spies and false brethren that are amongst you, especially of some priests trained by our enemies . . .

She suggested three means for her escape from Chartley and ended the letter with her thanks.

Whatever happens I shall be greatly obliged as long as I live for the offers you make to hazard yourself for my delivery.

God Almighty have you in protection,

Your friend forever.

Fail not to burn this quickly.

She gave the letter to Curle to put into cipher. "I shall not sign the letter. Note that I do not mention the six gentlemen, nor inquire into their plans. I wish to know nothing of the assassination, for my conscience does not approve it."

Though, God forgive me, my heart does . . .

IV.

A month later Sir Amyas said, "Your Majesty is looking more cheerful than usual. Do you feel well enough to hunt?"

She feared some cruel jest. "What do you mean?"

"Sir Walter Aston has invited Your Majesty to hunt in his park at Tixhall. He says the stags are fat."

"And you would actually let me go?" she asked, astonished.

"Aye, in my care."

He cannot know how much this means to me, Mary thought, or he would never permit it. To hunt! Free on a galloping horse, free in the wild green forest with the smell of trampled mint and sweetbriar and thyme. Old and rheumatic though I be, I warrant I'll handle my crossbow as well as ever. But even if my arrows miss their mark they will still soar gold in the sunlight and the hounds will bugle and my heart will store the day against the dark.

Foul weather delayed the hunt for several days, but on the morning of August 16th the sun streamed into Mary's bedchamber, and she summoned her ladies to dress her.

She stood at the mirror, tall, magnificently erect, the black pearled riding boots hiding her swollen legs, her great sleeves caught in points concealing her swollen arms. Plumes curled coquettishly from the brim of her hat matching the crimson of her lips.

"I could be thirty," Mary said, "by taperlight."

Marie said gravely, "I am nineteen and I am not ugly. But God help me should Your Majesty and I fancy the same man!"

They laughed and drank a toast to the day and trooped downstairs to the courtyard. Sir Amyas was unbelievably gracious in permitting Mary's servants to accompany her—secretaries Nau and Curle, Andrew Melville, Bourgoing and several of her ladies.

Preceded by the guards, Mary galloped at the head of the cavalcade, wishing it were twenty miles to Tixhall instead of three. The day was perfect and the heath fragrant from recent rains. She was momentarily so happy that she even turned in the saddle to smile and wave to Sir Amyas who was lagging far behind.

Nearing the gates of Tixhall Mary exclaimed at formal gardens hedged with hornbeam and a menagerie of painted and gilded griffins, unicorns and stags. It was long since she had looked upon elegance and her eyes were greedy.

"Madam." Sir Amyas rode up to her. "Here is Sir Thomas Gorge, a messenger from the Queen."

Mary checked her horse as a man in green habit swept off his hat and bowed.

"Your Majesty," Sir Thomas said, "the Babington conspiracy has been discovered and I am charged to arrest your secretaries. My mistress found it difficult to believe that you would intrigue against her and the state, but she has seen proof with her own eyes."

Mary gasped. "She is mistaken! I have not intrigued against her, but only for my release."

"She has proof," Sir Thomas repeated. He turned to Sir Amyas. "You know your orders."

Curle and Nau were trying to push toward Mary, but guards forced them back, and Sir Thomas rode off with them, followed by six horsemen. Mary, numb with terror, slumped in the saddle.

"Ride on, Madam." Sir Amyas' voice whipped her.

"Do we not return to Chartley?" she asked.

"I said ride on." He pointed to Tixhall, and she spurred her horse through the gates and up the long avenue. Bourgoing rode up to her, tried to comfort her, and assured Sir Amyas there had been a grave mistake.

"There has indeed," Sir Amyas said grimly, "And Queen Mary has made it."

Mary's thoughts were churning. How much did Elizabeth know?

Was she lying in saying that she had proof of the conspiracy? Had they tortured Babington? Would they torture her secretaries?

Followed by armed guards, Sir Amyas led Mary through Tixhall's great hallway up a carved oak staircase to a small bedchamber.

"Why am I here?" she demanded.

He said nothing, punching the bed's mattress. Dust rose like smoke from the moth-eaten gray velvet spread.

"For the love of heaven, bring me paper and quill and let me write to the Queen!"

"You shall write nothing."

He left her, locking the door. She heard Bourgoing outside in the corridor pleading to attend her, and Sir Amyas' curt refusal.

Suddenly she realized that the hunt had been a pretext to remove her from Chartley and search her apartments for incriminating evidence. Frantic, she tried to recall which papers she had burned, which were locked in coffers and desk. There was her will, leaving her royal rights to Philip. There were notes she had given Nau before dictating the long letter to Babington, but luckily she had not kept a copy of the letter itself. She had burned Babington's reckless letter to her and another less dangerous one. But what messages might arrive tomorrow when the brewer made his weekly delivery —messages she would never see?

She pressed her hands to her eyes. "*Jesu!*" The taunting letter she had written to Elizabeth was still in her desk. Even if Elizabeth could forgive the conspiracy, she would never forgive that venomous letter relating her vulgarities, listing her lovers. She would have been enraged had she received it privately, but now, aware that her searchers had read it, she would be doubly humiliated.

Mary clung to the faint hope that Curle or Nau had destroyed it without her knowledge, had burned the notes on the letter to Babington. But even if they had, Babington might have kept her letter and copies of his. And failing paper proof, there was the rack to force his confession.

She suffered on a mental rack for ten days, saw no one save Jane, Marie and an apothecary. Sir Amyas did not appear until the morning he escorted her back to Chartley.

At Chartley she found her chambers ransacked, the desk and three coffers gone, all of her silver plate and jewels missing. She had only the rings on her fingers, the crucifix and beads she had worn to Tixhall. From the floor she picked up a list, evidently forgotten in the searchers' haste, marked "Goods Stolen From the Queen of Scots." It included everything of value except her money, clothes, holy relics and a few trinkets.

She turned on Sir Amyas in a fury. "I cannot believe Her Majesty stoops to theft—but I can believe it of you!"

He shrugged and was silent.

Several times in the days that followed, she sent for Sir Amyas, repeatedly protesting her innocence of plotting Elizabeth's death, begging him for news of Babington and her secretaries. But he told her nothing.

Looking from her window one day, she saw Sir Amyas walking in the garden with his butler. Suddenly he laughed, slapped the butler's shoulder affectionately, walked on past the yew hedges, around the castle and out of her sight.

So the butler had not been dismissed. Probably he had been Sir Amyas' spy all along, taking messages from the beer casks and showing them to his master. Perhaps in that manner they had the key to her cipher from the start and made copies of every letter sent and received . . .

One morning while Mary was still abed, Sir Amyas came to her, ordered her women from the chamber and demanded the keys to her money cabinet.

"I will not give them to you," she said. "The money is for my funeral and for my servants. It will pay their expenses back to their homelands when I am dead."

"It will also pay bribes," he said. "Give me the keys or I'll break the cabinet."

"Oaf," she said contemptuously. But she told him where the keys were hidden, and he opened the cabinet and removed the canvas money bag.

"Two things you cannot take from me," she said haughtily. "My royalty and my religion. And I still do not believe Her Majesty ordered this theft. I shall write to her if I have to use blood on linen!"

"Save your strength, Madam. You are taking a journey."

"Where?"

"I am not authorized to tell you. We leave within the week."

The Tower, she thought . . . and the block.

V.

For three days Mary and her household traveled under heavy guard, stopping at inns overnight. They avoided large towns, and the names of the villages meant nothing to Mary. She had no hint of their destination. Vainly she begged information, looked about for a familiar road. They seemed to be riding north one day, south the next. Perhaps it was Elizabeth's plan to drive her mad.

It was late September and harvests lay plump on the land. Wild grapes ripened on country stiles and sumach reddened in the lanes. She sensed that it was her last autumn, that she would die with the year. Bravely, she hoped, and without self-pity. I have had more than most folk, she thought—love and grandeur, passion and power. I have missed only peace.

But peace she would have too. She would find it in prayer, in true repentance. Wherever they took her, there God would be.

At twilight on the third day she saw a castle towering black against a lilac sky. Monstrous, double-moated, it dominated the surrounding moors from the banks of a river.

"Fotheringay," Sir Amyas said.

Fotheringay . . . Mary caught her breath. A state prison so fearsome that Catherine of Aragon had begged on her knees for the Tower. In the dungeons the sound of dripping water to taunt the thirst of prisoners licking the damp stone . . . a new torture chamber with Spanish innovations—the eye wrench, the breast screw, thin rods for internal probing.

She noticed Sir Amyas watching her closely, expectantly. *He wants to report my terror to Elizabeth. He would delight in my tears.*

"Mon Dieu," she said, smothering a yawn. "I shall welcome a bed."

Violently he burst out, "You'll not sleep this night when I tell you what has happened." He checked his horse and she halted hers.

"Babington was seized and sent to the Tower. There he was confronted with a copy of his letter to you and your reply. He admitted both were criminal. He was tried and condemned with twelve other conspirators and executed at St. Giles-in-the-Field in London."

She listened, nauseated. Babington and the priest Ballard were cut down from the gallows while still alive, disemboweled and quartered after three hours of torture. Others had their sexual organs cut off and were allowed to bleed to death. Still others, more mercifully, were hanged until dead.

"And what of my secretaries?"

"They are prisoned in Sir Francis Walsingham's house and have fully confessed your crimes."

Poor wretches, tortured, terrified . . . She wondered what had happened to Gilbert Gifford who had instigated the beer barrel correspondence, but dared not ask for fear of betraying him.

"Who were the conspirators executed?" she asked.

Sir Amyas told her their names, but Gifford's was not among them. Strange, for he had been deep in the plot and, she guessed, one of the six gentlemen designated to assassinate Elizabeth. It seemed incredible that the others had not betrayed him under torture, but she was grateful that he at least was free.

"Then all the conspirators are dead?" she asked.

"All but yourself—Madam."

VI.

Mary's apartments were small and dismally dark, but she was grateful for an adjoining oratory. There she placed her wooden saints and holy pictures, laid upon the altar her lovingly embroidered cloths. There she prayed for courage.

Shortly after Mary's arrival, a messenger from Elizabeth brought her a letter marked "In Strict Confidence." Elizabeth asked her to admit her guilt in the conspiracy. "If you will do this by letter, in your own hand, as queen to queen and woman to woman, submitting to my personal judgment, you will not be tried in open court and I will find some means of lenience."

She offers me my life, Mary thought, but at too high a price. In admitting guilt I would betray my honor and the honor of my church, and give her the spurious glory of tolerance and mercy. In short, she wants me to debase myself and deify her to the world.

And so, "In Strict Confidence," Mary wrote her contemptuous refusal and from her window watched the messenger start south through the grain-colored fields of Northamptonshire.

During those two weeks she suffered cruelly from the pain in her side, but was cheered that her servants were allowed to attend her —physician, surgeon, and apothecary; Master of the Household Melville, her chef and her ladies. Their quarters were cramped, and she asked Sir Amyas why they could not have more space; she had seen large empty apartments on the way up the staircase.

"Those chambers are reserved for the lords of the Council and Her Majesty's commissioners who are coming here to question you." His voice suddenly turned soft. "If you will ask Her Majesty's humble pardon for your crimes, I will report to her—"

"No. Since I have committed no crime against her I cannot ask pardon."

"Then it will go ill with you. The evidence is all against you."

"Naturally," she said. "The commissioners will see to that."

They arrived October 11th. More than fifty, and an escort of two thousand horsemen. They brought her a letter from Elizabeth, addressed insolently "To the Scot," demanding that Mary submit herself to the commissioners and answer their questions.

Two days later, seven lords preceded by an usher bearing the Great Seal of England came to Mary's presence chamber. She received them with assumed serenity, trying to conceal her shaking nervousness. Cecil . . . Walsingham . . . men dedicated to her destruction.

Lord Chancellor Bromley said, "We are commissioned to examine Your Majesty on the recent conspiracy involving regicide and invasion. Neither your rank nor your condition as prisoner can exempt you from obedience to English law."

She said calmly, "I would rather die than acknowledge myself Her Majesty's subject or bow to her jurisdiction. It would betray the dignity of other sovereigns as well as my own. But I am willing to reply to all questions, provided I am interrogated before a free Parliament and not before these men, who have doubtless been carefully selected and who have probably condemned me unheard."

They protested that they had not condemned her.

"Nor has Her Majesty," Cecil said, eyes hard, voice wheedling. "She is anxious that your innocence be proven."

"Aye," Mary said with an ironical little smile. "As anxious as you are."

How bloodless he is, she thought, in his somber silvery velvet, his silver hair smooth as a cap, his eyes cold as blue-white ice. Sixty-six years old in cunning, and devious as a maze.

"Must I remind you of Her Majesty's generosity?" he asked. "She punished those who contested your pretensions to the crown. In her goodness she saved you from being judged of high treason with the Duke of Norfolk. She has protected you from the fury of your own subjects—"

"You stray from the point," Mary said. "I cannot be tried, for I am a queen and subject to no one. Remember too that the world is wider than the realm of England." She added, "I was about to dine. You will have the kindness to leave me."

They left. But later in the afternoon they returned, insisting that she must appear to answer charges.

"The statute under which you would try me," she said, "is the new 'Bond of Association' made expressly to convict me and dispossess me of my rights to the throne. I repeat, I am not subject to English law and it has no validity for me, because I am kept here by force."

Sir Christopher Hatton said gently, "You are accused of conspiring in our Queen's death. If you are innocent, you harm your reputation by evading trial. Lay aside the bootless privilege of royal dignity, appear in judgment and protest your innocence, lest you bear an eternal blot upon your honor."

I will be tried whether I am present or not, she thought. But if I agree to appear I establish a dangerous precedent for rulers throughout the world, weakening the inviolability of royalty. On the other hand, my absence will be taken for cowardice, my silence for guilt.

She turned to Walsingham. "I offer to stand trial upon one point alone—conspiracy against the Queen's life—for I swear I am innocent."

"Indeed, Madam," Walsingham said, "we shall consider that point alone and begin examination tomorrow."

She appraised him curiously, wondering if it was true that Elizabeth hated him for his bluntness, his lack of humor, his refusal to flatter her or flirt. He was not unattractive—dark, with great, deep-set black eyes and a pointed beard, hollow-cheeked, superbly groomed. But whatever Elizabeth's personal feelings, she held him in high favor as spy-master.

Walsingham removed a paper from his belt. "A letter from the Queen, Madam."

Mary dismissed them to read the letter in private.

You have planned in diverse ways to take my life and ruin my kingdom by the shedding of blood. I never proceeded so harshly against you but maintained you and preserved your life with the same care which I use for myself. Your treachery will be proved to you and made manifest in the very place where you are. And it is my pleasure that you shall reply to my nobles and to the peers of my kingdom as you would to myself were I present. I have heard of your arrogance and therefore I demand, charge and command you to reply to them. But answer fully and you may receive greater favor from us.

Elizabeth, R.

Mary summoned Bourgoing and showed him the letter. "I had made up my mind to stand trial, but now that she presumes to command me I shall refuse."

He said, "I am your physician, not your counselor. But I strongly advise you to stand trial. Otherwise they will try you without a word spoken in your defense."

She knew he was right. All night she stayed awake rehearsing what she would say, refuting probable charges. She knew nothing of English law, but even if they offered her counsel she dared not accept it. Better to risk her own mistakes than trust a lawyer provided by the enemy.

At nine o'clock in the morning, robed in black, a veil of white gauze flowing from her peaked coif, Mary entered the trial chamber, supported by Bourgoing and Andrew Melville. On benches at the right of the large room sat Lord Bromley, Cecil and the earls; on the left the barons and knights of the Privy Council, Walsingham, Hatton, Sir Ralph Sadler and others. Around a table sat six judges, two doctors of civil law, the Attorney and Solicitor Generals, notaries, lawyers and clerks.

Sir Amyas came forward and escorted Mary to a scarlet velvet chair. Above it on a dais stood a chair of state sheltered by a canopy emblazoned with the arms of England. Symbol of Elizabeth's presence, it dominated the room.

Looking up at it, Mary fancied that Elizabeth actually sat there in her crimped red wig, jeweled ruff, skirts spread over a monstrous farthingale. She imagined the long, oval, ivory-skinned face, the cheeks sunken from pulled teeth. A face ravaged by years of terrible decisions and more terrible indecisions, by screaming tantrums and fierce, frustrating loves. Small eyes, beaky nose, cruel red gash of a mouth—and liver-spotted hands clutching the scepter of justice . . .

"My place should be there," Mary said to Melville. Then she turned to face the assembly.

Lord Chancellor Bromley rose, and the room quieted. He went to the dais and knelt in obeisance to Elizabeth. Bowing backward, he paused before Mary.

"We are gathered here as Her Majesty's commission to examine the Queen of Scots, not in desire for vengeance but in duty to English subjects. Madam, you will hear the indictment."

"First," she said, "I wish to make it clear that I am not here as Her Majesty's subject and recognize no superior save God. I came to this kingdom on promise of her assistance and aid against my enemies."

Bromley denied that Mary had entered England on promise of Elizabeth's assistance.

"You are mistaken, my lord. I came here relying on her promises of friendship and aid in time of trouble." She drew Elizabeth's ring from her finger. "This she sent me in pledge—regard it well. Trusting to this, I came among you. All of you know how the pledge has been kept."

After hearing the indictment, Mary again protested the new law on which it was based. Then Gowdy, the Queen's Sergeant, described the seizure of Babington and the six men who had conspired to murder Elizabeth.

"What know you of this, Madam?"

"I knew nothing of the six gentlemen, neither their names nor their occupations, and have trafficked with none of them."

"But you knew Babington."

"No." The lie was safe, for Lord Shrewsbury had had no idea that his ward, then twelve years old, had conspired with Mary at Sheffield. "I never met him."

"But you wrote to him." Bromley pointed to papers on the table. "We have copies of your correspondence."

"Copies?" she said scathingly. "Then it is second-hand evidence and totally invalid. Why do you not produce the originals, so that I may compare them with the copies side by side?"

She stared at Walsingham, who found sudden interest in his signet ring. "Could it be," she asked, "that my ciphers have been tampered with?"

There was indignant babble, all of the men talking at once. She raised her hand for silence.

"I wish to examine this correspondence."

"It will be read to you," Bromley said, and instructed the clerk to read the letters aloud.

Babington's letter to her sounded like the original, word for word, as she remembered it.

"And now Your Majesty's reply."

It began as she had written it. Then, in horror, she heard an unfamiliar paragraph:

By what means do the six gentlemen plan to proceed? When affairs are prepared and forces in readiness both within and without the realm, then shall it be time to set the six gentlemen to work, that upon the accomplishment of their design I may be suddenly freed from this place . . .

She sprang from her chair, wincing at the pain in her legs. "I did not write that! I swear I never—"

"You will be seated, Madam," Bromley said, "and the reading will proceed."

The letter continued as she had written it, but a spurious postscript had been added:

I would be glad to know the names and qualities of the six gentlemen who are to accomplish the designment, for it may be that upon knowledge of the parties I can give you further advice. I wish to know the names of all such principal persons, and also from time to time how you proceed.

Dear God, she thought, my original letter was probably removed from the tube by Sir Amyas, delivered to Walsingham for these interpolations, and then sent to Babington to induce him to write me the names of all conspirators. Probably Gilbert Gifford was Walsingham's spy set to trap me by instigating the beer-barrel correspondence.

"I swear on my word as Queen I did not write the two portions referring to the six gentlemen," Mary said furiously. "It is easy to forge ciphers and handwriting." She glared at Walsingham. "I suspect this is your work and I demand to see the originals."

Again a babble of voices. When they quieted, she said, "I do not deny that I have done my utmost to escape. But I take God as witness that I have neither conspired against the life of your Queen,

[572]

nor approved such a plot. I confess I have written my friends appealing for their help to remove me from miserable prisons where I have languished for nearly nineteen years. I have also pleaded the cause of oppressed Catholics with the kings of Europe—I would gladly shed my blood for them. But I declare formally that I did not write the words produced against me. Can I be held responsible for the criminal projects of a few desperate men, which they planned without my knowledge or participation?"

"Babington confessed your full knowledge," Walsingham said.

"Why was he put to death without my confronting him? Is it because such a meeting would have brought to light the truth? Is that why he was executed so hastily?"

"Your two secretaries also confessed, Madam, stating that this letter was dictated by you and transcribed by them into cipher."

"I should like to see their depositions."

They handed her Nau's purported confession. It stated that Mary had directed many conspiracies against Elizabeth, though he had often tried to deter her.

"Do you claim that this deposition is in Nau's handwriting?" she asked Walsingham.

"He wrote and signed it with his own hand."

"Then his hand was cramped from torture. This is not his usual writing, and if you will send for members of my household they will bear me out."

"Naturally," Walsingham sneered.

"Then send this to France! Others will testify that he never wrote it."

"Others being your friends."

"Then why is Nau not here to testify against me? Why are he and Curle held in your house when they should be present as witnesses? What is it you fear, that they will repudiate confessions doubtless made under duress?"

"We will recess for dinner," the Judge said.

When I make points they cannot refute, they read an indictment, or evade a reply, or recess, she thought. In truth, they are not trying me for conspiracy in Elizabeth's murder, but as lay leader of Catholic Britain and for being the legitimate Queen of England. They are also trying me for the venomous letter I wrote to Elizabeth; but that is one document they will not dare produce, even in copy.

The trial continued through the long afternoon. Contrary to their promise, the commissioners brought up other charges besides Elizabeth's plotted murder, and Mary constantly led them back to the point. Repeatedly she demanded to see the original Babington correspondence, and always they avoided a direct answer. Lawyers hurled questions at her, and without waiting for an answer declared her guilty of deception and evasion. As many as seven or eight questioned her simultaneously, shouting one another down and drowning out her replies. By five o'clock she was fighting not only eleven furious lawyers but a compulsion to faint.

When the trial resumed the next day she said, "I find myself overwhelmed by advocates and lawyers, but if I must submit to them I ask at least to reply to each person and to each point separately, without confusion. And is it not against all justice that I am denied counsel, papers and notes, a secretary? It is easy for you to vanquish by force of words a solitary and defenseless woman. But there is not one among you, even the cleverest, who would be capable of defending himself were he in my place."

Cecil brought up the matter of her will. "You have transmitted to King Philip your pretended rights to the crown of England."

"Those rights are not pretense, as well you know," she said. "And though I have no kingdom to confer, I have the legal privilege to give what belongs to me."

"If the Spanish army had entered the country could you have answered for the Queen's life?"

"I am not bound to answer for Spain and am ignorant of the King's intentions. But I could have brought about an understanding between the two countries—as I have often wished to do." She thought of Philip's slowly building armada. "If you destroy me I warn you that you place England in grave danger."

The lawyers began shouting again, charging that in Rome Mary was publicly prayed for as legitimate Queen of England.

"If the Pope gives me the title of queen, it is not for me to correct him. He knows what he does much better than I," she said.

They shifted back to the Babington plot, insisting that she had approved Elizabeth's murder, a Catholic rising and her subsequent enthronement.

Wearily, she reiterated that she had not conspired in murder—only for her freedom. "If the Catholics offered their aid, it was to their own interest, since they are so wickedly oppressed here that they have fallen into despair . . ."

She seized the chance to plead for the thousands of Catholics in English prisons. But Cecil checked her eloquence.

"If it pleases Your Majesty, you may now withdraw and we shall conclude without you."

She rose. "I again demand to be heard in full Parliament, to see original documents and to confer personally with Queen Elizabeth. I am ready and willing to serve her. I desire no evil to anyone here, and I pardon all that you have said and done against me."

Slowly she walked to Walsingham and took him aside. "You know full well the world will brand this trial a farce. You break your own laws by providing me no counsel, by calling no witnesses and by presenting only copies of flagrantly falsified letters which no other court on earth would regard as evidence." She added disdainfully, "Send me to the block, but I promise you will see a martyr's death. You think me helpless, but time is on my side and the judgment of the future will brand your mistress a murderess."

He spluttered. "An empty prophecy."

"You know better. Tell your mistress to consider this: I face one man—the executioner. She must face the world's condemnation, and the contempt of millions yet unborn."

"You are no seeress."

"Persons facing eternity may sometimes glimpse the future." She smiled. "But I need no mystic powers to divine your verdict. It was made long ago."

"Your Majesty will hear our verdict by midnight," he said coldly.

But at midnight Sir Amyas informed her that Elizabeth had ordered them to suspend sentence until she herself had read a report of the proceedings, and commanded the commissioners to meet in the Star Chamber of Westminster in ten days and there decide Mary's fate.

"So you have ten days of grace," Sir Amyas said.

Ten days of prayer . . .

Sure of the verdict, she did not pray for her life but for the strength to yield it gallantly. For hours she knelt in her oratory in the incense-clouded candlelight. Gradually peace stole over her like slowly filtering sun and the terror of hellfire left her.

Close, closer to God than ever before, she whispered, "I repent . . ." Not her love for Bothwell, but her adultery, Not her righteous anger against Elizabeth, but her petty vengefulness.

"Teach me to pity her for she suffers more than I."

From the old disease of indecision. How many times has she signed my death warrant, then burned it to ash? How often during these ten days has she pronounced me guilty, then delayed the sentence? Always cursed by vacillation, she now must be in agony, for Cecil and Walsingham push her to the wall and demand she take final action. But she knows full well that if she executes me she sets a precedent dooming forever the inviolability of rulers. She gives her own subjects the right to judge and condemn her.

She suffers no less from guilt, for surely she is aware of forged evidence and false depositions. She fears Philip's vengeance, the world's censure, my martyrdom.

"Please, God, may I be brave . . ."

On All Saints' day she granted audience to Sir Amyas. With unusual courtesy he asked her how she spent her time.

"In prayer. With books. I am reading history and the lives of the saints."

He said gently, "Will you not plead guilty and throw yourself on Her Majesty's mercy? Confess your crime."

"Her Majesty cannot win my confession if she stretches me on the rack," Mary said. "There is no torture devised that can make me confess."

"Does your life mean nothing to you?"

"This life," she smiled, "means very little."

The ten days stretched into more than three weeks. Finally on November 20th Sir Amyas came to Mary with Lord Buckhurst, Sir Drue Drury and Master Beale, Clerk of the Council.

Mary received them graciously. "You may be seated, gentlemen."

Buckhurst opened his mouth, closed it, glanced at his companions. The room was silent save for the wind-gusted curtains and the bony arms of the oaks brushing the casement.

Mary's voice was steady. "You have brought me the verdict?"

Buckhurst did not look at her. "After long deliberation, Madam, Parliament has pronounced sentence of death."

She said, "I expected nothing else. You may tell Her Majesty that I rejoice that my troubles are ending, and thank her for my release."

"The Queen has not yet consented," Buckhurst said, "but since Parliament strongly urges her approval, she is unlikely to overrule the decision. She is aware that neither she nor the state nor the religion is safe so long as Your Majesty lives. Thus we have been sent to warn you to prepare for death. The Dean of Peterborough will be brought here for your consolation—"

"Let him console a Protestant," she said. "I do not want him. He shall not meddle with my last days. I wish to have a Catholic priest. And I beg that my money and jewels be returned to me."

Sir Drue said, "We shall ask Her Majesty." He stared at Mary curiously. "I marvel at your calmness, Madam."

"Why should I be troubled? My conscience is clear and I count it an honor to die for my faith."

"You persist in untruth," Lord Buckhurst said. "You do not die for your faith, but for conspiring in murder and overthrow of the government. Thus, Madam, you will not end as a saint or martyr, but as a criminal."

"Make your peace with God," Sir Drue said. "You may have little time."

Mary went to the window and drew back the draperies. A gray

November day, long shadows sliding along the fields, colorless save for pumpkins glowing between the haystacks.

She turned to them and smiled. "I have made my peace with God. And I have all of time."

From Fotheringay this 19th day of
December 1586

Madam:

. . . Lately on hearing the sentence given by your last assemblage that I should prepare myself for death, I begged them to thank you for such agreeable tidings and to implore you to permit me certain things, together with my money, which Sir Amyas Paulet assures me will follow. For this I wish to return thanks and to supplicate one last favor . . . In Jesus' name I require you to promise that you will permit my poor servants to bear my body to France for burial in holy ground near the late Queen my mother; because in Scotland the bodies of the kings my ancestors have been insulted and the churches pulled down and profaned . . . As I am told you have even conceded me a priest, I hope you will not refuse this, my last request . . . And because I fear the secret tyranny of some of those into whose power you have abandoned me, I beg you not to permit me to be executed without your knowledge—not from fear of the pain, which I am ready to suffer, but so that there may be reliable witnesses. I require that my attendants remain to be witnesses that I die in the faith of my Savior . . .

Do you wish me to return the jewel which you gave me now or later?

You will certainly have heard that they pulled down my canopy of state—by your order, they said. Later they confessed it was not done by your command but by some of the council. I praise God that such malice came not from you. I fear it has been like this in other matters and that is why they would not permit me to write you until they had taken from me all external symbols of dignity and power, telling me I was simply a dead woman.

. . . Do not accuse me of presumption if I remind you that one day you will have to answer for your charge . . . I pray that my blood and my country may be remembered in that time . . .

Mary, R.

VII.

December passed with no word from Elizabeth, and on January 12th Mary wrote her again: . . . *I require you, Madam, not to keep me longer in this miserable suspense which is more cruel than any certainty . . .*

Mary was certain that Elizabeth dreaded signing the death warrant, and feared she might secretly order assassination, thus escaping responsibility and at the same time depriving her of a martyr's death. Taking all possible precautions, Mary ate and drank nothing that had not been tasted. Men and women servants kept vigil in her bedchamber when she slept and guarded her when she ventured into the corridor for exercise. She never opened a letter or a parcel herself, lest her hands be pricked by a poison dart.

Sir Amyas read all messages addressed to her and, she felt sure, withheld most of them. She knew nothing of the world's reaction save what she could patch together from scraps of information overheard by her attendants. The people of Scotland apparently were infuriated by her plight. In Edinburgh her son was jeered and hooted on the High Street, the burghers demanding that he intercede for her life. Thus he had sent an envoy to Elizabeth, ostensibly to plead for Mary, actually to approve the death sentence.

Once she would have raged at such treachery. Now she accepted it sadly. In James, the gallant, reckless Stuart blood was subordinate to his craven Lennox heritage. Erudite he might be, and Elizabeth's match in guile, but he was Darnley's son, loving his drink and his hounds more than he loved his honor.

In her heart she forgave him, but she did not change her will in his favor. She left him the cloth of state now forbidden her and a piece of unicorn horn as antidote for poison. To her ladies she bequeathed her pitifully small possessions—clothes, a coral chain, a gold bodkin tipped with sapphire, a little silver heart, a bottle of sweet water, two ounces of musk. All of her servants would share in the sale of her furniture. She arranged for their transportation back to their homes and for their pensions. In behalf of those who were French, she begged her De Guise relatives to employ as many as possible and see to the needs of the old Archbishop of Glasgow in Paris.

Her will was nearly complete, her farewells written. The attire she would wear to her execution was assembled, even to the gold-bordered handkerchief that would bind her eyes at the block. She had done much of the sewing herself, embroidering a golden piety on the blood-red camisole, stitching the points of her sleeves, hemming the endless yards of her black robe.

There remained now only the need to strengthen her faith, and she blessed Elizabeth for permitting her a confessor, Father de Préau. But in late January Sir Amyas confined the priest to the far side of the castle and forbade Mary to see him.

"I demand to know whether Queen Elizabeth has commanded this," Mary said. "Surely it is my right to have spiritual solace."

"You have no rights, Madam. You are legally dead."

VIII.

The bedchamber curtains were drawn against the cold February day, and an oak fire crackled in the hearth. On a cushion by the fire, Jane Kennedy curled a wig and perfumed it with musk. At the window seat, Marie Paget played her lute, singing softly. Mary sat on a couch at the foot of her bed, trying to ignore the pain tugging at her side. She snapped her fingers to her white Highland terrier, who jumped up beside her, and she smiled and shook hands with his paw.

"Not too much musk on the wig," she said to Jane. "I wish to save most of the vial for you."

Jane's eyes sparkled with tears. "Ah, Madam, do not talk so. I cannot bear it! I fear I cannot bear another week, another day—"

"I know," Mary said. "You have mourned me these four months."

Marie broke off her song. "Damn Queen Elizabeth! I think indecisiveness should be a mortal sin!"

Gently Mary reproved her. "She is tormented as much as we. And you will speak of her with respect."

"How can I respect her when she treats Your Majesty so?"

"Because she is a queen. Because disrespect breeds anarchy."

"But she is wicked!"

"Not to her people. They worship her—"

There was a tap on the door, and Marie went into the presence chamber. After a few minutes she came back, her eyes enormous.

"What is it?" Mary asked, alarmed.

"A guard, Madam—a Scot! He whispered a message for you. It must be a jest in dreadful taste, for he says it is from the Earl of Bothwell, whose courier hides in the village."

Bothwell! Mary's heart wrenched at sound of the name. Then she realized this was his nephew Francis, son of his sister Janet Hepburn and Mary's half-brother Lord John Stuart. The lad—ah, no, a man now—had inherited Bothwell's title, and must be at least twenty-five.

"Lord Bothwell is no ghost, cherie, but my nephew. What is his message?"

"He asked your son to appoint him Ambassador to England, thinking to help you that way, but the King refused him. So he told the King plain out in council that if he allowed Your Majesty to suffer he deserved to hang."

Mary's laugh rippled. "He also inherited my husband's frankness."

"The King was nearly seized with a fit, and while the council poured wine down him, Lord Bothwell stalked out of Holyrood and rode to the Border, where he is trying to raise an army for your rescue. He says that he races time, but that should he fail you are to know this: On the day he hears of your death his dole-weeds will be armor, and he'll lead a raid into England to avenge you in blood."

"God keep him! Did he say anything else?"

"That he loves you with all his heart."

"Will the Scots guard return a message?"

"Yes, Madam."

"Tell Lord Bothwell that I send him my most precious possession." She removed Bothwell's ring from her finger, kissed it, held it to her cheek for a long moment. *Keep trust.* "Tell Lord Bothwell that I trust in him to guard Scotland as my husband did."

"Against his King?" Marie asked slyly.

"If need be, yes. According to his own conscience."

Marie took the ring. "God grant it reaches him safely."

"It will be safe," Mary said. "It returns to its own."

An hour later the Earls of Kent and Shrewsbury asked audience, along with Master Beale, Clerk of the Council. Mary received them in her bedchamber and they gathered about her couch. Only Shrewsbury had the courtesy to remove his hat. He had not attended the trial, pleading illness, and now he knelt painfully beside Mary, kissing the hand she extended.

"Rise, my lord, and be seated. Your gout—"

"It is not my gout that troubles me now," he said. "I wish with all my heart I did not have to bear this news . . . Her Majesty has signed your death warrant."

She had expected this for so long—daily, hourly. Yet now, aghast at her cowardice, she felt the terrible inner trembling and dared not speak lest her voice betray her.

While Beale read the death warrant, she struggled for composure. Elizabeth ordered the execution at a time and place agreed upon by Kent, Shrewsbury and four other earls.

Mary made the sign of the cross. From the table beside her she took her Bible and held it in her hand. "I swear that I am innocent—"

"You swear on a Catholic Bible," Kent said contemptuously.

"It is the Book in which I believe," she said. "Would my oath be more sincere if I took it on your Bible, in which I do not believe?"

"Jesuit sophistry," he muttered.

Ignoring him, she appealed to Shrewsbury. "I beg you to have my priest returned to me. I need him most desperately now."

"I did not know he had been removed, Madam. However, we have brought you the Dean of Peterborough—"

"I will not have him. In your house, my lord, I listened to learned Protestant preachers for nearly the whole of one Lent. I have read the doctrines of your most brilliant ministers. I find it all hollow. I implore that you allow me my own—"

"No!" Kent interrupted. "The Dean will convince you of the folly and abomination of Popery."

She ignored him. "Have any foreign powers interceded for me?" she asked Shrewsbury.

"Aye, Madam. But no one can show Her Majesty good reason why you should be spared."

No one threatens war, she thought, though Elizabeth is surely aware of Philip's shipbuilding.

"Will the Queen permit me to be buried in France?"

"Indeed not," Kent said brusquely.

She did not need to ask why. Elizabeth wanted no shrine on Catholic soil, no Catholic pilgrimages to her grave.

"Then where shall I be buried?"

"I know not."

Long ago she had considered asking burial in the little church of Faarevejle in Denmark, but decided against it. She did not want to lie near Bothwell's bones, but where his spirit would always remain.

"If it were possible," she said, dreaming aloud, "I would love a Scottish grave near Dunbar or Hermitage. But my enemies would pillage it."

Then she took a deep breath and glanced warningly at her ladies. Her eyes begged: Do not cry out, do not weep. Help me maintain my dignity. I have delayed this question until I had courage for it.

She tossed the words lightly with a tremulous little smile. "When am I to die?"

Shrewsbury's chin trembled and he turned from her. "At eight in the morning."

IX.

The Great Hall of Fotheringay was a gloom of black. Black serge draped the stone walls, covered the scaffold and the cushion at the block. But the flickering tapers caught pools of colored light from the cloaks and plumes of two hundred nobles, from the iron helmets of three hundred halberdiers, from the wine-red doublets of the musicians in the gallery.

Bulle, the headsman, tested the blade of the short-handled axe, then conferred with his assistant.

Mary lay at the block, her body flat on the floor, her long velvet petticoat flowing scarlet across the scaffold. Arms extended, she clutched her crucifix and buried her face in the cushion.

"God help me to forgive Elizabeth . . ."

For ordering this insulting music—a dirge usually played at the execution of witches. For the gravest humiliation of all—death by the axe. Thus do thieves die, knaves, the scum of England. In denying me the sword, she brands me the lowest criminal.

The music ended. The Earl of Shrewsbury signaled to Bulle, who stepped to Mary's side. As his assistant held her, he raised the axe.

Even now, she thought, I can escape. I have only to lift my head, tear off the handkerchief that binds my eyes and confess to conspiracy. For Elizabeth wants my confession far more than my death. She wants me alive, broken of pride and begging grace, a coward queen to throw in the face of the Pope . . .

She took a deep, shuddering breath and embraced the block with both arms, burrowing deeper into the cushion.

Bulle noticed that her arms were in the path of the axe, and he shifted them so that they rested straight at her sides.

"Madam," he said, "remove that ring."

"It is my marriage ring," she said, lifting her head. "I beg you to let me wear it. It has no jewels, it is of little value to anyone but me—"

"It is not allowed." Bulle tugged at her hand, and she sat up and worked the ring off her swollen finger.

"Please give this to my women."

"That is for Sir Amyas to decide. He will dispose of it as he sees fit."

She resumed her place at the block. *"In te Domine confido non confundat in eternum . . ."*

With her bound eyes deep in the cushion the darkness was absolute.

"In te Domine speravi . . ."

She heard thunder growl, roar, roll above the castle like cannon-fire. Then a tremendous crash in the garden as lightning struck.

"Bothwell!" She stretched her heart to him. *"Bothwe—"*

The axe hacked the back of her skull and blood spurted, but the head held fast. Sweat dripped from Bulle's forehead as he heard her moan. Again he swung, and her head moved sideways from the neck and hung by a tendon. A third time he struck—and the head rolled from the body.

Eager to show it to the crowd, Bulle gripped the wig by mistake, and the bloody white-curled head tumbled across the scaffold like a ball. He bent, picked it up by the hair and lifted it high.

"God save the Queen!" shouted the Earl of Kent. "So perish all the Queen's enemies!"

The crowd slowly dispersed. Bulle's assistant knelt to remove Mary's stockings, and found that her terrier had crept beneath her petticoat. It refused to leave her side and lay whimpering beside the body. Finally a page grabbed it and took it upstairs to be washed of blood.

Bulle placed the head on a platter and crossed the hall to a window where he held it out for the mob in the courtyard to see. Though drenched with rain, they clamored for the sight four times. Out of patience, Bulle cursed them and turned from the window. Carrying the head back to the scaffold, he placed it beside the body and wiped his hands on his apron. The Sheriff and his men were readying a litter for the corpse, and Sir Amyas strolled up to watch.

"She looks like a hag," he said, touching his lips with a handkerchief. "Full seventy years old."

Bulle stared at the head. "I've never seen the like. Fifteen minutes, and she still beats her eyelids and makes as if to talk."

"Aye," Sir Amyas chuckled. "She wants the last word, eh, Sheriff?"

The Sheriff nodded, laughing, then lifted the body and head to the litter. He instructed his men: "Take her upstairs to the third chamber on the left of the staircase. And be quick—the embalmers are waiting." The small procession moved off.

Bulle gave Mary's wedding ring to Sir Amyas, and he tossed it into a box on the floor.

The Sheriff turned to Sir Amyas. "What of her servants? Do they return to their homes?"

"They will be detained for some time. Her Majesty has no wish to harm them, but a free Catholic is a dangerous Catholic and we cannot have them spreading accounts of their mistress's 'martyrdom.' Here come her women now, bearing her clothes as if they were sanctified!"

Jane and Elizabeth approached the men and curtsied. "My lords," Jane said, "we promised to attend Her Majesty's body, and we beg leave to undress it."

"The surgeons will see to that," Sir Amyas said. "But there's work for you here." He pointed to the box on the floor. "There are her hose, shoes, garters and some Popish rubbish. Burn them, and those robes you hold. We want no relics of her wickedness."

Reluctantly they picked up the box, and crossed the hall to the fireplace. Mindful of the watching men, they tossed the Queen's clothing into the blaze. Then, crossing themselves, they let fall the Paternosters—all but one, which Jane hid in her bodice with Mary's wedding ring.

"Quick," she whispered nervously. "Let us go upstairs."

They hurried up the staircase to their room, which adjoined the embalming chamber. Marie was peeping through the keyhole, and turned a pallid face to the others. "I thought Her Majesty would want me to watch—but I cannot bear any more!"

Jane knelt and peered through the keyhole, then, wordlessly, gave place to Elizabeth. They prayed for a time, until Elizabeth broke off violently. "They are so rough, damn them! They treat her like a side of beef!" Her voice soared toward hysteria, and she began to laugh, tears streaming down her cheeks.

"Hush," Marie said, but the surgeons had heard, and one of them shouted through the door and stuffed the keyhole with paper. Elizabeth was still laughing, and Jane slapped her silent, then bent to kiss the wet cheek.

"Our nerves are tattered," she said, and poured wine for each of them.

As they seated themselves by the fire Elizabeth said, "Forgive me, but I could not help it. I never saw an execution so close nor anyone dead I loved so well."

"We must remember Her Majesty as she was in life," Marie said. "She was so—I loved her so—"

Rough, gulping sobs shook her shoulders, and the others wept too. After a while they quieted, dried their eyes on their long-flowing sleeves and talked of Mary through little gusts of tears.

The fire fell to embers, but they made no move to rekindle it. The gloom of the room deepened and the wind rose, shaking the casements. Marie shivered, eyes round under her frilled coif. "Do you think her ghost will walk tonight?"

"Silly child," Jane said sharply. "God knows she would not linger here. There are pleasanter places if she has a mind to walk."

"Last night," Marie whispered, "I peeped into her chamber as she was completing her will. And I swear there were *two* of her shadows on the wall."

"Two!" Elizabeth leaned forward. "What are you saying?"

"The wine befuddles her," Jane said. "She has no head for it."

"No, I swear it! It was past midnight and I looked through the door from the threshold. The Queen was at her writing desk, busy with quill and papers. Behind her there was a taper. And it cast two shadows of her."

"A trick of the light, perhaps." But Elizabeth's voice held no conviction.

The outer door closed in the next room, and they heard the tramp of feet down the corridor. "The surgeons have left," Marie said.

They listened for a moment. There was no sound.

"Her Majesty asked us to see her in her shroud and bid her farewell," Jane reminded them. "Perhaps this door is unlocked." She rose and tried the adjoining door, but it held fast. "Then perhaps the one in the hall."

But when she peered into the hall she saw that a halberdier guarded the embalming chamber.

"He will never let us in," Jane sighed.

Marie sent her a wan smile. "If Her Majesty had promised us this last service would she not have found a way?"

"But you know the guard will not permit—"

"Indeed," Marie said contemptuously, "no English oaf will keep *me* out."

She went to the corridor, sauntered up to the guard and curtsied. "Good day, my lord. I had not expected to see you here."

The guard looked puzzled. "What—"

"Oh!" Marie contrived confusion. "I mistook you for Lord Kent."

"Wearing these?" He laughed, pointing to his helmet and shabby doublet.

"It is dark here. But now I see you are much handsomer—I mean," she stammered, "much younger than he." She pushed a curl under her cap and fluttered her eyelashes. "How stupid of me. You are so much taller . . ."

Jane and Elizabeth poked their heads out of their room, surveyed the situation and withdrew. In a few minutes Marie was back with a key to the adjoining door. "It cost me a kiss for the guard." Angrily she rubbed at her mouth. "But we may go in if we are silent as mice. He will stand outside and raise a clamor if anyone comes."

One by one, holding each other's hands for courage, they tiptoed into the embalming room. Wind swept from the open windows and they shivered. The body of the Queen lay on the stone floor covered by a waxen winding sheet. Jane slipped Mary's wedding ring into its folds. "Farewell," she whispered.

Tall white candles in silver holders blazed at Mary's head and feet. Across her body lay the gold cloth of state, bearing the arms of Scotland and France.

"I hope she knows they returned it," Marie said.

"She embroidered it herself."

Elizabeth peered at the gold embroidery that traced a French phrase between thistles and lilies. "What does it say, Marie?"

" 'En ma fin est mon commencement.' " The candles flared and streamed upward. " 'In my end is my beginning.' "

AFTERWORD

THAT TRUTH IS STRANGER THAN FICTION is again made evident in the life of Mary Stuart. Many incidents in this book that may strike the reader as incredible are not products of a novelist's imagination—but true.

From the time Mary left France there were eerie portents. A ship *did* founder in Calais Harbor as Mary's galleys embarked and she cried, "My God, what omen is this?" A haar *did* shroud her entrance into Scotland. As Knox himself wrote, "In the memory of man that day of the year was never seen a more dolorous face of the heavens than was at her arrival. That forewarning God gave to us—but alas! the most part were blind."

It is true (if melodramatic) that Darnley stumbled upon Rizzio's grave in the darkness of Holyrood Abbey and that Mary vowed vengeance as she knelt by the mound: "I swear another shall lie as low before a year has passed." And it *was* precisely eleven months from the night of Rizzio's murder that Darnley was murdered at Kirk O'Field. Historians dispute whether the fifth or the fifty-fifth Psalm was read in Darnley's bedchamber during his last hours. Both are sinister—and one of them strangely *was* posted on St. Giles that day as part of the service. A raven *did* hover over Darnley's litter on the journey from Glasgow to Kirk O'Field and finally settled on his lodging. John Knox's prophecy that Edinburgh Castle would run like a sandglass and its commander be hanged against the western sun was fulfilled. And to this day in Mary's audience chamber at Holyrood, guards point out the inerasable stains of Rizzio's blood, now marked by a metal plaque.

In adhering to Mary's viewpoint throughout the book I was unable to include facts of which she was unaware, and thus have had to omit some fascinating material. We know that during her last weeks at Fotheringay Mary feared murder and took precautions against it. But she never knew how close she came to it—at Elizabeth's order. As historian Herbert Gorman states in *The Scottish Queen:*

"To her ministers she [Elizabeth] hinted . . . that the lean hand of the assassin might stretch out of the murkiness of London toward Fotheringay without her cognizance, that something secret and ultimate might happen to Marie before the warrant of execution was signed. . . . Before nightfall a special messenger was speeding to Fotheringay with one of the most monstrous letters that has ever been written:"

To Sir Amyas Paulet [Mary's jailer]

After our hearty commendations, we find by speech lately uttered by Her Majesty that she doth note in you both a lack of that care and zeal of her service that she looketh for at your hands, in that you have not in all this time . . . found out some way to shorten the life of that Queen, considering the great peril she [Elizabeth] is subject unto hourly, so long as the said Queen shall live. . . . And therefore she taketh it most unkindly towards her, that men professing that love towards her that you do, should in any kind of sort, for lack of the discharge of your duties, cast the burthen upon her, knowing as you do her indisposition to shed blood, especially of one of that sex and quality, and so near to her in blood as the said Queen is. These respects we find do greatly trouble Her Majesty, who, we assure you, has sundry times protested that if the regard of the danger of her good subjects and faithful servants did not more move her than her own peril, she would never be drawn to assent to the shedding of her blood. We thought it very meet to acquaint you with these speeches lately passed from Her Majesty, referring the same to your good judgments. And so we commit you to the protection of the Almighty.

> Your most assured friends,
> Francis Walsingham [Elizabeth's spy-master]
> William Davison [Elizabeth's Secretary]
> At London, 1st February, 1586 [old calendar]

[588]

A few hours later the nervous Davison, fearful lest the letter be made public, sent this postscript by a courier: "I pray you let this and the enclosed be committed to the fire, which measure shall be likewise meet to your answer after it hath been communicated to Her Majesty."

Although Paulet hated Mary, he dared not permit her murder lest Elizabeth use him as scapegoat and execute him for "negligence of his duty." Thus he wrote to Walsingham and Davison:

Your letters of yesterday coming to my hands this present day at five in the afternoon, I would not fail, according to your directions, to return my answer with all possible speed . . . with great grief and bitterness of mind, in that I am so unhappy to have lived to see this unhappy day, in the which I am required by direction from my most gracious sovereign to do an act which God and the law forbiddeth. . . . God forbid that I should make so foul a shipwreck of my conscience, or leave so great a blot to my poor posterity, to shed blood without law or warrant. Trusting that Her Majesty, of her accustomed clemency, will take this my dutiful answer in good part . . . I commit you to the mercy of the Almighty.

Your most assured poor friends,
A. Paulet
D. Drury.
From Fotheringay, 2nd February, 1586 [old calendar]
Your letters . . . seem to be meant as to Sir Drue Drury as to myself, and yet because he is not named in them, neither the letter directed unto him, he forbeareth to make any particular answer, but subscribeth in heart to my opinion.

Elizabeth, furious, called Paulet a "dainty and precise fellow" and finally signed Mary's death warrant though, she told Davison, "I do not like the legal method, as upon me alone will fall all the responsibility."

Most of the letters in this book are authentic, including two of the "Casket Letters" which Mary allegedly wrote to Bothwell—the long incriminating one from Darnley's bedside in Glasgow and the letter from Stirling indicating her collusion in

Bothwell's plans to abduct her. For four hundred years controversy has raged about these letters. Mary's defenders claim they were forgeries or that her enemies made interpolations in innocent letters. It is doubtful that we shall ever know the truth, for the original letters no longer exist and only copies remain. However, as Stefan Zweig points out in his biography, *Mary Queen of Scotland and the Isles:*

"Each time they were compared with Mary's writing . . . they were declared authentic and coming from Mary's own hand. More convincing still is that Elizabeth had the texts printed and circulated among the courts of Europe. Now although we have many reasons to distrust the actions of the Queen of England, we can hardly credit the assumption that she would compromise her high position by going to the length of forgery, since at any moment discovery was possible. . . . The only person who should have protested vehemently if the letters and sonnets were forgeries, namely Mary Stuart herself, was content to utter a feeble and quite unconvincing protest. . . . When writing to the Pope or the King of France and her other relatives she never mentioned a word about forgery of her letters."

I am inclined to agree with Mr. Zweig that Mary wrote them, for it was perfectly in her character to write foolishly and even dangerously. (No one has ever questioned the authenticity of her letter on page 553 reviling Elizabeth.) But if the Casket Letters *were* forged, who among the uncouth ill-educated Scots nobles was capable of forging them? Latin-scholar George Buchanan was an old man at the time, with a dry pedantic style. Lord James Stuart and Sir William Maitland of Lethington were men of culture but cold, practical, unromantic. Could they possibly have invented the passionate, turbulent, utterly feminine outpouring on page 346? It has the terrible truthful ring of Mary's own guilt and horror as she assures Bothwell that she will betray Darnley to his death.

Bothwell was so blackened by his contemporaries that for centuries historians have been convinced of his villainy, basing their judgment of his character on the propaganda of his enemies. Even Stefan Zweig presents Bothwell as a greedy, ambitious adventurer—until, carried away by his own description of Bothwell's behavior at the Battle of Carberry Hill, he exclaims, "A wonderful scene, and a wonderful man!"

It remained for Robert Gore-Browne to vindicate Bothwell in a superbly objective biography, *Lord Bothwell and Mary, Queen of Scots*. For seven years he probed, studied, traveled, weighed and analyzed evidence. His findings should embarrass future historians who try to use Bothwell as a scapegoat for Mary's ruin or who are too lazy or too prejudiced to seek new facts. As he wrote to me: "The novelists have taken more notice of my book than the historians, who go on and on repeating the same old story."

Though I do not agree in all particulars with Colonel Gore-Browne's version of the Kirk O'Field murder, I believe his is a brilliant reconstruction of a mystery that will never be solved, and I am deeply grateful for his wonderfully documented portrait of Bothwell.

I also wish to thank Miss Ruth Isaacs and Miss Flora Armitage of the British Library of Information in New York and Mrs. Nancy Browne of the Scots Ancestry Research Society in Edinburgh. My special thanks to Ronald Chisholm of London who drove me from Edinburgh through the winter-gripped Highlands to Inverness; to Don Forrest and Murdoch McIntosh. And had it not been for the kindness—and car—of Mr. and Mrs. Arthur King I would have missed much of the French chateau country.

Few tourists seek the lonely grave of Bothwell at the Church of Faarevejle near the ruins of Dragsholm in Denmark, where his body, mummified by the sea winds, may be seen under the glass lid of his coffin. But each year thousands visit Mary's tomb at Westminster Abbey. Close by lies Elizabeth. The Queens who never met in life sleep through the centuries side by side.

ELIZABETH BYRD

New York City, 1955

About Elizabeth Byrd

Most literary works of stature are born of long contemplation, and *Immortal Queen* is no exception. Miss Byrd's interest in Mary Stuart began at the age of seven when she learned that she was born on Mary's birthday and her mother on Queen Elizabeth's. (She points out, however, that she and her mother are still on affectionate terms.) Year by year she collected biographies of Mary and at twelve wrote a play about her which was produced at The Lincoln School in New York, where Miss Byrd was a student. Oddly, she chose for herself the role of Queen Elizabeth, which she says she performed "in a hoop-skirted costume borrowed from the Metropolitan Opera."

After high school Miss Byrd took writing courses at New York University, and turned thereafter to radio writing. In 1942 she conceived the original husband-wife breakfast-table chats, broadcast over station WMCA. Miss Byrd wrote the script and acted the part of the wife.

Thereafter she worked in New York literary agencies as critic and associate editor and resumed writing. Since 1945 many of her stories have been published in national magazines and she has written articles on fiction technique for a writers' magazine. She edited a women's magazine until she began work on *Immortal Queen*, then went to Europe in 1953 to complete her research.

"Surprisingly little fiction has been written about Mary," Miss Byrd says. "Biography, although extremely plentiful, is for the most part either distorted by religious bias or slanted to prove the author's prejudice for or against her. She was portrayed as martyr or devil, rarely as a woman with the elements of both.

"Mary's era was amoral and she herself had been trained in Machiavelli's theories that the end justifies the means. From childhood she must have been confused between his cynicism and the philosophy of Jesus. So her inner conflicts began long before she was swept into intrigue, adultery and murder. She was as much a victim of her era as of Elizabeth."

Miss Byrd has tried to be completely objective in regard to the religious controversies in the book. "I wanted only to show the Reformation as it was, to report rather than to propagandize. I have no 'message' save one that I think has validity for us today: If people would take to heart the sacredness with which Mary and Bothwell invested a pledge—if the phrase 'word of honor' could again be meaningful rather than a cliché—a cornerstone of morality would be restored to contemporary life."

Born in St. Louis of native Missourians, Miss Byrd was moved to New York in infancy. Her father's ancestors are descended from John Campbell, first Earl of Loudoun, Lord Chancellor of Scotland. They fled religious persecution in the early seventeenth century and went from Ayrshire, Scotland, to northern Ireland. In the eighteenth century Miss Byrd's great-great-great grandfather, Joseph Hunter, settled in Virginia, later joined George Rogers Clark and moved to the fort at the Falls of the Ohio—now Louisville, Kentucky. His daughter, Nancy Hunter, was a heroine during the Indian attacks on the fort.

Miss Byrd lives in Manhattan, where in her free time she does volunteer work for The American-Scottish Foundation, an organization devoted to the social and economic welfare of the Scottish Highlands. She is engaged at present on her second novel and several short stories. *Immortal Queen*, her first novel, will go far toward placing her in that rare group of historical novelists whose books are not merely factually accurate but alive as works of art and recreations of their periods.